STAR TREK
DEEP SPACE NINE®
MILLENNIUM

STAR TREK
DEEP SPACE NINE®
MILLENNIUM

THE FALL OF TEROK NOR
THE WAR OF THE PROPHETS
INFERNO

JUDITH & GARFIELD REEVES-STEVENS

Based upon *Star Trek*®
created by Gene Roddenberry,
and *Star Trek: Deep Space Nine*
created by Rick Berman & Michael Piller

POCKET BOOKS
New York   London   Toronto   Sydney   Singapore

POCKET BOOKS, a division of Simon & Schuster, Inc.
1230 Avenue of the Americas, New York, NY 10020

Star Trek Deep Space Nine Millennium Book 1: The Fall of Terok Nor
copyright © 2000 by Paramount Pictures. All Rights Reserved.

Star Trek Deep Space Nine Millennium Book 2: The War of the Prophets
copyright © 2000 by Paramount Pictures. All Rights Reserved.

Star Trek Deep Space Nine Millennium Book 3: Inferno
copyright © 2000 by Paramount Pictures. All Rights Reserved.

 STAR TREK is a Registered Trademark of Paramount Pictures.

This book is published by Pocket Books, a division of Simon & Schuster, Inc., under exclusive license from Paramount Pictures.

ISBN: 0-7434-4249-0

First Pocket Books trade paperback printing January 2002

10 9 8 7 6 5 4 3 2 1

POCKET and colophon are registered trademarks of Simon & Schuster, Inc.

Printed in the U.S.A.

These titles were previously published individually by Pocket Books.

To Denise & Mike and more adventures
in the 8th dimension

For Herman Zimmerman and all his talented artists
and designers in the *Deep Space Nine* Art Department,
who took "a strange, intriguing object in orbit of Bajor"
and made it the best-looking series on television

And last, though not least . . . since before our sun
burned hot in space, every writer of a *Star Trek* novel
or nonfiction book has had an unsung partner—a heroic
captain whose mission it is to keep them true to the *Star
Trek* universe, its history, its character, and its ideals. In
return, she's faced with *Star Trek* book writers (okay, like
us) who push her unmercifully on deadlines, who grumble
about her notes (especially when she's right), and who
rarely share with her the bottom-line truth: she makes
all of our books better. After sixteen of them,
we thought it was about time to come clean.

So, with respect, appreciation, and many, many thanks,
this one's for Paula Block.

bathlh Daqawlu'taH!h

CONTENTS

BOOK I
THE FALL OF
TEROK NOR

At that moment, before the sky was opened, it was all a flurry of this and that and the everyday. But with the Opening, there came a stillness, a pause in the endless avalanche of life, if you will, as if the stars themselves whispered for us to turn away from what troubled us and glimpse what waited at our journey's end. And the truth is, what the stars showed was no different from what we had already suspected: There were many paths to that final destination, and even in the Temple of All That Had Been and Was Still To Come, the place where all answers waited, it was up to us— to us—to choose our own way.

—JAKE SISKO, *Anslem*

PROLOGUE
In the Hands of the Prophets

"THERE WAS another time," the Sisko says.

"It is not linear," Jake answers. The twelve-year-old boy dangles his fishing line in the quiet water of the pond, rippling the reflections of towering trees, green fields, and the pure blue sky of Earth. The sun is strong, and the rich scent of the bridge's sun-warmed wood makes uncounted summers happen all at once for the Sisko.

"But it is, was, will be. . . ." The Sisko falters with the syntax of eternity. His father plays the upright piano in the restaurant in New Orleans as the Sisko plunges into the depths of the Fire Caves with Gul Dukat and first takes his captain's chair on the bridge of the Starship Defiant, all within a single heartbeat—the same heartbeat.

—The heartbeat of his unborn child, now grown, now fulfilling a destiny unimaginable to the Sisko, a destiny now known to him, now unknown.

The Sisko laughs at the wonder of it all.

"You're laughing again," Jean-Luc Picard tells him in the ready room of the Enterprise, in orbit of Bajor.

The Sisko looks down at the old uniform he wears at this moment. The texture feels so real to him, even as it dissolves beneath his fingers and he is in his bathing suit on the beach carrying lemonade to the woman who will be/is/was his wife—still at this same moment.

"*That is correct,*" *Solok confirms. The young Vulcan walks beside the Sisko on the path leading from Starfleet Academy's zero-G gymnasium to the cadets' residences.* "*All moments are the same.*"

"*In* this *time,*" *the Sisko says. He watches Boothby plant fall flowers by the statue of Admiral Chekov.* "*But there are* other *times. That's my point.*" *The gardener now prunes bushes for the spring.*

"*This is not logical,*" *Solok says. His cadet's uniform becomes that of a baseball player, and he tosses a small white ball into the air, then catches it with the same hand an infinite number of times.*

"*Logic has no place here,*" *the Sisko says. He reaches out and intercepts the ball even as Solok attempts to catch it.* "*Because logic is linear.*"

"*Some logic is absolute,*" *Sarah Sisko says. She stands by the viewport in the Sisko's quarters on Deep Space 9, the radiance of the opening doorway to the Celestial Temple filtering through her hair. Wormholes within wormholes. Temples within temples. An infinite regression. Or an eternal one.*

"*I think I finally know why I'm here,*" *the Sisko says.* "*Why you . . . had to be certain my mother would marry my father, give birth to me.*"

"*You are the Sisko,*" *Major Kira agrees. She stands at her station in Ops.*

"*You* need *me here,*" *the Sisko says.*

"*You are the Sisko,*" *Curzon Dax agrees, the vast spacedocks of Utopia Planitia orbiting with flawless precision beyond the viewport of his shuttle.*

"*You need me here to teach* you,*" *the Sisko says.*

Interruption.

The Sisko finds himself in the light space. Around him Sarah, Jake, Kira, Solok, Curzon, Worf, and Admiral Ross.

"*You have much to learn,*" *the admiral says.*

"*Then shouldn't I already know it?*"

"*Your language is imperfect for these matters,*" *Solok says.*

"*You have much to realize that you already know,*" *Worf says.*

"*That you have always known,*" *Jake says.*

The Sisko holds up a finger, and each of his observers watches it, as he knows they will.

The Sisko regards their expectant faces and laughs again. "*Look* at you all," he exclaims. "You want to know what I'm going to say next. Because you don't know!"

The Prophets are silent.

The Sisko thinks of a thing, of a time, of a moment, makes it real.

And they are on the Promenade of Deep Space 9, as it is the day the Sisko first sets foot upon it.

The Sisko can smell stale smoke, hear the clamor of work crews. Feels what the Prophets cannot feel, the . . . anticipation.

He leads them to the entrance of the Bajoran Temple.

"Since you do not know time, how can you know of other times?" the Sisko asks, so much that is hidden now known to him.

As he knows they will, the Prophets continue their silence.

The Sisko holds out his hand to them. "Welcome, Prophets," the Sisko says with a smile. "Your Emissary awaits you."

All enter the Temple then. Intendant Kira and Jadzia and Ezri, Jake and Kasidy, Weyoun and Damar, Quark and Rom and Nog, Bashir and Garak, Vic and Worf, O'Brien and Keiko and Eddington and Vash. All at the invitation of the Sisko.

It takes hours for them all to pass through, all in a single moment.

The last is the Sisko, poised on the threshold of the Temple.

He remembers his own words the first time he stands here.

"Another time."

An infinity of eternities in just two words. An infinity beyond the understanding of the Prophets.

Until now.

The Sisko enters the Temple.

Not to show them the beginning of things. Because that would be linear.

He enters the Temple to show them the end.

As it was.

As it is.

As it will be. . . .

CHAPTER 1

ON THIS DAY, like a beast with talons extended to claw through space itself, the Station stalked Bajor one final time.

Viewed from high above, from orbit, the dark, curved docking arms angled sharply downward, as if gouging the planet's surface to leave bloodred wounds of flame. And from each blazing gash of destruction, wave after wave of ships lifted from the conquerors' camps and garrisons, on fiery, untempered columns of full fusion exhaust.

As those ships exploded upward through the planet's smoke-filled atmosphere, the sonic booms of their passing were like the echo of the death-screams of the ravished world they left behind. The jewel-like sparkle of the departing ships' thrusters like the glittering tears of that world's lost gods.

On this day, on this world, sixty years of butchery and brutality had at last come to an end.

But on the dark station that was Terok Nor, with viewports that flashed with phaser bursts and shimmered with the fire of its own inner destruction, there was still far worse to come.

On this day, the Day of Withdrawal, the Cardassians were leaving. But they had not left yet . . .

• • •

Held within the cold and patient silence of space, the Promenade of Terok Nor itself was a tumultuous pocket universe of heat and noise and confusion.

The security gates that had bisected its circular path had by now collapsed, twisted by hammers and wirecutters and the frantically grasping hands of slaves set free. Glowing restraint conduits that once had bound the gates now cracked and sparked and sent strobing flashes into the dense blue haze that choked the air, still Cardassian-hot.

Hull plates resonated with the violent release of multiple, escaping shuttles and ships. A thrumming wall of sound sprang up as departing soldiers phasered equipment too heavy to steal.

Decks shook as rampaging looters forced internal doors and shattered windows. Among the empty shelves of the Chemist's shop, a Bajoran lay dying, Cardassian blood on his hands, Cardassian bootprints on his back, his collaboration with the enemy no guarantee of safety in the madness of this day.

Turbolifts whined and ladders rattled against their moorings. Officers shouted hoarse commands. Soldiers cursed their victims. In counterpoint, a calm recorded voice recited the orders of the day. "Attention, all biorganic materials must be disposed of according to regulations. Attention. . . ."

But on this day, the only response to that directive was the desperate, high-pitched shriek of a Ferengi in fear for his life. And in fear for good reason.

Quark the barkeep kicked and fought and shrieked again, as the Cardassian soldiers, safe in their scarred, hard-edged armor, dragged him from his bar, soiling and tearing his snug multicolored jacket.

Quark opened his eyes just long enough to recognize the scowling officer, Datar, a glinn, who waited for him with a coil of ODN cable. In the same quick glimpse, he saw the antigrav lifter from a cargo bay bobbing in the air nearby; he heard the soldiers as they mockingly chanted the last words he would hear before he stood at the doors of the Divine Treasury to give a full accounting of his life—

"Dabo! Dabo! Dabo!"

Yet even as he faced his last minute of existence, Quark still couldn't help automatically tallying the damages each time he heard a crash from his establishment as the Cardassian forces laid waste to it.

A sudden blow slammed Quark to the Promenade deck, and a quick, savage kick from a heavy leather boot forestalled any thought of escape.

But even as he cried out in pain, Quark wondered if his brother and nephew had made it to a shuttle, and if the Cardassians had found his latinum floor vault. He gasped in shock as he felt Glinn Datar's rough hand claw at the sensitive lobes of his right ear, the violation forcing him to his feet. In the same terrible moment, Quark found himself wondering just why it was Cardassians always had such truly disgusting breath.

"Quark!" the glinn growled at him. "You have no idea how it pains me to take my leave of you."

"All good things," Quark muttered as waves of incredible pain radiated from his crushed right ear lobe and across his skull and neck.

Datar's swift, expert punch to the center of his stomach doubled Quark over, his lips gaping in vain for even a mouthful of air.

"Relax, Quark," the glinn hissed, reaching out for Quark's ear-lobe again. "It's not necessary for you to speak—ever again!"

Quark felt himself hauled up until he stared right into Datar's narrowed eyes. He felt his poor earlobe throb painfully, already starting to swell.

"My men and I are going to make this a real farewell." The glinn nodded once and Quark felt huge hands forcibly secure his shoulders and arms from behind. Datar addressed his soldiers as if reading from a proclamation. "Quark of Terok Nor, you miserable mound of *sluk* scum: For the crime of rigging your dabo table, for the crime of watering your drinks, short-timing the holosuites, inflating tabs, and . . . most of all for the crime of being a *Ferengi* . . . I sentence you to *death!*"

Incredulous, Quark tried to plead his innocence, but his rasping exhortations were drowned out by the cheers of the surrounding soldiers. He tried to blurt out the combination of his floor vault, the shuttle access codes Rom and Nog were going to use to escape, even made-up names of resistance fighters, but the sharp cutting pressure of the ODN cable Glin Datar suddenly wrapped around his neck ended any chance he had of saying a word. Even the squeak that escaped him then registered as little more than a soon-to-be-dead man's choked-off wheeze.

Eyes bulging, each racing heartbeat thundering in his cavernous ear tunnels, Quark could only watch as two soldiers hooked the other end of the thick cable to the grappler on the cargo antigrav.

Datar slammed his hand on the antigrav's control and the meter-long device bucked up a few centimeters, steadied itself, then rose smoothly and slowly and inexorably, trailing cable until it passed the Promenade's second level.

The cable snapped taut against Quark's neck, yanking him at last from the grip of the soldiers who had held him. Kicking frantically, he felt a boot fly free. He grimaced in embarrassment as he realized his toes were sticking through the holes worn in his foot wrappings. Hadn't his moogie told him to always wear fresh underclothes?

Even Quark knew that was a foolish thought to have, especially at the moment in which he was drawing his last breath. His fingers scrabbled at the cable around his neck, but it was too tight and in too many layers for him to change the pressure.

Dimly through the pounding that now filled his head, Quark could hear the soldiers' laughter and hooting. Even as his vision darkened, he raged at himself for having failed to predict how quickly the end of the Occupation would come.

He had seen the signs, discussed it with his suppliers. Another month, he had concluded, perhaps two. Time enough to profit from the Cardassian soldiers being shipped out, eager to convert their Bajoran "souvenirs" to more easily transportable latinum. He had even already booked his passage on a freighter and—

—Dark stars sparkled at the rapidly shrinking edge of Quark's vision, as he mourned the deposit he had paid to Captain Yates. Just then the roar of something large approaching—something loud and silent all at the same time—swallowed the jeers of the Cardassians, and Quark felt himself fall, flooded with shock that he was not ascending to the Divine Treasury but apparently on his way to the Debtors' Dungeon. How could that be possible? He had lived a life of greed and self-absorption. How could he not be rewarded with eternal dividends? He wanted to speak to someone in charge. He wanted to renegotiate the deal. He wanted his moogie!

And then the back of the deck of the Promenade smacked into the back of his bulbous head and scrawny neck.

Through starstruck vision, he saw the glow of a phaser emitter node by his chin, felt a searing flash of heat at his neck, and then the constriction of the ODN cable was gone.

"Breathe!" a harsh voice shouted from some distant place.

"Moogie?" Quark whispered. His mother was about the only person he could think of who might have any reason at all for saving him from the Cardassians.

Then Quark was roused from his lethargy by four nerve-sparking slaps across his face.

He wheezed with an enormous intake of breath, then choked as he saw who was saving him from the Cardassians.

Another Cardassian!?

This new Cardassian, gray-skinned and cobra-necked like all the others, was someone Quark had never seen before. He wore an ordinary soldier's uniform but had the bearing and diction of an officer, perhaps even of a gul. All this Quark observed in the split second it took for the new Cardassian to haul him to his feet. As a barkeep, Quark was a firm believer in the 194th Rule, and since he couldn't always know about every new customer *before* that customer walked through the door, to protect his profits he had been required to become expert at deducing a customer's likely needs and desires from but a moment's quick observation.

This Cardassian, for instance, would order vintage *kanar,* and would always know if the Saurian brandy was watered. *An officer and a gentleman,* Quark thought admiringly. Reflexively he considered the likelihood of the Cardassian also needing wise and seasoned—and not inexpensive—investment help.

But then the gray stranger locked his free arm around Quark's neck to violently spin him around as he fired his phaser at two other Cardassian soldiers across the Promenade at the entrance to the Temple.

Quark flopped like a child's doll in the stranger's grip. He goggled in surprise as he saw the body of Glinn Datar sprawled on the deck nearby, smoke still curling up from the back of his head and adding to the blue haze that filled the Promenade. *Cardassians fighting Cardassians?* It made no sense. Especially when it seemed they were fighting over *him.*

Suddenly Quark's captor crouched down and twisted to return fire to the second level. Still held in a stranglehold, Quark squealed as with an ear-bruising thump he was whacked backside-first against the deck. Crackling phaser bursts lanced past him, blackening the Promenade's deck. The scent of burning carpet now warred with the stench of spoiled food wafting along from the ruined freezers in the Cardassian Cafe.

". . . I'm going to be sick . . ." Quark whimpered.

But clearly, the Cardassian stranger didn't hear, or didn't care.

Quark felt his gorge begin to rise. Under other circumstances, he woozily decided, he might wish he were dead rather than feel the way he felt now. But he seemed too close to that alternative already.

". . . I have a stomach neutralizer in my bar . . ." Quark mumbled hoarsely. He waved a hand vaguely in the direction of an area behind his captor. If he could just get back to his bar. . . .

But there was an abrupt lull in the phaser firefight, and the gray stranger jerked Quark to his feet. He pointed spinward toward the jewelry shop—or what was left of the jewelry shop. "That way!" he shouted. "As fast as you can!"

Protectively holding on to both of his oversize ears, Quark peered through the haze at what appeared to be other figures hiding among the debris in front of the gem store. Their silhouettes were unmistakable. *More* Cardassians.

"Could I ask a question?" Quark whispered.

The Cardassian glared at him, then shoved him down to the floor again and leaped to his feet, slamming both hands together on his phaser as he fired blast after blast at a group of Cardassians suddenly charging him from the other direction.

Quark risked looking up just long enough to see multiple shafts of disruptive energy blast his captor and send him flying across the Promenade. Alone now, Quark acted on pure instinct and did what any Ferengi would do.

He sped for his latinum, all injuries real and imagined forgotten.

Scuttling like a Ferengi banker crab, half crawling, half running across the deck, he finally reached the door of his bar.

Quark rolled through the door and jumped to his feet once he was securely inside his own domain. "Safe!" he cried out, then cursed as his one bootless foot trod on a piece of shattered glass.

Only after digging the glass out of his sole did he think of looking over his shoulder. The scene was one of mayhem. The Promenade had become a full-fledged war zone. Phaser fire streamed back and forth like lightning in the atmosphere of a gas giant. On the one hand, Quark had no problem with Cardassians killing Cardassians. Especially since it would be a few days before he could get his bar reopened, so a few missing customers wouldn't be noticed. On the other hand, could it be possible they were killing themselves over *him?*

"Get down, you fool!"

Quark whirled around at the guttural command. He had no idea where it came from, but the rough voice was unmistakable.

"Odo?" Quark asked.

Suddenly, a humanoid hand shot out of a dark corner behind the overturned dabo table, trailing a quasitransparent golden shaft of shape-shifter flesh.

For an instant, Quark felt as if he were about to be engulfed by a Terran treefrog's tongue, then the hand slurped around his already bruised neck and snapped him into the shadows.

With the enforced assistance, Quark somersaulted to a sitting position behind a tumble of broken chairs. Automatically, his barkeep mind tabulated the potential cost of the damage. Half of them would have to be replaced, at two slips of latinum each. Three, he could see, could probably be repaired for half a slip each. He might even be able to get a deal from Morn if he could be persuaded to stay on the station. But the way Morn was always traveling around, never staying put for two days in a row—

"Quark! Get your head down!"

Instantly, Quark flattened out on the floor beside Terok Nor's shape-shifting constable. Odo's half-finished humanoid face, with its disturbingly small ears, stared ahead toward the front of the bar, as if he were expecting an attack any moment.

"How long have you been here?" Quark hissed.

"An hour. Since Gul Dukat left the station."

Quark felt a rush of indignation. If Dukat was already safely evacuated, why were all these other Cardassians still here? "You were hiding *here* when they dragged me out *there?*" he said accusingly.

Odo looked at him, nothing to hide. "Yes."

"Aren't you supposed to be the law on this station?"

"I am a duly appointed law-enforcement official."

"Doesn't that mean you're supposed to protect law-abiding citizens?"

"Your point would be?"

"They were going to kill me!"

"Yes," Odo said again.

Quark fairly vibrated with outrage as he tried to find the proper words to express his fury and sense of betrayal. "Then why didn't you try to stop them?!" he finally said, adding sarcastically, "In your capacity, that is, as a duly appointed law-enforcement official."

Odo shrugged as best he could for someone lying on his stomach among a cluster of broken bar chairs.

"A shrug?" Quark said. "That's your answer? The law doesn't apply to people like me? You're not a law-enforcement official, you're the judge and jury, too, is that it?"

As usual, Odo's eerily smooth visage revealed no emotion, only the weary resignation of a teacher forced to repeat a lesson for the hundredth time. "Fifty-two hours ago, Terok Nor ceased to be a protectorate of the Bajoran Cooperative Government. Martial law was declared under the provisions of the Cardassian Uniform Code of Military Justice."

Quark waited . . . and waited . . . but Odo said nothing more, as if his most unsatisfactory explanation had been fully complete.

"*And?*" the Ferengi said in a state approaching apoplexy.

"Quark, I heard the charges the glinn read against you. You *have* rigged your dabo table. You *do* water your drinks. You short-time the holosuites *and* inflate the tabs you run for customers who have consumed too much alcohol to be able to keep track of their spending. Under military law, the Cardassians were within their legal rights to execute you."

Quark's mouth opened and closed silently as if the ODN cable were wrapped around his neck once more. The only words he managed to utter were, "But they were going to hang me for the *crime* of . . . of being a Ferengi!"

Odo shrugged again. "Even the Cardassians are allowed poetic license." Then Odo held a finger to his lips and nodded sharply at the main entrance to the bar.

Quark looked out to the Promenade. The firefight had stopped. It was too much to hope that both sides had killed each other. Which could only mean one side or the other had won. "I hope someone steals your bucket," he snarled at the shape-shifter.

His insolence, however justifiable, earned him a sharp jab in the ribs. Unfortunately in the very location where the brutish Cardassians had kicked him.

Then three figures stepped into the bar.

Quark recognized them at once. They were the same three he had seen silhouetted by the gem store. Which meant the loser in the fight he'd just survived had been the Cardassian who had tried to save *him.*

One of the three interlopers scanned the bar with a bulky Cardassian tricorder. It took only seconds for him to point to the mound of chairs by the overturned dabo table.

A second of the three stepped forward. "Ferengi. Constable Odo. Step into the open, hands raised."

Quark looked at Odo. The shape-shifter had the expression of an addicted tongo player calculating the odds of calling a successful roll.

"Step out now," the Cardassian threatened, "and you will have a chance to live. Remain where you are, and you will certainly die."

"I'm convinced," Quark said and pushed himself to his feet, in spite of Odo's accusatory glare.

He frowned at the angry shape-shifter. "Oh, turn yourself into a broken chair or something." Then he stepped forward, hands stretched overhead, wincing as his torn jacket sleeve momentarily brushed his injured earlobe.

As Quark limped heavily toward the three Cardassians, he actually heard Odo step out from cover behind him. But then his attention was diverted by another surprising observation that had escaped him on first seeing the three strangers: These Cardassians weren't in uniforms. They were civilians. Three young males clothed in drab shades of blue, brown, and gray, without even the identity pins that might establish them as members of the Occupation bureaucracy or diplomatic corps. Two of them, though—the ones in blue and brown—carried military-issue phase-disruptor pistols, the housing of each weapon segmented like the abdomen of a golden beetle.

What is it about Cardassians and bugs? Quark wondered. If he could just understand that about them, he'd know exactly what would tempt them to buy, and he'd corner yet another market missed by others.

But then Quark's soothing thoughts of profit were displaced by alarm as the gray-clad Cardassian shoved his tricorder like a weapon in the barkeep's face. This particular Cardassian was distinct from the others because he was bald. Quark had never seen a bald Cardassian before. In some ways, the sleekness of the Cardassian's skull made the alien look more intelligent. Except, of course, for his pathetically small ears. Not to mention the two secondary spinal cords running up the sides of his wide and flattened neck like cables on a suspension bridge. And the spoon-shaped flap of gray flesh on his forehead that made him look like a—

The light from the tricorder's small screen flashed a different set of colors across the bald Cardassian's face. "This Ferengi's Quark."

The Cardassian in the blue tunic gestured at Quark with his phaser. Quark noticed that his overgarment was torn at the shoulder and smudged with black soot, as if its wearer had ripped it on burning debris. "There are two other Ferengi on the station."

The Cardassian in blue didn't have to ask the obvious question for Quark to decide to answer it. There was no profit in withholding information for which they could easily torture him. "My brother and nephew. They left on a shuttle as soon as we heard what was happening on Bajor." Quark was confident he could carry off the lie. He had been dealing with the Cardassians—and the gelatinous Odo—long enough to have developed a reasonably effective tongo face.

The Cardassian in the torn blue tunic stared at Quark a few moments longer, as if he expected the Ferengi to suddenly break down and confess the real whereabouts of Rom and Nog. But since Quark had no actual knowledge of where his cowardly brother and confused nephew were at this precise moment, it was doubly easy to stare back with an expression of total innocence.

At last, his interrogator turned to the bald Cardassian with the tricorder. "What setting do we need to kill the shape-shifter?"

Quark stared hard at Odo beside him. *Let's see how you like it,* he thought peevishly.

But maddening as ever, Odo simply stared impassively at the three Cardassians, betraying not even a hint of emotion. The shape-shifter was as annoying, in his way, as a Vulcan.

"Wait." It was the third Cardassian who intervened now. The one in the brown tunic, so blatantly new it still bore the creases from having been folded on some display shelf, probably in Garak's tailor shop. This Cardassian was certainly not bald. His long black hair was drawn back in the same style as some soldiers Quark had seen. The new civilian clothes could mean he was a spy, but they could also mean he was a coward. Which one, however, Quark couldn't yet be sure. But because the brown-suited Cardassian didn't seem eager to kill Odo, Quark was leaning toward the latter.

"Can you take on the appearance of a Ferengi?" the Cardassian in the suspiciously new civilian clothing asked Odo.

Odo frowned. "If I had to."

Quark scowled at the constable. From the way the shape-shifter answered, it was obvious he'd rather change himself into a mound of garbage before he'd become a Ferengi.

"Would that work?" The question came from the Cardassian in the torn blue tunic, and was addressed to the bald Cardassian with the tricorder.

"We only have one Ferengi. If we need a backup. . . ."

"All right. We won't kill you. Yet." The imperious pronouncement from the Cardassian in blue made Quark think for the first time that the group had a leader. Whatever that information was worth.

"How generous of you," Odo replied with ill-concealed sarcasm.

Responding immediately, the Cardassian leader slashed his phaser across Odo's face as if to teach him a lesson in obedience.

Though Quark had seen it before, he still cringed as Odo's face rippled into a honey-like jelly at the moment of impact, allowing the phaser to slip through his mutable flesh as if passing through smoke.

An instant later, Odo's humanoid face had reformed, his expression still one of vague disinterest.

The Cardassian bared his teeth like a Klingon, as if he were about to attack Odo again and this time with more than a single blow. But the bald Cardassian put his hand on the attacker's shoulder. "We can't keep her waiting," he said.

Her? Quark thought. Now that *was* something new. Perhaps there was *another* leader. But who? And for what reason?

The Cardassian in brown gestured harshly with his phaser. "Turbolift 5's still working."

This time it was Odo who made the first move. He started forward, onto the Promenade, and Quark followed gingerly—with each step he could feel another sliver of glass he'd missed get driven deeper into his exposed foot. "Could I just get my boot?" he asked plaintively.

"Only if you want to die," the bald Cardassian growled.

Quark sighed heavily and gritted his teeth, stepping carefully around the sprawled bodies of the fallen Cardassian soldiers. "Interesting negotiating technique you've got there," he muttered.

"Faster," was the bald Cardassian's only reply.

Quark picked up his pace and followed Odo into the haze.

After they had passed a few empty shopfronts, Quark realized what was different about the Promenade. "Does it seem quiet to you?" he whispered to Odo.

Odo sighed. "Yes, Quark. *Too* quiet."

Quark snorted as he recognized the line Odo had quoted. "And I thought you didn't like holosuite programs."

"The next one of you who talks dies," a Cardassian snarled from behind them.

This time, Odo smiled nastily at Quark as if to say, Please continue. But Quark walked on in dignified silence.

As they stepped cautiously over the torn-down and sparking security gate leading to the Bajoran half of the station, Quark looked up to see a fourth Cardassian, also in civilian clothes, crouching on the second level. For an instant, their eyes met. It was Garak.

Quark was just about to call out Garak's name when he remembered the Cardassians' two phasers and the order he and Odo had just been given.

But the bald Cardassian had already noticed where he was looking, and now glanced up at the second level as well. Quark held his breath, but the bald Cardassian looked away, having seen no one. Garak had obviously jumped back, out of view.

Quark wasted no time trying to figure out why. No one had any reasonable explanation for why the Cardassians were leaving Bajor after sixty years of the Occupation. They were aliens, so in Quark's view—in the sensible, practical Ferengi view of things—they were obviously going to behave like aliens. As they should be allowed to do. Provided they paid their bills, of course. Alien or not, some laws were universal.

Turbolift 5 was on the Promenade's inner ring, just across from the small Bajoran Infirmary. Though the door to the Infirmary was open, Quark could see there was no sign of damage within. And why would there be? There had never been anything of value in it. All the medical supplies that came aboard Terok Nor were destined for the fully equipped Cardassian Infirmary across from his bar. The Bajoran Infirmary might just as well have been a barber shop for all the medicine that was allowed to be practiced in it.

Against all logic, the turbolift car arrived. Another event that made no sense to Quark. All the main lights on the Promenade were out. Only emergency glow panels were operating. And virtually all other equipment, from automatic firefighting systems to station communicators and the replicators were off-line. But not, it seemed, Turbolift 5.

The bald Cardassian scanned the waiting car with his tricorder, then stepped inside. The leader in the torn blue tunic waved Quark and Odo in without speaking.

Quark looked out at the Promenade as the lift doors closed. For a moment, he saw Garak again, huddled behind the rolling door of the disabled security gate across the main floor. At least, the figure had looked like Garak. But what would Garak have put on a uniform for . . . ? Quark couldn't identify the tailor's military-style outfit, other than that he knew it wasn't Cardassian.

Quark looked to Odo to silently inquire if the shape-shifter had seen Garak, but Odo was still pointedly ignoring him.

Quark decided he could play that game every bit as well as Odo, and looked straight ahead as the lift descended. The movement felt unusually rough, as if the power grids were under strain. Quark tried his utmost not to think about that. The last thing he wanted was to be trapped in a turbolift with three surly Cardassians. Unlike Odo, he couldn't count on conveniently escaping by liquefying and slurping out between the doors. . . .

Quark took another look at Odo as a sudden thought struck him.

Why *was* the shape-shifter still here? He himself was trapped, of that there was no question. But Odo had already had at least a dozen opportunities to make his escape.

As Quark pondered the shape-shifter's motives, that portion of his brain that constantly counted and calculated registered that they had descended precisely ten levels. Almost unconsciously, Quark braced for the turbolift car's change of direction as it would begin to move laterally along one of the station's spokes.

But the direction didn't change. The car kept descending past the level of the docking ring.

Quark began to feel again the clammy touch of panic. Up till now, he had been operating under the assumption that there was something these three Cardassians—and *she,* whoever *she* was—wanted him to do. The fact that they wanted anything at all meant, reassuringly, that he was in the middle of a business transaction. And when it came to business, Quark knew he was definitely fighting on home soil.

But now, once again, he was heading into unknown territory. As far as he knew, the lower core of the station was the site of the fusion reactors, the power transfer manifolds and basic utilities, and its few residence levels were little more than prison cells for Bajoran ore workers. It was a realm for engineers, not business people. Even worse, he was not aware of *any* docking ports off the lower levels. The only way out of the lower core would be back up through the turbolift shafts.

Or through an emergency airlock, he thought queasily.

Quark moaned as he realized the trap he was entering. Then moaned again when he realized he had been so thrown off-balance by the lift car's continued descent that he had actually lost count of the levels they had passed. And every fool knew that a Ferengi who lost count had lost everything.

The two phaser-armed Cardassians continued to stare at him, their weapons held loosely at their sides as if daring him to break the rules and talk. But, finally, Turbolift 5 reached its destination.

The stop was so sudden, Quark felt the car rise back up a few centimeters as if it had overshot the desired deck. Then the doors opened.

The level beyond the open doors was so dark, it looked to Quark like the void of space itself.

But the Cardassian leader in the torn blue tunic pushed him forward anyway, and Odo at his side, even before a welcome pool of light from a palm torch sprang to life ahead of them.

"Straight ahead," the Cardassian leader ordered.

Quark limped on, as told. Adding to his resentful discomfort now was the fact that the deck plates on this lower level weren't covered by any type of carpet. They were just bare hull metal as far as he could tell. And since the station's lower core was terraced like a towering cake built upside down, Quark realized with a sinking feeling it was entirely possible that boundless space was really only a few centimeters below his feet.

But then, why are the deck plates so hot? he wondered.

He decided he absolutely hated Terok Nor. He'd be glad to leave it.

Alive, he added quickly, in case the Blessed Exchequer or any of his Exalted Tellers happened to be listening in.

The long, curving corridor on this level was narrower than others on the station. The ceiling lower. And except for a pale patch of light which Quark was just now beginning to perceive ahead, it seemed that none of the emergency glowpanels was functioning down here.

The spot of light from the palm torch kept skittering ahead, leading the way. On either side it was too gloomy for Quark to make out the Cardassian directional and warning signs on the bulkheads, but every few meters he passed an inner door. Some of these were open, with total darkness beyond.

If I *were Odo,* Quark thought darkly, *I'd be through one of those doors so fast the light from the palm torch couldn't catch me.*

But most inexplicably, the shape-shifter remained at Quark's side, even letting the Ferengi's injured foot set the pace.

Finally, just as Quark feared he would fall to the floor in exhaustion, the Cardassian leader ordered them to turn right at the next intersection. It was a *cul-de-sac,* where Quark would normally expect to find a turbolift. But instead, he halted before three more Cardassians, all females this time. Two were in soldier's armor, crisp, unmarked, the composite surfaces gleaming in the way Quark had come to recognize only the most elite Cardassian units were able to maintain. And despite the cold level of threat the two uniformed females presented, there was no doubt in Quark as to which female his three captors served.

She was the one in the middle, the only one in a matte-black civilian outfit that clung, Quark appreciatively noted, to the ridges of her spinal cords like a second skin.

"This is the only Ferengi on the station." Surprisingly, it was not the Cardassian in the torn blue tunic who was the first to address the female. It was the bald Cardassian with the tricorder. But in any case, Quark knew they were now in the presence of the real leader of the entire group, male and female—*She.*

The female leader studied Quark as if he were livestock at an auction. Quark straightened up, smirking engagingly, but her widely spaced dark eyes turned to Odo. "Why is that here?"

The bald Cardassian's reply was instant. "I thought we could use him as a backup. He can take on the shape of a Ferengi."

Quark's evaluation of the female shot up in value with her skeptical response. "But can he take on the *brain* of a Ferengi?"

"Terrell," the bald Cardassian said deferentially, "with respect, we are running out of options. Dukat has left. The station will be under Bajoran control in hours."

Terrell frowned as she hunted for something in the engineer's case she wore at the side of her wide belt. "Unlikely. In fifty-three minutes, the station will be a debris field and navigational hazard. Dukat activated the self-destruct." She removed a palm phaser and without a moment's pause shot Odo.

The constable grunted and slumped to his knees, gasping painfully for breath. But to Quark's intense relief, Odo was only lightly stunned.

Terrell lowered her palm phaser and glared at the bald Cardassian. "Atrig, that thing is a *shape-shifter.* It could have escaped you whenever it chose. The fact that it didn't suggests it was spying on us."

The bald Cardassian's reaction to his leader's admonition was most revealing to Quark. It was definitely not that of a soldier. The Cardassian in the gray tunic merely clenched his teeth, glanced down, embarrassed more than anything else. Definitely not the response of a soldier. Quark's fuschia-rimmed eyes narrowed in speculation. If these two had come into his bar as customers, Quark would have instantly concluded that Atrig, Terrell's bald subordinate, was desperately in love with his superior, while Terrell considered Atrig as nothing more than a useful tool she might carry in her case.

"Of course," the bald Cardassian said, in almost a whisper, his head still respectfully lowered.

Terrell dropped the small phaser back into her case. "Just see you keep it stunned in case we do need it." Then she turned her attention to Quark. "*You* will perform a service for the Cardassian Union. If you succeed, you will have time to reach an escape pod before the station self-destructs. If you fail . . . ." Her smile was cruel.

Quark looked questioningly at Atrig. Atrig understood. "Now you can talk."

"What kind of service?" Quark demanded. *Let the negotiations begin,* he thought.

"A simple one." Terrell turned her back to him and faced a blank bulkhead. Though he couldn't see exactly what she was doing, Quark could tell she was operating some kind of small device, for the bulkhead began to move to one side, revealing an extension of the corridor.

Quark's first reaction was one of true surprise. His second was of true apprehension. Over the years he had mapped every hidden section of the station, to establish his network of smugglers' tunnels— but here was a corridor extension completely unknown to him. And beyond it, there was a light source, about ten meters past the bulkhead.

Quirk squinted at the light. It appeared to be emanating from a door whose center glowed pale pink.

"What's in there?" Quark asked nervously.

Terrell turned back to him. "Nothing for a Ferengi to fear." Then she nodded, and Quark felt himself pushed forward, toward the light, a phaser jammed between his shoulder blades.

Halfway to the door, he heard a sudden commotion behind him, then phaser fire. *Odo.* The constable must have tried to make his escape, and not been fast enough.

Quark chanced glancing over his shoulder and did a relieved double take. Odo was still staggering along behind him, supported by the Cardassian in the torn blue tunic.

But now the two armor-clad female Cardassians held a third stunned captive.

Garak.

The Cardassian tailor was no longer in the strange uniform Quark had been unable to identify, but was back in his usual civilian garb. Quark didn't stop to question the change. He had always suspected that Garak wasn't the plain, simple tailor he made himself out to be. All Cardassians were masters of conspiracy, duplicity, and deviousness. The only remaining mystery for Quark was how the contentious aliens had managed to occupy Bajor as a cohesive force for as long as they had.

Atrig grabbed Quark's shoulder, forcing him to a stop three meters from the glowing door.

Correction, Quark thought. The door wasn't just glowing. It was *pulsating.* The effect was difficult to define precisely, but to Quark it seemed as if the door alternately bulged out and relaxed in, as if it were the flank of some large creature slowly breathing. The glow intensified with each intake of breath, changing from rose-pink to dark red, and Quark saw now that the light it created wasn't uniform. Instead, the vertical surface rippled outward, like a rock-disturbed pool of water standing on its side.

But that shimmering surface wasn't liquid, Quark knew. It was a solid layer protecting those on the outside from something that these six Cardassians didn't want to face—or *couldn't.*

Yet for some reason, they believed a Ferengi could.

But why? Quark thought, even now still trying to find an angle to exploit. If whatever was causing the door to ripple and glow was some deadly form of radiation, the Cardassians could have captured anyone to . . . to do whatever it was they wanted done. It was a well-known fact to everyone on the station that no Cardassian officer would hesitate to order a fellow Cardassian soldier to face death.

So why do they need a Ferengi? And only a Ferengi?

"Garak," Terrell said with sarcastic condescension. "I don't know which surprises me more. That you haven't left the station already. Or that Dukat left you alive."

Quark looked back to see Terrell standing before Garak. The tailor's sagging body was held upright by the two female soldiers, each holding an arm. Garak shook his head as if to clear it.

"I was merely trying to warn you," the tailor said faintly. "I believe that Gul Dukat may have failed to inform you that for some reason the station's self-destruct system has been inadvertently activated. You should leave as quickly as possible."

Terrell patted the tailor's cheek. "Why, Garak, how noble of you."

"Terrell, my dear, given all that we mean to each other, I feel I owe it to you."

Interesting, Quark thought.

"And I owe you. So much."

Quark shivered at the unpleasant edge to Terrell's cool voice.

Garak merely nodded as he glanced at the glowing door. In the rose-colored light, his gray Cardassian skin took on an almost sickening, raw-meat color. "Well, I can see you're busy. So I'll be on my way."

"You'll leave with me, Garak. Interrogating you will help pass the time on the way back home." Now Terrell's voice was openly menacing.

Garak's careful civility gave way to cold rage. "You know I cannot go back to Cardassia."

"I do know," Terrell said. "That's why I'll execute you myself before we arrive." Then she turned toward the glowing door, her back to the Cardassian tailor as if he no longer existed.

Quark's eyes followed her movement to the door. He alone of the observers gasped at the change. It was as if Terrell now faced a vortex of glowing magma, blazing with light, yet producing no heat. Pulsating coils of red light snaked out from the rapidly deforming surface of the door. Some tendrils seemed almost ready to break free of the surface, as if whatever lay beyond was increasing its efforts to escape confinement.

Quark felt himself pushed forward again by the bald Cardassian.

"Terrell," Quark squeaked, his voice breaking in its urgency. "I'm going to need some information." More than anything else, he longed to run home. But he knew that wasn't possible. Perhaps he'd never see Ferenginar again. "What in the name of all that's profitable is in there?"

"A lab," Terrell said tersely. "What you're seeing is merely a holographic illusion. A new type of holosuite technology."

Quark couldn't be certain of the truth. He couldn't see any holoemitters in this hidden section of corridor. But then, they could be installed behind the illusion. Maybe—

Don't be a fool, Quark told himself.

Whatever was responsible for the phenomenon before him, it

wasn't an illusion, and it *was* dangerous. There was no other reason for him to be here.

"So what do I have to do?" Quark asked.

"Go into the lab—"

Quark couldn't help himself. *"Through that thing?! You're crazy!"* He flinched as Atrig shoved a phaser into his back. "My mistake," he croaked.

"We will open the door," Terrell continued. "You will go inside the lab, ignoring everything you hear, everything you see, except for the main lab console on the far wall."

"Everything I *hear?*" Quark asked, his voice trailing off as his imagination got the best of him.

Terrell ignored his apprehension. "On the main console, you'll see a . . . power unit. A . . . type of power crystal. Sixty-eight centimeters tall. Twenty-five wide at its top and bottom. Spindle-shaped. You can't miss it."

The corridor fell into momentary darkness as the door heaved inward.

"And you want me to bring it out," Quark said weakly.

Terrell nodded at him. "Very perceptive. It's in an open housing. Simply disconnect two power leads to detach it from the console, then carry the crystal out. As soon as you do . . . you'll be free to go."

Her very unconvincing smile confirmed the situation for Quark. He instantly knew that if he did succeed in retrieving the crystal from the lab, a minute later he'd be as dead as if he were still dangling at the end of an ODN cable on the Promenade.

Quark's agile mind raced to identify the loopholes in this transaction.

But he had run out of time.

"Open the door," Terrell ordered.

At once, the Cardassian with the torn blue tunic moved to place himself alongside the pulsating door, one arm stretched out before him. With one trembling hand, Quark shielded his eyes from the increasing red glare to see what the Cardassian was trying to do.

At the edge of distortion effect, Quark saw a door control. The Cardassian in blue touched it gingerly.

Incredibly, the door seemed to melt to one side, and Quark squinted as the light level reached an almost painful intensity.

"—YES—"

Startled, Quark looked around, trying to see who had just cried out.

It was Odo.

"YES! YES, I UNDERSTAND!" Odo shouted. He struggled in the grip of the Cardassian in the new brown tunic, the Cardassian who Quark suspected was either a soldier, a coward, a spy. *"I WILL—"* Odo screamed. Then the shape-shifter began to reach out his arms, stretching away from his captor toward the bloodred light of the lab.

"Stop him!" Terrell commanded.

Instantly, Atrig stunned Odo again and the shape-shifter slumped, as his semiconscious body slowly assumed its humanoid shape once more.

"What happened?" Quark demanded.

"You didn't hear them?" Terrell asked in return. "The voices calling?"

"What voices?"

Terrell's face blazed with reflected crimson light. "You'll do fine," she said. "Go! Now!"

Pushed relentlessly forward by Atrig, Quark swayed before the open doorway. He could see nothing in the lab except a swirl of light, a whirlpool of luminescence.

"Hurry!" Terrell shouted.

And then the light swirls fragmented before Quark, becoming writhing tendrils that seemed to reach out for him and—

"TERRELL!"

This time the outcry came from Atrig, as the bald Cardassian leaped through the air to meet the coil of light heading directly for the woman he loved. The light hit Atrig square in the back, hurling him across the corridor as if a battering ram had struck him.

Atrig's limp form crumpled to the deck, a glowing patch of carmine light flickering over him.

Quark ducked as two more tentacles of flame-red energy snapped out from the doorway. Beneath the crackle of their passage, he heard hideous screams. Saw the Cardassian in blue and the other in brown lifted up from the deck, wrapped in red light.

Their cries became muffled as the scarlet glow spread over them, flowing around them like a hungry wave. Then, horribly, slowly, their wildly flailing arms and legs ceased their struggle, as if the light itself were somehow thick and resistant.

Forgetting for a moment that Atrig no longer was behind him to prevent his escape, Quark stared at the faces of the two trapped Cardassians. Their gaping mouths were stretched in soundless wails. And then, like a plasma whip being cracked, the two were sucked back into the vortex of light, disappearing in an instant.

Odo—now held by no one—knelt on the deck and looked back at the light. Quark could see him silently mouth a single word, over and over—*Yes . . . yes . . . yes. . . .*

The two female soldiers still held on to Garak, showing no fear, but clearly ready to leave as soon as they were ordered.

Quark turned to flee, but Terrell blocked his way. Her palm phaser was aimed directly at his head. *"Hurry!"*

Quark stared at Terrell. It was madness to do what she wanted. It was guaranteed suicide. But as much as he hated to admit it, if he didn't do as she ordered, then that fool Odo would be on his feet and stumbling forward in Quark's place, into something that for some unknown reason the Cardassians believed only a Ferengi could survive.

Quark told himself it wasn't respect he felt for Odo. It was just that after so many years of being adversaries, he knew how the shape-shifter thought, knew his strategies. And most importantly, Quark thought, he knew how much *he* could get away with. And for some inexplicable reason, the shape-shifter had stayed at his side all the way from the Promenade, when he could have escaped and left Quark to his fate—alone.

Quark's chest swelled out as he drew in a deep breath. As the old Ferengi saying had it, Better the Auditor you know, than the Auditor you don't. *Sometimes,* he told himself, *you just have to sign the contract you negotiated.*

"Now!" Terrell ordered.

Quark released his breath in a mighty sigh, covered his head with his arms, and ran straight through the doorway into the blinding red light and—

—his cut and bleeding foot suddenly sank into a soft sludge of cooling mud.

It was raining. A soft mist, really.

Quark stood completely still, eyes tightly shut.

The air was sweetly perfumed with the fetid rot of a swamp.

The swamp.

Quark lowered his arms from his head. Opened one eye. Then the other. And then he gasped as through the dark silhouettes of reaching branches and hanging moss, he saw the soft and welcoming lights of the Ferenginar capital city shining through the distance and the dark of night.

"Home . . ." he cried, delighting in the magical way the word created a delicate puff of mist before him.

But Quark was no believer in magic. He needed to know how it was he could see his breath as a delicate puff of mist. There had to be another source of light nearby.

He looked around trying to figure out where the lab had gone, where Terok Nor had gone, if he had finally died.

But all questions were erased as he saw a sparkle of blue-white brilliance approaching through the swamp trees, as if a living diamond were floating toward him.

Quark was completely overcome by the beauty of the spectacle. He stood transfixed until . . .

"Quark? Is that you, son?"

Quark's mouth dropped open in incredulity. "Moogie?"

"Over here, Quark. . . ."

Quark shifted in the mud of his homeworld, and suddenly the glittering diamond was before him, held in his beloved mother's arms.

"Why didn't you tell me you were coming home," Quark's mother said crankily. "I would have made your favorite *mooshk.*"

Quark's mouth watered at the intense memory of his moogie's *mooshk.* And to see her right now, glowing as if she were a part of the crystal she held, her completely unclothed skin faceted with light.

"So the only thing I have to give you is *this,*" Quark's mother said. She held out the glittering jewel to him, until it seemed to float by itself, a shining, hourglass-shaped orb of promise and hope and everything anyone could ever want. "Go ahead, Quark. Take it. . . ."

Quark reached for the orb like a child reaching for a toy. Everything was going to be perfect now.

But as his hands closed on the object his mother was giving him, one tiny nagging thought came to him.

Small. Subtle. Barely worth mentioning.

Something that might occur only to a Ferengi.

"Moogie," Quark said. "Can I ask you a question?"

And as Quark's mother began her transformation, Quark shrieked louder than any Ferengi had ever shrieked, as he saw—

CHAPTER 2

—STARS FLASHED before Quark's eyes, and he slapped his hand to his expansive forehead, grimacing with pain.

"Who designed this *frinxing* bed . . ." he muttered, as he swung his feet over the edge of the narrow Cardassian sleeping ledge and tried once more to sit up, this time without banging his head on the underside of a utility shelf.

Then he looked around at the stark holding cell in Deep Space 9's Security Office and answered his own question.

"Cardassians. Ha!"

Quark had had it with Cardassians. In fact, even though the Cardassian Occupation had ended six long years ago, Quark had had it with this station. "Deep Space 9, Terok Nor . . . Federation bureaucrats, Cardassian secret police. . . . What's the difference? I ask you. . . ."

He stood in front of the holding cell's forcefield and checked to make certain the Security Office beyond was still empty. Though the lighting levels were low, set for DS9's night, the main door was still sealed and Quark remained safely alone. He cleared his throat. "Computer: Release the prisoner."

The security screen flashed with silver scintillations, then shut down. At least, it appeared to shut down. Quark wasn't a Ferengi to take anything for granted. He carefully flicked a finger toward the boundary of the forcefield, until he was certain the screen was off. Only then did he step over the lip of the cell doorway.

Quark trudged across the deck in his nightclothes, scratching where it itched. He came to the replicator, smacked his lips, then punched in his prisoner code for a cup of millipede juice, hold the shells. The cup appeared and Quark gulped the pale green bug squeezings down, looking around to check that he was still—

"Bzzzt—you're dead," Odo said, only one meter behind him.

Quark choked, then sprayed a mouthful of millipede juice, forcing Odo to step back out of range.

"Don't *do* that!" Quark sputtered indignantly, wiping bug juice off his sleep shirt.

Odo shook his head, not impressed. "Would you rather the Andorian sisters did that?"

Quark jammed the cup back into the replicator for recycling. "You're supposed to be protecting me. That's what this is, remember?" Quark waved his hands to include the entire security office. "Protective custody."

Odo pointed to the holding cell. "In there. Behind a forcefield. That's protective custody. Out here, you're fair game."

Quark rubbed at his temples, not knowing where the pain of his impact with the shelf left off, and his tension headache began. Twenty meters away, just across the Promenade, his bar was in the hands of Rom. *Engineer* Rom. Turned-his-back-on-everything-Ferengi, work-for-free, use-a-padd-to-total-all-bills, good-for-nothing *Rom*.

"Are you all right?" Odo asked.

"Do you care?"

Odo crossed his arms. "Not particularly."

Quark muttered a partially satisfying Ferengi epithet under his breath and looked around for a padd.

"Now what?" Odo asked

"I need something to read. Rom's driving me into bankruptcy and there's no way I can sleep."

"Actually, the bar has seldom been busier."

In a sudden wave of apprehension, Quark grabbed Odo's tunic. "He's cut prices, hasn't he? Go ahead, I can take it."

Odo firmly removed Quark's hands from his chest. "Rom is treating the customers fairly. Word must have gotten out, and so business is up. You should be happy."

Quark couldn't believe the foul language Odo was capable of using. " 'Fairly.' I'm . . . I'm ruined. I . . ." And then Quark could see no other way out. "All right, that's it. Protective custody is over. Thank you. I'm going to my—"

Odo didn't let him finish. And didn't let him leave. "It's not that simple, Quark."

Quark had been battling Odo for more than a decade. He knew what that tone meant. "What do you mean, not that simple? Being in here was my idea."

"It *was* your idea. Now, I'm afraid, it's mine."

Quark rocked back on his bare feet, studying Odo more closely in the dim light. "You *are* worried about me. I'm touched. But, I'm also running behind, so—"

Odo didn't move from Quark's path. "Please return to your cell."

Quark laughed derisively, smiled broadly. "Odo . . . you almost make it seem as if you're putting me under arrest."

Odo said nothing. He didn't have to.

"You can't be serious," Quark said. He knew his earlobes were flushing telltale red. "No, I take that back. You're always serious. What I meant was, you're joking. No, you don't do that, either. But what you *do* do is . . ." Quark's throat tightened. He couldn't bring himself to say the words.

Odo could. "Put people under arrest."

"For *what?!*" Quark demanded. His face creased in a disbelieving grin as he said the most outrageous thing he could think of. *"Murder?"*

But Odo's silence and unchanging expression made the grin fade.

Quark's head throbbed unbearably. "Odo, you know me. How many times do I have to say it? I did not kill Dal Nortron."

"That's right. I do know you, Quark. Which is why I don't believe that you planned and carried out the premeditated cold-blooded murder of your Andorian business partner."

Quark sagged with relief. "Well, at least we can . . ." He looked up at Odo with sudden fear. " 'Business partner'?"

"Did you honestly think you could keep it from me?"

"The Andorian sisters did it! *They* killed him!"

"And they say that *you* killed him. Imagine that."

"So you're arresting *me* on *their* word but you're not arresting *them* on *mine?!*"

Odo uncrossed his arms and shook his head. "Quark, we've been over this. If I arrest Satr and Leen while they are on DS9 as representatives of the Andorian government, they will file a diplomatic protest, I will have to release them, and I guarantee they will leave the station and my jurisdiction within the hour."

"Sure! Right! So that's why they can walk around the station free as a greeworm while I'm in here—"

"Where they can't get you."

"No!" Quark exploded. "Where *I* am under *arrest!*"

Odo looked away as if preparing to leave. Quark knew that was how the changeling preferred to solve most of his problems. By avoiding confrontation.

But then, Odo looked back at Quark, and there was almost an air of sorrow about him. "Quark, listen carefully. This time, you are in serious trouble. Two nights ago, Dal Nortron won a considerable amount of latinum from you."

"It happens, Odo," Quark said tightly. "That's why they call it gambling."

But Odo did not allow himself to be interrupted. "Two hours later, Dal Nortron died—"

"Of unknown causes!"

"Under mysterious circumstances. The latinum—gone."

"Odo, think about it. How long would I stay in business if I started killing everyone who won at my dabo table? Are you kidding? I give the winners presents! I give them unlimited holosuite sessions—even *free drinks!*" Quark shuddered at the thought of it. "I do whatever I can to get them to return to that table so I can win my latinum back. I don't kill customers!"

"Satr and Leen say you had an argument with Nortron."

Quark glared at the changeling. "I have arguments with you. And I haven't killed you. Yet."

"Quark—pay attention! If I hadn't put you in protective custody, the Andorians would have killed you for revenge. They see justice in rather more simplistic terms than I do."

Now the sorrow was Quark's, as well. "Justice? So you do think I'm a murderer."

Odo reluctantly confirmed Quark's conclusion. "There is the matter of Kozak—"

"Kozak?! That was almost four years ago. *And* it was an accident!"

"Exactly," Odo agreed. "As I said, I do not believe you *planned* to kill Dal Nortron. But accidents do happen. Especially in the heat of an argument between business partners."

Quark swung his hand at Odo as if trying to clear the air. "Why don't you just string me up on the Promenade and be—" He stopped speaking, suddenly overwhelmed by a powerful sense of *déjà vu*.

A few moments of Quark staring blankly into space was apparently all Odo could take. "Quark—?"

"I was . . . having a dream. Just before I woke up. Hit my head." Quark rubbed at his forehead again. The pain seemed diminished. He let his fingers trail to his throat and ran them lightly across his larynx, as if expecting to find rope burns there. "They were hanging me. . . ."

Odo frowned. "Guilty conscience?" Quark knew he'd get nowhere arguing this any longer with Odo. He started back for his cell.

"We still have a few things to discuss," Odo said. "I will need to know the details of your . . . 'business arrangement' with Dal Nortron."

Quark stepped over the lip of the cell. "Talk to my lawyer."

"You don't have a lawyer."

Quark shrugged. "Then I guess we have nothing to discuss until I do get one. Computer: Restore security field."

The air between Quark and Odo flashed with silver sparkles.

"Quark, don't make this more difficult than it has to be."

But by this point, Quark didn't care about making anything easier, especially not for Odo. "When is Captain Sisko back?"

"Tomorrow afternoon. If they don't run into any Jem'Hadar patrols." Odo's stern attitude softened. "That captain they were trying to rescue . . . she was dead."

"I suppose you think I killed her."

"She had been dead for three years. Apparently, an energy field around the planet she'd crashed on shifted the subspace signals through time."

"Odo, let's get our priorities straight. What does any of this have to do with me?"

"Please forgive me," Odo said icily. "I forgot with whom I was dealing. Pleasant dreams, Quark."

Odo turned like a soldier on parade and marched toward his office.

He had just reached the doorway when Quark called out to him. "Odo, wait."

Odo stopped, but didn't look back.

"Can I ask you something?"

Odo looked over his shoulder. "You can *ask.*"

Quark held his hand to his throat again, trying to recapture the elusive threads of his half-forgotten dream. "Those last few days on the station . . ."

"What last few days?"

"The end of the Occupation. When the Cardassians withdrew."

"What about them?"

"The Cardassians never liked me."

Odo turned back to face Quark. "Can you blame them?"

Quark struggled to find the words for what he knew he had to ask. "They destroyed so many things on the station . . . four Bajorans dead . . ."

"Your point, Quark?"

"Why didn't they kill *me?* I mean, that's what happens when governments fall. People like me are lined up and . . ."

"Shot?"

Quark saw an image of Ferenginar's capital city. He was there, doing something important in . . . in a swamp? "Hung," Quark said quietly. "Strung up on . . . on the Promenade . . . ?"

"Sounds almost . . . poetic," Odo said.

Quark stared at Odo, saw the glimmer of recognition in the changeling's eyes. "You've said that before. Or something like that. I can see it. I can remember it."

And then something went dark in Odo. "I don't know what you're talking about."

"Yes, you do," Quark said.

"I'll tell Rom you want a lawyer. When you're willing to talk about your business arrangement with Dal Nortron, we can talk again." Odo turned to leave.

"Where were you on the Day of Withdrawal?" Quark called after him. "You answer that and I'll tell you *everything* about Dal Nortron!"

Quark saw Odo hesitate. "Come on, Odo, admit it. There's only one way you can resist an offer like that."

The hesitation ended. Without another word, Odo disappeared through the doorway to his office. He *had* resisted.

And to Quark, that could mean only one thing.

Odo didn't remember what had happened to him on the Day of Withdrawal, any more than Quark did. . . .

CHAPTER 3

Lieutenant Commander Jadzia Dax stood on the deck of the *Starship Enterprise* with her back to the captain's chair. Because it was the first *Enterprise,* there was only one direction from which the final attack could come.

The turbolift.

Five minutes ago, when she had hurriedly studied the ship's schematics on the desktop viewer in the briefing room, she had found it difficult to believe that the most critical command center on the entire ship was serviced by only one lift. But in the memories of her third host, Emony, she found the explanation. The more than century-old *Constitution*-class to which the original *Enterprise* belonged had been designed primarily as a vessel of scientific exploration. The engineers of the twenty-fourth century might perceive its design idiosyncrasies, such as a single turbolift serving the bridge or fixed-phaser emitters, as design flaws. Dax's third host, however, considered such features to be the last echoes of the twenty-second century's charmingly naïve optimism toward space travel, inspired by the end of the Romulan Wars and the resulting birth of the Federation a mere two years later.

As a joined Trill possessing the memories of eight lifetimes, more or less spanning the past two centuries, Jadzia Dax understood she was more attuned than most beings to the similarities of every age. And the truth was that while technology might change, human hearts and minds seldom did. It definitely wasn't the case that life was simpler or human nature less sophisticated in the past.

But in the case of this ship, Jadzia couldn't help thinking, *the designers were behind the curve. They really should have known better.* After all, the first *Enterprise* had been launched a full twenty-seven years after the first contact with the Klingon Empire, a disastrous meeting that clearly proved that not everyone in the quadrant shared the Federation's belief in coexistence. And right now, the proof of that was about to face her in a life-or-death confrontation.

Jadzia heard the distant rush of a turbolift car approaching the bridge. She hefted the sword in her hand and with one quick step vaulted over the stairs to the upper deck of the bridge. She reflexively tugged down on the ridiculously short skirt of her blue sciences uniform, changing her balance to be prepared to spring forward the instant the doors opened. *If,* that is, she *could* spring forward in the awkward, knee-height, high-heeled black boots that were also part of her uniform.

The turbolift stopped. She held her breath as she faced the doors with only one thought in her mind . . . *Klingons—can't live with them, can't—*

The red doors slid open. The lift was empty! Then a sudden crash made her spin to see a violently dislodged wall panel beside the main viewer fly into the center well of the bridge. The wall panel had covered the opening of an emergency-access tunnel, and now from its darkness emerged her enemy, resplendent in the glittering antique uniform of the Imperial Navy, a blood-dripping *bat'leth* held aloft, ready for use again.

Jadzia straightened up, unimpressed. "Worf, that wasn't on the schematics."

Lieutenant Commander Worf leaped down from the upper deck and moved warily around the central helm console, eyes afire. "I am not Worf. I am Kang, captain of the *Thousand-Taloned Death.* And you are my prey!"

Worf lunged past the elevated captain's chair, swinging for Jadzia's legs with a savage upsweep of his *bat'leth.*

Jadzia expertly deflected the ascending crescent blade with her sword as she flipped through the air to land behind the safety railing that ringed the upper deck to her right. Although he had missed his target, Worf's momentum forced him to continue his spin until his *bat'leth* plunged deep into the captain's chair behind him, shorting the communications relays in its shattered arm and causing a spectacular burst of sparks to shoot into the air.

"Worf, I'm serious," Jadzia complained testily. "I was just in the briefing room. I specifically called up the bridge schematics."

Worf grunted as he struggled to tug his weapon free of the chair. "You should not be talking. You should be running for your life."

He turned away from her to give the stubborn *bat'leth* one final pull.

Jadzia saw her opportunity and took it. She leaned over the railing and swatted Worf's backside with the flat of her sword.

Worf wheeled around in shock. "That was *not* a deathblow!"

"I said, I checked the schematics. There *is* no emergency tunnel beside the viewscreen. You're cheating."

Worf flashed a triumphant grin at her, his weapon finally free. "If you did not see the tunnel on the deck plans, it means you did not use the proper command codes to access them. To the computer, you might have been an enemy, and so you were not shown the correct configuration."

"What?!"

"Defend yourself!" Worf shouted. He swung down to slice the safety railing in two, directly in front of Jadzia.

But Jadzia lashed out with her boot to slam Worf on the side of his head, at the same time she swung her sword against his *bat'leth* to send it spinning out of his grip to shatter the holographic viewer on Mr. Spock's science station.

"You never told me about needing command codes!" she protested.

Worf put one huge hand to the side of his head, looked at the pink blood on his fingers, flared his nostrils in what Jadzia, sighing, knew all too well was a sign of intense pleasure. There was nothing a Klingon liked better than a caring, loving mate who knew how to play rough. "You did not ask," he said, breathing hard, then leaped over the twisted railing to land heavily on the upper deck two meters from Jadzia.

"You're not playing fair," Jadzia told him.

Worf shot a glance upward at the center of the bridge's domed ceiling. "That is not the opinion of the Beta Entity," he growled.

Jadzia risked a sudden look at the ceiling as well. It was maddening to admit, but Worf was right. The amorphous energy beast that fed on the psychic energy of hatred and conflict grew brighter as she watched.

Worf took a step closer. Jadzia took a step back.

"Do not attempt to delay the inevitable. Escape is impossible."

Jadzia stood her ground, raised her sword. "Who said I wanted to escape?"

Worf took another step, arms reaching out to either side, eyes absolutely fixed on his quarry. "Ah, knowing you must lose, you choose to attempt to take your enemy with you. The w'Han Do. A warrior's strategy." Worf threw back his massive head and roared approvingly.

"Even better, I have no intention of losing, either." Then Jadzia slashed her sword back and forth in an intricate display of k'Thatic ritual disembowelment that had taken her past host Audrid more than eight years to master, and finished the motion by unexpectedly launching the sword across the bridge, where it crashed into an auxiliary life-support station.

Worf, who had been transfixed by Jadzia's dazzling swordplay, appeared shocked by what could only have been a careless mistake. He stared at her sword as it twanged back and forth in a shower of sparks from a shattered display screen.

The diversion worked exactly as Jadzia had planned it. As Worf puzzled over the sword, she slammed into him, shoulder first, elbow in the stomach, driving him back until he collided with a station chair and pitched backward, falling flat on his back.

In an instant, Jadzia was astride him, hands raised, fingers scooped in the strike position for a Romulan deeth mok blow to crush the larynx.

Worf fought for breath, the air in his lungs knocked out of him by the violence of his impact. The sweat and blood that covered his face gleamed as the energy beast pulsated above them.

". . . You can not defeat a Klingon with a pitiful deeth mok . . ." Worf wheezed defiantly.

"There's more than one way to skin a Klingon," Jadzia said.

Worf's eyes widened in alarm at the thought—and also, Jadzia thought, more than a touch of anticipatory excitement.

And then she swiftly brought both hands down to the sides of Worf's enormous ribcage and—

Worf howled with laughter. He frantically wriggled under Jadzia, ineffectually trying to slap her hands away as he gasped for breath.

"Give up?" Jadzia asked.

Worf's eyes teared as he snorted, "I will not surrender! I am Kang!"

"Ha! I knew Kang," Jadzia said as she dug in, effortlessly repelling his futile attempts to stop her. "Kang was a friend of mine. And *you* are no Kang!"

By now, Worf was totally incapable of speech. Any intelligent sound he attempted to make was overwhelmed by convulsive laughter.

Jadzia went for the kill. "Say *'rumtag,'* " she demanded as she drove home her attack, running her fingers over Worf's ribs at warp nine. "Say it!"

The word erupted from Worf like a volcanic explosion. *"Rumtag! Rumtag!"*

With a whoop of victory, Jadzia rolled off her husband and stretched out on the floor beside him, holding her head up on one elbow as she watched him struggle to catch his breath and regain his dignity.

His pitiful attempt to glare at her as he said, "You tickled me" made even Worf burst out laughing again. After a few more aborted tries, he took a deep breath and blurted out, suddenly deeply serious, "Now we are both in danger."

"Something else you didn't tell me?" Jadzia asked lightly.

She was suddenly aware of the light from the Beta Entity getting brighter, and then the creature was all around them both. She felt a mild electrical tingle over her body and tugged down on her short skirt again. Then the light winked out as the energy creature disappeared.

"What happens next?" she asked, more curious than alarmed.

Worf took an even deeper breath, in an obvious attempt to restore his warrior's concentration. "Nothing. We are both . . ." He fought to stifle an incipient giggle. ". . . dead." He snorted again and rubbed his ribcage.

"Say that again."

"The Beta Entity was not pleased with the change in our emotional mood. Thus, it enveloped us and drained us of our life energy."

Jadzia screwed up her face in confusion. "That's not right. I studied this mission at the Academy. The energy creature that captured Kirk and Kang and made their crews keep fighting to the death on the *Enterprise* fed on hate. When Kirk convinced everyone to stop fighting and to laugh, to express joyful emotions, the creature didn't kill anyone. It just . . . left."

Worf had finally regained his appropriately stern expression. "This is the Klingon version of the holosimulation. And besides, it was Kang who convinced the others to stop fighting."

Jadzia raised an eyebrow and playfully placed a single finger against Worf's side. "It was who?"

Worf smiled. "It was . . . your *rumtag!*" And then he was on her, running his fingers up and down her sides, until this time it was Jadzia who was reduced to helpless laughter.

Finally, exhausted, breathless, they both collapsed together on the lip of the upper deck, Jadzia sitting up, leaning against Worf's broad chest, Worf's fingers gently untangling the intricate weaving of her twenty-third-century hairstyle.

The bridge of the *Enterprise* was silent, filled with a soft haze colorfully lit by the shifting display screens that ringed the Trill and the Klingon, a ship out of time.

"It's almost romantic," Jadzia said softly, sighing. She remembered being on this same bridge—in reality—when she and Captain Sisko had taken a trip into the past. She thought of the legendary Spock again, how close she had actually come to him. She sighed again.

Worf ran a finger along the spots that trailed from her temple. "Perhaps we should return to our quarters."

Jadzia looked up at Worf and smiled teasingly. "Actually, I was thinking that maybe we could slip down to the captain's quarters. Imagine—James T. Kirk's bedroom. Think of the history."

Worf frowned. "I would rather not. Besides, we only have the holosuite for another five minutes."

Jadzia considered the possibilities of the bridge for a moment, but five minutes was more of a challenge than she was in the mood for right now. She ran a finger along Worf's sexily rippled brow.

"There's an arboretum a few decks down. Call Quark and book another hour."

"That is not possible, Jadzia. Odo has requested all the holosuites beginning at oh-seven hundred."

"All of them?" Jadzia sat up, away from Worf. "He's having a party and he didn't invite us?"

"It is for his investigation of the Andorian's murder."

"Ahh," Jadzia said, understanding. Once highly detailed scans had been made of crime scenes, they could be flawlessly recreated with holotechnology, and the computers could be used to call out various anomalies with great precision. "Does he have any new leads?"

Worf blinked at his wife. "Why would he need new ones?"

It took a moment for Jadzia to realize what Worf was actually saying. "Worf, Quark didn't kill the Andorian."

"All the evidence points to him."

"All the *circumstantial* evidence."

Worf got to his feet. "It is my understanding that the evidence is more than circumstantial." He adjusted his old-fashioned gold-fabric sash, then turned in the direction of the turbolift.

Jadzia jumped to her feet and grabbed his arm to stop him. "Not so fast, Kang." She forced her groom to turn to face her. "What evidence does Odo have?"

Worf rolled his eyes, replying like a five-year-old asked to recite logarithmic tables. "The Andorian businessman—"

"Dal Nortron," Jadzia said. "Let's concentrate on the facts."

"The Andorian businessman, *Dal Nortron,* arrived on DS9 last Sunday afternoon. Sunday evening, he won more than 100 bars of—"

"One hundred twenty-two bars."

Worf glowered at Jadzia. "One-hundred *twenty-two* bars of gold-pressed latinum—after *three consecutive wins* at dabo. That fact alone is enough to suggest that Quark had arranged to pay off the Andorian—Dal Nortron—through rigged winnings."

"Dabo's a popular game in this quadrant. There are two documented cases of gamblers winning seven consecutive dabos, which is within the statistical realm of probability."

"Not at Quark's," Worf said.

"Come on, Worf. Odo inspects the table every week. Quark doesn't rig it."

Worf let his opinion be known with a grunt.

Jadzia shrugged. "Go on."

"Two hours after Nortron left Quark's, he was found dead, and the latinum was missing."

"Stop right there. There's no logic to what you're saying." Jadzia waited for Worf to interrupt, surprised when he didn't. "If Quark had arranged to pay off Nortron with rigged dabo winnings, then why would he *kill* Nortron to get those winnings back?"

Worf shifted his considerable weight from one foot to the other. "Perhaps Nortron took advantage of the table once too often. Perhaps Quark wanted people to think he had settled a debt to Nortron and planned, when he had done so, *to* steal back his latinum. Perhaps he did not like the way Nortron was dressed."

"Oh well, now, that is motivation for murder."

"Jadzia, Quark is a Ferengi. Ferengi do not think the way other civilized beings do."

Even though Worf's sternly delivered pronouncement told Jadzia that her new husband was reaching the limits of his patience, she persisted. "Worf—this is the twenty-fourth century! That kind of stereotype belongs in the dark ages."

"The Andorian was found dead near the reactor cores in the lower levels. Security monitoring is limited there. Who else would know that better than Quark?"

"*You,* for one. Maybe we should suspect you. That makes about as much sense as suspecting Quark."

Clearly upset by her lack of wifely loyalty, Worf glowered at Jadzia. "I am DS9's strategic operations officer. It is my job to know the station's security weaknesses—just as it is in Quark's interest to know them because of his long involvement in smuggling operations."

Jadzia softened her tone and affectionately reached up to straighten Worf's sash. "There's a difference between smuggling and murder, Worf. Especially since some of Quark's smuggling operations benefited the Bajoran resistance as well as the Federation."

Mollified only slightly by her touch, Worf regarded her gravely. "He cares only for profit."

"Granted. But not enough to kill for it."

Worf brushed aside Jadzia's hand. "This conversation is useless.

You have not listened to me at all. You have already made up your mind about the Ferengi's innocence."

"Me? How about you? You've already made up your mind he's guilty."

Worf stared at Jadzia as if he really didn't understand what she was talking about. "Of course I have. Because he is."

"Worf! We don't even know if it *was* a murder!"

Worf's heavy brow wrinkled, and Jadzia could see he was waging an internal debate. She decided that he knew something she didn't and was wondering if he should tell her. Jadzia decided to help him make the right decision. There were better ways to defeat a Klingon than through combat.

She stepped closer to him, slipping her hand beneath his sash this time. The old Klingon uniforms had no armor, and the thin cloth of his shirt did little to interfere with the contact of her flesh against his. "Worf . . ." she whispered into his ear, "I'm your wife. We have no secrets from each other, remember?" Then she bit his ear lobe. Hard.

Worf took a quick breath, then spoke quickly, as if he was worried that he would change his mind. "Odo showed me Dr. Bashir's preliminary autopsy report. Dal Nortron was killed by an energy-discharge weapon. Odo believes such a weapon would be too primitive to show up on the station's automatic scanning system."

"How primitive?" Jadzia asked, stilling her hand on his chest.

"Microwave radiation. Extremely intense. It . . . overheated every cell in his body. A weapon without honor."

Jadzia swiftly reviewed everything she knew about microwave radiation. In this case, it was her own experiences as a science specialist that took precedence over the memories of Dax's previous hosts.

Microwaves were part of the electromagnetic spectrum, one of at least seven energy spectrums known to exist in normal space-time. In pre-subspace, EM-based civilizations—that converged toward rating C-451–45018–3 on Richter's scale of culture—the primary applications of microwave radiation were line-of-sight radio communications and nonmetallic industrial welding, typically with some half-hearted attempts to create first-generation beamed-energy weapons. On Earth, it had even been used for cooking food. Primitive was not the word for it. Prehistoric was more like it, right alongside stone knives and bearskins.

Jadzia took her hand from Worf's chest, amused in spite of the situation to see her groom only then resume easy breathing. "Be reasonable, Worf. Why would Quark use an old-fashioned microwave weapon when he could have disintegrated Nortron with a phaser?"

Worf glanced over his shoulder at the turbolift doors, as if worried someone was about to join them. He took a step back from her. "Phaser residue can be detected for hours after a disintegration."

But Jadzia curled one finger under his gold sash to gently pull him back to her. "Who would have known he was missing?"

Worf smoothed his sash again, trying to dislodge Jadzia's grip. "Perhaps Quark didn't want to put the latinum at risk."

"So . . . stun Nortron, take the latinum, *then* disintegrate him."

"Just because I believe Quark is a criminal does not mean I believe he is a *smart* criminal. And would you please stop that!"

Jadzia was about to raise the stakes when she was interrupted by an announcement from hidden speakers.

"Ladies and gentlemen, boys and girls and morphs, this simulation will end in thirty seconds. Thank you for choosing Quark's for your entertainment needs. Be sure to inquire about our half-price drink specials for holosuite customers when you turn in your memory rods. Now, please gather your personal belongings and take small children by the appropriate grasping appendage. And remember, Quark's is not responsible for lost or stolen articles or for damage caused by micro-forcefield fluctuations. Five . . . four . . . three . . ."

The bridge of the *Enterprise* melted from around Jadzia and Worf, retreating back into history. Now they stood in a simple unadorned room, its lower walls studded with the glowing green emitters of a compact holoprojector system.

"Please exit through the doors to the rear of the holosuite, and thank you for visiting Quark's—the happiest place in the Bajoran Sector."

Jadzia and Worf exchanged a look of shared puzzlement.

"That voice sounded like Leeta," Jadzia said.

"I have heard that Rom is introducing new policies during Quark's . . . incarceration."

"If Rom is next in line for the bar, I'm surprised you haven't started suspecting him of setting up his brother."

The holosuite door slipped open to reveal Odo and two security officers.

"Commanders . . . I trust I'm not interrupting," the constable said.

"We have finished," Worf said brusquely. He started for the door.

"No, we haven't," Jadzia countered.

"I'm sorry," Odo said, "but I do require the holosuites for assembling—"

"That's not what I meant," Jadzia interrupted. "Odo, Worf told me that Dal Nortron died of exposure to microwave radiation."

Odo frowned. "That is privileged information. At least," he added gruffly as he looked at Worf, "it was."

"Worf was conferring with me—security operations officer to science officer."

Odo did not look convinced. But then, he rarely did. "Go on."

"A microwave weapon seems such an unlikely choice to commit a murder, I was wondering if there might be another explanation."

"I am open to suggestions."

"Well, if the body was found near the reactor levels, have you ruled out energy leaks or power modulations coming from the power transfer-conduit linkages?"

Odo blinked. "I was not aware that fusion power-conduits could generate microwave radiation."

Jadzia shrugged. "Not directly. But there's so much other equipment on those levels, a fusion power surge could set up rapid oscillations in various circuits. That's all you'd need to generate an electromagnetic field. And if the field was strong enough or close enough to something that might function as a waveguide, it could reach microwave levels."

Odo looked off to the side as if reprocessing the data she had just provided. "Could traces of such a field be detected after the fact?"

Jadzia ignored her husband's disapproving frown. "Absolutely. You'd need to examine everything in the area for magnetic realignment, heat damage, even signs of electrical sparking between conductive materials.

"Electrical?" Odo made a sound in the back of his throat, then nodded. "Very well. I'll send a forensics team down at once. If they find evidence of anomalous energy discharges, I'll let you know."

"And if they don't?" Jadzia asked.

Odo gave her a grim smile, as if he had successfully led her on.

"Then it will be additional evidence that the murder was committed with a microwave weapon."

Jadzia was surprised when Worf suddenly grunted. "Unless," he said, and Jadzia could sense his reluctance, "the Andorian was killed by an anomalous power discharge somewhere else on the station and his body taken to the lower levels to confuse the investigation."

Jadzia was pleased that Worf had offered some support for her theory, despite his conviction that the guilty party was already in custody.

But Odo rendered Worf's suggestion unnecessary. "We can rule that possibility out, Commander. I do have enough security tapes and computer logs to establish that Dal Nortron took a turbolift to the lower levels approximately twenty minutes before he was killed."

"Before he died," Jadzia corrected.

"He was murdered, Commander. Of that I have no doubt."

Jadzia ignored Odo's increasing air of formality. "Do your security tapes and computer logs show that anyone else was in that area at the same time?" she asked.

Odo's hesitation answered the question for her.

"I didn't think so," Jadzia said.

"There's no such thing as a perfect crime," Odo said bluntly. "I've already connected Quark to Nortron. They were involved in a business dealing together. They had a falling out. Quark killed him. Accidentally, more likely than not. But it is definitely murder."

Jadzia studied Odo closely. She had seldom heard such emotion in the changeling's voice. Almost as if he were personally involved in this case.

"Odo, did *you* know Dal Nortron?" Jadzia asked.

"Of course not. Why would you even ask such a thing?"

Eight lifetimes of experience told Jadzia she was on to something. "No reason. But I'd find someone who did know him," she said. "Someone who can tell you why he came to DS9, and why he went down to the lower levels."

Now it was Odo who was losing his patience. "To meet Quark."

"But your own records say Quark *wasn't* down there."

"Records can be altered, Commander."

Jadzia smiled sweetly. Now she had led *him* on. "Exactly. Altered to take someone out. Or to put someone in. And if the records can be altered so easily, Quark and Dal Nortron could have met *anywhere* on the station without you knowing about it. And if they could have met anywhere, why did they choose the lower levels?"

Odo exhaled in frustration, but said nothing.

Worf tugged on Jadzia's arm. "We should let the constable get on with his duties."

"What's down there?" Jadzia asked again as she left with her husband. "You answer that question, Odo, and you'll solve the crime."

Odo did not respond, but Jadzia didn't care.

Eight lifetimes of experience gave her the answer she knew the constable didn't want to admit.

Somehow, in some way, whatever had happened to Dal Nortron, Odo *was* involved.

And the answer to *that* mystery was somewhere in the lower levels.

CHAPTER 4

THEY WERE CALLED *tiyerta nok*—literally, the life-flow of iron, or as the current usage had it, the arteries of the machine.

That was the term the Cardassians gave to the engineering access tunnels that riddled their mining station: a complex network of barely passable crawl spaces supporting a web of ODN cables, power conduits, waste-, water-, and replicator-mass plumbing, and air-circulation channels. But as soon as Starfleet had taken control and Terok Nor became Deep Space 9, the *tiyerta nok* inevitably became known as Jefferies tubes, a term some said had its origins as far back as the very beginnings of starship design. Others said even further.

But unlike DS9's other Jefferies tubes—most of which by now had been retrofitted with new, Starfleet-standard lighting sources and ODN upgrades—the Jefferies tube on this lower level was dark, cramped, and cut off from the station's main air-flow system. Not a whisper of a breeze passed through it, and Jake Sisko blinked as steady drips of sweat rolled into his eyes.

"You're crazy," Nog said. "It'll never work."

Jake was flat on his back at the end of this particular *tiyerta nok*, lifting his cramped arms directly overhead to work on the panel set into the uncomfortably low, sloping ceiling. The much shorter Nog was crouched at Jake's feet, where the tunnel height was a bit more generous, keeping a palm torch on the panel above Jake and passing along tools as Jake requested them.

"Nog, it's perfect," Jake insisted. He wriggled a multispanner against the flathead mini-tagbolt he had finally loosened, and the second of three U-shaped clasps holding the egress panel in place dropped free, hitting him right between the eyes. "Oww!" It was more a cry of surprise than pain. "These things never used to be so tight."

"Some of the old Cardassian subsystems are self-repairing." Nog spoke with apparent disinterest, though he added with a chuckle, "Did that ever surprise the Chief when he finally figured out why some of *his* repairs kept reverting to Cardassian configurations. But anyway, the plan can't work, because there's no way you'll ever get past the ambassador's bodyguards."

Jake carefully put the multispanner down beside him and groped for the intergrips. Three more minis to go. "That's what the diversion's for. When the bodyguards go to help the dabo girls, we slip into the ambassador's quarters, take the latinum—"

"What?! You never said anything about stealing latinum!"

Jake moaned and lowered his strained arms to rest them. "Technically, we're not stealing it, Nog, we're only taking it to confuse Odo about the motive. And even if we *were* really stealing it, so what? We're murderers, remember? Cold-blooded and remorseless."

Jake squinted as Nog aimed the palm torch directly into his eyes. "Jake, my friend, you have to start getting out more. *We're* not murderers."

"Okay, okay. You know what I mean. Quark and Morn are the murderers."

Nog put down the palm torch, but even with the suddenly increased darkness Jake had no trouble sensing how annoyed his friend was. "I thought you said you couldn't use their names."

"You're right. I mean 'Higgs and Fermion.' It's just that I've been thinking about this story for so long, and while you were on patrol Quark let me watch one of his smuggling transactions—"

"*Jake!*" Nog hissed. "I'm wearing a communicator!" The Ferengi teenager lowered his chin to his chest and spoke loudly and precisely for the benefit of any potential eavesdroppers. "And I'm certain my Uncle Quark would never be involved in smuggling, or any other type of illegal—or even questionable—activity. Perhaps he was just playing a joke on you by pretending that he was."

"Oh, forget it," Jake muttered. Then he went back to attacking the third mini-tagbolt. "No one ever told me writing was such hard work."

"What's so hard about sitting in front of a computer and talking?"

"Shine the light *here*," Jake said. "And that part's not hard. It's all the work you have to do ahead of time so you can *know* what to say to the computer. That's the hard—*owwh!*"

The third mini was much looser than the second, and left a dent in Jake's forehead when it fell.

"We could have used the transporter to get down here," Nog said.

Jake didn't know why he bothered to keep explaining things to Nog, but he tried again. "That would leave a trace in the station security log." He pried at the egress panel with just his fingers now; to his relief, it came out easily. "Huh. I thought that would have been stuck after all these years."

Nog, uncharacteristically, said nothing, and Jake looked back at him with renewed suspicion. "You sure you haven't been back here since the last time?"

Nog looked offended. "Why would I come down here?"

Jake smiled insinuatingly. "The 'Room,' remember?" Then Jake used his feet to push himself backwards until his head and upper body poked out through the wall-panel opening. A moment later, he had turned his body and swung his legs out and down, hung on to the edge of the opening, and then dropped lightly to the floor of a small stretch of corridor. The corridor was lit only by the reflected light coming in through a panel opening set high near the ceiling in the bulkhead behind him.

"Whoa . . . it's still not hooked up to the main power grid," Jake said.

Nog's voice echoed in the Jeffries tube before he stuck his head through the wall-panel opening and brought the palm torch up beside him, letting it play around the area. "With the war, the Chief's retrofit schedule lost its priority. Except, of course, when he needed to maintain critical functions."

Jake's eyebrows lifted in surprise. Starfleet had made the retrofitting of Deep Space 9 a high-profile project, and accordingly Chief O'Brien had been given the authority to set up a renovation-and-repair program that would eventually move through the entire station, from Ops to the lowest level. War or no war, it was hard to believe that after almost six years, *no one* on *any* of the retrofitting teams had stumbled upon this ten-meter stretch of corridor that somehow had been sealed off from all the other corridors on the level.

Jake glanced up at Nog. "Aren't you coming down?"

"I thought you said you just wanted to time how long it would take for Quark and—I mean, for 'Higgs and Fermion' to escape through the Jefferies tube."

That *was* the original reason why Jake had talked Nog into retracing their old routes through the Jefferies tubes. He had decided to put his semiautobiographical novel, *Anslem,* aside for the time being and try something more commercial. So the new crime novel he was working on, *The Ferengi Connection,* was going to be set on a fictional Cardassian mining station still in orbit of Bajor. For that reason, he wanted to be completely accurate about how long it would take his crime lords Higgs and Fermion to secretly move from one part of the station to another. When Quark had allowed him to observe the illegal sale of Denevan crystals last Saturday night, Jake had been most interested to learn that the Ferengi used a network of secret passageways different from the Jefferies tubes. That would allow him to move through the station without being observed by Odo. Unfortunately, Nog's uncle wasn't about to give Captain Sisko's son, of all people, any details about the network, so Jake had decided to base the tunnels in his novel on the engineering ones he and Nog used to play in.

"Well, we're here. You timed it. Let's go back," Nog said impatiently. He held out his hand to haul Jake back up to the panel opening.

"No," Jake said as he looked around. "I can use this in the story. A lost section of the station. . . . Maybe this is where Quark—*Higgs*—has his secret headquarters."

"Jake, did you ever stop to think that maybe this section was sealed off for a reason?"

Jake didn't understand why Nog was being so cautious. "Nog, we used to come down here almost every day after school. If there was anything dangerous, we'd already know about it. Now get down here."

Nog mumbled something in an obscure trading tongue that Jake couldn't make out. But the young Ferengi squirmed through the panel opening and dropped with a loud thump to the uncarpeted deck beside his friend. He got up awkwardly, brushed dust from his Starfleet uniform, then aimed his palm torch to one end of the short corridor. The beam of light found only a standard, DS9 bulkhead, a dull, burnished-copper color, ridged and scalloped like the skin of a gigantic reptile. Nog shone the light in the other direction, but his torchlight uncovered only more of the same. "You know, we really have to tell Chief O'Brien about this," he said.

Jake patted Nog on the back. "And what are we going to say when he asks us *when* we discovered a lost section of corridor?"

"We were children," Nog said. "If we told anyone what we had found back then . . . ." He laughed. "My father would have served me my lobes on a platter for playing in the tubes."

"And for playing with a *'hew-mon,'* " Jake added.

Nog frowned, and Jake knew why. Despite the cannibalism rumors that still refused to die, human-Ferengi relations had come a long way in the past decade; but those relations still weren't so secure that many Ferengi would be comfortable joking about them.

"Would your father have been any more understanding?" Nog asked defiantly.

Jake snorted. "If I had told him about the tunnels back then, I'd still be confined to my room."

"But . . . we are going to tell them now, correct?"

"Maybe not right this minute," Jake said.

"Jake, we don't have any excuse for keeping this to ourselves. In fact, it might be my duty as a Starfleet officer to tell my commanding officer that—where are you going?!"

Jake ignored Nog and his unfathomable anxiety, and walked toward the only door in the corridor. "Let's just see if it's still here," Jake said.

Nog darted past him and stood in front of the lone door. "It is. Now let's go to Ops and—"

Jake smiled at Nog and reached for the door control panel. "And *now,* let's see if it's still *working.*"

"It *is* working!" Nog bleated as he pushed Jake's hand away from the door control.

Jake regarded his friend with a slight frown. "Nog, is there something you'd like to tell me?"

"Let's go to Ops, find Chief O'Brien, and . . . and I'll tell you everything."

Even in the pale illumination from the palm torch, Jake saw Nog's large ears flush. The explanation came to him suddenly.

"Nog . . . you *have* been coming down here, haven't you?"

"No. Well, yes. But, not often. A few times. Five . . . maybe eight, ten times."

Jake stared at Nog, nonplussed. "By yourself?"

Nog's mouth opened and closed but nothing came out.

"Oh, I get it now." Jake shook his head with a laugh, the sound oddly muffled in the enclosed space. "So . . . if I open this door, just what am I going to see?" He tried to remember the titles of the 'special' holosuite programs they used to 'borrow' from Quark's bar, the ones Quark kept locked in the little box under the stale pistachios no one ever asked for. *"Lauriento Spa? Vulcan Love Slave?"*

At that, Nog started to laugh, too. *"Part One* or *Part Two?"*

There was only one answer to that question. *"Part Two,"* Jake said with a snicker. Then both friends completed the title at the same time: *"The Revenge!"*

That was enough to make both double over in fits of uncontrolled giggling, both recalling how they would take the adult holosuite cylinders and try to run the graphic subroutines through their personal desk padds. At best, they were able to call up mildly suggestive silhouettes of some of the holographic performers from the programs, usually obscured by blurred color and jagged outlines. But the two young friends, certain they were close to learning the secrets of the universe—and equally certain they were going to be caught by their fathers at any minute—had stared at those flickering images for hours, trying desperately to see in them what it was that adults found so compelling.

Eventually, the laughter faded and Jake caught his breath. "So, you really *don't* want me to open the door?" he asked.

Nog chewed at his lip. "And if I say no, as soon as we leave you'll be right back here to open it anyway, right?"

"Right," Jake agreed. That's exactly what he had decided to do.

Nog sighed in resignation. "Go ahead." He stepped aside.

Jake made a production out of pressing the door control. When the door slipped open, he comically placed both hands over his eyes.

Until he heard Nog say, "Hey, that's not my program. . . ." Jake took his hands away, looked into what had been the most exciting discovery of their childhood on Deep Space 9, something not recorded on any deck plan or technical drawing. A lost Cardassian holosuite.

Nog was already inside the room, standing on a slightly inclined rocky landscape. Beyond him, about a holographic kilometer away, Jake spied a collection of small stone buildings reminiscent of a primitive village. It was night on the holosuite, but the buildings and the land were lit by a cool, blue-green illumination. Jake couldn't detect the source of that backlighting, though it appeared, improbably, to be coming from somewhere behind him.

He stepped inside to join Nog, then turned around to look past the improbable cutout of the doorway to the DS9 corridor, to an astounding holographic vista of a night sky.

At once he identified the source of the blue-green light.

A planet filled almost a tenth of the sky in the holographic scene, the bright light reflecting from the green oceans of its sunlit half enough to wash most of the stars from the heavens.

Then he recognized the planet. "Hey, that's Bajor. . . ."

"Really?" Nog said.

Jake pointed skyward. "By the terminator . . . see those mountains?" The distinctive pattern created where three tectonic plates had collided to form a perfect X of intersecting mountain ranges was so well known as to almost be the galactic symbol for Bajor.

"Dahkur Province," Nog murmured. He looked around the holographic landscape again. "So this must be one of Bajor's moons. But I didn't program this."

"Neither did I," Jake said.

The two friends looked at each other, and Jake could see that Nog had just reached the same conclusion he had. "Someone else has been down here."

"Pretty dull program," Jake said softly. "I don't see a single Vulcan love slave."

They stood in silence for a few moments, listening to the holographic wind. Jake looked back at the village and saw flickering lights in some of the windows of the small buildings.

"Does it feel as if something should be happening?" Nog asked.

Jake shook his head. "It's not on pause. We've got wind, moving lights in that village."

"But why would anyone want a holosimulation of . . . of nothing happening on a Bajoran moon?"

Jake shrugged. "Maybe the program's caught in a loop. Or the holosuite's broken." He cleared his throat. "Room, this is Jake Sisko. Show me my fishing hole. . . ."

Unlike any other type of holographic simulation Jake had ever seen, the distinctive program switchover of the Cardassian holosuite now began. At first, the colors and the shapes of the Bajoran moon's landscape seemed to liquefy and swim into each other, and then, as if the plug had been pulled on reality, all the colors spun swiftly— dizzyingly—into a spiral vortex that made Jake feel as if he were about to be drawn down an endless tunnel. But, just as quickly as the vertigo of that transformation made itself felt, the spiralling stopped and with a strange optical bounce that Jake could almost feel, the new program took shape.

Jake and Nog were standing on a covered wooden bridge that spanned Jake's favorite fishing hole. It was his father's favorite, too, and six years ago, Jake had been delighted to discover that this secret Cardassian holosuite could access his father's programs from DS9's main computers.

Except . . .

"This isn't my program, either," Jake said to Nog. The perpetual summer sun wasn't shining. In fact, the day was overcast. In fact, it was actually raining."

"I, uh, sort of made some, uh, minor modifications," Nog confessed with a shrug. "The rain makes me feel more . . . at home. . . ."

Then Jake saw that he and Nog weren't alone. There were people *swimming* in the fishing hole. "Who are they?" He stepped closer to the bridge's railing, saw the impressive size and bulbous shape of the swimmers' bald heads. "Ferengi?"

"Uh-huh," Nog said in a strangled croak, as if his throat was slowly closing in.

The Ferengi swimmers saw Jake and Nog on the bridge, and started waving enthusiastically.

Then Jake saw how small their ears were, and he began to really understand. "Ferengi *females* . . ."

"I've never really been much for . . . pointed ears," Nog mumbled.

Two of the swimmers began climbing a wooden ladder at the side of the bridge. They were calling Nog's name, and as they stepped onto the bridge, leaving wet footprints behind, Jake was momentarily startled by the bulky, multilayered swimming costumes the Ferengi females wore. Other than their heads, their hands, and their feet, not a square centimeter of skin was exposed, not a curve of their bodies could be discerned.

Jake looked at Nog with a grin.

Nog's open-mouth smile was so broad, it almost made him look as if he'd just been stunned by a phaser. The Ferengi teenager stared at the two fully clad females without blinking.

"You're drooling," Jake teased.

Nog looked up at his friend. "Vulcan love slaves don't . . . wear any clothes," he said sheepishly. "Where's the fun in that?"

Jake took Nog by the arm, tugged him toward the door to the corridor. "Nog, you need to get out more. Let's go find Chief O'Brien."

Allowing Nog to wave a sad farewell to the Ferengi females, Jake pushed his glum friend out the door.

The Ferengi females—representing everything Nog could ever want—returned that wave sadly as Jake and Nog left, reverting to their true forms only when the door had completely closed, and the waiting began again.

CHAPTER 5

IF MILES O'BRIEN had his way, every starship, every runabout, every shuttlecraft, *and* every space station in the galaxy would be as smooth and featureless as his little son's bottom.

Not that DS9's chief engineer minded a turn in space. Perhaps because he was a happily married parent of two young, active children, O'Brien greatly enjoyed putting on an environmental suit and slipping out of the artificial gravity fields for an hour or two, just as he was doing today to float above the *Defiant,* relatively speaking, of course. And stolen moments such as these, when he could just drift peacefully among the stars, hearing only the rhythms of his own heart, his own breathing, he found those moments truly restoring.

But to *work* in space? In the twenty-fourth century? What was Starfleet thinking?

To O'Brien, who had given the matter some thought, the perfect spacecraft would be without surface texture—not one exposed conduit, not a single inset panel, and absolutely no components that could be serviced only from the outside of the ship. Instead, in his opinion at least, everything should be accessible from *within,* so that engineers and repair technicians could work safely in a breathable atmosphere, under controlled temperatures, in conditions where an unexpected sharp edge of metal would mean only a quick trip to the infirmary and not explosive decompression and a terrible, painful death.

Humans are far too fragile for space, O'Brien thought, not for the first time. Far too fragile for most things, actually. Which is why machines were so necessary. And why engineers in particular were humanity's best hope for a better future.

O'Brien smiled to himself just thinking about his engineer's dream of that better tomorrow. Gleaming starships, hulls like mirrors, blazing past the stars with their fragile cargo safely cocooned, and—

"You still breathing out there, Chief?"

The brisk voice in O'Brien's helmet communicator was as loud as it was unexpected.

"Who is this?" O'Brien demanded.

The short sharp burst of laughter that came in response to his startled request was enough to answer his question.

"Sorry, Major," O'Brien said. "I was . . . I was concentrating on the transionic power coupling."

O'Brien regretted the words as soon as he said them. He could picture the wry smile on Kira's face as she replied, "I'll say. You were concentrating so hard we could hear you snoring."

Blushing in spite of himself, O'Brien maneuvered gingerly around from the open coupling bay until he could look along the length of the *Defiant*'s upper hull, past the towering pylon and immense curve of DS9's docking ring and up to the Operations Module, as if there were viewports there through which he could see the major. "I'm running a level-six diagnostic," O'Brien explained. "There's not a lot I can do while the computer's working."

"Which is why I was wondering if you'd like to lend a hand to the PTC work crew," Kira said. The humor had gone from her voice. O'Brien thought he could detect the slightest undercurrent of concern.

"Have they run into trouble?"

"It's not trouble yet, Chief. They were almost ready to lift off a hull plate, but then they got an anomalous density reading."

Kira's news hit O'Brien like a shock of transtator current. "Tell them not to touch it!"

"I'm confident they know enough not to do that. Rom's leading the team."

"Ah, well, all right, then," O'Brien said, his sudden concern subsiding to a more tolerable level of wariness. Rom was one of the best junior technicians he had ever trained. The hardworking Ferengi could be counted on to take a conservative approach to repairs—and to O'Brien, the conservative approach was always the best. "Let me seal this bay and I'll join them." O'Brien tapped his thruster controls to move closer to the *Defiant*'s hull and the open coupling bay.

"Want me to beam you over?" Kira asked.

O'Brien gazed up through the top of his helmet, admiring the towering spires of the station's curved docking arms, picked out against the fathomless black of space by brilliant running lights. That a machine—an artificial construct built by intelligent hands—could even exist in this universe, could even dare to shine as brightly as the timeless stars, frankly thrilled him at such a visceral level that he couldn't care less if those hands had been Cardassian or human. "That's all right, Major. Looks like a nice day for a walk. . . ."

As DS9's chief engineer, O'Brien was well aware that, according to regulations, untethered spacewalks from one section of the station's exterior to another were strictly forbidden. The massive station's slow stabilization spin, almost imperceptible even at the outer edge of the docking ring, could induce in inexperienced personnel violent attacks of debilitating space-sickness. Poor Worf almost had to be prodded into his environmental suit for EVA drills.

But O'Brien had no such trouble with an exterior traverse of the station. In his mind, he saw the huge structure simply as a giant cog, moving within its perfect circle, wholly predictable, reassuringly stable. Thus, after the transionic coupling bay was safely sealed and the diagnostic readers placed on standby, he oriented himself to the station's local coordinates, correctly pointing his feet at the *Defiant*'s hull, and tapped his thrusters. Then he smoothly slipped above the ship, effortlessly adjusting his vector so he would rise above the gentle slope of the docking ring beside the pylon, level out, then drop over the ring's inner edge as if taking a ski jump into an infinite valley filled with stars.

O'Brien sighed with pleasure. He loved this view, the sensation of this movement. In an old-style system of measurement he had mastered in order to be able to read old engineering texts, the distance to the far side of the ring was almost a mile. Certainly, he now reflected, he had seen larger artificial structures in his career in space. The planet-sized Dyson Sphere, for instance, which Captain Picard's *Enterprise* had encountered when they had rescued the legendary Montgomery Scott. Contemplating that engineering feat still kept O'Brien awake at night, as he struggled to comprehend the staggering mechanical stresses on its hull components. But a Dyson Sphere was so enormous, he knew, that there was only one way to truly make sense of its size and scope, and that was through mathematical abstractions.

A mile-wide space station, though, that was something concrete, something that could be seen and felt. In fact, Deep Space 9 was about as large as an artificial structure could be built and still be comprehensible to unenhanced human senses. It was part of the reason he had enjoyed this assignment so much. In some ways, DS9 was the ultimate machine. And its size and complexity were just below the level at which engineers were forced to rely on artificial intelligence and data reduction in order to grasp the structure of what they built. But DS9—well, by now, O'Brien felt he knew it well enough that he could almost have built a duplicate of it by himself.

As he dropped, O'Brien's line of sight cleared the interior habitat ring. Now he could see the red glow of the fusion reactors' exhaust cone at the relative bottom of the station. There, the saucer-shaped module containing the station's main fusion reactors—of which only four had been certified safe enough to remain operational—was attached to the main core by a constricted airlock linkage. That airlock connector was what allowed the quick jettisoning of the module in an emergency with minimal loss of interior atmosphere.

The airlock connector, though, was strictly designed to allow only the passage of turbolift cars and life-support services. The end-product of the fusion reactor—power—was delivered to the rest of the station through six exterior power transfer conduits that extended from the top hull of the fusion module to the bottom hull of the lower habitat. Again, in an emergency they were designed to be quickly separated from the station. A single conduit could supply the station's minimal power needs for weeks.

But yesterday, when Odo's murder-investigation team had detected an inexplicable modulation in the output of power-transfer conduit B almost exactly where it entered the main station, jettisoning the conduit had fortunately not been required.

No Dominion warships were reported within tens of parsecs of the Bajoran system, so emergency conditions did not apply. O'Brien had called for a by-the-book shutdown of conduit B, using the remaining five to supply the station without requiring any power rationing. And once the conduit was cold, he had assigned an engineering team to open it up and remove all the exterior hull plates, so that they could conduct a visual inspection in addition to the molecular scanning. It was a time-consuming procedure to be sure, but also a conservative one. A chance to make repairs without danger of attack or risk of catastrophic disaster was something that came to O'Brien less and less these days. He found he was actually looking forward to helping Rom and his team.

There were three other engineers with Rom, floating by the top of the power conduit where it entered the lower hull of the main station. O'Brien could see they were each attached to the station by a memory tether—without them, DS9's rotation would move the conduit away from anyone in an environmental suit within sixty seconds.

O'Brien expertly maneuvered himself into position beside Rom. Rom was easy to identify among the engineering team because he was the shortest of the four, and he wore a modified helmet that provided more room for his Ferengi skull.

"Chief O'Brien," Rom said in greeting as he took O'Brien's arm, "I didn't mean for Major Kira to call you away from your important work."

"That's all right, Rom." From any other Ferengi, O'Brien knew that those words would be a reflexive and meaningless expression of the 33rd Rule of Acquisition. But in Rom's case, O'Brien believed that the Ferengi technician, gratifyingly enough, did consider anything the chief engineer of DS9 did to be of crucial importance to the station. Of course, it also was true that Rom always believed anything a chief of engineering did to be more important than what a mere assistant did. Unsure whether the Ferengi technician's belief stemmed from something in the Ferengi tradition of apprenticeship or from Rom's admiration for his chief's skills, O'Brien rather hoped it was the latter.

Grateful for Rom's steadying grip, O'Brien fired a memory tether from the mobility module around his right forearm. At once, the tether's tip sought out the nearest spinward positioning cleat on the hull and magnetically attached itself to the metallic surface. Now, O'Brien knew, the tether would automatically adjust its length and tension to keep him in position over the very same point—power-transfer conduit B, hull plate B-OF-186-9776-3. The Cardassians were nothing if not impressive record keepers.

"So what do we have?" he asked Rom.

Rom tapped some controls on his forearm padd, and they watched as a holographic display of a tricorder screen sprang up and took shape a half-meter in front of O'Brien's helmet.

O'Brien whistled as he interpreted the shifting, false-color display of a hull-plate scan. On a typical plate, the scan would show thirteen distinct color bars representing the thirteen composite layers used to form the station's skin. But on this display, O'Brien noted with a frown, several segments of the hull plate's interior layers were mixed together as if sections of them had melted into each other.

He checked the coordinates of the display. "You're sure this isn't reversed?"

"Yes, sir," Rom said earnestly. "See the outermost layer? Pure plasma-sprayed pyroceramic trianium."

Rom was right. The PSPT layer was for micrometeoroid protection, a final fail-safe for the station in case the station-keeping deflectors went off-line. Even more importantly, it was always and only applied to the exterior of the hull plates. Which meant the mixing of layers was definitely on the inside.

"Good attention to detail," O'Brien said. Even through his helmet he could see Rom's broad smile in response to his compliment. "A lot of engineers would have automatically concluded that the sensor was in error."

The smile left the Ferengi technician's face as quickly as it had appeared. "Oh, no, Chief—the whole team agreed that this was an anomalous reading."

O'Brien nodded. He didn't know if that were true or not, but he appreciated the fact that Rom took responsibility for his team—two Bajorans and a new Vulcan ensign who had just been assigned to DS9 from the Academy. "Well done, people," he said, with a glance that encompassed Rom's three assistants.

This time, all except the Vulcan smiled back in acknowledgment of the praise.

"All right, Rom," O'Brien said. "What do we do next?"

Though obviously startled that O'Brien wasn't taking over the operation, Rom rose to the challenge. "Well, the final decision will have to be based on an understanding of what has caused the mixing of the hull layers."

"Very good. What possibilities should we investigate?" O'Brien effortlessly reassumed his role as instructor for the station's engineering staff. It gave him real pleasure to see someone grasp and apply engineering concepts for the first time. Somedays, he even thought he might enjoy teaching at the Academy himself. Once the war was over, of course.

"Um, um . . ." Rom said as he gathered his thoughts. "Well . . . if we had found this kind of mixing on the *exterior* layers of the hull, we could conclude that . . . it was the result of an energy discharge. Maybe a stray . . . phaser hit from an old battle."

"That's one," O'Brien confirmed.

"And . . . if we open up the plate and find that the innermost layer is not disturbed—that is, it *appears* to be undamaged, then . . . we might conclude the mixing of layers is a manufacturing flaw."

O'Brien decided to challenge Rom once again. He frowned. "The Cardassians? Miss a manufacturing flaw as prominent as *this?*"

A look of momentary panic contorted Rom's face. From long experience, O'Brien knew that many students folded at this point, unwilling to appear to contradict their teacher's pronouncement.

But Rom swallowed hard and blurted out. "I really don't mean to argue but . . . ."

"But what?" O'Brien prompted, trying to keep a smile from his face.

"Well . . . Cardassian manufacturing standards fell drastically during . . . the last few years of the Occupation and if this hull plate was manufactured during that period and Bajoran slave workers were part of the quality assurance program then . . . then there's a chance—a little, tiny, barely-worth-mentioning *chance*—that a manufacturing flaw like this could slip through." Rom audibly gulped at his own temerity and the remainder of his words tumbled out in a rush. "But . . . you're probably right. Don't pay any attention to me."

O'Brien shook his head. "Rom, never be afraid to question the chief engineer."

Rom blinked in surprise. "Never? Really?"

O'Brien reconsidered. "Well, maybe not when you're under enemy fire. But this is a stable situation, so we might as well enjoy the luxury of exploring all the possibilities. In this case, you're right. It *is* possible we're seeing a manufacturing flaw."

Rom brightened like a puppy who'd been given a brand-new chew toy. O'Brien couldn't help himself. He had to smile.

"Thank you, Chief."

"But let's not get carried away." O'Brien was the teacher again. "I think there's one more possibility we should consider. What about you?"

Rom nodded quickly in his helmet, making his entire weightless body rock slowly back and forth around his center of gravity.

"And that possibility would be . . . ?" O'Brien said.

"Oh, uh, a power conduit rupture!"

"Exactly," O'Brien agreed. "Though because the hull plate surrounding the conduit isn't deformed. . . ."

Rom got it at once. "It would be a very small rupture."

"So given those three possibilities, what procedures do we follow to identify which one is the actual cause of the layer distortion?"

Rom looked off into space and recited the steps to be taken next, beginning with shutting down the power conduit—which had already been accomplished—to the final step of setting up a portable force-field in order to keep any possible debris contained once the damaged hull plate had been removed.

Timing his actions to coincide with the completion of Rom's list, O'Brien activated the memory tether override and used his thrusters to slip to the side. "Well, what are you waiting for, Rom?"

O'Brien chuckled at the expressions first of surprise and then delight that washed across Rom's face as the Ferengi technician realized he was being permitted to continue with the examination.

With renewed confidence, Rom efficiently directed the others in setting up the forcefield generator that Kira now beamed to the engineering team. Then he positioned his team at the connection points of the hull plate they were about to remove.

Elapsed time for these preparations was approximately twenty minutes, and O'Brien took full advantage of his position as an observer to use the time to watch the incomparable parade of the wonders of space: the steady shine of the untwinkling stars, the subtly shifting colorful filaments of the Denorios Belt, and the distant pure light of Bajor's sun, Bajor-B'hava'el—the brightest star in space for DS9, though distant enough from the station that it was simply a brilliant point of light, not a blazing disk.

"We're ready, Chief," Rom announced.

Even from his position, floating five meters away, O'Brien could see that Rom's team had properly installed the forcefield emitters and that the four engineers were correctly in position. "You're in charge, Rom."

Rom nodded and turned his attention to steadying himself on the multitorque defastener he had attached to the plate bolt, then gave a quick glance to reassure himself that each of his team members was also poised to use their own. "All right, everybody, on the . . . count of ten. One—"

"Uh, Rom?"

"Yes, Chief?"

"Why not make it the count of three?"

"Good idea. Everybody, forget what I said about going on the count of ten. That would take too much time and slow down the—"

"*One!*" O'Brien prompted.

Rom got the hint. "Uh . . . two . . . and *three!*"

O'Brien carefully monitored the spinning bits of each defastener as they counterrotated, detaching the hull-plate fasteners.

"Slowly . . ." Rom cautioned nervously. "Standing by to activate the forcefield . . . as soon as the hull plate is free. . . ."

Then a few puffs of gas vented, as the hull-plate seal was broken and the plate itself began to drift away from the curved pillar of the conduit structure, propelled by the centripetal force imparted by DS9's rotation.

O'Brien's attention focused on what would happen next—in the next minute or two. When the plate had drifted about a meter away from the surface of the conduit, Rom would activate the forcefield so that any debris behind the plate would remain in place. Then, when the plate was about ten meters from the conduit, Jadzia was standing by in Ops to grab the plate with a construction tractor beam and hold it safely out of the way.

As far as O'Brien was concerned, his credits were on the cause of the distorted layers being a tiny rupture in the power-transfer conduit that had allowed plasma current to leak out and melt the inside of the hull plate. And a ruptured energy conduit would certainly explain the anomalous readings Odo's people got from the lower levels when they were investigating the death of that Andorian businessman.

Then the loudest, highest-pitched Ferengi scream O'Brien had ever heard shoved every other thought from his mind as he slammed his gloved hands to the sides of his helmet in a useless attempt to block out the din.

"Computer!" O'Brien shouted. "Lower helmet volume!"

Instantly, Rom's squeal dropped to a more tolerable level, and O'Brien swiftly detached his memory tether and thrusted in to see whatever it was that had so upset Rom.

Dead bodies.

Two of them.

Cardassians.

Crammed into the insulating buffer zone between the power-transfer conduit's inner and outer hulls.

The arms of the two corpses were stretched out as if desperately reaching to freedom. Their black, shrivelled lips were drawn back exposing startlingly white teeth, their jaws agape in terror.

O'Brien shivered. The dessicated gray flesh still coating what could be seen of the two skeletons was fractured by deep-cut purple fissures, the result of prolonged exposure to the absolute vacuum of space.

"It's all right, Rom. Calm down. Breathe normally." O'Brien stayed out of Rom's reach in case the Ferengi panicked and started flailing. "O'Brien to Ops, lock on to Rom and prepare to beam him in on my order."

"What is it, Chief?" Kira asked.

"I'm locked," Jadzia's voice added.

O'Brien kept his voice deliberately neutral, setting a proper example for his staff. "There are two bodies in the insulating space between the hulls. Cardassians."

"Construction workers?" Kira asked.

O'Brien thrusted in closer. One of the skeletons was missing its hand—it had been severed cleanly at the wrist. "Don't think so, Major. They're not in environment suits. In fact, they look to be civilians. Been here quite a while, though. All the moisture in them's sublimated long ago."

O'Brien puzzled over the missing hand. He looked around to see if it had floated free.

It had. He could see it attached to the inside of the detached hull plate, as if it had been welded in position, exactly where scans had detected that strange mixing of the plate's interior layers.

"Chief," Kira asked carefully, "any chance they might have been put in there when the conduit was manufactured?"

O'Brien understood what the major was suggesting. The two Cardassians might have been victims of the Bajoran resistance—walled up in the conduit to die when it was carried into space. They certainly looked as if they had been in vacuum long enough to have been killed during the Occupation.

But the theory didn't hold because of one critical detail. "Probably not," O'Brien said. "These conduits were all assembled in space when the station was constructed. I don't know how the blazes they got in there."

Jadzia's voice came over the comm link next. "Chief, we should transport the bodies to the Infirmary for Julian. But I can't get a good lock on them. Is that conduit still live?"

"Dead cold, Commander. If you can lock onto Rom, there's no reason why you shouldn't be able to lock onto the Cardassians."

"Well, I can't," Jadzia replied, and O'Brien could hear her annoyance.

"How about I pull them out into the open?" O'Brien suggested.

"What a good idea," Jadzia said, with more than a hint of sarcasm.

O'Brien looked back at Rom. The Ferengi engineer seemed

calmer now. "Okay, Rom. Best thing to do is to climb back on the horse."

Rom's grimace of distaste was clear behind his faceplate. "There's a *horse* in there, too?!"

O'Brien didn't have the strength to explain. "Just give me a hand pulling them out so Jadzia can transport them."

O'Brien could see that the Ferengi engineer would rather start a fight with Worf than handle dead Cardassians, but he gamely tapped his thruster controls and moved into position beside his teacher.

"You get the one on the right," O'Brien said as he moved in to grab the arm stump of the Cardassian on the left. "And be gentle. They're apt to be a bit . . . brittle."

"Shouldn't a medical team come out to do this?" Rom asked as he tentatively reached for the Cardassian on the right.

Exercising caution, O'Brien took hold of the other corpse's arm. For a moment, he was disconcerted because the insulating gap was only about a meter and half deep, and he couldn't see where the dead Cardassian's legs were. But before he could stop to analyze the significance of what he saw, his hand reflexively gave his thruster controls a tap for reverse, and he abruptly tumbled away from the conduit, pulling the upper half of the dead Cardassian with him.

At the very same moment, Rom's renewed screaming in O'Brien's helmet informed him that Rom had discovered where the missing legs were.

He could see it for himself.

The corpse he'd been reaching for was only half there.

Severed at the waist, the truncated body spun around in empty space, slipping away from the conduit with the momentum O'Brien had transferred to it.

And the fate of the lower half was now apparent.

All that remained of it was a shiny discolored patch of merged flesh and metal on the inner hull of the conduit.

The lower half of the Cardassian's body had been fused *within* the metal hull plate of the station.

No wonder Dax couldn't get a clear lock on them, O'Brien thought. The poor devil must have been caught in the worst kind of transporter malfunction imaginable.

So bad that fifteen separate fail-safe systems made certain that such a tragedy could never happen by accident.

Which meant only one thing to O'Brien, as the gigantic station wheeled around his tumbling form.

Odo had two more murders to investigate.

CHAPTER 6

AN ENTIRE WORLD lay before Captain Benjamin Sisko.

Its visage was smooth and pristine, like the all-enshrouding ice caps of a frozen planet. And its unmarked surface held no hidden secrets, nothing lost or obscured in deep caves or folded valleys.

Only smooth, featureless mountains broke the Platonic ideal of that perfect sphere. One long, unending line of regular red stitches, interlocking the two halves of the skin of the world to make a single whole.

Yet from that unblemished perfection, from that balanced mass and absolute symmetry, unending diversity was born in unending combination. Like an omega particle exploding to become an entire universe of possibilities in which—

"Captain Sisko . . . ?"

Sisko looked up from the baseball he held in his hand to glance across his desk. He saw the questioning expression in Commander Arla Rees's eyes and instantly knew this was no time for excuses. This very serious young Bajoran Starfleet officer deserved the absolute truth.

"I apologize, Commander. I must have tuned you out and—"

"That's quite all right, sir. I read the report of your mission to save Captain Cusak. I understand it might take time to recover from such an encounter."

Sisko regarded the attractive young commander with new interest. He had returned from the *Defiant's* latest patrol—and the mission to save Cusak—to find that Starfleet had unexpectedly assigned him a new second-in-command to coordinate with Major Kira.

Kira's reaction had been explosive. She believed Starfleet was passing judgment on her performance, or the perceived lack of it. Fortunately, Sisko had been able to quickly confirm that Commander Arla was here only on temporary assignment. After more than a decade of intricate negotiation and elaborate construction, the Farpoint Starbase on Deneb IV was finally about to be activated and Arla was slated for the number-two position on the base's command staff. Given the complexities of Starfleet's relationship with the Bandi of Deneb IV, the staffing wizards at headquarters had decided that Arla could benefit from experiencing life on DS9, a living laboratory of cross-cultural complexity.

She'll need the benefit of a few other experiences, too, if she's to survive out here, Sisko thought as he contemplated the Bajoran newcomer before him, whose sharp edges had yet to be blunted by the realities of routine. But he remembered what he had been like when he was a freshly minted commander. He was willing to give her the benefit of the doubt. Jean-Luc Picard had done the same for him when Sisko had taken this assignment, though the captain of the *Enterprise* might not have realized it at the time.

"Thank you, Commander," Sisko said. "But that's no excuse for not listening to your report."

Arla offered him a padd. "You could read it later."

Sisko was tempted. The last thing he needed to hear right now was yet another report on Starfleet–Bajoran cultural referents in the workplace. But why was Commander Arla suggesting that she would be willing to forgo the official schedule? The scuttlebutt had it that Arla wasn't allowing anyone on the station to bypass standing Starfleet orders. Why was she willing to bend the rules for him?

"I appreciate the offer," Sisko said. He put his baseball back in its display stand on his desk and pushed it away so he wouldn't be tempted to reach for it again. "But you've worked hard on that report. I would like to hear it."

Arla nodded, and looked back to the padd, as if trying to find her place. Sisko was momentarily caught by the particularly elegant line of the epinasal folds on the bridge of her nose. There was a slight downward curve to them, which gave her an intriguing expression, as if she had just thought of a sly joke and was keeping it to herself.

Careful, Sisko cautioned himself. She had looked up without warning and caught him staring. Second time in this meeting alone.

"Captain? Is there something you wanted to say?"

Sisko shook his head, making a deliberate attempt to ignore her expression of shy amusement. "Please—continue." Then he leaned back in his broad-backed chair, tugged down on his jacket, and forced himself to listen to every word Arla Rees had to say about the time-and-motion modification studies that had arisen from observations of Bajoran and Starfleet personnel working together.

Regrettably, but inevitably, the thirty-minute presentation was followed by Arla's suggestions for overcoming the perceived difficulties of human-Bajoran interactions. Sisko struggled to give his full attention to each of her recommendations before responding.

"Very clearly thought out," he announced when she had finished. And he meant it. The new commander's report revealed exceptional intelligence. For just the briefest of instants, Sisko felt a rush of pride in knowing that someone with the potential of Arla Rees—who could have chosen virtually any career in the galaxy—had been inspired to join Starfleet.

"Thank you, sir."

"A most thorough analysis of the existing literature as well."

Arla's smile was tremulous, expectant.

Sisko wondered how far he'd have to go with this. "I'll definitely circulate it among the command staff." *That should do it,* he thought.

"And . . ." Arla prompted.

"And . . . I'll ask them to read it." Sisko didn't know what else she wanted of him.

Well, obviously that wasn't it, he thought as he saw Arla's crestfallen expression.

"Shouldn't we have a general meeting of all command staff to discuss implementing my changes? Sir."

Sisko leaned forward, trying to find the best possible way to put what he knew he had to say.

"Commander, truthfully, those are all very insightful observations about working conditions on DS9. And your suggestions for improving things are just . . . fine. But they're not necessary." Before Arla could respond, Sisko quickly added. "And more than that, they won't work. Can't work."

The dismayed young commander shook her head as if to be sure she had heard him properly, making the chain of her single silver earring sway against her olive-gold cheek.

"I beg your pardon, sir, but how can you know without trying?"

Sisko firmly reclaimed his usual air of detachment, settled back in his chair with a patient smile. "I have tried them, Commander. Everything you've suggested and more. And really, when it comes down to a choice between forcing everyone to do their work according to Starfleet's textbook definition of perfection, or having everyone do their work in their own way, with respect for other people's traditions and work habits, I have found it's better for people to find their own way than to have it forced upon them by an unseen bureaucracy."

Arla's chin lifted, in a way that reminded Sisko of Major Kira when she was not at all convinced of someone else's argument. "But sir, the literature clearly suggests ways that humans and Bajorans could be more efficient as team workers."

With a sigh, Sisko rose to his feet and waved a hand past the closed doors of his office, down the stairs to the lower level of Ops. "I have no doubt that's true, Commander—for humans and Bajorans. But look out there. What about Commander Worf? Commander Dax? And I have a half-dozen other races staffing this station. Should we make Bolians adhere to some form of Bajoran-human work ethic? Should we force Martians to celebrate the Bajoran Days of Atonement instead of Colonial Independence Day?"

Arla's almond-brown eyes met his. "Well actually, sir, one of my suggestions is that all group religious celebrations be banned from the station. Not personal expressions of faith," she hastily amended, as his look of consternation and lack of comprehension registered on her. "I'm not suggesting that. But for the good of the group, religious events really have no place in what is, after all, a military environment—which is what DS9 will be for the duration of the Dominion War."

Sisko concentrated on keeping his voice calm in the face of Arla's surprisingly insensitive conclusion. "Commander, war or no war, this station is first and foremost a civilian installation run by the Bajoran government. Starfleet's presence as an administrative authority is temporary, and strictly limited to security operations. In no way would we *ever* infringe on the religious rights of any culture—which makes your suggestion totally out of line."

Arla's face reddened. "Sir, I'm not suggesting Starfleet outlaw religion, just relegate it to private expression, off-duty. I . . . I don't think there's anything out of line with my suggestion."

"No," Sisko said slowly. "Not as a suggestion. But what surprises me, frankly, is that you—a Bajoran—are making it."

"We're not all religious fan—" and Arla hesitated, apparently rethinking her choice of words. "We're not all religious to the same degree, sir."

"So it would seem."

"I don't mean to offend you, sir. I mean, I know that many Bajorans believe that the wormhole aliens you've encountered are their Prophets."

"And you don't," Sisko said, not bothering to make it a question.

"Sir, with all due respect, I'd be much more inclined to believe that the Bajoran wormhole was a celestial temple if it didn't form with verteron nodes. I mean, if it's truly a home for gods, shouldn't it operate outside the normal laws of physics, instead of appearing as a natural phenomenon?"

Sisko sat down again and reached out for his baseball. He decided he was going to have to take a closer look at Commander Arla Rees's personnel file. He had met many Bajorans, with many different degrees of belief and many different traditions of worship. But he had never met one who so obviously rejected the idea that the beings in the wormhole were the Prophets.

"I have heard that argument," Sisko said, noncommittally, tossing the baseball from one hand to another while he waited to see what else the surprising young Bajoran would come up with.

Arla didn't keep him waiting, apparently most reluctant to accept such a neutral stance from him.

"Sir, do *you* believe the wormhole aliens are the Prophets? I mean, I know some people call you the Emissary, and I don't mean to offend you, but . . . you're an educated man."

"And as such," Sisko said lightly, "My eyes are open to the full range of wonder the universe contains."

Arla's spontaneous smile was full of quick, responsive humor. "You're not answering my question, sir."

Sisko stopped playing games. He placed his hands together as he thought for a moment. "Very well. What do I personally believe? I am sure there are entities who live in the wormhole. I have no doubt that these entities are the source of the Orbs which have had such a profound effect on your people's history and culture. I have no doubt that these entities are, indeed, what the Bajoran people call their Prophets. And I have no doubt that the Prophets are inextricably involved in the fate of your people."

"That's still not an answer." Now Arla, too, spoke in earnest. "And the question is so simple. Are . . . they . . . gods?"

"A wise man once said, 'Any sufficiently advanced technology is indistinguishable from magic.' Why should it be indistinguishable from the works of gods, Commander?"

"Sir, don't you think there's a difference—a *profound* difference—between having the *attributes* of a god, and *being* a god?"

If you only knew how many times I've asked myself that same question, Sisko thought wearily. "Yes," he said. "I do."

At that, Arla shot him a quick, almost triumphant look from beneath her improbably thick fringe of eyelashes. "So—what is the answer to my question?"

Sisko suddenly felt the need to bring an end to their conversation. "In all honesty, I don't know."

Sisko could see this disconcerting young woman didn't want their meeting to end with that pronouncement. But he could also see that she understood he did not wish to continue on this topic.

So, instead, she turned abruptly to look out the viewports in the main doors. Beyond her, in Ops, Starfleet uniforms mingled chaotically with Bajoran.

She glanced back at him. "So, ten races?"

Sisko reminded himself of his earlier resolve to give the young commander the benefit of the doubt. In her way she was, perhaps, trying to change the subject, to bring their discussion back to the work at hand. "And that doesn't count the civilian staff," he said.

Arla turned away from the viewports, glanced down at her padd, then hugged it close to her, as if she no longer had any intention of turning it over to him.

"I'm sorry, Captain Sisko," she said quietly. "It's all new to me but I was just . . . trying to help."

"Believe me, Commander, I understand."

Arla took an impulsive step closer to his desk, and Sisko couldn't help noticing that the young commander's stiff military bearing, formerly so reminiscent of Kira's, had suddenly relaxed. "You *do* understand, don't you," she said with an open, frank look of approval that reminded Sisko of earlier days, of his youth, when he, too, had been capable of uncomplicated emotion. "I . . . I felt you would from the moment I met you."

Sisko might have been distracted before, but he was on full alert right now. There was only one way of dealing with what was happening, what might happen. "We should have dinner," he announced, rising to his feet to meet her gaze directly, though he had to look up to do so. The young Bajoran was a half head taller than he.

Arla's smile of pleasure was instantaneous. "I'd like that."

"So would I. I'd like you to meet two very important people in my life. My son, Jake, and Captain Kasidy Yates."

Arla regarded him quizzically. "I don't remember a captain of that name from the Starfleet personnel lists."

"Ah," Sisko said, as he stepped around his desk and toward the main doors, moving close enough to trigger their sensors. "That's because Kasidy is a civilian. A merchant captain." The doors slid open and the noise of Ops filled Sisko's office like a current of power. "She is also the woman I love," Sisko added deliberately, knowing no better way to set the record straight than by a blunt statement of the facts.

He was greatly relieved to see Arla's shoulders come back into square and her posture return to that of an officer. "I look forward to meeting them both," she said politely.

"I'll check with Kasidy, but I believe tomorrow night is open."

Arla stood beside Sisko at the top of the stairs to his office. She handed him her padd after all, and as he took it, her long, slender fingers for the briefest of instants grazed his, generating a current of another kind. "Tomorrow night," she said.

Startled by his own response, Sisko took the padd, promptly removing his hand from contact with Arla's. He was about to dismiss her when his communicator chirped, followed by a familiar voice.

"Bashir to Sisko."

Sisko tapped his communicator. "Go ahead, Doctor."

"I've completed my preliminary scan of the two bodies Chief O'Brien found."

Sisko could sense Bashir's unspoken conviction that his captain wasn't going to like what he heard next.

"What's the bad news?" Sisko asked.

"The Chief was right," Bashir answered. "I'd say we're looking at two more murders. And at least from a preliminary analysis, it appears both were killed by the same type of weapon that killed the Andorian."

Sisko's jaw tightened, and he felt his back stiffen as he reached a conclusion he suspected Bashir was about to share with him. "I see. Does Quark have a connection to the Cardassians?"

"I've asked Odo to bring him over to the Infirmary. I think you should be here."

"On my way, Doctor." Sisko paused for a moment, and then made a sudden decision. "Speaking of interspecies relations, Commander Arla, have you ever seen a changeling and a Ferengi interact?"

"Oil and water?" she asked.

Sisko shook his head. "Matter and antimatter. And you're about to experience it firsthand."

CHAPTER 7

"QUARK, QUARK, QUARK . . ." The expression in Sisko's eyes revealed such an unsettling combination of exasperation and pity that Quark couldn't hold the captain's gaze. Instead, he glanced furtively around the Infirmary to avoid it—but everyone else present was looking at him, too.

Everyone except the two very dead Cardassians on the examination table.

What was left of them.

"Can't you . . . cover them up or something?" Quark finally asked. "It's disgusting."

"Hmm," Odo said.

"What 'hmm'?" Quark demanded. "And don't say it's another sign of a guilty conscience. I've never seen them before. My conscience isn't guilty."

"I wasn't aware you had one," Odo said.

"Besides, Quark," Dr. Julian Bashir added, looking up from his continuing inspection of the corpses, "after being blasted with microwaves, transporter-fused to hull metal, and exposed to vacuum for a few years, these two are so mummified that one of them could be Garak and you wouldn't be able to recognize him."

"However," Garak added with a polite cough from his position overlooking Bashir's shoulder, "one hastens to add that a simple process of elimination should serve to confirm that I am *not* one of the dear departed."

With open-mouthed disbelief, Quark watched the decidedly striking new Bajoran Starfleet officer who had entered the Infirmary with Captain Sisko turn to address DS9's sole Cardassian inhabitant. "Oh, are you Garak?" She held out her hand. "I'm Commander Arla. I've heard so much about you."

After a moment's hesitation, Garak shook the Bajoran officer's hand as if it were coated with a Brigellian nerve toxin. "I'm sure you have."

"Excuse me," Quark interrupted, "but can we get back to *me* for a minute?"

"That depends," Odo said gruffly. "Are you ready to make a confession?"

"That's it! That is absolutely it!" Quark bared his artfully stained fangs, which had cost his parents a small fortune in orthodontic bills to twist into such Ferengi perfection. "You people—oh, you take the spore pie, all of you. Two nights ago, an unexplained death, and what do you do? You play Let's Blame the Ferengi! And now, two more unexplained deaths—from *ten years ago*—and what do you do? *The same thing!* Well, I'm sick of it." He jabbed an accusatory finger at Odo. "I'm sick of being your one-size-fits-all answer to crime on DS9!" Then he pointed at Sisko. "And I'm fed up with Starfleet not standing up to Odo's lax standards and sloppy investigations!"

Odo bristled with predictable indignation. "Let's talk about 'sloppy' after we've discussed those Denevan crystals you sold to the Nausicaan last Saturday night. You thought I didn't know, didn't you?"

"Arrrghh! You're doing it again! Changing the subject! Every time I make a point in my own defense, it's as if you people don't even want to pretend you've heard me."

Quark turned to Captain Sisko. "When the Cardassians withdrew, *you* were the one who wanted me to stay on this station as an example to others. To keep the community together."

"As I recall," Sisko said calmly, "first I had to threaten to put Nog in jail."

Quark waved his hand dismissively. "Negotiations. That's all that was. The point is, I stayed, didn't I? Even in the middle of this war, the Promenade is thriving. Do you have any problem hiring workers to live on board these days? No. Because I've done exactly what you wanted me to do."

"Let's not forget you made considerable profit at the same time," Major Kira said pointedly.

Quark felt as if he were in a shuttle spiraling out of control. "Of course I'm in it for profit! I'm a businessman! But there are rules to business!"

"Two hundred and eighty-five. Isn't that right, Quark? Some of which have never been revealed to a non-Ferengi." Odo's condescendingly snide tone was utterly maddening to Quark.

Quark was so overcome by frustration, his voice almost rose to shouting level. "When the Dominion took over this station, I could have made immense profit by turning in the major and . . . and your son, Captain . . . and everyone else working in the Resistance. I could have become an honorary Vorta and ended up with a ship made of latinum. But I stayed here and I risked my life—and my business—for you people! And this—*this* is how you repay me. You should all be ashamed of yourselves."

This time, there was only silence in the Infirmary. Quark straightened his jacket, wondering if it just might be possible that he had finally managed to get through to these small-lobed, microencephalic aliens.

And then Sisko ruined it all by saying, "Why ten years?"

Quark sighed. "Didn't you hear a word I said?"

"Every one of them," Sisko confirmed. "And the two that concern me are 'ten years.' How do you know when these two Cardassians were killed?"

Quark's ridged brow crinkled in puzzlement. "Isn't . . . isn't that what Dr. Bashir said? That they were killed during the Occupation? That was ten years ago."

"Technically," Kira said, "the Occupation spans anywhere from six to sixty-six years ago. Though the station wasn't built until twenty-four years ago."

"All right!" Quark sputtered. "I confess! I took a number out of thin air! I was confused! I suppose the almighty Federation has laws against Ferengi businessmen being confused and I deserve everything I've got coming to me!"

"Calm down, Quark," Bashir said. "You're jumping to far too many conclusions."

"Me?!"

Bashir nodded. "The only reason I've called everyone in here is to see if we can't get some answers." He turned to Garak, who was still hovering behind the examination table on which the Cardassian corpses were displayed. "Garak, may I call upon your expertise?"

Garak regarded the doctor warily, the reptilian gray nobs of his forehead bunching together in deep furrows. "Oh, Doctor, I'm afraid that in matters of mysterious deaths, I am entirely bereft of experience."

Quark took some comfort in noting that no one in the Infirmary appeared to believe Garak any more than they appeared to believe him.

"I was speaking of your expertise as a tailor," Bashir clarified.

Now smiling expansively, Garak nodded graciously. "But of course. You'd like me to examine the clothes these two are wearing."

"Please," Bashir said. "They're carrying no artifacts, no currency, weapons, I.D. rods . . . all they have is their clothes."

Without further hesitation, Garak bent over the table as if he saw such grotesquely mutilated bodies every day of his life. The only reason Quark watched what happened next was because the thought had occurred to him that his freedom might be dependent on the outcome of Garak's examination.

Garak's sharp gaze traveled from one wizened corpse to the next. One body—the one truncated at the waist—was clothed in an undistinguished tunic of brown fabric. The other body, which had been severed approximately at the knees, wore a similar garment, this time of blue.

Quark held his position as Garak picked up a pair of medical tongs from the side of the examination table and pushed them through the slightly elastic resistance of the medical containment field that surrounded the bodies. No doubt Bashir had set up the field more to protect the sensibilities of his visitors than out of concern for medical contamination. That simple act, however, released a sudden and most unpleasant odor of charred flesh mixed with the sickly-sweet-smelling antiseptic spray the doctor had used to coat the bodies. Quark turned away, coughing and gagging, noticing that even the doctor held a hand against his mouth.

Garak, however, appeared impervious to the stench. Concentrating on his task, he delicately nudged the head of the body in the brown suit. Quark's eyes narrowed. The Cardassian tailor's handling of the tongs made it seem as if he was quite experienced with autopsy procedures. "Ah, here's your first clue, Doctor, and one doesn't have to be a tailor to see it."

Quark stopped breathing so he could take a closer glance at the gruesome mess on the table. He stepped back quickly, having seen nothing that told him what Garak was talking about. From his expression, neither had Bashir.

"His hair," Garak said. "See how long it is? The way it's tied? Very characteristic. This man was a soldier in the Invidian Battalion. They managed the southern provinces."

"Managed?" Kira repeated angrily. "They were a death squad."

Sisko put a hand on Kira's shoulder as if passing her an unspoken signal. "Then why is he in civilian clothes?" he asked.

Hew-mons, Quark thought, with a shake of his head. *Always changing the subject.*

"Perhaps he died on his day off," Garak said lightly, directing his answer to Kira. "Whatever his reason for choosing this attire, I'm sure his DNA profile will be on file at Central Records. Determining his identity should make it easier to discover his date of death."

"What about the other one?" Bashir asked.

Garak glanced over at the slightly more complete body in the blue tunic. He used the tongs to lift up a tattered flap of cloth from the corpse's chest. "This one . . . I believe he might have been in a struggle. See how the fabric is torn on the shoulder?"

Now everyone crowded around the table to verify the tear in the body's tunic, then just as quickly reeled back. With all of Garak's movement through the surface of the medical containment field, the distressingly sweet, cloying odors of death and disinfectant had become even stronger.

"Any way of dating the clothes?" Bashir asked, with a hand

shielding his nose. "The width of the lapels? Length of the sleeves?"

Garak cocked his head, as if puzzled. "Fashion is more a function of geography than time, Doctor. What is stylish on one world is hopelessly garish on the next. There are colony worlds in the Union right now where this brown tunic would be the latest word in male furnishings. And other worlds where a man wearing anything blue would be arrested for disrupting public morals."

"Can you at least make a guess as to *where* the clothes were made?"

Still holding the torn shoulder fabric in the tongs, Garak frowned in disapproval. "I'm afraid this tunic was replicated. It could come from thousands—tens of thousands of different suppliers across the quadrant." He released the fabric remnant, then turned his attention to the second corpse's brown tunic with an approving smile. "Ahh, but *this* is—or at least *was*—a hand-tailored garment of the finest quality." With his customary, fastidious touch, he manipulated the tongs to open up the tunic to examine its lining. "It should be possible to trace the fabric, and from there. . . ." Garak froze.

"Do you see something?" Bashir asked, though everyone, including Quark was aware that something had shocked the Cardassian tailor into utter stillness.

"The lining." The tone of Garak's voice seemed oddly flat to Quark.

The doctor looked over Garak's shoulder. "What about it?"

"I often used this fabric myself. It's from a very small mill on Argellius II. I . . . look at the exquisite workmanship of that cross-stitching . . . oh my." Garak looked up at the curious faces of the people who surrounded him. "This is one of mine."

"That's an enormous help," Bashir said to Garak. "Isn't it?"

"I'm . . . not absolutely certain that's true," Garak replied, almost haltingly.

Quark couldn't remain silent any longer. Did he have to do everything himself? "Are you kidding? The kind of records the Cardassians keep put Ferengi records to shame. And I guarantee you, if I had sold someone a hand-tailored suit *twenty* years ago, I'd still know the name of his mate, his offspring, *and* his pet vole."

Whatever honest reflection of mood that had been revealed in Garak's face disappeared as quickly as if an Ark had been closed on an Orb of the Prophets. From across the examination table, Garak delivered a withering cold glare in Quark's direction. "Ordinarily, I might say that the random sand scratchings of an unhatched *krimanganee* would put Ferengi records to shame, but alas, this is not the time for banter." Resentfully, Quark noted how the Cardassian tailor softened his expression as he turned to Bashir. "And again, ordinarily, I would have to agree with you, Doctor. It should be a simple matter to discover to whom I sold this tunic, because I, too, never forget a customer." Garak's face showed he was as in the dark as they were. "Unfortunately, though, it appears I have forgotten this one."

Kira voiced the next logical question before Quark could shout it out. "Is it possible someone else bought the tunic and gave it to this man as a gift? Or that he stole it?"

"No, no, Major, you misunderstand," Garak said with an exaggerated display of patience. "Obviously, I could not remember this customer by his features, given the condition he's in. What I meant to say is, I have no recollection of selling this tunic to anyone. In fact, I have no recollection of even making it. Yet it is unquestionably my handiwork."

While everyone else looked mystified, Quark suddenly saw the pattern that was emerging from the void of confusion. But before he could act to confirm his suspicions, he saw Odo looking thoughtfully at Garak.

Aha, Quark thought, *Odo sees it, too.*

The changeling's next question was proof enough.

"Garak, is it possible that you made or sold this tunic about the time of the Withdrawal?"

"The lining fabric is old enough. It's . . . possible," the tailor admitted.

But Quark had no intention of standing idly by while Odo proceeded with his typically, time-consuming, step-by-step approach to an investigation. It was as if the changeling had never heard of the 9th Rule and the value of acting on raw instinct.

"Garak," Quark quickly said, "tell me—can you remember *anything* that happened on the Day of Withdrawal?"

"Of course," Garak said forcefully. "Every detail. Why are you smiling at me like that?"

Quark shot a sideways glance at Odo. The changeling was frowning, but Quark knew it was for the same reason that he himself smiled.

Garak was lying.

And Quark and Odo knew it.

"Would you like to try answering that again?" Odo asked Garak.

Garak looked at Quark, looked back to Odo, drew himself up rigidly. "I would not. And now, since I appear to have answered everything I can about these garments, I have a business to attend to."

Then Garak turned and left the Infirmary without another word.

Quark grinned at Odo, daring him to tell the others about what they both knew to be true. "See? The same thing happened to him."

"Am I the only one who's missing the point of this conversation?" Sisko asked.

Odo said nothing so Quark moved immediately to exploit the changeling's reluctance. "Captain," he announced, "allow me. Because unlike Odo, *I* have nothing to hide. You see, neither Odo nor I can recall anything about what happened to us on the Day of Withdrawal. And I think it's obvious that Garak doesn't remember anything, either."

"It *was* a long time ago," Sisko said.

"Not to me," Kira interrupted.

"Not to any Bajoran," Commander Arla added.

"And certainly not to any Cardassian," Quark said, "*or* Ferengi, or *changeling* who was on the station at the time. I'd say we've got a real mystery brewing here."

Sisko rubbed at his goatee. Quark suppressed a shudder of distaste. Even though the captain had worn the look for several years now, Quark still thought it made him look half-Klingon. "Quark, why am I feeling that *you're* changing the subject now?"

"It's the same subject, Captain. Two Cardassians dead from ten—I mean six years ago. An Andorian dead today. Dr. Bashir says everyone was killed by the same type of microwave energy discharge. Now what you have to do is find someone with a link to all three victims."

"We have," Odo said firmly. "You."

Quark turned in a full circle, appealing to the rest of them. "Does anyone else find it suspicious that Odo is going out of his way to blame these murders on me?"

Odo leaned forward and put his hands on the edge of the examination table. "You're heading into dangerous territory, Quark."

"See?" Quark said to Sisko. "See how defensive he is?"

Odo's voice actually shook with anger. "Quark, I'm warning you. . . ."

But, undaunted, Quark pressed the attack. "So, where were *you* on the Day of Withdrawal, Odo? In fact, where were you when Dal Nortron was killed? By a weapon that couldn't be detected by your own security scanners, I might add."

"That's it! You're going back to your cell." The changeling made a move as if to vault over the examination table and its grisly contents.

To Quark's relief, Sisko intervened again. He held up a hand. "That's enough, Constable. This is an open investigation."

"Not with Odo in charge," Quark complained through clenched teeth. He turned to Sisko. "Captain, I formally request you take him off this case because of conflict of interest. *He* should be a suspect, too."

"I will do no such thing. As far as I'm concerned, I agree with Dr. Bashir. Too many people are jumping to too many conclusions on too little information." Sisko looked at the doctor. "I want you to prepare complete DNA profiles for these two bodies so we can identify them."

"Through Cardassian Central Records?" Bashir asked.

"That's right."

"I'll prepare the records," Bashir said, "but aren't we at war with the Cardassians?"

"For humanitarian purposes, Starfleet and the Cardassian Union have established unofficial lines of communication to facilitate the identification of war dead and the repatriation of remains. You give me the profiles, I'll handle the rest."

Then Sisko faced Odo. "As for you, Constable, I want a complete report on Dal Nortron's death on my desk within the hour. And I don't want to read any conclusions not supported by incontrovertible evidence. Is that understood?"

Odo's initial reply was terse. "Yes." But then he continued. "Unfortunately, I will not be able to provide a *complete* report because Quark has refused to co-operate with my investigation."

"Is that right, Quark?"

Quark squirmed under Sisko's intent gaze, but he remained defiant. "Why should I cooperate?" Quark said. "Odo's not interested in the truth."

The captain's reply was so loud, it echoed off the hard surfaces of the Infirmary walls and ceiling, and Quark reflexively covered his sensitive ear channels to protect them from the assault. "I am tired of this game you two are playing. Even if you don't think Odo's interested in the truth, you can be certain I am. Cooperate."

Quark knew a bluff when he heard one. "You can't order me to do anything," he countered.

"You're absolutely right," Sisko agreed. "But what I *can* do is decide that neither Bajor nor Starfleet has jurisdiction over the death of two Cardassian nationals. Which means, I could turn over these bodies to the Cardassians, along with our prime suspect, and let them settle this matter."

Quark swallowed. Hard.

"The choice is yours, Quark," the captain concluded. "You can either cooperate with Odo, or you can 'cooperate' with the Cardassians."

Quark frantically sought to extract some benefit from a deal he knew he would be forced to accept. "All right, but I want Odo to release me from custody, and to provide me with a bodyguard."

The look on Sisko's face told Quark that was the last thing he had expected the Ferengi to say. "What do you need a bodyguard for?"

"Dal Nortron's partners," Quark said. "The Andorian sisters."

Sisko looked at Odo for clarification.

"Their names are Satr and Leen. They claim to be representatives of a trade mission from Andor so they have limited diplomatic immunity. They both believe Quark murdered Nortron and have filed for the Andorian Rite of *Kanlee*."

"And just what is the Andorian Rite of *Kanlee?*" Sisko asked.

"Roughly translated," Quark said darkly, "it means kill the Ferengi."

Odo ignored the interruption. "It's an old Andorian tradition," the changeling told Sisko. "They believe Quark killed Nortron. To maintain the balance of good and evil in the universe, they want to kill him. They are . . . a passionate people."

For a very long moment, Sisko stared at Quark, and Quark could tell the captain was making his decision. Quark felt almost sure he could predict what it was going to be.

"Here's my offer, Quark. You cooperate with Odo in the investigation of Dal Nortron's death, answer all the questions he asks, and instead of being confined to your cell, you'll be under station arrest, with a bodyguard."

Sisko's terms were exactly what Quark had expected. He took it as a minor victory. "Thank you, Captain."

But also as he expected, Odo didn't approve. "What about the murder of these two Cardassians?"

"For now," Sisko said, "I'll handle that investigation." He glanced around the Infirmary once, as if to make sure no one else had anything to say, then concluded, "I think we're finished here."

"But—but—" Quark protested, "what about the Day of Withdrawal?"

"One investigation at a time," Sisko told him. The captain looked back at the incomplete bodies of the unknown Cardassians. "This is one mystery where time is no longer of the essence." Sisko then nodded at Kira and the new Bajoran officer. "Major Kira, Commander Arla, you're with me." Then the captain and the two Bajoran officers left the infirmary.

Odo gestured sarcastically toward the door. "Come along, Quark. You're with *me*."

But it appeared Dr. Bashir wasn't quite finished with either of them. "Just a minute, you two. Is it true what you both said about not being able to remember what happened on the Day of Withdrawal?"

"A complete blank," Quark said emphatically. "I remember starting to pack up the breakables in the bar when the first reports of the troop transport launches started coming through . . . and then . . . next thing I knew, Rom and Nog found me asleep in the storage room and it was the next day."

Bashir looked at Odo. "How about you, Constable?"

"Nothing so mysterious," the changeling growled. "I've been thinking more about it, and I do remember breaking up a fight outside the chemist's shop. I was obviously hit by phaser fire, and woke up a day later when the Bajoran provisionals arrived."

"You're sure that's what happened?" Bashir asked. "I mean, someone saw you get shot, or you confirmed there *was* a fight at the chemists?"

Odo nodded. "Now that you mention it, yes. I do recall looking into it over the next few days. When the fighting broke out, I went to the Promenade, and the next thing I knew I was waking up and the whole thing was over—the withdrawal, Gul Dukat's departure, I missed it all."

Quark hid a smile of victory. Odo had just told his biggest lie of the day—one that would be easy to disprove. At a time when it would be most profitable to do so, that is.

"Well," Bashir said, "a phaser stun would certainly explain a loss of short-term memory."

But Quark wasn't willing to let Odo escape so easily. "Tell me, Doctor, would Odo's getting hit by phaser fire explain why *I* don't remember what happened that day? Or why Garak doesn't remember?"

Bashir looked confused. "Garak said he remembered everything perfectly."

Quark rolled his eyes at the doctor's incredible gullibility. "Dr. Bashir, Garak *says* he's a tailor. You don't believe *that,* do you?"

Bashir hesitated, then apparently decided to sidestep Quark's question. "There are techniques available, completely harmless, that I can use to see if either of you—or Garak—might be suffering from some type of post-traumatic stress syndrome, perhaps causing you to block out some kind of unpleasant memory of the Day of Withdrawal. I'd be happy to . . . see if I could help."

"Thank you, Doctor," Odo said. "But I doubt if I have anything to remember other than being in a phaser coma."

"I'll get back to you," Quark said drily. He would need many more details about how Bashir's techniques worked before he allowed himself to be in a position where someone might have access to his safe combinations and account passwords.

Bashir seemed disappointed by Quark's and Odo's lack of enthusiasm for his suggestion. "Well, you know where I am."

With that, Odo escorted Quark from the Infirmary, and they both made their way along the Promenade to the Security Office. Quark was only too glad to leave the unsettling smell of death and disinfectant and return to the bustling life of commerce the Promenade represented. Appreciatively, he sniffed the sweet tang of frozen *jumja* mixed with the incense from the Bajoran Temple, all overlaid with the exotic perfumes of twice a dozen worlds. It all was pure magic to Quark. Because to him, the combination of all these scents from all these potential customers gathered together to shop in one place invariably coalesced into the sweetest scent of all— latinum.

His snug jacket expanded to the breaking point as he breathed in deeply, happily. Then he saw the crowds in his bar to the left and instantly his sense of well-being evaporated. His eyes widened in alarm. There was no way his idiot brother Rom could handle that kind of crowd. He started toward the entrance. "I'm just going to check in with—"

But Odo grabbed him by the ear. *"After* you've 'cooperated,' " he hissed, and pulled Quark after him.

It was only with immense effort that Quark kept himself from squealing in public. Odo *knew* how much that hurt. But Quark continued without protest, because in just those few seconds he had had to look in through the main entrance to his bar he had seen three people who he did not want to notice him in his current state of custody.

Two of the people were those Andorian sisters, together at a small table and leaning so close together in intent and sibilant conversation that their blue antennae almost touched.

But the third person, sitting at the bar, trying and failing to look interested as Morn prattled on and on and on to her, was far more important to avoid than either of the Andorians.

She was Vash, a human female who had traveled the galaxy not only with Jean-Luc Picard of the *Enterprise* but with the unfathomable entity known only as Q. She was also Quark's favorite archaeologist—the one potential business partner he constantly thought of with real regret, as the one who got away.

And if Vash had returned to Deep Space 9 ahead of schedule, then Quark had no doubt that the news of Dal Nortron's untimely end had already spread across the quadrant—and all of Quark's other 'special' customers were already on their way.

Unfortunately, for that exact same reason—Dal Nortron's death—Quark had been left with nothing to sell.

Which meant that over the next few days, the Andorian sisters were not the only ones on Deep Space 9 who'd be looking to kill a certain Ferengi barkeep.

CHAPTER 8

"ALL RIGHT," Sisko said to Kira and Arla as the turbolift began its short trip from the Promenade to the Operations Center, "who wants to start? The Day of Withdrawal."

Kira looked at Arla, who shook her head. "It only took a day on DS9," Kira said. "But it was more like a week of withdrawal on Bajor. The Cardassians pulled back to their garrisons and the spaceports in stages." She paused for a moment, clearly remembering scenes of devastating destruction, then doggedly continued. "Burning the villages, poisoning the land and the rivers. For the first few days, the Resistance didn't know it was happening everywhere. Each cell thought it was seeing the leadup to a concentrated regional bombing attack. The Cardassians had done that sort of thing before."

The lift rose up through the final deck and, as always, Sisko felt a familiar sense of coming home. Ops was the heart of Deep Space 9, as much so as the bridge of a starship. Even the harsh angles and bare metal of its towering Cardassian components had become an oddly welcoming sight to him.

He exited the lift car with Kira and Arla close behind him and headed off in the direction of the science station, where Jadzia was on duty. She was running a metallurgical analysis on her screens.

"Dax," Sisko said, "join us." He nodded at the short flight of stairs leading to his office. Jadzia rose from her station to follow him at once.

As Sisko started up those stairs, he asked Kira if she could remember exactly where she had been on the Day of Withdrawal.

She shook her head with a rueful smile. "I missed it. Twenty years in the Resistance, and the week the Cardassians left I was in a triage center in Dahkur, burning with fever and pretty much delirious. Lake flu. It swept through the whole province that year."

"No lasting effects, I hope."

Kira shrugged. "So do I."

Behind them, Jadzia stepped through the entranceway, and the doors to Sisko's office slid shut.

"What about you, Commander?" Sisko asked Arla. He was pleased to see that whatever air of overfamiliarity she had exhibited an hour ago, she was keeping it in check now.

"Oh, I was on the *Solok.*"

Sisko hadn't recalled that posting from his quick glance at the Bajoran newcomer's file. "The Vulcan science vessel?"

Arla nodded. "We were at *Qo'noS.* A very dull assignment to remap the Praxis Ring."

"So, you weren't involved in any of the events of Withdrawal, either?"

Kira broke in. "She wasn't involved in the Occupation. Period."

As if a ship had just decloaked before him, Sisko was suddenly aware of the tension between the two Bajoran officers, and realized with a start that it had been there since he had first seen them meet.

He exchanged a quick glance with Jadzia, and her subtle nod confirmed that she saw the same animosity. Sisko wondered how he had missed it. But he could guess what was behind it.

"Is that right?" he asked in as neutral a fashion as he could.

Arla kept her eyes on him, ignoring Kira. "My grandparents lived on B'hal Ta. A Bajoran colony world. When the Cardassians annexed Bajor, my family was able to relocate to New Sydney. That's where I was born."

"You were fortunate," Sisko said. He decided that that accident of fate was more than enough reason to account for the major's feelings toward Arla Rees. He knew that there were those on Bajor—especially those who had served in the Resistance like Kira—who believed that expatriate Bajorans who had not suffered through the Occupation, and who had not voluntarily returned to their home-world or taken up arms against Cardassia, were only one step removed from being collaborators.

"Yes, sir, very fortunate."

Sisko decided to bring the conversation back to the less-controversial present. "So, from your experience, Major, and from any research you might have done, Commander, can you think of any reason why personnel on board DS9 on the Day of Withdrawal might have suffered from memory loss, selective or otherwise?"

"Benjamin?" Jadzia asked. "Who's suffering from memory loss?"

Sisko quickly summarized for his old friend Quark's claim to be missing memories of the day in question, and the Ferengi's suspicions that Odo and Garak were similarly affected.

"Fascinating," Jadzia said. "The old name for it is 'Missing Time Syndrome.' On Earth, it goes back centuries, before first contact, when the Reticulii were conducting their genetic profiling of humans and didn't want anyone in the sample group to know they had been transported to the orbiting medical ships. Today, the Federation's own First Contact Office uses the same techniques if a duck blind's exposed or a precontact investigator is detected."

"In this case," Sisko said, "I think we can rule out any involve-ment by the Reticulii or the First Contact Office. What other possi-bilities should we consider? Medical experimentation?"

Kira shook her head. "The Cardassians conducted a horrendous amount of so-called medical research on Bajoran prisoners. Some of it involved mind control. But that was mostly in the camps. Up here, they kept the slave workers in line with force and random execu-tions. So I think it's unlikely anyone experimented on Quark—espe-cially since, if the Cardassians *had* experimented on him, their proto-cols usually called for the experimental subjects to be killed when the experiment was finished."

Arla looked hesitant, but now offered her own theory. "I don't know how relevant this is, but starships use anesthezine gas to dis-able intruders, and memory lapses are sometimes reported as a side effect."

Sisko looked at Kira. "We have a Starfleet anesthezine system installed on DS9. But there're also the remnants of a Cardassian neurozine gas dispersal network which, as I recall, was kept on hand in case of worker revolt."

Kira's voice was bitter. "Crowd-control inhalants like anesthezine are nonlethal. And nonlethality was never a concern of the Cardassians. They used neurozine at fatal concentrations, and if they had used it up here on the Day of Withdrawal, there would have been a lot more than just four Bajorans dead."

Sisko turned to Dax, who had so many times in the past been able to share the wisdom and experience of her past hosts. "Old Man?"

But she didn't look hopeful. "Benjamin, there're so many methods of blocking memories that I wouldn't know where to begin without more information."

"What kind of information?"

Jadzia pressed her lips together in thought. "Well, I'd like to know how much time Quark believes he's missing. Is it the same length of time that Odo and Garak can't account for? Is it the exact same period of time? Were they together on the Day of Withdrawal? Were they exposed to . . . a radiation leak? An unusual subspace discharge?" Her face brightened as if she had just had a sudden insight.

"Something just occurred to you," Sisko said.

"I talked with Odo yesterday about his investigation into the Andorian's death. He thinks a microwave weapon was used, but I think it's possible some sort of accidental energy pulse could have caused similar injuries."

Sisko smiled at Jadzia. "Old Man, you've been spending too much time in the holosuites with Worf. You were the reason we even found the Cardassians' bodies. Right after your talk with him, Odo sent a team down to the lower levels to look for energy anomalies. They found one where a power conduit entered the lower module. And Rom's team found that the cause of the anomaly was that the Cardassians had been transporter-fused into the inner hull plates, weakening the shielding."

Jadzia made a face at Sisko. After so many years of friendship, she was allowed more freedom with Starfleet protocol. "I knew that, Benjamin. I was standing by with the tractor beam when Rom found the bodies. I was just wondering if an anomalous *energy* event that resulted in microwave radiation could also be tied to an anomalous *temporal* event."

"An anomalous temporal event?" Arla said. "Those are incredibly rare."

"Not on DS9," Sisko said. "Unexpected time shifts are quite common in this region of space."

Jadzia confirmed it. "Actually, the odd temporal events we've experienced in the past almost all arise in some way out of our proximity to the wormhole. The structure of subspace is extremely twisted in this region. What's really surprising is that we don't experience even *more* jumps in time than we do. But on the Day of Withdrawal, the station was still in orbit of Bajor. And the planet's gravity well would have provided a great deal of shielding against almost any wormhole-related phenomena."

Sisko sat down on the corner of his desk, reached back, and picked up his baseball. "Okay, so we can rule that possibility out, too. But I still want this looked into.

"Major Kira," he said, rolling the ball back and forth in his fingers, feeling its comforting contours relax him as they always did, freeing him to think more clearly. "The constable seemed reluctant to discuss the Day of Withdrawal in the Infirmary. Perhaps he won't be as reluctant speaking with you. See if you can get him to talk about what he remembers from that day."

Kira seemed surprised by the request. "Captain, I'm not sure I feel comfortable doing that."

Sisko understood her reluctance. Everyone on the station knew about the love affair that had blossomed between Kira and Odo in the last month. And as their friend and colleague, Sisko was happy for both of them. "I'm not asking you to betray a trust, Major. Let Odo know that you're asking on my behalf. Let him know that I understand his reluctance to discuss what he remembers in front of Garak, but that I would appreciate a more forthright account that will remain confidential."

Kira nodded, accepting his argument.

Sisko tossed his baseball up a few centimeters, then caught it again. "Commander Arla, since I'm assuming you've had few if any dealings with Cardassians, I'm assigning you to question Garak."

Arla's eyes widened. "Question him about what, sir?"

"What Dax wants to know. I want a timeline of everything that

happened to Odo and Garak *and* Quark on the Day of Withdrawal."
Then he smiled winningly at Jadzia.

"Don't tell me," she said, pouting. "I get to talk to Quark."

Sisko's grin grew. "I can't imagine anyone else he'd rather open
up to."

"Captain," Kira broke in briskly, "can I ask why something that
happened six years ago is important enough for us to drop our other
duties and—"

"No one's dropping their other duties," Sisko said. "There's a
war on."

"Exactly," Kira agreed. "And I don't see the point of expending
extra effort just to solve the deaths of two Cardassians, especially
one who was in a death squad."

Sisko replaced his ball on his desk, then stood up to address Kira
and the others, not as their coworker and friend but as their commanding officer and captain of Deep Space 9. "Major, those two
dead Cardassians represent a mystery. And I will not have mysteries
on my station. Because until we find out how those Cardassians died,
and why Quark and perhaps two other people on this station had
their memories interfered with, I can't be certain if any of it might
happen again. And believe me, if an attack wing of Jem'Hadar fighters is bearing down at us, I want to know that my officers are not
suddenly going to develop a case of amnesia and end up fused into
the hull plates. Is that clear?"

Kira, Arla, and even Jadzia stood at attention. "Yes, sir," Kira
said.

"Right away, sir," Arla added.

"Ben, I'll speak to Quark as soon as Odo's finished with him,"
Jadzia confirmed.

Sisko could see that there was more that Jadzia wanted to say.
"Something else?" he asked.

"What about the Andorian?"

"Quark's many things," Sisko said reluctantly, "but he's no murderer. Though I do think Odo's enjoying this chance to make him
sweat. And at the same time, I think that by appearing to be convinced that Quark is guilty, Odo's making the real murderer feel
overconfident."

Arla seemed shocked by Sisko's statement. "Sir, do you honestly believe that the constable has the wrong man, and that the real killer is still free on the station?"

"That's exactly what I think, Commander."

"But . . ." Arla said, obviously disturbed by the thought, "isn't knowingly permitting the continued custody of an innocent man a violation of Starfleet directives concerning the application of local laws? And aren't you risking the real murderer escaping? Not to mention putting the other personnel on this station at risk of being killed?"

"Commander, Starfleet regulations are written by bureaucrats in comfortable offices back on Earth. As captain of this station, I do have the authority to . . . be flexible in how I choose to follow those regulations, whenever I feel a given situation is outside the parameters Starfleet considered when the regulations were written. Believe me, Commander, this entire station falls outside those parameters."

Jadzia smiled at Sisko, and then took the confused commander's arm. "Odo won't be through questioning Quark for a while. Why don't we get some *raktajino* and . . . we'll talk."

Sisko could see that Arla was flattered by Jadzia's request; she left the office with her, Major Kira following a moment later.

As Sisko stood in the doorway to his office watching the three officers head for the turbolift, he was pleased to unexpectedly see his son, Jake, just emerging from the lift on the main deck below. The love he felt for his boy, this anchor for him in the storm of events that regularly engulfed this station, filled Sisko with a transcendent joy.

But his sudden smile was undercut as he saw who stepped out of the lift behind Jake: Jake's best friend, Nog, and Chief O'Brien.

Jake looked up to wave at him, and Sisko returned the gesture, growing even more concerned as he noted Jake's halfhearted smile, Nog's nervous expression, and O'Brien's flushed cheeks.

"Hi, Dad," Jake called out as he took the stairs to the upper level, two at a time.

"Sir," Nog added crisply, just behind Jake.

Sisko frowned, and the three visitors froze where they stood. "You know, if this were six years ago and I saw you three coming up here like this, I'd think Chief O'Brien had caught you *boys* playing in the Jefferies tubes again. But you two young *men* are too old for that now, aren't you?"

O'Brien was wheezing slightly as he resumed climbing the stairs. "Funny you should say that, sir."

Sisko sighed. "Should we step inside?"

"Yes, sir," Jake said glumly.

Sisko followed the three into his office, suspecting he wasn't going to like what they had to tell him.

He was right.

CHAPTER 9

FOR THE second time in two days, Jake Sisko opened the small egress panel and slid it to the side of the cramped Jefferies tube.

"It's open," he said. Then he heard Nog's communicator badge chirp as his friend passed on the report to Chief O'Brien.

The chief's voice came back, echoing along the metal-walled tube. "According to your position on the station plans, you two lads should be facing another fifteen meters of unobstructed passageway."

Jake sighed. He and Nog had finally done what they should have done years ago, and told DS9's chief engineer about the hidden section of the station. Then, with an agitated O'Brien at their side, they had told Jake's father. And *then*—Jake was sure it was just to compound the humiliation he and Nog felt—Sisko and the chief had insisted they repeat their story to the forbidding, and strongly disapproving, Lieutenant Commander Worf.

But even though it was plainly evident through all the reporting that his father was keenly disappointed in him for having kept something like this a secret for so long, Jake could also see that neither his father nor the chief nor Commander Worf actually believed the story when they first heard it. So why were they upset? Not that they shouldn't be, because the story *was* true. It was just . . . Jake didn't know. He only hoped that in a million years or so, when he was his father's age, he would have a better grasp of a teenager's way of thinking.

Jake lifted his head to look back down the narrow Jefferies tube at Nog. "I don't get it. Do they still think we're making this up?"

Apparently, Nog's comm channel was still open because O'Brien answered. "No, I don't think you're making it up. I'm just telling you what's on the screen."

"Sorry, Chief," Jake said with a grimace. "I'm going to climb through the opening now."

Jake pushed himself up through the open access way just as he had before, then again swung his body around to free his legs so he could drop down into the dark section of corridor. Nog followed a moment later, much more quickly and smoothly than the last time. Once again, his palm torch was the only source of light.

"Tell them," Jake said.

Nog tapped his communicator. "We are in the corridor." Nog made it sound as if they were commandos who had just beamed in behind enemy lines.

A few seconds later, the short section of corridor lit up with the golden energy of the transporter effect, and three sparkling columns of quantum mist resolved into Jake's father, O'Brien, and Worf. Each of them carried their own palm torch. Jake wasn't quite sure why Worf had his hand on the phaser he wore. But then, Worf was like that.

Benjamin Sisko's expression was unreadable. "Chief?" was all he said. Jake had noticed that his father had a shorthand way of dealing with his command staff, almost as if they shared some low-level telepathic link.

Chief O'Brien's attention jumped back and forth between the corridor and the large engineering padd he carried. The padd was similar to the kind Jake had seen artists sometimes use for sketching. "This makes absolutely no sense," the chief said. "Look at the deck plan for this section."

As Sisko and Worf stood on one side of O'Brien to study the engineering display, Jake stood with Nog on the other.

On the padd, Jake could see four yellow dots representing the team's active communicators tightly grouped together, blinking in the middle of what a label identified as a storage room.

"This is clearly not a storage room," Worf stated in his deep, somber voice.

O'Brien nodded, pointing to various bulkheads that surrounded the blinking lights on the padd display. "I think I can see what's happened here. The Cardassians' own official plans have been altered to show that these two storage rooms, here and here—" O'Brien's finger touched the surface of the padd, "—have back walls that extend an extra three meters or so. Notice this relay room extends two more meters. And this heat-exchange conduit is . . . maybe a half-meter wider than it has to be. And the two corridor sections running to either side are the same. So I'm betting the conduits that are supposed to be running right above us have been rerouted to either side, too, probably passing through the deck plates instead of running through that Jefferies tube that just isn't there."

Jake was surprised by how seriously the three men were reacting to the unmarked corridor's existence. His father, especially, looked grim. "Why weren't these deviations noticed when the first retrofit team went through the station to confirm the Cardassian plans?"

O'Brien looked apologetic. "I'm betting they were noticed. But there are lots of discrepancies between the Cardassians' plans for the station and how they were executed. A project this big, there would have to be. I've noticed little things over the years myself—pipes in the wrong order, a junction box on the left wall instead of the right . . . it gets so you come to expect it. But they're usually not major enough to bother altering the plans to fit."

"Yet this stretch of corridor is . . ." Sisko swung the beam of his palm torch from one end of the section to the other. ". . . at least ten meters long, Chief. That's a lot of station to go missing."

"No argument from me, sir. All I can say is that this is a noncritical section of the station, so with the war changing our priorities, we just haven't had a full refit team down here yet. For what it's worth, we would have found this . . . missing space . . . eventually."

Sisko levelled his gaze at Jake. "For what it's worth, we should have been informed about this missing space six years ago."

Jake was about to remind his father how many times he had apologized already, when Nog nudged him in the side. Jake understood.

Nog had gone to great lengths to explain to Jake that their best defense was to behave like Starfleet cadets—limiting their responses to Yes, sir; No, sir; and most importantly, No excuse, sir. "It's a good way to avoid arguments," Nog had emphasized.

So Jake remained silent until his father said, "All right, then, where's this . . . hidden holosuite?"

Nog hurried ahead. "Right down here, Captain. It's the only door in that bulkhead."

The team followed Nog until they were gathered together by the closed door. Worf and O'Brien immediately scanned the door and the area beyond it with their tricorders—one set for engineering readings, the other for security.

Jake shifted his weight from one leg to the other, impatient with the delay. He wanted this over with. "Dad, there's nothing dangerous in there. We've been inside a lot of—"

Sisko cut him off with an icy glare. "And maybe you've been lucky. Before they left, the Cardassians booby-trapped all sorts of equipment and facilities in this station, *especially* anything with a military function. And the only reason I can think of for putting a holosuite down here is for training purposes."

"Yes, sir," Jake said dispiritedly.

"I detect no explosives or triggering devices behind the door," Worf announced as he lowered his tricorder.

"Captain," O'Brien added, "I'm not even picking up any evidence of power flow. The tricorder's telling me there's a room beyond the door, about five meters by six. But I don't think anything inside is even connected to the station's power grid." The chief made an adjustment on his tricorder. "In fact, I'm not even picking up any evidence of holo equipment. Either projectors or microforce-field emitters."

Nervously, Jake looked up and down the corridor to see if there was any chance they could somehow be at the wrong door. But just as every time before, there was only the one.

"You're certain it *was* a holosuite?" his father asked him.

"Dad, it could run our fishing hole program perfectly. Water and everything."

His father looked back to O'Brien. "Then it has to be a holo-suite, *and* for it to run a program from my own data library it has to have some type of interface with the station's main computer network."

O'Brien made more adjustments, then frowned. "If there is, sir, I'm going to have to make a more detailed scan. From inside."

Sisko nodded at Worf. Worf tapped the door control and the door opened.

Jake almost smiled as he heard Nog take a deep breath. His best friend was preparing himself for the embarrassment of having everyone see his adolescent modification of the fishing-hole program, complete with Ferengi bathing beauties.

But as the light from the palm torches stabbed into the room, it revealed . . . only a room.

Jake and Nog both tried to push ahead, but were held back by Worf.

"I've never seen that before," Jake said to his father.

"Sir, this holosuite has *always* been in operation," Nog added.

Sisko looked at O'Brien. "Any chance the holosuite ran on batteries and yesterday's visit finally exhausted them?"

O'Brien was skeptical. "No battery powerful enough for a holosuite goes completely dead that fast. I'd still be able to pick up some residual charge somewhere. And even taking a direct reading from the far wall, there are *no* holoprojectors on it or in it."

Sisko nodded at Worf again and he and the Klingon stepped into the room together. Jake watched as his father and Worf reached the middle, then turned slowly, playing their palm torches around in a circle like all-seeing scanners.

"It appears to be a lab of some sort," Worf said slowly.

"Maybe," Sisko said. "It does look as if they were building things in here. Maybe a machine shop? Chief O'Brien?"

O'Brien stepped in next and Jake watched him make the same careful examination of the room, this time giving a running inventory of everything he saw. "Circuit testbed, communications console, a Type-IV computer interface. . . ." He gave Sisko a significant look. "That's identical to Dax's science station in Ops." He returned to his assessment of the room. "A few storage lockers, maybe for lab coats or tools or lunches . . . None of them locked."

"What about that?" Sisko asked, aiming his torch to a corner of the room Jake couldn't see.

"Well, it's a console," O'Brien said. "But I don't recognize the configuration."

Sisko looked at both O'Brien and Worf. "Gentlemen, any energy readings?" he asked.

Worf and O'Brien replied at the same time. "No, sir."

Sisko motioned to Jake and Nog. "You two. In here."

Jake and Nog stepped over the lip of the door and into the room. In this nonoperational mode it was completely unfamiliar to Jake, and he could see the same lack of recognition in Nog.

"Really, sir. We never saw it this way," Nog said.

"You two said you were able to change whatever program it was displaying," Sisko prompted.

"That's right," Jake said. "I'll give it a try." He cleared his throat. "Room, this is Jake Sisko. Show me my fishing hole."

Jake unconsciously braced himself for the sudden swirl of holo-pixels and the odd optical bounce that had always followed that command.

But nothing happened.

"Anything?" Sisko asked O'Brien.

"I've set this at full sensitivity, Captain. If there were a single acoustical pickup in this room, I would have detected the current flow created when Jake spoke." He showed the tricorder's flashing face to Jake's father.

Sisko answered his own question. "Nothing."

Jake winced at his father's tone of voice. "Dad, this *was* a holodeck. We played in my fishing hole. And Nog had a really great Ferenginar adventure playground." The playground had been at the edge of a dismal, rain-misted swamp, Jake remembered, but the programmable swinging vines *had* been a lot of fun.

"What else?" Sisko asked sternly.

Jake shrugged, perplexed by what he had no way to explain, or prove. "A couple of other programs from our personal library. You know, the theme park at Tranquility Base, the Klingon Zoo . . ." He glanced at Nog.

"We could only ever run programs that were in your personal files or my father's," Nog said. "I mean, we could customize elements of them with voice commands, but . . . we never really figured out the room's full operating interface."

Sisko looked again at O'Brien and Worf as if silently soliciting their opinions.

In response, Worf asked the next question. "Are you certain you never saw a holoprogram that was Cardassian in nature? A military training scenario? Cardassian history reenactments?"

Both Jake and Nog shook their heads.

"Oh," Nog suddenly added. "There was the moon. The Bajoran moon."

"Which moon?" Sisko asked sharply.

Jake stared beseechingly at Nog, who shrugged. "Dad, I don't know. One of the inhabited ones. That was the program that was running yesterday when we came in. That's what made us think that someone else had been in here."

Sisko rubbed his free hand over his clean-shaven scalp. It was a gesture Jake had seen his father make a thousand times, most often when Dax was forcing him into checkmate in three-dimensional chess.

"Chief," Sisko said, "if we don't know what that console is, is there any chance it could be some radically different form of holo-projector?"

Jake took a look at the unidentified console as O'Brien walked over to it and the four palm torches in the room converged upon it.

The console was definitely Cardassian in design—a large, jagged boomerang shape, tilted slightly toward the operator, finished with the familiar dull-gray bonding metal. The flat-panel controls were unlit, though the light from the palm torches showed that the controls were arranged in standard Cardassian logic groupings. About the only detail that made the console unusual was that in the center of its slanting surface, a section had been inset in order to hold a flat shelf about a half-meter square.

Even to Jake's untrained eye, it seemed obvious that whatever had been connected to the console on that shelf had been ripped out. Two power leads dangled to either side, their interior component wires roughly torn apart. Jake could even see heat damage on the console just beneath the lead ends, as well as in the center of the shelf.

"Now, this is interesting," O'Brien said as he held his tricorder only centimeters from the damaged console.

"Was it a holoprojector?" Sisko asked.

"I doubt it," O'Brien answered. "But I don't think I've ever seen energy traces like this before."

"What kind of energy?" Worf asked.

"Hard to say, Commander. I don't think it's from a weapon. But . . . whatever was on this section here—" O'Brien pointed his tricorder at the console's inset shelf, "—it was radiating . . . something I haven't seen before."

Jake stepped back as his father moved in front of him and Nog as if to shield them from the console. "Dangerous?" his father asked.

"Not now, sir. And there's no way to know if what I'm picking up came about because it was a slow release of radiation over a long period of time—in which case, I don't think it ever would have been dangerous—or if it came in a sudden, explosive release, in a short time—in which case, it might have been." O'Brien snapped his tricorder shut with a practiced flip of his hand. "Sorry, Captain. But that's the best I can do with this. I'm going to need a full team to take it apart. Couldn't hurt to have Dax take a look, too."

"Maybe in a day or two," Sisko said. "I've already got her helping out with the dead Cardassians."

Jake was surprised to hear Commander Worf snort.

Sisko raised his eyebrows. "A problem, Mr. Worf?"

Worf looked up at the ceiling. "Sir, it is not any of my business."

"But . . . ?"

"For Quark to say that he has lost his memory to provide an alibi for his actions at the time the Cardassians were killed is . . . ludicrous."

"You're right," Sisko agreed. Jake was as surprised to hear his father say that as it appeared Commander Worf was. But then his father finished his statement. "It *is* none of your business."

"Yes, sir," Worf growled grumpily.

Jake caught the lightning-quick wink and a smile that his father meant just for him. Then he watched as his father tugged down on his jacket and transformed himself from Jake's father into a Starfleet captain again.

"Anything else you feel we should know?" he asked Jake and Nog. "Any detail, however small, you think might help us out?"

Jake and Nog looked at each other, shook their heads.

Sisko accepted their answer. "All right. You two can—"

"I have a question," Chief O'Brien suddenly said. "How did you two find this room in the first place?"

"We used to explore the Jefferies tubes," Jake said.

"I can understand that," O'Brien replied. "But what possessed you to go to all the trouble of opening up that access hatch? It couldn't have been easy."

Jake looked down at the deck, trying to remember the first day he and Nog had found the room. "I think it was because we had never seen one so small. It's not exactly a standard size."

Nog coughed. "We were . . . looking for hidden Cardassian treasure, Chief."

"Ah," O'Brien said. "For a couple of twelve-year-olds, that makes perfect sense. But then, when you came in here, to the room, for the first time, how did you know it was a holosuite? It couldn't have been running any of your own programs without your having given it a command, right?"

"Right," Jake said with surprise. He looked down at Nog. "What *was* running when we came in?"

Jake felt his father's hand on his shoulder. "Jake, do you have any sense that you can't *remember* the first time you came into this room?"

"I don't think so," Jake said, wondering why his father suddenly sounded so worried.

"Wait! I remember," Nog said.

Everyone looked at him. He looked up at Jake. "You didn't want to go inside, remember?"

Jake laughed. "Oh yeah. I was . . . I was afraid. I remember now."

Nog looked back to Sisko. "So Jake dared me to go in first."

"And what program was running?" O'Brien asked.

"That's what was so great," Nog said excitedly. "It was Ferenginar. The swamp outside the capital city. It was dark, and wet, and raining. I was *so* excited. I came out to tell Jake it was just like my adventure playground program, and when we both came back in, we found the playground just a few hundred meters away."

O'Brien looked at Sisko. "The room recognized him. Called up his favorite program from his father's personal library. And all in the space of time it took to open the door."

Jake looked at the serious expression that his father, O'Brien, and Worf all shared now. "Why's that bad?"

O'Brien answered. "Jake, there's no power coming into this room. There's no computer link through that Type-IV console or through any other piece of equipment in the room. Yet somehow this room had the data-processing capability to identify Nog and call up a program from his father's personal library in seconds. Not even the holodecks they use at Starfleet Academy have that kind of processing ability." O'Brien turned to Sisko as if making a formal report. "Sir, with this new information, I think it's reasonable to assume that this was a top-secret Cardassian research facility, probably involving advanced computers and holo-replication technology far beyond anything we have."

"I agree," Sisko said. "So why did the Cardassians leave it behind?"

"Perhaps," Worf said in a voice full of grave concern, "the equipment in here was too complex to be removed in time during the Withdrawal, and was considered too valuable to be destroyed."

Jake could see that his father was definitely intrigued—and disturbed—by that possibility. "You know," he said softly as if talking to himself, "Starfleet has never been able to come up with a satisfactory explanation for why the Cardassians didn't activate DS9's self-destruct system when they withdrew. I wonder if this room—this lab—is the reason. Did they achieve a breakthrough here that they hoped to keep hidden until they could return?"

"But they did return, Captain," Worf said. "Last year. Why did they not reclaim their equipment then?"

Sisko looked up, and Jake could see he was enjoying the challenge this room was presenting. "Perhaps the work being done here was so secret that only a handful of people knew about it. Perhaps they died during the Withdrawal, or shortly after. There could be a dozen reasons, Worf."

"But if the work was so secret and so valuable," O'Brien said, "then why was it being carried out *here?* In a mining station? In an occupied sector subject to attack by Bajoran resistance fighters?"

"I don't know, Chief," Sisko admitted, and didn't seem troubled by his lack of an answer. "But you can be sure there was a reason. We're dealing with Cardassians here, and they have a reason for everything they do." He looked around the room, deep in thought. "If this *was* a Cardassian research facility, then you can be sure that the reason it is *here* is because this is the only place it *could* be."

Jake saw that O'Brien didn't share his captain's sense of urgency for the problem at hand. "But, sir, why would that be?"

Jake could see his father was in his element now. His face was alive with new purpose. "Who knows, Chief. But one thing's for sure—even after six years, this old place still has a few surprises left in it."

CHAPTER 10

THE ONLY THING worse than a Ferengi with a headache was a Ferengi with an earache. And at this moment, in his darkened bar in the middle of DS9's night, Quark suffered from both—unquestionably the aftermath of the past eight hours he had spent with Odo.

And now his woes intensified as he saw the after-hours condition of his establishment. The chairs had not been placed on top of the tables. There were still glasses on the dabo table. And behind the bar, the replicator had been left on.

"Why do I even bother?" Quark said to the empty room. He gazed up at the vivid orange, red, and yellow stained-glass mural that dominated the first floor of his bar. All its backglow panels had been left on, too. "What about you, Admiral? Do you have an answer?"

The mural kept its silence, which was no great surprise. Quark shuffled over to the bar to pour himself a very large drink.

Exactly what the mural was, Quark really wasn't sure. For years, that same wall had been dominated by a large Cardassian *galor,* courtesy of Gul Dukat.

Quark seldom cared about politics, and if the commandant of Terok Nor had wanted his grandmother hung on the wall, it would have been fine with the Ferengi. So the lurid green, pink, and yellow symbol of the Cardassian Union, which looked to Quark like some improbable combination of the hooded Smiling Partner of Ferengi legend and a short-handled screwdriver, had remained proudly in place—until Gul Dukat had swaggered in one day to announce he had just won a spectacular work of rare and valuable art in a late-night game of tongo. And since Quark's was the only public facility on the station with a ceiling high enough to properly display this great treasure, Dukat proclaimed Quark's would be its new home.

At the time, Quark had cared as much about his establishment's decor as he did about politics. His was the only bar on the Cardassian half of the station—indeed, it was the only bar on the entire station, the closest thing to competition being the Cardassian Cafe. And if a tired Cardassian soldier or Bajoran trustee would rather eat replicated Cardassian *neemuk* without benefit of *kanar* to wash it down or the company of luscious dabo girls, then Quark was just as happy not to have those lackluster, boring slugs taking up valuable space in his bar.

So, Cardassian *galor* or Dukat's esteemed art treasure, it mattered little to Quark at the time what was on the back wall of his bar. True, he had had to shut down for two days while a team of Bajoran artisans were brought up to install the mural, and Subcommandant Akris had not granted Quark's request for a matching percentage decrease in the weekly kickback—that is, licensing fee—that Quark had to pay the station management office. But Dukat had more than made up for Quark's initial lost profits by pretentiously buying endless rounds for his staff on the night the mural was grandly unveiled—to mostly diffident though polite applause.

As Quark had worked the tables that night, he had overheard the Bajoran comfort women saying that at least the orange light helped bring a more Bajoran flush to the cold gray faces of the Cardassian officers they were forced to entertain. Quark himself liked the orange light, because it made it easier to use short measures in amber-colored drinks. And Dukat got to proudly trumpet on about the addition he had made to culture on Terok Nor—making the station an uplifting beacon of Cardassian light amidst the primitive darkness of the Bajoran sector.

It was just that no one seemed to be sure what the mural was supposed to represent—until finally, that first night, when much *kanar* had been consumed and two glinns had already been dragged off to the Infirmary after a particularly brutish fight (which fortunately had lasted long enough for Quark to take bets and clear five slips of latinum), Dukat toasted the mural in such a way that it was clear what *he* thought it was.

"To a mighty enemy," Dukat had proclaimed, "defeated at last, now sentenced to look on the works of the Cardassian Union and despair! Ladies and gentlemen, I give you the portrait of Admiral Alkene, late of the Tholian Assembly!"

After Dukat and his guests had left that evening, Quark and Rom and two Cardassian mining engineers had closed the place, leaning on the bar, staring thoughtfully up at what was now called the Tholian mural.

One mining engineer drunkenly offered up the observation that Tholians had faceted heads.

The other, in an equal state of disequilibrium, disagreed, maintaining it was the Tholian helmets that were faceted, and that the shape of Tholian heads was closer to the long and pointed sections included in the mural. Except that he was positive the mural had been installed upside down.

Rom had volunteered that *he* was fairly certain the mural was actually a version of the traditional good-luck banners that were always hung over the drinking troughs in what he delicately referred to as Tellarite mud-pits of ill repute. "Yep, they . . . make them by the hundreds on Tellarus," Rom had sniggered. "And you see that same crazy design on Tellarite scarves and pill boxes and . . . lingerie."

Quark remembered glaring at his idiot brother, demanding to know why the Tellarites would put a portrait of a *Tholian admiral* on *lingerie!*

Rom had simply shrugged and gone on to explain in excruciatingly precise and clinical detail that the shape in the mural was not that of a Tholian head at all, but of an entirely different, but equally remarkable part of Tellarite male anatomy.

Even as he began to laugh at Rom's hilariously ribald description, Quark had felt his heart actually stop beating as he suddenly remembered the presence of the two Cardassian engineers. Fortunately, both were so drunk that they didn't hear Rom dismiss the Gul's great work of art as nothing more than a big Tellarite . . . well, even in private, Quark had not been able to say the word, though he relished the aptness of the image.

For at least a year after that, he and Rom had shared a rare moment of rapport in their guilty, private pleasure every time Dukat came to the bar with whoever his latest comfort woman was and regaled her with the story of Admiral Alkene, ending with a grandiloquent toast and salute to the mural.

Only Quark and his brother knew to what the gul was really raising his glass, and they kept that knowledge to themselves. And if any other visitors to Quark's during those last years of the Occupation recognized what was hanging on the wall for what it was, they also wisely kept their expert knowledge—and their laughter—to themselves.

Though Quark had never been able to confirm Rom's saucy identification of the mural's subject matter, and for that matter had never been able to determine how his idiot brother had come to have such deep knowledge of Tellarite mud-pits of ill repute, it was always in Quark's mind that if the day ever came that the Cardassians left Terok Nor, he would celebrate that glorious occasion by shattering Gul Dukat's mural into ten thousand shards.

But that day had come and gone, six long years ago, and the mural remained, with both him and Rom still referring to it, in private, as the Admiral.

But the Tholian mural was of no importance this night, and Quark tried not to think of the disarray the bar had been left in—or the overtime it would cost him to get it back in shape for Morn's arrival in the morning. Instead, he poured himself a *snoggin* of Romulan ale.

And since old traditions are hard to ignore, he did hold up the glass to the mural. "To you, Admiral—or whatever you are. Because you're still here, and I'm still here, and I have absolutely no idea why that should be." He gulped down a mouthful of the ale, shivering as the blue fluid sliced through him like a protoplaser. "Except, that is," he coughed to finish his toast, "as some twisted reminder of the 117th Rule: You can't free a fish from water."

"Actually . . ." a distant, muffled voice interjected, "that's the 217th Rule. A lot of people make that mistake."

The empty glass slipped from Quark's hand and shattered on the counter of the bar as he stared at the mural. For just a split second, visions of latinum came to his mind as he calculated the increased business he could attract with a talking wall decoration that knew the Rules of Acquisition. But only for a split second.

"Rommm . . ." Quark sighed. "What are you doing back there?"

"Uh, up here, Brother." Quark looked up. Rom was standing on the second floor, holding a large tray stacked with dirty dishes. He carried a server's billing padd in his mouth, accounting for the muffled nature of his voice.

"My mistake," Quark said in exasperation, "what are you doing *up there?*"

"Uh, cleaning up." Rom started down the stairs, eyes fixed on the precariously balanced dishes before him. "We had three different parties in the holosuites tonight, sooo . . . things are still a bit messy."

Rom made it to the bar and put down his tray just as Quark lunged to catch the first falling glass. "Where are the servers?" Quark demanded. "Did they all quit? Or did you talk them into going on strike again?"

Rom took the padd from his mouth and wiped the edge of it on his sleeve. "Well, no. I . . . sent them home."

Quark shook his head, having a hard time believing he was actually having this conversation. "How could you send them home when the place looks like this?!"

"Because . . . it takes longer to clean up when we've been this busy—and then we have to pay them overtime."

Quark blinked. Had his brother actually said something sensible? "Wait a minute. You sent them home—to save money?"

Rom nodded excitedly. "Well . . . yes. You see, tomorrow's my day off from station duty, so I can stay up all night to clean the bar, and that saves us the overtime charges for the serving staff."

Quark snorted cynically. "Sure. So you can pocket that money for yourself."

"Uh, no, Brother. If we can keep overtime to a minimum for the next two weeks, then when we get our next beverage shipment, we'll be able to pay on delivery, and that will net us a one-point-six-seven percent discount for cash. Which, when you multiply by our standard adjusted gross markup, works out to an additional profit of—"

"I know what it works out to," Quark said. "Who gave you that idea?"

Rom looked around the empty bar and shrugged. "Uh . . . you've been saying we need to cut overhead, and that made me think of how Chief O'Brien tries to . . . optimize the station's engineering resources, so I used his Starfleet scheduling programs to examine the bar's operations. And . . . it worked! Didn't it?"

Whether it was the headache/earache assault, the exhaustion he felt after Odo's interrogation, or—more probably—the Romulan ale, Quark ran out of things to complain about. "You surprise me, Rom."

Rom grinned. "Uh, you surprise me, too. I . . . heard you talking to . . ." He started to snicker. ". . . the Admiral."

Quark poured another *snoggin* of ale. "I didn't know you were eavesdropping." Quark went to swallow the drink, but stopped when he saw Rom staring at him. "What?"

"I heard what you said, Brother. Why *is* the mural still here? I mean, you always said you wanted to . . . get rid of it as soon as the Cardassians were gone."

Quark took a deep breath, realized he had no answer, so he made one up. "I got used to it. It's the same reason you're still here."

Rom's gap-toothed grin was knowing. "Oh, I know *that's* not true. You're just tired after being in that cell for so long. I sent a message to the Nagus!"

Quark felt as if he had just been slapped awake. "About what?!"

"Well . . . Odo told Leeta to tell me that you said that you needed a lawyer."

"Doesn't *anyone* on this station know about negotiations?" Quark exclaimed in disgust. "You know, when you make an outrageous demand that you know won't be met, in order to counter the outrageous demand made by the other party?"

Now it was Rom's turn to look confused. "You mean . . . you don't need a lawyer?"

"No."

"But—"

"But what?"

Rom shrugged. "You killed that Andorian."

"Rom! I did not kill anyone!"

Rom blinked innocently. "You killed that Klingon."

"An *accident!* What are you? Working for Odo now?"

"But, Brother, if . . . you didn't kill the Andorian, why have you been under arrest for the past two days?"

"Because Odo is one of those rare individuals on this station who is actually more of an idiot than you are!" Even as the words were leaving his mouth, Quark could see he had hurt his brother's feelings. "I'm sorry, Rom. Really. I didn't mean it. It's Odo who's put me in such a bad mood." Quark set up a second glass. "C'mon, have a drink to celebrate my release."

Rom watched carefully as Quark poured more ale. "But . . . wasn't it supposed to be a good idea that you were in protective custody?"

Quark handed the glass to his brother. "It was, until Odo decided I really was guilty and made it a real arrest. He still thinks I'm guilty."

The two Ferengi clinked glasses and toasted the Admiral. Then Rom gaped like a drowning fish as the Romulan ale scorched his insides. "I . . . I don't . . . understand . . ." he gasped.

"You drank it too fast," Quark explained.

"N-no," Rom wheezed. "If Odo still thinks you're guilty, then why did he let you go?"

"Captain Sisko listened to reason. *Hew-mons* do that occasionally, you know, Rom. He made Odo release me *and* give me a bodyguard."

"What bodyguard?"

Quark pointed out to the Promenade. "That body—oh, for—"

The Bajoran security officer he had left standing watch at the main door to the bar was gone.

Quark crouched down and waved his hand at Rom. "Check the other door. Hurry!"

Rom jumped back to look spinward at the smaller entrance to the left of the bar. "Uh, there's no one there, either."

Quark's desperately racing mind tried to make sense of the situation. The bodyguard had been Bajoran, so he probably hadn't been bribed to abandon his post. And if Vash was making a move on him, she wouldn't kill an uninvolved party, so she had either stunned the guard and—

"The Andorian sisters," Quark hissed.

Rom nodded with a happy smile. "They're very pretty."

"They want to kill me!" Quark yelped from behind the bar.

Rom leaned over to peer down at his hiding brother. "But . . . that was only because they thought you killed Dal Nortron. And since you didn't . . ."

"But *they* still think I did!"

Rom nodded with understanding. "Oh . . . then you *are* in big trouble. Huge trouble. Gi*gan*tic trouble."

The only thing that stopped Quark from slapping his brother silly was his desire to stay down, out of the line of fire. "Thank you for figuring that out for me, idiot! Now listen carefully. . . ."

"Brother, I don't like it when you call me names. Chief O'Brien—"

"Shut up! Shut up and go to security. Get Odo. I don't care if you have to pour him out of his pail—"

"Uh, I don't think he lives in a pail anymore—"

"I don't care! It's not important! Just tell him his guard is gone and he needs to—"

A sudden series of swift knocks froze Quark in mid-command.

He mouthed the words, "Who . . . is . . . it?"

Rom mouthed back the words, "I . . . don't . . . know."

Quark made fists with both hands, and sputtered out loud, "Of course you don't know—you . . ." He caught himself, dropped his voice to a whisper. "You didn't look."

"Oh," Rom said, as if the concept of seeing who was at a door was startlingly new. "I can do that." He left the bar.

Quark sank deeper behind it, knowing there was nowhere to run. The closest entrance to his network of smugglers' tunnels was in a wall halfway across the bar. Then he brightened. The lights were out. Maybe . . . just maybe whoever was at the door who had come to kill him would think Rom was Quark, kill Rom, then leave. Quark chewed his bottom lip, trying not to jinx the possibility of good fortune by thinking too much about it. But it *was* possible. There could still be a happy ending to this tawdry mess after all.

"Hello?" Quark heard Rom speaking softly in the distance. "Is . . . someone there?"

Quark braced for the sound of a phaser. *My poor brother,* he thought. *How brave he is to risk his life for me.* He began to plan Rom's memorial party. He was sure he could get Chief O'Brien to pay for it.

"Hello?" Rom said again.

Quark heard the hum of the door inductors as they began to slide open.

"Is someone—*ah!*"

Quark grimaced as he heard his brother's death cry swallowed by the crackle of an energy discharge. *At least it was fast,* he thought. He'd be sure that his nephew Nog took comfort in that knowledge.

But then he heard footsteps—a sound so faint only Ferengi ears could perceive it.

Vash, Quark thought, outraged. She knew what he looked like. That *hew-mon* female had killed Rom out of spite. *You'd think spite would be enough for her.*

Then Quark heard a second set of footsteps. He stifled a groan. Two sets could only mean he was wrong about Vash. It *was* the Andorian sisters. They knew what he looked like, too.

Who am I fooling? Quark suddenly thought. It was one thing to sit back and hope for disaster to strike others in order to save him. But the 236th Rule said it best: You can't buy fate.

I have to be brave, he told himself. *I have to avenge Rom's brave sacrifice. I have to stand up for what I believe in.*

Slowly, Quark craned his head around and reached for the bottle of Romulan ale, grabbing it by its neck. In his mind, he painstakingly choreographed the moves he would have to make to go on the offensive—a sudden leap to his feet, smash the bottle to create a jagged makeshift weapon, then prepare for victory. If there were any other result, he wouldn't know it until he was on the steps of the Divine Treasury bribing the Nagul Doorman.

So be it, Quark thought with utter finality.

And then in a brilliant burst of speed and grace, Quark thrust himself to his feet, spun around like a dancer, swung the bottle of Romulan ale against the edge of the bar and—

—screamed in high-pitched mortal agony as the *entire* bottle shattered, slicing his palm with shards from the fragile neck.

"Frinx!" Quark squealed, as he clasped his bloody hand to his chest and looked out across the bar to see the last person he expected to see—

"Rom?!"

"Uh . . . sorry, brother . . . but there was nothing I could do."

Quark blinked through a haze of pain. Now his hand throbbed as badly as did his head and ears. "Nothing you could do about what?!"

"Well . . . he made me open the door."

Quark wrapped a bar rag around his bleeding hand, but that only drove the bottle shards in more deeply. And despite Rom's babbling, there was no one else present.

"Who made you open the door?!"

Rom looked down at something on his side of the bar. *"He* did. He . . . said you wanted to see him."

"Rom," Quark said as he rocked from foot to foot, "I can't see *anyone!"*

"Uh . . . because you're not looking?"

Quark sighed and trembled and wanted to cry, all at the same time. He leaned forward, looked over the edge of the bar, and saw—

—multicolored stars explode in his vision like the prettiest globular cluster he had ever seen.

As Quark fell into those stars, he heard what could only be the laughter of the much-maligned Tholian Admiral echoing in his poor wounded ears. And he suspected that the basic underpinning of his personal philosophy had been proven true once again.

No matter how bad things look, they can always get worse.

CHAPTER 11

SOMETIMES Sisko felt that he had never left the wormhole after his first meeting with the aliens. That after his first encounter with the Prophets in their Celestial Temple, everything that had happened since—or that *appeared* to have happened—was somehow already a memory. A memory he was merely reliving.

Standing before the sink in the tiny kitchen alcove of his quarters on Deep Space 9, Sisko whisked at the eggs in their copper bowl, smearing out the streaks of dark pepper sauce, frothing the egg mixture into a whirlpool just as the wormhole frothed the quantum foam of normal space-time.

How many times had he done this—made an omelette? How many times had he made *this* omelette? Or could it be they were all part of the exact same moment in time and—

—he was a child standing on a low wooden step stool in the kitchen of his father's New Orleans restaurant. His father—Joseph—stood behind him, his large, comforting hand guiding his son's small hand on the whisk as it swept through the eggs, teaching him as his father had taught him, and—

—he was a father looking over his own son's shoulder. Little Jake-O was standing on a low wooden step stool in the cooking corner of that cramped apartment he and Jennifer had rented in

San Francisco as they waited for the *Saratoga* to return to port so they could finally share their careers, and their dreams, as a family. He held Jake's small hand in his, guiding it as his father had guided him, as Jake might someday guide his own child's hand—

—all the *same* moment, these memories of things long ago and of things still to be, yet all bound up together in the soothing traditions of those kitchens.

He laughed, softly, caught up in his discovery.

"That sounds nice," Kasidy Yates said.

Drawn suddenly from all moments to *this* moment, Sisko turned to Kasidy Yates where she sat on a chair at the dining table set for breakfast. Her lithe form was draped in one of his caftans, a textured cotton with a bold brown and white blockprint pattern from Old Zimbabwe. Her long brown fingers gracefully cradled a cup of morning coffee, her soft dark hair still mussed from bed, her clear brown eyes not quite yet open. Her infectious smile transfixed him, as it had from the first day they'd met.

"I've missed that," he heard her say. "You laughing."

Sisko held the copper bowl against his hip as without conscious thought he continued to fluff the eggs. "I was thinking that the reason the Prophets made me their Emissary is because I already knew about nonlinear time."

Kasidy frowned, didn't understand.

Sisko's smile widened. "The kitchen!"

Kasidy nodded with sudden understanding. "Cooking does seem to carry you away," she said with an answering smile.

Sisko leaned over to give her a kiss on the forehead. "But it always brings me back to you." The light moment transformed when he did not move away.

Kasidy put down her coffee, Sisko his bowl, as Kasidy reached up to his face and kissed him as they had not kissed in weeks, in months, perhaps ever.

"I . . . thought I had lost you," she whispered, her breath soft against his cheek.

Sisko felt her body tremble, as if she were fighting back tears.

He knew why.

A week ago, they had been on the *Defiant*. Kasidy had volunteered to be a convoy liaison officer for Starfleet escort duty to Vega. So they could be together.

It had been a terrible mistake. And the mistake had been his.

In loving Kasidy, he had made her a part of his life that was separate from Starfleet and the Dominion War. In tearing down the barriers between his life and his duty, he had only succeeded in putting her in harm's way—at his side.

Once before, he had done that to the woman he loved, and it had cost her her life. Surviving the consequences of that mistake had taken him twelve years and the intervention of beings beyond human comprehension.

And he had.

Yet even now he could still see Jennifer, motionless on the deck of the *Saratoga,* her soul forever lost to him except in memory.

As protection from the cruel uncaring universe that might still end the existence of Kasidy Yates, Sisko now took refuge behind a different shield around his heart, a shield he had begun constructing the moment he and Kasidy had found themselves in active service together on the *Defiant.*

If Kasidy died under his command, the only way he could be certain he could still function to save his ship and his crew was to see her already among the dead, to mourn her before the fact, to be prepared for the awful day he might lose her. But even as he tried to reduce his vulnerability, Sisko knew it was impossible. He was in love and he was loved.

He stroked her hair, knowing how wrong it all was. First to put her at risk, and then to try to remove her from his heart.

"You can't lose me. Nothing will keep me from you," he murmured. For whether it was a memory of a past dream or a memory of something still to come, at the very end of whatever pain and whatever tragedy this universe and this war held for him, Sisko knew— *knew* with a conviction of faith and hope and love that would outlast the stars—he would *always* come back to the arms of Kasidy Yates.

And somehow, through some living bond still to be formed between them, he knew that Kasidy accepted his vow.

"Does this mean you're going to make me breakfast?" she teased even as her eyes told him she knew what he felt.

"Eventually." Sisko leaned down to kiss her again.

And as their lips met, their eyes closed, and time became nonlinear once again. Until—

A discreet throat-clearing cough.

Sisko opened his eyes at the same moment as Kasidy, brought back to *this* moment by—.

"Hey, guys."

Sisko couldn't resist reaching out a hand to tousle his son's hair as Jake, smiling sheepishly, skirted past them to the replicator. He remembered when he had had to bend down to touch the top of his son's head. Now it seemed he had to touch the stars to do the same.

"Hey, Jake-O," Sisko said as his son ordered and retrieved and drank in one gulp a tall glass of orange juice.

"I heard you went on a treasure hunt," Kasidy said.

Sisko saw Jake's swift glance at him, but he had no recriminations for his son. He and Jake had talked at length about Jake's actions—and his lack of action—last night. And Sisko had been deeply gratified to learn that almost everything he had to say to his son had already been in Jake's mind. Jake's and Nog's omission, not telling anyone about the mysterious Cardassian holosuite, was simply a leftover piece of business from when the two young men were little more than children.

Jake knew he had been wrong, and Sisko knew that doing the wrong thing and learning from it was what the process of maturing and growing was all about. All life was about such learning. What was important to Sisko, and what made him feel so proud of his son, was that for all the missteps the boy did make—and some days their number was truly astounding—he seldom made the same misstep twice.

As long as Jake kept that same spirit, Sisko could never really be angry with him—or disappointed.

"Buried treasure," Sisko said, picking up the copper bowl to give the eggs a final flourish. "Buried and forgotten." He set the bowl on the counter, cut a square of Imolian butter, and turned away to heat the empty omelette pan.

He could see that Jake heard and understood his tone of voice. The past was the past. They had moved on. They must always move on.

Jake pulled up a chair to sit down beside Kasidy at the table. "I was really surprised no one else had found that room by now."

Kasidy looked over at Sisko. "Do you think there could be other sealed-off sections in the station?"

Sisko dropped the butter into the hot omelette pan, then swirled it around to melt it evenly. "If there are, Chief O'Brien will know about them in a week. He's going to use the *Defiant*'s tactical sensors to conduct a full survey scan of DS9, then correlate that scan with the Cardassian's blueprints to look for deviations. He says he should have done it years ago."

"Any reason why the holosuite was sealed off?" Kasidy asked.

Sisko poured the beaten eggs from the copper bowl into the pan, tilting the pan expertly to lightly coat the top of the egg mixture with the melted butter. "We don't even know that it *is* a holosuite," he said.

"What else could it be?" Jake asked.

Sisko reached for a handful of grated jack cheese and trailed it perfectly along one side of the gently bubbling mass of eggs. "Just because we don't know the answer doesn't mean we have to settle for a guess." Biting his bottom lip in concentration, he sprinkled in chopped scallions, and then added a dusting of the secret ingredient in all the great recipes of Sisko's Creole Kitchen—the Cajun spices his father sent him on a more or less regular basis. "That would be too easy."

The door announcer chimed.

Sisko prodded the edge of the cooking eggs and glanced at his son. "I can't leave the pan now. . . ."

He heard the door to his quarters slide open just as he judged that the texture of his creation was perfect. With a rapid twist and a flip of the pan, he held his breath as he slid the golden disk toward the forward edge of the pan, then folded it expertly over on itself, achieving a half moon of Creole perfection.

"Uh, Dad . . ." Jake said.

Sisko looked up, saw Jadzia, was delighted. "Old Man! You're just in time for breakfast."

But Jadzia didn't share Sisko's enthusiasm—not today. She frowned. "Sorry, Benjamin, but . . . Quark's gone."

Sisko's sense of disbelief changed quickly to dismay, betrayal. "He's left the station?"

"I can't be sure. If he did, he did it in disguise. There's a chance he's simply hiding out here. But . . . well, maybe you should come down to the bar and . . . see for yourself. I think the situation's more complicated than we first thought."

Sisko's wrist jerked as he sharply snapped the pan again and the omelette flipped over with Starfleet precision. The bottom was an elegant combination of rich yellow and crispy brown. Sisko sighed. "Jake, it's up to you to uphold the family honor. You know what your grandfather always said." He slipped the omelette onto a plate already warmed by the inductor oven.

His son stepped into the alcove as Sisko stepped out. "No one leaves the table unsatisfied," Jake said.

"Do I have time to put on my uniform?" Sisko asked Jadzia.

She nodded. "This is going to be a Starfleet matter."

Sisko had been afraid of that. Somehow, when Quark was involved, situations always became more complicated.

Quark's bar looked normal for this early in the morning. The dabo table was silent. A rambunctious group of young Starfleet fighter pilots from the *Thunderchild* who hadn't yet switched over to station local time were ending their duty day around a large collection of bar tables they'd pulled together. A handful of the station's Bajoran morning-shift personnel were eating replicator breakfasts, a handful of night-shift personnel were eating replicator suppers. And faithful Morn was on his stool—so much a part of the place that he was sometimes easy to overlook, except for the nonstop droning of his voice.

"So far so good," Sisko said to Jadzia.

She gestured to the bar. "Let me buy you a *raktajino*."

They chose stools as far away from the loquacious Morn as possible. "When did you find out Quark was gone?" Sisko asked.

"Odo told me he finished questioning Quark early this morning, around four. So I went to Quark's quarters at nine—I thought I'd let him get some sleep."

"And?"

"He wasn't there. Isn't anywhere."

"Anything missing? Signs of a struggle?"

"Nothing I could see. Odo's people are going through it now."

"That's not like Quark."

Jadzia almost laughed. "Not like Quark to run away from trouble? Benjamin, that's exactly like him."

Sisko shook his head. That wasn't what he had meant. "He and I had a deal. And . . . Quark usually keeps his deals. At least with me." He saw Jadzia's look of amazement. "Oh, he'll look for and exploit every loophole he can find. And just *making* the deal can be . . . an adventure in frustration. But when all is said and done, Quark, in his own Ferengi way, is one of the most honorable people on this station. *Not,*" Sisko added quickly, "that I would ever tell him that to his face. It could undercut me in future negotiations."

"Let's hope there are future negotiations," Jadzia muttered.

A sudden worrisome thought struck Sisko. "He didn't run into trouble with the Andorian sisters, did he?"

Jadzia shook her head. "Odo has them under twenty-six-hour surveillance. They've been keeping to themselves."

"Then what is it you suspect, Old Man?"

His old friend merely answered his question with another. "Do you have your *raktajino,* yet?"

Sisko looked around. Though the establishment was open for business—he recognized the usual servers managing the tables—no one was behind the bar. Yet he had heard the rattle of glasses in the recycler trays, and the hum of the replicator. That was why he hadn't noticed the absence of anyone—because it still sounded as if someone was present.

"All right," Sisko said, "I'll admit it. I'm confused. Care to enlighten me?"

Jadzia nodded. Tapped on the bartop. "Barkeep! We want to order!"

Sisko blinked with surprise as a Ferengi jumped up into view from behind the bar.

A very small Ferengi.

His skull and features were the size of any other adult of his species, complete with an unusual black headskirt, but the rest of his body was dramatically foreshortened. A meter tall at most.

"What do *you* want?" he snarled.

"Benjamin," Jadzia said, "meet Base. Base, meet Captain Benjamin Sisko, commander of Deep Space 9."

"Yeah, yeah, right, whatever," Base snapped. "You want to order? Or you want to stop bothering me?"

"Two *raktajinos,* please," Jadzia said.

"You actually drink that crap?" Base gargled in disgust, then whirled around and dropped below the level of the bar again.

Sisko couldn't suppress his curiosity. He stood up and leaned over the bar to see that a series of stools had been arranged behind it, presumably so the small barkeep could jump up to serve—if that's what such an unwelcoming manner could be called—the customers.

Sisko sat back down. "Base?" he asked Jadzia.

"Rom says he's an old friend of the family, helping look after the family's interests during . . . Quark's troubles."

"Does Rom know where Quark is?"

Jadzia rolled her eyes. "Here's where it gets interesting. Rom claims that he didn't know Quark had been released. Odo, on the other hand, says that Quark told him he was going directly here after he *was* released. And all the servers say that Rom sent them home early last night."

"Ah," Sisko said, rubbing the fingers of one hand against his temple to forestall the headache that Quark could so easily provoke. "So Quark could have come here, and the only witness would have been Rom."

"Exactly."

Sisko sat up straighter with a sigh. "All right. I see how this might complicate matters. But why do you think it might be a Starfleet matter?"

"Base isn't your ordinary Ferengi."

Sisko gave Jadzia a look of mock surprise. "No."

"Settle down, Benjamin. He's a smuggler."

"A Ferengi smuggler. That *is* unusual."

"Who operates in the Klingon Empire."

Sisko toned down his skepticism, recalling that the dismemberment and vivisection penalties Klingons assessed on captured smugglers tended to keep most Ferengi from becoming involved in illegal shipping in that region of space. "That makes him either the bravest Ferengi I've ever heard of, or the stupidest."

"Or," Jadzia added, "the most desperate. He has a number of warrants outstanding among the Ferengi Alliance, so by law he can't conduct business with any other Ferengi."

"Yet he's here," Sisko said, drumming his fingers on the bartop.

There was still no sign of the *raktajinos.* "Presumably working for Quark."

" 'Helping Quark,' is what Rom said."

Sisko saw Jadzia staring at his fingers and forced himself to stop fidgeting. "Helping him do what, is the question. Clearly, he's not experienced in bartending. Is there any connection between Base and the Andorians?"

"Odo's working on it," Jadzia said. "Though I think he has other things on his mind." She nodded for Sisko to look down the length of the bar.

Sisko did, and this time he did not have to pretend to be surprised.

"Vash?!"

"The one and only."

The calculating archaeologist, known for her questionable ethics as much as for her beauty, was seated at the last stool at the bar, leaning forward and having an intense conversation with Quark's diminutive replacement.

"I bet she's not ordering *raktajino,*" Sisko said.

"Shall we?" Jadzia asked as she rose to her feet.

Sisko followed Jadzia down to the end of the bar, until they both stood behind Vash. At that same instant Base looked up and saw them. A fierce scowl darkened his face. "Go away, go way. I'll get your stupid drinks when it's your turn. I have other customers, y'know."

Her conversation interrupted, Vash turned around on her bar stool to see the cause of Base's displeasure.

Sisko caught the naked look of shock that illuminated Vash's pale face before she turned on her spectacular smile. *"Captain* Sisko, what a pleasure. I heard you'd been promoted."

His return smile equalled hers in sincerity. "And I'd heard the Siladians had put a price on your head for desecrating their burial moons."

"A misunderstanding," Vash said airily. "All the artifacts were returned."

"I'd heard that as well. Counterfeits, every one."

"They were counterfeits when I . . . retrieved them, Captain. The Siladians have been looting their own burial moons for generations, and replacing what they steal with replicas so they can keep the tourists coming. It's a rather clever operation."

"Or a rather clever story," Sisko said. He knew better than to trust a word she said. "Are you here on your own this time? Or . . . ?"

"No Q, if that's who you mean. He did come back a few times." For a moment, her face took on a strange expression, as if she were remembering things that were inexpressible. "But . . . I haven't seen him for . . . centuries, it feels like."

Sisko studied the wayward archaeologist thoughtfully. The way Vash said it, it sounded as if she really did mean centuries. He wondered what other types of adventures the superbeing known as Q had taken her on.

"Then what can we do for you?" he asked.

"I said, go away!" Base thumped the base of a glass tumbler on the bartop for emphasis.

"Why don't you look after your other customers?" Jadzia said with an easy smile.

"Why don't you and the captain take one of those barstools and—"

"Base!" Vash interrupted. "Captain Sisko is in command of this station. He can shut Quark's down anytime he feels like it."

"That barstool'd give them both something to feel," Base muttered, his small dark deep-set eyes burning into Sisko's.

"Why don't we take a walk?" Vash slipped off her bar stool and companionably took Sisko's arm in hers.

Jadzia locked eyes with the Ferengi barkeep. "Good idea, Benjamin."

"I'm still going to charge you for the stinkin' *raktacrappos!*" Base huffed as Jadzia and Vash walked out of the bar with him, one on each side.

Once out onto the Promenade, Sisko tugged at the collar of his duty jacket, puzzled by the Ferengi's anger—and over nothing. "How can anyone stay in business with an attitude like that?"

"He does business with Klingons," Jadzia reminded him.

"It's a bit more peculiar than that," Vash said as she quickly scanned the Promenade, both levels, right and left. "Did you notice Base's headskirt?"

Sisko thought back. "It was black. I don't often see that color."

Vash shot him a glance. "It isn't a headskirt. It's hair."

Sisko and Jadzia glanced at each other. "On a Ferengi?" Sisko asked. They had hair enough in their ears, Sisko knew, especially as they grew older. But he couldn't recall ever having seen a Ferengi that wasn't bald.

Vash's sharp eyes studied the customers at the gift shop. "Obviously neither of you is aware that on Ferenginar, the civil standardization authorities use Base as an example of what happens when pregnant Ferengi females travel in space and are subjected to radiation: They give birth to something like . . . well, Base."

"His mother left the planet?" Sisko knew that Jadzia's curiosity was warranted. Off-planet travel was still most unusual for a Ferengi female. Only in the past two months had Grand Nagus Zek introduced any gender-related reforms in Ferengi Society. Decades ago, when Base was born, it would have been almost inconceivable for a female to leave her family compound, let alone her homeworld.

Vash turned abruptly and began walking antispinward, leading Sisko and Dax toward what used to be the school, away from the gift shop. Sisko wasn't certain, but it was possible Vash had recognized someone at the gift shop. "Oh, Ferengi females leave the planet all the time," she said, in answer to Jadzia's question. "Always have. Otherwise, how would they have colony worlds?"

"By transporting their females in stasis," Jadzia said.

"And sometimes things go wrong." Vash gave Sisko a sly smile. "Stasis fields break down. A colony ship is raided on the outskirts of the Klingon Empire and one lone Ferengi female sets off on her own. Or, a lonely Ferengi businessman on a trip to *Qo'noS* decides to partake of the local pleasures. . . ."

"Are you suggesting Base is a Ferengi-Klingon hybrid?"

Vash innocently widened her eyes at him. "Captain Sisko, with the enmity between those two species, *and* their physical differences, that would be impossible. I'm surprised you'd even think such a thing."

"Then why go to such detail explaining Base's origins?"

"Just because something is impossible doesn't prevent people from speculating. You mentioned Base's attitude. Well, imagine how'd you feel if you were a Ferengi and everyone else thought you were half Klingon. You might have a bad attitude, too. Don't you think?"

"I *think* you're avoiding the question I asked back in the bar." Sisko looked at Jadzia and both of them stopped walking at the same moment. "How can we help you?"

Vash paused and Sisko saw her look past him, back in the direction they had come from. "Tell me, Captain, do you take such a personal interest in all the visitors to this station?"

"Only when they're thieves and scoundrels."

Vash nodded appreciatively. "Flattery will get you everywhere, Captain." She started forward again, turning toward the entrance to Cavor's shop.

Sisko put out a hand to hold her back, outside Cavor's display window. The featured floating antigrav balls were a popular attraction on the Promenade, and several other visitors were standing enthralled in front of the display. "I'm serious, Vash. We *are* in the middle of a war zone here, and I have no time for games. Either convince me that you are on DS9 for a legitimate reason, or you're on the next shuttle leaving for Bajor."

"Now who has an attitude?"

"You want to understand *my* attitude? Very well. Last week, three Andorians came to this station—Andorians with troubled legal histories involving smuggling. Then Base shows up in Quark's bar, and now you. The last time we had so many smugglers onboard at one time was, coincidentally enough, the last time you were here. When Quark was going to hold an auction of your stolen Gamma Quadrant artifacts."

"They weren't stolen," Vash said virtuously.

"Excuse me? What about the energy creature's crystalline off-spring?"

"Well, not all of them . . ." she amended.

Sisko turned to Jadzia. "I think I see what's going on here. Quark was going to hold another auction. Which means that either he came into possession of something he thought would be of interest to the likes of Vash, the Andorians, and Base—" He looked at Vash. "—And whoever else it is who's on this station that you seem to be so concerned about. Or that you, the Andorians, or Base, or whoever, have come into possession of something you want Quark to sell."

Vash's studied silence told Sisko he was close.

"Ordinarily," he continued, "I really wouldn't care about what you people are up to. I'd leave you all to Odo and the Bajoran authorities. But in this case, I have one Andorian visitor dead, and one Ferengi inhabitant of this station missing. And that makes what *you're* doing here *my* business."

Vash turned away from her contemplation of the window display. "Who's missing?"

Sisko kept his expression carefully neutral. He didn't even risk looking at Jadzia. "Rultan. One of Quark's servers."

Vash shrugged. "Don't know him."

"When are you and Quark supposed to meet?" Sisko asked, as if he had just suddenly thought of the question.

"I had no plans to see Quark," Vash said.

"Not even for old times' sake?" Jadzia asked.

Vash looked at Jadzia, looked back at Sisko, and it was as if Sisko could hear isolinear circuits at work in her mind. *"Quark's* the Ferengi who's missing?"

Sisko didn't see the point in continuing the deception. He nodded.

"How missing?"

Sisko didn't understand.

"Any sign of foul play?"

"Nothing apparent," Jadzia said. "But he disappeared last night—which is when Base appeared."

Vash shook her head. "Base wouldn't hurt Quark. There'd be no profit in it."

"Vash," Sisko said, "this is your last chance. What's going on here?"

The way Vash looked at him, he could tell she knew at least part of the answer. This woman was maddening in her infernal duplicity. What would it take for her to share what she knew?

But, first, Vash had a question of her own. "The Andorian . . . Dal Nortron? How was he killed?"

"Lethal exposure to microwave radiation," Jadzia answered. "Odo believes it was a weapon. I think there's a chance it might have been accidental."

Vash nodded and turned back to Cavor's window display.

Though it was a struggle, Sisko succeeded in keeping his patience because it appeared Vash was in the midst of thinking something through. Finally, she turned and looked directly into his eyes.

"Captain, do you believe what they say about Quark? That he killed Nortron?"

Sisko met her sharp gaze directly. "No." Believing that Vash was reaching her own moment of truth and would act on it momentarily, he offered no further qualifications.

"Do exactly as I say," Vash suddenly said in a low voice, confirming his supposition. "I'm going to walk away from you. I'm going to look angry. You're going to grab me and say that you don't believe me, and that you're taking me for questioning. Then do it, and make it look good. Understand?"

Sisko signaled his understanding by making no move to look around to see who might be watching. He felt certain that Vash knew who their charade was going to play for. So, he gave her the reason she needed to walk away. "That's not good enough, Vash," he said harshly. "I want answers."

Vash threw up her hands. "What's wrong with you people?! I've already told you everything I know! Now leave me alone!"

She spun around and started to walk away.

Sisko took two quick steps and then took her arm.

"Let me go!" Vash shouted. "You have no right to hold me!"

Jadzia took Vash's other arm. "Yes, he does."

Sisko hit his communicator badge. "Sisko to security. I need a team on the Promenade, Main Floor South, *now.*"

Vash tugged back and forth between Sisko and Jadzia. "You can't be serious! I haven't done anything!"

All signs were good that they were putting on a convincing show. By the time two Bajoran security officers hurried around the curve of the Promenade, they were surrounded by an inquisitive crowd that was growing by the minute.

"I want this woman held for questioning," Sisko said loudly. He let go of Vash as the security officers took her. And just in that brief instant, Vash slapped a hand to the side of her neck and staggered, losing her balance.

Startled, Sisko caught her as she began to fall. On the side of her slender neck, he saw a small bronze-metal dart, no larger than a fingertip. He grabbed it, pulled, and a half-centimeter-long needle emerged from Vash's neck, dripping a fluorescent blue fluid.

Vash shuddered uncontrollably as Jadzia called Worf for an

immediate transporter evacuation to the Infirmary. Sisko swiftly scanned the crowd, but there was nothing to see except the concerned faces of onlookers. Discovering whoever had fired the dart would have to wait until the station's security recordings could be studied.

"Quark . . ." Vash whispered urgently, her voice slurred. ". . . the auction. . . ."

Sisko bent nearer, cradling her as he waited for the transporter lock. "They're on their way, Vash. You have to hold on."

"Must listen . . . was going to sell. . . ."

Sisko leaned closer, put his ear to her lips. "What, Vash? What was he going to sell?"

Vash's eyes rolled up and her eyelids fluttered, and what she said next made Sisko's blood run cold.

". . . an . . . Orb . . ." Vash gasped. ". . . Jalbador. . . ."

And then the transporter took them.

CHAPTER 12

JADZIA SMILED as she watched Julian Bashir hold the neural dart up
to a light and examine it closely by eye. It was so typical of him, and
also what made him so endearing.

Here he was in DS9's Infirmary, a state-of-the-art Cardassian
medical facility that had been fully upgraded with the latest Starfleet
innovations, surrounded by scanners and sensors that could shuffle
through the dart's composition molecule by molecule and more often
than not identify the planet of origin for every mineral compound
used in its manufacture. Yet Julian *still* had to look at the dart himself, using his own hands and his own eyes to be certain no detail had
been missed.

It was so . . . well, Jadzia could find only one word to explain
that kind of self-absorbed conviction in the superiority of his abilities, and that word was "cute."

Bashir glanced over at her and returned her smile, but seemed
confused about why he was doing so. "What?" he asked.

"Nothing," Jadzia shrugged, lips still pursed in a smile. "Just
remembering something Emony said. It was more than a hundred
years ago."

"Ah." Bashir nodded as if that explained everything, and went
back to peering at the dart.

That was one of the advantages to being a Trill, Jadzia knew. In fact, except for Lela, the first, all of Dax's previous hosts had known it, too: A joined Trill could get away with the most outrageous behavior imaginable, and then simply explain it away by blaming it on a previous host.

Since most unjoined species could never even imagine what it must be like for two minds to share a single body and several life-times of experiences, they would accept such an explanation without question. What would be the point? To be honest, Jadzia thought, most people looked on joined Trills as some kind of zombie held in thrall to a neural parasite.

But the truth was that she herself had found that joining with Dax had been incredibly liberating. It was exhilarating to be able to decide to do anything at all—and that included indulging herself in harmless flirting with Julian right up to taking part in the most eroti-cally charged physical challenge in the quadrant, euphemistically called 'wrestling' Galeo-Manada style—and because she was joined, anything she chose to do was *all* acceptable.

Of course, part of the trick of deciding which passions and pas-times to explore came from trying to think of something that none of the other hosts had been familiar with—which usually meant that the more lifetimes a symbiont shared, the more idiosyncratic and eccen-tric its hosts became.

Personally, before she was joined Jadzia had always had a partic-ular curiosity about Vulcans, and had hoped that sometime during her career in Starfleet she'd have a chance to experience *Pon farr* on a more personal level than the textbooks allowed. But after joining, when she had instantly been able to look back on several *Pon farr* encounters—from both sides of the Teiresian veil, as it were—there was little there that remained mysterious to her, and that lost mystery had been the key to her fascination.

Oh, someday, a century or two down the road, the right Vulcan might come along at the right time for the Dax symbiont to decide it was time to travel down that road again. But for now, Jadzia was more than happy, deliriously happy in fact, with her sweet cuddly-bear of a Klingon mate.

Jadzia coughed to cover her sudden giggle, as she suddenly recalled the look on Worf's face when she'd startled him with the endearment at precisely the wrong moment—as if there were ever a right moment to call a rough, tough Klingon a sweet cuddly-bear. But fortunately, she'd been able to blame the transgression on her ever-useful past host Audrid.

Bashir gave her another perplexed smile. "Emony again?"

"Audrid. I'm sorry."

"No need." He placed the dart back in a small sample dish, then entered notes on his padd.

Jadzia admired the dark curls of Julian's close-cropped hair. *He was close,* she recalled with a sigh. If Worf had been unable to transcend his insular Klingon heritage enough to fully admit a Trill into his life, Jadzia had little doubt that her heart could have been won by Julian Bashir. That was the other advantage to being a Trill. Life's choices that could last a lifetime for others were not necessarily a limiting factor. Other lifetimes and other choices waited to provide near infinite possibilities.

Bashir stopped writing on the padd, then tapped the small device against his hand.

"You've reached a conclusion?" Jadzia asked.

He had. "A linear-induction dart. Centuries-old technology. So primitive the launch tube would never show up on the Promenade weapons scanners. Cardassian design, of course, like most assassination implements, but its manufacture, interesting enough, is *Andorian,* as is the neural toxin inside: bicuprodyanide."

Jadzia frowned. "That's fatal to Andorians."

"And Bolians," Bashir added. "In fact, it has near one hundred percent lethality in any species with a bicupric-based oxygen-transport metabolism. Which means almost anything with blue skin."

"But . . . it's not fatal in humans," Jadzia said, perplexed.

Bashir dropped his padd on his medical work station in a gesture of finality. "In a high enough dose it can be, Jadzia. Just from ordinary metal toxicity. But Vash, mind you, would have to have ingested a coffee mug–full of the stuff, and even then we'd have a good ten to twelve hours to treat her. As it is, with the few milliliters that actually got into her bloodstream, she'll only have a bad headache for a day or two. Nothing more serious."

"In other words," Jadzia said slowly as she worked it out, "whoever used the dart against Vash either didn't know about human bio-chemistry—"

"*Or,*" Bashir interjected, "was equipped to kill an Andorian and shooting Vash was an unexpected, spur-of-the-moment decision—"

"*Which,*" Jadzia continued, getting into Bashir's rhythm, "could indicate that the attacker was desperate to stop Vash from talking—"

"—so he struck as quickly as he could to render her uncon-scious—"

"—and he—"

"—or *she*—"

"—plans on coming back to finish the job before Vash wakes up—"

"—which should be in the next thirty minutes!" Bashir grinned at her, quite obviously enjoying the chance to play detective. "I must say, Jadzia, we make a wonderful team."

Being a Trill, Jadzia simply returned Julian's grin and said, "I've always thought so. But for now," she went on, "maybe we should have Odo post more guards?"

Bashir nodded, "Good idea. I'll call—"

"*Where is she?!*"

Major Kira burst into the Infirmary like an avenging Pah-wraith, fury expressed in every line of her being.

Jadzia could guess what had caused Kira's reaction, and it seemed Julian had also, because at once he took on the manner of someone outside the jurisdiction of both Starfleet protocol and Bajoran laws. He faced Kira as a physician with a patient in his care—a patient no one would be allowed to harm.

"If you mean Vash, she's still recovering," Bashir said firmly.

Kira took a swift look around the Infirmary, saw the analysis bed was empty in the treatment alcove and started for the surgery. "I don't care. I'm talking to her."

Bashir immediately stepped in front of Kira, to block her advance. "Not until she's awake, Major."

They were centimeters apart, neither one willing to yield. Kira's hands were balled into fists at her side. Restlessly, she shifted her weight from foot to foot. Her voice was demanding, belligerent. "Then wake her, Doctor. Use some of those magic potions of yours to bring her around now."

Bashir held his ground, unconvinced. "There is no medical need to do so."

With that, Kira's military bluster gave way to a plea of personal indignation. "Julian! She is involved in trying to *sell* an Orb of the Prophets. That is an *outrage!* To me, my world, to ten thousand years of Bajorans who have sought to follow the Prophets' teachings. I *demand* to speak to her."

Bashir still didn't move, though Jadzia was pleased to see Julian's attitude soften. "Major, first of all, Vash isn't going anywhere. And second, any questioning you conduct might be more useful if you had a few moments to . . . gather your thoughts, so it won't be . . . as personal."

"How can it *not* be personal?"

Bashir sighed. "Listen, Nerys, whatever Vash said to Captain Sisko, you have to remember she had just received a jolt of a disruptive neural toxin, almost directly to her brain. Maybe what she said did make sense. Maybe it didn't. But in any case, the captain said he couldn't understand everything she said. The point is, we won't know for certain until she wakes up."

Kira stared hard at Bashir. "A 'disruptive' neural toxin? Not a fatal one?"

"Fatal to Andorians, not humans. She'll be fine."

Jadzia saw the major's rigid posture relax as she stepped back from Bashir, lowering the level of confrontation, but not ending it. "You're surprised by that," Jadzia said to her.

Kira nodded, taking a deep breath to further compose herself. "I thought . . . I didn't have much time. That I might lose her before . . . . Why would someone try to kill Vash with an Andorian toxin?"

"To make it appear as if an Andorian is the attempted murderer," Odo said, startling everyone as he suddenly entered the Infirmary.

"Did you find something on the scanner records?" Jadzia asked. She knew that was what Odo had been doing for the past ten minutes: analyzing the security tapes taken of the crowds on the Promenade at the time Vash was hit by the dart. Normally, she knew, visual scanners weren't used in the public areas of the station on an ongoing basis. But there were few things Odo hated more than an unsolved crime in his territory, and Jadzia was aware DS9's security officer was determined to use every means he could to solve Dal

Nortron's death and erase what he would no doubt consider a personal affront to his abilities as station constable.

"No, I did not," Odo said gruffly. "Whoever the shooter was, he must have positioned himself just by the gym, under the banners. Precisely where there is a gap in the scanner coverage."

Bashir shot a sideways glance at Jadzia, clearly intrigued by Odo's reasoning. "That could indicate the shooter is someone with highly detailed knowledge of station security."

Odo folded his arms. "Just what are trying to suggest, Doctor?"

Odo's challenging tone seemed to unsettle Bashir. "I'm . . . suggesting nothing."

To divert Odo before he could directly accuse Julian of suspecting him, Jadzia bestowed a winning smile on the constable. "Odo, Julian and I were just trying to find a pattern to the . . . the clues in this case. So far, when you put them all together, they don't make a lot of sense, so any extra piece of information should be considered carefully."

"Of course they don't make sense," Odo said darkly. "Quark is involved."

Jadzia wasn't willing to let that stand. *"Maybe,"* she said.

Odo was silent, but the pained expression on his face conveyed his thoughts well enough.

"Well," Kira said, "the one person who might be able to make sense out of whatever *is* going on is still in there." She pointed to the surgery.

But Vash's doctor still wasn't ready to yield. "And she'll be waking up soon. Odo, just in case whoever attacked Vash tries to come back and finish the job, could you—"

"I already have three officers stationed outside the Infirmary, Doctor. And Worf has placed transporter-suppression shields around this section of the Promenade to prevent anyone or anything being beamed in or out."

"I certainly couldn't ask for more than that. Thank you, Constable."

Odo's stiff response told Jadzia that the constable wasn't swayed by Julian's attempt to create a more cooperative mood. "Don't mention it, Doctor. However, in the interests of full security, I would appreciate being in the room with Vash when she wakes up."

Before Bashir could answer, Kira added, "So would I."

"She's not going to be in the best of shape," Bashir warned.

But Kira was in control of her emotions now. "Julian, an *Orb of the Prophets.* Vash is no longer just a smuggler who can pay a fine and move on to the next system. Even an *attempt* to interfere with an Orb makes her liable to life imprisonment under Bajoran law. What she's done—or even planned to do—is so serious, I've reported it to Kai Winn. Three Vedek Inquisitors are already on their way."

"The Inquisitors function as a *war* crimes investigative tribunal." Bashir's voice betrayed his alarm.

Kira's jaw tightened. "Up until now, all missing Orbs were the result of Cardassian looting. We are talking war crimes."

Jadzia finally saw her chance to act as mediator. "Nerys, let's say Vash is involved in . . . oh, I don't know . . . some extralegal transaction involving obtaining an Orb from one of the Cardassians who stole it in the first place. If she were doing this so she could, say, *return* the Orb to the Bajoran people—the way Grand Nagus Zek returned the Orb of Wisdom—don't you think it possible that no charges would be brought? I mean, the Inquisitors didn't file charges against Zek."

"Are you defending her, Jadzia?" Kira's voice was incredulous.

"If she's done what you think she's done, not at all. But what I am trying to do is to point out that we don't know everything yet, and that there might be some alternate explanation. And if we keep that in mind, then maybe we'll be able to *talk* to Vash, instead of interrogate her. And maybe she can help us right now, instead of deciding to say nothing until her legal defender spends months negotiating an . . . accommodation with the Inquisitors. If we keep open minds, maybe we can get to the bottom of this much faster than if we jump to conclusions. That's all." Jadzia held steady under Kira's measuring gaze.

The major made her decision. She nodded to Jadzia. "All right, I won't threaten her with life in prison right away. And since you seem to be open to more possibilities than the rest of us, why don't you start the questioning—I mean, the conversation."

Odo cleared his throat. "In case any of you were wondering," the changeling said heavily, reminding them all of his presence, "I have no problem with Dax asking the questions. At first."

Now everyone looked at Bashir.

"Too much stress will delay her full recovery. A conversation will be much better than the third degree."

Kira blinked. "The third degree of what?"

"I'll explain later," Odo said.

But Kira wasn't willing to let it go. She frowned. "What are the first two degrees?"

"I'm sure 'interrogation' is what Julian meant to say," Jadzia said smoothly, glaring at Julian to stop him from adding anything else provocative. Jadzia could see that Kira was losing the fight to control her impatience. "So, Doctor, keeping our minds open, promising not to be a source of stress for her, is it possible you'll allow us to see your patient?"

"Yes. But . . ."

"But what?" Kira snapped.

Bashir raised his eyebrows. "Doesn't anyone think we should wait for Captain Sisko?"

"He's involved with Chief O'Brien," Odo said. "He'll be expecting a report from me, and from you, Doctor, when we're finished with the prisoner . . . that is, the patient."

"All right," Bashir shrugged. "Then just let me check on her first."

Odo bowed his head as if giving his approval.

Bashir went into the surgery.

Jadzia looked at Kira and Odo. "Why does it feel that we're on opposite sides all of a sudden?"

"We're not," Kira said testily as if offended even by Jadzia's question.

"I hope you don't think that Julian and I are insensitive to the Orbs, or to the Bajoran religion," Jadzia said.

Kira stared at a point over Jadzia's shoulder as she seemed to think over many different possible replies before she said, "Not intentionally."

Now Jadzia felt offense. "Then I apologize," she said tersely.

"No need."

"Well, obviously, something is needed."

Kira's gaze shifted. Her eyes met Jadzia's. Again, it seemed she struggled with finding the right answer before she muttered, "All right. It couldn't hurt for you to spend some time in the temple."

Jadzia felt her spots prickle, never a good sign when it came to her mood. "Major, since coming to this station six years ago, you know very well I have made the Orbs one of my chief areas of study."

Kira's smile was condescending, almost one of pity. "Dax, you've spent six years studying what you believe to be solidified energy vortices. And you can spend the next six hundred years doing the same, and you will learn absolutely nothing because they are not vortices, they *are* the Tears of the Prophets. And until you understand that, you won't—"

"She's awake," Bashir announced as he walked from the surgery. "Doing fine, as a matter of fact." He looked around uncertainly, as if he sensed residual traces of the argument that had just begun between Kira and Jadzia. "You can . . . come in now . . . if you still want to, that is. . . ."

Kira pushed straight past Jadzia into the surgery. A moment later, Odo gave Jadzia a small shrug, and followed after Kira.

Bashir stared at Jadzia. "I was only gone a minute."

"Around here, that's all it takes," Jadzia said drily. Then she followed the good doctor into the surgery, wondering what the *next* minute would bring.

CHAPTER 13

O'BRIEN SHIFTED uncomfortably in the center chair of the *Defiant*. It wasn't that he had never taken command of the ship before. But he had never done so when Captain Sisko was standing at his side.

"We're at fifty kilometers and holding," Commander Arla said from her position at the flight operations console. Beyond her, on the *Defiant*'s main viewer, Deep Space 9 was a distant, sparkling smear of jeweled radiance against the translucent lavender plasma wisps of the Denorios Belt. There was no atmospheric distortion in space to account for the constant flickering of the station's lights, O'Brien knew. Instead, it was DS9's slow rotation that caused lights to flare erratically from viewports and disappear behind defense sails and docked spacecraft, like the twinkling of stars.

"Um, what do I do now?" Arla asked.

It was obvious to O'Brien that the young Bajoran Starfleet officer was about as at ease as he was with their new assignment—which was to say, not at all. And for good reason. Apart from Captain Sisko, Arla and O'Brien were the ship's only crew for this mission. Arla claimed she hadn't piloted anything larger than a shuttle since she'd graduated the Academy, and now she was at the conn of one of the most over-powered, hard-to-handle starships in the fleet.

"Activate automatic station keeping," O'Brien told her. Reflexively, he looked up at Sisko to make sure he had said the right thing. The captain's nod told him he had.

"Relax, Chief. Worf is standing by at Ops. If anything even *looks* like it's about to go wrong, you can have a full crew beamed on board in less than a minute."

But the cause of O'Brien's unease wasn't the prospect of disaster. He couldn't resist the impulse any longer. He started to get out of the chair. *The* chair. "You sure you wouldn't feel more comfortable doing this yourself, sir?"

"The *Defiant*'s in good hands, Chief. Now sit down."

O'Brien sighed as he did. But it still didn't feel right.

"Are the tactical sensors reconfigured?" Sisko asked.

"As best they can be," O'Brien answered. "Though they really were never designed for this kind of detail. I mean, I had to modify the gravity generators to create an artificial inertial-matrix aperture for the—"

"I don't need a lecture, Mr. O'Brien," Sisko said gently. "Just your assurance that they're going to work."

"Oh, they'll work, sir. Just not as fast as if she were the *Enterprise*."

"How long then?"

O'Brien had already done the duration calculations, but he worked through them again just to be sure. "I'd say ten hours for the full sensor sweep. Maybe another hour for the computer to finish the comparison between the Cardassian schematics and the scan results."

"And then we'll have a complete interior map of the station—"

"—with all deviations from the original designs called out by the computer. If there are any more hidden rooms in there, we'll definitely find them."

"Very good," Sisko said. "Now I'm wondering if while you're conducting the station scan, you can look for something else that's gone missing."

O'Brien sat forward in his chair, apprehensive. "I can try, sir. What is it?"

"Quark."

O'Brien frowned at the viewer before him as he contemplated the computational effort that would be required by what the captain was asking of him. On the *Enterprise,* with her special-purpose science sensors and multiband hyperspectral arrays, O'Brien would have felt confident he could do a biosweep of Deep Space 9 and find an hour-old outbreak of mold on a single slice of bread in a neutronium-lined food cooler inside of fifteen minutes. Finding a full-grown Ferengi would have taken less than half that time.

But the *Defiant* wasn't built primarily for science. Her scanners and sensors were designed to locate and analyze targets first and further humanity's understanding of the universe second. To tune and focus sensor emanations to ignore all living matter in approximately two cubic kilometers of space, *except* for one Ferengi. . . .

A sudden thought struck O'Brien. "Captain, are you sure Quark's even on the station?"

"That's what I'm hoping you will tell me."

O'Brien's brow became deeply furrowed as he calculated his chances of success. "Is there any chance you might get all the other Ferengi to leave the station for the day?"

"As I said, I don't want anyone to know that any kind of a scan or a search is under way. That's why you and Commander Arla got the job. And only you two. Do you think you can do it, Chief?"

O'Brien nodded, his head already filling with a list of the adjustments he'd have to make to the sensor scan rates, the density-overlap mapping algorithms, even the power-output waveguides. The subspace resonance patterns would have to be tuned to the exact salt content of Ferengi muscle tissue and . . . . He suddenly realized he hadn't answered the captain's question because he'd already become caught up in the *how* of his assignment. Not to mention the *why*. "Yes, I can, sir. Is Quark in trouble, Captain?"

Sisko nodded gravely. "He might be."

O'Brien found himself wondering if Quark had become the victim of a kidnapping. If so, then his sympathy was with the kidnappers. "Then should I scan the docked ships, as well? Just in case he's on one of them?"

"Good idea, Chief. And keep scanning them as they dock, just in case someone's going to try to slip him onto one that's arriving later." Sisko tugged down on his jacket. "Anything else before I go?"

O'Brien reviewed the assignment again. "Well, it would help if I knew where Rom and Nog and all the other Ferengi staff from Quark's are, so I can rule them out as the sensors find them."

"Very well. I'll have Odo put someone on it. But I think it's a good bet that if Quark is on the station, he won't be on the Promenade. You'd be safe ruling out any Ferengi contacts you make there. At least, at first."

"Understood, sir."

"Carry on, Chief." Sisko touched his communicator. "Sisko to Worf. One to beam out."

O'Brien watched as his captain dissolved into light, and then the *Defiant* suddenly felt as if she were twice the size of any other starship he had ever been aboard.

But at least with no one around to tell him otherwise, O'Brien could finally get out of *the* chair.

He headed over to his familiar engineering station, settling into his own chair with a relieved sigh. He was home. "Computer," he said, "transfer command functions to the engineering station."

"Command functions transferred," the computer promptly acknowledged.

O'Brien took a few minutes to enter the standard biological assay parameters that would have to be implemented to search for Ferengi life-forms, then announced, "Activating sensor sweep," as if somehow the bridge was staffed by a full crew. He touched his finger to the 'initiate programmed sequence' control, and the display screen above his station changed its subspace-frequency-response graph to show that the scanning had begun.

"So that's it." He looked over at Arla.

The young Bajoran officer looked back at him. "Ten hours?"

O'Brien understood what she meant. "I'm afraid so."

"Afraid isn't the word for it. I mean, automatic station keeping, automatic sensor sweep. What are *we* doing here, Chief?"

O'Brien got up from his chair to walk over to the empty science station. He preferred to be on his feet anyway, rather than sit around waiting for things to happen. "Well, the one thing you have to expect in space is that nothing will ever go the way you expect it will. So, today we're the *Defiant*'s insurance and her last-ditch backup system."

As if restless also, Arla swung her tall form around in her chair to watch the Chief cross the bridge. "I want to run a starbase, not pilot a starship."

As if his hands had minds of their own, O'Brien leaned down to the science workstation and entered the commands that would start a level-four diagnostic running in the science subsystems. Just to be on the safe side. Couldn't hurt. He smiled as the science displays came to life, running through their paces. He glanced sideways at the young Bajoran officer, tried to remember what it was she had just said . . . Oh, yes. "It's good to know how to do different things, Commander. So in an emergency, everyone can trade off. Watch each other's back. That sort of thing."

"Would you call this an emergency?"

"I don't know what the captain knows." O'Brien kept his attention on the science displays.

"And that doesn't bother you?"

Arla's voice was serious. O'Brien sighed. "It's not my position to be bothered by it, Commander. But I can see that you are." He could see where this conversation would be going. He straightened up, deciding he might as well head back to his engineering station. If Arla was going to talk his ear off, at least he'd be comfortable.

Arla, it seemed, had come to a decision of her own. "Can I speak freely, Chief?"

Safe in his chair, O'Brien nodded, giving her a half-smile. "You're the commander, Commander."

"Captain Sisko, he's not the most orthodox commanding officer, is he?"

"Well, let me say that this isn't the most orthodox command. Y'know, before I came here, I served on the *Enterprise—*"

"Under Picard?" Arla asked, with true admiration in the way she said that famous name.

O'Brien appreciated that attitude. "The one and only," he said proudly. "And for a starship captain on the cutting edge of the frontier, out where no one's gone before, you need exceptional flexibility, because the situation's always changing. Picard was brilliant at that kind of give-and-take. Still is, from what I've heard. But, when I took this assignment at DS9, I thought I'd be settling back into a more normal routine, like being at a starbase."

"From what *I've* heard, I didn't think anyone ever got tired of serving on the *Enterprise.*"

"Oh, I didn't get tired." O'Brien chuckled. "I got married. Had a little girl. And all of a sudden, as much as I loved the *Enterprise . . . .*"

He thought back to those agonizing days, when he'd debated end-lessly with himself about putting in for a transfer. And the terrible nights, when he awoke from stomach-twisting nightmares in which the *Enterprise* ran afoul of Borg cubes, black holes, runaway warp cores . . . a thousand and one disasters that must never touch Keiko and Molly.

And how he'd felt when he read the reports of what happened at Veridian III, the ship blown from space to a terrifying crash landing, with all its crew and its families and the children . . . at the same time that he'd said a prayer for the survivors he'd thanked the stars that he and his wife and their daughter were safe and not with them.

"You were saying, Chief—as much as you loved the *Enter-prise . . . ?*"

O'Brien, still distracted, made an effort to retrace his thoughts. "What I meant to say was, Commander, as . . . as complicated as I thought commanding that ship was, I've found DS9 to be even more . . . challenging. I suppose that's the word. I mean, Captain Picard could take us to a planet in trouble, we'd show the flag, do what we could to resolve things, and then we'd move on, knowing that three other ships and half the Federation's bureaucracy would be in our wake to follow up on what we had done. But here," O'Brien looked at the young Bajoran officer, wondering if she could under-stand what he was trying to stay, with life experience so different from his own, "staying in one sector, dealing with the same worlds over so many years, there's no chance to move on. Captain Sisko has to live with the consequences of his decisions. It calls for . . . a very creative approach to command."

"Plus," Arla said carefully, "he's the Emissary."

"Ah, now, I wouldn't know about that." O'Brien knew his limita-tions, and this kind of discussion was not his strong suit.

"So you don't believe the wormhole aliens are gods?"

O'Brien knew the right way, for him, to answer this one. "Captain Picard told me an interesting thing one day. He said one of the best lessons he ever learned at the Academy didn't come from a class-room, or an instructor. It came from Boothby."

O'Brien waited a moment to see if that name registered with Arla. It did.

"The gardener?" she asked.

"Among other things, it seems. But the captain said that Boothby told him, and I quote, 'Jean-Luc, when you find yourself locked up on a ship hundreds of light-years from nowhere and with no chance of escape from your crewmates, there are three things you must never discuss: politics, religion, and another crewmate's spouse.' " O'Brien stretched back in his chair. "So, right about now is when I think it's a good time for me to follow old Boothby's advice."

Arla tapped her fingers on the edge of her flight console. "There are a lot of cautious people on Deep Space 9."

"Goes with the territory."

Arla nodded. "I had a long talk with Dax about Captain Sisko."

That didn't surprise O'Brien. Dax was the most experienced member of the DS9 crew, and she was never reluctant to pass on whatever help or advice she could. All anyone ever had to do was ask. "They've been friends for a long time, those two."

"She wouldn't answer my question, either. About the wormhole aliens being gods."

O'Brien felt he was going to regret being sucked into this debate, but he didn't see as how the young commander was giving him any choice. If Julian were here, O'Brien knew, the doctor would view the situation entirely differently. Julian would relish the argument. O'Brien didn't. But it was either join the discussion or spend the next ten hours watching level-four diagnostics run. "I take it, then, that you don't believe the entities in the wormhole are gods."

Arla shook her head, and O'Brien thought he could detect a hint of unhappiness. "That's why I'm trying to understand how it is that Captain Sisko, an educated, intelligent man, an *alien,* brought up without any cultural influence from Bajor—how could *he* accept that they're gods? I mean, someone born on Bajor—fine, I can understand that. I don't agree with it, but I understand. They don't really have a choice. The whole primitive Prophet belief system permeates every aspect of our culture. There's no escape."

"You escaped."

"I wasn't born on Bajor."

That explains a lot, O'Brien thought.

After a few moments of silence, Arla leaned forward. "You're not saying anything."

O'Brien shrugged, looked around the unnaturally empty and quiet bridge. "I don't see that there's a lot I can say. Obviously, the type of environment someone's born into has a lot to do with what they end up believing in life. Vulcans embrace logic. Klingons find honor in battle."

"So what do you believe, Chief? Not about the Prophets. But about . . . whatever faith you were raised in."

O'Brien relaxed. This was one of the questions he could answer, one that rarely caused offense. "Oh, I'm a great believer in IDIC, Commander. Infinite diversity in infinite combination. The beauty of it is that nobody's wrong. Logic. Battle. They're all facets of the same thing. As if the true reality of the universe, whatever final answers there are to be discovered—if they can be discovered—is like a hyperdimensional string. Look at it one way it's an electron. Another way and it's a proton. Yet another one, you see a verteron. But it's all the same thing, just different ways of looking is all."

As pleased as O'Brien was with his answer, he didn't like the way Arla was staring at him, as if she had heard those exact words too many times before.

"Well, I'm not afraid to say when something's wrong."

Oh, oh, O'Brien thought. *This is where it can get ugly.*

"I think," Arla proclaimed, "that my people's delusional worship of the Prophets turned them into the galaxy's biggest victims."

"Now, that's harsh, don't you think?" O'Brien asked.

"No, I don't. Do you know how old Bajoran culture is?"

O'Brien wasn't sure. He thought back to that lost city the captain had rediscovered. "Twenty thousand years, I believe."

"Try *five hundred* thousand years," Arla said. "Think of that, Chief. Half a million years of almost unbroken continuity of culture. No notable worldwide disasters. No great empires fell. No dark ages. And no natural ebb and flow to history like on so many other worlds. But one unbroken strand of culture that has lasted since before your species ever evolved."

"Quite impressive," O'Brien said.

Now Arla's sadness abruptly became disgust. "Quite a *waste.*" She stood up, started to pace. "Half a million years of utter, contemptible passivity! That whole time, we did nothing but pray and wait for the gods to guide us. And ten thousand years ago, when it finally looked as if some forward-thinking communities were at last going to throw off the yoke of stagnant religious belief, what happens?"

"I wouldn't know," O'Brien said nervously, though he could guess. He had heard the number ten thousand before. But somehow, he didn't think Arla was really interested in what he knew. She was working her way through some argument that had nothing to do with him. And one he wished that he knew how to deflect.

"The first Orb lands on Bajor." Arla's face twisted with loathing. "It was the worst thing that could have happened to my people."

O'Brien didn't like the hostility Arla was expressing. He wondered how anyone could get through the Academy with such negative views of an alien culture. Since Arla wasn't born on Bajor, he felt justified in thinking of the Bajoran culture as an alien one from Arla's perspective. "To be fair, Commander, I don't think you'll find a lot of Bajorans agreeing with you on that."

"Of course not," Arla said. "Because for the past ten thousand years, the wormhole aliens have been manipulating our culture, breeding us, in fact, to develop even greater passivity."

O'Brien couldn't believe what she had said. Even at the risk of provoking her further, he felt he had to object. "You're going to have to explain that, Commander. I've known too many Bajorans from the Resistance to think of you as a passive bunch."

"The facts are simple, Chief. Ten thousand years ago, humans were just getting ready to invent the wheel and the roads that go with it. Vulcans were bloodthirsty savages. Klingons were less than Vulcans. And Cardassians? Ha! They were still swimming in swamps catching fish in their mouths. But we Bajorans were peaceful, advanced, and shared a world government."

"What's your point, Commander?" O'Brien wondered if it were too late to make a call to Worf. Just to check in. That sort of thing.

"My point is, ten thousand years later, every other race in the quadrant is busy carving up the galaxy—*except* Bajor. Instead, we've been brutalized, terrorized, occupied, and looted. And do you know why?"

"No," O'Brien said, his hand on his communicator, "but somehow I know you're going to tell me."

"Because for the past ten thousand years, the wormhole aliens have dropped their Orbs on us, deluding us into thinking that there are gods above managing our fates. And since the gods are taking care of us, why should *we* bother taking care of ourselves?" Arla now stood in the center of the bridge, arms spread wide in frustrated anger. "Honestly, can you think of a better way to cripple a species than by telling them that if they just wait peacefully, everything will be *given* to them? There's no need to study, to learn, to explore. Or even to dream. Just sit down, make yourself comfortable, and wait for the next dispatch from heaven." She shook her head, oblivious to O'Brien now, caught up in her own speechmaking. "You humans, and the Vulcans, and Klingons, and Cardassians . . . you reached *out* to the universe. You built starships and went looking for your gods. But on Bajor, with those hideous Orbs, the gods kept coming down to us, telling us not to worry, and not to try to better ourselves."

Arla flung herself down in her chair as if exhausted. O'Brien regarded her warily, wondering if she would settle down soon. "The Prophets occupied our world long before the Cardassians ever did," she concluded bitterly. "And that makes them the biggest enemy of the Bajoran people."

"Commander Arla, I don't mean any disrespect. But I certainly hope you know better than to go spouting off like that in public."

Her frown wrinkled her epinasal ridges. "I do know. But I asked if I could speak freely. . . ."

"You did that, all right."

"Sorry, Chief," Arla said. "It's just that, coming to Bajor, seeing the shape my people are in, when I know how much more we could be capable of . . . ."

O'Brien nodded, relieved that her outburst was over, and that he hadn't had to alert anyone else. That he'd been able to handle the situation himself. Even Julian could not have done better. "That's all right. It's all off the record."

Arla nodded and turned her chair back to the board and the distant view of Deep Space 9.

"Someday, the Prophets are going to destroy us," she said quietly. "And the horrible thing is, sometimes I think I'm the only Bajoran who realizes it."

O'Brien didn't begrudge her having the last word, though he suspected there was something else the young commander wasn't telling him—whether about the Prophets, about her past, he couldn't be sure. But now was perhaps not the time to probe for it, not when the topic was so disturbing to her. There'd been enough emotional venting for now.

The Chief contemplated the next ten hours of silence with more equanimity than he had before.

It wasn't as if they had to be unproductive hours.

With his spirits already rising in pleasant anticipation, he asked the computer to run a level-*five* diagnostic on the engineering subsystems.

In all the confusing diversity of the universe, O'Brien knew he could always find his peace in the beauty of a well-constructed machine, operating according to the inalterable laws of physics.

He wondered where Arla and others who felt as she did would find their answers—their peace. And what might happen if they didn't find it soon.

CHAPTER 14

IN THE SURGERY, Vash was sitting up in the angled examination bed. She had shadowed circles under her large, expressive eyes and her lustrous skin was pale, but Jadzia could see no signs of trembling or weakness.

Vash's query was unspoken but obvious to all who observed her.

Kira started to speak but Odo coughed and she reluctantly turned to Jadzia.

"You're safe for now, Vash. Odo's using suppression screens to protect against unauthorized transportation." Jadzia moved to block Kira and Odo from Vash's line of sight. Julian was standing on the other side of the examination table with his hands behind his back, keeping watch on the Cardassian diagnostic displays above his patient. "And there are security officers standing guard outside the Infirmary."

Vash wasn't impressed. "Oh, I see. Being safe must be some new Starfleet term for being a prisoner."

Jadzia smiled. Sweetly. "You're not under arrest. Yet."

Vash's answering smile was just as sweet. "Why would I be under arrest? Is it against some Bajoran law to be the target of an assassin? Or did I obstruct traffic on the Promenade when I collapsed?"

Interesting, Jadzia thought. Of all the experiences of all Dax's

previous hosts she had to draw on, the ones she usually found herself
returning to least were those of Joran, her sixth. He'd been a mistake,
his existence still suppressed by the Symbiosis Commission to avoid
alarming the Trill public with the revelation that the selection
process was not perfect. Joran had been unbalanced. He'd committed
murder.

Jadzia now took the rare step of brushing lightly against the disturbing memories of that perverted mind and its hideous act.
Because she sensed a similar lack of equilibrium in Vash.

But could Vash kill? Jadzia wondered. Not in self-defense,
because almost anyone was capable of that. *Could she kill in the way
that Joran had, merely for sport, or lust, or greed?*

"On Bajor," Jadzia said severely, "even the *attempt* to traffic in
Orbs is one of the most serious crimes in their system."

Vash stretched and moved her shoulders as if verifying the health
of her body. "I told him that, huh? The captain? About Quark being
involved in selling the Orbs?"

Jadzia nodded, looking beyond Vash to see Kira now caught in an
impressive struggle to remain silent.

The archaeologist bent forward, rubbed gingerly at the side of
her head. "On the Promenade, when I got hit . . . I thought I was
dying, you know? I remember *wanting* to tell someone . . . the captain . . . something that might make it easier for him to find who
killed me." She gave a sudden, rueful laugh. "My bad luck I didn't
die." She twisted around to look over her shoulder at Bashir. "Why is
that, Doc?"

Bashir looked away from the Cardassian readouts. "The dart contained an Andorian toxin."

Vash suddenly laid back against the angled table, as if all the
strength had left her. "Satr and Leen. They've been after me for a
long time. Ever since the Mandylion retrieval."

Jadzia saw Odo shake his head 'No' at the possibility that the two
Andorian sisters were involved in the attack on Vash. But Jadzia had
already deduced the improbability of that for herself. Even if Odo
did not have visual records of whoever had fired the dart at Vash,
Jadzia was aware the Andorian sisters were under constant surveillance. If they had been anywhere near Vash at the time of the attack,
Odo's officers would have known it.

Right now there was no advantage to be gained in sharing that news with Vash. But if her cooperation were needed later, such information would be as valuable as latinum. So Jadzia did not contradict Vash's supposition. She merely said, "Odo's working on tracking the sisters' movements."

Then Jadzia added, as if the question were unimportant, "Anyone else who might be after you? Captain Sisko said he thought you saw someone you knew on the Promenade, just before the attack."

Vash stared up at the ceiling, frowning. "This'll sound crazy, but . . ."

"I know all about crazy," Jadzia murmured comfortingly. "Believe me."

"Yeah? Well, I thought I saw Dal Nortron following us. How's that for crazy?"

With that, Odo reached his breaking point. "Excuse me, ladies, but there are only two Andorians on the station, and had one of them been on the Promenade at any time close to the instant you were attacked, they'd stand out on the surveillance tapes like . . . well, like Andorians." Odo stepped back, a hand held up in apology. "I apologize for breaking in."

But the damage was done. Jadzia had seen a worrisome little flash of calculation in Vash, as if the archaeologist had just learned something of importance from Odo's outburst—such as the fact that the Andorian sisters had *not* been on the Promenade and thus could hardly be considered suspects.

"What I meant was, he was in disguise," Vash said, recovering smoothly, but not smoothly enough for Jadzia, who was on full alert, now. "Or altered or something. I mean, no antennae, sort of brown skin. He might even have had Bajoran epinasal ridges. Like I said, I couldn't be sure."

"We'll study the visual scans again," Jadzia said evenly, more and more determined not to let Vash control this interrogation. "But in the meantime—Quark and the Orbs. Let's talk about that."

"What's the point?" All sense of hesitation or unease gone, Vash sat up again and ruffled her hair into place. "If I do, I go to prison. If I don't, it's just something I said when I had a shot of bicuprodyanide bubbling in my brain. I think what I meant to say to Captain Sisko is, Damn, I'm sorry I'm dying before I ever got a chance to have Quark show me an Orb like he promised he would the last time I was on the station. There's one in the Temple on the Promenade, isn't there? Yeah," the archaeologist continued, staring brazenly right into Jadzia's eyes, betraying no guilt whatsoever, "I'm sure that's the one Quark said he'd show me. Did you actually think I'd deal in a stolen Orb when I know what they mean to the Bajoran people?"

Now it was Kira who was close to the breaking point. Jadzia heard her give a muffled exclamation, but the major said nothing more, keeping to her promise not to interfere.

Julian, on the other hand, was suddenly looking ridiculously pleased with himself. But all he did in reply to Jadzia's questioning look was grin foolishly, once again appearing much too cute for his own good. *A good Galeo-Manada workout would cure that in a hurry,* Jadzia thought.

"I can certainly see how your explanation of what you said to Captain Sisko *might* make sense," Jadzia told Vash. "Of course, part of the problem is that the captain didn't understand every word."

"I guess I was lucky to be able to say anything at all."

"One of the more interesting things he said you told him was that Quark was going to have an auction to sell an Orb."

"Did I say auction or action?" Vash suddenly seemed busy rearranging her tunic. "Sell an Orb, or see an Orb? I bet I wasn't too clear." She looked up and smiled brightly at her interrogator.

"And then there was a word you used, one he didn't quite get, maybe something . . . Bajoran?"

Vash stopped fussing with her clothing for a moment, looked thoughtful for a moment, then shook her head.

"Let's try it this way, then," Jadzia suggested helpfully. "What Orb was Quark going to show you at the temple?"

"Oh," Vash said. She swung her legs off the side of the examination table. "Sure, that was it. The Orb of Jalbador."

"What?" Kira sputtered. She moved so quickly to Vash's side that she was between Jadzia and the archaeologist before Jadzia had even realized what she was doing. Odo moved forward but Jadzia quietly signaled him to hold back. Perhaps Kira could shake something out of Vash. It was worth a try.

" 'Jalbador'?" Kira said to Vash. "Is that what you said?"

Vash shrugged, unintimidated. "Yeah, so?"

"Not one Orb, but the Lost Orbs? The Lost Red Orbs of Jalbador? Is *that* what this is about?"

"You should talk to Quark," Vash said. "But, yeah, that's what he said he'd show me. A Red Orb of Jalbador."

Kira hung her head and shook it, as if berating herself for being a fool. "That's it, we're done here." She turned away from Vash, as if she had lost all interest in the archaeologist.

"I beg your pardon?" Jadzia asked.

"This is . . . more than ridiculous. I have to contact the Kai at once."

"Major, why?"

"Because, Dax, the Red Orbs of Jalbador don't exist. They are . . . I don't know a non-Bajoran example. But, they're not part of any of the legitimate teachings of our religion."

"Apocryphal?" Bashir suggested.

"That's as good a word as any," Kira said. "But more than that, they're something that . . . fringe people and fortune seekers and . . ." She waved a dismissive hand at Vash, who made a face back at her. ". . . and petty thieves go after all the time. I mean, at least once or twice a year there's some unbelievable story about the Lost Orbs being found, hidden in the ice on Mount Ba'Lavael. Or deep in the Tracian Sea in the sunken ruins of B'hala."

"But Major," Bashir objected, "B'hala didn't sink in the Tracian Sea. Captain Sisko found it under the Ir'Abehr Shield."

"Exactly, Doctor. But until the Emissary found it, B'hala had been lost for twenty thousand years! That's twenty thousand years of legends and lies and outright fraud. Do you know how many people on Bajor—and on a dozen other worlds, I'm sure—have been bilked by swindlers who claim to have an ancient map that shows the location of B'hala or the resting places of the Red Orbs?"

"The Brooklyn Bridge," Bashir suddenly blurted out. It made so little sense to Jadzia and everyone else in the surgery that they all turned to look at him.

"On old Earth," he continued, his expression somehow conveying the impression that he expected everyone else to know exactly what he meant. "The late 1800s. People newly arrived in what used to be called New York City were offered deeds to the Brooklyn Bridge—a spectacular public works built and owned by the local government. To buy the Brooklyn Bridge became a colloquialism for gullibility." Jadzia winced as Julian enthusiastically adopted a broad dialect as he quoted, " 'Well, if you believe dat, buddy, then I have a bridge in Brooklyn I wanna sell ya.' "

No one said anything right away. But Odo finally broke the silence. "Excuse me, Doctor, but is this the same Brooklyn Bridge that's installed at the big amusement park on Earth's moon?"

"Why, yes," Bashir said eagerly. "Taking it apart, moving it in sections, rebuilding it—it was one of the most phenomenal engineering feats of the twenty-third century."

"In other words, eventually, someone really *did* buy the Brooklyn Bridge?"

Jadzia tried not to laugh as Julian's face fell.

"Well, yes, Odo, but the point is . . . ." He looked plaintively around the surgery, loath as always to accept that no one was really up to appreciating whatever his point was. "Never mind."

"I really have to go," Kira said abruptly. "Odo, forget everything I sent you on Orb law. As far as I'm concerned, you can charge this woman with being a public nuisance, or you can . . . ship her out to wherever she's planning on selling her 'Orbs' next. Jadzia. Doctor." Kira left.

"That's it?" Vash asked, slipping off the examination table to stand upright, without any signs of ever having been affected by anything.

"Apparently so," Jadzia said.

Odo stepped around so that Vash could see him without straining. "Tell me, Vash, what *are* your plans now?"

"Staying alive is always high on my list of things to do."

"Then obviously, staying safely behind transporter-proof shields and being guarded by my officers is agreeable to you?"

"That depends on what the price is."

"Quark," Odo said. "Where is he?"

"Frankly, constable, I don't know. I was surprised to hear he had disappeared."

"Where were you going to meet him?"

Vash cocked her head at the constable. "I already had this conversation with the captain and Commander Dax."

"That's not an answer."

"At the bar, Odo. Where else would I meet him?"

"And what were you meeting him about?"

"According to the major there, not much." Vash sighed at Odo's poorly concealed look of exasperation. "All right. This is everything I know. Quark put the word out that he had been asked to be the broker for a transaction involving . . . the Red Orbs of Jalbador." Jadzia was impressed by Vash's attempt to make it seem she was embarrassed to even say the name of the Orbs. Vash was really good.

"The broker," Odo repeated gruffly. "So, presumably someone else had possession of the Orbs—"

"And Quark asked me if I knew of any prospective buyers."

"And did you?"

"Are you kidding? Half the antiquarian collectors in the Alpha Quadrant would bankrupt themselves for a chance to own a Bajoran Orb. Odo, seriously, this was shaping up to be the biggest transaction since the Fajo collection went on the block. I'm talking big."

"Did you put those interested collectors in touch with Quark?"

Vash drew back in surprise that seemed genuine even to Jadzia, who was increasingly fascinated by the archaeologist's behavior. Her performance, filtered as it was through poor Joran, seemed to Jadzia as if it were being dictated by an already written script. Somehow, the archaeologist had manipulated the situation so that Odo was asking all the questions Vash wanted him to ask. The performance was brilliant.

"Did you?" Odo repeated.

"Be serious," Vash said. "If I brought in my . . . clients, the bidding would . . . well, you could buy and sell planets for what some people would be willing to spend. And my cut would only be ten percent of Quark's commission." Vash sat forward, as if suddenly excited by the prospect of such a deal. "But, if I kept my people out of it, well, Quark doesn't have the connections I do. The bidding wouldn't go anywhere as high, and . . . ."

"You planned to buy it for yourself," Odo said, "and then hold your own auction for the people who could really pay."

Vash held up her hands as if surrendering. "Guilty."

"My sentiments exactly," Odo told her. "You know, of course, what the penalties are for trading in Orbs. Not just in Bajoran law, but under the Federation's own protection-of-antiquities statutes."

Vash curled a finger at Odo, asking him to move closer. "Odo, remember what the major said? There *are* no Red Orbs of Jalbador. If someone wants to buy something he only *thinks* is illegal, that's not a crime."

Odo rocked back and crossed his arms. "Oh, you are a piece of work."

"I'll take that as a compliment."

For a moment, Jadzia's Trill-constant swirl of consciousness paused and then coalesced into the pattern she'd been seeking as she realized what Vash was trying to do. There was now only one last question for Odo to ask.

As if on cue, she heard the constable say, "One last thing. If all of this . . . confusion was brought about by the potential sale of an artifact that you and whoever else was involved knew was a fraud, why would someone want to kill you?"

Jadzia caught her breath as Vash delivered her answer: "I'm not the only one who deals in rare antiquities. My clients buy from several different sources, so . . . any one of them could have decided that the potential payoff was worth taking me out of the picture."

Odo gazed down at the floor and Jadzia knew exactly what he was going to say next. The only thing a man like Odo could say after the story he had just been told.

"Vash, I have far better things to do with my time than try to stop criminals from killing other criminals. I'll keep all the security precautions in place while you're in the Infirmary, but as soon as Doctor Bashir says you can be released, I want you off this station. Is that understood?"

For once, Vash seemed truly serious. "Yeah, I understand. And . . . it may not mean much coming from someone like me, Odo, but thank you for . . . the transporter shields and the guards. I'll be on my way as soon as the doctor says."

Odo nodded his head once, said his good-byes to Jadzia and Bashir, then left.

Vash turned to Bashir. "So Doc? How long have I got?"

Bashir studied the Cardassian readouts. "How's your head?"

"Like I've got Gorns playing ten-pin behind my eyeballs."

Bashir nodded as if he knew exactly what that felt like. "I thought so. At least another twenty-six hours of observation, then I'll make a decision." He reached into a tray by the table and brought up a hypospray. "In the meantime, this should take the Gorns down to five-pin, at least."

Vash smiled as Bashir touched the hypospray to the side of her neck opposite to where the dart had struck. She still had a small dressing on that wound. Bashir had not wanted to use a protoplaser to speed the healing of the puncture because any residual toxin might have been trapped in the new tissue growth.

"Are you a bowler?" Vash asked.

"I'm afraid darts are more my game."

Vash laughed softly, seductively, and being a young attractive woman herself, Jadzia did not need to call upon the experiences of any of Dax's previous hosts to know exactly what Vash was trying to do.

"Maybe we should play sometime," Vash said.

"Darts or bowling?"

"Or . . . something else?" Vash's smile was sly, knowing. "You can choose. I'm open to just about anything."

Jadzia rolled her eyes as she saw the sudden flush that came to Bashir's cheeks as he *finally* realized Vash was no longer talking about the same indoor sports he was. "You get some sleep," he said.

Vash reached out to touch his hand. "Thank you, Doctor."

Jadzia had to admire Vash's technique. The touch had clinched it. Bashir was definitely on the hook, though she knew him well enough that he would do nothing to pursue this new opportunity until after Vash was no longer in his care.

Bashir eased away from her hand. "Uh, you're quite welcome. I'll . . . check in on you later, then."

"I'll be here."

I don't believe it, Jadzia thought as she started for the door. *The silly creature actually batted her eyelashes at him.*

Then Jadzia hooked her arm around Julian's and guided him to the door at her side. "Come along, Doctor. You have other patients."

"I do?"

The surgery door slid shut behind them, and they were in the main work area. Without Vash.

Immediately, Jadzia said, "Julian, I'm surprised at you."

"Why me? On the contrary, I'm surprised at you and at Odo."

"That woman was . . . wait a minute. Why are *you* surprised at *me?*"

Bashir headed over to the workstation where he had left the neural dart. "Because you—*and* Odo—were falling for everything Vash said."

Now Jadzia was doubly surprised. "I wasn't falling for everything she said. *You* were." She batted her eyelashes at Bashir. "Oh, Doctor, I'm open to anything. Really, Julian."

Bashir gave her a look of amusement. "Could it be you're jealous?"

"I am a happily married woman, thank you. I just happen to be concerned for my friend."

Bashir rolled the dart in his fingers, as if looking for something he and the most sophisticated collection of medical scanners and analyzers this side of Starbase 375 had missed the first time. "Well, your friend is equally concerned about you." He brought up his other hand and adjusted the position of the dart. "So you should know that everything Vash was saying in there was a lie." He began rolling the dart again, as if trying to feel for some slight imperfection.

Jadzia sighed with relief. There was hope for Julian yet. "Thank goodness you were able to sense it, too. I really was getting worried about you."

Bashir looked as if he hadn't quite understood what Jadzia had said. He continued to roll the dart in his fingers. Jadzia eyed him with renewed concern. She didn't like the way he was handling the dart, and she trusted he wasn't going to do something stupid, like accidentally prick himself with the dart's small needle. "I didn't have to *sense* anything, Jadzia. I knew what was going on the instant she made her mistake."

"What mistake?"

"Dax! You musn't have been paying attention. Now I'm even more surprised."

Jadzia put her hands on her hips. "Julian, unlike Miss Batty-Eyes in there, I am not fond of this kind of game. What mistake did she make?"

"Bicuprodyanide," Bashir said happily, entirely too happily in Jadzia's estimation. "She said she had it bubbling in her brain, if you recall."

Jadzia thought back. Yes, she could remember Vash saying exactly that. "But what about it? She did have bicuprodyanide in her system, didn't she?"

"Absolutely. Except . . . I never told her that's what it was. All I said was she had been exposed to an Andorian neural toxin."

Jadzia tapped her forehead with her fingers. It had slipped right by her. But then she thought she detected a flaw. "Just a minute, Julian. Maybe it was a lucky guess. I mean, how many Andorian neural toxins can there be?"

Bashir held up the medical padd he had been working with earlier. "In common use or easily replicated with nonspecialized equipment, one hundred ninety seven. I have no doubt that Vash knew exactly what was in this dart, and because of that, there was no possible way she thought she was dying when she told Captain Sisko about the Red Orbs."

Jadzia was struggling now to deal not only with what Bashir was suggesting, but with the fact that he had jumped so far ahead of her own assumptions. "But Julian, how could she take the chance that her accomplice would be able to shoot her at the right time, with the right toxin, without being seen?"

Then Jadzia felt Dax lurch within her abdominal pocket as Bashir suddenly slapped his hand to the side of his neck, driving the neural dart needle into his flesh. *"Julian!"*

But Bashir's only response was to seem to pluck the dart from his neck and then roll it forward in his fingers so that Jadzia could see the needle had been removed. It was in his other hand.

"What better way to make us believe she's telling us the truth, than by making us think that someone would rather kill her than have us hear what she had to say?"

To Jadzia, that moment of revelation was as powerful as if an Altonian sphere had just turned monochromatic. She had become so caught up in the idea that Vash was manipulating the truth in the surgery that she hadn't stopped to consider that that manipulation might have started much earlier.

"She's been lying from the beginning," Jadzia said wonderingly.

"I think that's likely," Bashir agreed.

"Which could mean . . . she does know where Quark is—"

"—and she knows who claims to have the Red Orbs—"

Then Jadzia and Bashir hesitated as they drew the ultimate conclusion from what they had discovered.

"And the Red Orbs themselves . . ." Jadzia said slowly.

Bashir nodded. ". . . could very well be real." He smiled at Jadzia's look of concentration. "As I said, we could be a great team."

Even his persistence struck her as endearing. But she deflected him by saying, "Julian, we already are a great team."

He stepped closer to her. "So what does the team do now?"

"Now . . . we go see Benjamin."

She could see it in his eyes: It wasn't what he had wanted to hear her say, but he knew it was the right thing for her to have said.

What a sweet hopeless romantic Julian is, Jadzia thought with real affection as they left the Infirmary together. *Someday, the woman who gets Julian is going to be the luckiest woman in the quadrant.*

She wondered who that lucky woman would be.

CHAPTER 15

"YOU'RE CRAZY," Nog said.

Jake shrugged. "My granddad says that's not so bad in a writer."

"Then may I say your grandfather is crazy, too."

Jake straightened up from the safety railing on the second level of the Promenade. Years ago, when he and Nog had first met and made the first tentative steps in forging a friendship that would transcend the traditional boundaries of their respective species, they would sit on the deck here, letting their legs swing over the side until Odo or one of his officers told them they should have something better to do and it was time to move along.

But now, Jake realized there *had* been nothing better for the two of them to be doing than watching the parade of life that had passed by beneath them. Because those long hours of observation, speculation, and just plain talking had helped them become the young men they were today—the writer and the Starfleet officer.

It was from this vantage point by the safety railing that Jake first began noticing the intricate details of people's behavior: how some couples walked close together, some apart; how some people smiled secretly to themselves, while others fought back hidden tears. He'd seen the confidence of the newly arrived visitor, fresh from the shuttle, striding in to face the challenge of Quark's dabo table. Hours later, he'd watched the defeated shuffle of that same person as he crept away with only the clothes he wore.

Nog had learned no less than Jake. He had explained the Great Material River to his *hew-mon* friend, and how the Promenade was a perfect tributary of that mighty cascade that shaped the universe. On the shores of the Promenade—that is, its shops and kiosks—were pockets of accumulation, areas that had too much of one thing or another. Flowing between those shores were the rushing waters of customers—that is, those who had too little of what the shops had too much of.

On the other side of the equation, the shopkeepers had far too little latinum, and so an endless rebalancing of accounts ensued as the waters lapped at the shores, eroding a little here, building up a little there, always working to achieve a balance that forever remained out of reach.

Jake had been brought up in a Starfleet home and was fascinated by the Ferengi outlook on the universe. Nog, who had been brought up to accept the Great Material River as the only reasonable way to see the universe, had been equally fascinated to learn about Jake's alien perspective. The idea that it was acceptable—even desirable—to accumulate knowledge for no other purpose than to increase understanding, and the entire concept of helping others without *any* prospect of profit, were staggering to the young Ferengi.

But once both boys got over their initial dismissal of each other's viewpoints and began to truly try to see what the other meant, whole new vistas opened before them.

In Jake was born the need to see how other minds—not just human and Ferengi—viewed the universe, and then to illuminate those views for others through the written word. In Nog, a mad dream was born in which the precision of Ferengi thought could be applied to the romantic altruism of the Federation in order to create a new paradigm of galactic organization, one in which the most extreme imbalances in the Great Material River—meaning those that invariably led to conflict—would be forever eliminated, while still leaving ample opportunity for individuals to profit.

Thus Jake and Nog had set their lives' goals and directions, all in the idle pastimes of children, and all from this one corner of the Promenade.

Not that any of that made it easier for them to reconcile their differences today.

"You know what your problem is?" Nog asked.

"I don't get out enough?" Jake answered.

The Ferengi frowned. "No. It is that you are always trying to understand life in terms of a made-up novel."

"Nog, that's my job."

"How can it be a job if you make no money from it? Writing news articles is your job. Writing novels for no money, that is . . . an affliction."

Jake put an elbow on the safety railing and rested his head on his hand. "Nog, when you were at the Academy, did you make any profit?"

Nog reacted suspiciously to Jake's abrupt change of topic. "No. . . ."

"But someday you expect to profit from your Starfleet experience, don't you?"

Nog appeared to be selecting his words with extreme care. "I would hope that . . . many individuals, commercial concerns, and government agencies will profit from . . . what I will learn during my career in Starfleet."

Jake pounced as soon as Nog had cornered himself. "So you admit that—"

Nog realized the trap he'd been caught in and wouldn't let Jake finish. He did it himself. "Yes, yes, that I performed certain activities with no chance of immediate profit, but with the expectation of earning profit at a later time."

Jake's smirk let Nog know who had won this particular argument. "So, as I was saying, from the perspective of a made-up novel, there's something going on here on Deep Space 9. Something that your uncle's involved with. And something that's brought smugglers in from across the quadrant. And it's not what Vash told Dax and Odo."

"And as *I* was saying, you're crazy. You're drawing connections where none exist. You're trying to make my uncle into that Fermion character—"

"Higgs. Higgs is based on Quark. Fermion is based on Morn."

"—that *unbelievable* character in your novel. And he's not."

Jake stretched and straightened up again. A wave of new visitors was arriving on the Promenade from the turbolifts and airlocks. Not too many were Bajoran, so Jake decided the commercial cruiser from Sagittarius III had finally arrived. The Sagittarians were neutral in the Dominion War, and as a result their cruisers carried cargo and passengers from most of the nonaligned worlds. Whenever a Sagittarian ship docked at the station, there was always a good chance a rarely seen alien might be on board, and Jake found himself watching the crowd closely, hoping he might catch his first glimpse of a Nanth.

But he hadn't forgotten his friend, and even as his gaze remained on the lower Promenade level he said, "Nog, if I gave you ten crates of stem bolts, self-sealing or not, your imagination would run wild thinking up new schemes for selling them, or trading them, or . . . somehow turning them into latinum. When it comes to business, you won't accept any limits."

"Of course not."

"Then why is it you have no imagination when it comes to how *people* behave?"

After a few moments of silence, Jake glanced sideways to see that Nog was just staring at him, as if he could think of nothing more to say.

Jake sighed. "Let's try it again." He held up a finger. "First of all, Quark called in a group of smugglers to take part in the sale of a counterfeit Bajoran artifact." He held up a second finger. "Then, one of the Andorian smugglers was murdered." He held up a third finger. "And then, someone tried to murder Vash." He held up a fourth finger. "And despite Vash explaining the whole thing to Dax and Odo, there are still at least four smugglers on the station—Vash, the Andorian sisters, and that guy, Base." Jake waved his hand back and forth, trying to emphasize the importance of those facts. "So put all that together, and what do you have?"

"Four fingers."

Jake closed his eyes. "Nog, use your imagination."

"All right. I will now imagine the impossible." Nog put his hand over his eyes, a thumb on one temple, a forefinger on the other. "I am imagining that you are giving up this stupid line of reasoning. I am imagining that . . . that you are buying me lunch at the Replimat. I am imagining that—"

But by then, Jake's laughter had become contagious and Nog began laughing, too.

"I am *not* buying you lunch," Jake laughed. "It's your turn."

"That is why I was using my imagination," Nog said.

They both began walking toward the closest spiral stairway.

"Anyway," Jake said, undeterred by his friend's resistance. "I still think I'm right."

"That the counterfeit Bajoran artifact isn't counterfeit?"

They came to the staircase, and Jake waited for Nog to go first. "If it were all a scam like Vash said, the smugglers would have left by now, right? After all, Odo knows all about it, so what's the point of sticking around?"

"To obtain the counterfeit artifact and take it someplace where potential customers don't know it's counterfeit," Nog said.

They arrived on the Promenade's main level, and Jake was surprised by the noise and bustle of the new arrivals. Many of them were looking around as if they had never seen a space station before.

"That still doesn't answer the big mystery," Jake said as he and Nog started for the Replimat. "Why would professional smugglers get involved with murder for a counterfeit artifact? I mean, I understand the idea of trying to make a profit for low risk—"

"I would certainly hope so."

"—but to commit murder?" Jake said. "That's a high-risk crime. Which means the potential profits have to be equally high. Isn't that one of your rules? The riskier the road, the greater the profit?"

This time when Jake looked at Nog, he could see the Ferengi looking thoughtful.

"All right," Nog said. "You have a point. A small one. And it probably has nothing at all to do with what's really going on here. But . . . ."

Jake grinned. "But what?"

"It is probably good enough for *The Ferengi Correction.*"

"*Connection.* The title is *The Ferengi Connection.*"

"Whatever."

Jake stopped Nog by the directory monolith. "Okay. I'm being serious now."

"When aren't you serious?"

"I mean it, Nog. How am I ever going to be able to convince a reader that a story I write might be true, if I can't even convince *you* that what we're really seeing go on all around us *is* a story?"

Now Nog looked worried. "I do not have the slightest idea what you're talking about."

Jake took a breath, oblivious to the crowds of people passing by. "Given everything that's happened here over the past three days, what do *you* think is going on?"

"Anything other than what you think is going on."

"You're doing this on purpose."

"Jake, be reasonable. Let us say you are right. Let us say that Uncle Fermion—"

"Quark."

"—Quark is selling a real Bajoran artifact with a value worth killing for. First of all, what kind of an artifact is that valuable? I mean, the rarest Bajoran artifact that I have ever heard of was that icon of the city of B'hala. And nobody was trying to kill to get that. The Cardassians just . . . gave it back to Bajor."

Jake glanced up at the Promenade's high ceiling. Nog had a point. Even Jake had never heard of an artifact so valuable that—he had it! "Nog! It's an Orb!"

Nog reacted with outraged shock. "An Orb is not an 'artifact.' It is . . . an Orb. And my uncle would not be stupid enough to risk buying or selling an Orb, no matter how great the profit."

"But there would be incredible profit for someone not as . . . law-abiding as Quark? Like a real criminal?"

Nog clearly did not want to be having this conversation. "I suppose."

"All right. Then that's what it is. Thank you, Nog. You've solved an important story point. Quark—Higgs—is trying to sell an Orb. And since we haven't heard any news about an Orb being stolen, it's got to be one of the Orbs that went missing during the Occupation that the Cardassians haven't returned yet."

Nog looked disappointed. "So now you are suggesting that either a *Cardassian* is selling a stolen Orb or that someone with more lobes than brains stole an Orb from the Cardassians."

"Isn't there some Rule of Acquisition to cover this?" Jake asked. "You know, Profit plus more profit equals temporary insanity for a desperate criminal?"

Nog screwed up his face in concentration. "Perhaps in one of the reform editions. But not in the . . ." He frowned. "You are not being serious. There is no such law."

"All I'm looking for is a possibility. A willing suspension of disbelief. What's it going to take to convince you?"

"Really?"

"Nog, if I can convince you, I can convince anyone. Now, let me have it. What do you need to believe the story?"

Nog looked around at the milling crowd. "More smugglers. If someone's trying to sell an Orb, there should be a great many more than four smugglers on board DS9. There should be dozens, if not hundreds."

"Okay, I can live with that. Quark put out the word a few days ago. The closest smugglers arrive in a day or two. With more continuing to arrive. So there will be more by now, we just don't know about them. What else?"

Nog shrugged. "Cardassians."

"Why Cardassians?"

"They're trying to recover their stolen property."

That was going too far for Jake. "Nog, there won't be any Cardassians coming to DS9. We're at war with them."

Nog shook his head. "The *Federation* is at war with Cardassia. Bajor is not a member of the Federation. Technically, it has been given neutral status by the Dominion. And technically, this station is Bajoran territory."

"But it's *in* Federation space."

Nog held his hands out as if he had nothing more to offer. "You asked what it would take. I answered. Now you really do have to buy me lunch."

Jake started walking again, with Nog hurrying to keep up. "I don't have to buy you anything. I asked for help. You set up impossible conditions."

The Replimat was full, every table taken. There was even a line outside. The Sagittarians did not have a reputation for palatable food. Too many of their flavorings were self-organizing slime molds, which often tried to reconstitute themselves and then escape from whatever dish they had been mixed into.

"Not impossible," Nog insisted. "Necessary. As in necessary for me to accept your premise. Should we try the Klingon Cafe?"

"Impossible, because there's no way anyone will believe that Cardassians will come to DS9. Why don't we try Quark's?"

Nog looked uncomfortable. "That little Base . . . he makes me nervous. Did you know he has hair? On his . . . scalp? Uh, no offense."

"We'll eat upstairs."

"All right." Nog suddenly brightened. "Maybe Leeta will be on duty. Then we can negotiate a family discount!"

The young men left the Replimat and started back toward Quark's. "You have to pay to eat at your uncle's?" Jake asked.

"Exploitation begins at home," Nog said, as if quoting another of the Ferengi Rules. "And if the Orb is really an Orb and you want your story to be believed, then you have to do something dramatic so the reader will understand the stakes have been raised."

"What are you talking about?"

"Cardassians on DS9."

"Forget it. I'm not writing a fantasy. I'm writing a heist novel and there are rules I have to follow. And one of them is . . . ." Jake hesitated. Couldn't quite believe what he saw—whom he saw—stepping through the airlock across from Quark's, beyond the Infirmary.

"Is what?" Nog prompted.

"Cardassians," Jake said.

Nog sounded as confused as Jake felt. "That's a rule?"

Jake reached out, took Nog's shoulder, and pointed him in the same direction he was looking. "No," Jake said. "That's your proof."

Cardassians.

Three of them. Just outside the circular door of the airlock. One was female, the other two male. And one of them was unlike any Cardassian Jake had ever seen before: He was bald.

Jake felt Nog tense, and instantly the Ferengi tapped his communicator badge.

"Nog to Commander Worf. Security breach on the Promenade. Airlock Alpha. Three enemy personnel."

Jake wheeled to Nog. "Nog, they're not enemy personnel. Look at them—they're civilians. No weapons. No—"

Jake stopped talking as the crowd reacted to five columns of shimmering light that formed around the airlock stairs.

Jake stared in fascination as four Starfleet security officers beamed in with Worf and scattered the crowd. Each of the five had a phaser. Each phaser was aimed at the Cardassians.

"Isn't that a bit of an overreaction?" Jake asked.

"We are at war," Nog said.

Jake had tried, but he still didn't understand the military mind-set that had become so much a part of Starfleet in the past year. But the one thing he felt he did know was motivation, both in the characters he wrote about and in real life. And he understood the motivation that had led to the scene being played out before him right now.

"Okay, Nog—this proves my point," Jake said as Worf and his team took the Cardassians into custody. "What possible reason could three Cardassians have for risking a trip into *Federation* space to set foot on a *Starfleet*-controlled space station?"

Nog looked up at Jake, and Jake could see that this time his friend knew exactly what he was talking about.

"You said it yourself," Jake continued. "They want their Orb back. It's the only possible reason they could have for coming here."

Nog looked grim. "We shall see." Then he went to offer his assistance to Worf.

Jake remained behind. But as he watched the Cardassians being led away, he was filled with an overpowering sense of just being *right*.

He was the only person on Deep Space 9 who truly knew what was going on, and it was time to start letting people know it.

CHAPTER 16

"I AM LEEJ TERRELL," the leader of the Cardassian mission said in the relative calm of the Wardroom. "And these are our credentials."

Sisko accepted the articulated Cardassian padd she gave him. The excitement of the unannounced arrival of three Cardassians on a neutral cruiser had finally lessened throughout the station. But the security concerns remained.

As he took his seat across from his visitors at the conference table, Sisko studied the padd, comparing the identity dossiers it displayed as the station's computer automatically tested the authentication codes in the padd's memory.

According to the padd, Leej Terrell was the widow of a minor trade diplomat from Cardassia Prime. Her technical specialist, Dr. Phraim Betan, was a physician retired from the Cardassian Home Battalions. And her associate, Atrig, of no specified job function, was a businessman who ran an import-export company among the Cardassian colony worlds. The three Cardassians were, each dossier proclaimed, volunteers working for the Amber Star, with no official connection to the Cardassian government.

Sisko, however, didn't believe a word of the dossiers. For a diplomat's wife, Terrell was too clearly used to giving orders, not practicing diplomacy. Dr. Betan was too young to have retired from anything. And Atrig—perhaps the most striking Cardassian Sisko had ever seen—had not lost his hair nor been so badly scarred at the base of his neck and across one of his wide shoulder membranes ferrying goods from one world to another. Atrig had been in battle.

Decked out though they were with false identities, innocuous civilian outfits, and singularly hollow smiles, Sisko had no doubt he was seated across the table from three Cardassian soldiers. Three very active, and dangerous, Cardassian soldiers.

A Federation authorization window opened on the padd's display—the authentication codes had been confirmed. Terrell, Betan, and Atrig had been cleared for travel within the Bajoran sector.

But Sisko didn't really care. He placed the padd on the table as if it held nothing of interest or of value for him.

"So, you are traveling under the guise of a humanitarian mission," Sisko began.

"Not under the guise," Terrell replied easily. "We *are* a humanitarian mission, accepted by both the Federation and the Dominion during this terrible conflict."

Sisko folded his hands. "Then why didn't you make travel arrangements directly with this station? If you are permitted to travel through Federation space, why arrive unannounced?"

Seated directly across the table from him, Terrell matched Sisko's gesture, folding her own hands in a mirror image of his. "In times such as these," she said, "I often find it is more expedient to beg forgiveness than ask permission. If I had requested your approval to travel here, would you have given it to me?"

"No," Sisko said, registering Terrell's surprise at his decision not to hide the truth through the more standard practice of equivocation and diversion.

"Then I was right to do as I did," she said with a smile.

"Again, no," Sisko said, keeping his tone deliberately impassive and uninformative. "You have disrupted my station. You have raised many questions in the mind of my strategic operations officer. Whatever delay you might have expected if you had contacted me ahead of time you can be sure will now be even longer, as Commander Worf tries to uncover what you're hiding."

Sisko saw Terrell shoot a swift glance at Dr. Betan. And then as if the glance had been a signal for his action, the doctor spoke next.

"Captain Sisko, I assure you we have nothing to hide. We are volunteer workers of the Amber Star, private citizens aligned with no political group. We are merely here to repatriate the remains of the unfortunate Cardassians you discovered fused within the hull of this station. I'm sure you'll understand how this humanitarian act will at last bring closure to their families, as their fates are now known and the two unfortunates can be laid to rest according to their own customs."

"Ah, but I understand completely, Doctor," Sisko said. "And I am very pleased that the genetic profiles of the soldiers have allowed you to identify them." Hastily suppressed reactions from all three Cardassians informed Sisko that his statement had startled them, a suspicion Terrell quickly confirmed.

"I believe you have reached an incorrect conclusion, Captain Sisko. The dead whose remains we are recovering are not—were not—soldiers. Their identification files are in the padd, as well. You will see that they were civilian support staff for the Terok Nor mining operation. Low-level. Of course, they worked *for* the military in trying to restore order to Bajor—"

"Excuse me?" Sisko said, not sure he had heard Terrell correctly.

Undeterred by his interruption, Terrell proceeded silkily. "Captain, you know what a troubled world Bajor is today. Believe me when I say that in the past, it was even more so. Remember that the Bajorans endured centuries of petty political and religious squabbling. And almost sixty years ago, when we could see these poor people were about to allow those conflicts to erupt into the horrors of all-out world war, well, we had to act, didn't we? We're a compassionate people, Captain. If we had not brought order to these people—our closest neighbors in space, after all—when we did, Bajor would be a wasteland today."

Sisko clenched and unclenched his hands so vigorously during Terrell's vile tirade that the popping of his knuckles rang out in the Wardroom. "Parts of Bajor *are* a wasteland today, because of what *you* and your Occupation forces did to it."

"And we regret that," Terrell said. "If you could only know how it pained us whenever we had to discipline these people."

Terrell paused as if to let him take part in the conversation. But Sisko remained silent because he knew if he opened his mouth to say a single word, he'd end up screaming at these sanctimonious monsters.

"I understand what you're feeling," Terrell said with infuriating condescension. "I know how attached one can get to Bajorans. In a way, they're so much like children. In fact, our research has proven without doubt that the reason they remain so backward, and so dangerously unable to consider the consequences of their actions, is that their brains are not as developed as most other sentient creatures. Those parts of the neural structure responsible for higher-order thought are stunted, more like those found in less evolved animals such as—"

"That is quite enough," Sisko said through clenched teeth.

Terrell waved her hand as if what she had to say was of no real importance. "I know, I know."

Sisko could hear his heart thundering in his ears. He wanted nothing more than to end this meeting and escape from Terrell's presence. He put his hands on the table, prepared to stand, to . . . he saw the padd.

He forced himself to relax back into his chair.

Terrell had almost succeeded in perfectly deflecting him off the topic they'd been discussing.

He looked at her with new respect—as an adversary.

He decided it was time to deflect *her.* "To return to the topic at hand, your identification of the bodies as those of 'civilians' does not match other details we've obtained from our investigation." Now Sisko stood to end the meeting. "I can only surmise that the Amber Star has made some error, and so we will not be able to release the bodies until a more detailed analysis is completed."

Terrell was on her feet at once. "Captain Sisko, there is no error."

Sisko smiled. "I know an error would be unlikely coming from your military's Central Records. But as you said yourself, the Amber Star is a civilian organization. I'd prefer my medical staff continuing with—"

"I would be happy to be of assistance," Dr. Betan interjected. "There are subtleties to Cardassian biochemistry and physiology with which an alien doctor might not be familiar."

"Thank you, but it won't be necessary," Sisko said. "Our Doctor Bashir is one of the finest in Starfleet. And he has the advantage of working in a Cardassian medical facility." He gestured to the door. "I'm sure we'll clear this up in oh . . . a week or two."

Terrell gave no sign of leaving. Her voice turned harsh and her manner seemed more threatening. "Captain, do not turn this into a diplomatic incident. Whatever slim chance for peace exists now will be lost forever if the population of Cardassia believes the Federation would play politics with the bodies of Cardassian citizens. *That* they will not forgive."

"I don't understand," Sisko said.

Terrell's eyes narrowed. "That we care for and respect our honored dead?"

"No," Sisko said. "That you think Cardassia has anything to do with the disposition of this war." Sisko made no effort to disguise his pleasure at his Terrell's displeasure. "Admit it, Terrell, your world is as controlled by the Dominion as Bajor was controlled by you during the Occupation. In fact, I wonder how far down the evolutionary scale the Founders rank Cardassian neural structures."

"You are making a mistake," Terrell hissed.

Sisko actually laughed. "I'm not the one who's stepped into the middle of enemy territory." He turned his back on the Cardassians and walked to the doors. "The Sagittarian cruiser is departing tomorrow at fifteen hundred hours. You will be leaving with it. In the meantime, I'll have you escorted to guest quarters."

"Captain Sisko," Dr. Betan fluttered as he looked nervously at Terrell, "for the sake of galactic peace, please reconsider this deadly insult."

The doors slid open and Sisko looked up to see Major Kira approaching. He allowed himself a moment to contemplate what this meeting might have been like with Kira involved. The Cardassians would be badly injured or dead by now. Neither of which states would have been desirable.

"Captain," Kira said urgently, "we have a problem." Sisko was relieved to see that her attention was solely focused on him and not on his visitors.

"It's take care of, Major. I've dealt with the Cardassian delegation." It was safer not allowing the fiery Bajoran any contact with Terrell and her companions. If she did, a second front could open up right here on DS9.

But Kira was not interested in Sisko's visitors. She glanced back over her shoulder. "Not a Cardassian problem. A Bajoran one."

Sisko stepped out of the Wardroom to look down the corridor in the same direction Kira did. Past Worf's security detail. Where, surprisingly, four Bajoran monks were striding toward him in great haste.

"Didn't you say you contacted the Kai and the Inquisitors?" Sisko asked Kira. "That they were no longer needed because the Red Orbs of Jalbador don't exist?"

"These aren't Inquisitors," Kira replied. "And they aren't here about Quark's Orbs." She frowned at Sisko, lowered her voice. "Word got out about the Cardassians arriving for the bodies."

"Captain Sisko," the lead monk called out in a booming voice. "I am Prylar Obanak. It is most urgent we speak."

Sisko was doubly taken aback. First, by the fact that a Bajoran monk had addressed him without calling him 'Emissary.' And second, by the narrow band of red cloth the prylar wore tied around his forehead under his hood. Recent events had compelled Sisko to study a wide range of ancient Bajoran texts dealing with the fallen Prophets known as the Pah-wraiths and he had learned that a strip of red fabric was often worn by those who worshiped them. When the red cloth was worn about the arm, Sisko knew, it was a symbol of a Pah-wraith cult which had been around for years, but which most Bajorans treated as a joke. What the fabric meant when tied around a monk's head—well Sisko wasn't actually sure, now that he thought about it—but each of the three monks accompanying Obanak was also wearing one in that position.

Sisko was not anxious to become involved in a new distraction. He still had O'Brien's search to contend with, along with the mysteries of the murdered Andorian and the dead Cardassians. He tried to deflect Obanak into Kira's care. "You can discuss anything you'd like with Major Kira and—"

"This does not involve Nerys," the prylar rumbled. Even though he pitched his voice at normal speaking level now, its timbre was still remarkably deep and resonant.

And once again he had surprised Sisko. For a monk, it seemed to Sisko that the prylar was unduly familiar with Major Kira, addressing her as he had by her given name. But then, even before he had uttered a word it was clear to the most casual observer that Obanak was not a typical prylar. He was a full head taller than Sisko, and despite the loosely fitted robes he wore, it was clear the monk had the musculature of a plus-grav powerlifter. Whatever kind of religious he was, Obanak did not appear to be living a life of quiet contemplation.

Kira offered her own explanation to Sisko. "We were in the Resistance together."

Obanak bared his teeth in a fierce smile, revealing less than a full set. Sisko wondered if the missing ones had been knocked out in battle and if so, in the past or more recently. "And my followers and I consider ourselves to be in the Resistance today."

Now Sisko was thoroughly confused. "Resistance to—" But that was all he was able to say before being cut off by a deafening roar.

"*Murderer!*" Obanak raised his arm and pointed accusingly past Sisko and into the Wardroom.

To Sisko, there was no doubt that Obanak meant one of the three Cardassians behind him and, as captain of DS9, he acted swiftly to prevent escalation of a potential incident that could involve the entire station.

Setting aside any consideration of how deserving his visitors might be of Bajoran wrath, Sisko twisted the enraged prylar's arm down and pushed Obanak back against the far bulkhead of the corridor. At the same time, Worf's two security officers held back the other three monks. Meanwhile, Kira stepped in to keep the Cardassians safely in the Wardroom.

As he held Obanak in position, Sisko became aware of the monk's improbably massive biceps. The only reason Obanak wasn't moving was clearly because he chose not to—it was doubtful even Worf would have been able to stop the Bajoran prylar.

With order restored, Sisko spoke sternly to the four Bajoran and the three Cardassians that he and his staff now held apart from each other. "You are all guests on this station. Do I have your word you will not disturb the peace again?"

"Of course, Captain," Obanak said thickly. "I apologize. I was unprepared for the sight of such *kheet'agh* in this place."

Sisko frowned, but he released his grip on the prylar, whose only response, fortunately, was to adjust the position of his robes. Though the term Obanak had hurled at the Cardassians was unfamiliar to Sisko, he could guess it was not a flattering one. His own attention, moreover, had been caught by the prylar's omission of a term that he was accustomed to hearing from Bajoran religious figures. It now seemed somehow wrong not to be addressed as 'Emissary.' But that was the least of his concerns at the moment.

Sisko turned back to Terrell, Dr. Betan, and Atrig, who had yet to give their word that they would not cause trouble.

Atrig had moved into position directly in front of Terrell, as if to shield her from attack. His legs and arms were in an unmistakable fighting rest-stance. Now Sisko was positive that the bald Cardassian was no more a civilian than the two dead Cardassians in the Infirmary had been.

"I assure you, you are in no danger," Sisko informed his visitors.

Terrell stepped out from behind Atrig, though Atrig was still poised to defend her. "So you say, Captain," she said. "Of course, we've come to expect this sort of overwrought emotional outburst from Bajorans. It's not their fault, you know, any more than a beaten dog is responsible for snapping at its rescuer. It's that the Bajoran neural—"

A powerful voice drowned hers out as Prylar Obanak intoned dramatically: "Leej Terrell. Prefect of the Applied Science Directorate, Bajor Division. Personally responsible for the deaths of over two thousand Bajoran citizens during the conduct of medical implant experiments. It was said that even the Obsidian Order feared her for her ability to make opponents simply disappear."

The silence in the corridor lasted only a moment.

"Is that all?" Terrell said, unperturbed and now in command of herself again. "Surely you're not finished. There are so many more crimes I'm supposed to have been responsible for. Prefect of medical research. Commandant of a work camp on a colony world. In charge of mining operations here on Terok Nor. I think once someone claimed I was even responsible for the assassination of Kai Opaka."

"Kai Opaka wasn't assassinated," Kira said grimly.

"Of course she wasn't," Terrell agreed soothingly. "And neither was I responsible for any of the other crimes I supposedly committed. It's just that your people have a great deal of displaced anger, and you—"

"I think you should leave it at that," Sisko warned.

"Good idea," Kira added.

Terrell looked past Kira as if she didn't exist. "Captain Sisko, again I appeal to your humanity. Given the unwarranted hostility you can see we're facing here, and the unfortunate consequences that might ensue if it's allowed to continue, would it not be to everyone's advantage if you simply let us receive the bodies of our fellow citizens with dignity and—"

"They cannot take the bodies," Obanak thundered.

Terrell's cold glance flicked off the prylar. "Sir, be reasonable. No matter how your mind's been twisted against us, you can only kill a Cardassian once."

"Unfortunately," Kira muttered.

"That's enough, Major," Sisko said firmly. He turned to the Bajoran prylar. "Why is it any concern of yours what happens to those bodies?"

Obanak nodded his head in the direction of the corridor. "May we talk in private?"

Sisko gestured to Worf and Kira to maintain the separation of the remaining Bajorans and Cardassians. Then, together with the prylar, he walked away from the Wardroom and down the corridor, until not even Obanak's deep voice could be overheard. And it was then that the prylar dropped his posturing and made the case for his position.

"Captain, I don't know how much you know about what happened on this station during Withdrawal, but there were many deaths."

Sisko knew that wasn't the case. He braced himself for other untruths. "The official death toll was four."

"Four Bajorans," Obanak said. "Among the Cardassians . . . well, certain Resistance members undercover on Terok Nor saw the confusion of Withdrawal as their chance to strike a final blow against the enemy. At least one hundred Cardassians were killed on that last day."

"That's never been part of any account I've heard." Sisko could not recall Major Kira ever alluding to such an event. But then she did not readily discuss the dark days before the Federation had taken over Deep Space 9.

"Why would it be? If the Cardassian people ever learned that their troops were slaughtered during a retreat, don't you think they would demand retribution? Either against the Bajoran people or against the Cardassian leaders who accepted the slaughter without retaliation?"

Sisko could see the logic in that, though it was still not a full explanation. "But then why didn't the Bajoran Resistance publicize their great victory against the oppressors?"

"Captain, think of the consequences." Sisko couldn't help noticing that the Bajoran prylar out of the presence of the Cardassians was a most persuasive fellow who presented his arguments in a reasonable, not a rigid manner. "In the past," Obanak continued, "it would be quite one thing for the Resistance to take credit for wiping out one hundred Cardassians on patrol in some desolate mountain region. Under conditions such as those, it was next to impossible for the Cardassians to be sure which cell was responsible. But up here, as I'm sure you know, the situation was more tightly defined. Consider this: The names of every Bajoran on the station at the time of the Withdrawal exist in Cardassia's Central Records. Among them, inevitably, are the Resistance members responsible for those last acts of righteous revenge. So my point is this: If the Cardassians show no signs of making an issue over what happened, then why would any Bajoran risk calling attention to it?"

"All right," Sisko conceded. "I agree that both sides have something to gain from hiding the truth. But what does that have to do with Terrell and the bodies we found?"

Obanak paused and took a particularly long, deep breath. The action reminded Sisko of a stress-reducing Bajoran meditation technique Kira had once recommended he try. "As of now, Captain, those actions, those deaths . . . they belong in the past. The two bodies you found, chances are they are two of the hundred from the Day of Withdrawal."

Sisko saw a shadow pass over the prylar's face as he gave name to the terrible last day of the Cardassian occupation of the station. "Now, what happens when those bodies return to Cardassia and an investigation begins? We on Bajor believe that witnesses will be tracked down, events reconstructed, someone will remember that a certain Bajoran was the last to see a certain dead Cardassian. A few days later, that Bajoran will be murdered in his home by assassins hired by the grieving family.

"And we can't forget the possibility of physical evidence as well," Obanak added. "A physical altercation during Withdrawal might have produced a fleck of Bajoran blood, a scraping of Bajoran skin under a fingernail, or a single strand of Bajoran hair caught in the fabric of a dead man's suit. Each body could provide hundreds of different ways for Cardassian investigators to identify a member of the Resistance who may or may not have been responsible for a Cardassian's death." Coming to the end of his argument for Sisko's help, Obanak folded his arms within his robes. "If you allow that to happen, Captain, then the cycle of violence will continue."

Sisko studied the prylar. He still hadn't decided on a course of action. But he now understood Obanak's position. "What would you suggest I do?" he asked, truly interested in the Bajoran monk's answer.

"My followers and I will take the bodies and, in accordance with Cardassian rituals, we shall cleanse them, prepare them for their journey through their Divine Labyrinth, and then cremate them."

"Evidence and all?" Sisko asked.

Obanak nodded. "To keep the past in the past, where it belongs."

Sisko considered his options. Obanak seemed sincere but hopelessly naive. "Prylar Obanak, do you honestly believe I can convince Terrell and her people that you—a Bajoran monk—will perform any sort of Cardassian funeral rite with the proper respect?"

"We are incapable of doing anything except show the proper respect. Captain, my followers and I are not the type of religious with which you are familiar. I refer to the misguided ones who adhere to flawed texts imperfectly chosen from the long legacy of our world's relationships with the True Gods of Creation. Such misguided ones as might call you Emissary."

That explains his reluctance to call me by that title, Sisko thought. "You're right," he said. "I'm not familiar with your approach—"

"More than an approach, Captain. We follow the One True Way."

This encounter with Obanak was causing Sisko to feel both intrigued and uncomfortable. He was well aware that there were many sects on Bajor. Many different ways of interpreting holy texts, the Prophets, and their actions. But for all those different approaches, Bajoran religion was rarely, if ever, confrontational. All but a few Bajoran religions were based on the one central tenet of the

Prophets' undeniable existence. But past that point, any group was free to go its own way. Most accepted the guidance and leadership of Kai Winn. Some did not. And, at least in Sisko's experience, Bajor was unique among most worlds of the Federation in that in the face of such diversity, religious intolerance did not appear to exist. Of course, he had also thought that given that the proof of their gods' existence was so tangible—in the form of the Orbs—there wasn't room for much argument.

"You will forgive me," Sisko began as diplomatically as he could, "but I have seen on Bajor that there appear to be many ways to worship the Prophets."

"Many ways," Obanak agreed. "But only one way that is correct above all others."

Sisko looked back down the corridor toward the door to the Wardroom. Obanak's three companions were still waiting there with Worf's security officers. Kira was standing with them, apparently having no desire to remain in the Wardroom with Terrell and the other two Cardassians.

Cardassians, Sisko thought. Cardassians back on DS9. A Bajoran monk from a sect he had never heard of. Two murdered Cardassians from six years ago—perhaps from the very same day Quark, Odo, and Garak could not remember. One murdered Andorian from four days ago. Quark missing. Smugglers everywhere. Counterfeit Orbs and . . .

Where is the pattern? Sisko asked himself. He could envision all the separate pieces swirling around like flotsam on the steep sides of a whirlpool or like tiny runabouts tossed by the negative energy flux of the wormhole. Yet he couldn't help but feel that somehow, in some way, all those pieces should fit together—if not among themselves, then around some missing final piece.

"Captain?" Obanak asked.

Sisko returned his attention to the Bajoran monk, not quite sure how long he had been staring blankly down the hall in search of answers.

"Were you with them?"

"You mean, with the Prophets?"

Obanak nodded.

"No," Sisko said. "But I thought you didn't believe I was the Emissary."

"Clearly, you are not," Obanak said. His thick brow suddenly deepened over his large, dark eyes. "Do you believe you are?"

Sisko paused before answering. It was ironic, but that was exactly what Commander Arla—a Bajoran of no religious beliefs—had asked him. And now he was being asked the same question by someone on the exact opposite end of the curve of religious possibilities—a Bajoran who seemed to believe that all other Bajoran beliefs were wrong.

"That is what the Prophets call me," Sisko said. "And that is what many Bajorans call me. So I accept that that is what I am—to them. What it means, though, I really cannot say."

Obanak regarded Sisko gravely. Almost, it seemed to Sisko, with respect. "I must say I hadn't expected you to be so open-minded, Captain. Usually, when the False Prophets cloud an innocent mind, that mind remains closed."

"False Prophets?" Sisko was certain he had never heard a Bajoran use the word 'false' in the same breath as 'prophets.'

"Those that dwell in the *Jalkaree*. The Sundered Temple. What the unenlightened call the wormhole."

It was then that Sisko realized why the prylar wore the sign of the Pah-wraiths. "I see: you consider the Pah-wraiths to be the *true* Prophets."

Obanak touched the thin red cloth strip on his forehead. "Oh, no, Captain. Open your mind even more. This compulsion that exists for people to choose only one path or the other—that of the Prophets of the *Jalkaree* or of the Pah-wraiths in their prison of fire—it is a deliberate obstruction of the One True Way."

"And what way would that be?" Sisko asked, wondering if he would ever truly understand Bajorans and Bajoran belief systems.

Obanak held the edge of his robe like an ancient orator about to deliver a speech. "Not so long ago, the misguided believed that a long-prophesied confrontation took place on this very station—the Gateway to the Temple. Is that not right?"

"The Reckoning," Sisko said. He still had nightmares about that horrifying event, when a Prophet had inhabited the body of Major Kira and a Pah-wraith—Kosst Amojan, the Evil One—had taken over the body of his own son Jake in order to fight an apocalyptic battle between good and evil.

"The Reckoning," Obanak repeated. "First prophesied twenty-five thousand years ago. Yet what happened?"

"Nothing." Sisko had trusted in the Prophets and had been prepared to let the battle take place, no matter the personal cost. But Kai Winn had flooded the Promenade with chroniton particles, creating an imbalance in space-time and preventing the noncorporeal entities from remaining within their selected corporeal vessels. Thus nothing had been resolved.

"Exactly. And nothing is all that will ever occur as long as the different sides remain in conflict. No progress. No enlightenment. No rest. And no end."

"I still don't understand," Sisko said. Just what did this sect of Obanak's believe in or want to have happen for the good of Bajor? "What is the True Way?"

Obanak beamed at Sisko with an expression of almost transcendental bliss. "The One True Way is that path which shall be revealed when no other paths remain to be chosen."

Sisko stared at the monk, mystified. For a moment, he had actually believed he might be about to learn something new about Bajoran religious beliefs. But instead, Obanak had responded with a typically obscure pronouncement so imperfectly defined it might mean anything.

"I see you doubt me," Obanak said.

"I don't understand you," Sisko said truthfully. "There is a difference."

"Understanding is simple to those whose minds are open, Captain Sisko. When the Temple is restored, there will be no false paths to chose from. No False Prophets. No Pah-wraiths. No good. No evil. Simply the one True Temple. The one True Prophets. And the One True Way to a glorious new existence beyond this one."

Sisko shook his head. "That sounds just like what was supposed to happen after the Reckoning."

But Obanak was full of even more surprises. "The Reckoning," he said sternly, "was a petty conflict between the False Prophets and the Pah-wraiths of the Fire Caves. The True Way will be revealed when the False Prophets and the True Prophets are at last reconciled."

Sisko suddenly realized that Obanak might be referring to a *third* group of entities. He hadn't heard any discussion of that possibility before. "Are you saying that your True Prophets are *not* the Pah-wraiths?"

"Pah-wraiths and False Prophets and True Prophets . . . they are all one and the same, Captain. And in a long-ago time beyond measure, their home—their Temple—was sundered, and they were driven apart. Some to dwell in the *Jalkaree*. Some in the Fire Caves. And some in the *Jalbador.*"

"The Red Orbs," Sisko said with abrupt understanding.

"I beg your pardon?"

"That's why you're here?" Sisko said. "For the Red Orbs of Jalbador?"

Obanak shook his head. "Captain, really, what do you take me for? The Red Orbs of Jalbador are a child's bedtime story. They don't exist, they never have. Don't tell me someone's trying to sell them to *you*—the Emissary!"

But before Sisko could say more, he heard loud footsteps in the corridor, and saw Kira's compact form hurrying toward him, urgency expressed in every stride.

He called out to her, "What is it, Major?"

"It's O'Brien, sir. He has to see you."

"Why?"

He's found something with the scan."

"What is it?"

"He's refusing to tell anyone but you, sir. All he'll say is that it's something that just shouldn't be."

CHAPTER 17

"I KNOW ALL ABOUT the Orb," Jake said.

Jadzia Dax looked up at him from her science station in Ops and thought again how much Jake reminded her of his father. "I see. And which Orb would that be?"

Jake leaned in close, dropping his voice to a conspiratorial whisper. "You know. The one that was stolen from the Cardassians. The one that Quark's trying to sell. The one that all the smugglers are after." His eyebrows moved rapidly up and down as if to signal her that he was telling her something particularly special.

Jadzia found the rather juvenile gesture endearing, and she adored the feeling it gave her—that she was joining a game in progress. Her love of play had not been a characteristic of any one of her past hosts more than another. She shared it equally with all of them, because after a few centuries of life it had become obvious to the full series of Dax's hosts that opportunities for fun must be exploited at every turn. Over the centuries, such opportunities came by far too seldom.

Thus, Jadzia leaned even closer to Jake, made her own whisper even softer, and attempted to move her eyebrows up and down as he had. "This is for your novel, right?"

"No," Jake said. "This is for *real*. I've figured it all out, Jadzia, but I haven't been able to tell my dad yet. Do you know where he is?"

Jadzia sat back. Jake wasn't playing a game after all. "You just missed him. He beamed over to the *Defiant*."

"Beamed over? Isn't the ship docked?" Jake seemed troubled by her news.

Jadzia hesitated. She was well aware that Sisko made it a firm rule to never mislead or lie to his son. But Sisko's present mission was classified and he had left orders instructing that no one be given details about what O'Brien and Arla were doing with the *Defiant*'s sensors. So she compromised. "The Chief's testing some new equipment modifications," she said, neither lying nor telling the whole truth. "They're just fifty kilometers out."

"Can I beam over?" Jake asked.

"This wouldn't be a good time. Your dad's really busy."

"I know he is—because of the Orbs and the Cardassians and . . . well, everything. But I'm trying to help and—"

Jadzia held a hand up to forestall any further mention of the Orbs as she took a quick look around Ops. Again his father's son, Jake caught on right away and waited quietly for her next instruction. Jadzia's cursory visual sweep of the staff revealed to her that several of them were close enough to be half paying attention to what Jake was saying. Just in case he *was* on to something, she decided, his father's office would be a more prudent location for the details of whatever it was Jake had discovered.

Discreetly signalling that he follow her, Jadzia ushered Jake up to the steps and then escorted him to Sisko's office. The instant the door had closed behind them, she asked Jake how he knew about the Orb. "Did your father tell you?"

"No. I figured it out on my own. At least, I figured it out when I was talking with Nog. I mean, I heard that Vash was supposed to be after some rare Bajoran artifact. And I figured that the only type of artifact valuable enough to motivate people to commit murder—well, it had to be an Orb."

Jadzia sat down on the corner edge of Sisko's desk as she mulled over what Jake had learned on his own and tried to decide how much she should reveal to him, in turn.

"Well?" Jake asked. "Am I right?"

Oh, why not? Jadzia thought. Jake's very intelligent. He's even able to work out the convolutions of *Vulcan* murder mysteries—the true test of intellect. Maybe it was time she started thinking of him as an asset to the investigation and not merely as Sisko's son.

"All right," she said, "let's talk about this. But," she cautioned the eager youngster, "you can't tell anyone else what we've discussed except for your father. He'll let you know if you can tell anyone else. And that means Nog."

Jake nodded vigorously. "So, it *is* an Orb!"

"Yes and no," Jadzia said. "Vash said it was an Orb, maybe more than one. Something special called a Red Orb of Jalbador."

"I was right!"

"*But,*" Jadzia added, "Major Kira says the Red Orbs are just a legend. They don't exist."

Jake looked confused. "Why would Cardassians come to Deep Space 9 to get back something that doesn't exist?"

"The Cardassians say they are here to claim the bodies Rom and O'Brien found in the power conduit."

"A cover story," Jake said with a dismissive shake of his head.

"Maybe so," Jadzia allowed. "I didn't meet with them. But apparently a delegation of Bajoran monks also came aboard to demand that the bodies *not* be turned over, so *someone* thinks those bodies are important."

Jake's face took on a faraway look. He stared past her and through the large viewport behind his father's desk, muttering as if speaking only to himself. "So there's got to be a connection. . . ."

"Between what and what?"

"The Orbs and the bodies."

Jadzia sighed. A discussion of real facts and logical supposition was one thing. Making up fairy tales was another. "One major problem," she said as she eased off the desk and got to her feet. "The bodies are real, Jake. The Orbs still might not be."

Jake raised a triumphant finger. "Aha! My point exactly. A minute ago, you said that Major Kira said they *didn't* exist. But now you're saying they *might not* exist. What else aren't you telling me?"

Jadzia pursed her lips in admiration. The kid had her. "Well, you're not alone. Julian thinks the Orbs might be real, too."

Jake's shoulders went back and he straightened up to his full, impressive height. It was almost as if she were watching the actual inflation of Jake's ego. She could just imagine what he was telling himself—that he, a mere novice writer, had independently reached the same conclusion as DS9's genetically enhanced medical genius.

"Before you give yourself the Carrington Award," Jadzia said drily, "there might be a few more details to consider."

Jake's increased enthusiasm was all too evident to Jadzia. But it was too late to turn back. She had brought him into the investigation and now she would have to try to control his participation—for his own sake and hers. "Like what?" he asked, ready, it seemed, for anything she might ask of him.

"For one, where's Quark?"

"I've figured that out, too."

Jadzia sat back down, wondering if he had the ability to surprise her again, and half hoping he could. "Have you, now?"

"Sure. My dad knows exactly where he is, or Odo does or someone like that. Because otherwise, everyone would be looking for him. And since they're not . . . I don't know, maybe they're using him for bait to catch more of the smugglers."

"Sorry to disappoint you," Jadzia said, getting up from the desk. Jake's ideas were at the predictable level after all. "And remember you can't talk about this with anyone except your father—but that's exactly what the *Defiant* is doing right now: a complete tactical sweep of the station looking for Quark. And any more of those hidden sections you and Nog found."

"Damn," Jake said. Then quickly added, "Sorry."

Jadzia accepted his apology without letting him see how sweet she thought he was for offering it. She started walking toward the door, Jake following her as he recited a list to himself, "Orbs, Cardassians, bodies, smugglers . . ."

Jake gave Jadzia an intent look. "As long as I've promised not to talk about this with anyone else, is there anything else you think I should know?"

Her hand already on the door, Jadzia paused, considering, then deciding no harm would likely come from telling him a bit more, she turned back to face Jake. "There is one other mystery your father's contending with. And again, it's like the Orbs. It might be real or it might be . . . just a mistaken recollection."

"Great," Jake said. "What?"

"Quark claims he can't remember what happened to him on the

Day of Withdrawal. Odo claims he himself was knocked out by a phaser blast and missed the Withdrawal. And Garak says he remembers every detail, but . . . it's pretty clear there're some details he's completely forgotten."

"Whoa," Jake said. "Missing Time Syndrome."

Jadzia laughed. "You know about that, too?"

"Yeah, sure, I wanted to use it in a story some day. About a guy from way back in the twentieth century or so who gets involved in a Starfleet temporal operation and finds out about the future, so they wipe his memory, leaving him with Missing Time Syndrome. And the trick is," Jake said, the words all coming out of him in an excited rush, "the memory wipe isn't absolutely complete, and all these memories of the future come bubbling up in him, so he writes them down as if they're fiction. But they're real. And it's only now, looking back, that people today realize this guy actually did write about what was going to happen." He paused expectantly, as if waiting for her reaction.

Jadzia said the first thing that came into her head. "Sounds like a good children's story."

He frowned. "It's not for children."

Jadzia tried another approach. "The trouble is, the techniques the Department of Temporal Investigations use are foolproof. When they wipe a memory, it's gone. It won't even come back as a dream."

But Jake wasn't interested in talking about that story. "I'll think of some way around it. Tell me more about Quark and Odo and Garak."

"That's everything I know."

Jake clapped his hands. "Doesn't matter. I've got it! On the Day of Withdrawal, *they* killed the Cardassians and so . . . so the Bajoran Resistance wiped their memories so if they were ever interrogated, they'd really believe they were innocent!"

Jadzia put a hand on Jake's shoulder. "It's okay, Jake. This is real life. Not everything has to fit together that neatly. Sometimes things happen that just aren't connected to each other."

"Then why are all these things happening at once?" Jake asked. "There *has* to be some connection, Jadzia."

"Maybe the only connection is your imagination," Jadzia said, not wishing to sound condescending but definitely wanting to find some way to calm Jake down.

But Jake just shook his head, as if he'd just thought of something important. "No. The connection is the Andorian. Dal Nortron. His murder is what started everything."

"If it was a murder." The door slid open and Jadzia walked out into the small landing. But Jake wasn't behind her. He was still standing in his father's office, the expression on his young face grim.

"What is it?" Jadzia asked.

"Nothing," Jake said, unconvincingly. He stepped out into the landing to stand beside her. "Can I see the file on Nortron's death?"

"That might be pushing research too far, Jake. I think that's up to Odo, and I doubt if he would approve it."

Jake nodded without protest.

Her interest caught, Jadzia couldn't help asking. "If you did have access to Nortron's file, what do you think you might find?"

"I don't know," Jake said. "I was just wondering where exactly his body was found. It's not important."

Jadzia began walking down the stairs with him. "Well, you're coming up with some good thoughts," she said encouragingly.

"Even if they're wrong." Jake gave her a wry smile which Jadzia found reassuring, under the circumstances.

They came to the turbolift. She gestured to Jake to enter first. "The only way we learn is by gaining experience. And the only way we gain experience is by—"

"—making mistakes," Jake said as he stepped into the lift. "So at least now I know where my dad got that saying."

Jadzia hid her smile as she joined him. "After three hundred years, believe me—I've made enough mistakes to know what I'm talking about. As soon as your father gets back, I'll—"

The sudden scream of a warning siren interrupted her, as at the same time all the main lights in Ops began flickering.

Jadzia ran from the lift. "Worf, what is it?!"

Worf looked up from his security station, sweat already glistening within the deep ridges of his forehead. "The main computer has been compromised. All security subsystems are off-line."

Jadzia rushed for her own station, Jake forgotten behind her. "What the hell does that mean?" she demanded.

"Only one thing," Worf growled. "It is a prelude to attack!"

CHAPTER 18

"THERE," O'BRIEN SAID. "That's the hidden stretch of corridor with the holosuite. The one Jake and Nog found."

On the *Defiant*'s main viewer, a small red dot flashed in the lower section of a three-dimensional wire-frame schematic of Deep Space 9. Only a third of the station's outline was filled with detailed depictions of bulkheads and decks, conduits and waveguides, turbo-lift shafts and structural support beams. The other two-thirds of the station remained featureless. But that was to be expected. O'Brien had been conducting his tactical sweep for only a little more than three hours, and it was still under way.

Sisko watched as another pulsing light joined the first on the screen, a few decks higher and closer to the station's core. "What about that?" he asked, pointing to a second red dot. "Over there, two levels up."

"Ah," the chief said as he rotated the schematic on the viewer. "That's a deficiency we already knew about. The original plans called for that section to hold about ten additional living units. But the Cardassians never got around to finishing them, so they left it as one large room. The dock management people use it as a storeroom for unclaimed goods. Odo checks it for contraband every week or so."

A third red dot began flashing. Sisko leaned forward to get a closer look. "What about that one, Chief?" He tried to place the third location's features from memory. "Is that the water-recycling plant?"

"Yes, sir. That's the one I called Major Kira about. That's the part that just shouldn't be there."

Finally, Sisko thought. "I need an explanation, Chief."

Sisko watched as O'Brien expanded the schematic of the station until the viewer displayed a section only three decks tall, the third red dot now an irregular rectangle pulsing precisely where a network of pipes seemed to come to an end.

"Well, first off, sir, it *is* the water plant. I'm in there at least once a month for inspection. I know the specifications of all the pipes, the filters, the evaporators. And after six years of me crawling all over this station, well, if there were a single deviation or deficiency from the schematics, I'd know about it. And I can vouch for that whole section being spot on to the Cardassians' original plans." O'Brien paused to qualify his statement. "Of course, it does have documented upgrades from when the Starfleet Corps of Engineers rebuilt it three years ago. But I can vouch for those, too."

"So," Sisko said, "if you know that the physical layout of the water plant is in perfect agreement with the Cardassian schematics, then why is that flashing light saying the two patterns don't match?"

"Because they don't, sir."

Sisko turned to regard his chief engineer with growing impatience. He was vaguely aware of Commander Arla standing nearby, but the young Bajoran officer was wisely choosing to observe, not take part.

"You're confusing me, Chief," Sisko said. "And I don't like to be confused." But from the look he now saw on O'Brien's flushed, red face, it was clear that the engineer was as mystified as he.

"Sir, according to the tactical sensor sweep I've conducted, DS9's water treatment facility no longer even exists. Somehow, and don't ask me how, it's turned into a large, empty room. And that's why the red light's flashing."

"Correct me if I'm wrong, Chief, but if the water plant had truly disappeared, shouldn't we know about it?"

"Oh, we'd know about it," O'Brien said, perplexed. "We'd have a thousand calls in from the habitat ring about no running water. We'd have transporter venting of all the water being spilled into the plant from the severed pipes. The whole station would look to be floating in a cloud of ice crystals."

"And since it's not . . . ?"

"Someone's got to be running a sensor mask in the treatment facility," O'Brien concluded with a frustrated frown. "Something small, tightly focused, no appreciable power signature. Intended, I'd say, to defeat any tricorders being used to conduct a search. A tricorder that encountered that mask wouldn't register that anything was trying to jam its sensors. All it would show is that there was nothing in the room."

"In other words, that's where Quark is."

"Frankly, Captain," O'Brien said, "there could be a hundred Jem'Hadar hiding behind that thing and we'd be the last to know about it."

That was all Sisko needed to hear. He activated his communicator. "Mr. Worf, we have a probable target. Prepare transporter suppression fields and arm the anesthezine dispensers for the following coordinates."

Sisko recited four groups of digits, each corresponding to a specific location's deck, ring, corridor, and door number in DS9. But each number was offset by a different, predetermined amount, so that anyone listening in to his transmission would not be able to determine Sisko's real target. Only Worf had the key to the code, and his reply, as usual, was to the point.

"Understood. Implementing security measures. I will beam you to the perimeter of the location."

"No," Sisko said. He wasn't looking forward to any type of violent encounter around the equipment that supplied water to the station. "The Chief and I will beam to Ops. We'll leave from there with a full security team."

"Excuse me," Arla said. "You're leaving me here?"

Sisko didn't even glance at the Bajoran commander as he replied. "Regulations don't permit me to completely abandon a ship."

"But . . . I'm not rated for this class of ship. Not on my own."

Arla's qualifications or lack thereof were not one of Sisko's priorities right now. "Commander, trust me, all you have to do is sit. As soon as we're finished on the station, I'll have a crew beamed out." Sisko didn't understand why the young Bajoran officer was so troubled by the prospect of being alone on the *Defiant*. Most people in Starfleet dreamed of a chance to be the only person on a starship. It was a powerful experience, Sisko knew, to be the sole person in the presence of so much power and potential. But perhaps Arla Rees was better suited to flying a desk.

"Yes, sir," she said, and made her way quickly toward the lone flight operations chair as if she expected the artificial gravity to cut out at any second.

Arla's disappointing reaction to opportunity slipped from Sisko's thoughts almost immediately. He was anxious to get moving. "Status, Mr. Worf?"

"Anesthezine systems are on-line. I am now reconfiguring the interior security fields to—"

A high-pitched squeal blared from Sisko's communicator.

Sisko hit his communicator twice to reset it, tried opening a frequency again, and got nothing. In an instant he was on his way to the *Defiant*'s communications console, even as O'Brien scrambled to the tactical station.

It took only seconds for Sisko to see that all of DS9's communications arrays were dead: No carrier waves. No navigation beacons. No subspace repeater signals.

Sisko turned to face O'Brien. "Report!"

The chief didn't take his eyes off the madly flashing tactical displays he studied. "I have no idea what's going on. Massive power fluctuations. All external *and* internal communications are down. They're on emergency lighting, life-support, gravity . . . unless a quantum torpedo hit Ops dead center, I'd say we're looking at a total computer failure." The screens stopped flashing. O'Brien looked stunned. "Sir, there's not a single automated system operating on the station. It's as if the computer's disappeared."

"This is not a coincidence," Sisko said angrily. "Worf was adjusting the security fields. They were waiting for us to make our move."

"Who was?" O'Brien asked.

"Whoever's got Quark. Whoever put up that sensor mask so we can't see what's behind it. But they couldn't know we'd be on the *Defiant*." Sisko rushed back to the auxiliary engineering console. "Chief! We need to shut down the *Defiant*'s computers."

"What?!" O'Brien and Arla said it together.

"If the station's computer has been infected by a programming virus, or some type of disruptive radiation, the *Defiant*'s computers might be vulnerable, too. Let's move it!"

With O'Brien at his side, Sisko transformed the *Defiant* into little more than an inert chunk of dead mass within two minutes.

"Now what?" O'Brien asked.

"Now we're beaming directly to the water plant. Or, at least to the edge of that sensor mask."

Sisko saw O'Brien glance over at Arla, who was staring at the screen in front of her. Her olive-gold face was pale, her mouth hung slightly open. "Captain," the chief said, "I think I should stay here and keep the ship under manual control."

"I need you on DS9," Sisko said. That was the end of the argument. "Commander Arla, you *are* going to drift. But as long as you're moving away from the station, there's nothing you have to do."

Arla's words were rasping as if her throat were bone dry. "What . . . what if I do start drifting toward the station?"

"Use the docking thrusters to alter your trajectory," Sisko said sharply. He wondered how he had thought just a short time earlier that Arla was exactly the kind of officer material that Starfleet needed more of. The young Bajoran was not behaving as if she were even worthy of the command rank she now possessed.

"Just don't try to reverse course," O'Brien added. "With the impulse engines powered down, you don't have enough thruster propellant to manage it."

Arla's nod was hesitant. Incredibly, it seemed to Sisko she could not even control her appearance of nervousness. "And . . . if I'm heading for the wormhole?"

"It's going to take you a couple of hours to drift that far," Sisko said, trying to sound reassuring, when all he wanted to do was shout at her to pull herself together. "This'll be over by then."

"Captain," O'Brien suddenly suggested, "what if I just set a course for her now? Steer her away from the station and the wormhole. Only take a minute."

But Sisko shook his head. O'Brien was a good man, but he was needed elsewhere. "If there's anyone on that station keeping track of this ship, I don't want them to see Commander Arla changing course, because that will make her a target. I want them to think she's either disabled or abandoned. Commander—you have the conn. I suggest you sit back and enjoy the ride."

Then Sisko headed at double speed for the main doors and O'Brien followed just as quickly.

The *Defiant* was a compact ship, designed for the efficient movement of information and personnel in battle. It took only seconds to run down the corridor and reach the closer of the ship's two transporter rooms.

Sisko pushed through the doors before they had finished opening and headed directly for the equipment locker. "Set the coordinates, Chief. I'll get the phasers."

"Not rifles!" O'Brien warned as he entered beaming coordinates on the console. "None of the pipes in the water plant is shielded. Take hand phasers and don't set them for anything higher than force three. Otherwise, one miss and we'll all be swimming."

Sisko knew better than to question O'Brien's technical expertise. But he took four hand phasers along with two tricorders. One phaser he attached to the holster strips on his uniform along with a tricorder. One he held in his hand. And the other two phasers he handed to O'Brien, along with the second tricorder, the moment his chief engineer joined him on the transporter pad.

O'Brien attached one of the phasers to his own holster strips. "We'll materialize just to the side of the equipment transfer doors leading into the main treatment room," he told Sisko. "And brace yourself, sir. I don't know what the gravity's going to be like."

Then Sisko felt a momentary tingle like that of a cool breeze, as the *Defiant*'s transporter room turned into a spray of sparkling light. Almost immediately, the light faded to reveal a dark corridor ribbed and ringed by Cardassian struts. He and O'Brien had returned to Deep Space 9.

It took a few disorienting moments, and slippage of more than a few centimeters, before Sisko's inner ear caught up to the fact that the deck was slanted by four or five degrees. For his part, O'Brien made a series of small jumps, rising up from the deck only a centimeter or two each time. *Trust the chief to come up with his own way to measure an artificial gravity field,* Sisko thought.

"Okay, not that bad," the chief engineer said, confirming Sisko's guess about the reason for his impromptu athletic performance. "The station's gone to emergency gravity, and I'm guessing the old units in section 3 are barely holding on at fifty percent efficiency."

"What can we expect if they fail?" Sisko asked, phaser held ready as he made sure the short stretch of corridor was deserted.

"If the old units shut down all at once, it'll feel like the station's suddenly lurched a few more degrees."

Sisko didn't like the image. "Like an old sinking ship."

"At least we won't drown," O'Brien said. He looked at the closed doors to the water treatment facility. "I hope."

Sisko frowned, tapped his communicator. "Sisko to Worf." No response. "Sisko to Ops." Still nothing.

There was no time to waste. Sisko moved cautiously along the slanted corridor to the edge of the oversize water-plant doors. They had been designed to allow large pieces of equipment to be moved in and out, so they and the corridor ceiling were twice the height of most other similar structures in the station.

Sisko flipped open his tricorder and scanned through the doors for life-signs. But the readings indicated there were no life-forms in the facility.

He flipped the device shut and put it back on its holster strip. "I don't know what to expect in there," Sisko said in a low voice, "but since we're only using heavy stun, feel free to shoot first and ask questions later."

O'Brien gave a quiet chuckle. "Careful, sir, you're starting to sound like Worf."

Sisko tapped the door control.

The doors to the water plant remained closed.

Sisko tapped in his command override code.

This time the doors opened.

Then Sisko and O'Brien both moaned at the same time as the overwhelming stench of raw sewage enveloped them.

Sisko blocked his nostrils with one hand, but his action did nothing to diminish the awful smell.

"Must have been quite a spill when the gravity generators switched over to the backups," O'Brien coughed. "We should get used to it in a few minutes."

Sisko had to force himself to open his mouth to speak. "You have such a way of looking on the bright side of things."

Sisko led the way into the huge facility—one of the largest open spaces in DS9. It was three decks high, forty meters deep, fifty wide, filled with a maze of pipes, metal vats, and overhead walkways.

It also reverberated with the deafening roar of rushing water.

Sisko hadn't been down here for years, but he didn't remember it being so loud. He stepped closer to O'Brien so the chief could hear him. "Is it supposed to sound like this?" he shouted.

O'Brien nodded, then shouted back. "The sound bafflers must be off-line, or—" Abruptly, the chief engineer pointed up to the left. "Captain, over there!"

Sisko saw what he meant at once.

What appeared to be a silver flower had sprouted on the top of a five-meter-tall vat of dull, copper-colored metal emblazoned with a Cardassian warning glyph. The 'flower' was perhaps a meter across, with three pulsing blue lights on the tip of each of its five gleaming petals.

It was not Cardassian technology. Neither was it Starfleet.

"The sensor mask?" Sisko asked.

"That's my guess," O'Brien confirmed, then he took aim with his phaser.

Sisko could only hope that a force-three setting would be enough to overload whatever the alien device used for circuitry. Any phaser blast more powerful would risk puncturing the vat.

"Here goes," O'Brien said.

Then an object flashed through the air. O'Brien grunted as something hit his arm and his phaser went flying. Spun around by the impact, he collided full force with Sisko.

Sisko staggered back. Without stopping to think, he pulled O'Brien into the shelter of an immense pipe that emerged from the deck and curved away overhead. Pushing the chief down to a sitting position against the pipe, Sisko immediately reached out to examine O'Brien's arm.

"Careful," the chief gasped. The sleeve of his black jumpsuit was wet with blood where a slender gold dagger, a kind Sisko had never seen before, impaled the chief's forearm. A rivulet of blood was dripping from his cuff.

The golden blade was edged with a series of angled barbs, making for easy penetration but near-impossible extraction. Sisko kneeled down and leaned closer. He yelled directly into the chief's ear to be heard over the thunderous roar of the water. "I'm not going to be able to pull that out."

O'Brien nodded, sweat mingling with tears of pain on his cheeks. "It's going numb," he murmured weakly, and Sisko was only able to understand him by reading his lips. He knew at once the blade had to have been coated with some type of poison.

"Chief—I'm going to take out the sensor mask," Sisko shouted. "Keep trying to get through to Worf on your communicator."

He didn't like the way O'Brien looked blearily at him then, as if the engineer didn't believe that Worf was ever going to appear, or that he'd still be alive when Worf did.

"I'll—come—back—for—you," Sisko shouted, emphasizing each word as if that made his promise more valid.

Silently, O'Brien mouthed his response, "I know you will. . . ." And then the engineer's head slumped forward, eyes closed.

Filled with furious purpose, Sisko leapt to his feet, edged around the pipe until he could just see the silver blossom of the sensor mask emitter against the dark edge of the vat.

With the tracking precision of the *Defiant*'s sensors, he checked each catwalk, each potential hiding place for the enemy. But there were too many shadows, too many dark corners. He realized there was no way he could know where a potential enemy was hiding until a knife struck him just as it had the chief.

Sisko frowned. That particular choice of weapon troubled him. *Why a knife? One phaser burst and the chief would have been killed. One wide burst, and we'd both have been stunned.*

Again he used the tricorder to scan for life-signs, but it was useless. This close to the emitter its displays flashed erratically.

Sisko made his decision. He set his phaser to force six, medium dispersal. There was no time to take careful aim at the emitter as the chief had done.

He swung out and fired at once, ducking back behind the pipe even as a dagger clanged against it. The sensor mask emitter exploded in a shower of transtator sparks. The sensor mask was down.

Breathing hard, but feeling victorious, Sisko leaned back against the pipe, tried his communicator again. No response. But it didn't matter. Sisko knew that as soon as Worf was able to restore emergency communications in Ops, he'd be able to get through.

Suddenly, the thick odor of sewage intensified. Involuntarily gagging, Sisko stuck his head out to take a quick glance around the pipe and saw a gout of dark water spraying from the top edge of the vat where the sensor mask emitter had been. His phaser blast had obviously punctured the vat wall. And the vat had to be a waste separator, designed to send liquids to the recycling evaporators and solids to the replicator mass reclaimers.

Only now, both liquids and solids were splattering down on the metal deck of the facility, and because of the imbalance in the artificial gravity fields, the odiferous sludge from the vat was oozing toward the back of the cavernous water-plant room.

In a vain attempt to shield himself from the terrible smell, Sisko pulled the neck of his duty shirt up over his mouth and his nose. He had to keep going. At least now he knew where to go.

And with the emitter gone, his tricorder should be functional again. Sisko checked its display. It was. There were two life-signs twenty meters ahead.

Still keeping to the cover of the pipes, Sisko headed in the direction of the indicated life-signs, not certain what he was looking for.

But what he found wasn't surprising.

Quark.

In chains.

Hanging head down.

Over an open collection tank filled to the brim with dark, bubbling sludge.

Quark's hands were tied behind his back and thick black wires were cruelly clipped to the edges of his prodigious ears.

And the only way Sisko was able to tell that the Ferengi was even alive was because the tricorder said he was.

Sisko checked the reading again. "Damn," he whispered. One of the two life-signs had disappeared. Now there was only one—Quark. The other had moved out of range, or else had—

Pain seared Sisko's back as he was thrown forward to the slippery deck, his phaser and tricorder both tumbling away.

Throwing off the shock of the attack, Sisko rolled to his feet, leaping up to face whatever, whoever, had felled him.

An Andorian female. Three meters away. Crouched in fight-ready position, the stark-blue tendrils of her antennae jutting from her distinctive blue-white, Vulcan-short hair. In one blue hand, she held a golden dagger like the one that injured O'Brien.

His attacker was one of the two sisters Odo had been watching. But which sister, Sisko didn't know.

The Andorian moved closer, hypnotically waving her dagger in circles, her dark, blue-rimmed eyes absolutely fixed on his own. Sisko could see muscles ripple in her bare blue arms and midriff. She was dressed more for a workout in a zero-G gym than she was for any trade mission, wearing only a snug black leather vest, black leggings, and low-cut gripshoes.

A spasm twisted Sisko's back where the Andorian had kicked him. The fact she hadn't stabbed him as she had O'Brien meant she didn't consider him a worthy opponent. She intended to toy with him.

But Sisko was in no mood to be toyed with.

He slapped his hand down to his second phaser, ripped it from its holster strips, and—even as the Andorian launched herself at him with an ear-splitting shriek—fired point-blank.

She collapsed at his feet, her eyes rolled back, her body unmoving.

Sisko kicked the dagger from her limp hand, then twisted her over on her back to keep her nose and mouth clear of the sewage whose level was still rising. The movement of her chest attested to the fact that she was still breathing.

Sisko checked to be sure she had no other weapons, then started for Quark, who was still trussed and helpless, suspended from the ceiling.

Quark's mouth was moving at warp ten, but saying nothing Sisko could hear above the increasing din in the vast chamber. Sisko muttered to himself as he studied the chains from which the Ferengi dangled over the sludge tank. "Quark, I don't know what you did to those people, but—" Sisko stopped suddenly, remembering. *People.* And he whirled around just in time to be thrown against the sludge tank, as the second Andorian sister's hand stabbed at his neck.

This Andorian female was even more threatening than her sibling. While only slightly taller, she was much, much stronger. She wore almost the same outfit as her sister, but her long blue-white hair was pulled back tightly and braided, and the smooth blue skin of her left arm was intricately tattooed in black from wrist to shoulder.

With a shriek even louder than her sister's, she launched herself at Sisko before he had a chance to regain his balance.

Sisko tried to feint sideways, but stumbled.

The Andorian changed her angle of approach in midair, transferring her momentum into a spinning high kick that struck Sisko's shoulder, knocking him back against the edge of the sludge tank, so that his arm fell back into it.

Then the Andorian dropped to one knee beside Sisko, raised her hand to deliver a lethal punch-down blow to his chest.

But Sisko summoned all of his strength to fling his arm up, splashing raw sewage in her eyes.

The Andorian screamed as she shrank back from him, her hands clawing at her face.

Sisko twisted away, swinging one of his legs under hers, tripping her, so that she fell to the deck.

Ignoring his still-twinging back, he staggered to his feet.

In a heartbeat, the Andorian's body flexed powerfully, and she was once again standing upright before him, her blazing, dark eyes intent on revenge.

Sisko reached for his phaser, but it was gone.

The Andorian threw herself at him.

Instinctively, Sisko tucked and rolled *toward* her, forcing contact before she had anticipated.

He lost his breath in one explosive moment as her foot slammed into his ribs, but then the pressure was gone and he looked up, gasping, in time to see her flailing form flip over him and land in the sewage tank ejecting a fountain of disgusting liquid that struck and soaked Quark as precisely as if the Ferengi had been its chosen target.

Slowly, clutching his side, Sisko struggled to his feet, trying not to laugh because it hurt too much as Quark maniacally spun and sputtered and sprayed droplets of a dark substance whose origin was too terrible for Sisko even to contemplate.

"Calm down, Quark," Sisko finally managed to shout. "I'll get you down."

Quark screamed something indecipherable—two words? Sisko couldn't be sure. But the Ferengi was shaking and swinging back and forth on his chains, clearly panicked by something. Probably the fear of falling into the sludge tank, Sisko decided.

"What?" Sisko called up to Quark. The Ferengi's neck veins were now bulging as Quark screeched again. But it was impossible to hear him over the incessant rush and roar of the liquids in the pipes all around.

The second Andorian sister was trying to pull herself toward the edge of the tank, to drag herself out. She was moving so slowly, Sisko doubted she'd cause him any more trouble. He decided to leave Quark to Worf's security staff, and instead to go back to get O'Brien and deliver him to the Infirmary. Quark might be uncomfortable but he wasn't in any danger now.

He looked up to wave at Quark to somehow signal him that someone would come back for him, when he finally realized that the Ferengi wasn't looking at him, but at something beyond him.

With a sudden flash of alarm, Sisko turned about.

A moment too late.

A black shape enveloped him like a tidal wave sinking a ship, and the roar of the room fell away into silence as he drowned in a sea of darkness.

CHAPTER 19

"BEHIND YOU," Quark muttered as Benjamin Sisko collapsed on the filthy deck of the din-filled water-plant room. "I was *trying* to say, behind you. . . ."

But, as usual to Quark's view of things, no one ever paid him any attention until it was too late.

And it was much too late for Sisko, just as it was too late for those ghastly Andorian sisters.

Quark had absolutely no idea who it was who had struck Sisko down. All he knew was that Sisko's attacker was outfitted in a shiny black, wrinkled, class-two environmental suit, one designed to operate within normal life-support pressure and temperature ranges, and that such a garment was worn usually to protect against biological or chemical contamination. Knowing this did not make Quark feel any better.

Or smell better, Quark thought bitterly. Ever since something had happened to momentarily interrupt the station's gravity fields a few minutes ago, the water treatment facility had begun to stink worse that he most likely did, thanks to that clumsy Andorian female and her spectacular fall into the sludge vat. In fact, now that he thought about it, this place smelled even worse than a Medusan moulting pit.

Quark hung motionless in his chains, shutting out the cacophony of the incessant sound of rushing liquid, regarding the floor
and the latest interloper, as he stoked his internal fires of resent-
ment. Trust the Cardassians to economize by treating waste water
in a centralized location, instead of using personal recyclers. *I
mean,* Quark thought indignantly, *there's an understandable desire
for profit, and then there's being obsessed by it.* And right now,
suffering the disastrous olfactory consequences arising from the
imbecilic decision of whichever Cardassian genius thought he'd
save some latinum on Terok Nor's waste-recycling system, he
himself would actually be willing to trade a year's worth of profits
from his bar for just one last lungful of fresh air before the
stranger in black killed him as he had just killed DS9's chief executive.

Quark reconsidered the odds. After all, this close to the wormhole, one could never be too certain which prayers were going to be
answered. *Better make that six months' worth,* Quark amended as he
saw Sisko's murderer heading toward him, toward the sludge vat
above which he dangled helpless, headfirst, and beside which Satr
now lay, recovering her breath after climbing out of the vat.

Of the two sisters, Quark remembered thinking when he had
first met them that Satr was the cute one. And that the other,
Leen, was the smart one. But incredible though it now seemed to
him, he had been willing to overlook that classic character flaw in a
female. Instead, he had stupidly looked forward to seeing how long
he might be able to prolong negotiations with both Satr and Leen.
He'd been in the bartending business long enough to have heard
what they said about females with blue skin. And the chance to feel
four female Andorian hands on his lobes at the same time had
always been a little fantasy of his.

But then Dal Nortron had gone and got himself killed and spoiled
everything—he'd had to avoid the sisters instead of cultivating them.
Before long Odo had him in protective custody, *and then* had
arrested him, only to let him go just in time to be waylaid by that
miserable excuse for a Ferengi—Base. And all to be dragged down
here to meet Satr and Leen again.

Quark moaned just recalling the degrading treatment he'd been
subjected to. His head hurt like the devil, and it wasn't simply

because he had been left hanging by his heels like a Mongonian eel-bat for the past day and half.

He'd been a perfect gentlemen with those two Andorian monsters. Even after that ingrate Base had dragged him in a sack through the smugglers' tunnels and dumped him out in front of Satr and Leen, he'd made the two sisters a completely reasonable request in his most charming manner. Something along the lines of: "Ladies, such a pleasure to see you again. Is it time to do some . . . business?"

Satr's reply had involved a sharp elbow in his stomach, and Leen had trussed him up in chains like the Friday night special at the Klingon Cafe. It was then that Quark knew for certain that he had been betrayed by them *and* Base.

Base. The name should have warned him. The little insect had come into Quark's back office and launched into his oh-so-sincere sales pitch, about how he wanted to protect his investment in the Orbs, how he wanted to make sure Quark stayed safe before, during, and after the auction, how he planned to take care of Satr and Leen personally—and for only an extra eighteen percent of Quark's commission on the auction proceeds.

That percentage had been so out of line that Quark had actually spent twenty minutes negotiating a reduction, never once questioning why it was that Base should be on his side for eighteen percent, when the little gnat could kill him and have a shot at the full one hundred percent.

They had settled on nine-and-a-half. Plus Base could keep half the tips all the bar's wait staff earned during the days he replaced Quark as barkeep. In the meantime, Quark would be safe behind a sensor mask where no one could find him.

And worst of all, in Quark's recollection, was that the entire deal had been negotiated in front of his own idiot brother. Base had set the whole thing up so that when Quark disappeared, Rom would dimwittedly think that was part of the plan and would not be concerned. *No one* would be concerned.

As if anyone would anyway, Quark thought with a self-pitying half-sob.

And then, even more humiliating to recall, that conniving Base convinced him to put himself into the sack with an antigrav ballast, supposedly so he could be taken to a safe place deep within the station.

"Why the sack?" he remembered asking Base.

"For a stinkin' nine-and-a-half points," that little vole had squeaked persuasively, "no way you're going to find out about the perfect hiding place I figured out. But for twelve-and-a-half. . . ."

It had been the perfect argument. No hiding place on the station was worth an extra three percent, and like a *targ* to the Klingon wedding feast, Quark had climbed willingly into the sack, hugging the antigrav, until Base tossed him out on the deck of the water-plant room—and the four female Andorian hands went to work on him in a terrible travesty of his fantasy.

Now, suspended directly above a dark substance which was as good a metaphor for his life as any, Quark mulled over those he considered his enemies as if he were fingering a pocketful of well-worn worry stones.

First, Rom, his idiot brother who betrayed him by letting that half-sized, half-son-of-a-Klingon into Quark's bar in the first place. Second, Base. Third and fourth, Leen and—

Quark saw the black-suited figure below draw a small phaser and shoot Satr with a soundless flash of energy, then splash through the sludge-strewn deck to dispatch Leen next.

Wincing in commiseration for their bad luck, Quark amended his list of enemies, at the same time wondering where the Andorian sisters had hidden their latinum. It would be quite a tidy sum for someone fortunate enough to find it.

But not for him. His own luck, no matter how poor it had been, had obviously run out. It was his turn now.

The black figure, face completely obscured by a wrinkled black hood and a full-face breathing mask, looked up at Quark, then adjusted the small phaser's setting and took careful aim.

Even though he was resigned to his fate and determined to face it as a rational being, Quark instinctively reached back to his childhood lessons from the weekly Celestial Market classes his loving parents had forced him to attend. Trying not to breathe in any more of the noxious fumes that he had to, he reflexively mumbled the Ferengi prayer that was his people's traditional ward against impending disaster. "All right, this is my final offer. . . ."

But the shooter below was in no mood to negotiate.

He fired.

In one timeless instant, Quark realized that the shooter's beam wasn't aimed at him but at the chain that bound his feet.

A second timeless instant later, as he felt his stomach fall *up* toward his knees, Quark *dropped*—the chains melted through—straight into the bubbling vat of—

"Frinx!" Quark gasped, as a strong hand grabbed him just before he hit the liquid sewage.

Still in midair, he kicked wildly to be free of what was left of the chains still loosely draped around his ankles.

The figure in black deposited him on the deck, standing upright on his own two feet, right beside the motionless body of poor Captain Sisko.

Quark opened his mouth and let loose with a string of invective in the Trading Tongue such that his moogie would have scrubbed out his mouth with carapace gel if she had heard a single syllable—swearing like a philanthropist, his moogie would call it. Not that anyone could hear him in the roar of the outflow from the system pipes.

The figure in black regarded him impassively, then seemed to come to a decision, stepped back, and pulled off his breather mask.

Just as Quark bravely barked out, "I don't care who the *greeb* you are. If you're going to shoot me like the rest of them, go ahead—kill me and be done with it." He realized that once again—big surprise—the Choir of Celestial Accountants had been braying his name in jest.

The murderer wasn't male.

He was a female.

Vash.

She delicately wrinkled her button-like human nose at the stench of the place, then yelled out the sweetest words Quark had ever heard—not that he'd ever admit that to her. "Is that any way to talk to your new partner?"

"Just what I need," Quark muttered as he looked at the sprawled bodies of Satr and Leen. *"Another* new partner. . . ." Then relief flooded through him. Vash was no murderer. The odds were very good that both Andorians were only heavily stunned, not dead.

Vash snapped her breather back into place, then motioned for Quark to follow her.

But much as he wanted to get out of this foul pit, there was something Quark had to do first. He reached down and got a good grip on Captain Sisko's jacket to drag the unconscious *hew-mon* toward an open metal staircase beside the sludge vat.

When Vash saw what he was doing, she tried to pull him away, but Quark refused to let go of Sisko. Maybe Satr and Leen deserved to remain in the muck where they fell, and maybe the captain wasn't the best friend a Ferengi barkeep ever had, but Quark wasn't about to leave him to drown in such an undignified fashion.

With Vash's reluctant assistance, Quark hoisted Sisko up on a platform on the staircase, well above the steadily rising sewage.

Motioning to Quark to follow her across the room to the exit, Vash turned to look back at him, pulling aside her breathing mask long enough to shout, "I don't get it, Quark—what did *he* ever do for *you?*"

Breathing heavily as he dragged his boots through the disgusting deck debris—the *hew-mon* had been surprisingly heavy, and Quark's body was still telling him how badly abused it had been by its hanging ordeal—Quark looked back down at Sisko. "Nothing," he said, out of earshot of Vash. She'd never understand anyway. Not that anyone else ever had. Or ever would. "But he never did anything *to* me, either."

Even without looking at Vash, he could feel her suspicion, and he could almost hear her thinking, How could she trust someone who went out of his way to help a Starfleet officer?

Quark wearily cupped a hand to his mouth and yelled ahead to her, as he shook something unmentionable off his foot, "He owes me money!" The terrible thing was, he knew, that there had to be easier ways to earn latinum. But the even worse thing was that, all other things being equal, he hadn't found it. Yet.

"Stay still and keep your eyes closed," Vash told him.

In the dimly lit kitchen at the back of his bar, Quark did as he was told. "If you only knew how many times I imagined you saying those words to me," he murmured. Then he heard a frothy hissing noise and was suddenly engulfed in a thick foam. He started to protest, but the medicinal-smelling lather bubbled into his mouth the moment he tried to speak.

"And keep your mouth shut!" Vash snapped.

Quark suddenly felt cold. He started to shiver. As he did, he felt the foam begin to drop off him in clumps.

When his face felt free of bubbles, he risked opening one eye. Then the other.

Vash was in front of him, kicking off the last of her environmental suit, a large carryall duffel bag beside her, along with a pressurized tank and nozzle, dripping foam. Quark could see that portions of her protective suit were covered in rapidly evaporating bubbles as well.

And then he realized with delight that the dreadful stench of the raw sewage was gone. "What *is* that foam?" He looked down at his suit jacket. It was still wet, but there wasn't a single stain on it. Neither was there any muck on his boots or on the floor beneath them.

Vash leaned back against an inductor stove with a sigh. "A cleansing agent from Troyius. Their pheromonal systems are so volatile, they need something that will break down all organic waste completely and instantly—otherwise, they couldn't leave their planet."

"Well, that's *fan*tastic," Quark said admiringly. "Tell me, do they have a good distribution network?"

Vash gave him an odd, measuring look. "Oh, it's not what you'd call a perfect product. There are a few drawbacks."

"Really." Quark grinned. Anything that could eradicate all traces of what he had just been through smelled like pure latinum to him. "I can't imagine what they'd be."

"That suit of yours—replicated from synthetics?" Vash asked, curious. "Or is it natural?"

Stung by the insult, Quark smoothed the multicolored fabric of his snug tapestry jacket. "I am a successful businessman. Of course, all my suits are natural fiber."

Vash smiled. "You sure?"

Quark glanced down. *"AAAAAA!"* His jacket and trousers were in the process of melting, consumed by the same polyenzymic action that had neutralized the sewage.

The last curling streamers of his suit flickered out of existence

just as he ducked for cover behind a food locker. Quark found himself facing the bulkhead whose small access door led to the
unmapped tunnel through which he and Vash had escaped from the
water plant.

Leaning out from behind the locker, ears flushed, as naked as a
female in public, Quark blustered, "Well, don't just stand there,
woman! Get me something to wear!"

Vash looked up at the lighting panels on the kitchen ceiling. They
were dark. Only the emergency glowstrips on the walls were operating. "Bad timing, Quark. My guess is there's some trouble on the
station. I don't think Garak's will be open."

Quark pointed imperiously to the locker behind her. "The locker
by the door! Staff uniforms!"

Vash stuck her head in the locker and brought out a clothes
holder with a few wispy strands of glitter cloth. "Not your size," she
smirked, "but it'll bring out the yellow in your eyes."

Quark fumed. "That's a dabo costume. Give me a waiter's suit!"

"Oh, come on," Vash said as peeked at him through the almost
transparent cloth. "You wear something like this, I might stay at the
dabo table all night."

Quark couldn't help himself. "Really?" He ran the calculations
comparing how much someone could lose at dabo in a single night
against the irreparable loss of his self-esteem. It was a close call. As
the 189th Rule had it: Let others keep their reputation, you keep their
latinum. Maybe he had been hasty when he stopped having Female
Nights at the bar. Even though Rom had put up such a fuss over
wearing a dress the last time. . . .

"I'll take it under advisement," Quark said thoughtfully. "But
now, a waiter's suit?"

Vash pulled one out of the locker and handed it over to Quark,
making a show of covering her eyes. "Don't worry, I won't look,"
she said. "I just ate."

The pale-green jacket, brocade vest, and *ruksilk* shirt were too
large, the trousers were too long, and the boots were so large they
were almost unwearable. All in all, the lamentably unfashionable outfit reminded Quark of his years as a cabin boy on the old
Ferengi freighter, the *Latinum Queen*. But it would do for now. It
had to.

Decently covered, Quark emerged from behind the food locker, his steps necessarily mincing because of the unseen oversized shoes beneath the overlong trousers. "Now what did you say happened to the station?"

Vash looked him up and down with a broad grin as she hefted her strap-on carryall over her shoulder. But she merely opened the door leading to the main-level room of the bar without commenting on his appearance.

The room beyond was dark, but the light from the kitchen in which Quark and Vash stood revealed several overturned chairs, as if customers had run out of the bar in a hurry. There were still drinks and food dishes on the tables.

Quark stepped into the bar. He picked up a glass, sniffed it. Groaned. It had held a Deltan-on-the-Beach cocktail with a full measure of triple-proof Romulan ale. Was Rom trying to ruin him?

"Satr and Leen rigged a Pakled sensor mask in the water plant," Vash now told him, "so that if anyone went searching for you, you and they wouldn't show up as lifesigns on anyone's tricorders."

Quark looked around his bar. It looked to him as if it had been hit by something much more powerful than a sensor mask. "And that's not all they arranged," Vash said as she walked past him to open the closed doors of the bar.

Quark sighed. At least his idiot brother had remembered to lock up. Not that it mattered. Beyond the doors, the Promenade, lit only by emergency strips like his bar, looked deserted.

"I'm listening," Quark said, squinting to see what was in the shadows at the end of the bar, and frowning when he did.

"They also slipped a programming worm into the station's computer system," Vash said, turning to reclose the doors to the bar.

"Is that possible?" Quark began walking to the end of the bar.

"A little something they picked up on Bynaus," Vash said as she turned away from the door. "Until the worm detected someone setting up security screens around the water plant, trying to contain the area, the worm was dormant. The bad new is, once it was triggered, it reproduced so quickly it used up all available processing space. All the automatic systems locked up. They'd have needed a cold start to reset all the computers. The good news is there's no permanent harm done. DS9 should be up and running in about ten minutes or so."

"Good," Quark said, reaching out to touch what he had noticed in the bar's shadows. "I'd like to see Satr and Leen talk their way out of Odo's cell this time."

Vash's voice suddenly became tense. "Is someone at the bar?"

"Just Morn," Quark chuckled, affectionately. He poked at the lugubrious alien's shoulder. His voice became a stage whisper. "Mor-ornnn? Hellooo? Are you in there?"

The huge Lurian snuffled something unintelligible and shifted slightly on the bar stool, driving his massive head deeper into the crook of his well-padded arm, as he remained slumped facedown on the bar. Very faintly, he began to snore, each exhalation accompanied by the pungent perfume of Martian tequila. And judging from the strength of each puff, Quark calculated that at two slips a shot for the extra-premium blend, Morn had had enough this evening to more than pay for a bartender's brand-new suit—even if Rom hadn't properly watered the goods.

"Look at him," Quark crooned. "Sleeping like a baby. A great big, wrinkled, prune-faced baby."

"Well, wake him up and get him out of here," Vash said sharply. "We have business to conduct."

But Quark stood defensively in front of his first, best, and most treasured customer. "I'm sorry, but even *I* have to draw the line somewhere. If Morn wants to sleep on my bar, well then—may the Divine Treasurer bless him and keep him solvent all the days of his life—I am not going to be the one who says no. Besides, I can charge him half a bar of latinum for rent. *And . . .*" he added in a half-whisper, "if we wake him up now, he won't stop talking for hours." Quark smoothed his jacket, feeling better than he had since Base came into his bar. "If you want to discuss business, we can do it down there where we won't disturb . . ." His voice softened as he gazed down at the lovable lump of his constant and continuous consumer. ". . . the customer."

Vash eyed Morn's hunched-over and snoring body with distaste. She reached out to him, gave his bald scalp a sharp flick with one of her long nails. Morn's only response was to blow a series of small, quickly popping bubbles from his open mouth.

"Don't make him drool now," Quark warned. He took Vash firmly by the arm and led her to the other end of the bar. "Just think of him as part of the furniture."

"Now," Quark said as he took his usual place behind the bar, and placed both hands flat on the bartop. "What kind of business did my favorite archaeologist have in mind?"

Vash shrugged off her carryall, carefully lowering it to the deck, then rubbed at the spot on her shoulder where the carryall strap had been. "Not my business, Quark. *Your* business."

Quark blinked at her. "I'm not sure I follow. Would you like a reward for rescuing me? I'm sure I can work out an equitable payment schedule, though business has been slow and—"

Quark winced as Vash leaned over the bar and pinched one of his earlobes. Painfully. "Quark! I'm not talking about *new* business. I'm talking about the reason why I risked arrest in three systems to get here as soon as I did."

Quark's eyes widened nervously. He pulled back, but Vash did not release her grip on his ear. "You don't mean . . . ?"

"Yes, I do," Vash said. "The Red Orbs of Jalbador. You made it clear you were ready to deal. That's why I'm here. And that's why I saved your wrinkled Ferengi butt."

"You said you wouldn't peek!"

Vash increased the pressure on his ear. Quark had to stand on one foot, just to keep his balance, to spare his delicate earflesh. "Listen, Ferengi. I'm serious. When this station comes back on line, security's going to be all over the place trying to figure out what went wrong. And when they find out I'm not all cozy and warm in the Infirmary, they're going to come looking for me. And that's not going to happen, understand? Because I'm going to be on my way with what I came for. Now let's do it!"

Quark squealed as Vash suddenly yanked up on his earlobe, lifting him right off his feet. Then just as suddenly she released him, and he fell stomach first onto the bartop. His first thought was to look down the length of the bar at Morn, to make certain at least he wasn't disturbed. Then he flopped back, regaining his footing.

"It . . . it's not that easy . . ." he stammered, one hand to his injured earlobe.

Vash reached a hand inside a small pouch on her belt as if going for a knife. "Then I suggest you make it easy."

Quark waved his hands in a vain attempt to deflect whatever it was she was about to cut him with. "I'm just the middleman. The goods are with a . . . a third party."

"Then get him down here."

"I really wish I could. You have no idea. But, the fact of the matter is, he's dead."

Vash narrowed her eyes and Quark knew his other ear was doomed. Just knew it.

"Who?" Vash demanded.

"Dal Nortron. The Andorian who came here with Satr and Leen. Those heartless females were his bodyguards—and they killed him."

Vash snorted. "Bodyguards don't kill their clients. It tends to cut into repeat business."

Quark was outraged. "Base was *my* bodyguard, and he sold me out to Satr and Leen!"

Vash held the heel of one hand to her forehead and sighed. "Oh, *sleem* me. . . ."

Quark brightened. He sensed a slight lessening in her resolve to do something unspeakable to him. "Maybe your visit doesn't have to be a total loss. We can work out another deal."

"Another deal?" Vash leaned over, digging into her carry-all from the sound of it. Then she straightened up and slammed a spindle-shaped chunk of dark crystal on the bar. It was maybe two-thirds of a meter tall, a quarter-meter at its widest, top and bottom. And except for the fact that it was oddly dull in the way it reflected what little light there was, it looked exactly like—

Quark choked.

". . . Oh, no . . ." he whispered.

"Oh, yes," Vash said. "A Red Orb of Jalbador."

Quark could scarcely draw a breath. Shocked. Unprepared. "You mean . . ." he gasped, "they *are* real?"

"This one is." Vash leaned over the bar counter and in the same moment, Quark leaned back, thus ensuring the continued health of his other, as yet uninjured, earlobe. "But without the other two," she said in disgust, "it's worse than useless."

Quark's business sense quickened. He felt a strong sense of finality within Vash. There would be no more negotiations. He was right.

"Time's up, Quark. I want the map."

A commotion behind Vash made Quark's heart flutter like a grubworm on a toothpick, with no hope of escape.

"You mean, this one?" Satr hissed.

Vash wheeled around, phaser already in her hand and aimed behind her.

But the danger was above her, not behind. Satr and Leen— clearly recovered from whatever miserably low-setting stun Vash had used on them—were on the bar's second level, and the golden dagger Leen now threw down knocked the phaser directly out of Vash's hand before she could even fire it.

Instantly Satr flipped over the railing, her lithe, tattooed body spinning through the air, to land like a feline in a crouch, braced by one hand. In the next instant, the Andorian spun around on both hands and reverse-kicked Vash, sending her skidding across the floor of Quark's bar.

By the time the archaeologist regained her feet, Leen had slid halfway down the stairway railing to the main level and flipped over to land on her feet, a golden dagger in each hand.

The spectacle of fully clothed feminine physicality was too much for Quark, and he shivered with forbidden pleasure. Rather than slide the Red Orb off the bar, he continued to watch the action in anticipation of the three females' killing each other. Yet if even one of them survived, Quark had little doubt that he'd be the next victim.

Satr held up a slender cylinder of amber crystal. "We have the map, Vash. Without it, your Orb is nothing more than a sparkly rock. Let us buy it from you."

Vash was breathing hard, weaponless, holding her side where Satr had kicked her, but Quark suspected the resourceful archaeologist wouldn't admit defeat yet. And he was right again.

"Without an Orb, your map might as well be a Ferengi ear probe. Let *me* buy the map from you."

The one thing Quark never forgot was that he was Ferengi. He saw his opportunity and he acted upon it immediately. "Ladies, please . . . you each have something the other wants. What better situation could there be for striking a deal? A deal, I might add, I'd be glad to broker for just a small commission—"

Leen's bare blue arm flexed and a golden dagger flashed through the air to pin Quark's too-large jacket—with him inside it—to the wall.

"Or not . . ." Quark whispered.

Satr and Leen moved to flank Vash, one heading to either side of her. The archaeologist was forced up against the bar counter, with no way to escape them.

Leen drew a third golden dagger from the set of scabbards at her back, and once again held a wickedly sharp blade in each hand.

Satr tossed her crystal cylinder tauntingly, back and forth, from one hand to the other.

"You want the Orb, I want the map," Vash said, her eyes moving quickly from one to the other. "The Ferengi is right. We can work out a deal."

"Dal Nortron wanted to work out a deal," Satr sneered. "He hired us, so of course we supported his decision. And then the Ferengi killed him."

"*What?!*" Quark protested. "I didn't kill anyone! I thought you were all lying! That the map was a forgery!"

"You were willing to be the broker at the auction," Leen said.

"I make no representations as to the suitability of the product for the use to which the purchaser intends—"

"*Silence!*"

Quark knew much better than to argue with a blue tattooed female. Each intricate black scroll on her arm represented a man she had killed—after having had her way with him. And though Quark suspected he would not necessarily object to the second interaction, he would definitely have issues with the first.

He nodded, not even risking a single word to say he agreed with her.

"If *you* didn't kill Nortron," Vash said, "and the Ferengi didn't, then who did?"

"Do I look like the changeling?" Leen snarled viciously.

"We don't care who killed him," Satr said quickly, with a sharp glance at her sister. "The fact is, he's dead. We're not. So now we do things our way. And we want your Orb."

"It won't do any good without knowing where to use it," Vash countered.

Satr brandished her crystal wand. "This map tells us which world we must take the Orb to."

"And when we get close enough to the second Orb," Leen said triumphantly, "the first will glow to lead us along the final path."

"You actually believe that *kragh?*" Vash asked.

Quark caught his breath as Satr's head jerked menacingly forward like a striking snake. "If you didn't believe it, you'd sell us your Orb."

"You wouldn't believe what I went through to get this," Vash said, undaunted. "I'm not selling anything."

The three of them faced each other, drenched in sweat, ready to fight to the death, taut muscles rippling beneath the Andorian sisters' glistening blue skin, Vash's long, lustrous hair a dark fountain against creamy-white shoulders . . . Quark trembled, took a calming breath. He was falling in love, and he didn't care with which one.

A moment before he had been on the verge of slipping to safety and obscurity behind the bar. But now he paused, unsure.

"We're not selling anything, either," Satr said.

"Which leaves us only one alternative," Leen added.

"Exactly," Base squeaked. "It means I'll take both!"

"Oh, for—" Quark snorted in disgust, as Base jumped up on the bar waving aloft his comically puny *bat'leth*. The little betrayer could only have been hiding among the crates of glasses across from the replicator, waiting for his moment to strike.

Moron, Quark thought. Base would probably last about fifteen seconds against the blue sisters. And Vash would—

"What are *you?"* Satr said.

"Your worst nightmare, bluecheeks," Base chirped.

Leen hooted at the thought, then suddenly threw both daggers at the minute Ferengi.

And then, to Quark's utter astonishment, Base twisted his *bat'leth* in an expert blur and deflected both daggers. He hadn't even tried to duck.

"I can throw this a *skrell* of a lot faster than you blues can run," Base crowed. "Now bring me the map crystal," he said to Satr. Then he glared at Quark. "And you, you lobeless hunk of greeworm castings, you bring me the Orb."

Quark tugged at his jacket where its shoulder was still fixed to the wall by Leen's dagger, trusting Base would see that he was otherwise detained.

But Vash provided distraction enough.

"You backstabbing little *hardinak,*" she spat at him. "You're supposed to be working for me!"

"Ha!" Quark said, much that had been unclear at last becoming clear to him. "He was supposed to be working for *me!*"

"You're both fools!" Leen snarled.

"We paid him off so he'd work for us!" Satr added.

"Which begs the question," Vash said. "Who the hell are you working for *now?*"

Base shrugged his shoulders. "What can I tell you half-wits? With all the latinum you slugs gave me, I finally had enough to go into business for myself." Base jabbed his thumb against his small chest. "You'd better believe it. I'm pure Ferengi, in it for the profit and nothing else!"

That was too much for Quark. "Oh, will someone step on him and crush him flat."

Base squealed, enraged, as he whirled around to confront Quark, holding his miniature *bat'leth* high—relatively speaking—above his head with both hands.

Quark fought to wriggle out of his borrowed jacket, still pinned securely to the wall. The only way that pitiful excuse for a Ferengi would actually kill him was if he died first from embarrassment.

But Vash got to Base first, knocking him straight off the bar to the deck.

Squeaking in outrage, Base rolled to his feet, still waving his *bat'leth,* but in the wrong direction. Because Satr and Leen now attacked him from behind, Satr sweeping him up in the bare, muscled arms Quark thought had definite potential, Leen drawing her own well-exposed arm back to slap him, and then—

—Quark moaned as everything went wrong. Again.

Even though Base's *bat'leth* didn't have the finely honed cutting edges of the traditional Klingon weapon—and he certainly didn't have the skill to slice an artery or bisect a key muscle group—all he seemed to need to do to cause havoc was make contact between the blade and any part of his opponent's body, and Ferengi plasma-whip circuits did the rest. Which is just what he did.

Quark watched in disbelief as Base swung the *bat'leth* wildly at Leen until he provoked her sufficiently to reach out to swat it away.

At that precise moment of contact with Base's weapon, the blue Andorian flew back in a shimmering nimbus of disruptive neural energy.

Startled, Leen's sister dropped her prey; he took the opportunity to tuck, roll, and come up swinging, bashing Satr across the knees with his *bat'leth* so that she, too, collapsed in the throes of neural disruption.

Vash still hadn't regained her feet, and being at Base's level didn't have a chance. Quark covered his eyes with both hands, but peered through his fingers, appalled and fascinated at the same time.

After vanquishing his last female enemy with a glancing blow to the ankles, Base now threw back his head and cackled like a mad paultillian as he used his *bat'leth* like a vaulter's pole and sprang back up onto the bar.

He swaggered toward Quark.

Quark pulled and struggled mightily, but the barbs on the dagger just wouldn't let go. He was a sitting Grumpackian tortoise.

"Base, can't we talk about this?" Quark pleaded.

The little Ferengi spun his *bat'leth* around his wrist just like Bus Betar in the old Marauder Mo holos. The classic ones, not the remakes. "I don't think so, *frinx*-for-brains. For the first time in my life, it's winner-take-all." He stopped the *bat'leth* in midspin, tapped one pudgy finger against the tip of his weapon. "It's the 242nd Rule, after all . . . More is good, all is better. Prepare to meet your Accountant." Then Base raised his weapon. "The Orb is mine. The map is mine. *Everything* is mine! Do you hear me?! For the first time in my life, Base *wins!*"

"I don't think so, you miserable scrap of a sentient being!"

For a moment, Base stopped in midstride, staring at Quark as if those combative words had dared come from his intended victim's mouth.

Quark shrank down into his oversize green jacket, wondering if he *had* be stupid enough to utter those words. True as they might be.

And then, as the truth finally dawned on both hunter and hunted, Quark and Base both slowly turned to look at the person who had uttered them.

Morn.

No longer deep in his cups on the bartop.

Instead, the hulking Lurian was on his feet, a gigantic dark silhouette looming against the light filtering through the doors to the Promenade.

"Drop the *bat'leth*," Morn growled.

"Make me!" Base squeaked back in defiance.

"I will."

Quark's mouth dropped open in awe and respect. Not only was Morn his best customer, he was about to senselessly sacrifice his life in a tragic and doomed attempt to save *him*.

What a noble gesture, Quark thought. *A totally ineffective, inadequate, useless gesture.*

If he lived, Quark decided, he'd retire Morn's stool. Or—even better—charge people extra to sit in it.

"Prepare to die," Base yodeled.

Morn grunted. "Not today," he said.

And then, even as tiny Base raised his *bat'leth* for the attack, Morn swung up his huge arm and—

—*it snaked out along the bar like golden lightning,* until Morn's immense hand closed on the *bat'leth,* and crushed it, dropping the shards to the ground, and then snapped back like a tentacle around Base's scrawny neck, still eerily flowing like the pseudopod of a *hew-mon*-sized amoeba.

As Base gargled helplessly in Morn's unforgiving grip, Quark recovered his senses.

"Why didn't you wait until the little monster had killed me?" he snapped. "Wouldn't that have given you an even better reason to act, *Morn?*"

Morn shook his huge wrinkled head once, then softened, melted, into a gelatinous amber statue before resolidifying as Odo, though one Morn-like arm retained its grip on Base.

"Ohhh, you enjoyed that, didn't you?" Quark accused the shape-shifting constable. "Seeing me almost killed."

"As a matter of fact, I did," Odo said. "By the way, Quark, nice suit."

"That's not funny."

"And you'll notice I'm not laughing. Whatever else is going on around here—and I assure you, I did hear *everything*—Dal Nortron's still dead. And if you didn't kill him, and the Andorians didn't kill him, then there's still a murderer walking free on DS9."

Quark threw up his hands. "Finding murderers is not my job," he said piously. With much relish, Odo gazed at Base's stumpy legs kicking frantically as he held the snarling little Ferengi above the deck just high enough to keep Base from connecting with anything solid.

"Fortunately," Odo said gravely, "it happens to be mine. And in this case, I think my job has just become much simpler."

Quark saw where Odo was looking—directly at the Red Orb of Jalbador, still sitting on the counter of Quark's bar. Shocked and appalled, Quark realized he'd forgotten what a Ferengi must never forget. Profit and the potential thereof.

"As a wise man once explained," the constable said, "all we have to do now to solve the crime is follow the Orb. . . ."

CHAPTER 20

EMPTY OF ITS lifeblood of people, the station seemed a melancholy place to Sisko.

After five cold restarts, Dax's computer team still wasn't rid of whatever type of Bynar code Satr and Leen had input into DS9's computers, and all internal automated systems remained off-line. Even the main gravity generators hadn't been brought back into service. As a result, the banners decorating the Promenade all hung at the same skewed angle, and the deck itself was at a slant as if, impossible though it was, the entire station were listing in space.

The litter on the carpeted sections of the deck was a sad reminder of the hasty evacuation of all nonessential station personnel into the habitat ring. And aside from the dim emergency lighting, some fixtures of which were finally beginning to flicker after having been on too long, the only signs of life that remained were the faint sounds of chanting coming from the Bajoran Temple and the opening and closing of the doors to Odo's office.

Sisko now headed for the Security Office to join the others assembling there.

His ears still rang from the twenty minutes he had stood within the sonic shower, ridding himself of the malodorous sludge of the water-treatment facility, and every muscle in his body still felt the effects of the stun Vash had fired at him. But the physical disorientation he still suffered was not his biggest problem; it was his continued mental confusion. With the uncovering of each new piece of the puzzle—the seemingly unconnected and unexplainable events on the station, the one key element that would make sense of them all, was still missing. And that was annoying the hell out of him.

Halfway between the turbolift and the Security Office Sisko turned to see Bashir striding quickly along the corridor toward him.

"How is he?" Sisko asked. Despite every other threat to the station, O'Brien was his first priority. Worf and his security team had been beamed into the water plant the moment the transporter systems had finally been manually tuned. They'd found Sisko, just coming to, and O'Brien unconscious. Sisko had given the order to evacuate the wounded chief to the Infirmary first.

Bashir's report offered more mystery. "Interestingly enough, there was another Andorian toxin on the dagger that hit him. Not the same one Vash used on herself, but one intended to incapacitate almost any species. But don't worry," the doctor said quickly, seeing the anxious look that Sisko could not keep from his face, "it's not fatal. At least, not to Miles. He's too stubborn."

The doctor glanced around at the unsettling state of the Promenade as they walked towards Odo's office. "I suppose you've already thought about this—but what happens if the Dominion hears about our condition?"

Sisko *had* thought about that, right after Worf's team beamed the chief out to the Infirmary. "Admiral Ross has already dispatched the *Bondar* and the *Garneau* to provide us support."

"*Akira*-class," Bashir said.

Sisko nodded. "They'll stand up to anything the Dominion can throw at us. At least for the time being."

They'd reached the doors of the Security Office. Sisko paused before entering, gathering his strength.

"Something wrong, Captain?" Bashir asked.

Sisko shrugged. "There's something going on here I don't understand. And, to be honest, it makes me uneasy."

"For what it's worth," the doctor offered, "when I heard Vash actually had one of the Red Orbs, I thought that explained everything. I mean, I had halfway figured out for myself that the Orbs might be real. So maybe we should look at this as just another one of Quark's scams—albeit blown up to immense proportions because of the potential for . . . mind-boggling profit."

Sisko understood, but was unconvinced. "I hope you're right. A simple explanation is always the best."

"Unless it's the wrong one, of course," Bashir added with a charming, self-deprecating smile. Then the door to the Security Office slid open and he stepped through.

Instead of following the doctor, Sisko wheeled about suddenly, aware of eyes upon him. He looked down the corridor to the right, toward the entrance of the Temple where the large, solid, unmistakable form of Prylar Obanak stood in the doorway, arms folded within bright saffron robes, watching.

Both men nodded to each other in silent acknowledgment.

Then Sisko turned and entered Odo's office.

He instantly wished he hadn't.

A wall of sound assaulted his still-ringing ears. Odo and Quark were heatedly arguing in the front office. Satr and Leen and Vash were shouting at each other and at anyone who was close to their holding cells. And a particularly irritating high-pitched howl that Sisko had never heard before seemed to be coming from all directions at once.

To save what was left of his hearing, Sisko issued an immediate command prerogative.

"BE QUIET! EVERYONE!"

In the sudden silence, the fluctuating siren-like howl seemed even louder.

"Is there something wrong with a wall communicator?" Sisko struggled not to sound as cross as he felt.

"That's Base," Odo said gruffly. "Apparently he's claustrophobic."

Sisko lost his battle with his nerves. "Tell him if he doesn't stop that infernal squealing, I'll have him hauled off to an escape module. And then he'll know what claustrophobia really feels like."

Odo almost smiled as he headed for the holding cells off to one side of his office area.

"All right," Sisko said brusquely to Quark, "where's the Orb, and where's the map?"

Quark led Sisko and Bashir to the other side of the constable's office, where a small doorway led to a secure storage room. The outer wall of the storage room was lined with stasis safes, and one of the safes was open.

But Sisko's attention was on the storage room's center scanning table. On it was a spindle-cut chunk of what appeared to be randomly faceted red glass, and a small amber cylinder.

"That doesn't look like an Orb," he said, referring to the red glass-like object. All the Orbs of the Prophets Sisko had seen resembled shimmering hourglass shapes of solid light. They were so breathtakingly compelling, so disorienting, that ages ago Bajoran monks had fashioned jewelled arks to shield and hold them so that they could be carried among the faithful.

"Word has it, it's only supposed to glow when it's close to the next Orb," Quark explained.

Sisko picked up the faceted artifact to examine it more closely. "The next Orb?"

"Actually, there're supposed to be three," Quark said. "You use one to find the next one, then use those two to find the third."

Sisko touched the edge of the artifact, felt nothing, sensed no trace of the Prophets. "I see." He put the artifact down with a sigh. "And how much were you going to make by allowing this travesty of the Bajoran religion to take place?"

"Captain Sisko," Quark said emphatically, "I swear I had no idea the Orb was real. I thought I was going to be selling a map. This thing!" He picked up the amber cylinder from the screening table and held it out to Sisko. "That's all. I make my living from the Bajorans. Do you really think I'd risk my livelihood by insulting them?"

Sisko took the cylinder from Quark, turned it over in his fingers, still skeptical.

So, apparently, was Bashir. "Vash told Dax and me that an Orb could fetch the kind of money that can buy and sell planets."

Quark's eyes widened and he swallowed hard. "Really?" Then he recovered. "But I wasn't selling an Orb! Just the map! A treasure map! I must sell a half-dozen of them every year!" He faltered, then quickly added, "Not for Orbs, of course. But for the lost planet of Atlantis, missing ships, T'Kon portals, *Qui'Tu* and *Vorta Vor.* Classic stuff. Nothing more."

Bashir seemed to be convinced. "I believe him, sir. Especially since the penalties for dealing in Orbs cannot be plea-bargained."

"Exactly," Quark said with a shiver. "Why risk getting involved with a criminal-justice system that has such a rigid view of wrong and right when they're so many other ways to . . . uh, that doesn't sound right either, does it?"

"Quit while you're ahead, Quark." Sisko held up the amber map cylinder. "Tell me about this."

Quark shrugged. "I never saw it till Dal Nortron brought it to the bar the day he arrived. And I told that whole story to Odo just like you told me to."

"That's right," Odo said, making his appearance in the storage room just as Sisko noticed thankfully that Base's squealing had finally stopped. "According to Quark, the Andorian contacted him to arrange an auction for the map."

"Where did Nortron say he got it?" Sisko asked.

"He didn't tell," Quark answered. "And I didn't ask. There are some traditions in trade, you know."

"What's it a map of, Quark? Or did traditions prevent you from asking about that, too?"

"Captain, really. I had to write the promotional copy, didn't I?"

"And?" Sisko prompted.

Quark sighed dramatically. "According to the Jalbador legend, the three Red Orbs were scattered so they could never be brought together."

"Why not?" Sisko asked.

"It's a *legend*," Quark said testily. "Why three wishes? Why a magic greeworm? Someone told a bedtime story once and it got taken way too seriously, if you ask me."

Sisko waved a hand, realizing it was probably unrealistic to demand much more depth from Quark's explanation. "Continue."

"So—whoever hid them made a map of where they were hidden. End of mystery."

"Well, that makes no sense," Bashir complained. "If the Orbs aren't supposed to ever be found, why make maps? Why not just launch them into the sun?"

Quark rolled his eyes. "Bajorans didn't have space travel back then, all right? Now, do you want to hear this story or not?"

"It gets better," Odo pointed out.

"Thank you," Quark said. "So, the point is, the map Dal Nortron obtained—from *whatever* source—apparently reveals the world on which the second Red Orb is hidden."

"A world's a large place to hide something so small," Sisko said.

"Exactly, Captain. Which means, you need the first Orb to find the second. They react to each other, like a . . . a location beacon or something. And the thing is, I didn't know Vash had the first Orb."

Sisko handed the map cylinder to Odo. "Constable, is there any way we can see what's on this?"

Odo studied the transparent amber rod. "Looks like a standard Cardassian memory rod. . . ." He walked over to a wall display, pressed a control and a rod holder slid out.

"Quark," Sisko warned the Ferengi barkeep, "no games now. I'll accept that you're too smart to risk alienating the entire Bajoran population. But I need an honest answer." Sisko tried not to react to Quark's sudden look of panic at his use of the word 'honest.' "Who else—smuggler or collector or buyer—is on this station who might have been responsible for Dal Nortron's murder?"

Only Quark could look contrite, worried, and embarrassed all at the same time. "Captain, I don't know. The Andorian sisters. Base, of course. Vash. Those are the only ones my inform—I mean, they're the only ones I've seen."

"Here it is," the constable said from his position by the display screen.

Sisko left Quark, who likely had nothing more to offer, and walked over to join Odo and Bashir.

The amber cylinder did contain a map, but not of an entire planet. Instead, it outlined a city layout, of streets and dwelling blocks.

And nothing was labeled.

"That's not going to do anyone any good," Sisko said.

Odo studied the schematics on the display screen. "Maybe the legend was wrong. Instead of showing a world, the map shows a place *on* a world."

"But, Odo," Bashir said, "there are millions of worlds in the galaxy."

"Maybe there's another map that goes with this one," Odo suggested.

Sisko tried a different approach. "How old is that cylinder?"

Odo tapped a few controls, read a line of Cardassian script. "According to the manufacturer's code, five years."

"So this is a copy," Bashir concluded.

"Of a copy of a copy of a copy," Sisko added. "And if this truly dates back to ten thousand years ago, when the first Orbs started to appear, then the first version of the map would probably have been carved into rock or—" He stopped and then smiled broadly. "No. It *can't* be hidden on any one of millions of worlds." He turned to the Ferengi and exclaimed, "Quark! You're right!"

"I am?"

"You said it yourself. Ten millennia ago, Bajorans didn't have space travel. So the Orbs *had* to have been hidden on Bajor itself."

This time it was Bashir who seemed unconvinced. "But if the hiding place is Bajor, then why all the interest in a map that supposedly shows some *world* on which the orbs can be found?"

Sisko wasn't certain about that, himself, but he didn't think it was important. "The old Bajoran ideograms can be difficult to translate. They have so many meanings that change according to context. It could be as simple as the phrase '*the* world,' meaning the known world of Bajor, having been translated as '*a* world,' a few thousand years ago."

Sisko shook his head to ward off any other questions that could sidetrack them again. "In any case, the mystery that should concern us right now is who killed Dal Nortron."

"Hey, Dad."

Sisko turned, automatically smiling at the sound of his son's voice.

Jake and Jadzia stepped cautiously into the storage room of Odo's security office, neither of them comfortable with the sharply slanting deck.

"Jake-O, Old Man—who's minding the store?"

"Worf," Jadzia said with a playful smile. "We're running another diagnostic on the computer and I had to get away from those screens for a few minutes."

Under current conditions, Sisko could accept Jadzia's presence. But not Jake's.

"You know you shouldn't be here," he told his son. "The whole station's on gravity alert and I want you back at our quarters to look after Kasidy."

Jake looked at him as if he were hearing a deliberately bad joke.

"Like I'm supposed to look after the captain of an interstellar freighter. Sure, that's just the sort of job for a helpless female."

Sisko smiled but made his request again. "You know what I mean. I want my family out of harm's way."

Jake grinned. "Really? Family? Does Kasidy know about this?"

"Don't start," Sisko warned. "Now get moving, and don't use the turbolifts."

Jake hesitated, looked at Jadzia, and Jadzia coughed.

Something was obviously going on between them. "All right, you two," Sisko said. "I know a conspiracy when I see one."

"Benjamin," Jadzia said, "just before the computer was compromised, when you had just beamed out to the *Defiant,* Jake and I were having a . . . talk."

"You were in Ops?" Sisko frowned at his son.

Jadzia answered before Jake could. "He's been helping out with the computer restarts, copying files, shutting down subsystems."

Sisko relaxed, reminded of what he sometimes forgot these days, of all the time Jake used to spend with O'Brien. He gave his son the benefit of the doubt. "I take it this 'talk' was important?"

Jadzia exchanged glances with Jake. "Well, the budding novelist here figured out on his own that someone was trying to sell an Orb, *and* that the Orb was real. He had a few other interesting conclusions, too, so I thought maybe you could use his input while you're trying to put all this together."

Sisko sighed. "Okay. But let's do that *tonight,* Jake. Right now, things are still too much up in the air." He could see the disappointment in his son's eyes, understood how the boy felt, but for now, the station had to come first.

Jake nodded without protest. He wasn't the only one who was disappointed, though.

"Don't give me that look, Old Man."

"A good commander makes full use of all his assets."

"I see. The conspiracy is turning into a mutiny." Not for the first time, Sisko observed that Jadzia and Jake were alike in that they both knew exactly how far they could push him, and when they reached that point without success, they backed off without recrimination.

Almost without recrimination.

Jadzia leaned closer and whispered into Sisko's ear, "I'd watch out, Benjamin. Someday Jake's going to write a book about you and you do want to come off as one of the good guys, don't you?"

"Tonight," Sisko repeated firmly.

Jake said his good-byes to Odo, the doctor, and Quark and then, just before stepping out of the storage room, he glanced up at the display screen with a bright smile. "Hey, you got the interface going!"

Everyone looked at him in surprise, including his father.

"What interface?" Sisko asked.

"With the Cardassian holosuite." Jake pointed to the display screen. "Isn't what that is? It sure looks like the layout of the village Nog and I saw."

"What village?" Odo asked sharply.

"The one on the Bajoran moon."

Just for a moment, Sisko felt Deep Space 9 wheel crazily around him. And the effect had nothing to do with the canted slant of the deck or with failing gravity.

Without any logic or hard data, he suddenly was certain that the last piece of the puzzle had just fallen into place.

And the truly maddening thing was, it had been there all along.

CHAPTER 21

"THIS IS IT," Nog said. Then he looked up at Jake. "Wouldn't you say?"

Jake studied the holographic image that surrounded him and all the other onlookers in the holosuite at Quark's. As far as he could tell, it was a close reproduction of the primitive village he and Nog had seen in the distance four days ago, when they had entered the Cardassian holosuite. Fortunately, the computers that ran Quark's holosuites were separate from the station's, and were still fully operational.

The resolution, however, was low, the sky was an unreal shade of dark purple without stars or Bajor, and the re-creation was missing details like an evening breeze and the flickering of lights in the windows. But from the arrangement of the buildings and the sweep of the landscape, Jake would have to say Jadzia had done a great job of turning the two-dimensional map on the Cardassian memory rod into a three-dimensional simulation. Best of all, she had adjusted the gravity in the suite to compensate for the station's list, so that for the first time in almost two hours everyone was standing on level ground.

"I agree," Jake said. "This is the village we saw."

He looked over at his father, secretly pleased to be able to make an important contribution to the investigation. Especially after being so publicly dismissed in front of so many people—who were now here to see that he wasn't just the captain's kid, who had to be kept 'out of harm's way.'

Even his father looked impressed. He turned to Odo. "Constable? Theories?"

"I think it's obvious, Captain. Dal Nortron somehow knew about the Cardassian holosuite in the hidden section of corridor. He used it to create a simulation of this Bajoran lunar village, no doubt attempting to narrow down the location of the second Orb."

"And he was killed for his trouble."

"Undoubtedly."

"Which brings us back to Vash, Satr, and Leen as suspects. But how could any of *them* know about the hidden section of the station?"

"You might as well ask how could Nortron?" Odo said. "And again, I think the answer is obvious. The map is recorded on a Cardassian memory rod. That implies Nortron obtained it from a Cardassian source, and that it was a Cardassian who knew about what was hidden on Terok Nor and then told Nortron."

Even though everything Odo had said sounded reasonable, somehow it didn't strike Jake as right. There had to be another explanation for what had happened. He tried to think about how he would make everything come out if this were a novel he was writing, but unfortunately all that kept springing into his mind was the usual shock ending in which the station commander is revealed to be the killer.

Jake suddenly stared at his father, who turned to him as if he sensed the intensity of his son's gaze. "What is it, Jake?"

"Um, Dad, are we . . . still following the Starfleet changeling-detection protocols?"

Sisko shrugged. "All the time." Then he grinned as if he could read his son's mind. "Anyone in particular you suspect?"

"No, not really," Jake said diffidently.

"Jake," Sisko said, "if the Dominion was behind any of this, a Jem'Hadar attack wing would have started pounding us the instant our computers went off-line. The fact that we're still here means this doesn't have anything at all to do with the Founders."

But that didn't sound right to Jake, either. "But it *does* have something to do with the Cardassians, right? And they're part of the Dominion, sort of."

Jadzia looked at Sisko. "See? That's a good point."

"No, no, no," Major Kira suddenly interjected. She had gone off to walk through the simulated village and had just returned. "This reconstruction doesn't match *any* village on *any* of the inhabited Bajoran moons. It's a fake. A typical Quark forgery."

"I resent that," Quark said huffily. "My forgeries are anything but typ—never mind."

"Captain," Kira said, "we're wasting our time with this."

But Jake could see that Kira's argument had made his father think of something else. "Just a minute, Major. Let's accept that this simulation *doesn't* match an *existing* lunar village. But could it match an *ancient* one?"

"Lunar villages aren't that ancient, sir. The oldest ones, even going right back to the first landings, would only be a thousand years old."

Jake understood the reason for his father's quick smile. It didn't mean that he was taking what Kira said lightly. His amusement stemmed from the fact that Bajoran culture went so far back that a thousand years to them was like a long weekend to anyone else.

"Forgive me, Major." Sisko's apology was sincere. "Rather than 'ancient,' let's say 'old.' Could this represent an *old* lunar village?"

Kira turned around to stare back at the simulation. "Well, the architecture is right, even if the layout isn't. But if the Red Orbs are supposed to have been split up ten thousand years ago, how could one of them have been buried on a Bajoran moon *one* thousand years ago?"

"Maybe someone's keeping track of them," Jake suggested.

Kira shook her head. "Oh, no, Jake, you can't have it both ways. Either the Orbs are hidden or they're not. It doesn't make sense for anyone to be moving around Orbs that supposedly can never be brought together."

"Of course," Bashir said slowly, "there is *one* way for everyone to be right."

That the doctor suddenly had everyone's undivided attention was an understatement. Jake felt a little envious that Bashir and not he might be about to solve the mystery, but he was excited, too, to be here on the spot, as his father's murder investigation proceeded to its solution, step by step. All of this was vastly preferable to being sequestered somewhere safe while all the really interesting activities on the station were going on without him.

The doctor gave a little bow toward Major Kira. "What if these Orbs *are* forgeries, but ones manufactured a thousand years ago which would give them a certain air of authenticity. This would make them rare Bajoran artifacts that could have been hidden a millennium ago, and would mean they could still serve as a motive for murder today. At the same time, they would then also *not* be the legendary, and possibly, apocryphal, Red Orbs of Jalbador."

"Makes sense to me," Kira said.

"Except for that Cardassian connection," Sisko said. "I wish we knew what moon this was supposed to be. . . ." He turned to Jake. "Where was Bajor in the sky?"

Jake and Nog both turned and pointed away from the village. "Up there," Jake told his father.

"We were beyond the terminator," Nog added, "but we could still see part of the sunlit side."

"Computer," Sisko said, "add Bajor to the night sky, as seen from the Bajoran moon of Baraddo."

Jake looked up as the purple sky suddenly rippled and turned black, now dotted with twinkling stars. A few moments later, a full Bajor appeared against the stars, green oceans sparkling with the brilliant reflection of Bajor-B'hava-el.

"Too small," Nog said at once.

"That's right," Jake said. "It was twice that size at least."

Sisko nodded. "Computer, which moon of Bajor would correspond to an apparent diameter of the planet twice the width of what's displayed now?"

"Unable to comply," the computer answered. "Library access has been temporarily interrupted."

Jake knew that meant the computer had tried to contact the station's central computer banks, which were still off-line.

Sisko gave the challenge to Kira. "Major, pick a moon. There're only five that are inhabited."

Kira looked troubled. "But some have eccentric orbits. . . . Computer, adjust the sky as seen from the moon of Penraddo."

Jake watched as Bajor seemed to jump closer in the sky, almost doubling in apparent diameter.

"That is still not quite right," Nog said, frowning. "Is there any moon that orbits the planet even closer?"

"Not habitable," Kira said.

"You mean, not habitable *now!*" Sisko's smile was triumphant.

Jake didn't know what his father was talking about. But Kira apparently did.

"Jeraddo?" she said.

"If I wanted to hide something so that it could never be found," Sisko said, "what better place than a moon that will kill anyone who tries to land there? Computer: Show Bajor as it would have appeared from the moon of Jeraddo before the moon's atmosphere was converted."

Instantly, Bajor jumped even closer in the sky.

"Now *that* is the right size," Nog said.

Jake nodded.

But Kira wasn't convinced. "Jeraddo was only converted to an energy source five years ago, not a thousand."

Jake had a sudden flash of inspiration. "Which means," he said excitedly, "someone could have hidden the Orb on Jeraddo five years ago! To keep it out of the hands of whoever's been trying to find the Orbs and bring them together!"

Kira suddenly developed a pained expression. "Jake, where did that come from?"

Jake could tell that his interruption had surprised her. He was getting more and more used to that reaction. It was hard for the adults on the station to stop thinking of him as the little kid they'd always known. And it was hard for him to suppress the ideas he had about just about everything around him.

"Well," he began explaining enthusiastically, "Jeraddo was converted into an energy moon five years ago. The memory cylinder the map is on is five years old. So maybe the map isn't a copy— maybe it's only five years old. . . ." Jake could see Kira wasn't buying a word. And neither was anyone else. *Too bad,* Jake thought. *It would make a great conspiracy novel.* He could even use his father's suggestion and call it *The Cardassian Connection.* He could write a whole series. He could . . . see the almost pitying look on Major Kira's face. "Never mind," he said.

"I won't," Kira replied. She turned to Sisko. "Shouldn't we all get back to work?"

Jake could see his father wasn't ready to let go of this latest lead that he and Nog had provided. "Don't you have any curiosity for making an even more detailed simulation from the map? Maybe find out exactly where the Orb is hidden?" Sisko asked.

"Absolutely none," Kira said. "That Orb will never be found because it either doesn't exist, or if it does, because it's hidden on Jeraddo. Either way, that map means nothing."

Jake watched as his father's glance polled the rest of the group in the holosuite—Odo, Bashir, Quark, even Nog and him. No one else offered an objection to Kira's conclusion, so neither did Jake.

"All right," Sisko said. "We move on."

Jake braced himself for the return of the station's unbalanced gravity field.

"Computer," Sisko said, "end program."

But nothing changed.

"Computer," Sisko repeated, *"end* program."

The simulation remained.

"That Rom" Quark sputtered. "Computer, this is Quark. Implement safety override in holosuite C."

But again, nothing happened. Quark looked frantically back and forth at the unchanging Bajoran lunar village. "We're doomed," he said.

"Not yet," a disembodied voice replied.

Jake looked at Nog as everyone else scanned their surroundings, trying to find the source of the voice.

"Stay calm, and no one will get hurt," the voice said again.

Jake saw his father and Major Kira turn to look at one another at the same moment.

"Leej Terrell." To Jake, the way Kira said the name, it sounded like she was cursing.

Then something even more unusual happened. Jake was amazed to see the distant landscape shimmer just for an instant, as three Cardassians—one female and two males, including one who was bald and badly scarred—stepped *through* the holographic simulation to join the group in the holosuite.

Except they weren't here to play games.

Each held a Cardassian phaser.

"Thank you, Captain Sisko," the female said. "You finally found our missing Orb."

CHAPTER 22

SISKO STEPPED between Terrell and his son. *If she so much as aims her weapon in Jake's direction—*

The Cardassian seemed to recognize the reason for his move. "Noble, Captain, but unnecessary."

"How did you get in here!" Quark demanded of Terrell. "I demand to see your admittance receipt!" And he slapped at her bald associate as Atrig roughly searched through Quark's ill-fitting green brocade waiter's suit for possible weapons.

At the same time, Dr. Betan retrieved all communicators, along with Jadzia's tricorder and Jake's note padd. Sisko's holosuite party was now completely cut off from the rest of the station, captives of the three Cardassians.

Terrell stared at the indignant Quark. "You don't recognize me?"

Sisko saw the sudden flash of fear that moved through Quark, as if the Ferengi barkeep did recognize her, but was somehow terrified to acknowledge that fact.

"Should I?" Quark asked.

"I'm not the one to ask," Terrell said. She turned her attention to Odo. "How about you, shape-shifter?"

"What about me?" Odo growled.

Terrell seemed only amused by his attitude. "Some things never change." She casually lifted her phaser and shot Odo point-blank.

As the constable fell, Kira's attempt to run to his side was aborted by Betan's menacing sweep of his phaser in her direction.

Bashir knelt quickly beside Odo's fallen form to use his medical tricorder to check the constable's condition. He looked up at Sisko as Atrig relieved him of the device. "Just stunned."

"You had no need to do that," Sisko told Terrell.

But all the Cardassian said was, "You'd be surprised, Captain. Whenever Odo permits himself to be captured, I can't help but be suspicious."

Terrell spoke as if she knew Odo. That meant to Sisko that it was possible that she had been on DS9 before. Perhaps during the Cardassian Occupation of Bajor. He realized it was also possible that he was looking at yet another piece of the puzzle that involved his people and his station.

Sisko caught the eyes of the rest of his staff and shook his head, to instruct them not to try what Odo had done. He was aware of the frustration that tormented all of them—Jadzia, Bashir, Nog, Jake, and especially Kira. But even Quark would realize it was suicide to risk a frontal assault on three phasers.

Terrell approached Sisko. "We've been listening to everything you've discussed in here," she said. "All this talk about Orbs. Do they exist, don't they exist? Are they a fraud? A forgery? Apocryphal? You've been so caught up in the search for the real story about the Orbs that you've completely neglected the greater truth."

Sisko watched her closely, waiting for her to show the slightest inattention to her weapon. If he could get it, then the odds would be closer to even.

"What greater truth?" he asked. He didn't care what she gave as an answer. He only wanted to keep her talking, to increase the odds she'd be distracted. Having Jake here under these conditions was just as harrowing as when Kasidy had been with him on the *Defiant*. One way or another, these threats to his family had to end.

"Captain Sisko . . . *Emissary*," Terrell said mockingly. "You're familiar with the Orbs the Bajorans call the Tears of the Prophets. Tell me, where do those Blue Orbs come from?"

Sisko stared at her, measuring her, judging her. He would not play her game.

"That's right," she said, as if content to conduct both sides of the conversation herself. "The Celestial Temple. *Jalkaree.* The wormhole." Her narrow, gray face twisted into an unpleasant smile. "So, where do you think the *Red* Orbs come from?

"Correct again," Terrell said, without even waiting for Sisko to respond. "See how easy this is? They come from *another* wormhole. You see, Captain, it turns out you weren't the first to discover the wormhole in the Bajoran system. Or, rather, should I say, you weren't the first to discover the *first* wormhole. Because there are *two* of them. Care to make a comment now?"

Sisko shot a glance at Jadzia, but the scientist shook her head, her expression of disbelief confirming what he already knew. "That's impossible," he said.

"There can't be two," Jadzia added. "The entire Bajoran sector's been subjected to one of the most intensive subspace structural analyses the Federation has ever undertaken. I helped design the project. There *is* no second wormhole."

The Cardassian sneered at Jadzia, "I don't suppose that thorough analysis of yours included the effects of the three Orbs of Jalbador? No? I didn't think so."

"You're lying," Kira cried. "There is only one Celestial Temple and the Prophets are those who dwell within it!"

Without even glancing at her target, the Cardassian swept out her arm and smashed her phaser across Kira's face, knocking the Bajoran officer down beside Odo's still form. Blood trickled from the ridges of Kira's nose.

Sisko lunged forward, ignoring his own order, only to be stopped by a phaser burst at his feet and the realization that Atrig's next shot would hit Jake.

Bashir helped Kira to her feet as Terrell said coldly. "Spare me the superstitious prattle, Bajoran. Do you think yours is the first planet of simpletons who have been toyed with by a more advanced species? Your Prophets are exploitive aliens and they've treated your world like their own personal chessboard for twenty millennia. You people are nothing but their pawns. You've all been bred for ignorance and servility and—for all you know—pure entertainment."

"That is *enough!*" Sisko shouted. His voice was oddly flat in the dead air of the simulated holographic village, but it was loud enough to make his point.

Terrell's phaser swung back to cover him. "Of course it's enough. This dismal creature doesn't have the mental capacity to understand the truth. But you, Captain, and your Federation . . . you understand. You've always known about the corruption poised to consume the souls of those races that dare to think of themselves as gods. Why else would you have your Prime Directive except to spare yourselves that fate?"

Sisko shuddered as Terrell favored him with a look of approval. "That's one of the few things we Cardassians admire about your kind, you know. The Prime Directive. It shows that at some point you were like us—an ethical race. Your downfall, though, is that you lack the moral strength to distinguish between true sentient beings— like the Vulcans—and simple stock like the Bajorans, who have been so debased by their Prophets that—"

Kira pushed Bashir aside, launched herself at Terrell, arms out-stretched, her hands her only weapons.

She almost reached the startled Cardassian. But Dr. Betan caught her in time, spun her around, and shoved her forward, where Atrig stunned her with his phaser.

Kira collapsed instantly, her body sprawling awkwardly across the holographic rocks.

"The rest of you. Get down on your knees," Dr. Betan ordered crisply. "With your hands on your heads."

No one in Sisko's party moved, their eyes all on Kira. The stun had been a heavy one.

Dr. Betan pointed his phaser at Bashir's head, close enough that even a stun would be fatal. "We only need one of you to answer our questions. No loss to us if the rest have to die."

At that moment, Kira stirred and faintly moaned.

Thanking the Prophets, Sisko took action. He had to learn what questions the Cardassians needed answered. If there was anything he knew that they didn't, then in some small way he would have power over them.

Knowing his people had to be his first priority, Sisko knelt on the stones then, beneath the night sky and the brilliance of a full Bajor. And he placed his hands on his head.

The others immediately followed the example of their commander. "Ask your questions," Sisko said to Terrell.

She looked pleased at his compliance. "You and I are alike, you know. You've seen the Blue Orbs. You've contacted the wormhole aliens. In my way, I've shared those experiences."

"If you really had," Sisko said, "you would find it impossible to behave as you do."

Terrell cocked her head. "You surprise me, Captain. You know that's not true. You've devoted many of the scientific assets of this station to the study of the Blue Orbs. Each month I read an intercept of the latest installment of the never-ending report this Trill scientist of yours is compiling. And I want you to know, I understand. The Orbs are the artifacts of an advanced civilization. You're compelled to study them, just as we were when we discovered them on Bajor. But then again, we found more than just the Blue Orbs. We also found a red one. And do you know one of the things that distinguishes a Red Orb from a Blue? Other than the color, of course."

Sisko remained silent as before. The more she talked the more chance he had to learn what he knew that they didn't.

"Verteron traces," she said proudly. "That's what gives the Red Orb its color—a subspace-particle collision that traps chromic oxide atoms in a solidified energy vortex."

The sound of her voice rattling on while Major Kira lay untended not a meter away, made Sisko's head ache. How soon would it be before Worf would wonder why the meeting in the holosuite was taking so long?

"Not actually *solidified* energy, of course," Terrell said with a chuckle, "but one with a relativistic rate of temporal decay a billion times slower than the local inertial frame of reference. Am I boring you, Captain?"

"You'll never be able to leave this station," Sisko said challengingly. The safety of his people depended upon his keeping her off-balance, distracted until Worf could make his move.

Terrell's harsh, barking laugh was scornful. "My people *built* this station. We know more about it than you ever will."

The Cardassian waved her phaser at Quark, who ducked forward, lowering his head to his knees, his eyes tightly shut, expecting the worst. When it didn't come, he opened them one at a time to find Terrell regarding him with amusement. "Those smugglers' tunnels that you use for all your petty crimes, how do you think they came to be built, Ferengi? Because the designers of Terok Nor made an error? Or at the command of the Obsidian Order?"

Quark whimpered at the dreaded name and closed his eyes again.

"There is no Obsidian Order anymore," Sisko said.

Terrell shrugged, as if she were beginning to lose interest in their conversation. "They had outlived their usefulness. But rest assured a dozen other groups are now battling to see who will emerge as the Order's replacement on the Detapa Council."

Sisko strove to regain her attention. "Do you honestly think the Dominion will allow *any* group to attain the power of the Obsidian Order?"

Provoked, as he had hoped, Terrell threw the question back at him. "Do you think Cardassian patriots will allow their home to be enslaved by the Founders forever?" She shook her head in contempt. "In one guise or another, Captain, the Order *will* be reborn. Just as Cardassia will throw off her oppressors. And the key to this great new victory is the second wormhole in the Bajoran system."

"But what you're saying is impossible!" Sisko said quickly. Inwardly, he sighed with relief as the Cardassian picked up the challenge and began talking rapidly, intensely.

"Captain, *I* studied the Red Orb. Right here. On this station. That single Red Orb had verteron traces different from those of the Blue Orbs. We were able to tell from those traces that it had been exposed to multiple bursts of negative energy—exactly the energy signature created by the sudden intrusion of a wormhole into normal space-time. A form of hyperdimensional Cerenkov radiation, if you will. But where the Blue Orbs contained very slight verteron tracks—almost impossible to measure—the Red Orb had multiple tracks. And that meant that though it was possible the Blue Orbs might have passed through a wormhole once— whatever the Orbs were, wherever they had come from—there was no doubt the red one had been close to an opening wormhole *many* times.

"You can see why that Orb captured the interest of everyone in the rarefied assemblage of the Order's science directorate. Somehow, that Red Orb could be the key to actually *creating* a worm-hole."

Sisko's eyes widened with her next words. He tried not to look at Jake and Nog, praying that they would not speak or draw the Cardassian's attention to them.

"I set up my lab right here on Terok Nor," Terrell said. "In that hidden section of corridor you found. But it wasn't hidden from *you*. It was hidden from Gul Dukat, who never had a clue as to what I was doing here. And it was in that lab, with that Red Orb connected to a . . . well, let's just say, the right equipment, that I was able to release just enough of the solidified energy trapped within it. What I am saying, Captain Sisko, is that *I* was the first to create a wormhole precursor field—a thinning of the surface tension of space-time such that only a small push would be required to break through into a non-linear realm. The realm of—"

Sisko's arms dropped to his side. He regarded Terrell with amazement. "Are you saying you made contact with the Prophets?"

"The *aliens!*" Terrell snapped. She gestured with her phaser and Sisko placed his hands on his head again. "Wormhole aliens. Not face to face, but oh, they were in there. And they contacted us before we could contact them. Some of us could hear their thoughts. Almost all of us could see the images they created for us, enticing us into their realm as they opened doorways to whatever place it was we each most wanted to go. Disturbing, wouldn't you say? An alien race reaching into our minds, knowing our deepest desires like that?"

"Sounds like something only the gods would know," Sisko said softly.

Terrell's response was harsh and blunt. "It's also something that could be known by telepaths. Telepathic *aliens* with a perverted desire to make less-advanced beings worship them."

The Cardassian looked away from him, up to the holographic image of Bajor in the simulated night sky. "But even knowing what we were dealing with, there were those on my research team who heard the aliens' voices and . . . obeyed them, stepping through the precursor membrane."

Terrell closed her eyes for an instant. Sisko saw Atrig and Dr. Betan look at her with concern. "Most never came back."

Sisko seized the opportunity to make eye contact with Bashir and Nog, who gave him imperceptible nods of agreement. Even though they were on their knees, they were ready to move the instant he judged the Cardassians' weapons would not be a threat. Sisko wished there were some way he could signal Jake to run for cover ahead of time.

"And then, when we were so close—" Terrell was now so caught up in completing her story that she had begun to pace back and forth. The gaze of her two associates followed her as she continued to speak, "—when *I* was so close to finally controlling the Red Orb's energy, the order came to *withdraw* from Bajor. Who knows the reason? I think it was because the patience of the Cardassian people had reached an end. Here we had spent decades and the lives of so many good soldiers and trillions of bars of latinum to help restore some semblance of order to this ungrateful world, and still its pathetic natives resisted us. What was the point of continuing? If the Bajorans wanted to remain the playthings of the alien telepaths they called the Prophets, then at some point we had to say, 'Enough.' We can't save everyone. We couldn't save them from themselves. Any more than we can save you from yourselves."

Sisko shifted his knees against the rough stones, getting ready, still forced to listen to the Cardassian's self-serving, offensive recollection without objection.

"I knew I couldn't leave my lab behind for the Bajorans to discover," Terrell mused thoughtfully. "As challenged as they are, some of them have a certain natural, Pakled-like aptitude for machinery. They would never have understood the subtle complexities of subspace manipulation, but they might have been able to duplicate my equipment and quite by accident stumble upon a method for completing it. For that reason, the Obsidian Order gave the command to have the station self-destruct once all Cardassian personnel had been evacuated."

Sisko couldn't help the retort that rose to his lips. "So the station's continued existence is yet another example of the Order's effectiveness."

Terrell paused for a moment in her pacing, idly rubbed her thumb against the force selector switch on her phaser. Sisko heard the series of faint clicks that indicated the selector was dialling through its possible settings, like the spinning of a dabo wheel. "Captain, you're an intelligent being. The ability to open an artificial, stable wormhole between *any* two points in the galaxy, perhaps in the universe, would be the ultimate defense against aggression. Cardassian fleets could take off from Cardassia Prime and in minutes be in the atmosphere of any enemy's homeworld, having completely bypassed all that world's defenses."

Though he did not comment on what Terrell was saying, Sisko was perfectly aware of what wormhole technology offered the galaxy—or, in the eyes of some within Starfleet, how it threatened the galaxy.

"In a day," Terrell said calmly, "the Dominion would cease to exist. In a week, the Alpha and Beta Quadrants would begin an era of peace unsurpassed in galactic history."

Terrell now crouched down beside him. Sisko suppressed the urge to draw back from her in distaste. "You see, I know what drives humans to join Starfleet. I even know what you are, Captain. You're an explorer, a dreamer, someone who *needs* to propel his species beyond all limits of knowledge. In other words, you are just like *me* . . . like any other Cardassian."

"Don't count on it," Sisko said grimly. Surely Worf had had enough time to make his realization. He could feel the eyes of his own staff on him, expectant.

Terrell gave his shoulder an indulgent pat, and then stood up again. "You'll see. When the Dominion has been crushed. When the *Pax Cardassia* embraces all our worlds. When a bold new age of peaceful exploration and development of the galaxy has begun. I've no doubt you'll be there. On the bridge of a Cardassian science vessel or one of your own, it doesn't matter. Because we will all be joined in a common cause—"

"Never."

But Terrell was no longer listening to him. She was looking up once again at the simulated Bajor. "Computer, download current program to memory channel Alpha Prime. Authorization, Terrell, level 9, Green."

When the computer responded, Sisko was surprised to hear not the voice of Quark's holosuite management unit but the station's own synthetic voice.

Terrell smiled at his reaction. "The Andorians weren't the only ones to augment your station's computers with their own codes," she said. "Terok Nor will remain nonoperational until I have completed my mission."

"What *is* your mission?!" Sisko demanded. There was no time left for subtlety.

And, as if she felt the same way, Terrell finally told him. "The one thing that held back my work," she said, "was the fact that I only had one Red Orb. After all, Bajoran legends say that the doorway to Jalbador shall be opened only when all three are brought together. But in sixty years, the entire might of Cardassia could locate only one of those three. Until Quark so helpfully announced that he had a map to sell."

"This is not my fault!" Quark said vehemently.

"Calm down, Ferengi. You'll be a hero to my people if to no one else."

"So what?" Quark grumbled. "That and a slip of latinum aren't even *worth* a slip of latinum."

"So," Terrell continued for Sisko's benefit, "with the chance to find a second Red Orb—which could possibly provide the means to recover the Orb lost on the Day of Withdrawal—it was time for me to return to my old home.

"And that is my mission, Captain Sisko. To obtain the three Red Orbs. To wrest from them the secret of creating a translocatable wormhole. And then, finally, to destroy the aliens within it so its full power will be in the hands of the greatest force for galactic peace ever imagined."

Sisko heard the station's computer voice again. "Program-transfer completed."

"End program," Terrell said, and the crude reconstruction of the Jeraddon lunar village began to dissolve.

The familiar hardness of the holosuite's smooth deck replaced the rough stones previously beneath Sisko's knees. The lighting brightened. In the green glow from the standby holoprojectors, the three Cardassians resembled supernatural beings emerging from some alien pit.

But all Sisko was conscious of was that at last he knew what Terrell's weakness was. "You lost an Orb," he said, making his statement an accusation.

"I prefer to think of it as . . . misplaced," she said, her attention alarmingly now focused on Jake. "But the fact that your internal reports are full of references to the 'lost Cardassian holosuite' leads me to believe that the Red Orb is nearby, its residual power still with enough of a contact to my old lab to maintain the precursor condition."

Terrell poked Jake's shoulder with her phaser. "You weren't in a holosuite, young human. You were looking at visions of what you wanted most, created by the wormhole aliens to lure you into their realm." She looked back to Sisko, whose heart was pounding at the Cardassian's closeness to his son. "And if the Red Orb had still been connected to my equipment, your son might have stepped through the boundary layer into that realm and been lost forever."

And as quickly, as unexpectedly as that, it all came together for Sisko. Everything Terrell had said and, more importantly, what she had not said. He took a deep breath. "I know the questions you need answered," he said. He nodded at the other prisoners. "Let them go."

"And you'll tell me everything I want to know?"

"Yes," Sisko said. It was not a lie, and it was not capitulation. The truth was, he *could* answer her questions now, but she would not be able to use what he told her.

"Very well," Terrell said. She aimed her phaser at Jake. "But you will tell me everything I want to know *before* I let everyone go. Or I will kill them all, starting with this one."

It took all of Sisko's self-control not to respond automatically. He told himself her threat was hollow. After all, she could have killed everyone but him the moment she and Atrig and Dr. Betan made their presence known. But she didn't. *Could it be she actually does see herself as a force for peace?* he asked himself. *In her twisted mind, is there really some ethical compunction not to kill?*

He made his decision. "You don't want to kill them, Terrell. You told me yourself. You're a scientist, an explorer. All you really want is information. And I *will* give it to you. Once I know my son and the rest of my people are safe."

His eyes met hers without flinching.

"Terrell," Dr. Betan warned. "You can't trust him."

Terrell didn't turn away from Sisko's steady gaze. She motioned him to rise to his feet. "I believe I can. Computer: Run Odo Ital, One."

At once, the holosuite became a duplicate of the station's security office. Sisko looked around carefully, noting that it was not an exact duplicate. Some of the wall displays were different. And the Promenade beyond the transparent door panels was drab, washed out by dim blue light. Then he realized where he was, and when.

"Odo's office from the time of the Occupation," he said.

"Fitting, don't you think?" Terrell said. She gestured to Atrig and Dr. Betan to move the rest of their prisoners into the simulated holding cells.

Sisko heard Quark's indignant protest, "This is not one of my programs."

"The systems of Terok Nor are integrated in ways you can't imagine," Terrell said to Sisko in explanation.

"The Obsidian Order?" Sisko said, rather than asked.

"Precisely, Captain. As you know, to observe everyone all the time requires immense computational ability. Even these holosuites are connected to the station's main computers, though not by links any of your engineers would ever suspect."

The last prisoner to be locked up was Odo. By now, the constable had regained consciousness, though he was still groggy. Atrig and Dr. Betan pushed him into the last cell, then activated the force field.

Now, only Sisko and the three Cardassians were free.

Sisko stood outside the force field sealing the holding cells. He looked at Jake.

"Satisfied?" Terrell asked.

"How long will this simulation run?" Sisko asked.

"Thirteen hours. More than enough time for me to go where I need to go next, and for you to tell me what I need to know."

Sisko stiffened. She was changing the rules on him again. "Why don't I tell you what you need to know, and then you go wherever it is you have to go."

Terrell shook her head. "I'm willing to trust you, Captain. But only to a point."

She lifted her wrist communicator. "This is Terrell. Four to beam out. Energize."

And then, before Sisko could protest or even say a last word to Jake, he was lifted out of Deep Space 9, on his way to wherever it was that Terrell needed him to go.

CHAPTER 23

THE MOON OF Jeraddo was a seething crimson orb of gas wreathed in violent, thousand-kilometer filaments of blazing-blue lightning.

Three years ago, the moon's molten core had been tapped to produce power for Bajor, the world it orbited, an ingenious concept first developed by the Klingons. Decades ago, that initial concept's design flaws had caused the spectacular destruction of the Empire's main generation facility on the moon of Praxis. The flaws had since been corrected by assiduous Federation engineers focusing a low-level subspace inversion field on the moon's core. As a result, the normal convection of heat generated by the decay of natural radioactives had been accelerated a thousandfold.

In less than a year, the end result of the convection would have been to turn the entire moon into molten rock. But a clever feedback loop allowed the excess heat of the moon's core to be shunted into subspace and collected by orbiting conversion platforms. There, the enormous energy imbalance was transformed. Extremely high-frequency subspace waves were changed to more-easily-controlled midrange frequencies, which could be safely transmitted to Bajor's power grid.

The engineers who maintained the system likened it to setting off an antimatter bomb in a flimsy wooden box, and then only allowing the energy to escape through a very small hole in one side. The slightest miscalculation could result in the sudden release of *all* the energy at once, vaporizing the box—or, in this case, Jeraddo and whatever hemisphere of Bajor it was over at the time. But as long as everything performed according to specs, Jeraddo would be providing power to Bajor for the next thousand years.

And the only cost for that benefit was that what had once been an inhabited class-M moon, was now a class-Y demon world on which an unprotected visitor would live for less time than it took to draw a breath. Whether death would come from the toxic corrosive crimson clouds, the sudden atmospheric pressure waves of 1200-degrees-Celsius heat, or the wildly fluctuating gravity fields that were a byproduct of the subspace inversion at the moon's core no one could predict. Nor did anyone particularly care. All possibilities were equally unpleasant and equally fatal.

The ship that now took up a nonstandard orbit around the hellish moon appeared to be an ordinary Sagittarian cruiser, its gleaming yellow hull making electric contrast with Jeraddo's red clouds.

The cruiser was as long as the *Defiant* but no more than half its width. For redundancy—not efficiency—its back third was ringed by four half-size warp nacelles. Its middle third was covered almost completely with pressure hatches for twenty-four escape modules—one for every five passengers and crew, though each had seating and supplies for ten. And the front third was thick with ablative shielding on its forward surfaces. Any impact with an unexpected body would first be absorbed by the hull, then by the "crush zone" provided by the forward cargo storage holds. All was designed to protect the all-important passenger cabins amidships.

In short, it was a typical conservative, civilian ship, designed for safety above all else.

Which is why it looked so out of place this close to Jeraddo, a world where even establishing a standard orbit risked the survival of a ship.

Inside the cruiser, though, Sisko had a better sense of the vessel's survivability. Though it looked Sagittarian on the outside, it was pure Cardassian within.

"A *Chimera*-class vessel" Terrell had called it. She and Sisko both knew that in times of war, a neutral vessel could be a much safer means of transportation. Especially when it was liberally outfitted with hidden weapons and capable of outrunning almost any other ship in the sector.

"You actually plan to beam down there?" Sisko asked as he watched a false-color image of the moon's hidden surface scroll across the main bridge viewer of Terrell's cruiser. Though the thick clouds of the moon prevented any direct visual observation of its surface, the cruiser's sensors had no difficulty picking up ground detail.

"We've found the abandoned village," Terrell said. She was in the command chair—an imposing black structure that had the silhouette of a looming bat. Atrig was her navigator, seated at a forward console. Sisko didn't know where Dr. Betan was. "And from the details on that map, we can narrow down the Orb's location to perhaps a square kilometer of surface area, and search."

"I'm curious," Sisko said.

"I should hope so," Terrell replied.

"How did you manage to misplace an Orb on the station and have it turn up on this moon?"

Terrell stood up from her chair. Typical of Cardassian design, the chair was mounted on a meter-high platform so that the commander would always be above the crew. "It's not the same Orb, Captain. It's the second. When I find it, then I can return to Terok Nor and find the first."

"And then what?"

"And then, with Vash's Orb I will have all three, and I will not need equipment to open a wormhole. According to the ancient texts we've deciphered, I merely have to bring the three Orbs together . . . anywhere I choose." She stepped down from her command platform and walked forward to Atrig's navigation console to check the readings on his display. "We're coming up on the village now."

On the viewer, Sisko detected a grouping of primitive, blocky structures slide into view, arranged just as he recalled seeing on Dal Nortron's map. Though the crisp layout of the village seemed to be obscured, somehow.

"Is that debris?" he asked.

Terrell made more adjustments on the console and the sensor image of the village expanded on the screen and became more detailed.

"Some of the buildings appear to have collapsed," Terrell observed. "But with the winds and the gravity fluctuations, that's to be expected."

A door slipped open, and Dr. Betan walked slowly onto the bridge. He was wearing a bulky Cardassian environmental suit, shiny green-black in color, made up of curved segments to look even more like a beetle's carapace than any other Cardassian uniform Sisko had seen.

In his gloved hands, Dr. Betan carried the red hourglass-shaped crystal which Vash had brought to DS9. Sisko was startled to see that it wasn't as impenetrably dark as it had first appeared to be.

"See that?" Terrell said. "That glow inside?" She looked at Sisko. "It means it's getting closer to its missing mate."

"You seem to have everything under control," Sisko said.

"Not quite," Terrell said curtly. "You still have to answer my questions."

Sisko had known that was coming. "You won't like the answers."

"I think I will. Because if you're thinking of disappointing me, remember that Terok Nor is still running under manual-control conditions, and it will be several hours before anyone goes looking for your missing staff and your son. They are right where I left them—which makes them easy for me to find."

"All right. You want to know how to negotiate with the wormhole aliens," Sisko said.

Terrell nodded. "I know the science of wormholes. But the aliens are an X-factor. You've dealt with them and returned. My people never did. What's your secret?"

Dr. Betan pressed a small control on a side bulkhead and a panel beside a small transporter platform slid open to reveal four environmental suits in storage racks. Terrell gestured to them. "We don't have much time."

Sisko went to the suit Dr. Betan pointed out. It seemed to be the right size.

"There is no secret," he said. "The Prophets—the *aliens*—are in complete control the entire time. They initiate contact. They control the length of contact. And then they terminate contact." He stepped into the trouser section of the suit, and then watched as the imbedded pressure rings expanded to extend the legs to the proper length.

Terrell's voice was tense. "Then under what conditions could you see them refusing to let a traveler leave their wormhole?"

Sisko held up his arms so Dr. Betan could slide the chest piece over his head.

"Terrell, you told me I was too caught up in thinking about the Orbs. What if you're too caught up in thinking about the wormhole as simply another dimension?"

Terrell was more used to the suits than was Sisko. She was already dressed, needing only to attach her helmet. "Explain."

"The Bajorans believe their wormhole, the Blue Wormhole, is the home of their gods. In a sense, it's their heaven. But if you've truly discovered a second wormhole . . ."

"Don't even suggest it," Terrell threatened. "Heaven and hell, as you call them—supernatural realms of eternal reward and eternal punishment—are not worthy of scientific discussion or consideration." She strode over to Sisko and lifted a helmet from the rack behind him. "Life is everywhere in our universe, Captain. In the most unlikely ecological niche, on almost every world, we find something that qualifies as living matter. Why can't you accept that different dimensional realms also harbor life, without having to invoke superstition?"

"Just a suggestion," Sisko said. "The Prophets or aliens or whatever you'd like to call them can be unnerving, I'll admit. And I don't usually have any idea what it is they want when they contact me. But they've never kept me in their realm against my will. Why they, or beings like them, didn't allow your people to return, I can't say."

"Keep thinking," Terrell said tersely as she snapped Sisko's helmet closed and sealed it. The helmet was a hemisphere of something transparent that curved from a shell-like shoulder unit. At once, all sound was muffled except for the rasp of Terrell and Dr. Betan breathing over the suit's comm link, and Terrell's voice. "I'm sure you'll come up with something more useful in the next hour."

"Why an hour?"

"Because that's just about how long these suits will stand up to the corrosive atmosphere down there." She stepped up on the transporter platform at the side of the bridge. Sisko saw Dr. Betan do the same and followed.

Here we go, Sisko thought.

"Atrig," Terrell said tensely. "Energize."

And then Sisko dissolved into light, and reformed in absolute darkness.

CHAPTER 24

QUARK DIDN'T KNOW what made him feel worse. The fact that
Captain Sisko had been kidnapped by crazed Cardassians who might
soon have the means to conquer the galaxy, or the fact that his holosuites were wired into the station's main computers and apparently
had far more computational capability than he had ever dreamed of,
let alone charged for, in the past ten years.

He lightly moved his finger toward the open area at the front of
his holding cell and marveled again at the sudden shock of the simulated security forcefield. "Amazing," he said.

"Oh, be quiet," Odo grumbled.

The changeling was sitting on the edge of the bunk at the back of
the cell, holding his head.

"Well, I see you're back to being your old self," Quark said.

"Quark, I'm warning you . . ."

"No need. No need. In fact, I'm going to be especially nice to
you while we're in here."

Quark loved the way Odo looked up at him then. The constable
was so easy to bait.

"And why would that be?" Odo asked, sounding as if he already
regretted saying anything at all.

"Because we're finally in a position where everyone will have to listen to me, and you can't walk out, or threaten to haul me off to your office."

"You're babbling, Quark."

Quark went back to the cell opening and called out to the others. "Excuse me! Can I have everyone's attention, please?"

The cell across from Quark's held Bashir, Kira, and Jadzia. Jake and Nog were in the cell to the right. They all stepped forward to the limits of their own security forcefields to look at Quark.

"We're listening," Bashir said. The doctor sounded exhausted. Or frustrated. Or hungry. With *hew-mons,* Quark knew, it was difficult to tell.

"Well, I just wanted to remind everyone what Odo said about what happened to him on the Day of Withdrawal."

Quark heard Odo get to his feet and come up behind him.

"Let it go, Quark. I got stunned by a looter. I missed the whole day."

But Quark shook his finger at his nemesis. "Uh, uh, uh. Not so fast. When Dr. Bashir asked if you were sure, you launched into a most convincing story about how one of the things you missed was Gul Dukat scurrying off like a vole deserting a ship seized by bailiffs."

Odo glared at him, but said nothing. Quark knew it was because there was nothing he *could* say. Not now.

Quark finished the conversation by calling out to the others. "But even I remember when Gul Dukat left, because it was early in the day, *before* the fighting broke out. So if Odo remembers coming down to the Promenade to break up a fight, then he *has* to remember Dukat's leaving, so one way or another, he's hiding something— which means he's *lying* to us!"

"Happy now?" Odo asked.

"I'll be happy when you admit you can't remember what happened to you on the Day of Withdrawal."

"Then you'll never be happy again," Odo said, and walked back to the bunk and sat down with a grunt.

"Quark!" Jadzia called out to him. "This might not be the time to revisit the past. We should try and find a way to shut down this simulation."

Quark put his hands on his hips, thoroughly miffed. "Oh, I get it.

I get caught in a small white lie like, I thought you *wanted* me to keep the change, or, I logged the payment into your account yesterday—it must be the computer, and what happens? Everyone points their fingers at me like . . . like suddenly my pants are on fire. Typical Ferengi, you say. Isn't that just like Quark, you say.

"But catch Odo, our constable, our shining exemplar of truth, justice, and the Federation way, in a lie of supernova proportions, and what do you say?" Quark raised his voice in a not very convincing parody of Jadzia. "This isn't the time to revisit the past." He turned his back on everyone. "Well, I'm sick of it."

His ears tingled as he heard Jadzia sigh. Then she called out, "Anyway, Quark, you must have some kind of override on your holosuites. Can't you try shutting it down?"

Quark raised his hands to the simulated ceiling. "Don't you people get it? This isn't one of my holoprograms. *My* prisons have chains on the wall, metal rings on the floor, a complete selection of whips and restraints for every taste, and your choice of beverage. I have no idea where this came from."

"Could you at least *try?*" Jadzia asked.

Quark huffed with impatience. "Computer, end program. There, are you happy?"

"Try an override, please."

"Computer, this is Quark. I need an emergency shutdown in holosuite A."

"Please state your password," the computer voice replied.

Quark froze. How could he reveal his password to . . . *everyone?*

Odo seemed to be able to read his mind. "Quark, you can change your password later. We need to get out now."

Quark cleared his throat. "Computer . . . this is Quark. Password . . . and I don't want to hear any snickering," he suddenly warned his audience. "Password . . . Big Lobes."

Quark rolled his eyes as Nog covered his mouth and seemed to go into either a gagging or a coughing fit, Quark really didn't care to think which.

"Big Lobes authenticated," the computer confirmed. "Emergency shutdown procedure is not available."

"What?! Why not?" Quark demanded.

"Priority override is in effect during state of emergency. This simulation will run for an additional two hours, thirty-three minutes, or until terminated by Prefect Terrell."

Quark shrugged, totally defeated. His lot in life. "Well, that's that. The station's computer is controlling mine."

"But it can't be in *complete* control," Nog said with sudden inspiration. "For this simulation to exist, the station's computer *has* to be using subroutines from your computer."

"So?" Quark said.

"So," Nog answered as he stepped to the back of the holding cell he shared with Jake, "maybe one of those subroutines is the safety override, which means these forcefields might be just for show."

Quark wasn't impressed with his nephew's idea. "And how do you expect to find out if—"

"Nog!" The shout came from Jake as the young Ferengi charged forward to test his theory and—

—hit a full-power forcefield that threw him back against the far wall of the cell with twice the force with which he had launched himself.

Quark saw his nephew slide unconscious to the deck with a soft moan as his headskirt slid up the back of his head until it flopped forward to cover his face like a baby's sleeping bonnet.

Quark sighed. "That's Starfleet initiative for you."

He looked out past the Security Office to the doors to the Promenade. As gloomy as it was out there, in the abnormal blue Cardassian lighting Quark remembered so well and hated so much from the old days on the station, he could see simulated people walking back and forth. Bajoran slave workers and Cardassian soldiers, mostly. It was a very realistic effect, but it was still only window dressing. "If this simulation is so accurate, I wish we could get one of those pedestrians out there to come in," Quark sighed.

Odo snorted. "If it's an accurate simulation from the Occupation, no one will. This wasn't the favorite place on the station for Bajorans *or* Cardassians."

"Or Ferengi," Quark said.

And then the main doors slid open and someone entered.

"Anyone home?" a familiar voice shouted.

Quark stared in amazement, along with everyone else in the

holding cells, as a human in a tuxedo four hundred years out of style strolled into the cell area, smiling with blinding white teeth.

"Vic!" Quark burbled.

"Hey, gang," the holographic mid-twentieth-century lounge singer said as he gazed around the room. "Looks like you cats could use a cake with a file baked in it."

"I don't know what you're talking about, but I don't care," Quark said. "Ya gotta get us outta here!"

"I know, I know," Vic said calmly. "You're innocent, right?"

"We're more than innocent," Odo said. "We've been put here by the real criminals who are now running loose."

"Oh, I believe it, Constable. A straight arrow like you'd never end up in a joint like this." Vic looked over to see Kira and smiled at her. "Unless it was on accounta some dame. How ya doin', sweetheart? Stretch still treating you right?"

"Vic," Kira said, "how can you be here?"

Vic shrugged. "Ya got me, dollface. There I am, up on stage at my joint, singing my heart out for the blue-rinse set, next thing I know the lights start flickering and the power goes out. Well, management's not too upset, 'cause they've got lots of battery lights to keep the gaming tables going, but me, I got no mike. And the ice is starting to melt."

"Vic," Odo said, "I'm sure this is all fascinating, but could you go back to the center office, and open the little drawer to the left of the chair, right under the display screen."

"Is that going to help get the power back on?"

It was suddenly all too much for Quark. "How can you care about power when your program wasn't even running? When we came up here, all the holosuites were off except for this one."

"Quark, bubeleh, I keep hearing you people say the holosuite's off, how can I keep hanging around? But I gotta tell ya, Vic's is the original we-never-close baby. Now how that works, I don't have clue one. I'm just a hologram remember, and it sounds like you have issues you need to take up with the big guy upstairs."

"The big guy upstairs?" Quark asked.

"Felix," Vic explained. "My programmer."

"Vic," Odo pleaded. "The drawer."

"You got it, pallie. What exactly am I looking for?"

"An optolithic data rod," Odo said.

Vic held up his hands. "Whoa, slow down, Stretch. I'm strictly a twentieth-century hologram."

"It's going to look like a pencil," Jadzia suddenly said. "A fat, transparent, green pencil. Like it's made out of . . . oh, what was it . . . *Plexiglas!*"

"That new space-age plastic. Sure, I'm with ya." Vic stretched out his arms to make his white cuffs show against his black jacket. "Little drawer, ya said? On the left?"

"If you would be so kind," Odo said.

"Always willing to do a favor for the customers."

Vic walked out of the holding-cell area. Quark heard him whistle one of his twentieth-century songs. Something about "that old black magic . . ."

"How can this be possible?" Kira asked wonderingly.

"Vic's stepped into other holographic simulations before," Bashir explained. "If his program's being affected by all the computer disruption that's going on, it seems to make sense that he might go looking for a cause."

"The important thing is," Jadiza added, "that however he got here, he's going to get us out."

"Don't be too sure about that," Vic said. He was standing back in the doorway, holding the optolithic crystal in his hand. "I mean, this is something cats like me can only dream of." He paused, smiled at everyone until Quark almost screamed with frustration to have him get to the point. "A real captive audience," Vic said. "Badda bing!"

"Put the fat green pencil in the slot by the door frame," Odo said.

"*Captive* audience?" Vic asked. "Anybody? I know you're out there. I can hear ya breathing."

"Vic," Jadzia said. "If we don't get out of here as quickly as possible, there's a chance that the station's entire power grid could fail and—"

"I get the picture, Spots. The Big Lights Out." Vic went to the security operations control panel beside the door, held up the data rod. "Here?"

"That's it," Odo said. "Slide it in, then punch in this number."

Vic slid the rod into the memory reader, then scratched his head as he stared at the Cardassian control pad. "Punch it in where?"

Jadzia came to the rescue again. "What's the number, Odo?"

"Fifty-five, twenty-two, eight. Alpha," Odo said.

Quark repeated it to himself, then noticed Odo frowning at him.

"It's an *old* passcode. Big Lobes."

Then Jadzia carefully described the Cardassian symbols Vic would have to touch to input those numbers. "It's all Greek to me, doll," Vic said as he entered the final Alpha designator.

But at once the security forcefields flickered and Jadzia and Kira and Bashir jumped out of their cells to join Vic, while Jake carefully carried the still-unconscious Nog. Quark hung back to let Odo walk through their cell opening first. Once he knew it was safe, he quickly followed. By then Odo had left the others and hurried into the center office.

Vic rubbed his hands together. "So, whaddaya say you all come back to my place—drinks are on the house."

"We can't just yet," Jadzia said. "We still have to shut down this simulation."

Vic looked alarmed. "Hold your horses. You can't shut anything down while I'm in here."

"Can't?" Jadzia asked. "Or shouldn't?"

"Ya got me, Spots. I just said the first thing Felix put in my head. You people going to be okay, now?"

Odo appeared in the doorway holding a Cardassian phaser. "We will be soon."

"What kinda crazy pea-shooter is that?" Vic asked.

Odo adjusted the power setting on the weapon. "A Cardassian Model III phase-disruption weapon."

"Well, I'm glad you cleared that up," Vic said.

"Stand back, everyone," Odo said, then aimed the weapon at the far wall.

"What good is a simulated weapon going to do?" Kira asked.

"You don't spend enough time in the holosuites," Odo said. "Small props like these are usually replicated, not simulated. This should be a fully operational phaser, and as Nog was good enough to demonstrate, all safety protocols are switched off."

Quark groaned. "There goes my insurance. . . ."

"You might want to avert your eyes," Odo warned. Then he fired.

At first, it appeared as if the lance of energy shot out eight meters to hit a wall. But then, that half of the holding cell area began to waver, and finally winked out, as it now appeared that the phaser beam had hit a wall only half that distance away.

Quark grimaced as three clusters of green holoemitters exploded and the entire simulation of the security office disappeared.

"Someone's going to pay for that," he complained.

"Oh, be quiet, Quark."

Quark couldn't be sure who had said that, because almost everyone did. Then Quark saw Vic. It was not a pleasant sight.

The hologram was wavering, sparking with holographic scan lines, and going transparent.

"Y'know, gang, all of a sudden, I'm not feeling so hot."

Bashir went to Vic as if his medical skills might have some use for a hologram. "Maybe you should head back to the club, Vic."

"You're not just whistlin' Dixie."

"Uh," Bashir said, "is that a Yes?"

Vic nodded. "And I thought Rocket to the Moon at Disneyland was an E-ticket. . . ."

Quark looked at Odo who looked at Jake who looked at Kira who looked at Jadzia who looked at Bashir . . . but it was unanimous. Nobody knew what Vic was talking about.

Vic shuffled toward a wall of functional holoemitters and Quark was surprised to see a gray metal door materialize, with a red sign reading EXIT just above it. "See ya in the funny papers," Vic said, then opened the door and stepped through it. At once, his holographic body stopped shifting and he stood upright. From beyond him, Quark could hear laughter, the clinking of coins, and the sound of a twentieth-century band.

Vic spun around and pointed a finger at Quark. "Next time, pallie, pay the man the light bill." Then he gave them all a casual salute, the door swung shut, and he was gone.

"I have *got* to talk to Felix," Bashir said.

"That can wait," Jadzia told him.

It was Jake who explained why to Quark. "Now we rescue my dad."

CHAPTER 25

SISKO WAS IN HELL. It was the only way to describe what Jeraddo had become.

The ground was nothing more than stone and shifting ribbons of storm-driven dirt. The air was like something alive, one moment so thick that all Sisko could see was his own reflection in the curve of his helmet, then thin enough that the lights mounted on his shoulders stabbed ahead a few meters. He cringed as roiling crimson swirls and eddies of corrosive gas appeared like entrails, twisting all around him.

Sweat poured from Sisko's face and dripped from his beard. He tried to tell himself that the environmental suit had been set for Cardassian temperatures, but the temperature indicator on the narrow status display board at the bottom of his helmet showed an outside temperature of more than 800 degrees, with wild swings of several hundred more degrees every few minutes. He utterly failed to convince himself that the suit's insulation was as robust as the type Starfleet used.

"Stop, Captain!" Terrell's harsh voice crackled at him through his helmet speakers. The same subspace distortions that caused Jeraddo's gravity to intensify and weaken, as if Sisko were on the deck of a madly pitching sailing ship, also interfered with the suit's communicator. In the twenty minutes they had already spent on the surface, Sisko had calculated that the communicators wouldn't work past ten meters, and even then he and the Cardassians had to shout to make themselves heard over the static. He doubted Terrell's tricorder could extend past that range, as well. And the only way they could be beamed back to Terrell's disguised ship was because of the high-power, tight-beam transporter beacons they each wore.

But even if he managed to run off and get out of range before Terrell could fire at him, what good would it do him? Right now, his suit had forty minutes' worth of life in it. If he pulled off his beacon so he couldn't be traced, he still wouldn't be able to beam back to Terrell's ship. In less than an hour he'd become another featureless mound of Jeraddo debris.

Terrell and Dr. Betan stepped up on either side of Sisko, their own shoulder lights blinding as they converged on him.

Terrell pointed to the left. "In that building," she said.

Dr. Betan held up the Red Orb and swung it slowly toward the ancient stone wall to which Terrell pointed. The pale red light within the Orb intensified slightly, then died down when Dr. Betan moved it away again.

Sisko trudged ahead. By now, he didn't need to be told that he must always lead the way. Terrell had made it clear that she was not willing to turn her back on him. The building, perhaps a craft hall or a farmers' market a millennium ago, was larger than most in the village. The wind-eroded outer wall was made of giant blocks of local stone fitted together only with exceptional skill, not mortar.

The doorway through the wall was still in perfect condition, and Sisko did not have to duck down as he stepped through it, though he half-bent at the waist to aim his shoulder lights on what lay before him.

As he had suspected, the ground was littered with stones and tiles from the collapsed roof. There might have been wooden beams involved in the building's construction, but anything organic had been eaten away by the corrosive atmosphere years ago.

"Watch your step!" he shouted to the two behind him. "The floor is covered with roofing tiles." Then he stepped aside to let Terrell and Betan enter.

Though billows of red cloud still roiled through the building, the windblown dust and debris seemed lessened by the shelter of the walls. Sisko noticed that his shoulder lights reached a bit farther, and the buffeting of the gale-force winds that had threatened to topple him from time to time was no longer in evidence.

Terrell and Dr. Betan were discussing something. They had a comm-link channel separate from the one Terrell used with Sisko.

The glow of the Red Orb was much stronger now.

Sisko watched as Terrell used a tricorder, aiming it at the ground and showing the results to Dr. Betan.

"There's a chamber under this floor," she informed Sisko. "Dr. Betan's going to find a way down." Then Sisko and Terrell stood and waited while Dr. Betan walked carefully back and forth across the rubble-strewn floor, using the Red Orb as if it were some primitive dowsing tool. Sisko appreciated the chance to rest.

He looked over at the tall Cardassian, studying her through the flare of light reflecting from her helmet. Her dark eyes were wide. She was chewing on her bottom lip. But he didn't know if the gesture betrayed anticipation or nervousness. He wasn't at all sure that he could even come close to what was going through her mind, no matter how much she thought that he and she were alike.

"You don't need me down here," he shouted with some difficulty. His throat was becoming more and more raw. But he wanted to learn if she had any intention of allowing him back to her ship. If she didn't, then that might make it easier to . . . make sure no one else made it back, either.

"I will," Terrell shouted back. "Dr. Betan will keep Vash's Orb, but I need you to carry the second."

"Why?"

"Because you've survived contact with Orbs before. You of all people must understand the danger these artifacts represent."

"The Orbs of the Prophets have never put me in danger," Sisko shouted. The exertion provoked a brief coughing jag. For a moment, he wondered if his suit might already be leaking.

Terrell peered at Sisko through her helmet. Its transparent surface was already clouded from the corrosive atmosphere. "The Red Orb claimed seven of my researchers. I won't risk touching them."

"What about Dr. Betan?"

"He handled the first Orb years ago on Terok Nor. After that, he became addicted to neural depressants. By taking them, he can't hear the voices. But it has left him with . . . certain other deficiencies. His temper, among them."

"Have any of you thought that perhaps these Orbs aren't shaping up to be the best transportation system?" Sisko asked. "Especially if they're driving the people who use them insane or to drugs."

"There're ways around the Orb's psychic effects," Terrell said enigmatically. "That's why I had my soldiers save Quark from hanging on the Day of Withdrawal. That Ferengi owes me his life."

Sisko didn't understand. Terrell gave him the explanation.

"Because he's a Ferengi. They're resistant to most forms of telepathy. Even Betazoids can't get past those four brain lobes. Too complex? Too simple? Who knows? Who cares? But I needed to get my Orb out of my lab before the station self-destructed. So I told Atrig to bring me one of the Ferengi from the Promenade, and he brought me Quark—and Odo."

Quark and Odo on the Day of Withdrawal, Sisko thought. He saw another pattern forming.

"What about Garak?" he asked.

"Very good, Captain. Garak came on his own. He and I never really got along but Gul Dukat and he were involved in something . . . it's not important." Terrell frowned, as if remembering something unpleasant. "But he and Odo and Quark did enter my lab that day—along with the two soldiers whose bodies you found fused to the hull. I always wondered what happened to them." She fell silent, as if lost in thought.

Sisko touched her arm. "What happened to Quark and Odo and Garak?"

Terrell roused herself, checking ahead for Dr. Betan, who was still wandering back and forth with the Orb, then turned again to Sisko. "Twenty-two minutes before the self-destruct went off, the three of them staggered out of my lab. The precursor effect had already faded, and when I looked inside, the Red Orb was gone. At first, I was certain Quark had stolen it and hidden it somewhere. But then, why would he have come back to me? There wasn't any time for an investigation so I stunned them again and left the station. I thought everything would be lost when it autodestructed."

"But it didn't."

Even through her clouded helmet, Sisko could see Terrell's terrifying smile as she bared her teeth at him. "And if you knew how much time the Obsidian Order spent investigating why the autodestruct system failed . . . the record number of executions . . . . Even for the Order."

"Starfleet could never understand why you left the station behind."

"Well, now you know," Terrell rasped. "We never intended to."

Then Terrell turned sharply away from him, and Sisko realized she must have received a transmission from Dr. Betan, who was about fifteen meters ahead of them, pointing down at the ground and—

Sisko blinked as he saw Dr. Betan fire a phaser blast into the ground. Then he heard Terrell again.

"He's found a way down. The Orb's not far."

Terrell began trudging toward Dr. Betan. Sisko walked beside her. He checked his suit display. Thirty-two minutes of life remaining. If the Cardassian suit design could be trusted.

Halfway to Dr. Betan, Sisko caught sight of the liquid wave of rock that rose up behind the Cardassian, then swept forward, heading directly for him.

Instinctively he cried out, "GRAVITY WAVE!" then spun around to see Terrell beside him, screaming silently in her helmet to warn her associate.

Sisko dropped to his knees and wrapped both arms tight across his helmet. A moment later he felt as if he were falling, as the local gravity gradient dropped by at least ninety percent and then shot up by an almost instant tripling.

He was driven into the rubble so hard he felt stones push up into his flesh through all the insulating layers of his suit. Sisko lay unmoving on his back, instinctively holding his breath as he listened for the telltale hiss of atmosphere that would mean his death. But finally, all he heard was Terrell's harsh voice telling him to get up and hurry.

Apparently, Dr. Betan had also survived the sudden gravitational anomaly, but the hole the Cardassian had blasted into the stone floor of the building was now half-filled with rubble. Under one arm, Dr. Betan still held the Red Orb Vash had brought to the station. It glowed steadily now. The red light within seeming almost to pulsate.

"Down there," Terrell ordered as she aimed her shoulder lights into the pit Dr. Batan had created.

Sisko moved cautiously to the side of the opening, then peered down, awkward in his stiff suit. There was another stone floor about four meters below. Dr. Betan had already thrown a rope down to assist Sisko's descent. The other end was attached to an anchor loop on his belt, and Terrell stood beside him, coiling the rest of the rope in her gloved hands.

"Dr. Betan says that according to the way the Orb is glowing, the other Orb is no more than five meters in that direction." She pointed, and Sisko found a reference mark on the floor below. He took the rope in his clumsy Cardassian gloves and slowly edged himself off the side and into the hole.

Sisko dropped the first two meters at an alarmingly rapid rate before Terrell and Dr. Betan steadied him. A few seconds later, he was standing on the floor and looking around at—

Sisko gasped.

Across from him, in the direction in which the second Orb was supposed to be found, was a pristine wall carved with the largest Bajoran mural he had ever seen.

"What's wrong?" Terrell's voice crackled in his helmet.

"Nothing," Sisko shouted back. "If the Orb's down here, it might be hidden in a wall. I'll check it out."

Then he walked slowly over to the mural and lightly traced its exquisite details with his gloved fingers. He recognized some of the older word-forms that ran along the top and bottom of the mural and felt an odd combination of relief and disappointment when he could not find any reference to "the Sisko." But still, whatever events were depicted in the carving, they involved the Bajoran wormhole and the Prophets. Those word-forms and symbols he was able to read easily.

"Twenty-five minutes," Terrell's voice announced.

Sisko couldn't let this opportunity go to waste. He fumbled with the Cardassian tricorder built into his suit and programmed it for a full spectral scan of the mural. At the same time, he stepped back to see if he could find any place that an Orb might be . . .

There. In the mural. The distinctive Bajoran spiral that signified the opening of the Celestial Temple. Though this spiral curved the opposite way from most others Sisko had seen.

"I think I might have found something," Sisko called out. "Just a minute."

He moved closer to the stone block in which the spiral was carved. It didn't fit tightly to the other stones in the wall. He pressed his body against it.

The stone block swung up, little more than a slender slab of rock.

And behind it, in a hollow chamber no larger than an Orb Ark, a second Red Orb glowed brightly, throwing off small flares of red light, almost like the Blue Orbs Sisko had seen in the past.

"I've found it," Sisko reported to Terrell.

Her only answer was, "Nineteen minutes."

Carefully, Sisko removed the Orb from its protective shelter. As he did so, he felt no ill effects. Heard no voices. Sensed no sudden disorientation, the way he usually did at the start of an Orb experience. Whatever this thing was, it was not an Orb of the Prophets. At least, there was nothing in its behavior to suggest it was one.

Sisko carried the Orb back to the point at which he was below the opening Dr. Betan had made. He paused, half-expecting to hear Terrell tell him to tie the Orb to the rope for them pull it up, to be left here to spend the rest of his life—all eighteen minutes of it—to contemplate their betrayal.

Instead, Terrell told him to tie the rope to his belt, so they could pull both him and the Orb up.

Sisko did, keeping a tight grip on the Orb.

By the time he had emerged from the hole in the floor, both Orbs were blazing brightly enough that they couldn't be looked at directly. The brilliance of their internal light also made it clear how badly his own helmet had been scarred and etched by Jeraddo's atmosphere.

Terrell's helmet glowed as if lit from within by flames. Sisko couldn't see her face. "Excellent," he heard her say before she called out for Atrig. "Lock onto our beacons and energize."

In that split second, as he waited for the transporter effect, Sisko suddenly knew that Terrell couldn't be allowed to control the Red Orbs.

Almost without thought, he swung the Orb he had retrieved directly at Dr. Betan's helmet.

As the Cardassian doctor stumbled backward, horrified, dropping Vash's Orb to press his gloves to the rapidly growing network of cracks that spread across his corroded helmet, Sisko yanked his own transporter beacon off and threw it away.

Terrell was still fumbling for her phaser as she began to dissolve in the transporter beam.

Dr. Betan's helmet suddenly exploded like fine crystal an instant before he was beamed away as well. And then, a moment later, Sisko saw the pale glimmer of his own discarded transporter beacon as it also disappeared.

Sisko didn't stop to ask himself what he thought he had done. Instead, with only fifteen minutes of life remaining, he concentrated only on what he still had to do.

He tucked Vash's Orb under one arm, secured the second Orb under his other arm, then began to run.

He knew he had only fifteen minutes in which to hide the Red Orbs so they could never be found again. Not by Terrell, not by anyone.

Within seconds, Sisko was through a breach in the wall and onto a narrow path between two collapsed buildings. The Orbs, so close together now, were throwing off almost the same amount of light as his shoulder lights. But visibility was still less than a handful of meters. By now, he knew, with the subspace distortion Terrell's ship would never be able to scan for him.

In fact, Sisko realized, if he were Terrell, he wouldn't come chasing after him at once. Instead, he'd wait the fifteen minutes for his target to die and use the time to put on a new environmental suit, knowing that when his target's suit finally succumbed to the atmosphere, the Orbs would not be going anywhere.

Reasoning that he would not be pursued at once, Sisko paused to get his bearings, recalling that there was another large building to his left. One with a single standing wall. If he could place the two Orbs near that wall and somehow topple the wall onto them, with any luck he'd shatter one or both Orbs, or at least make certain they were buried under tonnes of rubble.

Terrell's cruiser couldn't remain in orbit of Jeraddo for too long. All Sisko had to do was introduce a delay.

This last mission would become his life's work. All twelve minutes of it.

Sisko hurried through the ground-level twisting, crimson clouds, the red of the atmosphere swirling around him merging with the red nimbus of the glowing Orbs he carried.

Finally, he located the wall, and made out the shape of a relatively flat paving stone on which he could place the Orbs. All that he needed now was some way to dislodge the wall, get it started falling in the right direction.

He decided to check out the far side. He couldn't afford to waste the time it would take to make his way around it. So he risked tearing his suit as he half-clambered over a pile of rubble at its side and—

—wedged his boot.

Sisko groaned.

He was trapped two meters above ground level, visible from any direction, with no place to hide the Orbs.

To die for a cause was something every member of Starfleet had to prepare for. It was part of their oath.

But to die for nothing?

Sisko trembled with frustration as he tugged at his boot. He picked up another rock and bashed the offending boot with it. But all he managed to do was wedge it in deeper.

"Warning," his suit's computer suddenly announced. "Loss of atmospheric integrity in three minutes."

"No!" Sisko roared. "You're wrong. I have ten minutes at least!"

But there was no arguing with his internal displays. The insulation field was within five minutes of failing. His backup air supply was completely exhausted, its tanks probably already dissolved by the acid air.

He wondered how far he could get if he took off his boot and decompressed. Maybe he could last thirty seconds. But would he even be able to move with his exposed foot contacting 800-degree rocks?

"No," Sisko whispered. And then there was nothing for him to do but to lift up the rock in his hand and smash it against the Red Orbs of Jalbador.

Again and again he brought the rock down.

His suit informed him that only two minutes remained before loss of atmospheric integrity.

Again he smashed the Orbs.

But the simple matter of normal space-time was no match for the solidified energy vortices of a nonlinear realm.

The Orbs withstood his attack. Untouched.

"One minute . . ." his suit announced.

Sisko absolutely refused to give up without achieving his last mission. He lifted one Orb over his head and with all his strength brought it down on the other Orb.

The light they both shed did not change in the least.

Sisko girded himself to try again. *Maybe I didn't do it hard enough,* he told himself. *Maybe it will work the next time.*

Again he lifted the Orb above his head, swung it down.

Again, nothing.

"Thirty seconds . . ."

The next time . . . it has to work the next time . . .

Once more he lifted. He swung. He lifted. He swung.

"Five seconds . . ."

With a cry of hope, rage, determination, he lifted that Red Orb as high as he could possibly stretch and—

—he couldn't swing it down.

His arms were locked in position. Something was holding them.

He twisted around in the bulky Cardassian suit to see a white shape glowing in the brilliance of his shoulder lights.

A luminous being.

Sisko gazed up at that form, at that being, and in that moment, without knowing what he saw or how it could be that he saw anything on this hellish world on which he was destined to die within an instant, he knew the Orbs were safe.

The luminous being moved closer to him, leaned down, details of its existence impossible to see through the clouded corroded surface of his helmet.

The luminous being put its arm around Sisko's shoulders, tapped itself once, then all was still.

And an endless eternity later, an endless moment later, a new light played over him as he stood locked in the embrace of the luminous being, in the depths of this inferno.

In the light of a transporter beam, Sisko could finally see through his helmet and the helmet of the angel who had come to save him.

Everything would be all right now.

It was Jake.

CHAPTER 26

"EMISSARY," KIRA SAID, "are you absolutely sure this is what you want to do?"

Sisko stood on the Promenade, outside the entrance to the Bajoran Temple. In each hand he carried a simple cloth bag. And in each bag was a Red Orb of Jalbador.

Less than twenty-six hours after his dramatic rescue on Jeraddo, Deep Space 9 was nearly back to normal, if not yet fully recovered. There was still a slight slant to the deck, but O'Brien had been released from the Infirmary and was now leading the gravity-repair teams himself.

While most automated computer systems were still off-line, Jadzia, with an unexpected assist from Garak, had finally located the long-hidden Cardassian override programs Terrell had activated, and was replacing all the individual isolinear rods on which they had been encoded. Nog was fully recovered from his run-in with the holographic forcefield and was in Ops with Jadiza and Garak, helping them with their restoration efforts.

Of Terrell's fate no one knew. There was no record of a Sagittarian cruiser breaking orbit of Jeraddo. The Bajoran Lunar Power Commission had searched its records and had found sensor traces of the ship's arrival. But preliminary evidence seemed to indicate a gravity disturbance might have pulled it into a deadly descent.

Sisko had told Quark, Odo, and Garak what Terrell had told him about what had happened to them on the Day of Withdrawal. Garak and Odo flatly refused to believe her account. But Quark had started talking to Jake about collaborating on a novel based on the incident—*Marauder Mo and the Treasure of Jalbador* Quark wanted to call it. Jake had already warned Quark there might be some copyright problems with his main character.

The *Defiant* was safely in dock again, after fielding the massive search party that had led to his discovery at the very last moment. Sisko had since learned that more than forty Starfleet personnel had taken part in the intensive search of the abandoned village.

Moreover, Sisko reflected thankfully, in the time since the *Defiant*'s return, Commander Arla Rees hadn't engaged him in a single discussion about Bajoran religion. Nor had she taken him up on his dinner invitation to meet Kasidy Yates. And Prylar Obanak and his followers appeared to have disappeared just as thoroughly as Terrell had managed to vanish over the clouds of Jeraddo. Though no doubt the group of monks had gone back to ground on Bajor.

"I'm sure," Sisko now said to Kira, satisfied that he was doing the right thing. "It's time to end it."

"We still don't know who killed Dal Nortron."

"Or who hid the Orb on Jeraddo," Sisko agreed. He lifted the bags. "But with these in safe hands, we'll have time to sort it all out at our leisure. The important thing is, the Orbs won't be in Cardassian hands."

"I'd still feel better if Vash were off the station."

"And Satr and Leen. And Base. But Odo's dealing with them. When it comes down to it, those four scoundrels are just petty thieves, led astray by what these Orbs represent."

Kira suddenly looked serious. "What *do* they represent?"

Sisko smiled at her. "Let's leave that to the experts." He entered the Temple, once again marveling at how each time he stepped through the doorway, it felt like the first time.

Kai Winn was there to greet him, and she bowed her head much too graciously. "Welcome, Emissary. It is always a pleasure to receive your summons and put aside all that I am doing to come and

see you here. I find the long ride from Bajor to be an especially pro-
ductive time for meditation and prayer."

Every once in a while, Sisko was sorely tempted to just tell the
Kai to stow it, but he let her play out her little game.

"And you, my child," Kai Winn said ingratiatingly to Kira, "how
fulfilled you must be to stand at the Emissary's side during these
important events, watching all that he does."

"Very fulfilled," Kira replied, not a trace of conviction within her
voice.

"And these are the artifacts?" the Kai asked, looking at the bags.

Sisko carefully pulled the Orbs from their wrappings and placed
them on a small table. The steady glow they had developed on
Jeraddo had now become a gentle pulsing, slowly dimming, slowly
brightening, three times each minute.

"Oh, my," the Kai said, "they are clever, aren't they? I could see
how many people might think they are somehow related to the Orbs
of the Prophets."

"I beg your pardon?" Sisko said. "These are the Red Orbs of
Jalbador."

The Kai smiled beatifically at Sisko. "Oh, Emissary, I know you
are new to our ancient traditions. Indeed, sometimes I wonder if anyone not born on Bajor could ever come to grasp the rich complexities
of our beliefs. But I am not here to discuss the wisdom of the
Prophets. Still, these . . . Red Orbs of Jalbador, they are but a legend
from a troubled time in our past." She shook her head. "And since
they do not exist, I do not believe that I, as a humble servant of the
people of Bajor, can accept them. It might lend an unwanted cre-
dence to their existence, and to other unfortunate legends best left in
children's storybooks."

Kira was outraged. "Kai Winn, you knew why we asked you up
here. These are the Orbs. Look at the way they're glowing."

"Child, though my ways are simple and I am certainly not as
worldly as some who look to me for guidance, I am no stranger to
the wonders of our age. I have seen many things glow, from phaser
beams to a child's glitterball. I am sure that as much as you and the
Emissary might want to believe in the tales of Jalbador, a few days of
study would reveal the secret of these objects to be nothing more
than some novel chemical reaction."

"Then perform that study," Sisko said. "In fact, I hope you do. Nothing could make me feel better than to know that these are some ingenious forgery."

"Emissary, again I think you overestimate my abilities. Which is not to say I am not flattered by your high esteem. But really, I believe it is here, on Deep Space 9, in a temple of secular science as it were, that the objects should be studied."

Sisko took a breath to calm himself. "Kai Winn, I am asking for your help."

The Kai was barely able to look at Sisko, as if she were embarrassed beyond words. "Emissary, you do me an honor for which I know I am not worthy. But in this matter, I truly have no help to give." She glanced disapprovingly at Kira. "May we speak in private?"

"Major Kira has my full confidence and trust."

The Kai's false smile became exceptionally brittle. "Very well. I only wish to point out that many people look up to the Emissary as a role model, a person who sets an example which can help them find their own paths to the Prophets. And, with all humility, Emissary, to express your belief in the legends of Jalbador, and in these so-called Orbs, well, that is not an example right-thinking Bajoran people would want their children to follow."

"I would think," Kira said angrily, "that the best role model for Bajoran children would be one who encouraged the search for truth."

The Kai blessed Kira with another blindingly insincere smile. "Why, yes, my child, that is what you'd think."

"Kai Winn," Sisko said before Kira could escalate the confrontation, "I'll make this simple. Take these Orbs to Bajor and subject them to examination, or I will find some other religious leader who will. And if these prove to have *any* connection to the Prophets, I promise I will make the Bajoran people know that you tried to stand in the Prophets' way."

That was the end of any pretence on the part of the Kai. She drew herself up, the perpetual smile gone. "Your acceptance of those objects as the Orbs of Jalbador marks your first step on the path to heresy. Do you understand? Do you think you can remain Emissary with half the population of Bajor believing you've become a religious fanatic?"

But Sisko knew this was an argument he couldn't lose. "You forget, Kai, I wasn't *elected* Emissary. For whatever reason, the Prophets *chose* me. And as their Emissary, I'm saying you don't have a choice. Take the Orbs."

The Kai's chin lifted in defiance. "Very well, if you are so certain these are the legendary Orbs, prove it. Find the third."

"It took sixty years to find these two. I have better things to do."

"But it cannot be difficult, Emissary. Look how they're pulsating with the fabled light of Jalbador."

Sisko wasn't sure what she meant and he could see that she knew it.

The Kai's cruel smile was predatory. "You mean you claim these are the Red Orbs—without knowing the whole legend?"

"Enlighten me," Sisko said.

The Kai clapped her hands together in delight, almost laughing at him. "Two Orbs *glow* when coming close to each other. But three Orbs *pulse*. It has been years since I read the legends, Emissary, but I would say that from the behavior of these . . . Orbs, the third one is quite nearby."

Sisko looked at Kira. "The one Terrell lost."

Kira couldn't resist adding, "You mean, the one Terrell thought Quark had stolen."

Sisko looked back at Kai Winn. "So if we find the third Orb, you will take them back to Bajor for study?"

The Kai's ingratiating smile returned in full force. "Oh, that will hardly be necessary, because you will be able to prove they are real right away. You see, when the three Red Orbs are brought together, the doors to Jalbador open freely, and then . . . well, it is all in the legends, Emissary."

"And then *what,* Kai?"

"Why then . . . the world comes to an end." This time the Kai really did laugh at him. "So you can see where a great deal of study would not be necessary. Either the objects are frauds, or they are real. And if they are real, Emissary, you will have the singular pleasure of knowing you have brought on the apocalypse." She sighed with pleasure. "Now you know why the stories of the Red Orbs are so popular with children and the unenlightened. They are quite . . . lurid, wouldn't you say?"

"I'm sure you'd know better than we would," Kira said. She gave

Sisko a conspiratorial wink. "What do you say? Shall we go on a wild Orb hunt?"

"You're not worried about the end of the world?" Sisko asked with a smile, accepting the Bajoran major's challenge.

Kira looked directly at the Kai. "Somehow, I don't think the Prophets would spend twenty thousand years trying to teach us about the universe and our place in it, and at the same time leave a big 'off' switch lying around."

Sisko picked up a Red Orb in each hand. "Kai Winn, we'll be back."

"Of course you will be, Emissary. Because there are no such things as the Red Orbs of Jalbador."

A few moments later, Sisko was standing on the slanted deck of the Promenade, slowly moving the Orbs back and forth.

"That direction," Kira said, pointing spinward toward Quark's. "The pulsing seemed to speed up a bit."

"Why, Major, I think you're enjoying this."

"What I'm going to really enjoy is helping the Kai carry three of these things onto her shuttle."

Then it was Sisko's turn to laugh as he walked up the center of the Promenade, swinging the Orbs to the left and to the right.

And he didn't need Kira to tell him that the pulsing increased the closer they got to Quark's.

Kira looked at Sisko. "Do you think he really did steal the third one?"

"Only one way to find out," Sisko said lightly, and he carried the Red Orbs of Jalbador into Quark's, where they proceeded to pulse faster than Sisko's suddenly racing heart.

CHAPTER 27

"OH, NO," QUARK SAID. "Not so fast! I don't want any of that in here!"

But he was too late, because Captain Sisko walked straight up to the bar counter and put both Red Orbs side by side on it.

"Captain, please, those things are more trouble than they could ever be worth. Things are—" Quark gave a strangled cry as he saw one of the most terrifying sights he had ever seen in his life!

Morn was running out of his establishment of business!

"Morn! Wait! Come . . . oh, for . . . now look what you did!" Quark threw his dish towel down on the bar in disgust. "My holo-suites are broken. My replicators are off-line. This stupid gravity imbalance is making people dizzy without the need to consume any drinks, no one wants to play dabo because the wheel won't spin straight, and now you chase off my best customer. If you've got a phaser on you, you might as well just shoot me now."

"Glad to see you, too, Quark," Kira said.

Sisko pointed to the Orbs. Quark had a hard time even looking at them because they were flashing like emergency strobe lights on Port Authority inspection shuttles. And that just unleashed too many bad memories.

"We have reason to believe the third missing Orb is in your bar and we want to take a look," Sisko said.

"I don't think so," Quark told him. "Unless we'd like to discuss compensation for what Odo did to my holosuite."

"Maybe we'd like to discuss an increase in rent instead?" Sisko suggested.

"For what?!"

"For what your inviting so many smugglers onboard is going to cost us." Sisko looked up at the ceiling. "Let's see now, we could begin with the bill for Odo's investigation. Then there's the replacement of the damaged hull plates."

"Oh, no—you can't blame that one on me."

"Oh, yes he can," Kira said.

"Oh, yes I will," Sisko added.

"This is blackmail!" Quark protested.

"Then we're in complete agreement," Sisko said. "You give us what we want—a few minutes to search the bar. And we'll give you what you want—peace and quiet."

"And no rent increase."

Sisko picked up the flashing Orbs again. "May I?"

"Oh, go ahead," Quark said. "And I hope if you find it, a Prophet jumps out and bites you."

Then Quark did the only thing he could do in the circumstances. He put an elbow on the bar, rested his head in his hand, and watched his customers leave in droves.

At any other time in his life, Quark might have found what Sisko and Kira were doing amusing. The *hew-mon* and the Bajoran were walking back and forth through the bar as if Odo had asked them to walk a white line.

But what wasn't amusing was that even Quark could see that every time Sisko passed through the center of the main level, the Orbs flashed faster and faster.

In less than ten minutes, all of his regular customers were gone. Instead, the bar was packed with Starfleet types. Dull, boring, root-beer-swilling slugs who wouldn't know a good time if M'Pella invited them up to her room for a nightcap. And they were all on duty, too.

Then, just to make matters worse—and lately, someone or something was always making matters worse—his idiot brother Rom chose this moment to walk in. With a construction team.

"Is it too much to ask what's going on?" Quark called out to anyone who might care to pay any attention to him.

Sisko came back to Quark. He pointed to the backlit glass mural on the wall facing the bar counter. "How long has that been there?"

"You mean the . . . uh, Admiral?" Quark asked, looking at the colorful artwork that was the centerpiece of his bar.

"Admiral?"

"Gul Dukat put it up. He said it was Admiral Alkene of the Tholian Assembly. Go figure."

Sisko studied the admittedly abstract portrait with a frown. "So it was here on the Day of Withdrawal?"

"You're not going to do something stupid, are you?" Quark asked nervously.

"I hope not," Sisko said.

Quark was getting the definite impression that the captain was deliberately tormenting him. Well, it took two to play that kind of game and, he wasn't one of them.

He closed the till, locked the order padds, then left the bar to join the Starfleet types at the base of the mural. The Orbs were now on the deck in front of it, flashing madly. Chief O'Brien and Rom were kneeling to either side, waving tricorders around like they knew what they were doing. Jadzia stood behind them, looking exceptionally lovely as always, Quark thought.

"Is there a problem?" he asked plaintively.

"I don't know," Sisko said. "According to the way these two Orbs are reacting, the third Orb is behind that mural. But according to the tricorders, it's just glass, plasma lights, and a cheap metal frame."

"It wasn't cheap, believe you me."

O'Brien got to his feet and joined Sisko and Quark. "If I didn't know better, I'd say there was a miniature sensor mask in there, just like the one Satr and Leen used in the water plant."

That was too much for Quark. "Why would anyone put a sensor mask inside a mural of a Tholian. . . ." He couldn't finish the statement. All he could think of was how much he hated the mural. How he had sworn he would tear it down the moment Gul Dukat left the station. And how, six years later, he still hadn't brought himself to do anything about it.

Almost as if he *couldn't* do anything about it.

"Something wrong, Quark?" Jadzia asked.

Quark shook his head. Wasn't there something Terrell had told him . . . not recently, but before . . . ?

"I'm so confused," Quark said. "I think I need to sit—"

A near-ultrasonic Ferengi scream pierced the bar.

Quark recognized it, and shoved aside Sisko and O'Brien to peer around the back of the mural to see—

Rom, on his knees, staring into a small open access panel at the back of the mural, his face bathed in a rapidly flashing red light.

"I . . . found it!" Rom squealed. "I . . . found the third Orb!"

Suddenly, Odo was behind Quark, arms folded, his attitude letting Quark know he was ready to make an arrest.

"Anything you'd like to tell me, Quark?"

"Odo, I didn't know it was there. I swear I didn't know!"

"According to Dr. Bashir, next you're going to try to sell me the Brooklyn Bridge."

But then Sisko was at Quark's side. "That's all right, Constable. I don't think he did know the Orb was there."

Odo snorted, disbelieving. "How could he not?"

"For the same reason," Sisko said, "you *and* Garak don't remember what happened to *you* on the Day of Withdrawal. Both your memories were tampered with. And so were Quark's. And before you ask why, I'll tell you right now I can't give you an answer. All I know is that it has something to do with Terrell and these Orbs."

"Hmphh," Odo said.

Quark stood closer to his new best friend, the great Captain Sisko.

"Well?" Kira asked, puzzling Quark but apparently not Sisko.

"Put the three orbs together?" Sisko suggested.

"Maybe that's not a good idea," Kira said.

"You think they might actually cause the end of the world?"

"What?!" Quark exploded.

"Calm down, Quark," Sisko chided him. "It's part of the legend of Jalbador that when the three Orbs are brought together, the Temple doors open and the world ends."

"I don't want the world to end in my bar," Quark said. "Talk about being bad for business."

"Probably not a good idea to get them *too* close together,"

O'Brien said. Quark could see the chief's attention was fixed on his tricorder. "I'm picking up a lot of neutrino flux. Almost as if some type of feedback loop is starting. That might explain the source of the light those things are producing. I don't think the world's going to come to an end, but we could get a blast of radiation that might do some harm."

"All right," Sisko said, holding up a hand that silenced Quark. "You call it, Chief. Five meters apart? Two meters?"

O'Brien made an adjustment on his tricorder, then showed it to Jadzia. "What would you say, Commander? Four meters should be safe?"

"Sure," Jadzia said. "And if you're going to send these back with the Kai, I'd recommend sending at least one on a separate shuttle. Just so an accident doesn't force them together."

Sisko smiled at Kira. "The *Kai*," he said. "Major, why don't you go back to the Temple and invite Kai Winn to visit Quark's."

Kira grinned fiercely. "With pleasure." Then she marched out into the Promenade.

"The Kai," Quark muttered. "In my bar. Might as well close early."

He watched anxiously as Sisko lifted the newly discovered Red Orb and carried it to the bar, keeping it well away from the other two still on the deck in front of the mural.

While everyone else packed away their tools and prepared to leave, Quark walked around behind the mural again. He looked inside the access panel.

"Uh . . . I never knew about that tunnel, brother."

Rom's sudden, without-warning appearance was enough to make Quark bang his head against the top of the opening.

"Neither did I," Quark said under his breath.

"But, it's a . . . good one to know about now," Rom said happily.

"Why not?" Quark said. "Everyone else knows about it now, too."

"Oh . . . yeah. I forgot."

Quark walked back to the front of the mural. He couldn't believe there was another maintenance tunnel coming into his bar that he didn't know about. Especially one that would have been so convenient for . . . he shook his head. For a moment, he thought he *did* remember the tunnel after all. But if he did, then why hadn't he been using it? And why hadn't *he* discovered the third Orb?

He was standing behind the bar when Sisko brought the second Orb up to the counter.

In a gesture of good will he knew would come back to haunt him, Quark started pouring mugs of root beer and passing them out to everyone for free. For Jadzia, he even hand-mixed a *raktajino.*

Then all three Orbs were on the bar, one at each end and one dead center, all of them flashing so rapidly that they almost appeared to glow with steady lights.

"I . . . think they're pretty," Rom said, beside him.

"I think I'd like them out of my bar."

"You know, brother, you . . . really should learn to take time to appreciate the wonders all around us every day."

"That's easy for you to say. You're married to Leeta."

"I'm serious." Rom pointed to the Orb in the middle of the countertop. "Just look at how . . . gloriously the light comes alive in that."

"Are you feeling all right?" Quark asked. Whenever Rom's babbling began to veer toward poetry, Quark worried about his sibling.

"You're not paying attention, brother. Look more closely." Rom started to push Quark forward, toward the Orb.

"Careful there, Rom," O'Brien warned. "Don't want to knock one of those things over."

Quark pushed himself away from his brother. "See the trouble you almost caused. These aren't playthings." Quark turned to the Red Orb directly in front of him. "They're . . ." He stopped as he tried to see what was inside the Orb.

There definitely was something inside. He knew because there had been the last time he had . . . "Oh, this is feeling too strange," he whispered.

"Brother?" Rom said.

Quark peered deep within the Orb. Yes. He could see it now. The city in the swamp. The glowing light approaching through the trees. The . . .

Quark popped open his eyes in Ferengi alarm.

"You're not moogie!"

He struck at the hideous monster before him, only at the last moment dimly realizing it was a reflection within a reflection within the sparkling red facets of the Orb.

"QUARK, NO!"

It could have been Captain Sisko who shouted. Or Jadzia or Chief O'Brien.

It might even have been Terrell or Odo or Garak, because they had all been there that day, in one way or another.

But by then it was too late, and Quark held the Orb in his hand and felt himself swung around through the air, as if he were dangling from a length of ODN cable stretching down from an antigrav high above the Promenade and then, when he let go and fell to the deck and looked up . . .

He had no idea what he was seeing.

Besides the Orbs, of course.

The three of them were floating in midair, just a meter or so above the deck, spinning and glowing, each just like an Orb of the Prophets, except their lights were crimson red, flame red, blood red.

The Orbs seemed to have moved themselves to the points of an equilateral triangle, and now twisting tendrils of light snaked out from each Orb to link up with the others. Defining the triangle's edges. Creating a . . . glow. A darkness. A distortion of some strange type. Exactly in the middle of their formation.

Quark felt Rom drag him to his feet.

He saw O'Brien try to touch one of the Orbs and be flung back in a flash of red lightning.

He saw Jadzia standing close to the floating Orbs, aiming a tricorder at them, a sudden strong breeze tugging at tendrils of her hair, which fluttered past her face as if flying right into the center of the Orbs.

"Do you feel that, brother?" Rom asked.

Quark braced himself against the deck. Somehow, it felt as if the deck were sinking in the center of his bar, drawing everything toward it.

The breeze was getting stronger. Now the flow of air blew *into* the bar, swirling napkins and debris into the center of the Orbs' pattern.

And that debris wasn't being blown back out.

"We've got intensive neutrino flux!" Jadzia called out over the intensifying wind. "A definite wormhole precursor!"

"Here?!" Sisko shouted.

Quark saw someone in a Starfleet uniform fire a phaser at one of the Orbs, but the beam suddenly doubled in width and flashed back at the shooter, disintegrating him.

And then Kai Winn and Major Kira were at the doorway of the bar, the Kai's saffron robes billowed around her.

"Emissary!" she cried. "What have you done?!"

And then Quark heard the deck creak as it seemed to distort even more and the station's pressure-failure sirens began to sound.

Quark could see Sisko tapping his communicator, giving orders, looking wild.

His brother Rom pulled on his arm, dragging him around the bar, giving the floating Orbs the widest possible berth.

Then the lights went out, as if the entire power grid had blown.

For a moment, the torrential wind died down and the red glow of the Orbs diminished. Quark and Rom stumbled and ran to join the last Starfleet stragglers fleeing his bar.

Outside in the Promenade, in the dim red glow that came from the three floating Orbs in the bar—the only source of light in the station, it seemed—Quark could see he was near to Captain Sisko. Without the roar of the wind, Quark discovered he could hear again, as well. O'Brien, at Sisko's side, was saying that the Red Orbs were drawing power from the station's fusion reactors. With the power failure, they, too, had lost power. If they could just shut down the reactors, the Orbs would be powerless.

"It's worth a try," Sisko said.

And then a dark shadow passed between Quark and Sisko, and Quark saw Sisko go down, struck by a sudden blow to the head by some crazed assailant.

"Abandon station!" Sisko suddenly shouted. "Chief! Jadzia! Pass the order on to abandon station!"

"What about the reactors?" O'Brien's voice was urgent.

"Now, Chief!"

Then the pressure alarms were replaced by a siren that Quark had only heard during drills. And never thought he'd live to hear.

Two long bursts. Two short ones.

The order to abandon the station had been relayed to Ops.

In the dim light and shadows, Quark saw Sisko push himself to his feet, rubbing at his jaw. The captain looked around in confusion, then tapped at his chest as he shouted more orders.

Suddenly new sources of light appeared on the Promenade.

Golden columns of quantum mist.

Emergency beam-outs.

"Uh . . . hold on to me, brother."

Quark felt Rom's fingernails dig into his arms. The wind began to rise again. The whole station seemed to creak and flex. The glow from the bar became brighter.

"Rom!" O'Brien shouted. "You're with me!"

Quark saw O'Brien lunge for Rom and grab his brother's arm just as Rom held on to Quark's.

"Chief!" Quark shouted. "What's happening?"

"There's a wormhole opening *in* the station!"

Quark felt his heart stop. A wormhole was opening in the *station?* A wormhole was opening in his *bar!*

Quark looked past Rom and O'Brien as it seemed his bar was lit by the literal flames of hell. Gul Dukat's pride and joy, the ridiculous mural of Tholian or Tellarite design, suddenly exploded into a spray of splintered glass, each glittering shard spinning madly as it was sucked down into the center of the triangle formed by the floating, glowing Orbs.

It was the last thing Quark saw before the station flickered out of existence before him in the swirl of the transporter.

But then, since he had lost everything, it was the last thing he ever wanted to see.

As far as he was concerned, the legends of the Red Orbs of Jalbador were true.

His world *had* come to an end.

CHAPTER 28

SISKO JUMPED DOWN from the *Defiant*'s transporter pad and ran into the corridor and to the bridge. He could already hear the ship's impulse engines coming on line as she prepared to undock from the station.

Worf was in the command chair and he stepped out as soon as Sisko appeared. On the main viewer, Deep Space 9 stretched out to the stars. But it was only a dark silhouette against the Denorios Belt. All station lights were out.

"How did you get the order to evacuate?" Sisko asked, slipping into his chair.

"It came into Ops through Jadzia," Worf said. He was already at tactical. "More than one thousand people are already away."

Sisko knew just how fortunate the inhabitants and crew of the station were. With the two *Akira*-class starships Admiral Ross had dispatched to help with the evacuation, more than twelve banks of transporters were operating at once. And the main personnel banks on the *Garneau* and the *Bondar* could retrieve more than one hundred evacuees every minute between them.

Jadzia and O'Brien were next on the bridge, followed by Bashir and Kira.

Bashir held a medical tricorder to Sisko and Sisko winced, suddenly realizing his jaw hurt.

"How's that feel?" the doctor asked.

"You should see the other guy," Sisko quipped. He didn't know with whom he had collided during the evacuation, but this wasn't the time to worry about it.

"Oh, Prophets!"

Sisko leaned forward with a smile. The exclamation had come from Commander Arla at flight operations, the least religious Bajoran he had yet to meet.

But before he could say anything to her about her apparent change in faith, he saw what she saw on the viewer and all sense of amusement fled.

A large glowing sphere of red energy blossomed over a section of the Promenade, just below Ops.

"What is *that?*" Sisko asked.

"The wormhole precursor," Jadzia replied. "It must have found a new source of power, because it's continuing to accelerate."

"Worf! What's the status of the evacuation?"

"Fifteen hundred people away," Worf reported. "But there is growing gravimetric distortion interfering with—"

Worf fell silent as a chorus of gasps filled the bridge.

The section of the habitat ring closest to the growing red sphere of energy was beginning to buckle, bending like a broken wheel.

Sisko stared at the screen in sickened fascination. "How many people are still on board . . . ?"

"Communications are down, sir. We must withdraw."

"Release the docking clamps," he ordered.

Arla fumbled with her console until Kira touched the young Bajoran commander on her shoulder and swiftly took over the position.

On the viewer, three escape modules launched from the habitat ring, but instead of flying free of the station they were drawn on perfect arcs into the red sphere.

"This can't be happening," Bashir said in shock.

The impact of the three modules set off a series of explosions that ringed the Promenade, and in a chain reaction they traveled up the central core to Ops.

"Jake . . ." Sisko whispered, as if an icy hand clutched his heart, then spoke more strongly, "Did anyone see Jake?"

"He's on board," Bashir said at once.

"What about Kasidy?"

Sisko's heart sank. No one had seen her on the *Defiant*. His hands tightened on the arms of his chair. Surely with the combined might of all the vessels using transporters now, Kasidy had been among the lucky ones.

A new wave of horrified gasps escaped those observing the viewer as a section of the habitat ring broke off and fell up into the red sphere.

"We are beginning to experience tidal distortions from an intense gravitational source," Worf announced.

Then Jadzia made her report. "It's a wormhole, Benjamin. For some reason it's opening about a hundred times more slowly than the one we're used to, but it *is* opening."

"Get us out of here, Major."

"Aye, sir."

On the viewer, the image of Deep Space 9—what was left of it— angled abruptly as the *Defiant* banked away.

And then the starship shook violently as the viewer flared with blue energy.

"We are under attack!" Worf shouted.

"Full power to shields!" Sisko ordered. He knew it had to be the Jem'Hadar. The Dominion had finally reacted to—

"You're not going anywhere," Leej Terrell said from the viewer.

Sisko leapt to his feet to face her. He recognized the bridge of her Sagittarian cruiser. "Mr. Worf, lock on all weapons," he said.

"I cannot acquire a target."

On the viewer, Terrell was a study in triumphant rage. She pounded a fist on the arm of her looming command chair. "Go back to your station, Captain. You found the third Orb. Now you must join it."

"I thought you wanted the Orbs for yourself," Sisko said, trying to goad her, as he had so recently, so long ago.

"If Cardassia can't have them, then no one can. Fire!"

Instantly the *Defiant* shook under another fusillade of phaser fire.

"Worf! Where is she!"

"Her ship is cloaked, sir! I can pick up a slight modulation when she fires, but not enough to extrapolate a course."

"Where did a Cardassian ship get a cloaking device?" Sisko demanded to know.

The *Defiant* trembled as another round of phaser fire found her.

Then Sisko heard the ship's own capacitors discharge with return fire.

"I believe I hit her," Worf called out. "I will continue to—"

The biggest blast yet hit the *Defiant,* and the ship spun on her axis.

Each time DS9 slipped past the viewer, the red sphere was larger. Now Sisko could see the rotating vortex was composed of red spiraling tendrils of energy. In form, it looked just like the wormhole he had seen open so many times. Only its color was different.

"Major Kira," Sisko said. "We need to be stabilized so Worf can return fire."

"She's picked her targets," Kira warned. "Our thrusters are off-line. Impulse is out. All we've got is warp and that's not powered up yet."

"Working on it, sir!" O'Brien volunteered before he had been asked.

"Can we get support from another ship?" Sisko asked.

"All channels are down," Jadzia said. "The other ships are withdrawing."

"How can that be? Surely they can see we're in difficulty!"

Jadzia turned from her science station to Sisko. "Benjamin, we're so close to that wormhole we could be within some kind of event horizon. Those other ships might not even know we're still here."

O'Brien chimed in. "That could explain why the wormhole seems to be opening so slowly. Those other ships might have seen it move as quickly as the blue wormhole does. And we might have been sucked in."

Sisko tried to follow the reasoning of his two experts. "So we're in some kind of temporal bubble?"

"Not necessarily," Jadzia said. "It could be straightforward relativistic time displacement. We should be able to warp out when the engines are ready, just like jumping out of a black hole."

"Thirty seconds to warp," O'Brien reported.

The *Defiant* shuddered as another volley hit her, then rang with her own phasers as Worf once more returned fire. "I think I may have hit her again," Worf said.

"Twenty seconds to warp," O'Brien counted down.

On the viewer, the red wormhole now obscured more than half of DS9. Sisko watched as the station's upper docking pylons begin to twist down to the red distortion, hull plates popping loose like autumn leaves in a storm. Then one of the pylons broke free entirely as an explosion engulfed its base. It tumbled into the wormhole, visibly breaking up into still smaller pieces. Then it disappeared.

Another explosion shook the *Defiant*. Transtator sparks erupted from Worf's tactical station and the Klingon had to jump back as the automatic fire-suppression system engulfed his console with anaerobic vapor.

"Ten seconds," O'Brien said.

"Major," Sisko ordered, "prepare to get us out of here."

Another hit.

"Shields at thirty-seven percent," Kira announced. "We can't take much more."

And then on the viewer, as if it were no more than a crumpled piece of tissue being pulled down a drain, Deep Space 9 fell in on itself, shattering like brittle ice, each shard drawn spinning into the endless, infinite tunnel of the red wormhole at its heart.

Sisko felt a part of himself vanishing into that ravenous maw, to be lost forever along with his station.

"They all got off in time," he chanted softly to himself, willing his words to be true. "They had to get off in time."

"We have warp!" O'Brien announced.

On screen, the red wormhole continued to expand, continued to open, its unwinding coils of negative energy now reaching out for the *Defiant*.

Sisko fell back in his chair, gripped the arms. "Now, Major!"

"Never!" Terrell's voice echoed from all the bridge speakers at once.

And then a final blast of phaser fire hit the starship just as she went to warp. And the first tendrils of the wormhole brushed across her hull to claim her.

No one on board the *Defiant* had a chance.

They were all engulfed in a red flash of overwhelming intensity, the sheer magnitude of which exceeded anything in their entire experience of existence.

And then each moment dissolved into the next.

Until there was only the silence and the darkness of endless infinite space . . .

CHAPTER 29

SHE TUMBLED dead in space. No running lights. No engine glow. Her only signature a faint infrared glow which testified to a barely functioning life-support system, and the fragile lives of the thirty-three people who still survived onboard.

There was no wormhole near her now. No sun. No planets.

And no hope.

Sisko awoke to the cool sting of a hypospray.

The bridge was dark, but enough display screens functioned for him to see Bashir kneeling at his side.

"Casualties?" It was any captain's first thought, first worry.

"Five dead in engineering," Bashir said. "A coolant leak. A dozen injuries. Nothing serious. And Jake's fine. He's helping clean up sickbay."

"Thank you, Doctor."

Sisko reached out, found the edge of his command chair, and used it to brace himself as he rose to his feet.

He could smell smoke and ozone, and the damp soapy scent of the fire-suppression sprays. But there were no wailing sirens. The ship was in one piece. They had survived.

Then he looked at the viewer, saw only stars there.

Closed his eyes. Saw Deep Space 9.

He found Jadzia. A small medical patch on her forehead.

"Your hair's a mess, Old Man," he said.

Jadzia smiled up at him, tightly. "Thank you, Benjamin. You know exactly what to say to make a girl feel her best."

"Any sign of Terrell?"

Jadzia shook her head.

"Communications back on-line?"

"There's no subspace distortion, if that's what you mean. But I'm not picking up anything."

Sisko looked back at the viewer with a sudden rush of apprehension. "Did we travel *through* the wormhole?"

The last thing he wanted was for the *Defiant* to become another *Voyager,* tossed tens of thousands of light-years from home.

"No. Those are local stars," Jadzia said. "But we are having trouble getting a fix on exactly where we are."

Sisko was suddenly aware of Major Kira beside him. Her face drawn, her eyes dark. She held out a padd. "I found out why our navigation charts aren't working." She handed Jadzia the padd. "It's not a question of where we are. It's *when* we are."

Sisko squinted sideways at the calculations Jadzia scrolled through on the padd. "We've travelled through time?"

Jadzia nodded. "From the drift in star positions . . . twenty-four . . . almost twenty-five years." She looked up. Her face held the same haunted expression as Kira's. "Benjamin, we've come forward to the year 2400."

Sisko exhaled in shock. "How can that be?"

"It has to be the wormhole," Jadzia said.

"Captain," Kira asked, "we will be able to go back, won't we?"

"Of . . . of course," Sisko said. "We can . . . we can slingshot back around a star. . . ."

"Not really, Benjamin." Jadzia seemed apologetic. "If we didn't travel here along a slingshot trajectory, we have no path to follow back."

"But there *has* to be a way, doesn't there?" Kira asked.

Sisko mind raced with possibilities. "We'll find a way. We'll contact the Federation Department of Temporal Investigations. Twenty-five years is a long time. There must have been some major breakthroughs in temporal mechanics. They'll be able to help us." Sisko turned to address his bridge crew. "Just remember, we have to follow Starfleet regulations to the letter. We can't afford to learn anything about the time we're in, so we won't alter the timeline when we—"

Sisko flew through the air as the bridge echoed with thunder.

"We are under attack again!" Worf said. "Cloaked vessel dead ahead!"

Sisko forced himself to stand. He could taste blood in his mouth from his fall. "Terrell . . . " he said. "However we got here, she came with us."

"I do not think so," Worf said as a collision alarm began sounding. "The ship is decloaking, and it is not hers."

Sisko stared at the viewer as a strange rippling checkerboard effect, unlike any cloak he had ever seen, distorted the stars until a ship became visible.

And though it was a class he didn't know, his apprehension became relief as he recognized the hallmarks of Starfleet design: twin warp nacelles set back for safety, a lower engineering hull, an upper command hull. Each element was elongated to an extreme degree, and the command hull had what appeared to be two forward-facing projections that resembled battering rams, but overall it was a welcome sight.

"That's quite a ship, Benjamin. It's close to a kilometer long, and I'm reading *eighteen* different phaser systems onboard. At least I think they're phasers."

Sisko smiled. "That's all right, Old Man. At least it's on our side. Commander Worf, open a channel."

"Channel open, sir."

"Attention, unidentified Starfleet vessel. This is Captain Benjamin Sisko of the *Starship Defiant.* My crew and I have been displaced in time and—"

"That's impossible," Kira said.

Sisko saw it, too. Didn't understand.

The huge vessel had come about so that its forward hull filled the viewer. And from that angle, the ship's name was clear.

U.S.S. Opaka.

"How could a warship be named for a woman of peace?" Kira asked, incredulous.

Sisko was uncomfortable with even seeing the details of the ship's design and learning its name. "Dax, degrade viewer resolution by fifty percent and disable recording. We can't take any of these details home with us."

He returned to stand by his command chair. "This is Captain Sisko of the *Defiant* to the captain of the *U.S.S. Opaka*. We are displaced in time. Under Starfleet regulations, we request that you do not communicate directly with us in order to allow us to preserve our timeline. We will require—"

"Incoming message," Worf interrupted.

"They have to know better," Sisko said. "We can't risk receiving it. Jam it, Mr. Worf."

"No good, Captain. They're using a type of multiplexing I have not—"

And then a familiar face formed on the viewer. His hair and beard were pure white, his features lined and wrinkled, but he was unmistakable to everyone on the *Defiant* who had encountered him four years ago—or twenty-nine years ago.

"Captain Sisko," the commander of the *Starship Opaka* began, "this is Captain Thomas Riker. Good to see you again, sir. And welcome back."

Sisko tried to make sense of the uniform Riker wore. It seemed to be closer to a Bajoran style, though in black and rust colors. Yet on his chest he wore a version of the classic Starfleet delta in gold, backed by an upside-down triangle in blue.

"Captain Riker," Sisko said. "I appreciate the contact, and I'm glad to see you're no longer in Cardassian custody. But by talking to us directly, you're making it difficult for us to go back to our own time."

Riker laughed. "I wouldn't worry about that, Captain. You can learn all you want about the future—because this is where you and your crew are going to stay."

Sisko squared his shoulders. "No, Captain Riker, we are not. One way or another, we want to return to our own time and our own lives."

Riker leaned to the side of his chair as if his back was sore. "Captain, I don't care what the hell you *want* to do. Your place is here and always has been. As for your ship and crew, every resource is needed for the war, and I'm not letting the *Defiant* get away."

"What war?" Sisko asked. Could it be possible that the Federation and the Dominion were still battling for control of the quadrant?

"Sir!" Worf suddenly announced. "Three ships approaching on an attack vector!"

"Cardassian?" Sisko asked. "Jem'Hadar?"

Worf looked up at Sisko in surprise. "No, sir . . . from their identification signals, they are *also* Starfleet vessels."

Suddenly a barrage of explosions surrounded the *Defiant,* shaking her badly.

On the viewer, Riker vanished and was replaced by an image of the *Opaka* firing needle-thin lances of silver energy at the approaching ships.

"All three of the new vessels have locked their weapons on us," Worf reported.

Riker reappeared on the viewer, eyes afire with rage.

"The War of the Prophets is coming! Choose your side, Emissary— because this is your war now!"

Then the bridge of the *Defiant* fell silent, as everyone turned to their captain.

And waited for Sisko to make his decision.

BOOK II
THE WAR OF THE
PROPHETS

There is linear in the nonlinear, so that neither exists one without the other. So it was with ANSLEM, *and all the multitudes that he held within himself, myself among them, in that place that was no place, obtained only by knowing the absence of hours in the hourglass. An* hourglass *as the entryway? Was there ever such a joke to make even a Vulcan laugh at those immensities and contradictions of meaning? Yet caught in that sea of sand, drawn toward the neck of that hourglass where both the Temples at last were aligned—well, what else could we do in those vast temporal currents but race time. . . .*

—JAKE SISKO, *Anslem*

PROLOGUE

In the Hands of the Prophets

"*THIS DOES NOT HAPPEN,*" *Captain Jean-Luc Picard says.*

The Sisko walks with him by the cool waters of Bajor. "It does not, but it did," the Sisko says. "Look around and see it for yourself."

They stand together on the Promenade, the Sisko and O'Brien and twelve-year-old Jake with his bare feet and his fishing pole, and with Kai Winn and Vic and Arla Rees and all of them, and they watch the Promenade die exactly as it dies the first time, deck plates buckling, power currents sparking, debris and trailing strips of dislodged carpet spiraling into the singularity that is Quark's bar—where the Red Wormhole opens the doors to the second Temple.

"There is no second Temple," Admiral Ross says.

He sits across from the Sisko in the Wardroom of Deep Space 9. Behind him, the casualty lists scroll endlessly as the war with the Dominion begins, ends, begins again.

The Sisko stands at the center of B'hala, in the shade of the ban-taca tower.

"But there was," the Sisko says.

"There is no was," Kira protests.

"Then explain this," the Sisko replies.

He is with them on the bridge of the Defiant *as Deep Space 9 is consumed by the Red Wormhole and the ship is trapped in a net of energies that pull it from that time to another yet to be.*

In his restaurant in New Orleans, the Sisko's father says, "That time is meaningless."

On the sands of Tyree, the Sisko's true mother says, "And another time yet to be is more meaningless still."

In the serene confines of the Bajoran Temple on the Promenade the Sisko's laughter echoes. "You still don't understand!" It is a marvel to him, this continuation of a state of being that should not exist without flesh to bind it. "I am here to teach you, *am I not?"*

"You are the Sisko, pallie," Vic agrees.

The Sisko makes it clear for them. "Then . . . pay attention!*"*

The Prophets take their places in the outfield as the Sisko steps up to the plate.

"Not this again," Nog says.

The Sisko is delighted. "Again! *That's right! You're finally getting the idea!" He tosses his baseball into the air. It hangs like a planet in space, wheeling about Bajor-B'hava'el, until there appears a baseball bat like a comet sparkling through the stars to—*

Interruption.

The Sisko is in the light space.

Jennifer stands before him, her legs crushed by the debris on the dying Saratoga, *her clothes sodden with her blood. "You keep bringing us back to the baseball game."*

The Sisko takes her hand in his. "Yes! Because now it is you—" *He looks around the nothingness, knowing they are all within it. "—all* of *you who will not go forward!"*

Jennifer is in her robes of Kente cloth, as she wears them on the day they are wed. "There is no forward."

The Sisko discovers he is learning about this place, as if when he falls with Dukat and his flesh is consumed by the flames of the Fire Caves, all resistance to the speed of thought is lost.

"If there is no forward," he argues, "then why are we not already there? Why do you not know everything that I tell you?"

"You are linear," General Martok reminds him, as if he could forget.

"So are you," the Sisko says.

And for the very first time, the Sisko now forces them *from the light space to a place* he *makes real, where from the mists of the* moon of AR-558 Jem'Hadar soldiers advance and Houdini mines explode all around them.

"What is this?" they plaintively chorus.

"This is death," the Sisko tells them. "This is change. This is the forward progression of time to an end in which there is no more forward. This is the fate of all beings—even your fate."

"Impossible," Kai Opaka says by the reflecting pool.

The Sisko leans against the bar on Space Station K-7, smiling as he looks down at the old gold shirt he wears with the arrowhead emblem that is only that, not a single molecule of communicator circuitry within it. "This is what has gone before," he informs the smooth-foreheaded Klingons at the bar.

The Sisko stands on the sands of Mars, before the vast automated factories where nanoassemblers fabricate the parts for Admiral Picard's mad dream—the U.S.S. Phoenix. "This is what is yet to be," he informs the Tellarite engineers at his side.

And now it is he who returns them to the light space. "And you are all part of that continuum from past to future, with an end before you as surely as you had a beginning."

"What is this?" Arla asks in despair.

"It is why I am here."

"You are the Emissary," Nog agrees.

The Sisko shakes his head. "I am not the Emissary. I am your Emissary."

"How is there a difference?" Grand Nagus Zek asks.

"Think to an earlier time. The first time I came before you."

"You are always before us," O'Brien says.

"I am before you now," the Sisko agrees. "As your Emissary. As one who has come to teach you what you do not know. But before that first time—you must remember!"

The Sisko brings them all back to the baseball game.

"Here—this first time—you did not know who I was!"

Solok looks at Martok. "Adversarial."

Martok looks at Eddington. "Confrontational."

Eddington looks at Picard. "He must be destroyed."

The Sisko throws a ball high in the air, swings, hits one out of the park, and all the Prophets turn to watch the orb vanish in the brilliant blue sky.

"Do you see?" the Sisko asks. *"How things have* changed? *The way you were* then. *The way you are* now."

The Prophets are silent.

Nineteen-year-old Jake steps forward from them all.

"This . . . does not happen," the young man says.

"Maybe you're right," the Sisko sighs. He sits at his desk in his 1953 Harlem apartment, pushes his glasses back along the bridge of his nose, flexes his fingers, then Bennie types on the Remington: Maybe all of this did happen . . .

The Sisko stands on Bajor, gazing up as that world's sun reacts to the proto-matter pulse set off by the Grigari task force eight minutes earlier and goes supernova, claiming all the world and all its inhabitants on the last night of the Universe.

. . . or maybe none of it happened, *Bennie types.*

"But still," the Sisko says as he tosses another baseball into the air, *"you want to find out what happens next because, for now, you just don't know."*

"We know everything," Admiral Ross says.

"Then answer me this," the Sisko says as another fly ball clears the home-run fence. *"When I first came to you, when you did not know me, why did you want to* destroy *me?"*

The Prophets are silent.

"Then see this, *and answer an even greater mystery,"* the Sisko says, as he returns them all to the bridge of the Defiant *just as Captain Thomas Riker delivers his ultimatum.*

"What mystery?" Weyoun asks, clad in his vedek's robes.

"I will show you the fate of the people who pray to the Prophets as gods. But then you must tell me: To whom do the Prophets pray?"

The Prophets still do not answer.

But they watch as the Sisko continues his story. . . .

CHAPTER 1

LIKE THE thirty-three fragile beings within her battered hull, in less than a minute the *Starship Defiant* would die.

Wounded. Space-tossed. Twenty-five years from home. Her decks littered with the bodies of those who had not survived her journey. And for those who still lived, her smoke-filled corridors reverberated with sensor alarms warning that enemy weapons were locked onto her, ready to fire.

Beyond her forward hull, the *U.S.S. Opaka* accelerated toward an attacking wing of three Starfleet vessels. But adding to the confusion of all aboard the *Defiant,* that warship, which was defending them—inexplicably named for a woman of peace—appeared to be a Starfleet vessel as well.

The *Opaka* was almost a kilometer long, and though her basic design of twin nacelles and two main hulls was little changed from the earliest days of humanity's first voyages to the stars, each element of the warship was stretched to an aggressive extreme, most notably the two forward-facing projections thrusting out from her command hull like battering rams. Now, as she closed in on her prey, needle-thin lances of golden energy pulsed from her emitter rings. Existing partially in the other dimensions of Cochrane space, those destructive energy bursts reached their targets at faster-than-light velocities, only to be dispersed into rippling patterns of flashing squares of luminescence as they were broken apart by whatever incomprehensible shields protected the three attacking Starfleet vessels.

In response, the *Opaka* launched a second warp-speed volley—miniature stars flaring from her launching tubes. The sudden light they carried sprayed across the *Defiant*'s blue-gray hull—the only radiance to illuminate her so deep in the space between the stars, for there was no glow from her warp engines.

Wisps of venting coolant began escaping from the *Defiant*'s cracked hull plates, wreathing her in vapor. Within the ruin of her engine room, at the source of the leaking coolant, the hyperdimensional stability of her warp core seethed from instability to uselessness a thousand times each second.

The ship had no weapons. Diminished shields. No propulsion. The most limited of life-support, and even that was rapidly failing.

But seconds from destruction, caught in a battle of a war that belonged only to her future, the *Defiant,* like her crew, was not finished yet.

"Choose your side!" Captain Thomas Riker screamed from the *Defiant*'s bridge viewer.

And within this exact same moment, Captain Benjamin Sisko was frozen—twenty years of Starfleet training preventing him from making any decision under these circumstances.

Somehow, when Deep Space 9 had been destroyed by the opening of a second wormhole in Bajoran space, the *Defiant* had become enmeshed in the outer edges of the phenomenon's boundary layer and, like an ancient sailing ship swept 'round an ocean maelstrom, she had been propelled into a new heading—almost twenty-five years in her future.

The year 2400, Jadzia Dax had said.

Which meant—according to Starfleet general orders and to the strict regulations of the Federation Department of Temporal Investigations—that it was now the responsibility of all aboard the *Defiant* to refrain from any interaction with the inhabitants of this future. Otherwise, when Sisko's ship returned to her proper time, his crew's knowledge of this future could prevent this timeline from ever coming to pass—setting in place a major temporal anomaly. Thus the source of Sisko's paralysis was simple: How could his ship and crew return from a future that would never exist?

With the weight of future history in the balance, Sisko could not choose sides as Riker demanded. Whatever this War of the Prophets was—and Sisko wished he had never even *heard* Riker say that name—he and the crew of the *Defiant* had to remain neutral. Starfleet and the FDTI allowed them no other option.

Sisko straightened in his command chair. "Mr. O'Brien. All power to shields—even life-support!"

Almost immediately, the lights in the bridge dimmed and the almost imperceptible hum of the air circulators began to slow. At the same time, Sisko felt the artificial gravity field lessen to its minimum level, and understood that his chief engineer had chosen to reply to his order through instant action in place of time-wasting speech.

Then the *Defiant* was rocked by a staccato series of explosive impacts unlike any Sisko had ever experienced.

"What was that?" Dr. Bashir protested to no one in particular. He was holding his tricorder near Jadzia, checking her head wound once again.

"Shields from sixty-eight to *twelve percent!*" O'Brien reported with awe. "From *one hit!*"

Sisko had already ordered the main viewer set to a fifty-percent reduction in resolution so that no one on the bridge—especially O'Brien and Jadzia—might inadvertently pick up clues about future technology simply by seeing what the ships of this time looked like. But the display still held enough detail to show the attacking Starfleet vessels flash by. The three craft, each twice the *Defiant*'s length and half its width, were shaped like daggers, the tips of their prows glowing as if they were nothing more than flying phaser cannons.

"Worf!" Sisko said urgently. "What are they firing at us?"

"Energy signature unknown!" Worf's deep voice triumphed over even the raucous, incessant alarms. "Propulsion systems unknown!"

Now the *Opaka* streaked by in pursuit. The viewer flickered with flashes of disruptive energy as once again the hull of the *Defiant* echoed with the thumps of multiple physical impacts.

"Worf?" Sisko asked. Under the circumstances, it was a detailed enough question for the *Defiant*'s first officer.

"Sixteen objects have materialized on our hull," Worf answered without hesitation. "They are attached with molecular adhesion. Sensors show antimatter pods in each."

"Contact mines," Sisko said, pushing himself to his feet. "Beamed through what's left of our shields."

Jadzia called out to Sisko from her science station. Her hair was still in uncharacteristic disarray. The medical patch on the side of her forehead obscured her delicate Trill spotting. But nothing could disguise the apprehension in her tone. "We're out of our league here, Benjamin. I think the mines were beamed in from those three ships, but I can't make any sense of their transporter traces. For what it's worth, they probably could've punched through our shields even at one hundred percent."

Major Kira didn't look up from her position at the helm. "The three attackers are on their way back. The *Opaka*'s still in pursuit."

Worf spoke again. "Sir, I am detecting a countdown signal from the mines on our hull. They are programmed to detonate in seventy-three seconds."

Sisko grimaced, trying to understand the logic of that. "Why a countdown? If they can beam antimatter bombs through our shields, why not set them to go off at once?"

Commander Arla Rees had the answer. "It's what the other captain said." The tall Bajoran spun around from her auxiliary sensor station. " 'Every ship is needed for the war.' He said he wasn't going to let the *Defiant* get away."

Sisko struck the arm of his chair with one fist. "Of course! The other side wants us, too, and they'll only detonate the mines if—"

He and everyone on the bridge involuntarily flinched, shielding their eyes from the sudden flare of blinding light that shot forth from the viewscreen faster than the ship's overtaxed computers could compensate for. At precisely the same instant, the deafening rumble of an explosion erupted from the bridge speakers as the *Defiant*'s sensors automatically converted the impact of energy particles in the soundless vacuum of space into synthetic noise, giving the crew an audible indication of the size and the direction of the far-off explosion.

"One of the attackers . . ." Kira said in disbelief. "It dropped from warp and *rammed* the *Opaka*." She looked back over her shoulder. "Captain, that ship had a crew of fifty-eight."

Now at Sisko's side, Bashir murmured under his breath, "Fanatics."

Sisko tried and failed to comprehend what such desperate action said about the Starfleet of this day.

"Forty seconds until detonation," Worf warned.

"Captain," O'Brien added, "our transporters are off-line. I can't get rid of the mines without an EVA team, and there's just no time."

Time, Sisko thought. And that was the end of his indecision. As a Starfleet officer, he couldn't risk polluting the timeline. But as a starship captain . . . his crew had to come first.

"This is the *Defiant* to Captain Riker, I am—"

The stars on the viewer suddenly spiraled, and the *Defiant*'s deck lurched to starboard, felling everyone not braced in a duty chair, including Sisko.

"Another ship decloaking!" Worf shouted as three bridge stations blew out in cascades of transtator sparks. "We are caught in its gravimetric wake!"

"Dax!" Sisko struggled to his feet. "Stabilize the screen!"

The spiraling stars slowed, then held steady, even though all attitude screens showed that the *Defiant* was still spinning wildly on her central axis.

Then, with the same dissolving checkerboard pattern of wavering squares of light that Sisko had seen envelop the *Opaka,* the new ship decloaked.

Again, Sisko had no doubt he was looking at a ship based on advanced technology. But in this case the vessel was not of Starfleet design; it was unmistakably Klingon—a battlecruiser at least the size of the *Opaka.* Yet this warship's deep purple exterior hull was studded with thick plates and conduits, with a long central spine extending from the sharp-edged half-diamond of the cruiser's combined engineering and propulsion hull to end in a wedge-shaped bridge module.

"Whose side is it on?" Sisko asked sharply, even as Worf reported that he could pick up no transmissions of any kind from the vessel. But Jadzia caught sight of something on the Klingon's hull and instructed the *Defiant*'s computer to jump the viewer to magnification fifty and restore full resolution.

At once, Sisko and his crew were looking at a detailed segment of the warship's purple hull. Angular Klingon script ran beneath the same modified Starfleet emblem Tom Riker had worn on his uniform—the classic Starfleet delta in gold backed by an upside-down triangle in blue.

"It has to be with the *Opaka*," Kira said.

Worf's next words unnerved Sisko. "And her designation is *Boreth*."

The *Opaka* was named for a Bajoran spiritual leader—the first kai Sisko had met on Bajor. And Boreth was the world to which the Klingon messiah, Kahless the Unforgettable, had promised to return after his death. The Starfleet of Sisko's day did not make a habit of naming its ships after religious figures or places. Something had changed in this time. But what?

"Thirty seconds," Worf said tersely.

Sisko faced the viewscreen. "This is Captain Sisko to Captain Riker and to the commander of the *Boreth*. My crew stands ready to join you. We require immediate evacuation."

"Course change on the two remaining attackers!" Kira announced. "Coming in on a ramming course!"

Sisko clenched his hands at his sides. He didn't understand the tactics. What about the antimatter mines? Their adversaries could destroy the *Defiant* without sacrificing themselves in a suicidal collision.

Sisko turned abruptly to O'Brien. "Mine status?"

"Only nine left! Seven . . . five . . . Captain, they're being beamed away!"

"The *Boreth*," Sisko said. That had to be the answer. But why?

He looked at Jadzia. "Any transporter trace?"

"Still nothing detectable, Benjamin."

"Ten seconds to impact with attackers!" Kira shouted. "The *Opaka* is firing more of those . . . torpedoes or whatever they are . . . five seconds. . . ."

Sisko reached for his command chair. "Brace for collision!"

And then, as if a series of fusion sparklers had ignited one after the other across the bridge, Dax, Bashir, and Worf—

—vanished.

One instant Sisko's senior command staff were at their stations. Then, in the center of each of their torsos a single pinpoint of light flared, and as if suddenly twisted away at a ninety-degree angle from every direction at once, the body of each crew member spun and shrank into that small dot of light, which faded as suddenly as it had blossomed.

"Chief! What happened!"

O'Brien's voice faltered, betraying his utter bewilderment. "I . . . some kind of . . . transporter, I think. It—it hit all through the ship, sir. We've lost fifteen crew. . . ."

Sisko strode toward Jadzia's science station, but Arla reached the Trill's empty chair before he did.

"The attackers have gone to warp, sir. The *Opaka* is pursuing. The *Boreth* is holding its position."

With an arm as heavy as his hopes, Sisko finally allowed himself to touch his communicator. "Sisko to Jake."

No answer. Sisko's stomach twisted with fear for his boy.

Arla looked up at Sisko.

"My son—he was in sickbay," Sisko said in answer to Arla's questioning glance.

"Communications are down across the ship," Arla offered.

And then a far-too-familiar voice whispered from the bridge speakers, with pious—and patently false—surprise.

"Captain Sisko, I cannot tell you what a privilege it is to see you once again."

Sisko forced himself to raise his head to look up at the viewer, to see the odious, smiling speaker who sat in a Klingon command chair, a figure clad in the unmistakable robes of a Bajoran vedek.

"Weyoun . . . ?"

"Oh, Captain, I feel so honored that you remember me after all this time," the Vorta simpered. "Though I suppose for you it is only a matter of minutes since you were plucked from the timeline and redeposited here."

Sisko stared at the viewscreen as if he were trapped in a dream and the slightest movement on his part would send him into an endless fall.

No, not a dream, Sisko thought. *A nightmare. . . .*

Because Weyoun's presence as a Bajoran religious leader on a Klingon vessel with Starfleet markings meant only one thing.

Sometime in the past twenty-five years, the war had ended.

And the Dominion had won.

CHAPTER 2

THE INSTANT the sirens began to wail, Captain Nog was out of his bunk and running for the door of his quarters, his Model-I personal phaser in hand. Then, barefoot, wearing only Starfleet-issue sleep shorts and no Ferengi headskirt, Nog slammed into that door. It hadn't opened in response to his full-speed approach.

Coming fully awake with the sudden shock of pain, he slapped his hand against the door's control panel, to punch in his override code and activate manual function. But before he could begin, the lights in his cluttered quarters dimmed, alarm sirens screamed to life and, with a stomach-turning lurch, Nog felt the gravity net abruptly shut down, leaving him bouncing in natural Martian gravity, still with all his mass but only one-third his weight.

Reflexively Nog slapped at his bare chest, as if his communicator badge were permanently welded to his flesh, then swore an instant later in an obscure Ferengi trading dialect. He darted back to his closet to get his jacket, only to pitch forward as the first shockwave hit Personnel Dome 1.

His cursing reduced to a moan of frustration, Nog jumped to his feet—and banged his head on the ceiling because he'd forgotten to compensate for the suddenly diminished gravity. Dropping to the floor once more, he yanked open his closet door, then ripped his communicator from the red shoulder of the frayed uniform jacket hanging inside.

He knew exactly what had just happened. The four-second delay between the loss of gravity and the arrival of the ground tremor made it obvious. The main power generators for the entire Utopia Planitia Fleet Yards had been sabotaged. Again.

Nog squeezed his communicator badge—a scarlet Starfleet arrowhead against an oval of Klingon teal and gold—between thumb and forefinger as he turned back toward the door. But all the device did was squeal with subspace interference—jamming, pure and simple.

Nog tossed the useless badge aside, then punched in his override code for the door. When the door still didn't open, he abandoned caution and protocol and blasted through it with his phaser.

A moment later his bare feet were propelling him with long, loping strides along the dark corridors of the shipyard's largest personnel dome. Multiple sirens wailed, all out of phase and echoing from every direction, a sonic affront to his sensitive ears. Flashing yellow lights spun at each corridor intersection. More shockwaves and muffled explosions rumbled through the floor and walls. But Nog ignored them all. There was only one thought in his mind, one goal as important as any profit he could imagine.

The Old Man.

As he reached the main hub of the dome—a large, open atrium—he could see thin columns of smoke twisting up from the lower levels, as if a fire had broken out at the base of the freestanding transparent elevator shafts.

Nog rushed to the railing, leaned over, and peered down to the bottom level. Glowing lances of light from rapidly moving palm torches blazed within the heavy smoke that filled the central concourse five floors down. Though he could see nothing else within the murk, his sensitive ears identified the rush of fire-fighting chemicals being sprayed by the dome's emergency crews. He could also hear the thunder of running footsteps, as other personnel bounded up the stairways that spiraled around the atrium, fleeing the fire below.

To the side Nog saw a disaster locker that had automatically opened as soon as the alarms had sounded. He ran to it and took out two emergency pressure suits, each vacuum-compressed to rectangular blocks no larger than a sandwich. As swiftly as he could, he tugged the carry loops of the compressed suits over his wrist, then charged up the closest stairway himself, pushing coughing ensigns and other Fleet workers out of his way while automatically counting each one, even as he also kept track of each set of twenty stair risers that ran from level to level. He was a Ferengi, thank the Great River, and numbers were as integral to his soul as breathing—fourteen times each minute, or approximately 20,000 times each Martian day.

Torrents of statistics flooded his mind as he ran, triggered by the people he passed. In this dome, he knew, most of the personnel were either Andorian (42 percent precisely) or Tellarite (23.6 percent), supplemented by a few dozen Vulcans (48) and Betazoids (42) who had been unable to find rooms in the respective domes set to their environmental preferences.

Of the six main personnel domes in this installation—hurriedly constructed after the attack of '88—none were set to Earth-normal conditions. After '88 it just hadn't made sense.

The Old Man's quarters, however, as befitted a VIP suite, had individual gravity modifiers and atmospheric controls, enabling flag officers and distinguished guests to select any preferred environmental condition, from the Breen Asteroidal Swarm frigid wasteland to Vulcan high desert. Those quarters were on the ninth level, just one below the topmost ground-level floor, with its common-area gymnasium, arboretum, and mess hall.

By the time he reached that level, Nog's feet were stinging from a dozen small cuts inflicted by the rough non-skid surface of the stairs. But mere discomfort had no power to slow him. He looked up once just long enough to see that all the clear panes of the dome's faceted roof were still intact, then headed away from the stairs to charge down the corridor leading to the VIP units.

Nog swore again as he saw the bodies of two guards sprawled on the floor by the shattered security door. Absolute evidence, he feared, that the sabotage of the generators was just a diversion, that the real target was alone and defenseless at the end of this final corridor.

Nog launched himself like an old-fashioned Martian astronaut over the knife-sharp shards of the shattered door. At the same time, like a twenty-fourth-century commando, he thumbed his phaser to full power. The pen-size silver tube bore little resemblance to the weapons he had trained with when he entered the Academy more than twenty-five years ago. But at its maximum setting this new model had all the stopping power of an old compression phaser rifle. For ten discharges, at least.

Nog finally slowed as he rounded the last corner before the Old Man's quarters. The sirens were quieter here, and only one warning light spun, presumably because security staff were always on duty here. But none of those alarms was necessary, because there was no mistaking the distinctive ozone scent of Romulan polywave disruptors—and that was warning enough that a security breach was under way.

He had been right about the true target of this attack, but the knowledge brought him no satisfaction. The Old Man was ninety-five years old—in no condition to resist an attack by Romulan assassins. The best Nog could hope to do now was to keep the killers from escaping.

Two more long strides brought him to the entrance of the Old Man's quarters. As he had expected, both doors had been blown out of their tracks, sagging top and bottom, half disintegrated, their ragged edges sparkling with the blue crystals of solidified quantum polywaves.

Phaser held ready, Nog advanced through the twisted panels, into a spacious sitting room striped with gauzy tendrils of smoke. The only source of light came from a large aquarium set into a smooth gray wall. The aquarium obviously had its own backup power supply, and undulating ripples of blue light now swept the room, set in motion by the graceful movement of the fins of the Old Man's prized lionfish.

Nog paused for a moment, intent on hearing the slightest noise, certain the assassins could not have left so soon. The shields that protected the shipyard's ground installations were separately powered by underground *and* orbital generating stations, and not even the new Grigari subspace pulse-transporters could penetrate the constantly modulating deflector screens. However the Romulans planned to escape, their first step had to be on foot.

Nog had no intention of letting them take that step—or any others.

As methodically as a sensor sweep, he turned his head so his ears could fix on any sounds that might be coming from the short hall leading to the bedroom, or from the door to the small kitchen, or from the door to the study.

He concentrated on the hallway. Nothing. Though that didn't rule out the possibility that someone might be hiding in the bedroom.

Next, the kitchen. Nothing.

Then the study. And there Nog heard slow, shallow breathing.

He began to move sideways, still holding his phaser before him, aiming it at the study door. There was just enough light from the aquarium to avoid bumping the bland Starfleet furniture. He flattened himself against the wall beside the study door, silently counting down for his own—

—*attack!*

His absolutely perfect textbook move propelled him through the study doorway in a fluid low-gravity roll, smoothly bringing him to his feet in a crouch, thumb already pushing down on the activation button of his phaser as he targeted the first Romulan he saw—the one on the floor by the desk.

But when the silver phaser beam punched its way through the Romulan, the Romulan gave no reaction.

For an instant, Nog stared at his adversary in puzzlement. Then reality caught up to him. His shot had been unnecessary.

The first Romulan was already dead.

So was the second Romulan, slumped on the couch. The gold shoulder of his counterfeit Starfleet uniform was darkened by green blood seeping from the deep, wide gash that scored his neck.

Then a tremulous, raspy voice came from the direction of the room's bookcases. The ones filled with real books. "There's a third one in the bedroom."

Nog slowly straightened up from his crouch. "Admiral?"

The Old Man stepped from the shadows, into the light spilling through the doorway behind Nog. He was a *hew-mon,* slightly stooped. His bald scalp was flushed a deep red, and his long fringe of white hair, usually tied back in a Klingon-style queue, sprayed across his bare shoulders. Only then did Nog realize that the Old Man was naked, his sharp skeleton painfully evident through nearly translucent, thin skin. The only object he carried was a *bat'leth.* It dripped with dark and glistening green blood.

But the Old Man's eyes were sparkling, and the creases around them crinkled in amusement as he also took a closer look at his would-be rescuer. "It appears you're out of uniform, Nog."

Nog laughed with affection. "Look who's talking, Jean-Luc."

Fleet Admiral Jean-Luc Picard—the beloved Old Man to his staff—joined in the laughter. "I was in the sonic shower when—" He doubled over, coughing.

Immediately, Nog pulled from the couch a blanket untouched by Romulan blood, and draped it carefully around the Old Man's sharp-boned shoulders. Fittingly, Nog saw, the blanket was woven with the old Starfleet emblem and the name and registration of Picard's last ship command: the *U.S.S. Enterprise,* NCC-1701-F.

Nog reached for the *bat'leth.* "Maybe I should take that."

The Old Man stared at the weapon for a few moments, as if wondering how it came to be in his hands.

"That's the one Worf gave you, isn't it?" Nog asked gently.

The Old Man seemed relieved. "That's right." He handed the *bat'leth* to Nog. "How is Worf? Have you heard from him on Deep Space 9?"

Nog kept his smile steady. He had already conferred with Starfleet Medical on this: The Old Man was in the secondary stages of Irumodic Syndrome, a degenerative disorder linked to a progressive and incurable deterioration of the synaptic pathways. The doctors had told Nog that the Old Man's short-term memory would be first to show signs of disruption, and that's just what had happened. It had become common this past year for the admiral to forget the names of the newer researchers who had joined Project Phoenix. But now, as the project drew nearer its absolute deadline and the unrelenting pressure mounted, it was distressing to see that the Old Man also seemed to be having more and more difficulty recalling events that had occurred years, even decades, before.

"Worf is dead, Jean-Luc," Nog said quietly. "When Deep Space 9—"

The Old Man's eyes widened. "—was destroyed. That's right." He licked his dry lips, pulled the blanket of his last command more tightly around his shoulders. "That's when it all started, you know."

Nog understood what the Old Man meant. Everyone in what was left of the Federation did. With the destruction of Deep Space 9 and the discovery of the second wormhole in Bajoran space, all the conditions that had led to this terrible state of siege had been set in place.

"I was there when it happened," Nog reminded him.

Late at night, the memories of that last day, that last hour on DS9, that last minute before he had been beamed out to the *U.S.S. Garneau,* were as vivid to Nog as if they had happened only hours earlier, as if he were still in his youth, still only an ensign.

Back then, back there, he had been working in Ops with Garak and Jadzia, painstakingly restoring the station's computers. Then something had happened in his uncle's bar. Captain Sisko had asked for Jadzia's help, for Chief O'Brien's help, even for Nog's father's help. But he had not asked for Nog's.

Less than an hour later, the gravimetric structure of space had suddenly distorted, and every warning light and siren in Ops had gone off at once as the order came to abandon the station. Even now, Nog was still unable to make sense of the readings he had seen at the time. Only after the fact had he learned that a wormhole had opened unnaturally slowly in his uncle's bar on the Promenade. After the fact, he had learned that a few survivors from the Promenade had been beamed aboard the rescue flotilla, with stories describing how the three Red Orbs of Jalbador had moved into alignment by themselves, somehow triggering the wormhole's appearance.

But in the confusion of those final moments, Nog had been left with the mystery of the sensors, watching uncomprehendingly as transport indicators showed the start of mass beam-outs, and—inexplicably—a handful of beam-ins.

Then, only seconds from the end, when the station's power had failed, plunging all of Ops into momentary darkness before the emergency batteries came on-line, Nog had heard Jake Sisko's voice as if he were calling out from far away. He remembered spinning around, already so close to panic that only Garak's eerily calm example had kept him focused on his work of dropping shields according to emergency evacuation procedures in order to permit as many transports as possible.

But when he had turned in answer to Jake's call—that was when Nog had screamed as only a Ferengi could. Because Jake was only centimeters behind him.

Jake had reached out to him then, silently mouthing Nog's name as if he were shouting as loudly as he could. To his perpetual regret, Nog had drawn back from his friend in fear. His abrupt move caused him to stumble back over his stool, begin to fall, and when he landed, he was on a cargo-transporter on the *Garneau.*

Two muscle-bound lieutenants had dragged him off the array so quickly, one of his arms had been dislocated, the other deeply bruised. And by the time a harried-looking medical technician had finally gotten to him, everything was over.

Deep Space 9.

The *Defiant.*

His father, his uncle, and his best friend, Jake.

Gone. Snuffed out. The void within him the equal of the one that had swallowed everyone he had loved.

"I was there when it happened," Nog said again. "When everyone died."

That sudden flash of a smile came to the Old Man again. "Oh, no. They didn't die, Nog."

But Nog knew that theory, too. And he didn't accept it. If there was any hope for the Federation, for the galaxy, for the universe itself, that hope rested instead with Project Phoenix and the brilliance of Jean-Luc Picard, however much that brilliance was compromised. What needed to be done now—the only thing that *could* be done—was something that only the Old Man had accomplished before; at least, he was the only starship captain alive today who had accomplished it. And Nog, and everyone else who had sacrificed and struggled to make Jean-Luc Picard's *Phoenix* a reality, continued to believe he could do it again. They had to believe.

Fifteen more standard days, Nog thought. All he had to do was keep the Old Man calm and stress-free for 360 more hours. Keep the Old Man's peridaxon levels up. Make sure he slept and ate as his medical team determined was necessary, and the *Phoenix* would fly and the nightmare would end. Failure was unacceptable—and unthinkable.

"Jean-Luc, Captain Sisko was lost with the *Defiant.* They were *all* lost. And now the Federation is counting on *you,* and science. Not some ancient prophecy."

The Old Man stood in the middle of his sitting room, shaking his head like a patient teacher addressing a confused student. "You know . . . you know people used to fight over whether or not a photon was a wave or a particle. Centuries ago they used to think it had the characteristics of both, and depending which characteristic an experiment was set up to find, that's the characteristic that was revealed."

It might have been a long time ago, but Nog still remembered the science history classes he had taken at the Academy. He was familiar with the muddled early beginnings of multiphysics, when scientists had first encountered quantum effects and had lacked the basic theory to understand them as anything more than apparently contradictory phenomena. He knew that the old physicists' mistake had not been in trying to determine the nature of light as particle or wave, but in thinking it had to be only one or the other. Fortunately, the blinding simplicity of the Hawking Recursive-Dimension Interpretation had taken care of that fallacy, and all apparent quantum contradictions had disappeared from the equations overnight, opening the door to applied quantum engineering for everything from faster-than-light communication to the Heisenberg compensators used in every transporter and replicator system to this day.

"The debate over the nature of light is ancient *history*," Nog said kindly. "Not science. Certainly not prophecy."

Another tremor shook the floor beneath them. Longer and more sustained than the others that had preceded it. Nog looked away from the Old Man as his ears picked up a distant, high-pitched whistle, something he doubted any *hew-mon* would be able to hear. To him, it could mean only one thing: The atmospheric forcefields were down.

"But the way the question was *resolved*," the Old Man insisted. "That's what's applicable today."

Nog quickly slipped one of the vacuum-compressed emergency suits off his wrist, tugged on the loop to break the seal, and in less than a second shook out a crinkly, semitransparent blue jumpsuit. "Here, Jean-Luc. We'd better put these on."

"Y'see," the Old Man said, as he stepped agonizingly slowly into one leg of the suit, then the other, "the conflict between particle and wave was resolved when it was discovered that the real answer united *both* aspects. Different sides of the same coin."

Nog slipped the blanket from Picard's shoulders and helped pull both the Old Man's sleeves on, making sure the admiral's hands reached to the mitt-like ends.

"Same thing with ancient prophecy and science," the Old Man explained.

Nog smoothed out the flaps of Picard's suit opening, then pressed them together so the molecular adhesors created an airtight seal. All that remained now was to pull up the hood hanging down the Old Man's back, seal that to the suit, then twist the small metal cylinder at the suit's neck, which would inflate the face mask to provide the admiral with ten minutes of emergency air while at the same time transmitting a transporter distress beacon.

Though he estimated the atmospheric pressure in the personnel dome would hold for the next minute or two, Nog didn't want to take any chances with the Old Man. Swiftly, he positioned Picard's hood, sealed it, then twisted the cylinder so that a clear bubble of micro-thin polymer formed around the Old Man's face.

"Science and ancient prophecy," the admiral shouted through the mask, undeterred by all of Nog's ministerings. "Look deeply enough, and who's to say both aren't different aspects of the same thing? Just like particle and wave!"

Even as Nog shook out his own suit, quickly donning and sealing it, the admiral's words had a chilling effect on him. The Ascendancy's propaganda had won it dozens of worlds already—fifty-two, to be exact, according to the latest intelligence estimates. If those false-hoods were to reach the workers of Project Phoenix, perhaps the project would survive. But if they infected Admiral Picard . . . Nog didn't even want to think of the consequences.

Nog hesitated before pulling his own hood over his head. For-tunately, the pressure suits were designed to fit up to a 200-kilogram Tellarite, so there would be ample room even for a Ferengi head and ears. "Jean-Luc, you can't allow yourself to be distracted by Ascendancy lies. You have to concentrate on finishing the *Phoenix.*"

"But they're not lies," Picard replied indignantly.

Nog put his hands on the Old Man's shoulders, and their suits crackled like a blazing campfire. "Jean-Luc, please. Remember what you've been telling us since the project began. The Ascendancy will do anything, *say* anything, to divert us from our course."

Picard patted Nog's hand on his left shoulder. "But that was *before,* Will."

"Before what?" Nog didn't bother to correct the Old Man. When

he was tired or confused, the admiral often thought Nog was his old
first officer from the *Enterprise-D* and *E,* Will Riker. Another casualty of '88.

"Before this attack!" The Old Man spread his arms grandly, and
Nog noticed that both his suit and Picard's had begun to expand
slightly, obviously in response to reduced air pressure in the dome.

Nog checked the ready light on the small metal cylinder on his
own suit. The emergency beacon was transmitting. The automatic
search-and-rescue equipment installed throughout the Utopia Planitia
Fleet Yards was designed to be activated by the first sign of falling air
pressure. By now, Nog knew, sensors throughout the domes should be
locking on to emergency beacons and activating automatic short-
range transporters to beam personnel to underground shelters.

"What's so special about this attack?"

"It's fifteen days!" the Old Man said. "Don't you see? It's no
coincidence they're attacking now! It's a diversion. To keep us from
the truth."

"What truth?" Nog shouted. The air outside his suit was thinning
rapidly, and the Old Man's voice was fading.

"They've come back!" the Old Man said. "It's the only explanation."

Then, before Nog could offer an alternate explanation of his own,
he was relieved to see the Old Man begin to dissolve in a transporter
beam, followed a moment later by the transformation into light of
the admiral's quarters. They were both being beamed away.

But as their new location took shape around them, Nog realized
with a start that they hadn't been beamed to safety in the underground shelters.

Martian gravity had been replaced by Class-M normal.

He and the Old Man were no longer in the shipyards, and the
people surrounding them were not Starfleet emergency-evacuation
personnel.

They were Romulans.

And this close to the end of the universe, Nog knew that Romulans could want only one thing.

The death of Admiral Jean-Luc Picard.

CHAPTER 3

SOMETIMES, Julian Bashir remembered what it was like to be normal.

But such bittersweet memories were suspect, because they were invariably mixed in with disjointed recollections of his early childhood, from his first faint glimmerings of self-awareness to age six. For the rest of his childhood—that is, everything beyond age 6 years plus 142 days—there were, of course, no disjointed recollections, only perfect recall. Because on the one hundred forty-third day of his seventh year of existence he had awakened in the suffocating gel of an amino-diffusion bath, with an illegally altered genetic structure. On that day everything had changed—not just within the boy he had been, but within the universe that had previously surrounded him.

In fact, sometimes it seemed to Bashir that the innocent male child who had been born to his parents thirty-four years ago had perished in that back-alley gene mill on Adigeon Prime, and that he—the altered creature who now called himself Julian Bashir—was in fact a changeling of old Earth legends.

Little Julian—the terrified boy who had been immersed in the diffusion bath with no idea what he had done wrong to make his parents punish him in such a way—had been undeniably slow to learn throughout his entire brief life. His environment had been a constant marvel to him, because so much of it was simply beyond his natural capacity to comprehend. His beloved stuffed bear, Kukalaka, had been no less alive to him than his mother's cruelly nipping and yipping Martian terriers. To little Julian, it had been obvious that the various computer interfaces in his home contained little people who could speak to him. And he had only been able to watch in wonder as the other children at his school somehow answered questions or accomplished tasks with abilities indistinguishable to him from magic.

One recollection that most often resurfaced when least wanted from those blurry, half-remembered days of dull normalcy, was of standing in his school's playroom listening to Naomi Pedersen chant the times table. To little Julian there had been absolutely no connection between the numerals that floated above the holoboard and the words that his classmate sang out. The disconnect had been so profound that Bashir clearly remembered his early, untransformed self not even attempting to understand what was going on: Naomi was simply uttering random noises, and the squiggles above the holoboard were only unrelated doodles.

From his present vantage point, Bashir regarded those days of simple incomprehension as the peace of innocence. They marked a time when he was unaware that life was a continuing struggle, a never-ending series of problems to be overcome by those equipped to recognize and solve them.

Now he recognized that same peace of incomprehension in most of the fourteen others with whom he had just been transported from the *Defiant,* and he envied them their unknowing normalcy.

But, incapable of giving in to what he suspected was their hopeless situation, Bashir still studied his surroundings. He and the others were standing together in what appeared to be a familiar setting: the hangar deck of a Starfleet vessel, complete with the usual bold yellow sign warning about variable gravity fields, and the stacks of modular shipping crates marked with the Starfleet delta and standard identification labels. Other than the fact that the lighting was about half intensity, and the air unusually cool, Bashir could almost believe he was on a standard Starfleet cargo ship in his own time. Only the Starfleet emblem on the crates confirmed that he and the others from the *Defiant* were still in the future.

Interestingly enough, that emblem, though understandably different from the one used in his time, was also different from the emblem Captain Riker had worn on his uniform, and that had been emblazoned on the Klingon cruiser. That identifying mark, Bashir recalled, had placed a gold Starfleet arrowhead against an upside-down triangle of blue. But here on this ship, the arrowhead was set within a vertically elongated oval, its width matching the oval's. The arrowhead itself was colored the red of human blood, the lower half of the oval teal and the upper half gold—as if the colors of the *k'Roth ch'Kor,* the ancient Klingon trident that was the symbol of the Empire, had been merged with the more recent symbol of Starfleet.

But rather than give himself a headache trying to fathom the political permutations that might have led to the two different versions of the Starfleet emblem in this future, Bashir set that particular problem aside. Instead, he directed his attention to the conversations going on around him—five now—and his mind was such that he could effortlessly keep up with each at the same time. In all except one of those conversations, Bashir heard relief expressed, primarily because of the familiar surroundings.

The single conversation that was more guarded was that between Jadzia and Worf. Klingon pessimism and the Trill's seven lifetimes of experience were obviously enabling the two officers to come to the same conclusion Bashir's enhanced intellect had reached: They were in more danger now than when the *Defiant* had come under attack.

Bashir wasted little time contemplating what might happen in the next few minutes. His primary responsibility was to his crewmates, and to the few civilians who had been evacuated from Deep Space 9 to the *Defiant* and then beamed here.

He rapidly assessed the fourteen others for obvious signs of injury or distress. Nine of them were either *Defiant* or DS9 crew members, six in Starfleet uniforms, three in the uniforms of the Bajoran militia. The other five, including—Bashir was surprised to see—the unorthodox archaeologist Vash, were civilians; three of these human, the other two Bajorans.

He also noted, without undue concern, that the medical patch on the side of Jadzia's forehead was stained with blood and needed to be replaced. Without a protoplaser he had been unable to close the small wound; the dense capillary network beneath a Trill's spots made them prone to copious and unsightly—though not life-threatening—bleeding as a result of any minor cut or scrape in the general area.

Close by Jadzia's side, Worf was uninjured and unbowed. His uniform was soiled by smoke, and one side of his broad face was streaked with soot. His scowl was evidence not of any wound to his body, but rather to his sense of pride and honor—outrage being his people's traditional response to captivity.

Bashir also observed that Jake Sisko, who was currently engaged in listening carefully to Worf and Jadzia's conversation without taking part, also seemed unharmed. The tall, lanky young man had been helping out in the *Defiant*'s sickbay when the group transport to this ship had taken place. It was a blessing, Bashir thought, that at least none of the *Defiant*'s surviving crew or passengers had required critical medical attention before their doctor had been kidnapped.

Then again, the last he himself could recall from his own final moments on the *Defiant*'s bridge was that there were still some antimatter contact mines attached to her hull, so there was no way of knowing if the ship or any of the crew and passengers not transported here still survived.

Then a hoarse female voice interrupted his thoughts. "This isn't good, is it?"

It was Vash, and automatically Bashir reviewed her condition. The last place he had seen her had been in Quark's bar, when the three Red Orbs of Jalbador had moved themselves into alignment and somehow triggered the opening of a second wormhole in Bajoran space.

Vash, an admittedly alluring adventurer and archaeologist of questionable ethics, was still in the same outfit she had worn in the bar—no more than an hour ago in relative time—as if she were prepared to trek across the Bajoran deserts in search of lost cities. She no longer toted her well-worn oversized shoulder bag, though. Bashir guessed it must be either back on the *Defiant* or left behind in the mad rush from Quark's and the subsequent mass beam-out to the evacuation flotilla.

Vash waved an imperious hand in front of his face. "You keep staring at me like that, I'm going to think one of us has a problem. And it's not me."

"Sorry," Bashir said, flushing. "I didn't see you on the *Defiant*. There were some injuries from the evacuation, and . . ." He shrugged. It was pointless to say anything more. It was quite likely Vash was used to people staring at her, for all the obvious reasons.

"I was hustled into the *Defiant*'s mess hall right after I was beamed aboard." Vash frowned. "What the hell happened?"

Bashir told her as succinctly as he could. The old, apocryphal legends of the Red Orbs of Jalbador had turned out to be correct, at least in part. A second Temple—or wormhole—had opened, though since they were now twenty-five years or so into the future the part of the legend about the opening of the second Temple causing the end of the universe was clearly and thankfully not correct. Bashir was about to describe the attacking ships and what Captain Thomas Riker had said about the War of the Prophets, but Vash interrupted.

"Twenty-five years? Into the *future?*"

Bashir nodded. "It happens."

"Not to me."

"Think of it as archaeology in reverse."

Vash's eyes flashed. "This isn't funny, Doc. The longer we stay here the more likely it is we'll learn about the future, and the less likely we are to have someone let us go back." She looked over at the crates. "Especially if some bureaucrat at Starfleet has anything to say about it."

"That's true," Bashir agreed. He glanced at the main personnel doors leading into the interior of whatever vessel they were aboard— one of the two surviving attack ships, he had concluded. "But on the plus side, no one from this ship has attempted to communicate with us. That could suggest they're also following Starfleet regulations, and want to keep us isolated for our return."

"You don't really believe that."

"And why not?"

"If they wanted to keep us isolated, why beam us off the *Defiant?*"

"We were under attack. The *Defiant* might have been destroyed."

"Attacked by who?" Vash asked, and Bashir told her the other half of the story, about Thomas Riker in the *Opaka* and the three attacking Starfleet vessels.

"That makes no sense," Vash said when Bashir had finished.

"Things change. Twenty-five years is a long time."

"How things have changed has nothing to do with our current situation," Vash told him. "If this is a Starfleet vessel, how long do you think it would take some technician to run a search of the service record of the *Defiant?*"

"Your point?"

"C'mon, Doc. Did that strange transporter scramble your synapses? If the historical record shows the *Defiant* disappeared with all hands when DS9 was destroyed, then we're not going back. It's that simple."

Bashir bit his lip. Vash had reached the same conclusion he had. There were a few unresolved issues, however. "This ship we're on was probably one of the ones involved in the attack. If it's been damaged, the *Defiant*'s service record may not be available. The delay in any attempted communication could be a result of having to wait to hear back from Starfleet Command."

Vash looked skeptical. "I never took *you* for much of a dreamer."

Before Bashir could reply, Jadzia, Worf, and Jake had joined them.

"Julian," Jadzia said teasingly, "a dreamer? Like no other, complete with stars in his eyes."

Bashir did not respond to Jadzia's banter. She had been trying to act as if nothing had changed between them since she had married Worf. But it had. Though until these last few weeks, when Jadzia and Worf had sought his counsel on the likelihood of a Klingon and a Trill procreating, Bashir had almost convinced himself that Worf was only a temporary inconvenience, not an insurmountable barrier. In time, he had reasoned, Jadzia would tire of her plainspoken Klingon mate and begin to seek more sophisticated company. But knowing her as he did, even he could not fantasize a time when Jadzia would tire of her child-to-be, or deny that child a chance to know its father.

So there it was. His heart was broken, and his success at hiding his misery from Jadzia was one of the few advantages of having an enhanced intellect: Only his ability to master advanced Vulcan meditation techniques was sparing him public and personal humiliation.

"Vash is concerned that the longer we wait here," Bashir explained, "the less likely it is we'll be allowed to go back to our own time."

"Allowed?" Jake asked in alarm.

Jadzia put her hand on the young man's shoulder. "To go back, Jake, we're going to need access to advanced technology."

Jake looked confused. "What about temporal slingshot?"

Jadzia shook her head. "We didn't get here by slingshot, so we don't have a Feynman curve to follow back to our starting point. Any attempt we make to move into the past will result in a complete temporal decoupling."

Jake stared at her, not a gram of understanding in him.

Worf took over. "It would be like entering a planet's atmosphere at too shallow an angle. Our craft would skip out, away from the planet, never to return."

"Though in our case," Jadzia continued, "we would skip out of our normal space-time and . . . well, then it becomes a question of philosophy, not physics. But if you think about it, if anyone with a warp drive could go back in time wherever and whenever she wanted, half the stars in the galaxy wouldn't exist. I mean, a century ago Klingons would have gone back in time a million years and dropped asteroids on Earth and Vulcan to eliminate the Empire's competitors before they had ever evolved."

Jake glanced at Worf. "Really?"

Worf shifted uncomfortably. "It was a different time. But yes, I have heard rumors of the Empire dispatching temporal assault teams to destroy . . . enemy worlds before the enemy could arise."

"What happened to them?" Jake asked.

"We do not know."

But as Bashir anticipated, Jadzia found so simple an answer unacceptable. "As far as we can tell," she said, "the physics of it is pretty straightforward. Any given time traveler moving from one time to another at a rate greater than the local entropic norm, or on a reverse entropic vector, *has* to move outside normal space-time along a pathway called a Feynman curve. Now, if the past the traveler goes to is not disrupted, the Feynman curve retains its integrity and, provided the traveler can find it again, the way is clear to return to the starting point. However, if the timeline is significantly disrupted, the Feynman curve collapses, because its end point—that is, the traveler's starting point—no longer exists. It's like cutting the end of a rope bridge."

Bashir was curious to see how Jake's imaginative mind would

tackle Jadzia's elegantly defined problems of temporal mechanics. Though strict causality did not exist at the most fundamental levels of the universe, it *was* the defining characteristic of macroscopic existence. Indeed, that was one of the chief reasons why the warp drive and time travel took so long to be discovered by emerging cultures. Even though both concepts were rather simple, requiring little more than a basic atomic-age engineering capability to demonstrate, the ideas of faster-than-light travel and time-like curves independent of space could not easily be grasped by minds narrowly conditioned by primitive Einsteinian physics—any more than Newton could have conceived of relativistic time dilation.

Jake's young face wrinkled in concentration. "Hold it . . . it sounds as if you're saying that the Klingons *could* have traveled back in time and destroyed the Earth."

"There's no reason why they couldn't," Jadzia agreed. "In fact, several of the temporal assault missions Worf mentioned could have succeeded. It's just that if they did destroy the Earth in the past, the present they came from—in which the Earth had not been destroyed—no longer existed, so they could never return to it."

"But . . . ," Jake said uncertainly, ". . . the Earth *does* exist."

"In this timeline," Jadzia agreed. She smiled indulgently at Jake. "What you're struggling with is what they used to call on Earth the grandfather paradox. It was a long time ago, before anyone thought time travel possible. Yet early theorists imagined a situation in which a time traveler could go back in time and kill his grandfather before his father was conceived. No father meant no son. No son meant no time traveler. But no time traveler meant that the grandfather hadn't been killed, so the father was born, the son became the time traveler, and . . ." Jadzia smiled as Jake finished the paradox.

". . . and the grandfather was killed." Jake's expression was thoughtful. "But . . . you're saying that *can* happen?"

"There's nothing to prevent it. The difference between what the Einsteinian-era physicists thought and what we know today, from actual experimental demonstrations, is that no paradox results."

"How's that possible?"

"Two solutions are suggested, but neither is testable—so both have equal validity. One solution is that if you, say, went back in time and killed your grandfather, a temporal feedback loop would be established that would collapse into a hyperdimensional black hole, cutting the loop off from any interaction with the rest of the universe. The end result would be as if the events leading to the feedback loop never happened. The second solution states that the instant you killed your grandfather, you'd create a branching timeline. That is, two universes would now exist—one in which your grandfather lived, and one in which he died."

"But if he died, then how could I go back and kill him?"

"You can't, Jake. Not from the new timeline. But since you came from the old one, there's no paradox. However, because the Feynman curve you followed no longer exists, you are trapped in the new timeline you created, with no way to get back. In effect, you're a large virtual particle that has tunneled out of the quantum foam."

Jadzia put her hand on Worf's shoulder, a gesture of familiarity that caused an unexpected tightness in Bashir's throat. "A few years ago," she said, "when Worf was on the *Enterprise,* he encountered a series of parallel universes that were extremely similar to our own. Some researchers suggest that those parallel dimensions have actually been created by the manipulation of past events by time travelers."

Vash put her hands on her hips and sighed noisily. "Do the rest of us have to know this for the test? Or does *any* of this hypothetical moonshine have anything to do with *our* situation, right here and now?"

Bashir sensed Jadzia's dislike of Vash in the Trill's quick reply, though her words were polite. "It has everything to do with our situation, Vash. From *our* perspective, we've traveled into our future. But from the perspective of the people who live here, we're intruders from the past who—if we return—could prevent this future from ever existing."

"It wouldn't just be a split-off, parallel dimension?" Jake asked.

"It might be," Jadzia allowed. "But then again, this present might just wink out of existence, along with everyone in it. Remember what happened on Gaia, to the people who were our descendants? If this was your present, would you be willing to risk nonexistence for the sake of a handful of refugees from the past?"

As Jake thought that over, Worf added, "Several years ago, the *Enterprise* encountered the *Bozeman*—a Starfleet vessel that had been caught in a temporal causality loop for almost a century. Once we broke the loop, the crew of the ship was in the same situation we face now."

"What happened to them?" Jake asked.

Worf frowned. "Historical records stated that the *Bozeman* had disappeared without a trace. Since it had never returned home in our timeline, Starfleet could not risk sending it back. Under Starfleet regulations, her captain and her crew were . . . resettled in their new time."

"And that's what's going to happen to us?" Jake said, dismayed.

"That appears to be the most likely outcome," Bashir said, when no one else offered an answer to Jake's question.

"Not for me," Vash said. "I'm not Starfleet. I'm going home."

"Really? How?" Jadzia asked. Bashir could tell she intended her challenge to reduce Vash to inarticulate silence.

But Vash merely issued her own challenge. "I thought *you* were the big expert on the Bajoran Orbs. You've never heard of the Orb of Time?"

"She's right!" Jake said.

Vash smiled dazzlingly at Jake. "Okay. I've got one partner. Anyone else?"

Bashir shook his head, refusing to play Vash's game.

"Too dangerous," Jadzia said. "We didn't get here through the Orb of Time, so there's no Orb-related Feynman curve connecting back to our own time."

Vash rolled her eyes. "C'mon! You're a scientist—think outside the warp bubble. Let's say you hadn't reached this time period on the *Defiant*. You could have lived through the past twenty-five years, easy. Are you telling me that under those conditions you couldn't use the Orb of Time to slip back twenty-five years?"

"Of course I could," Jadzia said, and Bashir could hear the growing annoyance in her tone. "Because the subatomic chronometric particles bound within my molecular structure would be in perfect synch with the current universe's background chronitronic radiation environment. I would *belong* in this time. But all of us are out of phase, Vash. We can't establish a second Feynman curve in this time because we're already connected to the first curve, stretching from our own time. Either we go back the way we came—by traveling through the boundary region of the wormhole that brought us here—or we don't go home at all."

Vash groaned in frustration, her expression becoming almost that of a wild creature held against its will.

Bashir leaned forward, lightly touching Vash's arm. "We're still simply speculating," he said in his most reassuring tone. "Starfleet might send us back at any moment."

"And if they don't?" Vash retorted.

Bashir took a deep breath and said what he knew someone had to say. "Then considering all the possible timelike curves we might have followed, perhaps twenty-five years isn't all that bad."

"What?!" Vash exclaimed.

"You said it yourself. This time period is within our natural life-times. People we know will still be alive. The places we know won't have changed all that much. It will be easier for us to adapt than it was for the crew of the *Bozeman*."

This time Vash grabbed his arm, and her tone was not at all reassuring. "Is it that easy to make a quitter out of you?"

Bashir peeled her hand off his arm. There were larger issues at stake. "Are you that willing to risk the lives of the billions of beings alive in this time who might be wiped from existence by a single act of selfishness on your part?"

Vash's cheeks reddened as her voice rose in anger. "I didn't ask to be beamed to the *Defiant*. I didn't ask to . . . oh, I *hate* you Starfleet types. The good of the many . . . it makes me sick!" Then she whirled around and marched off toward the main personnel door leading from the hangar deck.

Bashir resisted following, but he called out to her, "Vash! If you go out that door, you only increase the odds they won't send you back!"

Vash's pace did not lessen.

"Don't worry," Jadzia said. "The door will be sealed."

Just then the status of the door ceased to be important, because Vash suddenly collided with—nothing.

Bashir saw her come to a sudden stop, as if she had run into a slab of transparent aluminum, undetectable in the dim light of the hangar deck. Vash stepped back and rubbed at her face, then reached out and slapped her hand against something that was solid, yet absolutely invisible.

"She's hit a forcefield," Jadzia said.

"Unusual," Worf commented. "Most forcefields emit Pauli exclusion sparks when anything physical makes contact."

"Whatever it is, I don't think it's anything to worry about," Bashir said. He watched Vash turn and begin to walk across the deck, sliding her hand as she moved along the forcefield's invisible boundary. "I mean, even if it's a forcefield, it's not delivering a warning shock. I think it's further evidence that they want to keep us from interacting with . . ."

He stopped as a throbbing vibration began to sound through the deck, and he heard the rest of the *Defiant*'s crew begin talking excitedly as—

—the main hangar door slid open to reveal stars streaming past to a vanishing point.

Bashir reflexively held his breath. The ship was traveling at warp, and only the hangar deck's atmospheric forcefield was preventing the fifteen of them from being explosively decompressed into the ship's warp field.

"I think someone's trying to get our attention . . . ," Jadzia said lightly.

Bashir turned as he heard the quick hiss of an opening door.

Three Vulcans stood in the corridor beyond, two females and a male, their impassive faces offering no clue as to their intentions.

One after the other, the three Vulcans stepped onto the hangar deck, and Bashir took some solace from the fact that the uniforms they were wearing reflected Starfleet traditions. Their trousers and jackets were made of a vertically ribbed black material, with the entire left shoulder of each jacket constructed of a block of contrasting fabric in a traditional Fleet specialty color, in this case red on two of them and blue on the third. In the center of each colorful shoulder was what could only be a communicator badge, identical to the modified emblem on the crates and complete with the colors of the Klingon *k'Roth ch'Kor.* Only one element was completely new to Bashir: Two of the Vulcans—those with the red shoulders—were wearing large clear visors over their eyes, like some kind of protective shield.

As the three figures halted at the boundary of the forcefield, Bashir took the chance to study their uniforms more closely for rank

markings. He found them on small vertical panels, a centimeter wide
by perhaps four centimeters long, centered on their jackets just
below their collars. Instead of the round pips that Bashir wore, these
uniforms used square tabs, though he felt it was likely the number of
tabs would carry the same meaning.

"The woman on the right, with the blue shoulder," Bashir said
quietly to Jadzia and Worf. "The captain?"

The Vulcan in question had four square tabs in her rank badge,
and seemed older than her two companions. Her skin was a warm
brown, almost the same shade as Jake's, and a few strands of gray
ran as highlights through her severely cut black hair. Since the specialty color on her shoulder was blue, Bashir guessed that either blue
was the current color signifying command or this was a science vessel with a scientist for a captain. She was also the only one of the
three not wearing a visor.

Bashir looked at Worf. "Commander, we should probably follow
the temporal displacement policy to the letter, and you are the rank-
ing command officer."

Worf gave Bashir a curt nod, then stepped toward the silent
Vulcans.

"I am Lieutenant Commander Worf of the *Starship Defiant*. I
have reason to believe these people and I have been inadvertently
transferred approximately twenty-five years into our future. Under
the terms of Starfleet's temporal displacement policy, I request
immediate assistance for our return to our own time."

The Vulcan captain put her hands behind her back as she began to
speak. "Commander Worf, I am Captain T'len, commander of this
destroyer, the *Augustus*. You and your people have been positively
identified by your DNA signatures, obtained from transporter records.
As you have surmised, you have traveled in time almost twenty-five
years from what was your present. The current stardate is 76958.2."

She paused, and Bashir concluded it was to let her confirmation
of their fate sink in. "As I suspect you have also already surmised,"
she then continued, "the historical record shows that the ship on
which you made this temporal transfer was lost with all hands on
stardate 51889.4, concurrent with the destruction of the space station
Deep Space 9. Under these circumstances, Starfleet regulations are
clear. Do you agree?"

Worf's voice deepened. "I would like to examine the historical record myself."

Captain T'len raised an eyebrow. "That would be a waste of time and resources. If you do not believe me, logic suggests you will not be able to believe any historical transcript I provide."

Bashir was slightly surprised that T'len wasn't aware that Klingons preferred physical proof to logical inference. "Then I wish to be put in contact with officials from the Federation Department of Temporal Investigations."

T'len's deep sigh—a most atypical expression of emotion, unless Vulcans in this future were somehow different—strongly suggested to Bashir that the Vulcan was under some undisclosed yet incredible strain.

"Commander," she said almost wearily, "your personnel records indicate you are a reasonable being. Indeed, the records available for most of the other non-Bajorans with you indicate a high degree of probability you can still be of use to Starfleet in this time period. All you need to know now is that the Federation Department of Temporal Investigations no longer exists. Twelve years ago its responsibilities were assumed by Starfleet's Temporal Warfare Division. I assure you that under current conditions the personnel of the TWD are most unlikely to expend any effort in trying to convince you that this present is everything I say it is. You must either accept my word, or not."

Worf's grim expression betrayed his struggle to maintain composure in the face of what he obviously considered a threat, though it was as yet of an unspecified nature.

"What *are* the current conditions?" Worf asked, immensely pleasing Bashir. That was exactly the question he would have asked first, to be quickly followed by inquiries about the exact nature of the ominously named Temporal Warfare Division and what the Vulcan captain meant by her cryptic reference to the Bajorans among them not being useful.

"The Federation is at war with the Bajoran Ascendancy. And my crew and I have no more time to waste with you than does the TWD. Therefore, I put it to you and your people as straightforwardly as I can. The non-Bajorans among you may now take this opportunity to reaffirm your loyalty to the Federation and to Starfleet, and to join us in our war. Those who comply will be allowed to leave the hangar deck and will be assigned to suitable positions within the fleet.

Those who do not comply will remain on the hangar deck with the Bajorans until the atmospheric forcefield is dropped, in . . ." T'len tapped her communicator badge twice. ". . . three minutes."

Immediately, yellow warning lights spun across the deck and bulkheads as the familiar Starfleet computer voice announced, *"Warning. The hangar deck will decompress in three minutes. Please vacate the area."*

All around Bashir, the other captives began to talk in groups again, their mutterings and exclamations full of anger and shock. But Worf, interestingly, seemed only to become calmer, as if now that he understood the challenge he faced, he could focus all his energy on overcoming it.

"Am I to believe," the Klingon growled, "that in only twenty-five years Starfleet has degenerated into a gang of murderers?"

"Believe what you will," T'len replied crisply. "We are fighting for more than you can imagine. Logic demands that we waste no time or resources on anything—or anyone—that does not help us in our struggle. Commander Worf, your choice is simple: Join us in our war against the Ascendancy, or die with the Bajorans among you."

"Warning, the hangar deck will decompress in two minutes, thirty seconds. Please vacate the area."

Worf turned to face the fourteen others who looked to him for leadership. He was about to speak when it suddenly came to Bashir what the Vulcan was actually doing. He held up his hand to stop Worf from saying anything more.

"She's bluffing, Worf."

Worf's heavy brow wrinkled as he considered Bashir's emphatic statement, but T'len spoke before he could.

"Dr. Bashir, Vulcans do not bluff."

Bashir's response was immediate and to the point. "And Starfleet doesn't kill its prisoners—war or no war."

The captain held his gaze for long moments, then without a sign, suddenly wheeled and walked back toward the personnel door. "You know what you have to do to survive," she said without looking back. "The prisoner containment field is now deactivated. This door will remain open until five seconds before decompression." Then she and her two companions stepped through that door and were gone.

"Warning, the hangar deck will decompress in two minutes. Please vacate the area."

Vash started for the unseen edge of the forcefield. "Hey! You didn't ask me! I'll join up!"

But Bashir moved forward and pulled her back. "Get back here!"

Vash twisted out of his grip, slapped his hand away. "Look, all due respect to your Bajoran friends, but I don't plan on getting sucked out into hard vacuum!"

"We are in no danger," Bashir said forcefully. He looked around at the others. "Captain T'len will not decompress the hangar deck!"

"How can you be sure?" Worf asked.

"Because she is a Vulcan, and there is no logic to . . . to killing Bajorans, even if somehow they are enemies of Starfleet in this time. And there is absolutely no logic in killing *us*. We're completely contained on this hangar deck. We're no threat to anyone. And you heard what she said about confirming our identities through DNA scans—she knows that none of us is involved in . . . current conditions."

"Then why is she threatening us?" Jake asked.

"Warning, the hangar deck will decompress in one minute, thirty seconds."

Bashir registered Jadzia's and Worf's matching expressions of less-than-full confidence in his argument, as well as the outright look of fear on the five Bajorans, now standing apart from the others. "She's testing us."

"Where's the logic in that?" Jadzia asked.

Bashir knew he lacked a definitive answer. "Maybe what she said about DNA scans wasn't the truth. If they really don't have a way of confirming our identities, they don't really know who we are."

"And why would that be important?" Vash snapped.

But then Jake snapped his fingers. "Founders can fool a DNA scan, right?"

Bashir nodded, equally impressed by and grateful for the young man's quickness. "That could be it. If this . . . Bajoran Ascendancy is a result of the Dominion establishing a foothold in the Alpha Quadrant, Starfleet could still be at war with the Founders. For all Captain T'len knows, we might all be shapeshifters who've impersonated the lost crewmembers of the *Defiant*."

Jadzia narrowed her eyes. "Then why didn't they just strap us down and cut us to see what happened to our blood?"

Bashir winced. She was right. Though the Founders could mimic almost any living being down to the level of its DNA, once a single drop of blood escaped from that duplicated form, it immediately reverted to the Founders' normal gelatinous state. As his Trill colleague had just pointed out, there were easier, more direct methods of being certain Worf and the others weren't changelings.

"Warning, the hangar deck will decompress in sixty seconds. Please vacate the area."

"T'len!" Vash shouted. "I'm on your side! Beam me out!"

"If this is a test," Bashir said sharply, *"you* are most certainly failing."

"Me?" Vash hissed. "I'm the only one acting like a human being. I want to live!"

"Forty-five seconds to explosive decompression," the computer warned.

"Commander Worf!" Everyone turned to the Bajoran who had called out. He was an ensign no older than twenty, face pale with fear, the looped chain of his silver earring trembling. "You can't all die because of us." Bashir saw the other four Bajorans beside the young ensign nod nervously. Apparently they had discussed this act of sacrifice and he spoke for them all. "Do what the captain wants. Save yourselves. We . . . we'll trust in the Prophets."

"Thirty seconds to explosive decompression."

"Y'see?" Vash urged. "Even they don't want any false heroics!"

"It is not false!" Worf barked at her. Then he faced the Bajorans and stood at attention. His words were calm and deliberate. "Ensign, your courage brings honor to us all. But as a Starfleet officer and a Klingon warrior, I cannot abandon you to an unjust fate." Worf placed his arm through the ensign's, taking his stand beside the Bajorans. Jadzia promptly followed his example. Then Bashir, Jake, and all the others, except for one, stood together on the hangar deck, their fates as inextricably linked as their arms.

Only Vash stood alone.

"Fifteen seconds. . . ."

"Captain T'len!" Worf's voice rang out across the cold, dark hangar deck. "If Starfleet has forgotten the ideals for which it once stood, then let our deaths remind you of what you have lost."

Bashir watched Vash rub a hand over her face, almost as if she was more embarrassed than afraid to be so obviously on her own.

"Oh, for . . . ," she muttered, then hastily crossed the few meters to link her arm through Bashir's.

"Ten seconds . . . ," the computer announced.

"Happy now?" Vash asked Bashir.

"We're in no danger," Bashir answered. "I don't know why, but I'm still convinced this is a test."

"I'm convinced you're insane."

With a loud bang, the personnel door guillotined shut.

"Five seconds."

Bashir detected an instant increase in his heart's pumping action at the same time as beside him he heard Vash say, "Oh, what the hell," and he felt her hands on his face as she pulled him around and kissed him as deeply as he had ever been kissed, just as the computer announced, *"The hangar deck will now—"*

Then the rest of the warning was swept away in the sudden roar of rushing wind and the hammering of his heartbeat—and for all his enhanced intellect, Bashir couldn't tell if he was reacting to the threat of sudden death, or to Vash's thrillingly expert kiss.

CHAPTER 4

NOG JUMPED in front of the Old Man to block whatever weapons the Romulans might have, but before he could do anything else, the ribbon-like discharge from a polywave disruptor smeared across his chest.

Instantly Nog felt his entire body numb, then he collapsed to the floor, slightly puzzled by the fact that he was still alive. At maximum power, polywaves could set off a subatomic disintegration cascade that was far more efficient than disassociation by phased energy. He had seen Starfleet's sensor logs of the aftermath of polywave combat—the ghastly scattering of limbs and partial torsos left behind by the tightly bound polyspheres of total matter annihilation.

Yet at the moment, whether he himself lived through such an assault or not was of no importance to him. Because if the Old Man had been hit with even the same type of low-intensity paralysis beam, it was extremely doubtful that the elderly *hew-mon*'s fragile body would survive the shock.

Nog lay absolutely still on the floor—he could do nothing else, no matter what had happened to the admiral. Unlike a phaser stun, the polywave version left its victims completely alert but completely immobilized.

His vision began to blur. He was incapable of blinking, and the flow of air through his emergency breathing mask was drawing moisture from the surface of his eyes. His hearing was also becoming less acute, as if the small muscles connecting to both his primary and secondary eardrums were losing their ability to function. The only sound he could hear clearly was the slow thud of his own heart.

But . . . there. Somewhere in the increasingly indistinct background noise, Nog thought he heard the Old Man speaking. Though how could the *hew-mon* do that if he'd been paralyzed as Nog had?

Suddenly, Nog's field of vision shifted and shook as someone raised him up, ripped open his emergency hood, and peeled back the air mask. At once his vision cleared, and the first thing he saw was a young Romulan woman in the bronze chainmail of the Imperial Legion waving a small device in front of his face. The device, Nog realized, was a dispenser that sprayed a moisturizing mist, to keep his eyes clear.

"Ferengi," the Romulan said, her voice distorted and muffled as if she spoke from behind a door. "I am Centurion Karon. You are on board the Imperial cruiser *Altanex.* Though you cannot respond, I know that you can hear me. Your paralysis will begin to lessen within an hour. There is usually no permanent damage."

Usually?! Nog thought with alarm.

The Centurion shot a second cloud of mist into his eyes. "To answer what I suspect are your most pressing questions, the crew of this ship are no longer allied with the Ascendancy. We need to talk to Admiral Picard. We presume you are his bodyguard or attendant. When we have concluded our discussions, if either or both of you desire, we shall return you to a secure Starfleet base."

If either or both desire? To Nog, it almost sounded as if Karon expected that he and the Old Man might be persuaded never to return to Utopia Planitia. What could she ever say that would make that even a possibility?

Karon misted his eyes again. Though Nog could still only look straight ahead, he now saw the Old Man, hood removed, being led away by two other Romulans without sign of force or struggle.

The Centurion recaptured his attention with her next words. "No matter what decision you ultimately make, neither you nor the Admiral will be harmed. Two bions will now take you to our sickbay. When your paralysis has ended, we will speak again."

Nog tried his utmost, but failed to make a single sound of protest. *He* wasn't the one who needed sickbay—the Old Man was.

Her statement delivered, Centurion Karon slipped from his view, as once again Nog realized he was being moved. And only full polywave paralysis prevented his drawing back in disgust from the . . . things that moved him.

Bions.

Starfleet Intelligence had examined captured bions, and Nog had read the classified situation assessments with horror. Bions were supposedly artificial life-forms, created by Romulan science and now used as workers and soldiers throughout the Star Empire. Though the creatures were disturbingly humanoid, the Romulans insisted bions had no capacity to become self-aware. They were simply genetically engineered organic machines, no different from the myriad forms of mechanical devices that served the Federation, from self-piloted shuttlecraft to nanite assemblers. The only difference, the Romulans maintained, was that instead of being built from duraplast and optical circuitry, bions were self-assembled—that is, *grown*—from proteins swirling in nutrient baths. Or so, Starfleet warned, the Romulans would have the galaxy believe.

As far as Starfleet was concerned, there was a reason why bions had begun to appear shortly after the Romulans had allied themselves with the Ascendancy, and the first battles had been fought in the undeclared War of the Prophets. Bions, Starfleet's biologists had concluded, were not genetically *engineered* artificial life-forms; they were genetically *altered* prisoners of war.

Nog shuddered inwardly, if not outwardly. The Romulans were now doing to their captives what the Borg used to do with theirs. Except in the case of the bions, the Borg's biomechanical mechanisms of assimilation had been replaced by strictly biological processes.

The underlying technology was, without question, Grigari. And if only for that reason—the unconscionable alliance with the Grigari Meld—Nog fervently believed the Ascendancy deserved to be wiped out.

Nog was grateful he could not see the dreadful mutants that carried him now. Without constant misting his vision had blurred again, and he was able to form only the vaguest impression of green metal doors sliding open before him, a surprisingly narrow corridor moving past him, and, finally, an oppressively small medical facility, where an angular treatment bed emerged from a dull-green bulkhead, the display screen above it glowing with unreadable yellow Romulan glyphs and multicolored status lights.

He was maneuvered onto the treatment bed, and almost immediately his vision cleared again. This time the ocular mist came from an overhead pallet of medical equipment. Just in time to give Nog a brief, shocking glimpse of a bion.

Its face—for the bions were neither male nor female—was unnaturally blank, its severe features nearly obliterated by the camouflage effect of its bizarrely mottled skin, a dizzying patchwork of Andorian blue and Miradorn white, Orion green, Tiburonian pink, and Klingon brown.

Even more disconcerting, its mouth was a tiny, lipless gash intended to do little more than ingest nutrient paste. The creature had no real nose, only two vertical slits that pulsed open and closed like the gills of a fish.

Yet the real problem for Nog was what had happened to the bion's ears. Despite years of working with *hew-mons* and Vulcans and other cartilaginously challenged species, Nog knew he still had difficulty abandoning the old Ferengi presumption equating intelligence with ear size. And the same ruthless efficiency displayed in the bion's other minimal features had reduced its ears to mere vestigial curls of flesh that protruded from the jaw hinge like the wilted petals of a flower. On a purely visceral level, it was as if he was looking at creatures whose skulls had been flayed open and were empty—that they could even stand upright with such minuscule ears, let alone carry out useful tasks, was unnerving.

Hostage within his own still body, Nog could only watch now as one bion reached above him. Its two fingers and thumb identified it as a common worker unit. Other versions, Nog had read, had up to seven fingers for delicate mechanical repairs or complex weapons operation. No doubt other details of the bion's specific capabilities were indicated by the markings on the front of its tight gray jumpsuit and by the pattern of green stripes ringing each of its sleeves. Perhaps even the identity of the captive species from which it had been created was encoded there.

Another spray of mist clouded the air for a moment, and at the same time the gray-suited bion moved to position its face directly in front of Nog's unblinking eyes.

The bion's eyes were humanoid in size and placement, but the portion of the eyeball that was typically white in most species was a lustrous black. Nog didn't know if that color provided a specific, engineered advantage; he suspected it was a cosmetic detail designed to remove any sense of personality from the bions. Even a Vulcan's placid eyes could convey emotion. But bions had eyes that revealed nothing. Whatever secrets the pitiful creature's brain held, its flat gaze betrayed no trace of any individuality or past life.

The bion mercifully stepped back out of Nog's sight.

Nog waited for whatever would happen next, thinking of the Old Man, worried about where he had been taken and what their captors had done with him.

Long minutes passed without sign of anything else moving in the medical facility, and Nog concluded he had been left alone. He willed peace upon his racing mind. There was nothing he could do until his paralysis ended except meditate on the Great Material River, and hope that somehow it would take from him his mental clarity—of which he had no great need right now—and, just for a few hours at least, transfer it to Jean-Luc Picard, who most certainly did.

After all the effort these Romulans had expended in order to contact the the admiral, Nog didn't want to think what would happen when they realized that their prize captive was not the great man of years past, only a man.

Nog's thoughts paused. Hadn't someone once said something about that condition? But whether it was exhaustion or the effect of the polywaves, he no longer recalled who.

Another *lost memory,* he thought, troubled, as his consciousness finally sank into the Great River. In time, he supposed, that would be the fate of them all.

CHAPTER 5

HE WAS ONLY NINETEEN, but Jake Sisko already understood the inevitability of death. And on the hangar deck of this Starfleet vessel of the future he was, in his way, prepared to die.

Or so he told himself.

But even as the computer's warning was drowned out by the explosive burst of air that rushed over him, tugging him back against the linked arms of his fellow prisoners, Jake still didn't believe that the time of his death was near.

Part of the reason for his confidence in his survival came from his half-felt suspicion that the Bajoran Prophets might intercede, or that, at the very least, their existence implied that death might not be the end of his own awareness.

But as to whether it was faith in the Prophets or faith in Dr. Bashir's logical assessment of their situation—that they were merely being tested by the Vulcan captain of this ship—or simply the fire of his youth that at this moment made him unwilling to accept the final extinction of his intellect, Jake wasn't certain.

All he knew was that when a *second* blast of air rushed over him, and he realized that the ship's atmospheric pressure had been maintained and that he could still breathe—he wasn't really surprised.

Smiling broadly like most of the others at their close call, Jake glanced over in Bashir's direction. What he saw then *did* surprise him. The doctor was engulfed in an embarrassingly passionate embrace with Vash. Jake couldn't help gawking as a handful of excited conversations began around him and he saw Vash draw back from the doctor, look around, and he heard her say, "Guess you were right, Doc." Bashir was looking decidedly flustered, and Jake felt himself experiencing an unexpected pang of jealousy. Vash was extremely attractive, in a dangerous, older sort of way.

Then his and everyone's attention was diverted to the personnel door as it opened once again and Captain T'len reappeared, accompanied by her two visored officers in the black Starfleet uniforms with red shoulders.

"Is the test over?" Bashir asked. Jake appreciated and mentally applauded the defiance in his tone.

"It is," T'len replied.

But the doctor wasn't finished. "May I ask what the purpose of it was?"

"It was necessary to see if you had been altered by the Grigari. No Grigari construct yet encountered is capable of facing a life-or-death situation without attempting to bargain for its life."

Jake vaguely recalled Kasidy Yates telling him stories of the Grigari, though she'd seemed to imply that few experts believed that the fabled lost species was real—merely a name given to an amalgam of legends that had accumulated over time.

Bashir was nodding at Vash, who was still standing beside him. "Not a very convincing test. Vash here was ready to bargain with you from the beginning."

Jake regarded Bashir anxiously, wondering if it was a good idea to say anything that might provoke the captain, but the Vulcan seemed unperturbed by the doctor's identification of a logical flaw in her test.

"Vash is not a Starfleet officer. Her reaction was in compliance with historical records of her personality."

At that the archaeologist broke away from the group of captives, heading straight for T'len. "Yeah, well what about *this* reaction?" she said threateningly, leading Jake to half-expect she'd try to deck the Vulcan captain when she reached her.

But before Vash could cross more than half the four meters that stood between her and T'len, what looked to be a phaser beam shot out from the visor worn by the officer on the captain's right. The silver beam hit Vash dead center, and she immediately crumpled to the deck as if stunned.

"Whoa . . . " Jake whispered. Then, as Bashir, Worf, and Jadzia rushed to Vash's aid, he took a closer look at those special clear visors of T'Len's officers, what he had at first thought were a type of safety eyewear. After a moment, he realized that if he looked slightly away from the two officers, he could just make out a pattern of glowing lights on their visors' surfaces, as if the visors were generating some sort of holographic display for their wearer. On the officer nearest him Jake also noticed a narrow black wire that ran from the arm of the visor and hooked over the Vulcan's pointed ear. The wire disappeared into the collar of the officer's uniform.

Not bad, Jake thought. *A phaser that doesn't require anyone having to waste time to draw and aim it.* He had no idea how the odd silver phaser beam could have been generated in such a thin device, but he decided it was reasonable to assume that twenty-five years could have led to at least a few technological breakthroughs. He reminded himself to be on the alert for other hidden marvels of the day. They'd make for interesting details in the novel he planned to write after he returned to his own time. Because, just as he had not been ready to believe he was going to die, he was somehow sure that eventually he *would* return. All he needed to do was work out the details—or be sure that Dr. Bashir, Jadzia, and Worf worked them out.

For now, the doctor and the Trill were helping Vash to her feet. From what Jake could see of her, the archaeologist was unharmed, though the way she staggered made it clear she was still suffering from the effects of the stun.

Captain T'len continued coolly as if nothing unusual had just happened. "As I explained, your identities have been confirmed by DNA analysis. But do not think that changes your status on this ship."

"Just what is our status?" Bashir asked. He had his arm firmly around Vash's shoulders to support her.

"Refugees," T'len answered. "But that can change."

"How?"

"The decision is not up to me." The Vulcan captain then went on to explain that they would be taken from the hangar deck and given quarters, to which they'd be confined until their arrival at Starbase 53. During their confinement they would be provided with limited computer access in order to familiarize themselves with their new time period. "Make no mistake," T'len concluded. "This time period will be your new home."

As the refugees fell silent in the face of that blunt statement, Jake took advantage of the moment to shout out, "What happened to the *Defiant?*"

Captain T'len's dark eyes immediately sought him out, and Jake surprised himself as he held her intense gaze. "Your ship was captured by the Ascendancy. To answer the rest of your questions which must logically follow: So far as we know, the *Defiant* was captured intact. Though we do not have definitive knowledge, it is logical to assume that the crew has been captured. Whether or not they are subsequently harmed will depend on the degree of resistance they offer."

"Then we should attempt to rescue them," Worf said bluntly. "It is unacceptable to retreat."

T'len's gaze shifted from Jake to Worf, but her next words had the teenager's full attention. "I can assure you that a rescue attempt will be made. Starfleet has no intention of letting the Ascendancy keep Benjamin Sisko in custody."

Jake experienced a huge upswell of relief upon hearing the captain state Starfleet's objective so authoritatively, though he couldn't help also wondering why his father would have such importance in this time. But before he could get up his nerve to ask for clarification, one of the Bajorans changed the subject.

"Who are the Grigari?"

The captain's enigmatic response was ominous. "You'll find out." She gestured to the open door, and Jake followed the rest of T'len's prisoners as they began their long march.

To Jake, T'len's ship, the *Augustus,* seemed half-finished. The dull-gray floors of the cramped corridors had no carpet—the decks were simply bare composite plates. And no attempt had been made to hide the ship's mechanical components. The cluttered ceilings were lined with so many differently colored pipes and conduits that Jake doubted there was a single Jefferies tube on the vessel. ODN conduits were everywhere, running along bulkheads and punching through decks and ceilings almost at random. At least, Jake *assumed* they were ODN conduits. Who knew if optical data networks were still being used in this future?

The ship appeared to have no turbolifts, either. He and the other fourteen prisoners from the *Defiant* had to change decks by using steep and narrow metal staircases that rattled alarmingly as so many pairs of feet pounded down them. For a ship of the future, the *Augustus* was reminding Jake more of the old walk-through exhibit of the *U.S.S. Discovery,* a *Daedalus*-class ship more than two hundred years old, at the Starfleet Museum in San Francisco. But even that old veteran, one of the first ships commissioned by the newly formed Starfleet, had had more room.

The environmental controls also seemed to be less precise than the ones Jake was used to. The hangar deck had been cool, but the first corridors the refugees had been led through were uncomfortably hot. On their enforced march they had already encountered a few more of T'len's crew, and they had all, without exception, been Vulcan. That made the heat make sense to Jake: It reflected the crew's normal and preferred ambient temperature.

But then, trudging along in the line of captives, Jake stepped off a stairway into a corridor that was so cold its gray metal walls were rimed with frost. With a shiver, he abandoned his earlier theory of acclimation for a Vulcan crew, and decided that the unsettling changes in temperature merely meant that the ship's environmental controls were faulty.

Finally they reached the end of their march, and their destination turned out to be a series of personnel cabins—they certainly didn't deserve to be called quarters. Jake was assigned to one that was little bigger than his bedroom on DS9 but which was crowded with two bunks, a fold-down desktop, what seemed to be a limited-capacity food replicator, and—crammed into one corner with no privacy screen—a small toilet-and-sink unit that appeared to be able to double as a sonic shower enclosure. Everything was in the same depressing shade of muddy gray.

Jake's roommate was Ensign Ryle Simons, a young human from Alpha Centauri with an almost pure white complexion topped by a startlingly bright-red crewcut. Simons was fresh from the Academy and had been on Deep Space 9 for only two days, waiting to join the crew of his first ship, the *Destiny*. After taking less than a second to assess the cramped nature of their room, both Jake and Simons peppered the Vulcan lieutenant who stood in their doorway with questions.

"How long will it take to get to the starbase?" Simons asked.

"And where's the computer terminal?" Jake added.

The Vulcan stepped past the two young men and folded down the desktop so that it blocked the doors of the storage lockers that took up one bulkhead. "Our transit time is classified," she said, then busied herself with the desktop.

The surface of it was a large control surface, and the Vulcan swiftly tapped in a series of commands that quickly created what Jake recognized as a Starfleet computer input tablet not too different from the ones he was familiar with. What was different, though, was that the computer had no physical display. Instead, a holographic screen appeared a few centimeters above the desktop. For now, the modified Starfleet emblem appeared in the center of it.

No time like the present, Jake thought. "Lieutenant, why did the ship from the Bajoran Ascendancy also have a Starfleet emblem?"

The Vulcan frowned as she assessed him, shaking her head once. "The explanation is in the history briefings that will be made available to you."

"Then the explanation isn't classified?"

"No."

Jake refrained from showing amusement at the Vulcan's poorly disguised impatience. "So there's no reason why you *can't* tell us, is there? It would be more efficient."

"Then the efficient answer is: propaganda." The Vulcan abruptly stood up and moved toward the open door.

"I don't know what you mean by that," Jake said truthfully.

The Vulcan hesitated on the threshold, then looked back at Jake and Simons. Apparently she made some sort of decision, for she then delivered her explanation rapidly, without pause. "At the time the Ascendancy was formed, it initially sought new members from those worlds waiting to accept admission to the Federation, just as Bajor had been. One of the chief advantages to Federation membership is the opportunity to take part in Starfleet operations and to benefit from its defensive forces. Thus, in its attempt to sway the governments of the nonaligned worlds, the Ascendancy claimed to be the new political master of Starfleet. Since many Ascendancy vessels had been pirated from our fleet over the years, in a limited sense the claim was correct."

"Now I *really* don't understand," Jake said seriously. "How could any group simply *say* they're the ones responsible for Starfleet?"

"Following the destruction of Earth," the Vulcan said, her expression remaining completely neutral, "Starfleet's lines of command and control took several weeks to be reestablished. In some regions where political turmoil further complicated communications, some task forces and battle groups were cut off from command for months."

Jake couldn't speak, let alone think of any new question. Which was just as well, because the Vulcan had no intention of answering further inquiries.

"Use your computer," she said. "All your questions will be answered." Then she stepped back into the corridor, and the narrow door slipped shut and locked.

Jake looked at his roommate. The Centaurian ensign's white cheeks were splotched with red, while the rest of his face was almost luminescent in its paleness. "That . . . that can't be true," Simons said faintly.

But Jake knew better. The Vulcan had had no problem refusing to answer a question when the answer was classified. Thus, she had no motive for lying to them. "Let's check the computer," he said. He went to the desktop and placed his hand on the flashing yellow panel labelled USER IDENTIFICATION. At once the panel turned green, and the holographic display switched from a static image of the Starfleet emblem to that of a Bolian in the new version of the Starfleet uniform. Jake checked the square tabs on the Bolian's rank badge and saw that the blue-skinned alien was an admiral.

"This briefing," the Bolian admiral began, "has been prepared for the refugees rescued from the *Starship Defiant*. It consists of a twenty-two-minute presentation of the key events that have occurred since the destruction of Deep Space 9 and the loss of your ship until the present day, focusing on those events which have led to what is commonly known as the War of the Prophets. At the end of this briefing, you will be given an opportunity to examine files detailing the current status of any relatives you may have in this time period. The briefing will commence on your verbal request."

Jake stared at the image. "I don't get it," he said, turning to Simons. "We only showed up here less than two hours ago. How did they have enough time to make a briefing tape for us?"

Simons shook his head, puzzled. "Their computers are faster?"

Jake wasn't convinced. But he folded his arms across his chest and prepared himself for the worst. "Computer: Start the briefing."

The image of the Bolian admiral disappeared, replaced by that of a Starfleet sensor-log identification screen announcing that whatever images were about to be shown had been recorded by the *U.S.S. Garneau* on stardate 51889.4, in the Bajoran sector.

Jake felt his chest tighten even before the sensor log began.

He recognized the date.

He was about to see the events that, according to history, had led to his death.

CHAPTER 6

"WHAT'S WRONG WITH HIM?" Centurion Karon demanded.

Nog awoke with a start. He instantly moved his hand to the side of his head in response to a dull pain in his temple. Then he reacted to the shock of realization that the little finger of his right hand was broken. And then to the fact that he could move at all. Until he remembered where he was and how he had come here.

The Romulan centurion's voice was insistent. "Admiral Picard. Has he been injured?"

Nog pushed himself up on the medical bed. He rubbed at his head again, this time careful to keep all pressure off his broken finger. "Irumodic Syndrome," he said. His throat was painfully dry. He started to cough.

But Karon wasn't interested in his discomfort. *"Tash!"* she snarled.

Nog didn't know what that word meant, but from the way the sharp-featured Romulan had said it, he could guess. And he could also guess that it meant she knew very well what Irumodic Syndrome was.

"Does that mean Starfleet's not serious about Project Phoenix?" Karon asked.

"I am not answering any questions until I see Admiral Picard."

Karon's dark eyes considered him. Their highlights seemed to shine out at him from the shadows of her deep brow and precisely cut black bangs. "Who are you?" she asked.

Nog hesitated. Considering his present circumstances, he could be a prisoner of war, which meant he should say nothing, even though he knew his eventual fate would be to become a bion. Then again, it was possible that Karon had been truthful when she said the crew of this ship no longer supported the Ascendancy. Romulans had been the Federation's allies in the war against the Dominion. Was it possible they could be allies again? More to the point, Nog wondered, this close to the end, was there really anything to lose?

"I'm the Integrated Systems Manager for Project Phoenix," he said. "Captain Nog."

Karon looked gratifyingly impressed. "So you're in charge," she said with a slight incline of her head.

"I *manage* the project," Nog replied. "The Admiral is in charge."

Karon pursed her lips and nodded. "I understand personal loyalty. Odd to see it in a Ferengi, though. Perhaps our mission hasn't been wasted after all."

"What mission?" Nog said, deliberately ignoring her insult. It was the fate of the Ferengi to be misunderstood by all but their own kind.

Karon's cool gaze swept over him. "Perhaps you'd prefer getting dressed."

Nog looked down and felt his ears flush. He was still in his sleep shorts. His pressure suit had apparently been removed as he slept. "Yes, I would," he said stiffly. "But more than that, I would appreciate having someone look at this." He held up his little finger, trying not to grimace as he saw the strange angle it took from his hand.

It required an agonizing twenty minutes to get his finger straightened and set in a magnetic splint, and Karon apologized for the *Altanex* carrying no tissue stimulators suitable for Ferengi biology. Her explanation for his injuries seemed quite reasonable—that he'd broken his finger and bruised his temple when he fell to the deck after being paralyzed.

Once he'd been treated, Karon offered him a change of clothing, and Nog quickly pulled on a Romulan utility uniform—gray trousers, a tunic unfortunately intended for a taller person, and black boots that were, surprisingly, the perfect size. Then the Romulan centurion escorted him to Admiral Picard's guest quarters.

To Nog's relief, the Old Man was asleep, not in a coma or dead. And in response to his pointed questioning, Karon assured him that Picard's interrogators had not used any force or psychological pressure, especially—here Karon paused and fixed Nog with a measuring look—when it had become so quickly apparent that the admiral was not in full command of his legendary faculties.

With the Old Man's condition confirmed, Nog allowed Karon to lead him to a situation room three decks up. As he followed the Romulan, Nog studied what few details the short passage revealed about the vessel he was in. He wasn't certain what class of ship the *Altanex* was, but it was obviously cramped and confined, and the paltry number of crew members they passed suggested that it was also extremely small.

Lacking any other ready source of information, Nog had no reservations about directly asking his escort about her ship.

"We're a listening post," she explained, as she adjusted the replicator in the small situation room to display its menu in Ferengi tallyscript. "Our current position is within this system's main asteroid belt."

"Ah, a spy vessel." Nog glanced around the spartan room, trying to identify any obvious recording sensors. But all he saw was a blank tactical screen, a conference table with nine chairs, and on the table a small packing crate with reinforced locking clamps.

Karon didn't confirm or deny his definition of her term. "High-speed multiple transmorphic cloaks. But limited shields and weapons."

Nog was impressed. "With transmorphic cloaks you don't need shields. I had not realized you had perfected them."

A grim expression flashed across Karon's stern features. "Our engineers found they could solve their impasse with certain . . . biogenic components."

Nog understood and shared her distaste. The Romulans had again employed Grigari technology. Which meant the ship's state-of-the-art cloaking device was controlled in part by engineered tissues taken from captives.

Then, without preamble Karon said, "The Star Empire is collapsing."

Startled, Nog attempted to hide his shock the only way he could. He looked away from her, to the replicator.

"Are you surprised?" Karon asked.

"By the news? Or by the fact that you are telling me?" Nog concentrated on the replicator's talleyscript. There were no Ferengi selections available. The only non-Romulan food and drink he recognized were Vulcan, and he wasn't enamored of Vulcan cuisine. There were never enough beetles.

"You don't believe me." Karon folded her arms and drew herself up, making her posture even more erect than it had been. She was a few centimeters taller than Nog but very slight, even in chainmail. Nog had grown to his maximum height as a teenager on DS9, but he knew a decade of desk work had added more than a few kilograms of bulk to his small frame, giving him a much more substantial presence than Karon.

Nog saw little risk in answering her truthfully. "I haven't decided," he said. "For a collapsing power, you did not seem to have much trouble overwhelming Utopia's defenses."

"It was a Tal Shiar operation. They are the last to feel the deprivations of the Empire's eroding capabilities."

Nog allowed his face to reveal a slight degree of interest at her mention of the feared Romulan intelligence service. But the revelation was a calculated one, to make her think that he appreciated her candor. The centurion might believe she was engaged in a frank conversation with a fellow warrior, but to Nog, he and she were engaged in negotiations—everything was always a negotiation. And sometimes—most times—it was best not to let the other party know it.

"Why did the Tal Shiar want to kidnap Admiral Picard?"

"They didn't," Karon said. "The Utopia Yards are your last major shipbuilding center. The Tal Shiar wanted to cripple them. My . . . group saw a chance to make contact with Admiral Picard during the confusion."

Nog made a note of her hesitation at mentioning whom she was working with. That could mean she hadn't yet determined if she could trust him. It could also mean that there was no group, and that she and the handful of crew on this ship made up the whole of the Romulan resistance.

"Two questions," he said. "First, if the Tal Shiar accepts the Ascendancy's teachings, why bother attacking the yards this late?"

Just for a moment, it seemed to Nog that Karon sensed he was hiding something from her, but if so, it did not stop her from answering him. "This was one of fifteen attacks scheduled to . . . to keep the Federation off-balance. We know about Project Phoenix and Project Guardian. Even Project Looking Glass. But we can't be sure you don't have other last-moment operations planned."

Now Nog really was impressed. For obvious reasons, Project Phoenix had been impossible to completely hide. But Guardian was one of the most highly classified operations in Starfleet's history. Even he had been told only a few details about it, and those only because of how they might relate to the timing of the *Phoenix*'s mission. As for Looking Glass, that was a code name even he had never heard before.

Karon seemed to understand that Nog wasn't going to order anything from the replicator, so she reached past him to punch in some selections of her own. "As to what the Tal Shiar does or does not believe, I don't know anymore. I think at first our politicians considered the Bajoran Ascendants to be fanatics. The reason the Star Empire supported them was because the Ascendants' goal was to destabilize the Federation—always a worthy endeavor in Romulan eyes."

"But now?" Nog asked, trying not to let his voice sound too eager for details.

A tray with two tall glasses of brown liquid appeared in the replicator slot. Each glass was topped by a froth of foam.

"I don't know how much access Starfleet Intelligence has to events on Romulus, but as the Federation and the Klingon Empire suffered outright acts of terrorism and overt military strikes, we ourselves suffered from key politicians succumbing to mysterious diseases and accidents."

The centurion handed him a glass. "You were being attacked from without. We, from within."

Nog sniffed at the drink in surprise. Root beer. It smelled delicious. "By the Ascendants?"

"You said you had a second question." Karon held up her glass in an age-old gesture of salute, drank deeply from it, then wiped the foam from her upper lip.

Nog took a tentative sip from his glass. The subtle interplay of sarsaparilla and vanilla was missing, of course. In years of study, he had yet to find a replicator version of the drink that could match that made on Cestus III. In fact, he had been surprised to learn that root beer had not been invented there, considering that the versions from everywhere else were but a pale imitation.

But he wasn't here to discuss brewing methods. He set his glass down on the tray. "Why did you want to speak to the admiral?"

Karon sighed. "We know about the *Phoenix.*"

Nog made his shrug noncommittal. Such knowledge was not surprising. Almost everyone knew something about the ship. "You said that."

"We know its mission."

Perhaps in general, Nog thought, still unconcerned. It was unlikely even the Tal Shiar had managed to uncover all the details of the audacious plan the Old Man had put in motion almost five years ago.

"And we know that mission will fail."

Nog picked up his glass again to cover his shock and took another quick sip of its aromatic liquid. Swiftly, he considered all the possible reasons Karon might have for telling him this. His first thought was that she was also part of the Tal Shiar and it was an attempt to sow disinformation. But then, he reasoned, why hadn't she just killed him and Picard? Surely their deaths would have a greater chance of disrupting Project Phoenix than would their being swayed by her influence.

"For whatever it might be worth to you," he said carefully, "there are those in Starfleet who believe the same."

Karon shook her head. "You misunderstand. I did not say we *believe* your mission will fail. I said, we *know* your mission will fail."

Nog drank the last of his root beer and regretfully placed the empty glass on the tray. "How is it possible to *know* the fate of something which has yet to happen?"

He meant his question to be a challenge, and expected the Romulan centurion to respond in kind. But instead—surprisingly— Karon pulled out one of the chairs and sat down at the conference table. Her whole being seemed to Nog to be enveloped in an air of inexpressible sadness.

"Captain Nog, twenty-five thousand years ago, three Bajoran mystics set down their visions: Shabren, Eilin, and Naradim. All except the tenth of Shabren's prophecies have proved true, and that one can be read as a warning and not a firm prediction. The Books of Eilin unequivocally describe the rediscovery of the Orbs of Jalbador, just as it occurred twenty-five years ago. And Naradim's Eight Visions—"

"Are ancient poetry," Nog interrupted, as he took a chair facing her. "All the writings of the mystics are. Written with allusions and veiled references that every generation has reinterpreted and applied to their own unique circumstances."

Karon's gaze settled on Nog so intently he had the unsettling feeling that she had some alien power to read his mind. "You really *don't* believe that any of what's happened this past quarter-century has been foretold?"

Nog emphatically shook his head. "Of course not," he said firmly. "What has happened is the result of secular fanatics who have appropriated obscure religious writings in an attempt to justify brutal oppression and bloody conquest. The so-called War of the Prophets is a war of politics—not religion."

Karon's hands betrayed her inner tension as she twisted them together tightly, and she leaned forward, urgent. "But you work for Admiral Picard. *He* understands what's happening."

Nog spoke with pride. "Admiral Picard is a scientist. An explorer. A historian. Of course he understands."

"Perhaps not, it seems, in the same way you do. Captain Nog, are you aware that Naradim's Third Vision has been fulfilled?"

Nog groaned with impatience. He'd thought his presence here might give him a chance to launch a new attack against the Ascendancy. But instead, it appeared even the Romulan resistance was as caught up in religious nonsense as the fanatics who had enslaved Bajor and now threatened the universe.

"To be honest," he said, "I can't keep that drivel straight. What *is* Naradim's Third Vision?"

"It's the reason why the Tal Shiar launched fifteen attacks against the Federation and Starfleet in the last five hours."

Nog frowned. "To keep us off-balance, you said."

Karon drew back, studying him, puzzled, as if amazed that he still didn't understand her. "Captain, Admiral Picard understands even if you don't. He *told* us that he told you what had happened."

"What?" Nog rubbed at his aching temple. The centurion wasn't making any sense at all.

"The *Defiant,* Captain. It reappeared in deep space near the border of—"

"What!" Nog suddenly had trouble breathing.

"—the Bajoran Central Protectorates."

It was as if she'd shot him with a polywave all over again. "Is . . . is anyone on board?"

Karon's hands were still now. They lay flat on the table between them. "You know there's only one person who counts. And yes, *he* is on board. Benjamin Lafayette Sisko. Emissary to the False Prophets."

Nog felt the sharp heat of anger in his cheeks and ears, compounding the shock he felt. "Captain Sisko was one of the greatest beings I have ever known."

"For the False Prophets to have chosen him—indeed, if the new findings from B'hala are true, for them to have *arranged* his birth—how could he be anything else?"

Nog gripped his splinted finger in an effort to use the distraction of pain to regain his focus. "Who else?" he asked. "Who else is on the *Defiant?"*

"We haven't been able to intercept a complete list. Apparently, there's at least one Cardassian—"

"Garak?"

"I wasn't given names. Also a changeling—"

"Odo!"

"Eighteen in all."

"Eighteen . . . ?" Nog took a deep breath. The number was appallingly small. More than two hundred people had been reported missing when Deep Space 9 was destroyed. "Are there . . . are there any Ferengi on the ship?"

"I don't have that information."

"What about Captain Sisko's son?"

"Captain Nog, how do you know these people?"

Nog told her.

"That explains a great deal," Karon said when he had finished.

"You served under Sisko. You traveled many times through the false wormhole. You even have experienced a temporal exchange on your trip to Earth's past."

Her tone made Nog uncomfortable. "What does that explain?"

"I apologize in advance, Captain. But by your own admission, you have had several encounters with the forces of the False Prophets. I believe that could explain why you remain so resistant to the truth."

Nog clenched his fists, despite his splinted finger. "My mind is open!"

"Captain Nog, given the power of the Prophets, true or false, how would you know if it were not?"

Nog jumped to his feet, knocking his chair back. "This discussion is over. I want you to return Admiral Picard and me to the closest Starfleet facility."

"You haven't heard my proposition," Karon said, looking up at him.

"I am not interested."

"Are you interested in stopping the Ascendancy? Saving the universe? Preserving the memory of the great Jean-Luc Picard?"

That last question stopped Nog. Twenty-four years ago, just after the destruction of Cardassia Prime, he had been assigned to the *U.S.S. Enterprise* under then Captain Picard. That was when the Old Man had become his mentor, and had given him the new direction he had so badly needed after the loss of so many people who had been close to him. In truth, Nog admitted to himself, his career today was as much dedicated to Picard as it was to Starfleet.

"How can you do all that?" he asked the centurion.

"By myself," Karon said, as she pushed back her chair and got to her feet, "I cannot. But together, we can accomplish all that and more."

Nog held her gaze. "My question stands. How?"

The centurion spoke slowly and deliberately, as if the words she were about to say were the most important she had ever spoken. "Give us the *Phoenix*."

Nog stepped back in shock. "Never."

He saw Karon's lips tremble, as if she were restraining some great emotion. Then she turned sharply away from him and tapped her finger on the keypad of the small packing crate. With a hiss of mechanical movement, the thick locking clamps released and the crate opened to reveal a battered, discolored sheet of coppery-colored metal, a hand's breadth high and slightly wider.

Nog leaned closer. The metal sheet was supported in a nest of semitransparent packing gel. Two of its edges were smooth, and a jagged break showed where it had been shattered, so that it seemed that at least half of it was missing.

Karon reached into the crate, lifted out the metal, and gave it to Nog. Even as she did so, he realized he was looking at a starship's dedication plaque.

"Read it," she said quietly.

Nog turned the metal over, and felt as if the gravity web had failed again.

He had seen this plaque a thousand times before. The last time— three days ago—was when it had been pristinely mounted on the bulkhead beside the primary turbolift on the bridge of Jean-Luc Picard's greatest achievement. U.S.S. PHOEN . . . the remaining letters read.

Beneath that, in smaller type: FIRST OF ITS CLASS.

Beneath that, a list of the engineers and designers Nog had worked with every day.

And then, at the bottom, the ship's simple motto, chosen by the Old Man himself: ". . . *Sokath, his eyes uncovered.* . . ."

Nog spoke without thinking. "It's . . . a bad forgery."

But Karon's next words seemed to come to him from a terrible distance. "Captain Nog, that plaque is twenty-five thousand years old."

The plaque shook in Nog's hands. How could anyone know the target date? "Where . . . where did you . . . ."

The Romulan centurion completed his question. "Find it? At the bottom of a methane sea on Syladdo."

Nog shook his head. The name was unfamiliar.

"Fourth moon of Ba'Syladon."

Nog's pulse quickened. "The Class-J gas giant. . . ."

"The largest planet in the Bajoran system. Correct." Karon's eyes remained fixed on him. She was making no attempt to take back the plaque. "And twenty-five thousand years ago, the *Phoenix* died there, *before* her mission could be completed."

"You can't know that. Not . . . absolutely."

"We can know that. We *do* know that. We can show you sensor records of all the wreckage recovered to date. Wreckage that includes enough of the deep-time components to know they were never deployed as planned."

Nog looked down at the evidence in his hands. The metal plaque burned his fingers, froze them, the confusion of sensations occurring all at once.

"Don't let the *Phoenix* die uselessly, Captain. Don't throw away Jean-Luc Picard's greatest dream on a mission that cannot succeed."

And then he finally understood. "You want the ship for another mission."

"When the ship is completed. Yes. We do."

Nog looked up to meet her gaze. Realizing that what he held in his hands was the proof that everything he had struggled for in these past five years on Mars, everything he had sacrificed, had been for nothing. Nothing.

He could barely speak the words. "You are asking me to betray Starfleet, the Federation—everything I believe in."

"No, Captain, I am offering you a chance to save those very things. The only chance you have. We came here to put this question to Admiral Picard, but his time has passed. So I put it to *you,* Captain Nog. In all the universe, you are the only one who can save it now. Will you join us?"

It took Nog a long time to make his decision.

And time was the one thing he no longer had.

CHAPTER 7

IF SISKO CLOSED his eyes, he could almost believe he was on Bajor, in the kai's temple, in his own time. The gentle splash of water on stone in the meditation pool. The sharp peppermint-cinnamon smell of the *b'nai* candles. Even the cool breeze that brought with it the rich, loamy scent of the contemplation gardens. All these sensations brought back to him the world he had hoped someday would become his adopted home.

But even these sense memories faded when he opened his eyes and looked out through the curving viewports of the *Boreth*'s observation deck to see the *Defiant* being pulled through the stars at warp speed, ensnared in the purple web of a tractor beam and trailing half a kilometer behind the angular engineering hull of the advanced-technology Klingon battlecruiser.

At his right, he saw in Kira a reflection of his own distress at the sight of their ship—so distant, so powerless. At his left the tall, lean form of Arla Rees stood rigid, tense, though Sisko knew the defeat of the *Defiant* could not inflict the same emotional toll on her. The Bajoran commander had only served on Deep Space 9 for a few weeks, and she had not served on the *Defiant* before the events of the station's last day—or of the last twenty-five years.

"How do you think it happened?"

Sisko knew what Kira was really asking him. His conclusion—
that the Dominion had won its war with the Federation—had been
shared by all the others on the *Defiant* once they saw or heard of
Weyoun's appearance in vedek's robes. And now, the fact that they
had been been transported to Weyoun's Klingon ship and had discovered a Bajoran meditation chamber reconstructed to the last
detail in its observation lounge was more proof. There could be no
doubt that in this future the Dominion had won the war, and had
assimilated the cultures of the Alpha Quadrant as omnivorously as
had the Borg.

"Maybe it was Deep Space 9," Sisko ventured. "Once the station
was gone, Starfleet had no forward base to guard the wormhole."

Kira sighed. "So we really were accomplishing something. This
isn't the way I'd like to find out, though."

Arla turned away from the *Defiant*. "I thought the wormhole was
no longer an issue in the war, because the aliens kept Dominion
forces from using it."

Sisko saw Kira stiffen at the Bajoran commander's casual use of
the term "aliens" to describe the beings in the wormhole.

"The *Prophets,*" Kira said emphatically, "chose to stop *one* fleet
of Jem'Hadar ships from traveling through their Temple. But if the
Bajoran people failed in their duty to protect the Temple's doorway,
then it is entirely possible that the Prophets withdrew their blessing—just as they did when the Cardassians invaded."

Arla persisted. "Major, if the wormhole *aliens* are gods, how
could they let the Cardassians inflict such evil on our world?"

Kira's smile was brittle. "I won't pretend to understand the
Prophets, but I know everything they do is for a reason."

Before Arla could further escalate what was for now merely a
discussion, Sisko intervened to keep it at that level. This argument
could have no end between the two Bajorans of such dissimilar background and belief.

Kira had been born on occupied Bajor. She had grown up in relocation camps, and had fought for the Resistance since she was a
child. The only thing that had enabled her—and millions of other
Bajorans—to survive the horrors of the Cardassian Occupation of
their world was a deep and unquestioning faith in their gods—the
Prophets of the Celestial Temple.

But Arla Rees, only a few years younger than Kira, had been born to prosperous Bajoran traders on the neutral world of New Sydney. She had enjoyed a life of privilege in which the Cardassian Occupation, though an evil to rally against, had never been experienced firsthand. For Arla, now a Starfleet officer, as for many Bajorans of her upbringing, the Prophets were little more than an outmoded superstition perversely clung to by her less sophisticated cousins on the old world.

Sisko knew that as fervently as Kira believed in the Prophets and their Celestial Temple, Arla held an equally strong belief that the Bajoran wormhole was inhabited by aliens from a different dimensional realm, and that their involvement in the history of Bajor had been more disruptive than benevolent.

He himself had been wondering of late if reconciling these two opposing beliefs was one of the tasks that he, in his ill-defined and unsought role as the Emissary to Bajor's Prophets, was supposed to be able to accomplish. If so, then he was still unable to see how one could ever be reconciled with the other.

"That's enough," Sisko said to both Kira and Arla. "This debate is nothing we're going to resolve here and now."

"Oh, but we are," Weyoun proclaimed from behind them.

Sisko and the two Bajorans turned as quickly as if shot by disruptors, to see that the Vorta had apparently beamed into the observation deck behind them, just beside the meditation pool. Across the deck, the doors to the corridor were still closed, and there was no other obvious way in.

"Captain Sisko," Weyoun purred, "Major Kira, you have no idea how delighted I am to meet you again after so many years. And Commander Arla, it is such a pleasure to make your acquaintance." The Vorta smiled ingratiatingly at his guests and clasped his hands eagerly before him. "I trust you've found your quarters to your liking."

Sisko forced himself to control his initial impulse to angrily demand an explanation for everything that had happened to them. Weyoun's irritatingly obsequious manner had simply—like everything else about him and his species—been genetically programmed by the Founders in order to better serve the Dominion as negotiators, strategists, scientists, and diplomats.

In this sense, this latest version of Weyoun had changed not at all over the past twenty-five years. The clone's thick black hair, brushed high above his forehead, showed no trace of gray. His smooth, open face, framed by dramatically ribbed ears that ran from his chin halfway up the sides of his head, showed no sign of age-related lines or wrinkles. Indeed, the only aspect of the cloned Vorta that *had* changed from the time Sisko had last crossed his path was that this Weyoun now wore a Bajoran earring, complete with a gleaming silver chain.

But at the moment none of these details was important to Sisko. There was only one thought that claimed his mind. "What happened to my people who were beamed off the *Defiant?*" He did not add that his son Jake had been among them.

"Sadly," Weyoun began mournfully, "we must consider them dead. The attackers are not known for taking prisoners. And those they do take do not live for long."

Kira's outraged question filled the terrible silence that followed the Vorta's pronouncement. "What are you doing in those robes?"

Weyoun glanced down at his saffron-and-white vedek's robes, as if to be sure his clothing hadn't changed in the last few seconds. "Why, they were a gift. From the congregation of the Dahkur Temple. I believe that's in your home province, Major."

Kira's face tightened in disbelief. "None of the monks I know would ever accept a Dominion lackey as a vedek."

Weyoun gazed at Kira in hurt sadness, as if her words had wounded him cruelly. "The Dominon," he said, almost wistfully. "A name I have not heard in many years."

Kira's quick glance at Sisko revealed her lack of understanding, but he was unable to offer her any of his own.

"Why not?" Sisko asked Weyoun. "Did the Founders change its name?"

"Founders," Weyoun repeated, as if that word hadn't crossed his lips for a long time, either. "To be honest, I don't know how the Founders reacted to their loss."

"What loss?" Sisko asked. Now he needed enlightenment.

"Of the war, of course," Weyoun answered. "With the Federation."

Kira shook her head. "Wait a minute. The Dominion *lost* the war?"

Weyoun looked troubled. "In . . . a manner of speaking."

"And what manner would that be?" Sisko demanded.

Weyoun nodded thoughtfully. "I understand your confusion, Captain. Twenty-five years *is* a long time. And I will see to it that you have access to briefing tapes that recount the thrilling historic events you've missed. But for now, simply to put your minds at rest, I will try to . . . get you up to speed. Isn't that what you say?"

"Just start at the beginning," Sisko said. "Who won the war?"

The Vorta's smile was vague. "In a technical sense, no one—but the war *is* over," he hastened to add, as Sisko took a step toward him. "In fact, it ended almost one year to the day after the loss of Deep Space 9 and the beginning of your . . . miraculous voyage."

Sisko was no longer interested in even pretending to be patient. *"How* did it end?"

The Vorta pursed his lips. "With the destruction of Cardassia Prime, I'm sorry to say. A terrible battle. A terrible price to pay for peace. But the Cardassians were a proud people. And Damar and the Founder he served refused to surrender. Then, when—"

Arla interrupted suddenly. "What do you mean, the Cardassians 'were' a proud people?"

Weyoun fixed his remarkably clear gray eyes on hers. "I don't play games with my words, Commander. At all times, you can be sure I mean exactly what I say. Today, the Cardassians as a species are virtually extinct. Cardassia Prime. The Hub Colonies. The Union Territories. All destroyed."

"Destroyed?" Sisko repeated. "We *are* talking about planets?"

Weyoun nodded. "Entire worlds, Captain. Laid waste. Uninhabitable. A death toll in the tens of billions. . . . A mere handful of Cardassians left now. Traders. Pirates." He paused, then added with unexpected anger, "Madmen."

Kira sounded as shocked as Sisko felt. "But you—you somehow escaped all that destruction?"

Weyoun's facial expressions disconcertingly flickered back and forth between an overweening smile of pride and an exaggerated frown of sorrow. "No, Major. In a sense, *I* brought about that destruction."

Now Sisko, Kira, and Arla all began to speak at the same time. But Weyoun ignored their questions and protests alike.

"No, no, no," he said, tucking his hands within the folds of his robes. "Whatever you think of me, you're wrong." He stood with his back to the observation windows and their backdrop of warp-smeared stars. "Captain Sisko, you must believe me. I begged Damar to accept the inevitable. I implored the Founder to accept that it was time she and her kind accepted their fate to be partners in a new cause, not the leaders of a dying one. Yet—"

Sisko regarded him with disbelief. "Are you saying you turned against the *Founders?!*"

"But . . . they were your gods," Kira said.

Weyoun shook his head. "The only reason the Vorta believed the Founders to be gods was because that was programmed into the basic structure of our brains. Our belief in the Founders was achieved through the same genetic engineering that raised us from the forests of our homeworld."

"But you've always known about your programming," Sisko said.

"True. And our belief, engineered or not, did sustain the Vorta—sustained *me*—through the most difficult times. But then . . ." Weyoun withdrew his arms from his robes and spread them wide, as if to embrace Sisko and the others. ". . . The day came when those difficult times ended and . . . and *I* met the *true* Gods of all creation—the Prophets." His transformed face shone with bliss.

Sisko stared at the triumphant Vorta. "You . . . met the *Bajoran* Prophets?"

Weyoun nodded, his beatific smile never wavering.

"Through an Orb experience?" Kira asked doubtfully. "Or—"

"Face to face," the Vorta said in a humble voice. "In the True Celestial Temple. I traveled through it. A desperate expedition to see if it led to the Gamma Quadrant." He laughed quietly to himself in remembrance. "The Founder herself ordered me to go. Two Cardassian warships. A wing of Jem'Hadar attack cruisers. Yet . . . I was the only one to return."

And then, an icy hand gripping his heart, Sisko made sense of Weyoun's astounding story. "You traveled through the *second* wormhole."

The Vorta held a finger to his lips. "Oh, Captain, I must caution you. I have a very devoted, very religious crew. We don't call them . . . 'wormholes' anymore."

"*Two* Temples, then," Sisko said. "Just like the legend of the Red Orbs of Jalbador."

Weyoun stared at Sisko, abandoning all traces of the false veneer of a genetically engineered negotiator he had always maintained in their previous encounters. "In your time," he said seriously, "the legend of Jalbador existed in many different forms, distorted by the inevitable accumulation of error over the millennia of its retelling. But in essence, Captain, each variation of that legend possessed a fraction of the truth. A truth which you helped bring back to a universe that had lost its way."

"And that truth would be?" Kira asked grimly.

Weyoun's response was uncharacteristically to the point. "The Prophets are the Gods of all creation, and the True Celestial Temple is their home."

Then, pausing as if to compose himself, the Vorta studied his audience of three before focusing his attention on Arla. "Now I know this is not what *you* believe, Commander. I overheard what you were saying before I joined you. If the Prophets are Gods, then how can they let evil exist? That is a valid question. And it has a valid answer."

Weyoun stepped closer to Arla, addressing her as if Sisko and Kira were no longer present in this reconstruction of a meditation chamber. "You see, Commander, the Prophets do not wish their children to be afflicted by evil. But uncounted eons ago, when the universe was a perfect ideal contained within the Temple, some Prophets rebelled. Oh, they believed they had a just cause. They thought that a universe within the Temple could only ever be a reflection of perfection, not perfection itself. And so they fought to free creation from its timeless realm. And in that great and terrible battle—beyond the comprehension of any linear being—the One Celestial Temple was—" Weyoun clapped his hands together unexpectedly, startling his three listeners, "—split asunder!"

The Vorta smiled apologetically at Arla. "The battle between the two groups of Prophets ended then. But the damage had already been done. The stars, the galaxies, the planets . . . everything the Prophets had created in their image of timeless perfection spilled out into the void created by the Temple's destruction. And in that void, perfection was unattainable. Evil was loosed upon the face of creation. And all because of the pride of one group of Prophets, who thought they knew better."

"The Pah-wraiths," Arla whispered.

Weyoun brightened at Arla's response. "Ah, so you have had *some* religious instruction, Commander. Yes, of course. But the Pah-wraiths you know from your time are those poor beings who spilled from the Temple at the time it was torn in two. They could not carry on the fight in the False Temple, neither could they join their fellows in the True Temple. Instead, they sought shelter near the entrance to both shards of the One Temple, deep in the Fire Caves at the core of Bajor, lost and abandoned by both sides."

"This is all blasphemy!" Kira protested. "There was no battle in the Temple! There are no fallen Prophets! There is no second Temple!"

Undisturbed, Weyoun pointed an accusing finger at the livid major. "Then how do you explain your presence here *and* now, exactly as foretold by Naradim's Third Vision as recorded on the tablets of Jalbador?"

"What do you mean 'our presence' was foretold?" Sisko asked quickly, before Kira could interrupt Weyoun again.

"Behold," the Vorta intoned as if reciting from some ancient text, "you shall know the final prophecy of Jalbador is fulfilled when the False Emissary shall rise from among those that did die in the destruction of the gateway, to face the final battle with the True Emissary of the Prophets, and to bow before his righteousness at the time the doors shall be opened and the One Temple restored."

Weyoun's voice trembled with ecstasy as he concluded, "And by his return, and by his defeat, this shall you know as the True Reckoning, which shall come at the end of all days, and the beginning of that which has no beginning."

Sisko was unable to restrain Kira from another outburst. "More Pah-wraith heresy!" she exclaimed. "The Reckoning took place less than a month ago! And Kai Winn stopped it!"

Weyoun regarded her with pity. "Major, do you really believe any corporeal being could defy the will of the Prophets? Especially a nonbeliever such as Winn?"

Sisko could see the conflict in Kira. Winn was not the religious leader she had preferred, but neither did Kira doubt that the Kai had faith. "Kai Winn is not a nonbeliever. She is . . . sometimes misguided in her attempts to reconcile her spiritual duties with her political ones."

"Was," Weyoun corrected her. "Winn *was* misguided."

"She's dead?" Kira asked in a disbelieving voice.

"One of the first to be hung."

"Hung?!"

Weyoun sighed and bowed his head. "You missed so much. The end of the war. The Ascendancy of Bajor. The collapse of the Federation—"

Sisko, Kira, and Arla all said, "What?" at the same moment.

"*Near*-collapse," Weyoun amended. "Oh, there's still a council that meets . . . somewhere. Ships here and there that claim to be part of Starfleet. But all of it is little more than the twitching of a corpse, I'm afraid."

"What about those ships that attacked us?" Sisko asked.

"Oh, they weren't attacking you, Captain. They were attacking Captain Riker's ship in order to capture yours. Or, more to the point, to capture *you.*"

"Why me?"

"Isn't that obvious? Without you the True Reckoning can't take place."

Sisko stared at Weyoun, afraid to draw the only conclusion that seemed logical.

Weyoun nodded as if reading his mind. "That's right, Captain. *You* are the False Emissary. Risen from among those who died at the destruction of the gateway to the Celestial Temple, that is, your late lamented Deep Space 9."

"But if I'm the False Emissary . . ."

"Exactly." Weyoun bowed. "*I* am the True Emissary to the True Prophets of the One Temple, now Kai to all the believers of the Bajoran Ascendancy."

"*Kai?!*" To Sisko, Kira sounded as if she were about to choke. "You're a pawn of the Pah-wraiths!"

Weyoun's smile faded. "True, I am their servant. But consider this, Major. Even in the fringe beliefs you cling to, when was evil visited upon the universe?"

Whatever uncertainty Kira felt, it didn't prevent her from standing up to Weyoun. "Bajorans don't presume to speak for the universe. But evil came to Bajor when the people first turned away from the Prophets."

"And when was that? In your beliefs?" Weyoun added condescendingly.

"I don't think anyone knows the actual time period."

"Then *approximately* . . . how long ago?"

Kira shrugged. "At the . . . the very beginning of our time on our world."

Weyoun leaned forward, his manner suggesting to Sisko nothing so much as a spider about to complete its web. "Exactly. At the very beginning of time. And what will eliminate evil from the universe— or, at the very least, in your beliefs, from the people of Bajor?"

Sisko couldn't help feeling that the Vorta was about to spring his trap, and it seemed by the slowness of Kira's reply that she sensed the same possibility. "When . . . when all the people of Bajor return to the Prophets and . . . accept them as our Gods."

The Vorta nodded as if Kira had just answered her own question. "Then I ask you, Major, what better way to bring the people of the universe—or of Bajor—back to the Prophets than by bringing them back to the One Celestial Temple? And in all the 'blasphemous' and 'heretical' text that you refuse to accept, what is the one thing the Pah-wraiths always want to do?"

"Return to the Temple," Kira said reluctantly.

"Because by doing so the One Temple will be restored, and all the people will be returned to the Prophets."

"But the texts clearly state that the Pah-wraiths want to *destroy* the Temple!" Kira insisted.

Weyoun's reply was unexpected. "I agree. That's what your texts—inspired by the False Prophets—say. Because the False Prophets don't want the Temple to be restored. The False Prophets want to delude the people of Bajor into thinking that the Pah-wraiths are demons." The Vorta's voice began to rise accusingly. "But answer this, Major: Why is it that the Prophets you worship hide themselves in their Temple, refusing to come out, refusing to do anything except sow confusion with the Orbs they inflicted upon your world, while the Pah-wraiths—*even in your own texts*—are known to walk amongst the people of Bajor and to constantly struggle to open the Temple doors?"

"Lies!" Kira said. "I refuse to listen to more of your lies!"

"Listen to yourself, Major. Where are your arguments, your reasons? You are simply denying the truth out of habit." Weyoun was almost taunting her. "I expected so much more of you."

"Heretic!" Kira shouted as she rushed forward to strike Weyoun.

Sisko lunged after her but before he could reach her—

—a brilliant flash of red light flared from around Weyoun, and Kira was thrown back onto the flat stones that covered the deck.

Sisko dropped to his knees, supporting Kira as she gasped for breath, her dark eyes wide and unfocused. Arla moved to Sisko's side to add whatever aid she could give.

Weyoun's voice floated over them. "Forgive me. Major Kira's attack was quite unexpected, and in the years since we last met I have perfected my control of . . . telekinesis, I suppose you would call it. A little too well, it seems."

Sisko turned to Weyoun, who still stood in front of the observation windows. "Do you have a medkit or a tricorder—anything?" Kira shuddered in his arms, each hard-won breath shallower, as if her throat were closing.

"I'm afraid we have no medical equipment of any kind on board this vessel," Weyoun said apologetically.

Sisko was appalled. Klingon ships were not known for their medical facilities, but still they carried some supplies, if only for the command staff. "Then beam us back to the *Defiant!*" He felt Kira's body arch, then go rigid as she opened her mouth and made no sound, as if her airways were now totally obstructed. "She's dying!" Sisko shouted at Weyoun.

Weyoun moved away from the windows and leaned down to observe Kira. "No, she's not." He waved one arm free of his robes, then placed his thumb and forefinger on the lobe of Kira's left ear. "Her *pagh* is strong. She did not journey all this way to die so close to the end. . . ."

And then Sisko watched, uncomprehending, as shimmering red light sprang forth from the Vorta's pale hand and spread across Kira's distorted features, until suddenly her entire body trembled, she inhaled deeply, and—

—went limp, breathing easily as if she had merely fallen asleep in his arms.

Sisko looked up at Weyoun, and for just an instant saw the Vorta's eyes flash red as well.

"Yes, Captain?" Weyoun said, as his eyes returned to their crystal-gray clarity.

Sisko looked down at Kira, whose eyes remained closed. Her chest rose and fell with normal regularity.

"What did you mean . . . 'so close to the end'? The end of what?"

The Vorta smiled like a child with a secret. "Why, not the end, Captain. The beginning. Didn't you hear what I said? The reason you've been returned from the dead is so the final prophecy of Jalbador can be fulfilled."

Sisko struggled to recall the exact words Weyoun had used when he seemed to be reciting sacred text to Kira. "The end of all days, and the beginning of that which has no beginning?"

"Exactly," Weyoun said, beaming as if at his favorite pupil. "When we shall all be returned to the Temple, and this imperfect creation shall at last come to an end."

Had he heard anyone else speak in that way, Sisko would have assumed the speaker was insane. But he had seen the red glow in Weyoun's eyes. The same glow that had been in Jake's eyes when a Pah-wraith had possessed his son's body and controlled his son's mind.

Arla got to her feet, her voice uncertain, colored by fear. "You're both talking about the end of the universe, aren't you?"

Sisko felt the chill of madness fill the room, as Weyoun bestowed a smile of blessing upon the Bajoran Starfleet officer. "Oh, Commander, nothing as drastic as that. Merely the end of material existence. But at that time, you—" The Vorta smiled at Sisko. "—and the captain—" He brushed his fingers along the side of Kira's face. "—and even the nonbelievers will ascend to a *new* level of existence, wrapped for all time in the love and the wisdom of the Prophets."

Glow or no glow, Pah-wraith or no Pah-wraith, for Sisko, Weyoun had gone too far. He eased Kira onto the floor and stood up to face the Vorta. "You're insane," he said.

Weyoun merely shrugged. "Of course that's what you must think. It is demanded of your role as the False Emissary. But rest assured that even you will ascend to the Temple when you fulfill the final prophecy and acknowledge the True Prophets."

"Never," Sisko said. But even as he spoke, Sisko was aware that not even he, the Emissary of Kira's Prophets, knew what he must do next to stop Weyoun and the Pah-Wraiths from whatever terrible action they were planning. He still needed to learn more about this future before he could help anyone change it.

"Ah, but never doesn't mean what it used to," Weyoun replied. "Not when all you have left is fifteen days."

"Fifteen days . . . till what?" Arla asked.

Weyoun closed his eyes, as if at total peace with himself and the universe. "Fifteen days until the doors of the two Temples shall open together, and the final battle of good and evil shall be fought . . ." He opened his eyes, sought out Sisko as he continued, ". . . and won, and this cruel, imperfect universe shall at last pass, and we shall all ascend to the Temple for eternity."

Apprehension swept over Sisko. It was obvious that despite the complete insanity of Weyoun's proclamation, the Vorta believed every word he spoke.

And when the universe did *not* end in fifteen days, Sisko did not doubt there would be, quite literally, hell to pay.

CHAPTER 8

IN THE SMALL, low-ceilinged briefing room on the *Boreth*'s main cargo deck, Elim Garak read the sensor-log identification screen on the main wall-viewer, and felt nothing.

He didn't have to be paranoid to know that he and the seventeen other crew and passengers removed from the *Defiant* were under close observation. But from what he had already deduced about the state of this time period in general, and of the Bajoran Ascendancy in particular, being paranoid would stand him in good stead.

The large irregularly shaped Klingon viewscreen on the far bulkhead flickered once, then displayed an image of Deep Space 9 as it had existed on stardate 51889.4, as seen from the vantage point of the *U.S.S. Garneau*. The *Garneau* was—or had been—one of two *Akira*-class Starfleet vessels dispatched when the station's computers had fallen victim to some rather clever, if disruptive, Bynar codes inserted by two vicious Andorian sisters intent on obtaining the Red Orbs of Jalbador.

At the time, as he had helped Jadzia Dax eliminate the codes from Deep Space 9's Cardassian computer components, he had been impressed by the meddlesome Andorians' audacity—though given the results of their endeavors and how they had affected him personally, he would happily eviscerate them now, very slowly.

On the viewscreen, the image of Deep Space 9 grew as the *Garneau* closed in. This moment of calm before the inevitable temporal storm to come gave Garak the chance to admire once again the stately sweep of the Cardassian docking towers and the profound balance in the proportions of its rings to its central core. To his trained eye, the station was an exquisitely compelling sculpture, majestically framed against the subtly shifting energy cascades of the Denorios Belt, and it spoke to him of his long-lost home.

None of this would he reveal to others, of course. Instead, keeping his expression deliberately blank, he checked the timecode running at the bottom of the image. In terms of his own relative perceptions—and what other perceptions could there be that were as important?—the time it indicated was barely a day ago. He had been in Ops at that moment, still working on the computer though curious about what was going on in Quark's, where so many others of the station's personnel had congregated.

Not that he would admit to being curious, either. Far better to be aloof, he knew. Far better to be unconcerned. Far better to be so unremarkable and innocuous that the passing crowd could do nothing but ignore him.

At last, something happened in the recording. A faint red glow pulsed through three or four of the observation portals ringing the Promenade level. Garak decided that must have been the moment when the three Red Orbs of Jalbador were brought into alignment in the Ferengi's bar, beginning the process of opening the second wormhole in Bajoran space—and in the middle of Deep Space 9.

The alignment had been quite a sight—or so he had been told by one of his fellow passengers, Rom to be precise. The lumpish but loquacious Ferengi repair technician had described how the three hourglass-shaped orbs, indistinguishable from the better-known Orbs of the Prophets—except for their crimson color—had levitated, as if under their own control, until they had described the vertices of an equilateral triangle. Suspended in midair less than two meters above the floor of the bar, they had proved impossible to budge.

Garak sighed as if stifling a yawn. But inwardly he was anything but bored. No wonder dear, sweet Leej Terrell had been so eager to obtain the Orbs for herself—and for Cardassia. The Cardassian scientist had been his lover once, his nemesis many times, and was one of a scattered and secretive handful of highly skilled and exceedingly ruthless operatives who had survived the Dominion's obliteration of the Obsidian Order.

With the three Red Orbs in hand, Garak had no doubt that Terrell had believed she would have the secret to creating a translocatable wormhole. If anything could break Cardassia free of its devil's bargain with the Dominion, the ability to open a wormhole connecting any two points in space would be the ultimate deal-breaker. No planetary defense force would be able to stop a Cardassian fleet that could launch from the homeworld and within seconds appear in the atmosphere of the enemy's home. Terrell's trio of orbs and that second wormhole would be the key to a *Pax Cardassia,* bringing order to a troubled galaxy.

But at the same time as Garak fully supported Terrell's passion for freedom and admired her patriotism for Cardassia's sake, he also secretly hoped for *his* own sake that this sensor log would show her vessel's destruction. In detail.

On the viewscreen, the red emanations in the Promenade's observation portals had become a constant glow, slowly increasing in brightness. Garak noted a handful of escape pods already breaking free of the habitat rings. Then, almost obscured by a docking tower, the *Defiant* released her docking clamps and began to slip back from the station, moving out of the optical sensor's field of vision.

It was just about now, Garak realized, that he had been unexpectedly beamed from Ops into the confusion of the *Defiant,* then roughly pushed out the door and toward the mess hall. And he could see that the timing of his rescue had been perfect.

Because now on the viewscreen, the red glow had infected a full quadrant of the Promenade module. Silent explosions ran along a docking pylon. And then, the habitat ring began to bend like a wheel warping out of true, as if an immense gravitational well had formed in Quark's.

As it had.

Garak continued to watch events unfold without displaying the slightest interest in or outrage at what transpired next. More escape pods shot free of the station, only to be drawn back to disappear into the opening maw of the red-tinged wormhole.

Like the mouth of the human hell, Garak thought. *How fitting. How poetic.*

And then, faster than the sensor log had been able to record, the image of Deep Space 9 shrank and was gone, replaced by what could almost pass for the opening to the Bajoran wormhole. Except that that swirling mass of forces always seemed to have a blue cast to the energies it released, and this second wormhole was most definitely color-shifted to the red half of the visible-light spectrum.

Captain Sisko's voice disrupted the silence in the briefing room. "That wasn't how we experienced the station's collapse."

Sisko, Major Kira, and Commander Arla were seated up front in the first row of hard Klingon chairs, to which they had been escorted by Romulan security guards only moments before the briefing began. Garak could understand why the captain of the *Defiant* had been separated from the other passengers and crew when they had been beamed to the *Boreth*. But he didn't know why the major and the commander had been taken with him, unless it was because they were the only two Bajorans among the eighteen. He would, however, endeavor to find out. Though Garak knew he would never admit to curiosity—at least, not in a public sense—he was fully aware that he lived his life in a perpetual haze of it.

Sisko continued his correction of the sensor log's account. "We saw the collapse of the station proceed more slowly while we were under attack by Terrell's ship."

How very *interesting,* Garak thought, only his long years of training allowing him to keep his face completely composed.

A young Romulan who stood at the side of the briefing room, improbably outfitted in a poorly fitted variation of a Bajoran militia uniform, switched on a padd so that his angular face was illuminated from below. Then he looked over to Sisko and said, "That tends to confirm the hypothesis that the *Defiant* was caught within the boundary layer of the opening wormhole. Your ship would then have been subjected to relativistic time-dilation effects."

"Then shouldn't the same have happened to Terrell's ship?" Sisko asked.

Garak waited eagerly for the answer. But the Romulan was not forthcoming.

"There are no records of that ship as you described it—" The Romulan looked down at his padd again. "—A *Chimera*-class vessel disguised as a Sagittarian passenger liner. In any event, the *Defiant* was the only vessel to emerge into this time period."

Pity, Garak thought. He would have enjoyed one final meeting with Terrell. He would have liked to have seen her face when she learned that their precious Cardassia no longer existed. Its history, its culture, and all except a handful of its people erased from the universe, as if they had been nothing but a half-remembered dream.

He himself had learned the fate of his world just a few hours earlier from two young Klingon soldiers, also in badly tailored Bajoran uniforms. He had noted their intense interest in observing him, and upon questioning them had learned that they had never encountered a Cardassian before. Then they had told him why.

At that precise instant, Garak had to admit—if only to himself—he had felt a true pang of regret. But only for an instant. Immense relief—not sorrow—had immediately followed. In this time period, there was now nothing left for him to fight for. His struggles were over.

It was, he had decided, a quite liberating experience.

A Bajoran colonel now appeared on the main viewscreen, obviously reading from a script, droning on without much clarity of detail about the events of the few weeks that had followed the opening of the second wormhole. Apparently, the space-time matrix of the Bajoran sector had been altered in some obscure technical way by the second wormhole's gravimetric profile. Garak couldn't follow what the implications of that were, nor was he particularly interested. But supposedly the behavior of the first wormhole had become more erratic because of those changes. It had rarely opened after that, and travel through it had proved impossible.

Then, the Bajoran colonel recounted at tedious length, with the Cardassian-Dominion alliance mounting a major offensive throughout the region, a small battle group had broken through Starfleet's crumbling lines and reached the Bajoran system.

Garak covered his mouth with his hand and yawned outright. This time it wasn't an affectation. The briefing room was getting uncomfortably hot. He glanced at the unfinished metal walls, willing himself to see them move away from him and not close in. His claustrophobia—again a personal idiosyncrasy he avoided revealing to any other being—was becoming more noticeable of late. He redoubled his efforts to suppress it.

Another new sensor-log screen appeared on the viewer, and Garak welcomed it as a distraction from the heat and closeness of the room. This next recording had apparently been made by the *U.S.S. Enterprise,* also in the Bajoran system, on stardate 52145.7.

The new sensor recording began, and for a few seconds all Garak could see was streaking stars and lances of phaser fire. Then the image stabilized, and he was able to make out a tightly grouped formation of three *Galor*-class Cardassian warships surrounded by a cloud of Jem'Hadar attack cruisers, purple drive fields aglow. In the background, Garak could once again see the shifting energy curtain of the Denorios Belt, so he had a reasonably good notion of what he was watching: the departure of Kai Weyoun's expedition.

Kai Weyoun, Garak mused. He almost felt sorry for poor Major Kira, having to deal with that corruption of her deeply felt religion. *Almost* felt sorry. The major was a Bajoran, after all, and they were a far too sensitive people, regrettably quick to find fault or take offense. And judging from how they had created an entire religion around a few sparkling artifacts discarded by a more advanced species, rather easy to deceive as well.

The new sensor log continued, and Garak's conclusion was confirmed. Just as the *Enterprise* swooped in on what seemed to him to be a rather remarkably risky attack—which nonetheless resulted in the loss of a Cardassian warship—the red wormhole popped open, just as the blue wormhole so often had. At that, the two remaining *Galor*-class ships and their Jem'Hadar escorts vanished into the red wormhole, which then collapsed. Though the *Enterprise* continued on a matching course, unlike the blue wormhole the red wormhole did not open again.

Very selective, Garak noted. Which meant it was quite likely that the red wormhole was also home to an advanced species, or was otherwise under intelligent control.

The current sensor log ended, and the boring Bajoran colonel returned to the viewscreen to explain that the Weyoun expedition had been intended to traverse the new phenomenon and attempt to discover if it had a second opening in normal space, as did the existing phenomenon.

Garak's eyes began to close. Really, the colonel was almost soporific. Even he could guess that the *unstated* goal of the expedition had been to determine if the new wormhole led to the Gamma Quadrant.

But then Garak's eyes opened abruptly. The colonel had not referred to the wormholes as wormholes. He had pointedly called them *phenomena*. Why?

Listening more closely now, Garak heard the colonel go on to say that although it usually took less than two minutes to travel through the existing phenomenon, the Weyoun expedition remained in the new phenomenon for more than three weeks. At which time, of the 1,137 valiant soldiers who had made up the expeditionary force, only Weyoun managed to return. Though he brought with him new allies.

Now another new sensor log began running, this one from a Bajoran vessel, the *Naquo,* beginning with a rapid sweep across the Denorios Belt to catch the red wormhole in the process of opening. And then, from that cauldron of hyperdimensional energies, Garak saw seven ships appear.

Despite himself Garak leaned forward in his chair, as if those few extra centimeters might help him better understand the nature of the seven ships.

Are they transparent? he wondered, for certainly he could see the glow of the wormhole and the Belt through their elongated, ovoid shapes.

But as the sensor log displayed a progression of increasingly magnified views, Garak realized that the seven ships were little more than skeletons—collections of struts and beams, each vessel slightly different from the rest but with no obviously contained areas that might correspond to crew quarters.

A sudden flash of light from one of the ships ended the sensor recording. Sitting back once again, Garak decided the flash of light had been weapons fire. Wherever the second wormhole had reemerged into normal space, it was clear that Weyoun *had* returned with allies.

Once again, the Bajoran colonel returned to the screen. This time Garak did not feel at all sleepy.

The colonel now stated that the new phenomenon had connected the Bajoran Sector to a region in the farthest reaches of the Delta Quadrant. There, Weyoun had made contact with the Grigari, who returned the Vorta when the rest of his expedition had been lost.

Garak waited for more details, but the colonel offered none. An omission Garak found distinctly amusing in its circumspection. He himself had heard rumors of the Grigari most of his life. Though he could recall no convincing report of direct contact with the species, their medical technology was often traded at the frontier, having been obtained from other, intermediary species. Furthermore, that particular type of medical technology was banned on virtually every civilized world in the Alpha and Beta Quadrants.

He recalled once reading a report outlining the results of the Obsidian Order's analysis of a Grigari flesh regenerator, which some had hoped would enable certain torture techniques to be used for longer periods of interrogation. The Order's conclusion: too dangerous.

If but one contraband Grigari device had been deemed by the Obsidian Order to be too dangerous, then it was daunting to consider the damage a Grigari fleet might be capable of inflicting. Clearly, what the Bajoran colonel was not saying in this sanitized briefing was that Weyoun's expedition—Jem'Hadar and Cardassian alike— had been utterly decimated by the Grigari. Which begged the only questions worth asking: How had Weyoun survived, and why had the Grigari come through the wormhole under his command?

Garak repressed the hope that threatened to surface as a smile on his face. *A universe of mystery to explore,* he thought. It could actually be that there would be no one here he could bribe, threaten, or seduce into taking him back to his own time. And if so, he might grow to like it here.

He settled back to see what else would unfold from this selective presentation of the past twenty-five years, and what answers, if any, might be forthcoming. So far, it seemed, for each mystery described and explained two new ones were being revealed and left enigmatic.

As the briefing continued, the ever-curious Garak was not disappointed.

CHAPTER 9

WITH SEVEN LIFETIMES of experience to draw on, Jadzia Dax recognized a dying starship when she saw one, and the *Augustus* was dying.

It obviously had been launched before completion—its environmental controls were malfunctioning. The nature of the vessel's exposed wires, pipes, and conduits also told her that redundancy and self-repair capabilities were nonexistent. And there were appallingly few signs of any attempt to make the ship a secure home for her crew. Even the earliest starships had used paint and colored lights to vary the visual environment and prevent boredom from setting in on long voyages or tours of duty. Yet even those simple grace notes were missing from this ship.

And just as the yellowing of a single leaf can indicate the failing health of a tree, Jadzia was further convinced that the decline of the *Augustus* was not an isolated event. It was a symptom of a greater disease, one that must infect all of Starfleet.

None of these conclusions had she shared with Worf, however. Even as she had walked with him through the narrow, unfinished corridors of the ship escorted by Vulcan security guards, each wearing phaser-visors, Jadzia had remained silent, as had he. Now, with little more than a look exchanged since she and her husband had been escorted to the cramped cabin that was to be their prison cell, Jadzia knew that Worf had reached the same conclusion she had.

They were under surveillance.

The fact that the Vulcan captain of this vessel could subject them to the barbaric test of their humanity on the hangar deck was proof enough that this Starfleet had deviated from the ideals that had drawn Jadzia to serve in it. The computer briefing she and Worf had watched on the holographic screen had been further evidence of whatever disease was responsible for the decay around them.

Whether the briefing had been a complete lie or not Jadzia couldn't be certain. But she was convinced that it had not been the complete truth.

She had seen that same realization in Worf's eyes as well.

Because no matter how limited Starfleet's ship construction and maintenance capacities had become, no matter how brutal and arbitrary its commanders, Jadzia could not for an instant believe that in a mere twenty-five years Starfleet and the Federation had degenerated to the point that they would take part in a religious war. It was unthinkable.

Yet according to the computer briefing, that's exactly what was under way—the War of the Prophets.

Somehow, since the destruction of Deep Space 9 a new religious movement on Bajor, centered on the beings discovered to live in the second wormhole, had become a rallying point for a new interstellar political entity—the Bajoran Ascendancy. If the briefing was to be believed, the Ascendancy had early on launched a series of unprovoked attacks against Federation territory that had resulted in years of tense negotiations and border skirmishes, each side accusing the other of ongoing acts of terrorism.

Had that been the end of the story, Jadzia might have understood how a state of war could come to exist, with the Ascendancy attempting to take over new systems and the Federation attempting to maintain its borders.

But according to the briefing that was not the point of the undeclared war.

The goal of the Ascendancy was not to acquire new territory. It was simply to prohibit the passage of non-Ascendancy ships through the Bajoran Sector, including the homeworld system and the four closest colony worlds. In Jadzia's time—in fact, throughout the existence of the Federation—Starfleet had always respected the sovereignty of independent systems. The Prime Directive permitted it to do nothing less.

But according to that same briefing, which Jadzia had found to be a particularly deplorable piece of propaganda, long on emotion and short on facts, the goal of Starfleet in this war was not to defend Federation territory, not to contain Ascendancy forces within their own boundaries, but actually to invade the Bajoran home system and destroy the second wormhole, ending the new Bajoran religion.

Even seven lifetimes had not prepared her for the utter revulsion she felt for the Starfleet of this time. What had happened to the Prime Directive? What had happened to the Fundamental Declarations? For a moment the Trill had even found herself wondering if, in addition to traveling through time, the *Defiant* had somehow crossed over into a parallel universe, one closer to the horrors of the Mirror Universe than to the one she had lived in.

Their Vulcan captors had told them that the briefing would answer all their questions. But so many new ones had been raised in Jadzia that she had come to feel liberated. When she had entered the Academy, she had pledged herself to uphold the ideals of Starfleet and the Federation. When she had graduated, she had taken her oath as an officer to do the same. As a result, she felt no conflict in her present resolve to behave according to that pledge and that oath—both made to the Starfleet of the past and not to this hollow, dying version that did not deserve its name.

All she needed now was an opportunity to take action, and that opportunity came the moment she and Worf set foot on their third metal staircase. The ship's decks, doors, and intersections were labeled only by alphanumeric code, but Jadzia knew they were now on a deck higher than the hangar deck, which suggested they were moving closer to the bridge.

Worf and she—the tactical officer and the science officer—had been "invited" to a meeting there. And that strongly suggested that Captain T'len and her own science officer were now on the bridge, waiting for their "guests" to arrive.

Which means, Jadzia thought, *they won't be expecting—*

Two steps from the top of the staircase and the waiting Vulcan escort, she drove her fist upward into the man's stomach, and as he doubled over she smashed her other hand up against the visor he wore, seeking to damage it as much as its wearer.

Reflexively, the Vulcan guard reached out for her shoulder, seeking the nerves that would bring instant unconsciousness. But he was still off-balance, and Jadzia swept his outstretched hand aside and slammed his head against the metal handrail.

That was the telling blow, and with a groan the guard fell to the metal deck.

Only then did Jadzia turn back to see how Worf had fared, confident that he would have been looking for the same opportunity she had, and that he would have made his move in the same instant.

Sure enough, Worf was crouched at the bottom of the stairway, removing the phaser-visor from the guard who lay sprawled there. A thin thread of green blood trickled from the Vulcan's nose, which looked considerably flatter than it had a few moments earlier.

Jadzia leaped up the last few steps and pulled the phaser-visor from the guard she had felled. A thin black wire ran from the device into the collar of the guard's uniform. She pushed him onto his side and traced the wire down his back until it reached his waist. She pulled up on his jacket and discovered that the wire disappeared into a belt that was studded with various components, and which she concluded was the power supply and control mechanism for the weapon.

The belt had a twist lock that opened easily, and by the time Jadzia had donned it over her own uniform and was adjusting the visor to her head, Worf had run up the stairs with surprisingly little noise and had stopped beside her, his own phaser-visor already in place.

"Looks good," Jadzia told him. But looking through her own visor was like looking through transparent aluminum. She saw no holographic displays or any other indication of how the visor should be operated.

"Mine does not work, either," Worf said.

Jadzia tried pulling her loose belt tighter. "Maybe they're keyed to each individual user."

"Or they could require low-level Vulcan telepathy."

Jadzia realized there could be a dozen safeguards built into the visors, and even if she and Worf could get past them, they'd still not know how to aim and fire. "Okay, for now they're just fashion accessories."

Worf frowned. "This is not a time to joke."

Jadzia couldn't resist smiling at her mate. She knew that as far as Worf was concerned there never was a good time for a joke. "Good work taking out your guard. I knew you'd be thinking the same thing I was."

Something flashed through Worf's eyes that suddenly made Jadzia doubt he had been thinking the same as she had.

"Weren't you?" she asked.

"There were two earlier opportunities to attack. When you missed them both, I decided that *you* had not reached the same conclusion *I* had."

"So I took my time," she said. She most definitely intended to learn what the missed opportunities had been, but this wasn't the time for a debriefing. "But we're thinking the same thing now, right?"

"I hope so," Worf said seriously. "You are planning on locating the second hangar deck where they undoubtedly keep the shuttlecraft that were missing from the hangar deck we were beamed to."

"You want to hijack a shuttlecraft?" Jadzia asked incredulously.

"It is the best way to escape and find a source of information about this time that we can trust."

"I agree with the second part, but there's a much better way to escape than by taking over a shuttle."

Worf gave Jadzia a look she knew all too well—the one that said he was the warrior in the family and she was the scientist. "What better way?" he asked, and his tone suggested that he knew whatever she was about to say was wrong.

"We take over the ship."

"The two of us?"

Jadzia grinned. "If you'd like to go back to our quarters and rest, I can take care of it."

Worf grunted. "How?"

"First, we don't linger near the scene of the crime." She looked up and down the corridor, then started to run forward. Unlike all other Starfleet vessels she had been on, the *Augustus* had no maps or display boards in the corridors. And since the identification labels did not progress in any logical sequence, she decided to assume that the ship had been deliberately designed to make it difficult for any hostile boarding party to know where they were and where they should go.

But from what she recalled of the elongated shape of the vessel as she had seen it on the *Defiant*'s viewscreen, the odds were good that the bridge was ahead and no more than one or two decks higher.

Within two or three running strides, Worf had caught up to her, and together they ran to the next intersection.

Jadzia stopped in the middle of it, glancing port and starboard.

"How can you be sure we will not run into other guards?" Worf asked.

"Look at the ship's condition. It's filthy, poorly maintained. I bet they're running with less than half the crew they're supposed to have. That means double shifts, so everyone's either at their station or sleeping."

Worf adjusted the visor he wore—his prominent brow kept it from fitting securely across his face. "It is still dangerous to run without—"

Jadzia cut him off by pointing to a nearby door. "That one!" She ran to it, and as she looked for a control panel the door obligingly slid open before her.

"An unlocked compartment is not likely to contain critical components," Worf complained. But he dutifully followed her inside.

As the door slipped shut behind them, three small lighting fixtures flickered to life. Another sign that the *Augustus* wasn't operating at peak efficiency. The energy used to light the interior of a starship was usually negligible compared to what was required to run the warp engines or the replicators. But this ship was obviously set up to conserve even that insignificant amount of power.

"Why are we here?" Worf asked as he surveyed the room. It was almost the same size as the cabin they'd been given, but there was no furniture, and its walls were lined with conduits and cables.

"There!" Jadzia pointed to her quarry—a computer screen and control surface. "That won't have restricted access."

She went to the screen, and in only seconds she had called up a schematic of the ship. It was *Tiberius*-class, and seemed to have evolved from the *Defiant*. Almost three-quarters of its volume was devoted to warp engines and weapons systems. Only the central core of the ship contained significant life-support areas.

"This is good," Jadzia said as she made calculations based on the size of the habitable volume of the ship. "I'd say the regular crew complement wouldn't be more than fifty. So we're probably facing no more than thirty. That's just about two to one, and you're good for at least ten, so . . ." She looked back at Worf, but he wasn't paying attention to her. He was looking down at the deck. "Am I boring you?"

Worf was looking at the far bulkhead, and a sudden shaft of silver energy lanced from his visor to crackle against a bare spot between two conduits. "I have found the 'on' switch," Worf announced as he reached over to show her where her visor's activation controls were located, on the upper edge of her belt. Suddenly a rainbow collection of virtual squares appeared before her eyes, each about a centimeter across, and appearing to hover in mid-air a meter in front of her.

Then Worf touched another control on her belt and the squares seemed to float closer, until she could read their labels. Some corresponded to phaser controls. Others to tricorder functions.

"A combination phaser and tricorder?" she asked.

"Extremely efficient," Worf confirmed with approval. "It leaves both hands free to use a *bat'leth*."

Jadzia looked past the holographic controls to give Worf a wry smile. "Exactly what I was thinking." She refocused on the controls, noticing that whichever one she looked at brightened. "How do you actually get it to fire?" she asked.

Worf quickly briefed her on the visor operating system, explaining that it appeared to be similar to the helmets worn by Starfleet warp-fighter pilots in their own time. After enabling the phaser functions, firing, it seemed, was as simple as looking at a target and blinking the right eye.

"This is better than I had hoped," Jadzia said.

Worf sighed. "Do you really think we have a chance at taking over their bridge? Even armed with these?"

Jadzia patted Worf's expansive chest. "We're not going to take over the bridge. Chances are it has defenses we can't even imagine. I had something different in mind."

This time Worf's sigh was even louder. "It is obvious we do *not* think alike, because I have no idea what you mean."

Jadzia was about to wink at Worf, then thought better of it, considering her visor's capabilities. Instead, she pointed to a spot on the ship's schematic that indicated a large cabin just down the corridor from the bridge. "What's more important than the bridge of a starship? Or should I say, *who* is more important?"

At last Worf smiled. Trill and Klingon, bound by love and duty, they were finally both sharing the same thought.

They waited in darkness—and they did not have to wait long. The door to the captain's stateroom slid open only minutes after Jadzia and Worf had easily bypassed the lock. For all the advanced firepower the *Augustus* carried, her designers had left out a considerable number of security amenities, including a weapons-suppression system, computer control of all interior locks, and a personnel-locator network. The only reason for the omissions Jadzia could imagine was that their absence made the ship simpler and faster to build. But what did the concepts of simpler and faster have to do with a construction project undertaken by robotic assemblers? All the mysteries in this time period were making her uncomfortable.

With the door opening and the lights coming on, Jadzia trusted that several of those mysteries might soon end.

As planned, the instant the door had slid shut again, Worf leaned out from his position sprawled behind the bunk and stunned Captain T'len with a blast from his triphaser.

The stun intensity was at the lowest setting, and T'len's hand fluttered toward her communicator as she slumped on the deck, semiconscious. But before the captain could report, Jadzia was at her side and removed her communicator badge. Then Worf tied the captain's hands and feet with lengths of fabric he ripped from the sheets on the bunk and carried her to the room's lone chair.

As T'len slowly regained awareness of what had happened to her, Jadzia studied the stateroom to see if she could build up a picture of what sort of person the captain was. But almost everything in it was Starfleet issue, not a hint of individuality anywhere. No paintings or framed holos. No books. Not even a Vulcan IDIC placed as a meditation aid.

Jadzia's examination ended with T'len's blunt statement. "You will not survive this attempt to take control of my ship."

"We've survived this long," Jadzia said easily. "We'll make it through a few more minutes."

Worf stood so that he was midway between the closed door and the captain, and he kept his gaze firmly on the door to challenge anyone who might come through it. "Captain T'len, what is our estimated arrival time at Starbase 53?"

"Eighteen hours, fourteen minutes."

"What will happen to us when we arrive?"

"To you? Nothing. Because you will be dead. To your fellow refugees, I cannot say. It was anticipated that they would be given a chance to demonstrate their suitability for continuing their service with Starfleet. However, if your actions are typical of what we can expect from them, they will be imprisoned."

"You knew we were coming, didn't you?" Jadzia said. It was the only explanation for how quickly the briefing program had been made available. It had been created for the crew of the *Defiant,* the Bolian admiral had said.

T'len nodded. "Several years after your disappearance, Starfleet researchers went back to the sensor logs recorded at the time of your disappearance and discovered clues suggesting the *Defiant* might have been pulled along the equivalent of a temporal-slingshot trajectory around the mouth of the second wormhole. The trajectory was calculated and the time of your reemergence into the timeline plotted."

"Why did we reemerge in interstellar space?" Worf asked.

Jadzia expanded the question. "Shouldn't we have reappeared around the wormhole?"

"You did not travel *into* the wormhole. You traveled *through* a region of space-time that was significantly distorted by the wormhole. The Bajoran system has moved on in the past twenty-five years, through a combination of its own relative motion and the rotation of the galaxy. Since the space-time distortion caused by the wormhole is not constant—as would be the case with the gravity well of a star—the absolute region of space you passed through was unbound, and moved at a different rate."

Jadzia felt vindicated. "Given your knowledge of the second wormhole, I'd say Starfleet has done considerable research into it."

"These are desperate times," T'len said, looking down at the torn sheets that bound her hands and feet together.

"A Vulcan admitting to desperation?" Jadzia asked.

"You saw the briefing that was prepared for you," the captain replied. "Logic is in short supply at this time."

"Exactly what I was thinking," Jadzia agreed. "Now tell me—what *wasn't* on the briefing?"

"That question is too broad."

"I don't believe the Federation would enter into a war against any system just to wipe out a religion."

"Perhaps not in your time."

"Are you serious?" Jadzia asked, hating the implications of T'len's answer. "This War of the Prophets *is* what the briefing described?"

T'len looked up at the ceiling, an odd gesture for a Vulcan to make. "Starfleet's objective in this war, undeclared or not, is to gain entry into the Bajoran system and destroy the red wormhole and any and all artifacts of importance to the subset of Bajoran faith known as Ascendant."

Jadzia could see that even Worf looked shocked by T'len's words. "What about the Prime Directive?"

"It is no longer operative."

Jadzia stared at T'len. "I can't believe I heard a Starfleet officer say that."

"Commander Dax, this is a war of survival. Either *we* destroy the Ascendants, or they *will* destroy us."

"Because of their religious beliefs?"

"Precisely."

Worf shared Jadzia's incomprehension. "You will have to explain to us how a belief based in personal faith can pose a danger to the Federation."

"Not just the Federation," T'len said grimly.

"Captain," Jadzia asked in sudden apprehension, "*what* exactly do the Ascendants believe?"

The captain's explanation did nothing to make Jadzia more comfortable.

CHAPTER 10

ON SIX SWIFT LEGS, the Cardassian vole scurried along the overhead power conduit mounted near the top of the bulkhead just outside the *Boreth*'s main engineering station. Visually indistinguishable in color from the stained Klingon structural panels that lined the ship's corridor, the diminutive orange creature froze in the shadows near the ceiling, almost as if to avoid being heard by the sensitive ears of the two Romulans passing by below.

But when the two stopped, and each reached out in turn for the engineering security panel, the vole's tiny head jutted forward, its spine nobs pulsing in time with its rapid breathing, the hairless flaps of its bat-like ears flattening close to its skull, its glittering, bulbous eyes focusing on each move the Romulans made as they tapped out their individual security codes.

The engineering doors slid open.

In the same instant, the vole released the opposable claws of its two front pairs of legs and dropped from the conduit, straight for the Romulans—

—who didn't even bother to look up as the annoying buzz of a Klingon *glob* fly swerved around them, then vanished into the cavernous upper levels of the largest open area on the *Boreth*.

Seconds later, before the Engineering doors could close, the

Cardassian vole gripped the edge of a second-level safety rail with its claws, then vaulted to engineering's upper deck and slipped through the narrow gap between two heavily shielded quantum-wave decouplers, both aglow with flickering status lights. Just then, an exhausted Romulan technician who had been working all shift to trace the source of an intermittent photon leak near the decouplers glanced away from her padd toward the gap. And saw a dim orange blur streak by.

A momentary frown creased the technician's face. The *Boreth*, however, was a vast ship and contained a veritable secondary ecosystem of parasites and vermin, so the sighting of the occasional pest was not worth reporting. Thus duty won out over curiosity. The photon leak was real. The technician dismissed the fleeting sighting.

And far back in the twisted labyrinth of barely passable access paths that ran behind the wall of power relays that supplied the ship's Romulan-designed singularity inhibitor, the vole stopped, and after looking all around took a deep, squeaky breath and began to *expand.* . . .

In the shadows of engineering, Odo watched carefully as his humanoid hands sprouted from the sleeves of his Bajoran constable's uniform. Unlike the other, more common shapeshifting creatures in the galaxy, changelings such as he had the ability to alter their mass as well as their form. Though it was a completely instinctive process, Odo's first mentor in the world of solids, Dr. Mora Pol, had theorized that Odo's ability to alter the shape of his molecular structure actually enabled him to form four-dimensional lattices in the shape of hyperspheres and tesseracts—geometric shapes that could not exist in only three dimensions.

In effect, this allowed Odo to shunt some of his mass into another dimension, depending on the requirements of the form he assumed. Odo acknowledged that as a scientific problem his innate ability was interesting, and that Pol's theory, if true, made some sort of sense. Yet because of Dr. Pol's belief that changelings faced the risk of inadvertently pushing too much of themselves into that other dimension and disappearing altogether, Odo still experienced unease when attempting to reduce his mass to a matter of micrograms. As a result he had seldom dared push his shape-changing ability to the extremes of becoming anything as small as a Klingon *glob* fly, a creature only half the size of a Terran mosquito.

Since learning more about his true nature from his fellow changelings in the Great Link, Odo had learned that Dr. Pol's fear resulted from his misunderstanding the shapeshifting process; still, old habits died hard, and Odo still felt uncomfortable transforming himself into anything smaller than voles or creatures of similar size.

Relieved at his uneventful reversion to normal humanoid mass and size, Odo now turned to the one or two details still requiring his attention.

On his reconnaissance mission he had observed that almost all crew members of the *Boreth* wore uniforms apparently modified from something similar to the one he had customarily worn on Deep Space 9. Except that the *Boreth* crew uniforms featured slightly different shades of brown-and-tan fabric and had a single swath of a contrasting color running across the chest from shoulder to shoulder, instead of the two seemingly separate shoulder pieces his own uniform displayed. Also for some reason, Odo recalled, the *Boreth* crew uniforms were an invariably sloppy fit, as if the ship's clothing replicators no longer had accurate measuring capabilities.

Still the changes were simple, and as he now formed a mental picture of himself wearing a new uniform, Odo sensed the familiar rippling and shifting of his outer self as his external uniform updated itself to the new standard appearance, its surface even sagging and bunching to suggest a bad fit. Then, just to further the illusion should he be seen in engineering, Odo gave his head a shake, and his sleek, brushed-back hair—a near duplicate of Dr. Pol's own style and color—slithered forward to become black Romulan bangs. At the same time his simply shaped ears elongated slightly to form Vulcanoid points, and his brow became more pronounced. Odo knew that under normal lighting conditions there would still be an unfinished look to his features (despite his ability to duplicate every vane of every feather on an avian species, the far less demanding details of a humanoid face had always remained such a difficult challenge for him he sometimes wondered if his people had engineered a sort of facial inhibition into him when they'd adjusted his genetic code, to make him long to return to his homeworld). At least, he reasoned, his new Romulan form would offer some protection during his passage through engineering, while he committed the acts of sabotage so painstakingly planned by O'Brien and Rom.

Captain Sisko, of course, had given his express approval for the operation. From the briefing the survivors from the *Defiant* had received only a few hours ago, it had become obvious to all that despite the Starfleet emblems that adorned this vessel, the institution served by the crew of the *Boreth* bore no allegiance nor resemblance to the Starfleet of twenty-five years past. The emblems, in the captain's judgment, were a lie. Odo and the other survivors suspected the briefing was also.

Odo directed his attention to an exposed bulkhead between two large and unidentifiable cylindrical housings, where he found a power-relay switching box surrounded by a nest of conduits. The box itself was a meter tall, no more than a half-meter wide, and labeled with a Bajoran identification plate that had been haphazardly attached over a Klingon sign. From what Chief O'Brien had seen of the *Boreth*'s power-distribution system as he was led through the corridors, he had told Odo he was confident that the switching mechanisms in the ship would not have changed significantly since their own time. Odo studied the Bajoran plate more closely, confirming for himself that it did use the same terminology with which he was familiar. Still, when he swung open the access panel, he was relieved to see that the layout of the box's interior was indeed very close to what Rom had described.

At any given time, Odo was aware from experience, a starship generated a constant amount of power for internal use, though the demands on that power varied according to what subsystems—from replicators to sonic showers—were operating from second to second. Thus, a ship's power-distribution system was constantly adjusting the amount of power, available as either basic electricity or the more complex wave-forms of transtator current, that moved through specific sections of the ship's power grid and prevented localized surges, brownouts, and overloads. Odo knew that interfering with that system would, as a matter of course, make such interruptions in the flow of power more likely. And a properly timed interruption that affected engineering could have the desired result of forcing the *Boreth* to drop from warp. That, in fact, was Odo's goal.

Sisko had admitted that it was a risky plan, but the captain had also thought it likely that, given the speed with which the vessels of the other Starfleet had attacked the *Opaka,* if the *Boreth* were to lose warp propulsion in deep space, it would also come under swift attack.

Odo concentrated on transforming his fingers into right-angled wiring grippers in order to disconnect an inline series of transpolar compensators. He trusted that Kira would be as successful with her half of the mission: obtaining a Bajoran combadge from one of the guards watching over the *Defiant's* rescued crew and passengers. His Deep Space 9 colleague had taken the challenge because, whatever the truth of this future, as Bajorans Kira and Commander Arla were not subject to the same level of scrutiny as the other survivors. Consequently, Kira and Arla had each been given separate staterooms, while the remaining sixteen . . . *prisoners,* Odo decided was the best term for them . . . had been grouped into four main barracks-type rooms, each room featuring enough tiered bunks for twenty-one crew. O'Brien had identified the holding areas as enlisted men's communal quarters—a living area typical of some Klingon warships.

Whatever the barracks' original purpose, Odo had been pleased enough to have been placed in so large a confinement chamber. It had made it easier to move to the back of the room nearest the sanitary facilities and discreetly transform himself into the Klingon insect capable of escaping through the door with the departing guards. While he had originally planned to reach engineering through the ventilation shafts, the Chief had been quick to point out to him that various environmental systems on the ship employed charged grids specifically designed to incinerate unwanted pests.

Odo gave a final twist to the secondary connector ring, and the status lights of the compensators winked out. One down, five to go. By O'Brien's calculations, if he could compromise at least six relay switches within engineering, and then short-circuit a seventh, he'd be able to cause a surge that would interrupt power to the ship's warp generators long enough to trigger an automatic safety shutdown. Although the chief engineer had doubted it would take the crew of the *Boreth* more than ten minutes to bring their ship back into warp, if Kira had her communicator and Rom *was* able to reconfigure it and there *were* real Starfleet vessels nearby, Odo reckoned that ten minutes might be just long enough to bring the *Boreth* under attack.

Whether that attack would result in the rescue of the *Defiant's* survivors now held prisoner on the *Boreth* was a risk everyone had accepted. Action, in Odo's experience, was always preferable to imprisonment.

First changing the right-angled grippers at the end of his arm back into a hand, he carefully shut the access panel and glanced around his cramped work area. In the dim light, there appeared to be another power-relay switching box four meters along the bulkhead, mounted between two large vertical pipes. Odo approached the switching box, located the release latch for its cover and, just as he was about to open it, heard a soft voice in his ear murmur, "Odo. You can stop now."

Startled, Odo stepped back, unsuccessfully scanning the shadows and darkness for the source of the voice. He couldn't be sure, but it had sounded like Weyoun. Either Weyoun himself was here, or his voice had been relayed through an overhead communications speaker. It was unclear which.

Odo quickly decided against staying long enough to find out. He took a breath, formed a mental image of a vole, and—

—nothing.

Odo tried again.

And again. But his shape appeared to be locked in his half-formed Romulan disguise.

"Such a useful precaution," Weyoun's voice said breathily, from nowhere and from everywhere, "the inhibitor."

Odo simultaneously blinked and stepped back, as a small cylindrical device suddenly appeared to be hovering a few meters in front of him. One end was segmented like a series of stacked golden rings, the other bore a black panel dotted with sequentially flashing lights.

"The original was developed by the Obsidian Order." To Odo, it was as if Weyoun were speaking from the unsupported device, and he wondered if antigravs had actually been miniaturized to such an extent. "A very long and arduous process, as I'm sure you know. Then Damar had it further refined. I believe he was planning on betraying the Founder . . . once the Dominion-Cardassian alliance had proved victorious over the Federation, of course."

And suddenly Weyoun's pale face appeared in midair, smiling with a distracted expression, near the floating inhibitor. Then, with a series of jerky movements, the rest of Weyoun's body came into view.

Odo stared in amazement, as a flurry of small energy discharges revealed the Vorta before him in his entirety, half-dressed in a vedek's robes, half in what could only be an isolation suit with its cloaking field switched off.

"Also a most useful device, wouldn't you agree?" Weyoun said as he stepped neatly out of the bulky red suit and let it fall to the deck. "I'm surprised you people forgot about it. It was a Starfleet invention, after all. Apparently, something called Section 31 reverse-engineered the Romulan cloaking device on the *Defiant*. Quite illegal. It's fascinating what the passage of time brings to the release of secret documents."

Odo had no idea what Weyoun was talking about, and didn't care to know. "Turn off the inhibitor," he said.

Weyoun looked at the device in his hand, shrugged. "I don't think so."

Odo regarded him sternly. "I gave you an order."

"So you did."

Odo was uncomfortable with what he had to say next, but in this one limited case, surely the end justified the means. "Weyoun, I am your god. Do as I say."

Unexpectedly, Weyoun moved toward him, holding out the device as if making an offering of it. "Odo, do you realize you've never spoken to me like that before," the Vorta said as if concerned for his welfare. "I don't believe you know how much it has always troubled me to see you so conflicted, refusing to admit what you are, what you have meant to me."

"Well, I don't refuse to admit it any longer. Turn off the—"

The cylinder struck Odo's face like a club, knocking him to the deck.

Odo held a hand to his all-too-solid face. The pain was intense, and he looked up at Weyoun in shock. The Vorta appeared to be trembling in the throes of nervous excitement.

"I can't tell you how many times in the past twenty-five years I've wondered if I could do that. Did it hurt?"

Slowly, Odo got to his feet, only now recalling Sisko's warning that Weyoun had somehow overcome his genetic imperative to regard changelings as gods. "Yes."

"And that was just a simple blow. Imagine what it must feel like . . . to die."

Odo braced himself. Not only did Weyoun's attack confirm that the Vorta was capable of striking one of the beings he used to worship, it seemed he was preparing himself to kill. Only one explanation was possible. Weyoun was a clone and this one was defective.

"I'm not defective," the Vorta said before Odo could state his conclusion. "I prefer to regard myself as restored. Cured. Freed?" The Vorta shrugged. "The important thing is, I can finally think for myself."

"Perhaps," Odo growled, "you've just been more effectively programmed."

Weyoun merely grinned. "I wondered that myself, Odo, after I returned from the True Temple. After all, if some minor realignment of my amino acids were responsible for my former belief that you and your people were gods, I realized I really couldn't rule out the possibility that some other agency might have made a further modification in my program."

"And what answer did you find?" *As if I don't know,* Odo thought sourly.

As if delighted to share a confidence with one who would truly understand, Weyoun favored him with an intimate smile. "First, I returned to my own homeworld, as it were. To the Dominion cloning facilities on Rondac III. I awoke one of the other Weyouns. And you know, the most sophisticated medical scans showed that there was absolutely no difference between myself and him. Except in our thoughts and beliefs."

"Weyoun Eight believed the Founders were gods."

The Vorta sighed. "To the end, sadly."

Odo snorted. "You mean, you killed him."

Weyoun pursed his mouth, pious. "He was defective, Odo. It was a mercy."

"And what happens when the next Weyoun tracks you down and decides *you're* defective?"

"There is, there will be, *no* next Weyoun," Weyoun said firmly. *"I* am the last. The cloning facility, you see, had . . . outlived its usefulness."

"You mean, you destroyed it."

"You know very well it was in Cardassian territory, so—technically—the Cardassians must take the blame for its loss, because they would not surrender. Believe me, Odo, I would have preferred to have kept at least some other Vorta around to help me through these difficult years."

"You're sure you're the last of your kind?"

Weyoun nodded. "Just as you are the last of yours. At least in the Alpha Quadrant. Isn't that reason enough that we should be united in our purpose?"

"And what purpose would that be?" Odo steeled himself to continue the discussion with the odious creature before him. The more Weyoun babbled on, the more information he would supply that might suggest a way out of this intolerable situation.

"Think of the suffering you've endured, Odo."

Odo loathed the false concern in Weyoun's oily voice, but gave no outward indication of his feelings, waiting to see what the Vorta really wanted from him.

Encouraged, Weyoun warmed to his argument that he and Odo were soulmates. "Cast out by your own people. Forced to become a plaything of Bajoran and Cardassian scientists. Never really belonging to any world, even your own when you returned to the Great Link. But you and I . . . we share so much pain. Isn't it right and proper that we should dedicate our lives to eliminating pain forever?"

"Pain is a necessary part of life," Odo said gruffly. "It enables us to appreciate pleasure."

Weyoun gazed at him thoughtfully. "I never knew you had such a philosophical streak in you."

"Do you really want to end my pain?" Odo asked skeptically. "And the pain of all the others from the *Defiant?*"

Weyoun bowed his head as he had done countless times in Odo's presence, but not this time to Odo. "The cessation of pain, the onset of joy . . . that is the will and the one goal of the True Prophets," he intoned.

"Then free us," Odo said.

Weyoun sighed, lifting his head. "You're not being held prisoner here. You're being protected."

"It seems some words have changed their meanings in the past twenty-five years."

"Not words, Odo. The galaxy has changed. The Federation has become an abomination. Starfleet an organization of brutal murderers. If I gave you a shuttlecraft and sent you to . . . to Vulcan . . . or Andor, do you know how long you'd last?" Weyoun didn't even pause before answering his own question. "They'd shoot you out of space before you finished opening hailing frequencies."

For no distinct reason he could articulate, Odo was beginning to feel that he really wasn't in immediate danger from Weyoun. It was obvious that the Vorta had been changed in some way. Whatever set of neurons in his brain had been programmed to revere changelings had somehow been reconfigured to revere the Pah-wraiths instead. Recalling that once even the Ferengi Grand Nagus Zek had been altered beyond recognition, having entered the first wormhole, only to reemerge as an altruist determined to give away his fortune. As a result, Odo now had little doubt that alteration of fundamental personality traits was well within the capability of wormhole beings.

But still it somehow also appeared to Odo that Weyoun maintained a type of residual respect for him. The Vorta seemed anxious that he talk with him, listen to him, perhaps even come to understand him. And just as Weyoun's worship of him had been advantageous in the past, Odo decided that in this situation, it was still worth capitalizing on any remaining shadow of that behavior, no matter how distasteful it was.

"Weyoun," he began, without a trace of his previous challenging attitude, choosing instead to play along altogether with whatever Weyoun was up to, "I acknowledge there is a great deal about this time I don't understand. But if there is just one question you can answer for me now, then tell me: Why are the people from the *Defiant* so dangerous to the Starfleet of this time that they would kill us on sight?"

Odo was gratified by the effect of his changed tone on Weyoun, who responded by lowering the inhibitor and no longer making a point of threatening him with it. "Rest assured it's not you, Odo. It's Captain Sisko."

Odo kept his surprise to himself. "Why him?"

The Vorta regarded Odo earnestly. "Because he's the False Emissary to the False Prophets. And according to prophecies of Jalbador, the One True Temple cannot be restored until the False Emissary accepts the True Emissary."

Weyoun's face became grave. "There are those in Starfleet who have determined that if they can prevent Captain Sisko from being present when the two halves of the Temple at last open in conjunction, the Day of Ascendancy will be postponed for millennia."

It was beginning to make sense to Odo. "So everyone knew that the *Defiant* hadn't been destroyed along with DS9. That the ship had been caught in a temporal rift."

Weyoun nodded. "Not at once, of course. But as the Ascendancy regained its rightful position of primacy on Bajor—oh, I tell you, Odo, no world has ever seen such a cultural flowering. You would not believe the treasures those Bajoran monks concealed over the centuries, because they contradicted the teachings of the False Prophets. It is only now that ancient texts thought lost forever have been brought out into the light. Together with all of the writings and prophecies that . . . that the world had forgotten even existed, all of them hidden in caverns, walled-up in temples. . . ."

Odo forgot himself for a moment. "And these texts, these writings, described the *Defiant*'s return, did they?"

But Weyoun just smiled, and waggled a finger at him. "I hear that skeptical tone. And, no, the ancient texts didn't say that a twenty-fourth-century starship named the *Defiant* would be caught in a temporal rift only to reappear twenty-five years later."

"Didn't think so."

"Ah, but several texts did say that the False Emissary would arise from those who had perished at the fall of the gateway, just as I explained to Captain Sisko. The three great mystics of Jalbador—Shabren, Eilin, and Naradim—they had to describe their visions in the context of their time, you know."

"Weyoun," Odo said, choosing his words with care, "I have no doubt that ancient mystical texts can be interpreted to support recent events. Humanoids have been doing that for millennia on hundreds of worlds. What I find troubling is that you say Starfleet has also accepted these interpretations."

"What's left of Starfleet. Yes."

"Then what I don't understand is why Starfleet would accept that the writings on which you base your faith are true, yet not then also accept your faith."

Weyoun's smile faded from his face, and for just an instant Odo thought he detected the flash of a red shift in the Vorta's clear gray eyes. "In the final battle to determine the fate of the universe," Weyoun said passionately, "Starfleet, for reasons which no sane mind can comprehend, has chosen to support the wrong side. Could we say they are afraid of that which they don't understand? That they're afraid of change? Or is it something simpler, Odo? Can we simply say that in a universe in which all sentient beings have been given free choice, some, invariably, will choose evil?"

The Vorta paused as if in contact with something or someone of which Odo was unaware, and then disconcertingly began speaking again as if there had been no interruption in his speech. "These same questions have been asked since the True Prophets created sentient beings in their own image, and I doubt we will answer them here in engineering."

Even though he sensed Weyoun becoming threatening again, Odo pushed on.

"Weyoun, all things being equal, how can I know that it's not you who've chosen . . . evil?"

The Vorta studied him for a moment before responding. "You know, if my crew had heard that question come from you, Odo, not even I could have acted fast enough to save your life. If anyone else had asked that question, I would not even try to save him. But you and I . . . ?" Weyoun sighed deeply. "I will make allowances. But just this once. Do you understand?"

Odo nodded. "I understand I'm not to question you like that again."

An appreciative smile touched Weyoun's mouth. "Spoken like a Vorta." And then he was deadly serious again. "If you truly want to know who has allied themselves with the forces of evil, consider this, Odo: *My* forces rescued you and your ship from a Starfleet attack wing."

"Only," Odo interjected, "because you need Captain Sisko to fulfill your prophecy."

"Exactly!" Weyoun said, apparently unoffended by the interruption. "I do need Captain Sisko alive. But the ancient texts say nothing about you, Odo. Or about the others I saved with your captain. If I were serving some evil purpose, would it make sense for me to keep you all alive? Or would I simply have you killed? Just as those Starfleet ships tried to do?"

The Vorta held up his inhibitor device and checked its energy level. "It's time for you to go back to the others now, Odo. Tell them what we've talked about. Be especially sure to tell Captain Sisko that if this ill-conceived escape attempt by some unimaginable set of circumstances had worked, all he would have been escaping from was *my* protection, while at the same time delivering himself up to those whose only goal is to kill him."

Weyoun twisted a control on the inhibitor and, shockingly, Odo felt his outer surface instantly begin to lose its integrity, shifting from his Romulan disguise to his usual humanoid form.

Weyoun waved the inhibitor at him. "I think you would agree, Odo, that my scientists have made a great many advances in the time you've been gone. Just remember I can use this to turn you into a cube of duranium and have you thrown out an airlock if I have to."

Odo shivered in spite of himself. In a way, the experience of forced transformation had been like being in the Great Link. But in *that* surrender of individuality he himself had made the choice. Weyoun's machine had just chosen for him.

Weyoun's voice again filled his ears. "Tell Sisko what I've told you," the Vorta said with finality. "If you want to live, I am the only hope you have."

CHAPTER 11

IT HAD BEEN two years since he had had a new uniform. These days, replicator rations for nonessentials were nearly impossible to obtain. But while the words "nearly impossible" might be a roadblock for some Starfleet captains, to a Ferengi Starfleet captain they were a challenge. So two days ago, beginning with a priceless bottle of Picard champagne—vintage 2382, the last great year before the Earth's destruction—Nog had begun a complex series of trades that had not only resulted in his obtaining enough priority replicator rations to requisition ten new uniforms, but he had also acquired use of one of the last remaining private yachts in Sector 001.

Technically, the *Cerulean Star* was the property of the Andorian trade representative in New Berlin. But since the trade mission didn't have access to adequate civilian antimatter supplies, the yacht had not been used in ten months, and the New Berlin representative was certain that no one at her consulate would miss it—provided Nog returned it in three days and left enough Starfleet antimatter in the ship to reach Andor.

Given his transit time to Starbase 53, that left Nog thirty hours to pick up his passengers and warp back to Mars. There would then be ten days left until the end of the universe.

"But at least I'll face it wearing a new uniform," Nog said aloud.

He stood in the surprisingly large stateroom of the Andorian yacht, in standard orbit of a heavily shielded Class-B asteroid in the lifeless Largo system, checking his virtual reflection in the holographic mirror that circled him. Over the past year, he had noticed how his old uniforms had begun to fray, but not how the color at his shoulder had faded. This new uniform was an impressively rich black—it showed every speck of dust and lint—and its shoulder was a vivid, saturated crimson. Not quite a dress uniform, but it would do. Because for what he was about to attempt, he was determined to look his best.

Satisfied that the uniform was as perfect as he had time to make it, Nog donned a matching crimson headskirt and tapped his combadge.

"Captain Nog," he said. "One to beam down."

There was no verbal acknowledgment of his request, but he was on schedule, and three seconds later the Andorian stateroom dissolved into light, then reformed as the transporter room in Starbase 53's main ground installation, deep within the asteroid's core.

As Nog had arranged, Captain T'len of the *Augustus* was waiting for him.

"Captain," Nog said as he stepped down from the pad, "it is good to see you again."

T'len kept her hands folded behind her back. "This is most irregular."

Nog hid a smile. He liked Vulcans. They never wasted time—an attribute he had come to appreciate during his Starfleet career. "I agree," he said.

T'len raised an eyebrow. "I refer to your request, not the overall situation."

Nog was ready for that. "If it were not for the overall situation, I wouldn't have made my request."

T'len angled her head slightly in the Vulcan equivalent of a shrug. "Point taken." She gestured to the door, and Nog hung back a step to let her lead the way. Though they shared the same rank, T'len was also a starship commander, and in the subtle, unwritten traditions of the Fleet, that gave her greater privilege.

Nog followed in T'len's wake as she turned left outside the transporter room and walked toward the turbolift. Automatically, he noticed yet discounted the poor state of repair of the walls—sizable dents, repair patches of differing colors, irregular stains from cracked conduits that had leaked in the past. Starfleet had been operating under extreme wartime conditions for more than ten years. Mere appearance, like frayed uniforms, was not at the top of anyone's list of problems to solve.

"How have they adjusted?" Nog asked T'len, as they neared the turbolift alcove.

"Impossible to characterize except on an individual basis."

"So, some of them have adjusted better than others?"

Nog caught T'len's swift sideways glance at him. "If their state of adjustment varies according to each individual, then logic suggests that of course some have adjusted better than others. You will find out for yourself in just a few minutes."

"I'd like to be prepared."

The Vulcan seemed to accept that explanation. "Then you should be prepared for the human civilian Vash. I have recommended that she remain in custody here, until . . . the end of hostilities."

What a euphemism, Nog thought, and he wondered who had first used it. Hostilities would end in less than two weeks, either with Starfleet's being successful in obliterating most of Bajor or with the end of the universe. At the end of hostilities, either Vash would be released, everyone would have new uniforms, walls would be painted, planet-wide celebrations would be held . . . or else nothing would ever matter again.

But the end of the universe was not a topic of conversation in which Starfleet officers engaged. Quite properly, official directives stressed that all personnel were to focus on the mission, not the consequences.

"What's Vash likely to do?" Nog asked. "Escape?"

"In a manner of speaking. She is intent on returning to her own time."

Nog knew better, but couldn't resist. "Would that be so bad?"

T'len stopped and turned to him. "If Vash returned to her time and revealed what she had learned of our time, history would be changed."

"I ask the question again: Would that be so bad?"

Nog was not naive enough to interpret T'len's expression of surprise as evidence of her abandonment of all pretense of Vulcan self-control. "Captain Nog, you are the Integrated Systems Manager for the *Phoenix.*"

Though not quite sure why T'len was stating something so obvious, Nog waited, gambling on her explaining herself without his having to interrupt.

"Thus you understand the logic of time travel," she said.

Nog frowned. "Some would say there is no logic to time travel."

T'len looked away for a moment as if gathering her thoughts—as if a Vulcan ever needed to do that. "If Vash—or indeed, if any of the crew of the *Defiant*—are allowed to return to their present, only two end results are possible. One, Vash changes the past, and we will no longer exist as we are, and the billions of beings born in the past twenty-five years will likely never exist at all. Two, Vash changes the past, and in so doing she creates a new timeline while we remain in ours—exactly as it is, unchanged."

Nog shook his head. "Think of the billions who have died in the past twenty-five years," he said. "Think of Earth. Of Cardassia Prime."

T'len eyed Nog with what Nog felt could only be disappointment. "Captain Nog, in each generation are born a mere handful of great beings. Your Admiral Picard is surely one of them. Perhaps one other starship captain in all of Starfleet's history has matched his accomplishments. But if only one example of his brilliance is required, then we need look no further than Project Phoenix. To change history *without* changing our timeline is a concept as revolutionary as Hawking's normalization of the Heisenberg exceptions."

Suddenly, T'len's attitude, however subtly, seemed to Nog to soften. "Even as a Vulcan," she said, "I do understand what you are about to experience will be fraught with emotion. You are about to open a door to your own past. But do not allow yourself to be trapped by it. Jean-Luc Picard has given us a true phoenix. Trust in him, Captain. As a Starfleet officer, you can do no less."

"Trust *me,* Captain," Nog said emphatically. "I have no intention of doing anything else."

Nog's eyes deliberately met and held the Vulcan's as steadily as if he were negotiating difficult delivery dates with a recalcitrant supplier. And he was certain that Captain T'len in no way detected the lie he had just brazenly uttered.

It's good to be a Ferengi, Nog thought proudly, and not for the first time in his long Starfleet career. His people's four-lobed brains were resistant to most forms of telepathy, and negotiation skills continued to be taught to Ferengi youngsters at an age when most other humanoid babies were only learning to say their first words.

T'len nodded once as she led the way to the turbolift, and they rode the rest of the way to the conference room in silence. It was the Vulcan way. And Nog was glad of it.

In the command conference room of Starbase 53, Jake Sisko knew he was the most nervous of all the temporal refugees from the *Defiant.* Which wasn't to say that tension wasn't high for all the other survivors—officers and civilians, humans and Bajorans alike.

At first, this trip into the future had been just an adventure. High-risk and demanding, but when hadn't space exploration been that way?

But that had all changed only hours after he and the other survivors on the *Augustus* were shown the suspicious briefing tape. Right after viewing that tape, he and the others had been called to another briefing, this time at the request of Worf and Jadzia. The revelations in that second gathering had concerned the past twenty-five years' worth of history in this timeline that they had missed. Suddenly, all that had been left unsaid in the first briefing came into focus for Jake.

In the bluntest of terms, what the people of this time faced was nothing less than the impending end of the universe.

Until the moment Jadzia and Worf and Captain T'len had related this incredible news, almost every pair of captives on board the *Augustus* had already been engaged in planning an escape or an attempt to seize control of the surprisingly deficient ship. Because Worf and Jadzia had been first to take action, they had been the first to learn the truth.

Now no one was planning to escape. Except maybe Vash.

What appeared to be holding the others together at this moment, in Jake's view, was the shared opinion that if the end of the universe were approaching, it was because of what had been done and not done by all present during the last days of Deep Space 9. Although no one was talking about this upsetting conclusion, Jake felt certain that everyone believed in its truth.

Which meant in a way, he realized, that the fifteen temporal refugees from his time were now feeling responsible for everything that had happened in this time during the past twenty-five years, and which was now leading to disaster. How could they not stay here, in this time, to do everything they could to try and reverse what they had set in motion?

"So, you know this big shot?" Vash suddenly asked him.

Jake knew his uncertain smile betrayed his nervousness. He had always known that Nog would do well in Starfleet, and he was gratified to learn that his childhood Ferengi friend was a captain now. But he was having some difficulty thinking of Nog as a "big shot." And it was odder still to think that in just a few moments the doors were going to open and his old friend was going to step through them. *Twenty-five* years older.

"He's—he was—my best friend," Jake told Vash.

"Really." Vash ran her hands along her newly supplied gray-and-black uniform. The gesture was clearly meant to be provocative.

"Nice uniforms, hmm?" she said with a smile, as his eyes involuntarily followed the seductive movement of her hands.

Jake snapped his eyes back to Vash's face with an effort. All fifteen refugees had been given Starfleet uniforms of the day to wear. The Starfleet officers among them had received their equivalent rank and specialty markings. The Bajorans and civilians had been given a variant of the uniform that reminded Jake of what cadets used to wear. Instead of being mostly black, the main uniform was a ribbed gray fabric, leaving only the shoulder section black. The supply officer had explained that the uniform identified them as civilian specialists within the Fleet, subject to Fleet regulations.

Jake had been surprised that the uniforms were issued from a storeroom and not a replicator station, and even more surprised that nothing fit as well as it should—though he supposed that was to be expected when clothes weren't replicated with the benefit of a somatic topography scan.

But whoever had given Vash her specialist uniform must have expended some extra effort in determining her size, because to Jake it fit her to perfection. And she obviously knew it.

"Sorry," Jake stammered, having no idea what to say next. "I . . . yeah, Nog's my best friend." *What an idiot I am,* he thought.

"How old are you?" Vash asked with a frank grin.

"I'll be twenty next month."

"Nineteen . . . what do you think your father would say if we . . ." Vash let her voice trail off suggestively.

Is there even a chance? Jake thought in amazement. He, like everyone else who knew them, had assumed that Vash and Dr. Bashir were . . . He abruptly stopped that line of thought and shifted direction. "Um, I . . . uh, dated a dabo girl once. A couple of years back. That was okay with my dad . . . he even made us dinner."

Vash studied him as if she were really listening to him. "A dabo girl. How educational for you."

Jake nodded, watching her carefully for any signs that she was making fun of him. It actually had been, but not in the way Vash meant. Or did she—

"And after dinner," Vash continued, "was your date arrested, or did she just leave the station?"

Jake frowned. "Uh, Mardah left, yeah. She was accepted at the Regulus Science Academy."

"Let me guess. Your *father* wrote her a great letter of recommendation."

Jake sighed. "Look, I didn't mean to—"

"It's okay, Jake. We'll be friends. We'll go to . . . dinner a couple of years from now. We won't invite your father."

Jake nodded, half-disappointed, half-relieved, then suddenly added, "A couple of years from now. . . . So you think we're going to make it through this?"

Vash pointed to someone standing behind Jake. "Don't ask me. Ask him."

Jake turned to see whom Vash meant. A Ferengi standing in an open doorway beside Captain T'len. A Ferengi who looked like Nog, but wasn't.

This man was about five kilos heavier, with even larger earlobes, and his face seemed drawn, the brown skin weathered and wrinkled around the careworn, sunken eyes and—

"Jake," Nog said in the voice Jake remembered from only four days ago on DS9, "it *is* me."

Jake suddenly felt even more uncomfortable than when Vash had teased him into staring at her. He just knew that a look of shock had swept over his face, with his realization that this grizzled veteran *was* his friend, and that his friend was now so . . . so *old*. In the waves of emotions that broke over him, the strongest was one of sorrow. For all the time passed and not shared.

"Nog. . . ." Jake couldn't say anything else. His throat was suddenly swollen shut.

But Nog shook his head as if in understanding, and stepped forward and hugged him strongly, slapping his back, then looked up at him, beaming. "Just as I remember you. Not a day older. Not a *day* . . ."

Jake saw Nog's old-young eyes begin to glisten as if filling with tears. But then his friend looked away, bared his artfully twisted fangs and called out, "Dr. Bashir! Commander Dax!"

Jake broke away from Nog as his friend greeted all the others, the Ferengi's salutations ending with an awkward pause as he came face-to-face with Worf.

"Commander," Nog said formally, "Starfleet has missed you. And so have I."

"You are a captain," Worf replied gravely. "You do honor to your family and to your father."

And then Starfleet formality between Klingon and Ferengi broke down as Nog spread his arms again and Worf embraced the diminutive officer in a bearhug that Jake knew could fell a *sehlat*.

Finally Worf released his grip, and Nog dropped a few centimeters to the floor, then tugged down on his jacket and turned to face everyone. He cleared his throat noisily. "My friends . . . oh, my friends . . . I almost don't know where to begin."

But Jadzia did. "Captain T'len," the Trill officer said, "has been very efficient in bringing us up to date. We understand the danger threatening . . . everything. And we know that you're here to make a proposal to us about how we can help Starfleet destroy Bajor."

Jake grimaced. Intellectually, he knew he was in a different time, with a much different Starfleet. But emotionally, he was still having a very hard time understanding how anyone from Starfleet could say something like that. His thoughts flew back to when he was a small child in San Francisco and his mother and his father had first explained the Prime Directive to him. He remembered his favorite interactive holobooks, in which Flotter and Trevis had helped children discover the need for the Prime Directive in the Forest of

Forever. But in this future—Nog's future—it was as if the Prime Directive had never been issued.

"Still," Jake heard Nog say to Jadzia, "I can imagine how strange, even upsetting all of this must seem to you."

"We are Starfleet officers," Worf said simply. "What is your proposal?"

Nog immediately turned to Captain T'len, and now she stepped all the way into the conference room so that the doors to the corridor slid shut. Then she entered a code into the wall panel, and Jake saw a security condition status light on the panel begin to glow. He had once thought that DS9 had become overly militarized during the course of the Dominion War. But what had happened to the station in no way compared with the battle conditions under which the *Augustus* and Starbase 53 operated.

Nog wasted no time in beginning. "The art of making fancy speeches has declined in the past few years," he said crisply, "so I will state my proposition plainly. You do not belong in this time. Starfleet will not attempt to send you back to your own time. However, given your situation, Starfleet *is* willing to allow whoever among you wishes to volunteer, a chance to make another journey in time."

"That's not possible," Jake blurted out. He looked at Jadzia. "Didn't you say we couldn't establish a second Feynman curve from this time?"

Jadzia nodded to him, but then turned back to look at Nog. It was obvious to Jake that she was interested in what more Nog would say to them.

The Ferengi smiled at him. "Jake, I . . . don't remember you as a scientist," he said.

"Jake and I have had discussions recently," Jadzia said quickly, before Jake could respond, "about the possibilities of going back."

"I see," Nog said. He paused, a thoughtful expression on his face. "Then—in terms of your using a different time-travel technique to return to your own time—yes, that's right. You could not slingshot around a suitable star and expect to survive a transition back to your starting point in 2375."

"So," Jadzia said, "you're obviously proposing a transition to a different time."

"Correct," Nog agreed.

"But doesn't that entail the same risk to us?" Jadzia asked.

Nog shot a sidelong look at Captain T'len, and Jake could see that twenty-five years older or not, his "old" friend was nervous about what he was going to say next. "Not if the temporal length of your second Feynman curve is sufficiently greater than your initial starting point."

Jake didn't have the slightest idea what that meant. He looked to Jadzia for some explanation. She was nodding her head as if she understood, even if the frown on her face indicated to Jake that she did not agree with Nog's reasoning.

"For what you're suggesting, Nog—Captain—the temporal length of our second transition would have to be longer than our first by a factor of . . ." Jadzia looked up at the conference room's ceiling, as if performing a complex calculation in her head.

"A factor of three," Dr. Bashir unexpectedly said.

Jake felt his stomach tighten. That couldn't be right. "Twenty-five *thousand* years?" He stared at Nog in disbelief.

But his best friend merely shrugged. "That's exactly right."

Now all the temporal refugees around Jake were exchanging looks of unease. Murmurs of protest began to fill the Starbase 53 conference room.

"It's called Project Phoenix," Nog said, waving aside their concerns. "Created by Admiral Jean-Luc Picard."

The name alone brought silence to the group.

"Jean-Luc?" Vash asked. "Is he still . . . ?"

"Yes," Nog confirmed. "He's frail. In poor health. But . . . he has given us hope that the Ascendancy can be stopped before . . . before it's too late."

"Even assuming you have the technology to send us back twenty-five thousand years—" Jadzia began.

"And we do," Nog said, but Jadzia kept talking.

"—any change we make in the timeline to prevent the Ascendancy from arising will either erase this current reality, or create a parallel one, leaving this one unchanged and still facing destruction."

"Ah, but that's where you're wrong," Nog said triumphantly. "There is a *third* solution. Admiral Picard's solution. A way to go back into the past and make a change that will not take effect until *after* the ship has departed, thus *preserving* our timeline."

Dr. Bashir suddenly laughed. The unexpected sound was almost shocking to Jake, as was the observation he so clearly stated next. "A time bomb. You want us to place a literal time bomb."

And Nog confirmed it.

"Basically, that is correct," the Ferengi said. "In the past five years, Starfleet has expended enormous effort on the two critical components of the admiral's plan. The first is the *U.S.S. Phoenix*— the largest Starfleet vessel ever built in your time *or* ours. The second is the deep-time charges, made of a brand-new ultrastable trilithium resin together with advanced timekeeping mechanisms of incredible accuracy."

"So we use the *Phoenix* to go back twenty-five millennia," Bashir said, "plant the deep-time charges on Bajor, and some time after we leave for the past, the charges detonate. Presumably destroying the Ascendancy."

Like everyone in the room, Jake watched and listened as his best friend outlined the unbelievable mission.

"—And also destroying Kai Weyoun, the Red Orbs of Jalbador, and the center of Ascendancy rule," Nog said.

In the utter silence that followed Nog's list of targets, one of the Bajoran civilians gasped, and the following instant Jake understood why. "B'hala . . ." the civilian said. B'hala was the most sacred city on Bajor. It had vanished from Bajoran knowledge twenty thousand years ago, until Jake's father discovered it buried deep beneath the Ir'Abehr Shield.

"Again, correct," Nog said. "Admiral Picard's first love is archaeology, and he has researched the matter in precise detail."

The Ferengi pressed on, even though the flood of details was beginning to sweep over Jake like a thought-smothering wave, and he knew the overload had to be affecting the other survivors of his time the same way.

"We know," Nog continued, "that the first structures of the city known as B'hala were built approximately twenty-five thousand years ago. Approximately twenty thousand years ago, general knowledge of the city's location was lost for about five thousand years. Then, about fifteen thousand years ago, the last temple was built on the site, and it was swallowed by landslides. Until," Nog nodded at Jake, "Captain Sisko rediscovered it less than thirty years ago.

"According to our latest intelligence estimates, less than one-third of the city has been excavated under the Ascendancy, which means whoever goes back to the city's beginning will know exactly where to hide the deep-time charges in the remaining two-thirds to ensure that they will not be discovered over the millennia to come."

A question broke through the fog of disorientation in Jake. "Nog, why twenty-five thousand years? Why not go back ten years? Or a hundred?"

"A fair question," Nog said. "First of all, the *Phoenix* would have to go back at least a thousand years, to be sure that no early Bajoran space travelers or astronomers detected the ship arriving at warp speed or orbiting the planet for the three weeks it will take for the deployment of the deep-time charges."

"Okay, then go back *fifteen* hundred years," Jake said.

"And you wouldn't need a large starship for that kind of trip," Jadzia added.

Nog shook his head at the both of them. "No. The point is not merely to go back in time and deploy the charges. It's to go back and deploy them without introducing *any* changes in the timeline. That means B'hala must remain a lost city until Captain Sisko finds it in 2373.

"Remember—a team of Starfleet engineers will be working in the Ir'Abehr Shield for three weeks, and they have to be able to do so without attracting *any* attention. Admiral Picard has told us that the only way to be sure that our activities won't inadvertently lead to the early discovery of B'hala is to go back to a time *before* B'hala."

At that, Captain T'len stepped forward as if she were impatient. "The targeted time period is most logical."

"And what about the choice of crew?" Worf asked sternly. "Is that also logical?"

Jake saw something in Worf's eyes that made him think there was more to the question than there appeared to be. Captain T'len's hesitation in answering confirmed his suspicions.

"That argument can be made," she said at last.

Then Bashir again articulated what Worf must already have guessed. "It's a one-way trip, isn't it."

Nog drew himself up, a gesture at once like and unlike the Nog familiar to Jake. "Most likely," the Ferengi said stiffly—but proudly, too, Jake thought. "Yes."

"Most likely?" Bashir repeated incredulously.

Nog's voice took on a more determined tone. "The *Phoenix*, Doctor Bashir, is the largest starship ever constructed. It *will* survive a twenty-five-thousand-year temporal slingshot. But all our simulations show that neither her spaceframe nor her warp engines will survive the stresses of a return trip."

That was when Jake saw the logic of it for himself. He and the others from the *Defiant* were already misplaced in time. So what would it matter if they were misplaced somewhere—some*time*—else?

And he wasn't the only one to reach that realization.

"So we're expendable," Vash said angrily. "That's it, isn't it? We're a danger to you in this time, so you want to send us off on some high-risk wild *norp* chase and get rid of us." She leaned forward to jab her finger against Nog's chest. "Well, you can tell your Starfleet admirals that I'm not going."

With a forcefulness Jake knew the Ferengi would never have attempted in Jake's time, four days ago on DS9, Nog grabbed the anthropologist's hand and pushed it aside. His answer to her was almost a growl. "It is a *volunteer* mission."

"Captain," Jadzia said quickly, diplomatically defusing the sudden increase in tension in the room and returning their attention to what must be faced, "there still has to be more to the mission than what you've described. Once the charges are deployed, what are we . . . what is the crew of this new supership—the *Phoenix*—supposed to do? They certainly can't interact with any culture in the past."

"Absolutely not," Nog agreed, with a grateful glance at the Trill officer. "But Admiral Picard did suggest a course of action that might allow you, or perhaps your children or grandchildren, to return to the present." He looked over at Bashir. "As I said, Doctor, it is *likely* that the mission of the *Phoenix* will be one way. But it is not certain."

Then Jake, together with the others, listened intently as Nog described Picard's plan as confirmed, he said, by extensive studies conducted by the Federation's leading surviving experts in archaeology, biology, and ancient astronomy.

The essence of it, Jake realized, was that almost fifteen hundred years ago—and 7,000 light-years from Earth—a main-sequence star had gone supernova. The expanding gas cloud from that awesome burst of energy became known to Earth astronomers as the Crab Nebula. But to the astronomers of Erelyn IV, that same cosmic explosion was the last thing they or their fellow beings ever saw.

Erelyn IV itself was a Class-M world, home to a race of humanoids that was one of the first to develop interstellar travel—though not warp drive—in the present epoch of the Alpha Quadrant. But—and Nog emphasized this point—the planet was only twelve light-years from the Crab supernova, and the radiation released by that star's explosion had been lethal to all life-bearing planets within *fifty* light-years.

Jake remembered learning about Erelyn IV in school. His instructors had referred to the lifeless, crumbling cities and vast transportation networks of that planet to stress the importance of exploration and discovery. Because the radiation had sterilized Erelyn IV without destroying the buildings, libraries, and technology of its people, the Vulcan archaeologists who had studied the planet for generations had been able to reconstruct Erelynian history in unprecedented detail.

Sadly, the Vulcans also learned that at the time of the supernova, the Erelynians had a prototype warp engine under construction in orbit of their world. Had the funding battles their scientists fought against their world's shortsighted politicians been successful only a few years earlier, faster-than-light probes to the Crab star would have revealed the existence of the supernova before the radiation had reached their world, giving them time to construct underground radiation shelters. Had Erelyn IV's politicians permitted warp research to proceed a mere fifteen years earlier, that would have been enough time for the Erelynians to establish colonies on planets outside the sphere of lethality and to build shelters.

Fifteen lost years. The lesson had been taught to all children in the Federation: that such a short period of time could be all that might stand between planetary extinction and survival. The moral had been clear: Between thinking about one's next term in office and thinking about the next generation was a difference in attitude that could save an entire world—or condemn it.

The people of Erelyn IV had paid the ultimate price for their leaders' lack of vision. But they had left a poignant treasure trove of almost ten thousand years of their history—including, Nog explained, a complete map of the Crab star's solar system as it had existed before the supernova, as charted by sublight robotic probes.

"The Crab star had seven major planets," Nog now explained. "The second from the star was Class-M. The Erelynians' long-range scans showed a standard Gaia-class oxygen atmosphere, indicating a biosphere. But the scans they made also showed no signs of industrial pollutants; nor did they record any electromagnetic or subspace communications."

"So *that's* where you want us to go," Bashir said. He wasn't asking a question, and Nog didn't bother to do more than nod in response.

It was clear to all present that Nog was coming to the final part of the plan.

"The *Phoenix* will be able to make the voyage between Bajor and the Crab star in under two years. The ship is stocked with industrial replicators, nanoconstructors, and complete plans for building a duplicate vessel to bring you home."

"How long?" Worf asked bluntly. "For the nanoconstructors to build a ship without a shipyard and Starfleet work crews."

Jake saw an almost invisible wince twist Nog's features. "Our best estimate is . . . forty-eight years."

Now Jake understood why Nog had said their children or their grandchildren might make it back.

"A great many things can go wrong in forty-eight years," Worf said.

"Which, obviously, is why they picked that world," Bashir said lightly. "If something goes wrong and we can't travel back to this present, then even if our descendants spread out across the world, in the year 1054 C.E. everything turns to superheated plasma in any case when the sun explodes. As long as we stay on that world, we will have no interaction with the march of history throughout the rest of the galaxy."

"Exactly," Nog said. He turned to Captain T'len, as if he had said all that was necessary for now.

But Worf had another question. "You have not thought of every eventuality. What if we fail to build a second *Phoenix,* and our descendants first revert to more primitive ways, then develop a spacefaring civilization of their own. Twenty thousand years is more than enough time for that to happen, and for our descendants to travel to Qo'noS or Earth and change history."

"Commander Worf," Nog said with what Jake thought was an odd formality, "I assure you that we *have* thought of every eventuality. And what you describe cannot happen."

Jake didn't understand, but it seemed Bashir felt he did. "There's another bomb in the *Phoenix,*" the doctor said. "Set to go off . . . a century . . . ?"

Startled, Jake looked from Bashir to Nog. His friend's face was sad but resigned. Bashir's guess was true.

". . . After we leave," the doctor said slowly as he spoke his thoughts aloud. "Probably something that would set up an energy cascade in the atmosphere of the second planet, killing all higher animal life-forms in that world, but leaving the bulk of the ecosystem unharmed."

But now Jake was thoroughly confused. "But . . . why would we leave the *Phoenix* anywhere near the planet if we knew it could kill us? Or our descendants?" he added.

"Because," Captain T'len said with a stern glance at Nog, "everyone who takes part in this mission will understand and accept the importance of not changing the timeline. As Commander Worf stated, many things can go wrong in forty-eight years. Thus the crew of the *Phoenix* will leave their ship in close orbit of the planet as a fail-safe backup, to ensure that none of their descendants survive to form their own civilization."

The room fell silent once more, and Jake knew that everyone in it was contemplating as he was the enormity of what was being proposed to them.

After a few moments, Nog spoke again. "Admiral Picard set this all in place almost five years ago, and the plans have been continually refined and perfected ever since."

Jake looked over at Bashir, but the doctor seemed not to have anything more to say. Everyone else from the *Defiant,* with the exception of Vash, was making silent eye contact with their fellow temporal refugees. Vash simply glared at Nog and T'len as if they were personally responsible for thwarting her.

"Captain Nog, we would like time to consider your proposal," Worf said.

"I understand," Nog agreed. "But I would ask that you make your decision within the next fifty hours, so we can arrange passage to Utopia Planitia and I can begin your training."

Jake heard something odd in Nog's voice then. "Nog, are you going?"

"On the *Phoenix?* Yes."

"So you think it's going to work."

For the first time in the session, Nog smiled broadly. "I have absolute faith in Admiral Picard. I have reviewed all the operational plans and contingencies. I have no doubt that the mission of the *Phoenix* will succeed, and there will be no need to worry about the safeguard time bombs. I am completely confident that someday I and the crew . . . or our descendants . . . will be able to return to the present and the universe we will have saved."

Nog then said his good-byes, explained that he had meetings to attend, and hoped that he could meet everyone again at 1900 hours for a meal. Then, with the unsmiling Captain T'len at his side, he left.

Instantly a buzz of responses filled with new hope swept through the room. But Jake didn't join in, although Nog's presence on the *Phoenix* did change the equation for him personally.

Jake was in the midst of trying to comprehend the best thing to do.

Because he had seen his Ferengi friend give that same assured smile at least a thousand times in the past. And it had always meant only one thing.

Nog was lying.

So the *Phoenix* was already doomed.

And with her the universe.

CHAPTER 12

"CAPTAIN SISKO! You've been ignoring me!"

Benjamin Sisko snapped out of his reverie and sighed. He was sitting at an uncomfortable Klingon work station in his uncomfortable Klingon quarters on board the uncomfortable Klingon vessel, the *Boreth*. Kasidy Yates was looking out at him from the work station's main display screen. Her image was a stern, unsmiling portrait; it was the one that had been attached to her merchant master's license.

The annoyed voice haranguing him belonged to Quark. It came from the open doorway to Sisko's quarters.

"This isn't the time, Quark," Sisko said quietly, and meant it. Nevertheless he heard the sound of Quark's brisk footsteps as the Ferengi crossed over his threshold.

"In case you haven't noticed, time is what we're running out of." The irate barkeep was now at his side, hands on hips, looking quite ridiculous in his Bajoran penitent's robes of brown and cream.

"Everything will work out," Sisko said, still not raising his voice, surprised at how little irritation he felt at Quark's ill-timed intrusion. Then again, he wondered, was it even possible that he would ever feel anything again?

"How can you say that?!" Quark exclaimed. "The whole universe has been turned upside down! Did you know the entire Ferenginar system has been under an Ascendancy trade blockade for the past seven years? No one on this *frinxing* ship will even let me *try* to get a message through to *anyone* back home."

Sisko bowed his head, took a breath so deep he knew it would strain his chest, but still felt nothing. "Quark, we are all struggling with similar difficulties."

"Ha," Quark said. He pointed to the display. "At least you can access some sort of database to find out about . . ." Quark's verbal assault on Sisko suddenly ceased.

Sisko glanced up at him and saw that the Ferengi was reading the screen.

"I'm . . . sorry," the Ferengi said quietly, all bluster gone from him. "You know, I . . . I always liked Captain Yates."

Sisko nodded. "She was only one of many, Quark. So many people died when Earth was destroyed." He closed his eyes then, but Kasidy's face was still before him. At least, the old report said, she had gone out a hero, during her *fifth* run through Grigari lines to evacuate survivors.

"Captain . . . ?"

Sisko opened his eyes, looked up. "Yes, Quark."

The Ferengi mumbled a few words that were unintelligible before finally getting to the point in a sudden rush. "We need you."

Sisko contemplated Quark, curious. He couldn't remember ever having seen the Ferengi so uncertain, so obviously worried.

"I appreciate the vote of confidence," he told the Ferengi barkeep, "but if you listened to Odo's report about his run-in with Weyoun, I am the one person among us all who you definitely don't want."

Quark rocked back as if surprised by the statement. "Are you saying you *believe* Weyoun about Starfleet wanting to kill you?"

Sisko pushed his chair back from the workstation and stood up, leaving Kasidy's image still on the display. He wasn't yet ready to erase it. The act would carry with it too much finality.

"Starfleet vessels were waiting for us when we reemerged from the timeslip," he said, shifting uncomfortably in his own awkward and confining robes, orange and brown like a vedek's, like Weyoun's. Weyoun. Sisko sighed. He must have been over the Vorta's words to Odo a thousand times in the past two days. "Starfleet vessels attacked us."

"So did Riker in the *Opaka*," Quark argued.

"The *Opaka* and the *Boreth* chased the Starfleet vessels away."

With that reminder, Quark began to pace back and forth in frustration. "But I talked with Chief O'Brien. He said the Starfleet mines that were beamed onto the *Defiant*'s hull had countdown timers."

Sisko watched as Quark stopped his pacing and stared up at him, challengingly. "If Starfleet really wanted to kill you, then why didn't they use mines that exploded on contact?"

Silent, Sisko gazed at Quark, and the Ferengi slowly nodded, as if satisfied he finally had the *hew-mon*'s undivided attention.

"Captain," Quark said emphatically, as if to a novice who needed remedial training, "there's an old negotiating tactic that's even more basic than the Rules of Acquisition. If you can't convince a customer that your product is better than the competition's, then at least convince the customer that the competition's product is lethal."

Sisko shook his head.

Quark threw up his hands in renewed frustration. "Oh, for—it's like when customers at my bar complain about the menu prices," he sputtered, "and I tell them about the food-poisoning deaths at the Klingon Cafe."

Sisko felt a wry smile tug at the corners of his mouth. Really, the Ferengi barkeep was shameless. "As far as I know, Quark, no one's ever died of food poisoning at the Klingon Cafe."

Quark beamed with relief. "There you go, Captain. I'm so glad we finally understand each other."

Before Sisko could say anything more, the work station buzzed peremptorily. He turned to it in time to see the unsettling transformation of Kasidy's image into that of Weyoun.

"Benjamin," the Vorta simpered, speaking as usual with far too much familiarity, *"may* I call you Benjamin?"

As usual, Sisko ignored the request. "What do you want?"

Weyoun's smooth reaction was as if Sisko's own response had been nothing but a polite exchange in return. "We'll be arriving at Bajor within the next few minutes. I thought you might like to join me on the bridge. To see your adopted world in this glorious new age."

The last thing Sisko wanted to do was to spend more time in

Weyoun's company. But he was aware that a chance to examine the bridge might provide useful information about the organization methods and technology used by the Ascendancy . . . or whatever Weyoun's name was for the group that served him and ran this ship.

"Should I wait for an escort?" he asked.

But Weyoun shook his finger as if he'd just heard a clever joke. "Oh, my, no. As I'm sure you've realized by now, my crew has established an exceptionally comprehensive internal sensor system. Someone will be watching you the entire way, to be certain you don't get . . . lost."

"Then I'll be on my way."

Weyoun smiled expansively. "Very good. I do look forward to sharing your company again. Perhaps I can help you see Quark's lies for what they are."

Discovering that Weyoun was aware of the conversation he had just had with Quark was not at all surprising to Sisko. He doubted there was a word any of the people from the *Defiant* had said on this ship that hadn't been recorded by internal security sensors.

With a slow and deeply respectful bow of his head, Weyoun faded from the workstation display, to be replaced by Kasidy.

With a sudden flash of anger, Sisko hit the display controls, turning the screen black. He wished he could weep for Kasidy. That would be the appropriate response to his loss. But his chest felt empty, as if it no longer contained his heart. Only an unfeeling void where love had once reigned.

"If you'll excuse me." Sisko moved past Quark, heading for the open door to the corridor.

But Quark apparently did not feel their conversation was over, and he moved to block his escape. "Captain! I don't care if that puny-eared sycophant heard every word I said *and* every word I thought. He's lying to you about Starfleet and who knows what else!"

Sisko stared down at the Ferengi who stood between him and the door. "Thank you for your input, Quark. I think you should join the others."

"The others," Quark muttered, defiantly holding his ground. "A crazed Cardassian, a frustrated changeling, my idiot brother . . . don't you *get* it, Captain? You're the only one who can get us out of this!"

"Quark, are you aware of the 85th Rule?"

"Of course I am," Quark answered testily. "Never let the . . . oh." His shoulders sagged beneath his robes. "Right. Never mind."

Quark stepped to one side. The way was now clear.

"I'll see you with the others," Sisko said, turning around in the doorway.

"Right," Quark said darkly, shouldering his own way past Sisko and entering the corridor. "Maybe I'll organize a tongo tournament. That should help raise spirits."

Sisko watched the Ferengi stomp off along the dark, rusty-walled Klingon hallway.

Never let the competition know what you're thinking, Sisko thought, completing the 85th Rule.

Perhaps Weyoun *was* lying to him about Starfleet.

Perhaps it was time to fight back with a few lies of his own.

He turned in the direction opposite the one Quark had chosen and headed for the bridge, fully aware that unseen eyes watched him, as always, keeping his thoughts to himself.

The *Boreth*'s bridge was larger than Sisko had expected, at least three times that of even a *Sovereign*-class vessel. Even more unexpected, there was little to it that seemed Klingon. All the sensor screens and status displays he could see were, in fact, Bajoran, as were the muted metallic colors of the wall panels and friction carpet—perhaps the only part of the ship not marred by typical Klingon oxidation stains.

The main viewer, which showed computer reconstructions of stars passing at warp, took up most of the far wall. On the bridge's lower level, at least fifteen duty officers were seated at three rows of consoles facing the screen.

At present, Sisko was on the bridge's upper level where the turbolift had deposited him, and where Weyoun was awaiting him in his command chair, its outlines indistinguishable from those of a command chair that might be found on any Starfleet vessel. Unsurprisingly, Weyoun's throne took center stage. What did surprise Sisko was the fact that he wasn't Weyoun's only guest.

Standing beside the Vorta were Major Kira and Commander Arla. Like everyone else who had been captured with the *Defiant,* the two women were wearing robes typical of a Bajoran religious order. From the collar folds of the white tunics visible beneath their outer robes, Sisko guessed Kira and Arla had been given clothing of the rank of prylar. Their nearly identical expressions of discomfort indicated that neither woman was pleased with the outfit forced upon her, either.

Weyoun turned slowly in his chair, both hands upon its wide arms. Sisko caught the gratified smile that momentarily flashed across his host's face.

"Splendid—just in time." Weyoun gestured for him to come closer. "Please, join us."

Sisko glanced at the wall alongside the turbolift, where three stern Romulans stood, each with a hand on a long-barreled energy weapon holstered at his side. They made no move to stop him, so Sisko went to Weyoun, stopping beside Kira and Arla.

"We have just been having the most *fascinating* conversation about ancient Bajoran beliefs," Weyoun said pleasantly.

"Is that so?" Sisko answered. His eyes kept moving around the bridge stations, finding so much that was familiar, so much that was different in this time.

"Major Kira was describing various punishments that some of the earlier, more . . . strident, shall we say, Bajoran sects would visit upon those whom they viewed as heretics."

"Really," Sisko said, only half listening.

"Really," Weyoun agreed. "And it seems that two or three thousand years ago, at least in some sections of Bajor, I would have had my beating heart cut from my body as I watched. As punishment for professing belief in the True Prophets."

Kira smiled tightly. "In some ways, our ancestors were more advanced than we are."

Weyoun gave Kira a pitying stare. "Really, Major, how droll."

Sisko brought his gaze and attention back to the center of the bridge and Weyoun. "Tell me," he said, "what punishment do *you* inflict on those heretics who profess a belief in the Old Prophets of Bajor?"

Weyoun studied Sisko for a few moments before replying. "This may come as a surprise, Benjamin, but we inflict no punishment at all."

"That is a surprise," Sisko said mildly, "considering that you told

Odo your crew would have killed him if they had heard a question he had asked about you choosing—"

Weyoun held up a hand to cut off Sisko before he could finish.

"Really, Benjamin. You should know better. Despite my best intentions, there are always those devoted few who sometimes act in the heat of passion rather than restrain themselves in the cool cloak of the law."

Sisko felt rather than saw Kira bristle at that. Her dynamic presence had always been able to charge a room.

"Oh, really?" she retorted. "So everyone on Bajor is free to follow her own heart in choosing which religion to follow?"

"Of course," Weyoun said testily. "The True Prophets created sentient beings in their own image. That doesn't mean shape or size or number of grasping appendages, it refers to our possessing free will. The one true religion of the True Prophets couldn't very well claim to *represent* the True Prophets if it had to *enforce* its beliefs on everyone, could it?"

"But isn't that what you're doing?" Sisko seized the chance to build on the emotion provoked by Kira. "By destroying whole worlds that don't agree with you?"

Weyoun's lips trembled. Sisko hoped the movement sprang from anger, however tightly controlled. An angry opponent could become vulnerable. "I cannot be responsible for what other people—other worlds—*believe,* Benjamin. By the dictates of my own conscience and the command of the True Prophets, I must allow everyone to come to the right decision—or not—by their own free choice. All I ask in return is that those who don't believe as I do allow my followers and me to adhere to our own faith. A simple request, really." Weyoun's voice became calmer as his own words reassured him if no one else of the truth of his beliefs. "One that fits in nicely with that Prime Directive you used to be so proud of.

"Believe me," the Vorta said piously, "the only time the Bajoran Ascendancy has been forced to prevail against other systems or groups of systems has been when our right to pursue our own beliefs has come under attack. We are quite capable of acting in self-defense."

"Self-defense?!" Sisko said. "Is that what you call the destruction of the entire *Earth?*"

Weyoun sat back in his command chair, frowning as he picked at the skirts of his robe. "That, I fully admit, was a mistake."

Kira snorted in what seemed to be a combination of disbelief and disgust.

"A mistake," Sisko repeated.

"The Grigari trade delegation was not expecting the sensor barrage to which they were subjected. Their commanders thought they were under attack, and . . . they didn't realize that Earth's planetary defense system wasn't able to handle their warning shots. One thing led to another, and . . ." Weyoun held up empty hands. "It wasn't the first time a first contact has gone wrong."

"I don't believe you." Sisko made no attempt to lower his voice as he challenged Weyoun. He felt it might do some good if the Vorta's crew could hear what others thought of him.

But the Romulan guards gave no reaction, and Weyoun only adopted a look of profound sadness, a false expression like so many he affected. "And that is your right. Though in only ten more days, you—and everyone else in creation—will have the chance to learn the truth."

"Weyoun," Sisko said, "the universe is *not* coming to an end in ten days."

"Of course not," Weyoun agreed. "It will enter a new *beginning*. I knew you'd come to see it my way."

The first thought that came to Sisko then was how much he'd enjoy simply punching Weyoun in his sanctimonious face. *It would feel so good,* Sisko thought. And then he remembered how he had felt when he had read of Kasidy's death, the shocking numbness, and the fear that he might never feel anything again.

Except, it seems, rage, Sisko told himself. Perhaps that was all that was left to him in this era. Rage against those who had caused him such loss, and, perhaps, anger at himself for all that he had left undone.

"Are you all right?" Weyoun inquired.

"What do you think?" Sisko asked.

Just then a voice behind him said, "Emissary?" and Sisko turned to see a Romulan in an ill-fitting Bajoran-style uniform hold up a gleaming metallic padd encased in what appeared to be gold.

"Yes?" Sisko and Weyoun said together.

The Romulan was speaking to Weyoun. *"Emissary,"* he said more emphatically, "we are entering our final approach."

Weyoun smiled at Sisko as he gave his response. "Standard orbit."

The Romulan bowed his head in respect.

Sisko felt his stomach twist.

"Please," Weyoun said with a wave at the main viewer. Then he turned his chair around to face it.

Turning in the same direction, Sisko saw the streaking stars slow. Then a single point of blue light in the center of the viewer suddenly blossomed into an appreciable disk. Next, with only the slightest change in the background hum of the *Boreth's* engines, the stars abruptly froze in place and the planet Bajor grew until it filled the screen.

Sisko saw Kira's mouth open slightly, and he thought he knew why.

The sphere on the viewer, caught in the full glory of her sun's light, looked little different than it had in their own time. Bright blue oceans sparkled with brilliant light. Elegant swirls of white clouds traced the shores of the northern continent. A dark pinwheel flashing with minuscule bolts of lightning showed a tropical storm building majestically in the South Liran Sea.

And across the continents, verdant forests painted the land in an infinite shifting palette of greens. There was no trace of the dark scars left by the Cardassian Occupation and the final scourging they had inflicted on the Day of Withdrawal.

"Magnificent, isn't it?" Weyoun said. "Bajor restored. Reborn. Unblemished once more."

Sisko wouldn't give the Vorta the satisfaction of a reply. But he was right. Bajor had never looked better, or more compelling.

"Keep watching," Weyoun said.

The terminator passed through the screen, and a dozen cities were called out from the night by the blazing constellations of their streets and buildings. All of them seemed somehow bigger than in Sisko's memory.

"Is that Rhakur?" Kira whispered in amazement.

Sisko saw a sprawling web of light wrap around the distinctive dark shoreline of the inland Rhakur Sea. But the city was twice the size he remembered.

"It is," Weyoun confirmed. "The universities there have attracted scholars from across the two quadrants, and the expansion of facilities has been most gratifying."

Sisko turned his attention from the viewer to Kira. Her eyes glistened with moisture, as if she were about to cry. And again he knew why.

All her life, her world had been crippled and scarred.

Yet here it was before her, healed by time itself.

Sisko knew it was the future she had fought for, always dreamed of, yet never really expected to see.

But he refused to let the magnificent vision beguile her. She had to know the price her world had paid for such healing.

"And this is the world you want to destroy," Sisko said to Weyoun.

The Vorta looked over at him, puzzled. "The Prophets will destroy nothing. This world will be transformed, along with all the others of the universe, into a true paradise, and not just a mundane and linear one."

Sisko saw Kira abruptly rub her eyes, and he felt confident he had broken the spell of the moment. He glanced next at Arla, expecting to see a less emotional reaction, since Bajor had never been her home. But to Sisko's surprise, tears streaked the young woman's face.

"I never knew," she said.

Weyoun nodded. "Of course, you didn't. Keep watching."

In the middle of the main viewer, a new source of light slid into view and recaptured Sisko's attention. He squinted at the screen. It was as if a hole had been cut in some vast curtain to let an enormous searchlight bring day to the middle of night.

"Where's that light coming from?" Kira asked before he could.

"Orbital mirrors," Weyoun said smugly. "Bajor-synchronous, tens of kilometers wide, constantly refocused so that the sun will never set on . . ."

"B'hala," Arla breathed.

Weyoun shot a triumphant look at Sisko. "The jewel of Bajor Ascendant," he said. "Home of our culture, the revelation site of the first Orb to be given to the Bajoran people. Lost for millennia, then rediscovered exactly as prophesied, by the Sisko. I hope you appreciate the importance of what you have given the Bajoran people, and the universe, Benjamin. Everything that has happened these past twenty-five years, everything that will happen in the days ahead, is all because of you."

The Vorta inclined his head in Sisko's direction as if worshipping him.

Sisko's hands were balled into fists within the folds of his robes. "I refuse to accept responsibility for your perversion of the Bajoran faith."

Weyoun tried and failed to restrain a sudden fit of amused laughter. "Even your obstinacy in the face of truth was prophesied by the great mystics of Jalbador—Shabren, Eilin, and Naradim. Your life, your deeds, your great accomplishments—an open book, Benjamin. As if the mystics had stood at your side through all of it. Your protest is quite futile, I assure you."

And then B'hala, bathed in perpetual sunlight, slipped from the viewer, and only a handful of small oases appeared, tiny clusters of lights strung out across the vast stretch of the mountains forming the Ir'Abehr Shield.

"Torse," Weyoun said in a brisk, businesslike voice of command, "that's enough of the surface. Change visual sensors and show our guests our destination."

Sisko looked back over his shoulder to see the Romulan with the golden padd, Torse presumably, obediently turn to a sensor station and make rapid adjustments to the controls. Then Sisko heard both Kira and Arla gasp, and he turned back to face the viewer.

To see Deep Space 9 again.

Ablaze with lights. Surrounded by a cometary halo of spacecraft of all classes. Each docking port filled. Each pylon connected to a different starship. He even recognized one of those ships as Captain Tom Riker's *Opaka.*

Sisko stumbled to voice his swirling thoughts. "The logs . . . on the sensor logs . . . DS9 . . . I saw it destroyed. . . ."

Weyoun stood up and with a flourish freed his arms from his robes. "Never doubt the power of the Ascendancy, Benjamin." His face creased in warning. "Never."

Staring at the home he had shared with his son and with Kasidy, and which he had never expected to see again, Sisko felt Weyoun's light touch on his arm. "As it was written so long ago: Welcome home, Benjamin. We've been waiting for you."

CHAPTER 13

JULIAN BASHIR felt as if he were caught in a dream. The sense of unreality that had begun to envelop him as he had watched the briefing tape on the *Augustus* had become more than a minor sense of unease at the back of his mind. Now that he was on Mars, his apprehension was like a cloak that covered him completely, weighting each breath he took, obscuring his vision, masking his powers of analysis.

Even worse, at times he only felt human.

Of the fifteen temporal refugees who had heard Captain Nog's proposal at Starbase 53, nine had volunteered to join Project Phoenix and lose themselves even more thoroughly in time.

Of the six who had declined, five had been the Bajorans among them—three members of the militia and two civilians. In all good conscience, they had honestly explained that they could not take action against B'hala and their own people, though they understood why Starfleet felt it must. They requested instead that they be allowed to spend the next few weeks in prayer, so that they might put all their trust in the Prophets.

To Bashir's relief, the Bajorans' request had caused no consternation among Nog and his staff. Arrangements would be made, the Bajorans were told. Despite the War of the Prophets, their refusal had been accepted as simply as that. Some sense of Starfleet's original decency, it seemed, still existed in this time.

The last holdout to refuse the mission was—to no one's surprise—Vash. And also to no one's surprise, the volatile archaeologist was not allowed to go anywhere or do anything except accompany the others to Utopia Planitia. Nog informed her that she would not be forced to join the crew of the *Phoenix,* but neither would she be released from custody until the end of "hostilities."

Bashir recalled cringing at that euphemism, though he realized that the Ferengi captain had also felt uncomfortable using it. Under current conditions, such a term could refer to the approaching end of the universe as much as to the end of the great undeclared war against the Ascendancy.

Nog had subsequently left Starbase 53 on the same day he had first met with the temporal refugees, after an oddly tense dinner he shared with them. The spirited, private conversation Jake Sisko had with his aged childhood friend before they were all seated in the officer's mess did not go unobserved by Bashir. Clearly there was some conflict between those two.

By itself, Bashir did not find such discord remarkable. No doubt there would be abandonment issues on both sides of the friendship: Why was it that Nog was left behind on the day that DS9 was destroyed? Why was it that Jake had apparently died, yet now lived again, full of the energy of youth, which Nog as a middle-aged Ferengi no doubt missed?

Yet something more had passed between the two friends and Bashir, for all his intellectual powers, had to admit his frustration that he had no way of determining just what that something more was.

Three days later, everyone had arrived at the Utopia Planitia shipyards aboard Captain T'len's *Augustus.* Like all cadets, Bashir himself had toured the facility in his second year; from Mars orbit, both the constellation of orbital spacedocks and the vast construction fields on the planet's surface were larger than he remembered them being. In the support domes, though, it seemed to Bashir that the corridors and rooms at least were almost identical to his memories of them. Except, of course, for the pervasive and somewhat depressing lack of maintenance and repair.

Upon their arrival at Starbase 53, he and the others were told that fifteen different Starfleet outposts throughout what was left of the Federation had been subjected to terrorist attack on the same day the *Defiant* had reappeared. Reportedly, Utopia Planitia had been one of the hardest hit, with more than 200 personnel injured and 35 dead. When the pressure shield of his habitat dome had been breached, Nog apparently had managed to save both himself and Admiral Picard by taking shelter in a waste-reclamation pumping room that had its own atmospheric forcefield.

Recalling the account they had been given, Bashir couldn't help but feel a bit of pride at how Nog had turned out. Everyone on DS9 had taken a hand in helping mold the youth from the petty juvenile thief he had been at the beginning to the fine officer he had so clearly become.

But to Bashir, a terrorist attack still didn't explain Utopia's torn wall coverings, out-of-service lifts, cracked and damaged furniture, and a thousand other deviations from the ordered, precise Starfleet way of doing things in which he, like all those in Starfleet, had been trained. Though the operational areas of the shipyards still seemed outwardly as functional and as fully maintained as before, he couldn't help but see how attention to detail was sliding. And that unspoken sense of desperation in this beleaguered version of Starfleet was contributing mightily to the overwhelming unreality of this experience for him.

Which is why, he supposed, on this his second day in the shipyards he wasn't at all shocked when, while going from his quarters to the mess hall, he recognized a familiar figure, unchanged by time, walking toward him.

"Doctor Zimmerman?"

The bald man, whose quick, intelligent eyes were defined by distinct, dark eyebrows, halted a few meters from him. At once, Bashir felt himself subjected to an intense visual inspection. It was as if he were being compared to the contents of some sort of computer library file that only the bald man could see. Suddenly he snapped his fingers and exclaimed, "Julian Bashir! Of the *Defiant!*"

Bashir was puzzled by the way in which Zimmerman chose to identify him. He and the doctor had met on DS9 after all, when the doctor had been developing a long-term medical hologram. Zimmerman, however, didn't appear to have aged at all in the past twenty-five years.

"That's right," Bashir said, and he closed the distance between them to shake Dr. Zimmerman's hand. He checked the Starfleet rank insignia in the middle of the man's chest and smiled politely. *"Admiral* Zimmerman. Very good, sir. And very deserved, I'm sure."

The man before him returned his smile, but it was a rueful one. "Actually, Doctor Bashir, Lewis Zimmerman passed away several years ago."

In his shock, Bashir kept both his hands locked around the bald man's hand. "I beg your pardon?"

"Your confusion is understandable." Still smiling but without real conviction, the admiral who wasn't Dr. Zimmerman pulled his hand free from Bashir's grip. "In appearance, I was modeled after him."

Bashir still felt the heat of the man's hand in his. But if he had heard correctly, there was only one possible explanation for what he was seeing. He looked up to the left and the right of the corridor, where the stained walls met the ceiling.

"There are no holoemitters," the admiral said.

"But . . . are you . . ."

"I *was,*" the admiral said in a tone of resignation. "An EMH. Emergency Medical Hologram."

Bashir took a step back. He had known there would be technological advances in the past twenty-five years, but *this?*

"You are a . . . a . . ."

"Hologram," the admiral said perfunctorily. "Yes. Though obviously a type with which you are not familiar."

"I . . . I am astounded that such an incredible breakthrough has been made in only two and a half decades."

The hologram sighed. "It actually took more like four hundred years, but what's a few centuries among friends? Now, a pleasure to meet you, but I really must be—"

Bashir interrupted him, suddenly intrigued by a construct that was even more than an apparently self-aware, self-generating hologram. The artificial being's comment about "four hundred years" instantly raised a subject of great medical interest. "Excuse me," he said, "but if you meant it took four centuries to develop the technology that's freed you from holoemitters, are you referring to alien technology, or rather to something obtained through time travel?"

The hologram's eyes crinkled not unpleasantly. "My specifications are on-line and, if I might say, make for fascinating bedtime reading. But right now, I am—"

Another voice broke in, completing the hologram's statement. "Doctor, you are late."

"That's what I was just telling this young man."

Bashir turned, looking for whoever it was the hologram was addressing, and his eyes widened as he saw a tall and striking woman, no older than forty, striding purposefully toward him. She had an intense, almost belligerent expression; her pale blonde hair was drawn back severely, and she wore a Starfleet uniform with a blue shoulder and—like the holographic doctor—the rank of admiral.

She also had an unusual biomechanical implant around her left eye, an implant that Bashir was startled to think he recognized.

"They are waiting for us in briefing room 5," the woman said to the hologram.

Bashir couldn't keep his eyes off the ocular implant. He offered his hand. "I'm Julian Bashir of the *Defiant*. Admiral . . . ?"

The woman looked at Bashir's extended hand as if she were Klingon and he was offering her a bowl of dead *gagh*. She made no attempt to offer her own hand in return.

"Seven," she said flatly. "You are one of the temporal refugees."

"That's right," Bashir said. *Could it be possible?* he wondered.

"And you cannot stop staring at my implant," the admiral said.

"I'm . . . I'm sorry," Bashir stammered. "But . . . well, I know I'm twenty-five years out of date, but . . . it looks like Borg technology."

"It does because it is," Admiral Seven said.

Bashir felt as if he were falling down a rabbit hole. *"You* are . . ."

The admiral placed her hands behind her back and stared at Bashir with impatience. "I am Borg. My designation is Seven of Nine. My function is Speaker to the Collective. You must now allow us to continue with our duties. Admiral Janeway does not like to be kept waiting."

Bashir started at the mention of that name. "Admiral Jane—do you mean, *Kathryn* Janeway?"

"Yes," the hologram said as he stood beside the Borg, "and believe me, it doesn't pay to make her angry. So—"

"Voyager made it back?" Bashir said.

The Borg frowned at him. "Obviously."

"But . . . how?"

The hologram and the Borg exchanged a look of shared commiseration. Then the hologram said to Bashir, "It's a long story. We really do have to go."

Before Bashir could utter another word, the hologram and the Borg marched off together. And just before they turned the corner into the corridor leading to the briefing rooms, Bashir was stunned to see the Borg reach out to hold the hologram's hand as she leaned over to whisper in his ear as both of them broke out laughing like any young couple in love.

"Oh, brave new world that has such things in it," Bashir said to no one in particular.

Twenty minutes later in the mess hall, Bashir was still mulling over the significance of the beings he had met, and using a padd to review the stunning ten-year-old alliance between the Federation and the Borg Collective as engineered by Admiral Seven of Nine and a Borg whose designation was given only as "Hugh."

Though a great many details of the Treaty of Wolf 359 appeared to be classified, it was becoming apparent to him that technology exchanges were at its core. The Federation had and was providing expertise in nanite-mediated molecular surgery techniques to the Borg, while the Borg were providing transwarp technology which, Bashir concluded from reading between the lines, was the basis of Admiral Picard's *Phoenix*.

"Incredible," Bashir muttered to himself.

"What is?"

Startled, Bashir looked up to see Jake Sisko. How had he missed his approach? Even his enhanced senses seemed to be subject to his bewildering state of confusion these days. "The Borg," he said. "The Borg appear to be our allies now."

Bashir nodded as Jake gestured with the tray of food he held, to ask permission to sit down with him.

"I heard that, too," Jake told him, taking the seat opposite Bashir. The tall youngster leaned forward across the small mess table and dropped his voice. "But I can't get anyone to tell me what happened to the Klingon Empire. Are they part of the Federation now? On the side of the Ascendancy? People either ignore the question or they tell me the information's classified."

Bashir looked around the mess hall. At full capacity, it might hold three hundred personnel. But right now, perhaps because it was between shifts, there were only twenty-three others eating meals or nursing mugs of something hot. Twenty of these other diners were Andorians, the other three Tellarite.

"Have you seen another human here?" Bashir asked Jake.

Now Jake looked around the mess hall. "Well . . . wasn't the lieutenant who showed us our quarters human?"

Bashir shook his head. "Vulcan."

Jake frowned. "At Starbase 53 there were humans. The medical staff."

Bashir held up two fingers. "Two technicians. On a staff of fifteen."

Jake tapped his hands on the sides of his food tray. "So humans *and* Klingons are missing?"

Bashir shrugged and turned off his padd. "There's a lot they aren't telling us about what's going on."

Intriguing to Bashir, Jake immediately dropped his eyes to his collection of reconstituted rations and busily began peeling off their clear tops. When he had first visited the mess hall, Bashir had been interested to notice that what he thought were replicator slots lining one wall were actually small transporter bays with a direct connection to a food-processing facility a few kilometers away. Replicator circuitry and power converters were considered a critical resource and used for only the most important manufacturing needs.

"So, how's Nog?" Bashir asked, trying to keep his tone innocuous, but wondering why Jake had chosen not to react to his statement. He took a sip of the tea he had requisitioned. It was too cold, too sweet, and tasted nothing at all like tea.

"Different," Jake said, frowning at the contents of the containers he had uncovered. Again, it was not clear to Bashir if the frown was directed at the food or at his question.

"To be expected, don't you think?"

Jake gingerly dabbed a finger into the red sauce that covered a brownish square of . . . something, then tentatively licked his finger. He grimaced. "I actually miss the combat rations on the *Augustus.*"

Bashir smiled in commiseration. Vulcan combat rations were logical and not much else. They consisted of tasteless extruded slabs which were mostly vegetable pulp compressed to the consistency of soft wax. Accompanied by packets of distilled water and three uncomfortably large supplement pills to compensate for the differences between Vulcan and human nutrient requirements, 500 grams of pulp were sufficient to maintain a normal adult body for thirty hours. Vulcans were proud of the fact that their rations only had to be ingested once a day, and that the process could be completed in less than two minutes. How much more efficient could eating become? All of the temporal refugees had lost body mass during their voyage on the *Augustus.*

It was also possible, though, that Jake's joke might have another purpose—to change the subject. Bashir didn't intend to let such a ploy go unchallenged.

"Were you having an argument with Nog?" he asked. "Before we all had dinner at the starbase?"

He saw the answer in Jake's guilty expression. "Jake, it's bad enough that Starfleet is keeping secrets from us. We can't keep them from each other, too." Bashir dropped his own voice to a near whisper. "What did he tell you?"

Jake's shoulders sagged. "It's more what he didn't tell me . . . tell us."

"About what?"

Jake dropped his napkin over his untouched food. "He was lying to us."

Bashir felt the unwelcome touch of alarm. He had considered that possibility himself. "About the *Phoenix?*"

"No . . . I don't think about all that. Like, the *Phoenix* and going back twenty-five thousand years and the deep-time charges in B'hala . . . I really think that's what Starfleet's planning. Or *was* planning. But . . . when he told us he had no doubt that the mission would succeed . . . that was a lie."

Bashir put down his padd. "Considering the rather audacious nature of the mission, I'm not really surprised. It's perfectly understandable that Nog might harbor some doubts about the possibilities for success."

But Jake shook his head emphatically. "I'm not talking about doubts. Or being nervous. I mean . . . look, it's as if Nog already knows the mission *can't* succeed."

"Did he say that to you? Is that what you were arguing about?"

Jake looked right and left, obviously concerned about anyone overhearing their discussion. "That was part of it. But he didn't have to tell me. Not flat out."

"I don't understand."

Jake shifted uncomfortably. "He's been my best friend for . . . well, we *were* best friends for a long time. And I can tell when he's lying. He does this thing with his eyes and . . . his mouth sort of freezes in position."

Jake was obviously developing some skill in observation. "They call it a 'tell.' Or they used to," Bashir corrected himself, "a few centuries ago. In gambling and confidence games, some people develop a nervous habit which gives away the fact that they're bluffing. You're very observant."

Jake shrugged. "Not really. Uh, Nog sort of told me himself. His father and uncle kept giving him a hard time about it. They, uh, they claimed he had picked it up from me . . . a filthy human habit that would hold him back in business." Jake smiled weakly. "He tried to run away from the station a couple of times."

"I didn't know," Bashir said truthfully.

"I . . . talked him out of it. But anyway, he's still doing it. And he was definitely lying to us."

Bashir sat back in the flimsy mess-hall chair and mentally called up a Vulcan behavioral algorithm to try to calculate the odds that Jake was correct in his conclusion of Nog's truthfulness. Once the Vulcans had realized the failure of their early predictions that any species intelligent enough to develop warp drive would of course have embraced logic and peaceful exploration as the guiding principles of their culture, they had developed complex systems for modeling and predicting alien behavior as a form of self-survival. It was a difficult set of equations to master, but one could always count on a Vulcan to figure the odds for just about any eventuality.

Bashir completed his calculations. In the limited way he had trained himself in the Vulcan technique, he was forced to conclude that given the relationship between Jake and Nog, Jake was more likely than not correct in his assessment of his friend. Since there was nothing to be gained from questioning Jake's conclusion, the only logical course was now to determine the underlying reasons for Nog's behavior.

Bashir began the requisite series of questions. "Did you tell him that you knew he was lying?"

Jake nodded. "That's when he got mad at me."

"But did he deny lying?"

"How could he?"

"Did he say why?"

Jake appeared to be more profoundly unhappy than Bashir ever recalled seeing him before.

"All he told me was that I should keep my . . . my ridiculous *hew-mon* opinions to myself. And then, well, he sort of let me know that it was really important that I not tell anyone what I thought."

"With what you know of him, Jake, is there *any* reason you can think of why Nog would lie to us about the success of the mission?"

Now Jake looked positively haunted. "I . . . I think so."

Bashir leaned forward to hear Jake's theory about how Captain Nog was really going to save the lives of the temporal refugees—and the universe.

And what he heard was utterly fascinating, and at the same time utterly horrifying.

CHAPTER 14

"YOU KNOW HOW stardates work," Commander Arla Rees said.

"Of course." Sisko nodded, distracted, wondering about what was beyond the windowless hull of the small travelpod they were riding in. It reminded him of a two-person escape module, though he could see no indication that it carried emergency supplies or even flight controls. According to Weyoun, transporters were not permitted to operate anywhere within the Bajoran system—though he had provided no explanation why—and all travel here was carried out by pod, runabout, or shuttle. Thus, the survivors from the *Defiant* had been sent off from the *Boreth's* hangar deck two by two, in these tiny pods with no means by which to observe the somehow restored Deep Space 9 as they neared it.

"Seriously?" Arla persisted. "You've actually looked into how the stardate system was devised?"

Sisko looked across the cramped pod—or down the pod, or up it. There was no artificial gravity field, and no inertial dampeners, either. Essentially, he and the commander were the only passengers in a gray metal can with two acceleration seats with restraint straps, a pressure door, and four blue-white lights, two at their feet and two at their heads. Sisko even doubted if the simple vessel had its own engines or reaction-control system. He guessed they were being guided from the *Boreth* to DS9 by tractor beam.

"I've studied timekeeping."

Arla frowned. "When? They don't tell you a lot in the Academy."

"Actually, I had reason to take an extension course a few years ago. I even built a few different types of mechanical clocks on my own." Sisko tried to lean back in his acceleration seat, but of course there was no gravity field to aid his maneuver—only the two chest-crossing straps that kept him from floating out of the seat.

"Did your course deal with how the system got started?"

"Some of it. As I understand it, Commander, the impetus behind devising a universal—or, at least, a *galactic*—standard time- and date-keeping system was primarily religious."

From her seat beside him, Arla nodded her head in agreement, though Sisko didn't understand the reason for the odd smile that accompanied that nod.

He continued, not knowing what she was looking for in his answer. "There's certainly precedent for it. Many of the religious festivals and holy days celebrated on Earth are tied to the calendar."

"More often than not the lunar calendar, I believe," Arla said.

"That's right," Sisko said. Though he still didn't know why they were having this conversation, it seemed harmless enough. He decided to run with it. The commander would give him her reasons when she was ready, and that was fine with him. "Now if my memory serves me right, when the first outposts were set up on Earth's moon, since everyone lived underground and the moon is less than a light-second from Earth, timekeeping wasn't a problem. But when the outposts on Mars were established, and it was common for people to spend years there with their families, I recall learning that it became awkward trying to reconcile Martian sols at twenty-four-and-a-half hours with Earth days at just under twenty-four. So a council of religious scholars on Mars came up with the first stardate system—Local Planetary Time—based, I believe, on the look-up tables and charts the Vulcans had been using to reconcile their star-ships' calendars with their homeworld's."

"The Vulcan system was based in philosophy," Arla said, as if making some important point, "not religion."

"I . . . suppose you could say that," Sisko said amiably. "Now, for most people, once you have a few thousand starships and outposts and a few hundred colonies, it gets too cumbersome to keep using look-up tables and charts. But," Sisko smiled, "not for Vulcans. It's no secret they have no problem keeping forty or fifty different calendar systems in their heads at the same time. But humans, we freely admit, tend to place more cultural and religious importance on specific days."

"Just like Bajorans," Arla said as she turned to him, her eyes filled with a passion Sisko didn't recall having noticed before. She then paused expectantly, as if she had still not heard what she needed to hear.

"Is there some point to this conversation?" Sisko finally asked.

But Arla's answer merely took the form of another question. "What happened next? According to the extension course you took."

Sisko sighed, tiring of their exercise. He wondered how long it would take for the pod to drift over to the station. He was surprising himself with his need to touch the metal walls and feel the decks of DS9 beneath his boots again. And with his desire to have someone tell him how it was that he could have seen DS9 destroyed, and yet see it now restored. Weyoun had been of little help. All he would answer in reply to Sisko's questions was, "In time, Benjamin. All will be explained in time."

Only because there was absolutely nothing else to do at the moment, Sisko continued to humor Arla. This time his answer came straight out of the Academy's first-semester text file. "The underlying principle of the universal stardate system is that of hyperdimensional distance averaging."

"Which is?"

Sisko grimaced. The last time he had had this basic a conversation with anyone about stardates, Jake had been five and sitting on his knee, struggling to get his Flotter Forest Diary program to work on the new padd Sisko had given him for his birthday.

"If you insist." Sisko then rattled off the requisite information. "Any two points in space can be joined by a straight line. The length of that line, divided by two, will yield the midpoint. If the inhabitants of both points convert their local time to the hypothetical time at the midpoint, then they both have an arbitrary yet universally applicable constant time to which they can refer, in order to reconcile their local calendars." He paused before continuing. "You know, of course, it's the exact same principle developed on Earth when an international convention chose to run the zero meridian through Greenwich, establishing Greenwich Mean Time. It was a completely artificial standard, but a standard everyone could use."

"And . . .," Arla prompted.

"And," Sisko sighed. The Bajoran commander's persistence was fully up to Vulcan standards. "Any two points can be joined by a straight line. Go up a dimension, and any three points can be located on a two-dimensional plane. Go up another dimension, and any four points in space can be located on the curved surface of a three-dimensional sphere. Any five points can be found on the surface of a four-dimensional hypersphere, and so on. The standard relationship is that any number of points, n, can be mapped onto the surface of a sphere which exists in n minus one dimensions. And that means that all of those points are exactly the same distance from the center of the sphere. So, just after the Romulan War, the Starfleet Bureau of Standards and the Vulcan Science Academy arbitrarily chose the center of our galaxy as the center point of a hypersphere with . . . oh, I forget the exact figure . . . something like five hundred million dimensions, okay? So theoretically, every star in our galaxy—along with four hundred million and some starships and outposts—can be located on the surface of the hypersphere and can directly relate their local calendars and clocks to a common standard time that's an equal distance from everywhere. Just as everyone on Earth used to look to Greenwich." Sisko gripped his restraints and pushed himself back into his acceleration couch, trying to compress his spine. The microgravity, not to mention his traveling companion, was giving him a pain in the small of his back, as his spine elongated in the absence of a strong gravity field. "Is that sufficient?" he asked sharply.

"What do you think?" Arla replied.

A sudden shock of pain pulsed through Sisko just above his left kidney. He remembered the sensation from his microgravity training decades ago in the Academy's zero-G gym. He forced his next words out through gritted teeth. "I think it's a damn simple system. One that works independent of position and relativistic velocity. And since it's based on the galactic center it's blessedly free of political overtones." Sisko smiled in relief as his back spasm ended, as suddenly as it had begun, and as he at the same time relived a sudden memory of the one sticking point Jake—like most five-year-olds—had had when it came to learning stardates. "And once a person gets used to the idea that stardates can seem to run backward from place to place, depending on your direction and speed of travel, it becomes an exceedingly simple calculation to convert from local time to stardate anywhere in the galaxy.

"So—if you're asking me if I'm in favor of stardates, Commander, yes, I am. Now what does this have to do with *anything?*"

Arla's expression was maddeningly enigmatic, and Sisko could read no clues in it. "So you consider the system to be completely arbitrary?"

"Any timekeeping system has to be. Because the universe has no absolute time or absolute position. Now would you please answer my question."

"Then how is it—" Arla said, and Sisko's attention was caught by her tone. The commander was finally ready to make her point. "—nine days from now, when the two wormholes are going to open in the Bajoran system only kilometers apart from each other and . . . and supposedly end the universe, or transform it somehow, that that completely arbitrary stardate system is going to roll over to 7700.0 at the same moment that Earth's calendar starts a new century with the first day of 2401 C.E.?"

Her question was so incredibly naive, Sisko couldn't believe the Bajoran had even asked it. "Coincidence, Commander." Now it was he who was expectant, waiting for her to say something more, to somehow explain herself.

"Coincidence," she repeated thoughtfully, obviously not accepting his answer. Sisko regarded her with puzzlement.

"Did you know," Arla said, "that an old Klingon calendar system reverts to the Fourth Age of Kahless on that same date? That the Orthodox Andorian Vengeance Cycle begins its 330th iteration then also? That that very same date is the one given in Ferengi tradition when some groups celebrate the day the Great Material River first overflowed its banks among the stars and, in the flood that followed, created Ferenginar and the first Ferengi?"

As Arla recited her list, Sisko observed her gesticulate with one hand to emphasize her words, and was fascinated to see the sudden action in microgravity billow the commander's robes around her like seaweed caught in a tidal current, pulsing back and forth in time with the slow, floating motion of her earring chain.

"*Seventeen* different spacefaring cultures, Captain Sisko. That's how many worlds have calendar systems that either reset or roll over to significant dates or new counting cycles on the *exact* same day the two wormholes come into alignment. Two systems coinciding is a coincidence. I'll give you that. Maybe even three or four. But *seventeen?* There must be some better explanation for that. Wouldn't you agree?"

Sisko took his time replying. He wished he knew the reasons behind the Bajoran commander's sudden obsession with the timing of events and timekeeping systems derived from religious traditions. When he had first met her on DS9, he remembered being impressed by her intensity and by her drive to do the best possible job. True, there had been an awkward moment when he had realized that she was discreetly communicating her interest in getting to know him on a more personal level, but she had responded properly and professionally the moment he had made her aware of his relationship with Kasidy.

He had had no doubt that Arla would make her own mark in Starfleet. Though she had little interest in taking command of a ship and had opted instead for a career track in administration, some of Starfleet's best and most forward-thinking strategic leaders had come from that same background.

But most of all, Sisko knew that Arla had been one of the rare few Bajorans who were completely secular. By her own account, she had no faith in the Prophets. To her, she had maintained to him, they were merely a race of advanced beings who lived in a different dimensional environment, one which rendered communication between themselves and the life-forms of Arla's own dimension very difficult. And she had told him emphatically on more than one occasion that the Celestial Temple was simply a wormhole to her, worthy of study, not for religious reasons, but because it was stable and apparently artificial.

So how did someone like that, he now thought, *suddenly become so interested in comparative religion? And even more intriguingly, why?*

Sisko decided to change tactics. "Do *you* have an explanation?" he asked.

"I don't know," Arla answered simply.

"A theory then? Something that we could put to the test?"

A frown creased Arla's smooth forehead. "A week ago, if you

had asked me about the stardate standard, I would have given the same answer you did. That it was an arbitrary timekeeping system. That absolute time didn't exist any more than absolute location." A fleeting smile erased her frown. The smile seemed slightly nervous to Sisko. "What's that old saying, Captain? Everything's relative?"

"That's true, you know," Sisko said.

The Bajoran commander shook her head vehemently in disagreement. "No . . . those other timekeeping systems . . . Terran, Bajoran, Klingon, Andorian . . . they're *not* really arbitrary. They all share a common underpinning—not relative but *related.*"

"Commander." Sisko spoke in his best authoritative tone. "The calendar systems you refer to date back thousands if not tens of thousands of years, to a time before star travel. There is *nothing* to connect them."

"But there is." Arla's voice was rising with an urgency that was beginning to concern Sisko. The source of whatever had upset her was still not clear to him. "Don't you see? They all came out of *religion.* They're all based on some form of creation story. And maybe . . . maybe life arose independently on all those worlds, but maybe it also all arose at the same time—from the same cause."

Sisko's concern changed to indignation. It appeared the Bajoran commander was simply guilty of sloppy thinking. "Commander, for what you're proposing—something for which there is no conclusive empirical proof, by the way—you might as well credit the Preservers with having seeded life throughout the quadrant, as much as invoke a supernatural force. There's about the same amount of evidence for both theories."

Sisko couldn't help noticing Arla's hurt expression, as she came to the correct realization that he considered her idea to be totally without merit. "Captain, I was just trying to explain why I disagreed with the commonly accepted belief that all the timekeeping systems were arbitrary. If they all stem from the same act of creation by the Prophets, then it makes sense that they all come to an end at the same time."

"Then what about stardates?" Sisko asked. "Without question, that's a completely artificial system based in the necessities of interstellar travel."

But Arla was not giving up so easily. "No, sir. You said it yourself. The need for stardates arose in part from the religious need to chart Earth's festivals and holy days on other worlds. How do we know the religious scholars of the time didn't build into their time-keeping system the same hidden knowledge that underlies all the other systems in the quadrant?"

Sisko shifted in his accelerator seat, feeling the restraints securing him in place. He felt trapped in both the conversation and the pod. It was all too obvious that he wasn't going to prevail in this argument. As soon as anyone brought up anything like "hidden knowledge," all possibility of a debate based on available facts flew out the airlock. "I take it your religious views have changed in the past few days," Sisko said in massive understatement.

"I don't know," Arla said, her voice declining in intensity. At last, even she was sounding weary now. Sisko knew how she felt. "What I do know is that there has to be *some* sort of explanation," she said. "And as someone trained in the scientific method, I have to keep my mind open to *all* possible explanations, even the ones I might think are unlikely."

Sisko was aware that the Bajoran commander was chiding him for apparently closing his own mind to the possibility of supernatural intervention in the affairs of the galaxy. But he felt secure in his approach. After all, he had dealt with the Prophets firsthand. And though explanations from them were often difficult to come by, subtlety was not their style. If there had been some sort of connection between the Prophets and worlds other than Bajor, Sisko felt certain that strong evidence for it would have turned up much earlier than now.

"An admirable position," he said in deliberate tones of finality, hoping that Arla would understand and accept that he wanted no more part in this conversation.

Just then the hull of the travelpod creaked, and a slight tremor moved through the small craft.

"Tractor beam?" Arla asked.

"Or docking clamp. Do we seem to be slowing down?"

Immediately, Arla held out both her arms, and watched them as if trying to see if they might respond to a change in delta vee. But except for the undulations of the sleeves of her robe, her arms remained motionless. "Some tractor beams have their own inertial dampening effect," she said. "We could be spinning like a plasma coil right now and not know it."

Sisko knew that was a possibility, though he didn't see the point.

From what he'd learned so far, the Ascendancy, for all its apparent capabilities, seemed to be in favor of not expending any effort or supplies unless absolutely necessary.

The lights suddenly flashed with almost blinding intensity, and there was another scrape and a stronger metallic bang, followed by the sound of rushing air. Sisko looked to the pressure door.

"That'll probably be an airlock sealing against the hull," Arla said.

"Not on DS9," Sisko said. "If we were at a docking port on a pylon or the main ring, we'd be within the artificial gravity field."

Arla was looking at him with concern. "Then where did we go? To another ship?"

"I don't know," Sisko said. He braced himself against his restraints and half twisted in his chair to face the door. He debated the wisdom of releasing the restraints, but if a gravity field did switch on suddenly, he couldn't be sure in which direction he might fall.

A new vibration shook the hull—something fast, almost an electrical hum.

"We're changing velocity," Arla said.

Sisko saw the chain of her earring slowly begin to flutter down until it hung beside her neck. But whether it was the effect of acceleration or the beginning of a gravity field there was no way to tell. Einstein had determined that almost five hundred years ago and that, too, was still true.

And then both he and Arla were abruptly shaken as a loud bang erupted in the pod. The sound seemed to come from the direction of the door.

The next bang was even louder but not as startling.

The third deformed the door, and Sisko tensed as he heard a hiss of air indicating that atmospheric integrity had been lost around the door's seal.

But when the pressure within the pod didn't seem to change appreciably, Sisko revised his deduction. They had docked with or somehow been taken aboard another vessel whose atmosphere was slightly different from the pod's.

A fourth bang rocked the pod. The door creaked and swung open.

Beyond the pod's simple portal Sisko glimpsed a pale-yellow light fixture shining within a dark airlock. He could just make out the curve of a Cardassian door wheel in the gloom.

"This *is* the station," he exclaimed. He touched the release tabs on his restraints and pushed himself from the chair. His feet gently made contact with the floor of the pod. Automatically, Sisko estimated gravity at about one-tenth Earth normal.

He nodded at Arla, who then released herself to stand on the floor, still holding the loose restraints to keep herself from bouncing into the pod's low ceiling.

With extreme caution, Sisko began moving toward the open portal. The glare from the single dim light fixture in the airlock prevented him from seeing through the viewport in the far door. All he could be sure of was that whatever was beyond, it was in the dark as well.

He stepped from the pod into the airlock, almost falling as normal gravity suddenly took over.

The moment he regained his footing he took hold of Arla's arm. "Careful. They must be able to focus gravity fields better than we could."

"Who?" Arla asked, as she cautiously entered the more powerful field.

"Knowing Weyoun, this is probably some game he's devised."

"Or a trap."

"He already had us," Sisko reminded her. He pushed his face against the viewport, cupping his hands around his eyes to shield his vision and squinting to see some sort of detail in whatever lay beyond. But the darkness there was absolute.

A sudden mechanical grinding noise caused him to spin around. He saw the other wheel door roll shut, cutting off any chance of their returning to the pod. In any event, with the pressure door damaged— *by what?* Sisko suddenly wondered—the pod would not be the safest place to be.

Another rush of air popped his ears. Oddly enough, the effect made Sisko feel better, because he knew it meant that when the second wheel door opened there would be an atmosphere on the other side.

He turned to check on Arla. "Are you all right?"

Silent, she nodded, slowly raising her hand to point toward the second wheel door, her eyes wide with alarm.

And then just as the second door began to roll Sisko caught sight of what had disturbed her. For just an instant, through the moving viewport, against the darkness of what lay beyond, two eyes glowed red.

"It's Weyoun," Sisko said in disgust. Though what the Vorta was attempting to accomplish with this bit of theater was beyond him.

Then a sudden wind of hot, damp air from beyond the airlock swept over him in a rush, and he gagged at the sweet, fetid stench that accompanied it. Behind him, Arla did the same.

Sisko looked up, eyes watering, the sharp taste of bile in his mouth, knowing that whatever else lay in the darkness, there were organic bodies, rotting.

Then, from out of the darkness, the two red eyes approached him.

Sisko's vision was still blurry in the assault of that terrible smell, but with a sudden tensing of his stomach he realized that the shadowy outlines of the figure who was entering the airlock indicated someone taller than Weyoun. And those shoulders—

It was a Cardassian!

Arla cried out in fear behind him.

A powerful hand closed around Sisko's throat, its cold grip unnaturally strong. Red eyes of fire blazed down at him.

And Sisko recognized the creature who held his life in one gray hand.

It was *Dukat!*

CHAPTER 15

"WHERE ARE MY PEOPLE?" Worf growled.

Normally, Jadzia didn't like to see her husband give himself over to typical Klingon confrontational techniques. But in this case, as Worf glared down at Captain T'len Jadzia was in full agreement. There were too many unanswered questions and too little time to use diplomacy.

T'len stepped back from Worf, her Vulcan features revealing no outward sign of intimidation. Her gaze, however, moved almost imperceptibly to the closed door leading from the planning room to the corridor, as if checking for a path of retreat. *Good,* Jadzia thought. Here was where having three hundred years of experience paid off. And her experience was telling her now that there was seldom a better person to negotiate with than a Vulcan who had a logical reason to cut negotiations short.

She watched as T'len tugged down on her black tunic. "If you wish to determine the fate of your family members," the Vulcan captain told Worf, "you have been instructed in accessing Starfleet computers for all pertinent personnel records."

Jadzia hid a smile as Worf slammed his massive fist down on the table beside him, causing a large schematic padd to jump several centimeters into the air and spilling a coffee mug onto the floor.

Klingons could be so messy. It was one of their most endearing traits, she thought as she regarded her mate with loving pride.

"I am not talking about my family," Worf shouted. "I know my parents have passed on to *Sto-Vo-Kor.* I know my brother died in the evacuation of Lark 53. I am asking, What happened to the Klingon *people?* And I want an answer *now!*"

T'len narrowed her eyes, in what was to Jadzia a rather startling and misguided display of unalloyed Vulcan defiance.

"Or you'll do what, Commander?"

Worf didn't hesitate an instant. Jadzia expected no less of him. Once her mate made up his mind to do something, she knew little could dissuade him.

"Or I will kill you where you stand," Worf said.

T'len raised a dark, sculpted eyebrow. "You wouldn't dare."

"I would rather die battling my enemies than wait passively for the universe to end."

T'len looked past Worf at Jadzia. "Will you talk sense into your husband?"

Jadzia took a moment to enjoy the undercurrent of fear in T'len's voice. It was so satisfying when people had their worldviews turned upside down. As she had discovered in her many different lifetimes, on a personal level few events proved more rewarding. Though it might, of course, take some time for the person caught in such turmoil to realize it.

She shrugged as if completely powerless in this situation, though she and Worf had carefully rehearsed the moment—and this confrontation. "What can I say? You know how willful Klingons can be."

T'len's chin lifted, and she turned again to face Worf. She was backed against a central engineering table that flickered with constantly updating engineering drawings of the *Phoenix.* "Commander, I am not your enemy."

"If you do not tell me the fate of the Klingon Empire in this time period, then I have no choice but to conclude you are somehow responsible for the destruction of the Empire. That makes you my enemy, and deserving of death."

In what Jadzia could only consider a Vulcan's last-ditch retreat into pure desperation, T'len thrust her hand forward in an attempt to give Worf a nerve pinch.

As Jadzia knew he would, Worf caught the Vulcan's hand before it had traveled more than half the distance to his shoulder. Then he began to squeeze it. Hard. "You have attacked me," Worf announced in stentorian tones. "I am now justified in defending myself." At the same time, he began to bend T'len's hand backward.

"I *order* you to release me!" T'len said.

Worf was implacable. He continued without pause. "I do not recognize your right to order me. In my time, the Empire and the Federation were allies. Since you do not support the Empire, to me that makes you an enemy of the Federation. Either explain to me why and how conditions have changed, or prepare to take passage on the Barge of the Dead."

Jadzia could see T'len beginning to tremble in her effort to resist Worf's grip and to control the discomfort she must be feeling in her stressed wrist and hand.

"Vulcans do not believe in Klingon superstition," the captain said, her voice wavering despite her attempts to keep it steady.

"It will not remain a superstition for long," Worf said grimly. "In less than a minute, I guarantee you will have firsthand knowledge."

T'len raised her other hand to try to slap her communicator. But Worf caught that hand, too.

Jadzia judged the time was right. She stepped forward. "Captain, you know we want to help the cause. Isn't it logical that you provide us with the same information that inspires *you* to fight?"

"This is not your concern," Worf snapped at her, exactly as Jadzia had suggested he do. "The Trill homeworld is still within the Federation. But for all the information Starfleet is willing to give me"—he bent down until his fangs and glaring eyes were only a centimeter from T'len's tense features—"the Empire might as well have been destroyed."

"*It was!*" T'len suddenly exclaimed. "There! Does that satisfy you?!"

Jadzia could see the surprise in Worf's face. Almost as an afterthought he released the Vulcan's hand, and she immediately hugged it to her chest, rubbing at her wrist.

"Why could you not tell me at the beginning?" Worf said accusingly. "Just as you told the humans about the destruction of the Earth."

"Because the Earth was destroyed by the Grigari," T'len said sharply and, Vulcan or not, the bitterness in her was clearly evident. "But the Empire destroyed itself."

At once Jadzia moved to Worf's side then, to keep him grounded in this moment, to prevent his descent into the full rage of battle at T'len's revelation. She put her hands on his arm and his back.

"You—will—tell—me—how." Through the touch that connected them Jadzia felt the visceral struggle each word cost her mate.

T'len's answer was slow in coming. "Project Looking Glass," she said with a wary look at Worf and Jadzia. "The Klingons were so proud of it. While the Federation fought a holding battle against the Ascendancy, the Empire was to prepare a safe haven from the destruction of the universe."

Jadzia stroked her mate's back to calm him. "Isn't that a contradiction in terms?" she asked.

"Not if the safe haven is another universe," T'len said.

As quickly as that, Jadzia understood. "Looking Glass," she said, stepping away from Worf.

Because Worf understood, as well. "The Mirror Universe."

T'len nodded, and Jadzia relaxed, detecting the subtle change in the Vulcan captain's stance in response to Worf's more measured tones.

"In that universe," T'len added with greater assurance, as she sensed that Worf would not respond physically to her unwelcome information, "the Klingon-Cardassian Alliance was in disarray and easy to overcome once the Prime Directive was suspended. The total population was much lower. There were sufficient worlds in which to create new colonies. And the best physicists concluded that the destruction of our own universe would have no effect on the Mirror Universe. It appears that the Prophets—or the wormhole aliens of Jalbador—don't seem to exist there."

Jadzia knew Worf would not accept T'len's characterization of Klingons, no matter which universe they existed in. And he did not. "It is not like my people to plan for defeat," Worf growled.

T'len promptly deflected his objection. "That was just a contingency plan, Commander. The original intention was to send a Klingon fleet into the Mirror Universe, fight its way to Bajor, then reappear in our universe behind the Ascendancy's lines."

Worf grunted approvingly. "A worthy deception. It sounds like the work of General Martok."

"Chancellor Martok," T'len corrected. "And it *was* his plan."

Jadzia could see from the way Worf's eyes flashed that he already knew how the plan had ended.

"How did it fail?" he asked.

The hesitant manner in which T'len answered suggested to Jadzia that the plan's outcome still baffled the Vulcan captain. "I assure you, Commander Worf, the first exploratory and reconnaissance missions were flawless. Every replicator in the Empire and most of those throughout the Federation were requisitioned to create transporter pads, to transfer goods and warriors to the other side. That effort alone took two years. We still haven't replaced all the replicators we expended. But in time our forces were ready."

T'len's eyes lost their focus and became opaque, as she relived the moment. "The fleet—the Armada—moved out from the Empire in the Mirror Universe, heading for Bajor, while at the same time in our universe, to counter any suspicions, Earth entered into trade and treaty negotiations with the Grigari. But the Grigari fleet attacked Earth without warning, and with so many ships committed to Looking Glass—which we were certain had not been detected by the Ascendancy—there were no reinforcements to save that world."

T'len's eyes cleared, and she looked squarely at Worf. "When word reached the Mirror Universe that the Grigari had attacked *here* before the Klingons could attack *there,* the Fleet turned around to come to Earth's defense. And when it was in that state of confusion as its mission changed, a second Grigari fleet attacked there as well."

Jadzia took an involuntary step forward, then stopped herself as Worf's head bowed in sorrow.

"But how . . . how could the defeat of the Armada lose the *Empire?*" he asked T'len.

"All those transporters," T'len said quietly. "They had been used to send untold trillions of tonnes of supplies and equipment between the universes. Enormous complexes of them were on all the major worlds of the Empire."

"And the Grigari—" T'len paused for a moment before continuing. At that moment, Jadzia realized that in her way the Vulcan captain was trying to be kind to Worf, as she succinctly completed her account with little elaboration of the devastating consequences of the plan's failure.

"The Grigari used those same transporters to move weapons from the Mirror Universe into ours, weapons which detonated in place and tore apart worlds, rendered atmospheres unbreathable and collapsed entire ecosystems.

"The end result . . . was that we learned that the Grigari had known exactly what we had planned and had prepared a perfect series of countermoves against us. According to our best estimates," T'len concluded, "there are slightly more than one million Klingons left alive in this quadrant."

Worf's broad chest heaved, and if not for the presence of the Vulcan Jadzia would have reached out and drawn him close to her, to share his terrible grief.

When he finally spoke, Worf's voice was low but steady. "Why would you not tell me this before?"

"Because Starfleet needs every warrior who can serve. And that includes you, Commander. Also"—Jadzia felt T'len's gaze upon her—"we were concerned that if . . . *when* you found out about the fate of your Empire, you would do what so many other Klingons have done—go off on a suicidal mission to assuage survivor guilt and die in battle. Or that you would attempt to accomplish some great victory, in order to ensure that a relative lost in the destruction of the Armada might find a place in *Sto-Vo-Kor*."

The sounds of Worf's deep breathing intensified, but he did not respond further.

"What will you do, Commander?" T'len asked. "Abandon Starfleet? Abandon the *Phoenix?* Go off and die in glorious battle?"

Jadzia held her breath. This time, not even she knew what Worf's answer would be.

It seemed forever to her before her mate again spoke. "How did Chancellor Martok die?"

"He was with the fleet," T'len said simply, "on the flagship *The Heart of Kahless.* But they were wiped out to the last warrior. I do not know precisely how he died."

"He died with honor," Worf growled fiercely in what Jadzia knew was a challenge. "Of that you can be certain."

Jadzia tensed. The Vulcan captain stared up at Worf for a moment before making her decision. "I am," the Vulcan said.

Worf nodded once, then said, "I am a Starfleet officer. I see no conflict in fulfilling that duty and behaving honorably as a Klingon warrior. But you must no longer keep secrets from me, or from any of us. Either we are your fellow warriors and your equals, or we will leave you to fight on our own. Is that understood?"

"Yes," T'len said.

Jadzia had a question of her own for T'len. "Why are there so few humans left?"

Once again, T'len's voice betrayed an un-Vulcan-like emotional turmoil, but now Jadzia was realizing that more than just institutions had changed in this time. So had the people. She would have to remember that, and not depend on perhaps irrelevant assumptions derived from centuries of experience in other times. The knowledge gave her an odd feeling of freedom from the past lives she remembered. Whatever she and the others faced in this time would require her to make observations uniquely her own.

"The Klingon colony worlds," T'len explained, "were used to create the Armada in the Mirror Universe. In contrast, human colony worlds were used to establish emergency communities, survival camps really . . . in case Starfleet and the Empire were not successful in stopping the Ascendancy. And the same type of transporter facilities were installed everywhere from Alpha Centauri to Deneva. At sixty percent efficiency, with the facilities we established on fifty colony worlds, we would have had the capacity to transfer up to thirty million people a day into the Mirror Universe. In these past five years, we might have saved—evacuated—almost sixty billion people."

The Trill understood at least one reason for the Vulcan captain's distress. Sixty billion was a vast number, yet it would only have accounted for slightly less than ten percent of the total population of the Federation. And factoring in the populations of the nonaligned systems and all the other beings who must exist elsewhere in the galaxy and throughout the universe, sixty billion was as inconsequential as a raindrop in an ocean.

But there was another possible reason.

"The Grigari used those transporters, too, didn't they?" Jadzia asked.

"Nanospores," T'len said with distaste. "Nanites, which exist only to disassemble living cells to make other nanites, which then spread to other life-forms and begin the process again. They can't be screened through biofilters. There are no drugs to which they will respond. Neither are they affected by extremes of temperature. Whole populations were . . . were dissolved. Entire worlds stripped of their biospheres. And Starfleet had to maintain quarantines around all of them, to incinerate any ship that attempted to leave." T'len's dark eyes bore into Jadzia's. "Do you really want to know *more?*"

Jadzia touched Worf's arm, giving it a gentle squeeze. Felt no response in return. "Not now," she said. "I think we need to be alone for a while."

"We tour the *Phoenix* at 0800 hours tomorrow morning," T'len said, by way of agreement.

Jadzia nodded. T'len sighed as she gave a last rub to her strained wrist, then left the planning room.

As soon as the Vulcan captain had moved through the doorway and out of earshot, Worf turned to Jadzia, looked down at her. "This future *cannot* be permitted to happen," he said.

"But it already has, Worf."

Worf shook his head angrily. "We are still connected to our past. To *our* present. We must go back somehow and prevent this."

It was unfortunate, Jadzia thought, that the direct Klingon approach was not always the best—not even in this time, she would wager. And it was always so difficult to explain that to her mate. She put both hands on Worf's shoulders. "Worf, the only way we can go back to our present is by retracing our slingshot trajectory around the red wormhole, and that wormhole is in the middle of the Bajoran system. There's nothing Starfleet can do to get anywhere near it. We *have* to accept that there's nothing more we can do to change the past. But with the *Phoenix,* we do have a chance to change the future."

"I refuse to accept that."

Jadzia made a playful fist and lightly tapped her knuckles against Worf's heavy brow ridges. "Just as I thought," she said. "No evidence of brain matter. Solid bone throughout."

Her mate glared at her. "This is not the time for levity! The universe is trapped in a nightmare and we are the only ones who can restore it!"

"I agree," Jadzia said, drawing her fingers along Worf's cheek. "But what do I always tell you when you make such grand and glorious plans?"

Jadzia hid her smile as Worf's bluster became uncertain.

"I . . . do not remember," he said.

Jadzia didn't believe that for an instant. "We can do anything that we choose to do . . . *say* it. . . ."

Worf grimaced, as if he knew there was no escape this time. And this time, Jadzia thought, she would see that there wasn't.

"We can do anything that we choose to do," he repeated without conviction.

"Very good," Jadzia said, as she lowered her hand to caress his broad chest. "But sometimes, we do not have to choose to do it *now*."

She looked up at Worf, knowing what it was they both must do to prepare for the battle ahead, just as the first Klingon male and female had done before they had stormed heaven and destroyed the gods who had created them.

"The Empire must be avenged," Worf said.

"I know," Jadzia agreed. "But first we must prepare for battle."

Worf nodded his assent, placed both powerful hands on her arms.

"Computer," Jadzia said clearly, "seal the planning office door. Security request gamma five." She smiled at Worf, glad she had reviewed the security manuals for the shipyards.

Something clicked inside the door, and the security condition light changed from amber to red.

Right at that instant, Worf leaned down and kissed her, his full embrace of her powerful, charged with the emotion of the moment and not tempered by concerns that had gone before or would be faced in the future.

But that was Worf's way, not hers. There was still something that troubled Jadzia. She pulled back from him, but did not look away.

"What?" Worf asked roughly, his voice thick with passion.

"Something Captain T'len said. About . . . getting into *Sto-Vo-Kor*."

Worf threw back his head proudly. "An easy matter. I have eaten the heart of an enemy."

"There's more to it than that."

"Of course. A warrior must die in glorious battle."

"But T'len said that some Klingons were trying to fight to get their relatives into *Sto-Vo-Kor*."

Worf sobered, became thoughtful. "There are many qualities a warrior must possess. Among them is the ability to inspire great actions in the hearts of others. So, if a great warrior does not fall in battle, he is not necessarily denied the reward of *Sto-Vo-Kor.* If those who know him dedicate their own great battle to him, then there will be a place for the fallen among the honored dead."

Jadzia felt a wave of thankful relief for her mate's generous nature. In its way, the Klingon religion was also humane, in that there were many chances for personal redemption, even after death.

She gripped Worf's hand tightly in both of hers, and with perfect warrior's inflection she said in Klingon, "Then know this, my husband. That if you should die outside of battle, I will dedicate each battle I fight for the rest of my life to your honor and to your place among the honored dead."

Worf trailed his fingers through her long dark hair. "You are the most romantic female I have ever known," he whispered gruffly.

Jadzia took that hand as well, and lightly bit his fingers. "And will you fight for me if I fall outside of battle?"

Worf kissed her forehead. "That is not your destiny. You will die an old woman with long white hair, secure in your bed, surrounded by your grandchildren, and it will be our sons who will win glorious victories for us both, that we might sit at the table of *Sto-Vo-Kor.*"

Jadzia felt tears well up in her eyes as her love for Worf grew even stronger. She smiled at him, knowing that the time for words, no matter how beautiful, was coming to an end.

"Our *sons?*" she asked teasingly.

"At least ten," Worf murmured as he crushed her in his arms.

"Ten?" Jadzia laughed. "Then we'd better get to work. . . ."

They didn't speak past that, and afterward, content in the arms of her warrior, Jadzia drifted off to sleep, dreaming of sons—and daughters—and scores of grandchildren, and the perfect love she knew would last for decades to come.

Which meant, she dreamily realized, that the universe would *not* end as everyone feared.

She slept soundly, knowing that the future was secure, and that it would be many years before she came to the gates of *Sto-Vo-Kor.*

CHAPTER 16

"Do you BELIEVE?" Gul Dukat shouted, and his voice echoed in the darkness of the charnel house that was Deep Space 9.

Sisko fought to breathe as the Cardassian's deadly chokehold tightened on his throat. He struggled to get a grip on his attacker's arm, but it was as if Dukat's hand were forged from neutronium, and Sisko began to despair of surviving this possessed creature, who was something other than an ordinary life-form.

"DO YOU?" Dukat spat into Sisko's face, his foul breath so much stronger than the malodorous air surrounding them that it seemed to Sisko the Cardassian himself could be the source of the terrible stench. *"Before you are thrown into the Fire Pits to burn for your sins, will you not confess your unworthiness?"*

Sisko flailed uselessly, at last pointing to his gasping mouth, trying to form the words, "Can't speak," before he lost consciousness.

Dukat's glittering eyes flickered. He angled his head. His hand began to reduce its pressure on Sisko's swollen throat. Sisko's heartbeat no longer thundered in his ears.

And then something dark streaked through the air above Sisko's head, and he heard a thick thud of impact as Dukat's hand released him, and the Cardassian fell back into darkness.

In the same moment, Sisko collapsed to his knees, gulping air, gagging, massaging his bruised throat. In his relief to finally get a breath into his strained lungs, the air no longer seemed as dreadful as it had earlier. Breathing almost normally, he looked up to see Arla at his side, the arm of one of the pod's acceleration chairs balanced in her hand like a club—the weapon she had used against Dukat. She was peering into the dark shadows of the station, the only light on her the backglow from the pale yellow light in the airlock behind them, and beyond that the distant light from their travel pod.

She looked down at Sisko. "Are you all right, Captain?"

Sisko nodded and forced himself to his feet, half-stumbling on the ill-fitting robes he wore.

"Was that Gul Dukat?" Arla asked.

His throat still burning, Sisko shook his head in agreement.

And then a shriek came from the darkness. ". . . *Unbeliever.* . . ."

"Dukat!" Sisko croaked. "We don't want to fight you!"

"Then that makes it much easier for *me!*" Dukat screamed back, and from nowhere a solid fist struck Sisko in the side of the head, knocking him away from Arla, toward the open airlock.

Before Sisko could recover his balance, a shaft of bloodred light sprang from the open palm of Dukat's hand and reached out to engulf Arla, five meters away, in a scarlet corona of energy.

The tall Bajoran cried out as sparks flew from her earring and she was *lifted* into the air, her body writhing, arms swinging, legs kicking furiously.

"Leave her alone!" Sisko jumped to his feet again, commanding Dukat to obey him.

The Cardassian turned and stared at him, head still cocked, its outline framed in a wild frothing spray of white hair in the radiant-red backscatter of energy pulsing from his outstretched hand.

"Emissary," Dukat intoned ominously, "you know I can't do that. She's Bajoran."

"She's no threat to you!"

Dukat drew his hand back and its red halo of energy cut off as if a switch had been thrown. Arla's body fell at once, striking the deck heavily. She moaned, then lay still.

Sisko moved quickly to her side, checked for a pulse, felt it flutter in her neck.

Then he became aware of Dukat towering over him. Sisko looked up, for the first time noticing the red armband the Cardassian wore, and understood what it meant.

"Follow me," Dukat ordered. For now his hollow eyes were shadowed, dark.

"Why?" Sisko said, cradling Arla in his arms.

The white-haired figure shrugged. "Because, Emissary, you have already come back from the dead, just as I have. What more can I do to you that the Prophets have not already done? Yet think what you might *learn*. . . ."

Then, with a flourish of the dark robes he wore, the Cardassian whirled around and walked into the shadows. The movement caused a rush of evil-smelling air to wash over Sisko, and he swayed back beneath its force. Recovering, he glanced at the open airlock, though he knew the damaged travelpod could not be used again.

He had no choice now.

He lifted up Arla's unconscious form and followed after Dukat, the path taking him deeper into the unknown darkness of a Deep Space 9 he did not know.

Sisko emerged onto what once had been the Promenade, though there was little now that was familiar to him.

In the half-light of a handful of flickering yellow fusion tubes, Sisko could see no sign of any stores or kiosks, only a circular sweep of bare metal deck puddled here and there with dark liquid and framed by empty, open storerooms.

And there were the corpses, too, of course. The reason why the air was so awful here and throughout the station.

From what was before him, Sisko guessed at least a hundred had died, more if the scattered, haphazard piles of robed figures were the same in the other sections of the Promenade that he couldn't see.

And the slaughter must have gone on for some time. A few of the bodies were little more than skeletal remains. Some were still covered with flesh, though that was black and shriveled. And others were only a few days old, fresh like those to be found on battlefields, already swelling with the potent gases of decay.

The only thing they shared, other than the silence of the dead, was a thin band of red cloth, tied around each arm—just like Dukat's.

"My congregation," Dukat proclaimed proudly.

He stood on a platform, a pulpit that was little more than a hull plate balanced on top of a battered metal bench and half-covered by a filthy white cloth.

"Can you hear the applause?" Dukat cried as he closed his eyes briefly in bliss. "The cheers and the joy?"

Sisko shifted his deadweight burden, trying to change Arla's position within his tiring arms, to ease his aching back. The Bajoran was half a head taller than he was, and well muscled. And heavy. She stirred and gave a faint cry, but he didn't want to put her down here. There was no clear space that had not been fouled by the dead.

He called out to Dukat. "Do you follow Weyoun? Or does Wey—"

"*SILENCE!*" Dukat thundered, and a ruby bolt of fire shot from his hand to scorch the deck at Sisko's feet. In an instant, the dark metal there turned dull red with heat and a nearby puddle of unidentifiable liquid became steam, filling the air with a choking, noxious cloud of what smelled like sewer gas.

"Weyoun." Dukat spat the name out contemptuously. "The Pretender. The Puppet. A mindless plaything of those unfit to dwell within the Temple."

Sisko looked around, confused. Whatever Dukat had been up to here, it had been going on for months at least, if not years. So why had Weyoun brought Sisko and the other survivors from the *Defiant* here? Unless . . .

"Dukat—where are we?"

Dukat gestured grandly to each side of his makeshift pulpit. "In my domain: as it was, as it always shall be, Terok Nor without end. Amojan. Can I hear an Amojan?" He peered down at Sisko, his eyes aflame once more, his terrible gaze stopping on Arla. "Ah, I see you've brought a sacrifice. An innocent. To die like all the others you condemned so long ago, to bless this station."

"No," Sisko said quickly. He nodded at the bodies that surrounded them. "Is that who these people are? What they became? Sacrifices?"

Dukat held out his arms, hands cupped, as if seeking and receiving the adulation of a crowd. "Can you not hear them, Emissary? They have such courage to resist the beguiling promises of the False Prophets. As you well know."

"Which Prophets are those?" Sisko grunted, as he had to let Arla's body slip down, resting it full length against his to support her upright though still unconscious form. "Weyoun's Prophets from the red wormhole? Or those from twenty-five years ago, in the blue wormhole?"

Dukat reeled back, as if startled by the question. Then he leaped down from his platform, advancing on Sisko, his scaly, bare feet splashing through the murky pools of liquid on the metal decking of the Promenade.

"You still don't know, do you?" Dukat crowed in amazement.

"Know what?"

Dukat's gap-toothed smile was almost a leer. This close to his old adversary, Sisko now saw how cruelly the years had treated him, not only turning his hair white but deeply furrowing his skin, whose loose folds now hung from his chin and jowls, emphasizing his gray reptilian knobs and plates.

"I've missed you," Dukat sneered. "Oh, the times we had, the places we've been."

"You were going to tell me something."

Dukat nodded gravely. "I *was* going to kill you. Back then. Before the war was over. I had traveled so far, learned so many things, and then I returned. Did they tell you that? I returned to Damar and Weyoun, determined to obtain from them a simple carving . . . a trifling piece of wood, really. But it had the power to drive the False Prophets from their Temple. To restore Kosst Amojan and the Pah-wraiths to their realm of glory. And to *destroy* you so utterly. . . ." Dukat's grin was terrifying. "So imagine my surprise when Damar told me you were already dead, swallowed by a wormhole. End of story. End of revenge. End of everything.

"Do you understand the irony of that moment?" Dukat snickered, and spittle flew from his open mouth. Sisko turned his face away to avoid breathing the same air. "I came back with plans for my ultimate triumph, but you had already taken it from me, defeating me before you even knew the battle had begun. And then, just to prove that the False Prophets have a sense of humor like no other, since Damar had no other use for me, he had me arrested. For treason."

"But not killed," Sisko said, drawing Arla closer to him. "How merciful."

Dukat reached out to pat Sisko's shoulder and trail a horn-like fingernail along Arla's insensate cheek. "Oh, I've died a thousand times since then, Captain. I'm dead now. In a way, I suppose, I always have been." He frowned at Arla. "Isn't she tiring you? I could take her if you'd like."

"I can manage. Why was Weyoun bringing me to see you?"

Dukat exploded with laughter. This time there was no way to avoid the spray. Sisko closed his eyes just in time. "He was doing no such thing, Emissary! He needs you to end the universe. But I saved you! Brought you here, out of his reach. And as long as you stay here, the universe *cannot* end. It's such a simple plan, don't you think? And all you have to do . . ." And here, Dukat's voice dropped deeper, became louder. ". . . *is remain here forever, like all my congregation.*"

Sisko edged back, keeping Arla close to him, as the red light in Dukat's eyes began to grow in intensity.

"Do not be afraid," Dukat commanded, raising his hands so that Sisko could see the sparks of crimson that were beginning to crackle across his fingers and palms like milling insects of light. *"I have eaten the heart of Kosst Amojan. I have crushed the foul Pah-wraiths who dwelled in the Fire Caves. I am on your side now, Emissary! We serve the same lost Prophets!"*

Then double rays of red light slammed into Sisko and Arla, driving her inert body into his so the two of them fell backward and into a slushy mound of soft bodies.

In the explosion of decomposed tissue and fluids that erupted around them, Arla slipped from Sisko's grasp. But the pungent smell finally awoke her, and she flailed about in the ghastly detritus as, half-conscious and confused, she tried and failed to get to her feet.

Dukat ignored her and held out his fiery hand to Sisko. *"Join me,"* he roared in his demonic voice, *"and the universe shall be saved for all time!"*

And despite the absolute horror of Dukat's temple and the nightmare world that Deep Space 9 had become, Sisko at last heard something in the ghastly Cardassian's entreaty. Something offering hope.

Sisko took a deep breath. Why couldn't he join Dukat? Why couldn't he reach out to the Cardassian's hand and thereby change the fate of the universe?

After all, Sisko thought, *I already know I'm lost.* Everyone who had come forward in time with him on board the *Defiant* was lost. And if things continued as Weyoun and even Starfleet seemed to believe they would, then all of existence was lost as well.

It would be so simple. So easy. So . . . *worthwhile.*

Sisko got to his feet, took a step forward.

"HERETIC!"

The cry had come from Arla. Sisko had forgotten she was even present. "What are you saying?"

Stained and disheveled but standing once again, the Bajoran pointed a shaking finger at Dukat. "Look at him, Captain," she shouted accusingly. "He's wearing the robes and armband of a Pah-wraith cult."

Sisko stared incredulously at Arla. *He* knew about the Pah-wraith cults because of what had happened to his son when the Reckoning had played out on Deep Space 9. But how did *Arla,* a nonbeliever, know about such things?

"She's a lost child," Dukat crooned. "You don't have to pay any attention to her. Take my hand, Emissary. Take my hand and save existence."

The Reckoning, Sisko thought wildly. So many questions swirled through his mind. Why couldn't he voice at least one of them?

"You'll be able to hear them cheering," Dukat said silkily as he gazed at the bodies around them. "You'll be able to feel their love. . . ." His eyes flashed scarlet, went dark, flashed again.

Love, Sisko thought hazily. He had lost Kasidy. He had lost . . . "My son—what about Jake?"

"He's a lovely boy," Dukat said. "And he's waiting for you. Take my hand. . . . You'll see him for yourself."

"You can't believe him, Captain," Arla warned.

"Whose side are you on?" Sisko demanded of her. He looked at Dukat. "Whose side are *you* on?"

"The side of truth," they both answered together.

Then they looked at each other and hurled the same word at the same time, *"Liar!"*

Sisko stepped back again, clarity suddenly freeing him. "I know where we are!" he exclaimed. "The wormhole!" He looked from Dukat to Arla. "This is some sort of Orb experience! You're . . . you're both Prophets!"

Dukat howled with scornful laughter. "Really, Emissary. How naive. Can Prophets *die?*"

And then, as if brushing dust from his robes, Dukat lifted his hand and a blast of energy felled Arla. She crumpled with a terrible finality to the floor. A thin trickle of blood trailed from the corner of her mouth.

"No one's had an Orb experience since Weyoun returned from the second Temple," Dukat said in the awful silence. "You must accept the truth, Emissary. It is *now,* and you are very much *here.*"

"I don't believe you," Sisko insisted, feeling dazed and doubtful. Arla wasn't dying, *couldn't* be dying, not in the wormhole. "There was a flash of light in the travelpod," he told Dukat. "Like an Orb being opened. That's when all this started."

"True," Dukat agreed. "Except that the light was my transporter, not an Orb."

Sisko fell to his knees and placed a hand on Arla's throat. Nothing. No pulse this time. He struggled to remember something Weyoun had said. "But transporters aren't allowed in the Bajoran system."

"Have you asked yourself why that should be?" Dukat asked. "What Weyoun is really afraid of?"

"He's afraid of attack." Sisko didn't know why he felt compelled to answer the madman—unless it was the influence of the Prophets.

The light in Dukat's red eyes flared again. "Or is he afraid of escape?"

"Escape to *where,* Dukat?" Sisko asked in frustration. Then Arla's pulse quickened to sudden life under this hand. "You see," he said in triumph, "she's *not* dead!"

"Emissary, I can't believe you're being this obtuse. Look where you are."

"Deep Space 9!"

"Yet that station was destroyed, was it not?"

"The *Defiant* was restored! Obviously the station was, too."

Dukat shook his head ponderously. "But it wasn't."

Sisko had had enough. Arla was alive. So was he. Where there was life there was something to fight for. "Then how can we be here?"

Dukat's eyes glowed with insanity. "It's as easy as looking into a mirror and—"

A silver beam sliced through the air, smashing Dukat to one side.

Sisko recognized a directed-energy weapon attack when he saw one, and reflexively he grabbed Arla and pulled her back, to shield her.

But she fought in his grip. "Let go of me! You're no better than—"

Her body stiffened. Her protest ceased. She saw what Sisko saw.

For all around them, in the ruins of what once had been Sisko's Deep Space 9, from every dark shadow and alcove . . .

The dead walked.

CHAPTER 17

IN THE COMPANY of Dr. Bashir, Jake walked along the corridor of the Utopia personnel dome heading for the planning room, where they were to meet Jadzia and Worf.

The doctor had said little since the mess hall, where Jake had told him about Nog's lie. At least what Jake had suspected was a lie.

For once he had seen Bashir's reaction to what he had described, once he had realized the danger they all faced because of it, Jake had gone over his last conversation with his friend, reconsidering, worried that he might have jumped to an unwarranted conclusion.

"What if he's not lying?" Jake asked Bashir.

The doctor kept walking briskly. "I was waiting for you to say that."

"No, really," Jake said as his long legs kept easy pace with Bashir. "What if Nog's changed in the past twenty-five years? What if . . . if I misread the signs?"

"Think of it this way, Jake. There comes a time when each of us has to trust our instincts. And I trust your instincts from a time when you had no idea what the repercussions of your observations would be *more* than I trust your rather predictable second-guessing of yourself now that you're aware of the danger in which you've placed your friend."

Jake was intimidated by Bashir. He knew the man was genetically enhanced, like some latter-day Khan Noonien Singh. How could he argue with someone whose brain was the equivalent of a computer?

But he had to.

"Dr. Bashir, I'm not doing this to save Nog."

Without breaking stride, Bashir shot him an amused smile that let Jake know that was exactly what he was doing.

"Look!" Jake finally said, and for emphasis he stopped dead.

"I'll . . . I'll go tell Nog myself what you're—"

It took a few steps before Bashir realized Jake was no longer beside him. The doctor turned and came back to him, looking irritated. "You will do no such thing!" Bashir hissed. "I know what it's like to lose a friend, Jake. But you have to accept that after twenty-five years you *have* lost Nog. You don't know what pressures he's been exposed to, what compromises he's had to make, all the little capitulations and loss of ideals that accompany adulthood. The fact is, you don't know Nog anymore. You *can't* know him."

Jake felt his face grow hot. "Then why should you accept what I said about his maybe lying to us about the *Phoenix*'s chances?"

"Because that wasn't a conclusion based on friendship," Bashir said. "It was a straight observation, devoid of emotion."

"You mean, like I was a Vulcan," Jake said, depressed at the turn this conversation was taking.

"Say what you will, but Vulcans make the best witnesses. Now— shall we go?"

Jake gave up and then fell into step beside the doctor again. He supposed Bashir had a point, though the guy was awfully cynical about the process of becoming an adult. What sort of compromises would an adult *ever* have to make? Kids—even nineteen-year-olds— were the ones who were trapped by society and convention. Anyone could tell them what to do, force them to go to school, restrict their entertainment choices, and even, on the frontier where it was used, keep hard currency out of their hands.

But adults, it seemed to Jake, had none of these restrictions. Sure, there might be pressures associated with their jobs, but don't forget those pressures were taken on by choice. That choice, in his opinion, was the key difference between someone his age and someone Bashir's.

As they neared the planning room, Jake took a sidelong look at the doctor's face, trying to remember his real age.

Bashir paused beside the door. "What now?"

The guy has eyes in the side of his head, Jake marvelled. "I was just wondering . . . how old are you anyway?"

Bashir sighed. "By our standards, or in this time?"

"By our standards, of course," he said. He knew that technically everyone from the *Defiant* was twenty-five years older than they had been a week ago.

Bashir seemed to hesitate. "How old do you think I am?"

Jake couldn't resist the opportunity the doctor had just given him. "I don't know," he said with a perfectly straight face. "Fifty?"

Bashir's face twisted into an incredulous look. *"Fifty?* I'm thirty-four, Jake."

"I said I didn't know," Jake said innocently. "You made me guess. I guessed."

"Fifty . . ." Bashir rolled his eyes skyward, then punched in his code to open the planning-room door. Jake kept his smile to himself.

The security condition light was still red. It didn't change to either amber or green. Then the computer voice said pleasantly, "This facility is sealed. Operating conditions gamma five."

Bashir flashed a knowing smile at Jake. "Fortunately, I've read the security operations manual. Computer: Permit access to this facility, authorization Bashir, Julian, operating condition beta one."

This time the security light obediently turned from red to amber.

Jake whistled, impressed. "How did you get a security clearance?"

"I'm a physician," Bashir said smugly as the door began to slide open. "It comes with the job. Automatically, it seems."

A sudden crash and a strangled cry from inside startled them both.

Bashir didn't wait, so neither did Jake. They both threw themselves at the door before it was fully open and pushed their way into the room where—

—Jake felt his legs threaten to give out as he suddenly found himself facing Lieutenant Commander Worf and Lieutenant Commander Dax, both of whom were, to put it politely, out of uniform.

Bashir instantly spun around and with a quick apology literally leaped back into the corridor.

A second later, open-mouthed, Jake felt Bashir's hand on his arm as he was hauled out as well.

With a thunk, the door slid shut behind them. Only then did Jake risk looking at Bashir.

"Well," Bashir said tersely, and Jake thought it was odd that a medical doctor would be disconcerted by the scene they'd just encountered, "they are married, after all."

"I'll say," Jake added. He wanted to say something more. He wanted to ask if Dr. Bashir had known Jadzia's Trill spots went all the way down to . . . but something in Bashir's face told him that *not* talking about what had just happened was what adults did. If only Nog were still his age and—

The door slid open again.

"You may now enter," Worf growled at them.

Jake set his face on neutral and followed Bashir into the planning room. Worf and Jadzia were both back in uniform, and the large schematic padds were back on the planning table.

"Sorry to have . . . intruded," Bashir murmured.

Jake had a sudden flash of inspiration, as he decided that part of the reason for the palpable tension in the room was that Bashir had always been after Jadzia for himself. Now *that* was a complication of being an adult that was exactly the same as being a teenager—always wanting what couldn't be had. *Maybe there isn't all that much difference between us after all,* Jake thought, as he suppressed the nervous grin that threatened to expose his unseasoned youth. He filed the revelation in his mind for accessing later, when he could more comfortably turn this extraordinary experience into something for a book. He was already full of ideas about how he could incorporate the whole scenario of traveling into the future into *Anslem,* the mostly autobiographical novel he had put aside a few years ago and to which he still returned sporadically when inspiration hit him.

"We have reviewed the schematics of the *Phoenix,*" Worf said stiffly.

A half-dozen different jokes sprang up unbidden in Jake's mind, but he pushed them down, followed Bashir's lead, and said nothing.

"Its weapons systems are impressive and adequate," Worf continued. "However, its propulsion characteristics are . . . unusual."

"They're Borg," Bashir said.

"Transwarp?" Jadzia asked without the slightest trace of embarrassment in her manner or voice. Obviously, being a conjoined Trill had its advantages, Jake thought enviously.

"That's not how the engines were called out in the specs," she said.

"Then maybe it's something beyond transwarp," Bashir suggested. "But believe it or not, an hour ago I met a Borg in the corridor. She's a Starfleet admiral."

"They're our allies," Jake volunteered as he saw Worf's and Jadzia's surprised reactions. "They signed a treaty with the Federation."

"Well," Jadzia said after a moment's thought, "if the *Phoenix*'s warp engines are based on Borg transwarp principles, then from the time they attacked Earth we know they've already demonstrated the ability to channel chronometric particles for propulsion. I would guess the ship is sound."

Then Jadzia looked from Jake to Bashir, as if somehow her Trill senses or experience told her that the two of them could tell her something more about the *Phoenix*. "I'm going to guess you two have data we don't," she said.

Bashir turned to Jake. "Mr. Sisko, tell it to them exactly as you told it to me."

There was no way out, at least none that Jake could think of. So he told the same story he had told Dr. Bashir in the mess hall, about how he could always tell when Nog was lying, how he had sensed Nog was lying about his confidence in the mission of the *Phoenix*, and most importantly, that he thought he knew *why* Nog might have lied.

"And why is that?" Worf asked.

Feeling like a traitor and a turncoat, Jake stared down at the dirty floor of the planning room.

"I think Nog . . . I think Nog actually *believes* that the universe will end."

No one responded to this statement, and after a few moments Jake glanced up to see that they were all waiting for him to go on.

"Just before that dinner we had," he said, "at Starbase 53. I went up to him."

"I remember that," Jadzia said. "I thought you were having an argument."

"We were. Sort of," Jake confirmed. "Anyway, I told him that . . . well . . . that he hadn't really changed all that much in twenty-five years. That he was still the same old Nog—" Jake smiled briefly as he remembered that part of the conversation. "—well, *older* Nog. And that it was like things hadn't changed—I could still see when he was . . . well, he used to call it adapting the truth to close a sale."

Bashir interrupted. "Jake—you told me that you told him flat out that he was lying."

"I know," Jake said defensively. "Okay, so that's what I told him. I told him I could tell he was lying to us when he said he had confidence in the *Phoenix* completing her mission."

"And his response?" Jadzia prompted.

"I . . . I wish I could remember the exact words, Commander. He kind of got mad at me then."

"Told you to keep your ridiculous *hew-mon* opinions to yourself?" Bashir prompted.

Jake nodded. "Yeah, something like that. And that there was really nothing to worry about. Then something about how he had seen how the river flowed, and that the balance could be restored."

"Was that a reference to the Great Material River of Ferengi myth?" Worf asked sharply.

"I don't think they call it myth," Jake said. "It's more like their religion."

"And in their religion," Jadzia said, "to say someone has seen how the Great Material River *flowed* is the same as saying they've seen the future."

"That's right," Jake said.

"And restoring the balance," Bashir added, "is what happens when the River returns to its source, having completed its course. It's nothing less than the Ferengi apocalypse. The end of time, as it were."

"Maybe . . . ," Jadzia offered. "Maybe Nog's just feeling discouraged."

"It doesn't matter what he's feeling," Jake said glumly. "It's that he made a prediction, that he claimed to see the future."

"I do not understand," Worf said.

Jake didn't know where to begin. But Jadzia apparently did.

"Everyone knows the Ferengi culture is steeped in business customs," she said to Worf. "Well, part of business is the ability to predict future market trends. So a Ferengi's business prowess—which would be the equivalent of how Klingons judge their own ability in battle—is one of those characteristics that gives him his reputation. As a result, Ferengi usually only make definitive predictions about the future— about how they've seen the 'river' flow—when they're absolutely certain what the outcome will be. And from the Ferengi point of view, the best way to know the outcome is to . . . well, stack the deck."

Worf narrowed his eyes at Jadzia. "You seem to know a great deal about Ferengi culture," he said heavily.

Jadzia shrugged. "So I dated one once. Some of them are kind of . . . cute."

Worf grunted. Then he glared at Jake. "Do you really believe your friend Nog will sabotage the *Phoenix* in order to ensure the universe is destroyed?"

Jake held up his hands as if defending himself from a physical rather than a verbal attack. "Hey, I didn't say anything about sabotage!"

"But that's the only logical conclusion we can draw from what you've said," Bashir said. "If this was one of your stories, Jake, what other motive could Nog have for what he said?"

Jake shook his head. "I . . . I don't know. But sabotage? That's different from just going into something without expecting it to succeed. Isn't it?"

Bashir patted Jake's back. "Look, that's all right. You've told us what you needed to tell us, and . . . if you're uncomfortable, you can go."

All at once, Jake felt as if he were eight years old again and his father was putting him to bed just as the dinner party conversation was getting interesting. He felt his face heat up again, but this time in annoyance, not embarrassment.

"I'm not a kid anymore, Dr. Bashir. I want to get back home or stop this or do *something* as much as the rest of you."

Jadzia put a restraining hand on Bashir's arm, and earned an annoyed look from her mate. "Jake, you do know that we *can't* go home, don't you?"

"Yeah, I know."

"So the *Phoenix* is the best option we have for stopping the Ascendancy's plan," Worf said with a touch of impatience.

"You mean, it might be," Bashir cautioned. "First we have to be absolutely certain about Nog's motives."

Jake rubbed his hands together in frustration. "If all of you are going to talk about motives, then what about this? If Nog had some plan to sabotage the *Phoenix,* why would he go to all the trouble of warping out to Starbase 53 to see us and then invite us onto the ship as its crew? I mean, we're a complication, aren't we?"

"That's a good point." Jadzia looked pointedly at Bashir.

"Unless we are also a good cover for Nog's plans," Worf said.

"We still don't know for sure what those plans are," Bashir countered.

"We could argue about this for hours," Jake said, looking at each of them in turn with frustration. *Adults!*

"We *have* to be certain about our next step," Bashir told him.

"But why waste all this time and effort?" Jake persisted. "Why don't we just *ask* Nog what he's going to do?"

"You said you had already tried that," Worf said.

"No. I said I *thought* he was lying. I didn't ask him why. And even if I had, there was no reason for him to give me a truthful answer."

"If he had no reason to tell the truth to you then," Jadzia asked, "what makes you think he'll tell the truth when you ask him again?"

"Because," Jake said, "if we wait till tomorrow morning we'll be on his ship. And that will give us all the leverage we need. Tell the truth or . . ."

"You would propose to sabotage the ship yourself?" Worf growled.

"Commander," Jake said seriously, "I don't believe that's what Nog is planning to do. So I do believe that he will do everything he can to keep us from damaging the *Phoenix.*"

"Everything he can," Jadzia said thoughtfully. "Even tell the truth?"

"It's like my dad says," Jake told her. "All we can do is hope."

"That is not an inspiring plan to entrust the survival of the universe to," Worf complained.

"No, it isn't," Jadzia said as she slipped an arm around her mate's waist. "But for now, hope is all we have."

Worf grunted again. "If that is true, Jadzia, then the universe is doomed."

CHAPTER 18

IN THE NIGHTMARE of the defiled ruins of Deep Space 9, now more like an ancient decaying fortress of war than an orbital station, Sisko felt Arla shudder in his arms.

He understood why.

The dead of this mad prison were coming to life.

Skeletal creatures emerged from the shadows, their gaunt torsos little more than cages of skin-wrapped bones, curved ribs that swept from a central exposed spine to encompass . . . nothing.

Bone feet clattered on the Promenade deck. Bone joints and bone hands creaked and clicked as the dead came ever closer, trudging over bodies that had not yet stirred.

"Is that the best you can do?" Dukat's voice suddenly echoed.

All the skeletons in Sisko's view stopped at the sound of that challenge. Each of their heads snapped to the side, the dark eye sockets of their inhumanly elongated skulls seeking the source of Dukat's voice.

And then Sisko noticed something that had no place among a walking army of the dead.

The skeletons were carrying weapons—sleek rifles, long and fluid, shining like cooled and captured strands of melted silver.

That was when Sisko realized these beings were not remnants of the dead, nor were they exactly dead.

They were Grigari.

A flash of red light set the shadows aflame, and a Grigari near Sisko flew apart violently. A skeletal arm fell at Sisko's feet, bending and flexing, leaking a thick yellow liquid from a web of coolant tubes—or were they blood vessels? Sisko couldn't be certain.

Whether Grigari were alive or dead, machine or animal—such questions had not been answered in his time, and he doubted they'd been answered in this one.

The remaining Grigari lifted their weapons and fired. Silver lightning pierced the air with high-pitched static. More red bolts sought out white-boned targets, dropping one after another of the walking skeletons in shattering explosions of flying limbs and dripping components.

As the battle raged, Dukat stalked through it, invulnerable, defended by a flickering ovoid of red energy that responded like a starship's shields, intensifying in color wherever Grigari weapons fire connected with it.

Sisko crouched down, and then dragged Arla off with him to find refuge in an alcove on the outer ring of the Promenade. The silver and red blasts of energy flew back and forth nonstop now, illuminating the darkness like lightning, causing the metal to sing in time with their impact strikes.

But the battle was ultimately one-sided. The Grigari weapons could not penetrate Dukat's personal shield, nor did they appear to be weakening it.

"I don't understand," Arla muttered as she huddled by Sisko.

"A minute ago, you seemed to understand everything," Sisko said.

Arla looked at him, confused. "Did I?" She shook her head so that her earring chain swayed. "I remember Dukat attacking you by the airlock . . . I know I swung at him . . . and then . . . we were here. Is this the Promenade?"

Sisko didn't try to explain what he couldn't yet explain. Instead he kept his eyes fixed on Dukat. The Cardassian was now standing in the very center of the Promenade concourse firing energy blasts at the attacking monstrosities as if he were a living phaser cannon. And

Sisko still had no idea where he and Arla were, or why Weyoun would deliver him into Dukat's hands.

A familiar glimmer of light at the far curve of the concourse caught his eye. Then another and another. And then Sisko comprehended just where the Grigari were coming from. *Not* from among the piles of dead bodies as he had first thought. They were being *beamed* into the station. But from where?

Sisko involuntarily blinked as a second intense source of crimson energy joined the Grigari fusillade of silver beams, and Dukat was blasted from behind by a meter-thick shaft of translucent fire that deformed the ovoid shield surrounding him.

The Cardassian stumbled forward, recovered, spun around, reached out both hands and shot his own energy blasts back toward the source of new attack.

Weyoun.

The Vorta was striding purposefully along the concourse, encased in the same type of flickering personal forcefield that protected Dukat and firing the same type of red energy bursts from each outstretched hand.

"BETRAYER!" Dukat screamed, as he seemed to gather his strength to withstand Weyoun's onslaught.

"MADMAN!" Weyoun shouted in reply.

Like sorcerers of legend, the two beings advanced on each other on an unstoppable collision course, energy shields blazing with power, energy beams crisscrossing the air in spectacular bursts.

And the eyes of both Vorta and Cardassian glowed with the red madness of the Pah-wraiths.

Ricocheting shafts of energy leaped from the two forcefields— searing piles of corpses, setting still-fleshed bodies on fire, and mowing down the relentlessly marching rows of Grigari, whose weapons' silver fire embroidered the air of the red-blasted battleground.

Dense smoke began to fill the Promenade, replacing the breathable atmosphere. Sisko knew he and Arla had to make their move now. Their eyes met in complete understanding, though each knew there was nowhere to go on the station.

A new glimmer of light appeared behind Arla, and two Grigari materialized. Sisko pushed her aside, tensing, ready to leap, stopping only in shock as he recognized a third figure now joining the Grigari.

Tom Riker.

But he was a surprise that Sisko did not intend to question.

"Come with me!" Riker shouted.

Sisko could barely hear the words above the lightning-like crackle and sizzle of the energy exchange on the concourse, but he had heard enough. He yanked Arla around to show her Riker and gestured for her to run ahead of him, behind the two Grigari guards. Then, before he followed after her, Sisko took one last look back at the concourse.

Now Dukat and Weyoun were locked in physical combat, encased within the *same* ovoid shield of red energy, both bodies inexplicably rippling and distorted by intermingling layers of flame. Their tangled bodies tumbled and spun like an airborne gyroscope, as if gravity were no longer of any importance to them. Their single shield trailed bright cascades of sparks and oily smoke wherever it struck the walls and decks of the Promenade.

Sisko called out to Riker ahead of him. Perhaps he would have the answers. "What's happening?"

The answer that floated back to him was less than satisfying. "That fight's been going on for millennia, Captain. It won't end here." Riker stopped to allow Arla and Sisko to catch up to him and his Grigari guards. Then he reached down to his side, and Sisko saw a slender silver tube attached to Riker's belt. "Take hold of me," Riker instructed. "Both of you."

Immediately Sisko gripped one of Riker's arms, Arla the other; Riker nodded at the two Grigari, and the guards marched forward like machines, adding the fire of their own weapons to the lethal struggle still continuing undiminished.

Now it seemed to Sisko that half the infrastructure of the Promenade was melting, coagulating into glowing pools of super-heated hull metal, reflecting blazing pyramids of corpses. Yet the joined forms of Dukat and Weyoun were still locked in battle, glowing hands around each other's throats, the two opposing forces oblivious to the destruction they were causing.

"Has *this* happened before?" Sisko asked, tightening his grip on Riker's arm.

Riker tapped a control on the silver cylinder. Lights on it began to flash, slowly at first, then faster. "Not here," Riker said cryptically.

"We were surprised that Dukat had actually brought this station within range. It seems you were the perfect bait to force his hand."

"What do you mean, bait?"

But before Riker could answer, everything flashed around them, and then Sisko and Arla and Riker were standing on—

—the Promenade again.

A different one.

Brightly lit. Carpeted. With clean, breathable air.

Storefronts lined the outer and inner rings. Customers—all Bajoran—walked slowly by the storefronts, looking at Sisko, Riker, and Arla, curious but not breaking their pattern, as if strangers beamed into their view every day.

And then Sisko remembered Dukat's words about looking into a mirror.

"That other station," he said to Riker, who was paying close attention to what appeared to be the small medical scanner he held close to Sisko, then to Arla. "It was in the *Mirror* Universe."

"That's right," Riker said, distracted, reacting with surprise to something he evidently saw on the scanner's small screen. "Dukat used his energy beam against you?"

Arla, still groggy, frowned at Riker's question. "Yes. Is there long-term—" But she didn't have a chance to finish her own question. Riker had touched the medical scanner to her neck, and after a soft hissing noise, she at once fell backwards.

Sisko caught the Bajoran before she could hit the deck of the Promenade. He glared at Riker. "Hasn't she been through enough?"

Riker slipped the scanner back into his belt. "We take possession very seriously around here. She wasn't showing signs of being currently inhabited by a Pah-wraith. But she has been. Quite recently. Probably a low-level transference when Dukat attacked her."

Sisko rubbed at his temples, as if by doing so he could rid his brain of the disturbing thoughts Riker's news provoked in him. Possession. "I thought you people *worship* the Pah-wraiths."

Riker regarded him with surprise. "Not the ones from the Fire Caves. There was a reason why Kosst Amojan and those who followed him were expelled from the True Temple."

"And that would be?" Sisko asked wearily, angrily. Would no one tell him what was going on here?

Riker declined to enlighten him. "Something for you to discuss with the Emissary." He nodded at Arla, supported once again in Sisko's arms. "Let's get her to the Infirmary."

Sisko struggled to control his impatience as he followed Riker along the concourse, distracting himself by trying to identify landmarks from his past. But the layout had completely changed from his day. The Infirmary was where Garak's tailor shop had been, and all the equipment within it was Bajoran. In fact, except for the basic architecture, *everything* about the station now was Bajoran in design and color.

Riker had Sisko put Arla on a diagnostic bed, then turned her over to the care of a young Bajoran physician.

"Now what?" Sisko asked, as he followed Riker to an office area near the Infirmary's entrance.

"We wait for the Emissary."

"If he survives."

Riker smiled grimly. "He always does. The struggle among the Pah-wraiths is as old as the war between the Pah-wraiths and the False Prophets. It won't end until the universe ends."

Sisko wanted to grab Riker by his white beard and shove his face against the closest wall. Weyoun's followers were insufferable. This entire situation was insufferable. He longed for his own time. His son. Kasidy. His station. His life.

Riker appeared to sense Sisko's mood. "You have a problem with that?"

"I didn't think the universe was ending," Sisko said bluntly. "I thought it was being . . . transfigured."

Riker kept his eyes locked with Sisko's. "You've spent time with the Emissary. What do you believe?"

"I believe the Emissary is insane."

Riker appeared to consider Sisko's statement for a few moments, as if trying to uncover hidden subtleties, then he withdrew his medical scanner again and moved it around Sisko's face, then around the sides of his head.

"What are you looking for now?" Sisko demanded.

To his surprise, Riker leaned closer as if to read the scanner's display screen, and whispered, "I'm working for Starfleet. The *real* one."

Sisko's anger vanished at once. He caught Riker's eyes, and in an

instant an unspoken, blessedly sane, and understandable communication had flashed between them.

Tom Riker had just placed his life in his hands. And Sisko knew
he wouldn't—couldn't—betray that trust.

After an awkward moment, Sisko looked at the small medical
scanner. "Is everything all right?"

"No sign of possession," Riker said loudly. "Of any kind."

"Good to know." Sisko waited before saying anything else, hoping Riker would give some clue as to how they were to proceed.

But Riker gave none.

Sisko gestured at the station around them, not knowing what else
to say. "Can I ask how the station was restored?"

Riker looked puzzled.

"Deep Space 9," Sisko said.

"Oh! No, no," Riker answered. "This isn't Terok Nor. It's Empok
Nor. The Emissary had it towed here from the Trivas system. One of
the prophecies of . . . I believe it was Eilin, was that the True
Emissary would restore the Gateway. So . . ."

Sisko needed to act on what Riker had told him, but it was clear
that Riker felt they were under some type of surveillance.

"I'm not familiar with the prophecies of Eilin," he said carefully.

Riker didn't seem to think that was too important. "How about
Shabren?"

Sisko nodded. Shabren's Fifth Prophecy was one with which he
was especially familiar.

"Eilin was a contemporary of Shabren. And of Naradim. The
three great mystics of Jalbador. Though Eilin and Naradim were considered apocryphal by the religious leaders of your time. Until
recently, most of what they wrote was known only to scholars."

Despite his earlier relief, Sisko felt now as if he were drowning in
a sea of small talk. He looked around the Infirmary, trying to see
where surreptitious sensors might be hidden. "But not Shabren."

Riker smiled. "People used to say that Shabren's writings were
never censored because no one could be certain what he was saying."

Sisko didn't want this to go on any longer. "When will Arla be
released?"

"That will be up to the Emissary."

"Where are the rest of my crew and the people from the *Defiant?*"

"The Emissary has made arrangements for them all to be quartered here, until . . . the ceremony."

Sisko stared at Riker until Riker acknowledged the unspoken question.

"At the end. When both halves of the Temple will open their doors at the same time and in the same place, and . . . they will be rejoined, praise be to the True Prophets of the One True Temple."

"In what now—nine days?"

Riker nodded.

"How'd you come to work for Weyoun?" Sisko asked. "And not Starfleet?"

"When Cardassia fell, the camp I was imprisoned in at Lazon II was liberated by the Grigari. It was Starfleet that abandoned me to that camp. Starfleet cowardice and—"

"As I recall," Sisko interrupted, "you willingly sacrificed your freedom to save your crew and the *Defiant.*"

Riker's eyes flickered in warning. "That's not how it happened and you know it. Starfleet tricked me into that camp, and the Emissary freed me. And the more I studied the Bajoran texts, the more I realized that the Emissary was right. I owe him everything. We all do," he said emphatically.

From Riker's overly intense response, Sisko realized that the man must have created an elaborate cover story to gain Weyoun's trust. And if Weyoun's supporters had undertaken any efforts to double-check that story, then it must be that Starfleet had altered its records of Tom Riker's attempt to hijack the *Defiant* from DS9 and his subsequent selfless surrender, in order to confirm his story. To Sisko, that suggested that Riker was supported by the highest levels of Starfleet.

Sisko looked past Riker to Arla. She was still unconscious. The Bajoran physician was in the midst of meticulously arranging blinking neural stimulators on Arla's forehead and temples. "Where's your . . . your brother, I suppose you'd call him these days?"

"You mean my transporter duplicate," Riker said. "He made captain finally. The *Enterprise.* Took over from Picard."

"The *Enterprise* is a fine ship."

Riker frowned. "It's probably not the one you're thinking of. The E was lost in the Battle of Rigel VII. An unknown terrorist group attempted to alter the gravitational balance between Rigel and its moon. Caused them to collide. Starfleet claimed it was agents of the Ascendancy, but we don't do that kind of thing. It was probably Starfleet agents attempting to make us look bad.

"Anyway, no one told Picard about Starfleet's involvement, and he sacrificed his ship to destroy the gravity generator. Reconfigured the deflector dish or something, so that the ship and the generator together formed an artificial black hole."

Riker cleared his throat. "Starfleet held another hearing—three starships is an awful number to have lost—but there were precedents, so they gave Picard the *Enterprise*-F. First of its class, for once. Incredible ship. Think of the *Defiant* to the tenth power. Multivector assault capability. Built specifically to fight the Grigari. Fired the first shot in the . . . unfortunate miscommunication incident that resulted in the Sector 001 disaster—"

"You mean the destruction of Earth," Sisko said, appalled that such a hideous event should be referred to as an "incident."

"Completely avoidable," Riker said. "But my transporter duplicate seemed to be looking for a fight that day. First hint of trouble he went to battle stations, fired at the Grigari flagship, and—the *Enterprise*-F lasted all of three minutes in battle."

"So . . . he's dead," Sisko said.

"They all are. Troi. La Forge. Krueger. Tom and B'Elanna Paris. Torres. My duplicate's wife. End of an era."

"End of a world, you mean."

Riker nodded almost subliminally, as if to let Sisko know that he shared the captain's outrage, though he could not admit it publicly.

Sisko knew he and Riker had to talk free of surveillance. "I want to find out more about what happened on Earth," he said. "Is there a time we could talk again?"

Again, Riker's signal to him was barely perceptible. "There'll be time enough for study after the Ascension," Riker said. "Every being will have all questions answered then. I think a better use of your remaining time in the linear realm would be to visit B'hala."

"Would that be permitted?"

"I believe it's demanded." Riker held Sisko's gaze. "Portions of the city have been restored to what they were tens of thousands of years ago, exact in every way. No computers, no communications systems . . ."

No surveillance, Sisko thought, understanding. "I'd like to see that," he said.

"I think the Emissary has already started making plans."

Frustration swept over Sisko again, because there seemed to be nothing more to say. Yet if Riker was telling the truth with his revelation about working for Starfleet, then both he and Riker were committed to stopping Weyoun before the Vorta could merge the wormholes.

After a few minutes of silent waiting, the Bajoran physician joined them to let them know that Arla would recover from Dukat's attack. And then he asked them to turn their backs, because a new patient was arriving.

Riker complied with the physician's instruction at once. After a moment, Sisko followed his lead. Then the glow of a transporter filled the room, and Sisko detected the sounds of quick movement among the medical staff along with the irregular, rasping exhalations of someone having difficulty breathing.

Sisko risked a quick, surreptitious glance over his shoulder in time to see Weyoun—floating in an antigrav field, his naked body in a glistening coat of blood, his flesh disfigured with gaping wounds and charred patches of tissue. As his face turned to one side, Sisko saw that one of Weyoun's long ear ridges was missing, ripped out of place.

Frantic Bajoran physicians clustered round the Vorta's body, working rapidly, their huddle preventing Sisko from seeing exactly what treatment they were attempting to apply, though he caught glimpses of them cleaning out the gashes, abrading crusted skin, and wiping off blood.

Sisko felt Riker tap his arm, saw him shake his head in warning, as if he shouldn't be watching. But just then the physicians stepped back, and Sisko clearly saw Weyoun's most damaging wounds decrease in size until they were little more than minor skin scrapes any home protoplaser could heal.

And then even those signs of battle damage faded. Weyoun had been *restored.*

To Sisko, what he had witnessed was like watching Starfleet sensor logs of Borg ships undergoing self-repair.

He suddenly became aware that even Weyoun's hoarse breathing had eased. And with that realization, he saw the Vorta's head slowly turn in his direction. Then Weyoun's eyelids fluttered opened, and the Vorta looked at him—into him—as a soft red glow pulsed once in his eyes.

Sisko didn't look away.

Weyoun smiled.

"What is he?" Sisko asked Riker.

"No one knows," Riker replied in a low voice, "unless he's like the Grigari."

Riker's words made sudden, terrible sense to Sisko.

Defeating Weyoun had just become much harder.

Because how could Sisko stop an enemy who was already dead?

CHAPTER 19

Nog adjusted his tunic, checked to see that his combadge was on straight, then—out of habit—turned to the automated transporter console and said "Energize," as if the *U.S.S. Phoenix* actually needed a transporter technician for such a simple task.

Ten columns of light swirled into life on the elevated transporter pad, then coalesced into the temporal refugees snatched from the *Defiant,* including his friends: Jake. Lieutenant Commander Worf. Lieutenant Commander Dax. Dr. Bashir. Nog also noticed three others in the group who were unfamiliar to him—a young Centaurian ensign and two other Starfleet officers—as well as two *hew-mon* civilians. And, of course, Vash.

He wasn't at all surprised that it was Vash who spoke first, complaining as always.

"I said I didn't want to volunteer for this stupid mission!"

Nog watched, amused, as the archaeologist angrily pulled away from Bashir, who was vainly trying to calm her. But then Vash jumped off the pad to confront *him.*

"You!" she snapped. "Who's in charge up here?"

Nog resigned himself to the confusion someone like Vash could bring to a ship as complex as the *Phoenix.* As he saw it, he really had no choice. Even the conscientious objectors from Bajor who thought they'd be spending the rest of their lives—and the life of the universe—in prayer chambers on Mars would be brought aboard this ship soon enough. And they wouldn't be any happier about it than Vash was.

"I am," he told her.

Vash laughed mockingly. *"You. In charge of all this?"*

"As far as you are concerned, yes." Nog regarded her with some annoyance. His schedule didn't allow for annoyance. By now, T'len might already know the refugees were missing.

"Well, I want off." Vash said.

"That is not going to happen."

"You can't kidnap me like this!"

Nog sighed. The universe was scheduled to end in a little over seven days. "It's not as if you have time to lodge a formal complaint."

Vash made a threatening fist. "Then I guess I'll just have to lodge this up your—"

"Enough!"

Worf's commanding voice froze every movement in the transporter room. Though the Klingon stepped down to a position beside the belligerent archaeologist, he still towered over her. "As we agreed with Captain T'len, you are in our custody until we depart on the *Phoenix.* You will then be held in your quarters in the personnel dome until . . ." Worf stopped speaking, as if embarrassed to continue.

"Yeah, right," Vash sneered. "Until the 'end of hostilities.' " She glared at Nog. "Don't think I don't know what's going on in that swollen little skull of yours. You have no intention of letting me off this ship, do you?"

Nog kept his expression completely neutral. "Of course I'll let you off. Everyone will return to Mars today for further training. The *Phoenix* is not due to depart for another forty hours."

And then, knowing he had delivered another adaptation of the truth, Nog couldn't stop himself from glancing at Jake.

He saw the frown on Jake's face. Did he know? Had he guessed?

Nog turned away. He *knew* he wasn't that transparent. How could he have succeeded as a Ferengi if any . . . manipulation of the facts he resorted to was that easy to detect? No, there wasn't anything wrong with *him.* It was Jake. Had to be. Either Jake was upset about something completely unrelated to Nog's action, or his frown, if it indicated he was on to Nog, was the result of some non-*hew-mon* blood in the Siskos' family history. Something that could give Jake some kind of . . . of telepathy. *That's it!* Nog thought. The only way Jake could know for sure what Nog was doing was if Jake were a mind reader—even of Ferengi minds. And that was just impossible.

Feeling much better already, Nog clapped his hands, motioned toward the door. "Well, let's get this tour under way. I'm sure you'll find the *Phoenix* is a most impressive vessel."

The doors slid open to reveal the wide corridor beyond. Like every other habitable area on the *Phoenix,* the bulkheads, deck, and ceiling were unfinished, in keeping with Starfleet's wartime priorities.

"We already know the ship's impressive," Jake said, hanging back as the refugees entered the corridor. "We've seen the schematics, remember?"

Vash halted beside Jake, folded her arms defiantly. "Yeah, the kid's right. Why do we even need this tour anyway?"

Nog sympathized with Jake as he saw the resentful look that had settled on his friend's face at that "kid" reference. But being no kid himself, Nog addressed Vash sternly. "In case you haven't noticed, all the shipyard's holodecks are off-line. To understand this ship, you have to see it firsthand."

It didn't matter to Nog that neither Vash nor Jake believed his explanation. The important thing was that Jake, for whatever reason, had yet to challenge anything he had said so far.

But if he really is a mind reader, Nog thought, *then at least he'll understand why I* have *to do this.*

Vash, on her part, was whining so much about everything that no one was even listening to her anymore. Nog wished he didn't have to, either.

"Let's join the others," he suggested in a firm voice, and led the way without waiting for a response.

As they made their way toward a bank of turbolifts, Nog told his followers about the ship's construction. For all its great size, interestingly enough, the *Phoenix* had less habitable space than the *Defiant.* In fact, eighty-two percent of the ship's volume was taken up by its power generators, including an unprecedented array of forty-eight linked transwarp engines, any thirty-six of which would be sufficient for their voyage into the past.

As he and his party waited for the lift cars to arrive, Nog heard Bashir say, "I find it difficult to believe that a ship with forty-eight engines could even get out of spacedock with a crew of only twenty-two."

Nog smiled expansively. This was something he could explain. "Actually, Doctor, the *operational* crew is even smaller—fourteen. The other eight crew members are the engineers who will deploy the deep-time charges at B'hala. Or at the site of what eventually will become B'hala."

"Fourteen," Bashir said. "Even with full automation, how is that possible?"

The lifts arrived. "It's possible," Nog said, "because forty-four of the engines are designed to be used only once. Repairs and mainte-nance won't be necessary, so neither is an engineering crew."

Nog ushered the refugees into two different cars, joining Jake and four others in one of them. "Bridge," he said. The doors closed, and with a sudden jolt the car began to move.

"Don't you have inertial dampeners?" Jadzia asked him.

Nog coughed nervously. "The structural integrity field is still being aligned," he said. "So the dampeners are off for the moment." This time, he didn't dare look at Jake.

With another jolt, the car stopped and the doors opened onto the bridge of the *Phoenix*.

Nog stepped out, and though it was so familiar to him, he tried to see the bridge through the eyes of the temporal refugees. Certainly, he thought, they would recognize its near-circular layout, despite the fact that most of the wall stations were still obscured by tacked-up plastic sheets and dust shields. And there was a main viewer dead ahead, switched off for now, providing a central focus for the overall layout.

But the chairs and workstations would be different to old eyes, he knew. Almost alien, in fact.

There were fourteen chairs in total on the bridge, one for each of the operational crew, arranged in wide rows facing the viewer. Unlike the simple seats his guests would remember from their star-ship duties, these were enclosed units, with curving sides and tops, full body-web restraints, fold-down consoles, and holographic dis-plays.

Worf was the first to deliver his assessment of the design. "This is not a ship built for battle."

Nog knew that the Klingon meant that by confining the crew within those chairs, he could see there was little chance for carrying out the swift replacement of injured personnel.

"But twenty-five thousand years in the past," Nog told Worf, "there will be no one for us to fight."

Worf didn't look at all convinced. "We must still get to Bajor in *this* time."

"And to do that, we will be protected by the largest task force Starfleet has ever assembled," Nog said.

"Hold it," Jake said suddenly. "I don't understand. If this ship can take us into the past, why don't we just slingshot around *Earth's* sun, go back twenty-five thousand years, and *then* go to Bajor without having to fight *anyone?*"

"It's a question of temporal accuracy," Nog said stiffly to his childhood friend, who was still so close to childhood. "The farther we are from Bajor when we travel back in time, the greater the error factor we introduce into our final temporal coordinates at Bajor itself. Stardates aside, time really is relative to different inertial frames of reference. If we were to follow exactly a twenty-five-thousand-year slingshot trajectory around Earth's sun, we might only travel back twenty thousand years in regard to Bajor—and land when Bajorans had already settled the B'hala region."

"Then let's go back *fifty* thousand years," Jake said. "A twenty percent error would still bring us to a time before the site was settled."

As Nog tried to think of the best way to answer, Jadzia came to his rescue. "Jake, I think they're facing two difficulties with that idea," the Trill said helpfully. "First, I don't think anyone could build a ship capable of going back much more than thirty thousand years. Not without a radical new theory of temporal physics. And second, just from the geological data I've seen describing the proposed placement of the deep-time charges, I'd say the B'hala area was subjected to severe earthquakes or volcanic disruptions a thousand years or so before it was settled, significantly disturbing all the underlying strata. Is that right, Captain Nog?"

"Exactly," Nog said. He held his hands together as he took over the explanation for Jake. "You see, Jake, we're actually trying to arrive within a very narrow *window* of time. We can't arrive any later than twenty-five thousand years, because someone might see us. But we can't arrive any earlier than twenty-*six* thousand years, because before that there *were* a series of powerful crustal upheavals that would probably destroy the deep-time charges. That means we're attempting to achieve an error factor of plus or minus two percent on our first try. To even have a chance at that level of accuracy, we have no choice but to slingshot around *Bajor's* sun—and no other."

"You people are just crazy," Vash muttered.

"Excuse me, but we are attempting to save the universe," Nog said.

"Yeah, in the most bureaucratic, bungling Starfleet way you can." Vash threw her arms in the air. "What's wrong with you people?! Don't any of you get it? Do you know how many things have to go right for this ridiculous scheme to work?"

"It is not ridiculous!" Nog said.

Vash stared at him long and hard. "You know what, Captain? I don't believe you. Your heart—or your lobes or whatever it is you Ferengi invest with meaning—just isn't in it."

Nog was terrified. Was Vash a mind reader, too? Or could *every-one* tell what he was thinking? "I suppose Q gave you the power to read my mind," he said sarcastically.

"No one can read what passes for a Ferengi mind," Vash said with a rude smirk. "And I don't *have* to be a mind reader to know that you're not on the level. Oh, I've negotiated my share of deals with Ferengi. I know how you operate."

Thoroughly rattled though he was, Nog knew he had to act quickly. He couldn't risk any of the others following Vash's line of reasoning, even if there didn't seem to be much reason to it for now.

"Vash. Please. I understand what's really upsetting you and I guarantee you'll be able to leave the ship."

Then Nog was aware of Jake stepping to his side. "Nog," his friend said in a low voice. "We have to talk."

"Frinx," Nog sputtered. "What's wrong with you people?!"

"That's what I said!" Vash chimed in.

"STOP IT!"

Everyone stopped talking and stared at Nog.

Nog felt the sweet rush of power. He had given an order and had it obeyed. Instantly. Just like Worf.

"Much better," he said. "Now, to continue our tour, I'd like everyone to take a chair." He directed Worf to tactical, Jadzia to main sensors, Bashir to life-support, his chest swelling with pride as all three complied without protest. He then quickly polled the Starfleet personnel on their specialties and assigned them also to appropriate chairs.

Soon only Vash, Jake, and the three civilians were left without places.

"Can we go home now?" Vash asked without much conviction.

Nog pointed to the back of the bridge, where a series of padded half-cylinders were inset into the bulkhead.

"There's an awful lot of crash-padding on this ship," Vash said darkly as she backed into one cylinder, then jerked as autorestraints snaked around her. "What the hell's going on, Captain?"

"Our trajectory around Bajor's sun will be very rough. I want everyone to get a chance to try out the restraint devices."

Vash glared at him, but she was firmly secured against the bulkhead.

Nog looked around the bridge. Now he was the only one standing. It was going to work.

"Don't worry. We'll have plenty of time to talk later," he said to Jake as Jake adjusted his cylinder's restraint harness. Then he said "Very good" to everyone else as he walked around to the front of the bridge, where they'd be able to see him. "Now we're going to try out the holographic displays. You'll be able to see the status of any station on the bridge without leaving your—"

With a rush of static and a sudden glare of light, the main viewer came on behind Nog.

Nog felt his lobes shrivel. It could only be one person.

"Captain Nog, what are you doing on the *Phoenix?*"

As Nog expected, T'len's face filled the viewer. Judging from the equipment behind her, she was in the main flight-control center deep below the nanoassembler facilities on the surface. Nog took that as a good sign. She'd be on the bridge of the *Augustus* soon enough.

"I'm conducting a familiarization tour for the crew."

"They'll have two days for that en route to Bajor. Why have you pulled the work crews from engineering bay four?"

"Their work was done," Nog said, with what he hoped was the proper amount of surprise.

"Not according to the computer records," T'len said.

"It's not unusual for the records to lag," Nog pointed out.

"Report to me at ground control at once."

He held up his hand. "May I finish the tour first?"

"At *once*," T'len repeated. She reached for something out of sight, and the viewer went dark.

Nog turned back to face his crew. "Well, I think that brings this part of the tour to a close."

He braced himself for the first complaints.

"Captain Nog!" Worf said indignantly. "The restraints will not release."

"That's odd," Nog said in what he hoped was an offhand manner. "Let me check with the master control."

Nog walked quickly to the side of the bridge, straight to the transporter control station. The small clusters of transporter pads to either side of the bridge had been his contribution to the design of the *Phoenix*. He'd remembered how convenient it was to have similar facilities in Ops at Deep Space Nine. So much time had been saved. Like now.

Nog put his hand on the control station's security plate. "Computer, run Nog Five and Nog Alpha. Command authority Alpha Alpha One."

The starboard pads came to life first, and the five Bajorans from the past suddenly appeared. Civilians and militia alike, they were all in believers' robes. Two were kneeling in prayer. Everyone looked confused by what had happened.

"Quickly!" Nog commanded. "Go back to the crash cylinders!"

The other temporal refugees, who by now could have no doubt that Nog was acting on his own, started calling out to the Bajorans to release them.

But Nog slapped a red panel on a tactical station, and instantly a siren sounded and red lights flashed as the ship went to General Quarters.

"Hurry!" Nog shouted at the Bajorans. "We're under attack!"

Then the port pad flashed into life, and Nog was running for it, even before the frail form of Admiral Picard had fully materialized.

"My word," the Old Man said, as he half-stumbled from the pad. He was in his uniform, but it was wrinkled, as if he'd been asleep in a chair. "Is everything all right, Will?"

"Perfect," Nog said. He looked up at the graceful sweep of the illumination ceiling. "Computer: activate all shields. Rotating pattern Nog One." Gently he guided Picard to the captain's chair and helped him settle in. Nog also took the precaution of disabling the control console.

Now everyone was secure, and the *Phoenix* was impenetrable to attack. Nog knew that there was no turning back.

He was stealing a starship.

The only starship that might save the universe.

He ran back across the bridge, ignoring the clamor of the sirens and the shouted protests of those trapped inside their crash chairs. According to a time readout on the navigation substation, he had three minutes left to clear the spacedock and go to transwarp. In three minutes and one second, every simulation he had run for this operation had ended with the arrival of a Starfleet task force that could keep the *Phoenix* pinned in position until commandos came aboard.

Nog swiftly checked to see that the shields were still flashing off and on in the preset pattern, then began overriding the security codes on the transwarp station. He gave fervent thanks that given his position as Integrated Systems Manager it was not a difficult procedure—merely a time-consuming one.

Then the navigation displays came up, free of security blocks. Nog checked the time. Ninety seconds. He was going to make it. All he had to do now was wait for—

Nog squealed, as a large hand gripped his shoulder and yanked him away from the bridge station. He tumbled head-over-heels and came to a stop, sprawled on his stomach, watching as Worf's huge boots clomped toward him.

"No!" Nog gasped. "You don't understand!" He looked over at the chair Worf had been confined to and saw smoke rising from its cracked protective covering. Obviously a redesign would be in order.

But Nog's protests did no good, because Worf's powerful hand was already crushing his right ear, dragging him back to his feet as he squealed again.

"For your betrayal, you have brought dishonor not only to your house, but to your species," Worf thundered at him.

"I haven't betrayed anyone!" Nog squeaked. "You really *don't* understand!"

"Do you deny that you have joined the Ascendancy?"

"No-o!" Nog's hands scrabbled ineffectually at Worf's, vainly trying to dislodge the Klingon's brutally painful grip on his sensitive lobe. His entire head throbbed with agony. The intense pain robbed him of all reason.

"Then why are you attempting to steal this starship?"

"I can explain later! I *will* explain later!"

Without even seeming to expend any physical effort, Worf lifted him high in the air until their faces were a centimeter apart. "You will explain *now*."

Even to his own ear, Nog's voice was reduced to the high-pitched yowl of a cat. "Commander, please, you have to put me down before—" Nog started gagging, the pain was becoming unbearable.

"Before *what?*" Worf bellowed deafeningly.

And before Nog could answer, before Nog could warn Worf about what was about to happen—

It happened.

Nog saw three flashes of light flicker in the Klingon's dark, enraged eyes. He saw Worf look up, past the Ferengi in hand, and react in shock.

Then three more flashes reflected from Worf's sweat-covered skin. The odd rhythm of the light's appearance, Nog knew, was matched with the pattern of the rotating shields, timed to create transporter windows every few seconds.

Worf looked at Nog with unbridled disgust, then threw him to the deck.

Nog shivered with relief as he rubbed his crushed ear. He saw Worf slowly raise his hands as if in response to an unspoken order.

"I'm sorry," Nog croaked, but his throat was too raw for his voice to be heard over the GQ sirens that continued to blare.

And then Worf pivoted suddenly and launched himself to the side and—

—was hit on three sides by disruptor beams.

The Klingon fell heavily to the deck, his massive body motionless, smoke curling from each beam's impact on his uniform.

Nog shuddered. Everything was all wrong. It wasn't supposed to have happened like this.

Another hand took hold of his arm, pulled him to his feet.

Nog looked up. He was getting tired of this. Everyone tugging him one way, then another.

Then he recognized the person who stood before him.

Centurion Karon.

Three more Romulans beamed in behind her. They quickly ran to join the five others scattered around the bridge.

"How much time?" Nog gasped.

"Twenty seconds to spare," Karon said. "Congratulations, Captain. By turning over this vessel to the New Romulan Star Empire, you have guaranteed there will be a future."

Nog nodded, dazed. Then he felt a sudden drop in the deck as the inertial dampeners came on.

"Transwarp is enabled," a Romulan called out over the sirens.

"Activate," Karon ordered. "Transfactor twelve."

A deep rumbling came through the deck and reverberated through the bridge.

"Screen on," Karon said, as if she had flown this ship for years.

The main viewer came back to life, and on it stars flew past in stuttering flashes of color, too fast for the ship's computers to render in smooth lines.

"We have decided to call this vessel the *Alth'Indor.*" The Romulan centurion smiled at Nog again. "It means 'phoenix.' We have the same story in our mythology."

Nog no longer cared—and he was sure his expression showed it.

"Don't worry," Karon said briskly, as if she also had no trouble reading his mood, if not his mind. "You have done the right thing."

That sentiment Nog could agree with, even though he knew his reasons were not the same as hers.

The stars sped by even faster.

The ship sped toward its journey through time.

Some of those on board the *Phoenix* would survive, Nog knew. That much was inarguable.

But not even Nog knew who those few would be.

CHAPTER 20

GARAK SAVORED the satisfying crunch his boots made as they crushed the ancient stones of B'hala. They had something of the same consistency as sun-bleached bones. At least so he had heard, and now, happily, he could confirm it for himself.

In this future, he thought, Bajoran boots had very likely walked through the rubble of Cardassia Prime, as the Bajorans had reveled in the destruction of his world. Somehow, that made his sense of anticipation for the coming destruction of everything else more reasonable. Especially this holy city, which had unleashed on the universe the ultimate means to the ultimate end.

"Garak? Are you all right?"

Garak turned and held up his hand to shield his eyes from the excruciating glare of the space mirror, which was low on the horizon and in his line of sight. At any given time, he recalled being told, there were two of those mirrors illuminating B'hala, making the city always appear as if it were high noon on a world with binary suns, even in the dead of night. The double shadows were disconcerting, giving as they did to everything the unreal look of artificiality. There was, however, another apparition that was even more unusual.

Garak smiled at the sight of Odo in penitent's robes. "Tell me,

Odo. Are those robes part of you? Or did our charming hosts make you put them on like the rest of us?"

Odo adjusted his robes with impatience. "The ones I formed weren't proper, I was told. I am actually wearing these. I don't know how you solids stand it."

"Ah, if I had known you were amenable to wearing clothes, I would have offered you a discount at my shop. Believe me, there is nothing like the kiss of Argelian silk to soothe the troubles of the day."

Odo folded his arms—an oddly bulky gesture, Garak observed, given what the changeling was wearing. "Don't think I haven't noticed that you've changed the subject," Odo said gruffly.

Garak bowed his head in a sign of respect. And he did respect Odo. In a way, as an adversary, more often than not. Though sometimes as an ally. The apparent contradiction did not trouble Garak. He was quite comfortable with the fact that his relationships with others were often as fluid as the politics of Cardassia. What was life, after all, but change?

"I am fine, Constable. And I do appreciate your concern in asking."

Garak could see that Odo was unlikely to accept his statement as the final word in the matter. While he waited patiently for whatever it was that Odo would decide to do next, Garak turned his attention to the surrounding restored buildings of heavily eroded stone blocks, noting that no structure appeared to be more than two or three stories high, and that most were still supported by crude wooden scaffolding lashed together by vegetable-fiber rope. Intriguingly, it was as if he and Odo were thousands of years in the past. Except for the weapons carried by their Grigari guards, who had taken up positions far in the distance, Garak could detect no sign of technology or any other indication that this city was the wellspring of an interstellar movement that had brought the Federation to its figurative knees.

Odo coughed. From experience, Garak knew the awkward gesture was the changeling's way of changing the subject. Odo wasn't much of a conversationalist.

"Garak, I really don't know any way of saying this that doesn't sound completely inadequate, but I am sorry for your loss."

Garak felt quite sure that Odo's statement was false. The

Cardassians had never been a friend to Odo. But social discourse did require the lubrication of lies.

"Thank you, Odo. I appreciate your good wishes, as well."

Odo cleared his throat. "If I had heard my world had been destroyed, I don't think I'd be taking it like you."

"What would you have me do, Odo? We're all terminal cases. Even our cultures. Even our worlds. A hundred years for an individual and he's gone, only a memory for a hundred more, at most. Perhaps longer if he's someone to whom they build statues. But after a thousand years, whom do we really remember? Garak shrugged, enjoying the rustle of the robes he wore. On some backward worlds of his acquaintance, such garments would be considered quite fashionable.

"You must remember that as nation states rise and fall, each one is always eager to erase its predecessor from the records. I doubt if Cardassian historians even knew the names of more than a few of the warlords who ruled our world, or parts of it, at least, one after the other. And each of those worthy souls fought mighty battles, brought death to tens of thousands, gave life to tens of thousands more. Yet their empires are gone, their deeds forgotten.

"And worlds, my dear Odo, are no different from people or countries. Had the universe continued, Cardassia's sun would have swollen into a red giant, or gone nova someday. And then the whole planet, the sum total of every pre-spaceflight Cardassian who had ever lived, warlords and rabble alike, would have returned to the elemental gas from which the planet had condensed in the first place. Five billion years from now, perhaps some of my parents' atoms would come back to life in the bodies of aliens we can't imagine. Aliens who would never know of the glories of Cardassia, because they would be too busy fighting mighty battles of their own. The same would happen to Earth. And to Vulcan. Even to your Great Link."

Garak smiled at the changeling. "Death is never a surprise, Odo. Only the timing of it."

Odo snorted. "I wish I had your blunt outlook on life."

"No you don't," Garak said amiably. He pointed ahead, to where the others were gathering around an excavation site with Sisko and Weyoun. "Shall we continue? The Emissary did say he had something of interest to show us. I can't imagine what it might be."

"We'll continue," Odo said. "For a while at least."

Garak appreciated the changeling's flair for the dramatic. So many people lacked it these days.

As they walked on together, Garak decided that Odo would be an ally today. At the same time as he made that decision, he found himself idly wondering which number was greater—the grains of sand that covered B'hala or the number of stars in the sky, somewhere beyond those infernal space mirrors.

He took a moment to contemplate, in honest wonder, the idea that something—some physical process as yet unknown and undefined—might actually have the power to erase every star from the heavens.

The very concept was astounding.

And to be present, to see it actually take place . . .

In truth, the possibility was making him feel privileged, even humble.

And considering how few things had actually had that effect on him in his lifetime, the experience was novel, and one he fully intended to enjoy exploring.

As far as exploring other things, however, it appeared Weyoun had been a busy Vorta.

He had obviously invited all eighteen prisoners from the *Defiant* to see B'hala before the end. Garak recalled that back in his present, B'hala had been merely a series of tunnels deep beneath the mountains. But here and now, the great lost city was exposed to the sky— at least, according to the briefing they had been given, a third of it was exposed. The rest apparently was still buried, and was destined to stay that way until the end of time.

Despite the fact that the end of time was only seven days and some few hours away, Garak couldn't help being fascinated, as he and Odo approached the other prisoners who stood beside Weyoun, that the Bajoran workers under the Vorta's command were diligently continuing their digging and tunneling, and recording every detail of the flayed site—as if any of it would or could matter anymore.

But the latest excavation in B'hala was a very special one, or so Weyoun had said when he had offered his invitation.

Right now, in fact, the Emissary to the True Prophets was crouched down at the lip of the deep pit—its opening was almost twenty meters across—peering with great interest into its depths, which were crisscrossed by wooden ladders and catwalks and only dimly lit by flickering combustion torches. The angles of the space mirrors appeared to be set too low to provide any appreciable downward illumination.

Behind the kneeling figure of Weyoun, Garak recognized Captain Sisko, Major Kira, and Commander Arla. Their only apparent guard was Captain Tom Riker. He was also the only member of this gathering who was not wearing religious robes. Instead he was dressed in what Garak considered to be a most inelegant uniform, a hodgepodge of Starfleet severity and Bajoran pomp.

All it would take is one gentle push, Garak mused to himself, as he and Odo joined the outer edges of the group. A simple nudge and Weyoun would tumble into the depths faster than Riker could run forward to save him. In his mind's eye, Garak watched the Vorta's arms thrashing, heard his wheedling voice receding in a doppler shift of death.

If Weyoun could only be removed from the events to come, it was entirely possible the universe could be saved.

Garak was familiar enough with Sisko and Kira to know that both possessed the courage to take such action—even if it meant immediate death. So the fact that they were choosing not to take advantage of their opportunity revealed to Garak that the two knew something he didn't. Most probably, that Weyoun *couldn't* be stopped by a fall.

"Such a fascinating time," Garak said aloud.

"I'm sorry?" Odo asked.

"A private musing, Odo. Not important. What do you suppose is down there?" Garak gestured to the yawning pit.

"With our luck," Odo grumbled, "more red orbs."

Garak nodded. How interesting. He himself hadn't thought of that. "Now, that would be a delightful complication."

Beside him he heard Odo sigh.

Then a shout echoed up from the excavation floor. Someone reporting that "it" was under way.

As Odo leaned forward to stare downward, frowning, Garak amused himself by turning to study the other prisoners clustered beside them. People had always been of more interest to him than things.

And the most interesting grouping was that of the two Ferengi—Quark and Rom—with the human engineer, O'Brien. These three had single-handedly come up with the plot to escape from the *Boreth,* sending Odo out on his fool's errand to overload the ship's powergrid. Garak had tried to explain that no one in their right minds would put all of their hostages in one location *without* arranging surveillance. But humans had this hopeless notion, that if they whispered softly enough no one would overhear what they were saying.

Surprisingly, Odo had not been executed. In fact, Weyoun had taken no reprisals against the prisoners at all. In Garak's experience, that was a sign of a sloppy leader, or perhaps of someone who could not conceive of anyone's challenging his authority. From events that had transpired since, Garak was leaning towards presuming Weyoun to be one of the latter. No one who could command Grigari could be considered sloppy.

Someone in the crowd jostled Garak, as several of the prisoners edged forward to the lip of the excavation and began pointing down. With a sigh, Garak pushed forward to look down into the gloom as well.

And saw Weyoun staring down at a large object, perhaps four meters long and two meters across, that was rising from the depths. Given the absence of ropes and pulleys, Garak concluded that the Vorta had relaxed the rules of B'hala's restoration to allow the use of antigrav lifters.

A few meters down from the lip of the excavation, it became apparent that the object was nothing more than a large boulder, the same pale color as the sand and stones that surrounded everything here.

"It must have some special significance," Odo said expectantly.

"After all this work, I should hope so," Garak said.

They watched with the others, as the enormous rock floated easily upward from the excavation, then shifted sideways through the air to a barren clearing to one side of the spectators. By the time the boulder had settled—without the slightest disturbance of the dry soil beneath it—Weyoun had scaled its summit so that he could speak to his audience.

As he did so, Bajoran workers swarmed the base of the rock, detaching from it blue devices the size of Garak's forearm—obviously the antigravs.

"My *dear* friends," Weyoun said. "What we are gathered here to witness today—or should I say, tonight—is the last preparation we must undertake before the ceremony of the Ascension can begin. Now, I know this rock doesn't look like much. It's certainly not a sacred stone, and there are no mystical carvings upon it. But it has fulfilled a very special function for us all.

"You see, the events that will lead to the transformation of the universe are—and always have been—very well known to Bajoran scholars. True, in the past those scholars made misguided attempts to censor the revealed truths of the True Prophets, and were reluctant to share their knowledge of the transformation with the people who trusted in them.

"But we have changed all that. Now we know the steps that must be undertaken before the transformation can begin."

Here Weyoun pointed down at Sisko. "First, the False Emissary must rise from the dead who fell when the Gateway vanished—and I'm so glad to have your own Captain Benjamin Lafayette Sisko with us here today." In a moment which Garak felt was amusingly surreal, Weyoun began to applaud, gesturing for his audience to join in. But no one did.

Weyoun made a show of adjusting his robes before continuing. "In the days ahead, I can promise you all that there will be further ceremonial activities conducted here in B'hala, and eventually up on the Gateway—and then at the doors of the sundered Temple itself." The Vorta smiled broadly, and Garak could see he was trying to make eye contact with every prisoner. Garak nodded in acknowledgment when Weyoun's gaze fell upon him. But he heard Odo's harrumph of disapproval, and saw the changeling look down when the Vorta's attention settled on him.

Garak caught the flicker of disappointment that touched Weyoun's face at Odo's dismissal of him. How strange that someone with such power could still want for something.

"In these troubled times," Weyoun began again, "we of the Ascendancy must admit that we have enemies. Doubters we can accept. Nonbelievers we can coexist with. But enemies . . . they're not interested in either our acceptance or coexistence, only in destruction. *Our* destruction, my dear friends.

"To date, I can tell you that our enemies have tried to destroy our ships, our worlds, our places of prayer. So we have fought back, as is our right. While our enemies have used their most sophisticated weapons against us, filled subspace with their lies, even tried to subvert us from within."

Garak was intrigued to see that at this point in his speech Weyoun bestowed a most meaningful look on Sisko, although even Garak could not understand how anyone could accuse the captain of duplicity. Sisko had never made any effort to disguise his fierce opposition to Weyoun and the Ascendants.

"But, dear friends, we have withstood their assaults, and in only seven days we will never have to endure them again." The Vorta paused, as if allowing time for his audience to cheer his words, but again there was no response.

"However," Weyoun said after a moment, "these next seven days bring special risks. Because the enemy will now be provoked into using its most fearsome weapons against us. And one of their greatest perversions of technology is the ability to travel through time itself."

A current of reaction raced through the gathering. It seemed to Garak that all but Sisko, Kira, and Arla were whispering to each other. He himself glanced at Odo, and the two of them silently shared their sudden interest in whatever it was Weyoun was building up to.

"In fact," Weyoun said, his voice ringing across the excavation site, "the scientists of the Ascendancy have said that it is even possible that our enemies would go so far as to travel *back* in time to before any of *this* existed." He spread his arms wide, and Garak knew the Vorta's reference was to the city of B'hala, revealed and unrevealed.

"And there and then," Weyoun said, "they could bury bombs of immense destructive power . . . bombs that would be hidden through the ages among the lost treasures of B'hala . . . bombs that would not detonate until *after* their timeships had set off on their blasphemous journey, so that our enemies could falsely claim that they had not wreaked havoc with the timeline."

"What an absolutely splendid concept," Garak murmured admiringly to Odo. "To change the past without changing the present . . . only the future. I'm truly taken aback with admiration. I wish I had had a chance to employ a similar technique when—"

"Be quiet," Odo hissed.

Undeterred, Garak cast his eye across the group again, wondering who the specific audience for Weyoun's performance was. Because that's exactly what this invitation to the excavation was—a performance, pure and simple, for the benefit of one or two of the prisoners.

His eye fell on Rom. Certainly the midlevel Ferengi technician had astounded everyone with his *savant* abilities in engineering. In fact, after Rom had come up with the audacious technology of self-replicating mines, seemingly in defiance of the laws of physics, Garak himself had even gone so far as to risk contacting some of his old . . . business acquaintances. He'd been curious to find out if any brilliant Ferengi scientists had disappeared in the past decade, perhaps predisposed to find a new and simpler life in some kind of disguise.

But this investigation had turned up no evidence regarding the possibility that Rom was something other than what he claimed to be, though Garak still had his suspicions.

However, he reminded himself, even if it was Rom who had conceived of the delayed temporal warfare Weyoun had described, it still seemed improbable that Starfleet could have moved on the idea so quickly, or that someone as lowly placed as Rom could have passed word to the correct authorities to begin with.

And that problem of communication likely ruled out Chief O'Brien as well. A stolid, boring sort of fellow to be sure, but also dedicated and forthright. Just the sort to have under one's command in case a grenade someday came through a window and required someone to throw his body upon it and save his betters. People like O'Brien had their uses.

But not in this case.

Which meant, Garak reasoned, that Weyoun's performance could only be intended for the one person present who could have had ample opportunity to be in contact with Starfleet—the *real* Starfleet—in time either to suggest preparing an attack in the past or to have learned that such an attack was planned.

Captain Thomas Riker.

Someone who—beyond any doubt—would be dead before this gathering was over.

Garak straightened his robes, pleased with the realization that of all the people here, only he knew what Weyoun was thinking.

Garak's attention returned to the Vorta, who was still emoting up there on his rock. Effortlessly picking up the thread of Weyoun's speech in progress, Garak wondered precisely how many heartbeats Riker had left. Such a fragile thing, life.

"Of course," Weyoun whined self-righteously, "knowing our enemies' plans, we had to take action. Yes, we could have sent our own forces into the past, to set up a shield of justice around our world. But the possibility that some unforeseen accident might change the past made us rule against it. Instead, our scientists concluded that we should let our enemies do their worst: Let them stand revealed as the monsters that they are.

"Let them take their sordid voyage into our history, plant their bombs, and be done with them, but"—Weyoun broke off unexpectedly to wave to a group of workers who had been waiting at the far edge of the excavation—"be certain that whatever cowardly action they take in our past cannot be hidden from the eyes of the Prophets."

The Vorta's smile was smug. "Which brings us to this rock." He stamped his foot against it. In seeming response to Weyoun's action, a few of the workers below him gathered around one end. They all held small tools, whose purpose Garak couldn't quite make out.

"A year ago, dear friends, our scientists constructed this rock— that's right, *constructed*. And then a group of brave believers traveled back through the Orb of Time to an age before the founding of B'hala, and there buried this rock in stable ground."

Suddenly the workers jumped back from Weyoun's pulpit rock, as a section of it fell off with a loud pop as if something under pressure had just opened. Garak leaned forward with the others to see the hollowed-out area now visible in the boulder.

"You don't suppose . . ."

"Will you be *quiet*," Odo said.

Weyoun was still atop his pulpit. "As you can see, this is not just a rock. Instead, our scientists carved into it with microtransporters and then installed within it the most stable and precise passive sensors. Sensors that could not be detected by our enemies' scans. Sensors that for almost twenty-six thousand years have waited patiently for us to reclaim them."

Weyoun slid down the artificial boulder to join the workers at its open end. He glanced over at Sisko, and then spoke loudly enough for the rest of the prisoners to hear. "Now, I can tell what you're worried about, Benjamin. What if *we're* altering the timeline by opening this prematurely? Could we be setting a predestination paradox in motion?" The Vorta shook his head. "Of course not. The Ascendancy has far more respect for the natural order of things than does your Starfleet."

Weyoun's workers busied themselves removing long, metallic cylinders from the boulder's interior. The silver objects gleamed in the blinding light from the space mirrors, as if they were freshly minted and not millennia old.

Garak was exhilarated by the spectacle the Vorta had provided for their enjoyment. But he decided against sharing his delight with Odo. Really, the changeling just had no idea how to enjoy the moment.

"No, Benjamin," Weyoun proclaimed. "The reason we are opening the deep-time sensors today is because *yesterday,* Starfleet's timeship began its voyage. And interestingly enough, your son was on it. Jake. Should give him something interesting to write about, don't you agree?"

It was impressive to Garak just how well Captain Sisko was controlling his anger. The human had never appreciated his offspring's involvement with the more difficult events on Deep Space 9. Garak wondered if he would have an opportunity to remind Sisko that perhaps it was for the best that Jake escaped the coming end of everything by being safely ensconced in the past.

"So," Weyoun said triumphantly; Garak was relieved to sense the Vorta was finally coming to his conclusion—despots so rarely understood there were a few occasions on which less was more. "What Starfleet has done was done long ago, and because of our patience the timeline is intact. And as we play back the sensor records of the past, we will be able to chart the location of each bomb the crew of that ship placed beneath us—here, in the unexplored regions of B'hala. And though Starfleet's plan was undoubtedly to ignite those bombs during the final ceremony to be held here, destroying half of Bajor in the process, even now ships of our own Ascendant Starfleet are in orbit above us, waiting to transport each bomb away and disperse it into deep space."

Weyoun bowed his head in pride. Held his fists to his shoulders. "Praise be to the True Prophets, may they show our enemies the errors of their ways." He looked up and nodded at the workers with the sensors. "You may examine them now."

"This should be very interesting," Garak said to Odo.

"Why? Because Weyoun has figured out a way to stop a last-ditch plan to save us all?"

"The plan's not ruined yet," Garak admonished the changeling. "After all, if *I* had designed the bombs Weyoun is looking for, I'd have buried them in pairs so that any chance observation would make someone think there was only one to each location. And then I'd make certain they were *all* set to go off the instant any of them was hit by a transporter beam. This entire city could be reduced to molten slag any moment now—a bracing thought, wouldn't you agree?"

Garak relished the sudden look of consternation that disturbed Odo's smooth features.

"Oh, relax, Constable. If we do go up in a fireball of apocalyptic proportions, at least you'll have the satisfaction of knowing that the universe has been saved."

"You're right," Odo muttered acidly. "I feel so much better."

"That's the spirit." Garak beamed as he watched Weyoun's workers hold all manner of tricorders and other devices near the deep-time sensor arrays. From time to time, he glanced over to see Sisko in intense conversation with Kira and Arla.

Rom and O'Brien were also engaged in a fevered conversation, no doubt reverse-engineering the sensors just from their appearance and Weyoun's description of their capabilities. But Quark was looking positively bored and stood to one side, alone.

"What a remarkable day," Garak said aloud, not intending the words for anyone but himself. "What a remarkable life."

"Has anyone ever told you how obnoxious you are?" Odo asked.

"Often," Garak conceded. "Though after we've discussed it in private, it turns out they always have meant it in jest. Interesting how people can be persuaded to change their minds, wouldn't you say?"

Odo rolled his eyes, obviously not willing to be baited. Garak joined him in watching the work on the sensors.

It was over in less than twenty minutes.

And then Weyoun turned to Sisko with an expression of sadness, and again spoke loud and clear for posterity. "Oh, dear Benjamin, I am so sorry. But the sensors show that no bombs were ever planted here. There are no transporter traces, no residual tractor-beam radiation trails, no sudden alterations in the gravimetric structure of the region . . . nothing. It appears that Starfleet's mission has failed, and your son Jake . . . well, I *am* so sorry. But the wages of disbelief are—"

Sisko threw himself at Weyoun, and Garak's pulse quickened. There was nothing quite so uplifting as seeing what a parent would do for its child.

But before Sisko could reach the Vorta, Riker had tackled the captain, bringing him down in a cloud of dry dust.

The two humans wrestled for a few moments on the edge of the excavation, but it soon became disappointingly apparent to Garak that Sisko was merely venting anger, and that Riker had no desire to make an example of him.

In less than a minute, Riker was back on his feet again, brushing sand from his atrocious uniform. Sisko sat still on the ground for a moment.

And then, quite unexpectedly—or so Garak thought—Weyoun went to Sisko and offered him his hand.

It also appeared that Weyoun was saying something to the captain, but this time the Vorta's words were intended only for Sisko. And most unfortunately, the angle of Weyoun's face was such that Garak couldn't read his lips.

"What a charming gesture," Garak said, annoyed. The Vorta was playing by the rules.

But then, predictably, Sisko rebuffed Weyoun's offer of help and pushed himself to his feet without assistance, in a whirl of dancing dust.

Garak's eyes narrowed as the Vorta reacted graciously by simply clasping his hands to his chest and bowing to Sisko, as if to say no offense had been taken.

But just then a giant gasp arose from all the prisoners and the workers, as Captain Tom Riker threw himself across the two-meter distance between himself and Weyoun and propelled the Vorta howling into the pit—

"Well done!" Garak exclaimed. He'd underestimated Riker.

Transporter hums filled the air, and waves of Grigari soldiers suddenly materialized, surrounding the area. Their bone-spur claws dug into the prisoners' robes, forcing all back from the pit that had claimed Weyoun and Riker.

"So much for Ragnarok," Odo said.

"A bit anticlimactic, though," Garak observed critically.

And then Weyoun rose up from the depths of the excavation, floating, arms outstretched, supported, it seemed, only by a softly glowing halo of red light.

"What is that?" Odo asked in shock.

Garak frowned. "What else? A Pah-wraith inhabiting the vessel of a linear being. Riker should have anticipated that."

Predictably, Odo glared at him. "A good man has died trying to save us!"

Garak was hardly in the mood for an argument. But then, neither did he intend to let Odo have the last word. "That 'good man' once worked for the Maquis. And knowing what I know about the Pah-wraiths, he is not dead yet."

As if on cue—a happy accident of timing but which Garak much appreciated all the same—Weyoun then dropped a hand to the pit below, gesturing as if giving a command for something else to arise.

That something was Tom Riker. Breathing hard. The bright blood streaming from a long gash on his head turning his white beard red.

Riker's left leg was also not hanging straight, and Garak could see a small, sharp glimmer of white against his dark, red-stained trousers.

"Compound fracture of the femur," Garak explained helpfully to Odo, who of course lacked any bones whatsoever. "Quite painful, I believe."

Weyoun drifted to the side of the pit and stepped gracefully onto solid ground. Riker remained suspended in midair, above the pit, his body in spasms, bubbles of blood forming at the corners of his mouth. A possible punctured lung, Garak thought. He turned to share this observation with Odo, but the changeling was looking elsewhere.

Sisko had his hands on Weyoun and they were having a heated conversation. At least, the human was heated. The Vorta looked detached.

But it seemed even a Pah-wraith did not have unlimited patience, and finally Weyoun flicked his hand at the human and a blinding flash of red light sent Sisko flying backward into the sand.

Then Weyoun imperiously gestured again into the pit, and a moment later a red strand of rope shot up and coiled out of it like the unfurling tongue of an immense unseen amphibian. Another rapid hand movement from the Vorta, and the sinuous rope snaked around Riker's neck.

The floating human grabbed at the rope, tore at its tightening coils, his one good leg kicking out for freedom.

A gasp from the horrified onlookers caught Garak's ear and he turned to see Quark suddenly stagger back, hands at his own neck. The Ferengi was obviously reliving some unpleasant memory. Garak frowned. An interesting development to be sure, but not in the end as intriguing as the one featuring Weyoun and Captain Riker. He turned his back on Quark.

To see Weyoun raise his hand high and Riker float higher, his struggles lessening, the mysterious rope looping in the air beside him.

Weyoun dropped his hand, and Riker dropped but the rope did not. It flexed and snapped tight, breaking only as its burden was sundered at its weakest point, and Riker's head and body plunged into darkness—separately.

"Showy, but no subtlety," Garak murmured.

Odo's face leaned menacingly into Garak's. "I don't want to hear another word out of you!"

Garak sighed. He had been intimidated by experts, rarely successfully, and certainly never by a mere changeling sworn to uphold justice. Swearing such an oath, in fact, had worked to undercut a great deal of Odo's authority, Garak had always believed.

"What I meant, Constable, is that there was no need for Weyoun to behave so crudely. After all, he has won. He can't be killed. And Starfleet's attempt to travel through time has obviously failed. He could have left Riker at the bottom of the pit to bleed to death in a dignified fashion. Instead, we've all been treated to a quite unnecessary look inside a troubled mind."

Odo stared at Garak in disgust. "You see something like . . . like *that* and *analyze* it?"

"Someone has to," Garak said. "And I do think it might be worth pointing out to Captain Sisko that Weyoun clearly has a weak spot in his personality. One that might conceivably be exploited to our benefit."

"And what weak spot would that be?" Odo growled, as if he couldn't believe he was engaged in this conversation.

"I think it might be wise to let the emotions of the moment dissipate," Garak said kindly. "You've been through a considerable strain."

Odo drew back as if he'd been slapped. "And you haven't, I suppose?"

Garak was tired of being questioned in this way. Tired of Odo's attitude. He looked from side to side and put on his best bland face—the kind that struck such terror into poor, sweet, gullible Dr. Bashir. "Odo . . . whatever we saw here today, remember this. I've seen worse."

Odo clenched his jaw, clearly wanting to say something more but just as clearly unable to bring himself to.

And Garak, oddly, found himself struggling not to add the words *And so have you—on the Day of Withdrawal.*

Now, why would I think that? he wondered. There was no way *he* could know what Odo might have seen or not seen when the Cardassians had withdrawn from Bajor. *Unless . . .*

"No," Garak said aloud.

Odo looked at him, not understanding.

But even Garak didn't understand this time.

The universe was coming to an end.

Nothing mattered anymore.

Not the death of Tom Riker.

Nor the Day of Withdrawal.

Nor even how his own lost memories from that final day on Terok Nor—

—when the Obsidian Order had come for him . . .

—when Terrell had taken him to the room . . .

—where . . .

"Garak?"

Garak stared at Odo, and for a moment it was as if the changeling was wearing his old clothes, the short cape and rough fabric from the time before he had donned the uniform of the militia, from the time before . . .

"Garak? What's wrong?"

"Nothing." Garak forced himself to smile. "A touch of vertigo. Nothing a good apocalypse can't extinguish."

Odo's eyes narrowed. "It seems you're not as tough as you let on."

"I'm not," Garak said firmly. "I'm tougher."

And then Weyoun summoned the Grigari guards to come for them and the other prisoners, to lead them away from the pit back to the shuttle that would return them to Empok Nor, the restored Gateway.

And Garak, who knew there was no point in thinking of the future, and who could not think of the past, devoted himself to thinking about only the moment and the glorious view of Bajor, as the shuttle climbed above the clouds and into space.

There might well be many good things in this universe, he knew. But in his experience, bad things had far outweighed them.

The end of everything would be a good thing.

He would finally be free of the horrors of his past.

Maybe he wouldn't tell Sisko about Weyoun's weak spot after all.

CHAPTER 21

NOG DROPPED a battered piece of metal onto the table in the unfinished conference room of the *Phoenix.*

It was a dedication plaque.

Its significance was lost on Jake, who looked at Jadzia and Bashir to see if they understood.

From the expressions on their faces, they apparently did.

Jadzia was the first to pick up the plaque and study it closely.

Jake noticed that Karon, the Romulan centurion at the head of the table and the leader of the team that had taken control of the *Phoenix,* was studying Jadzia just as intently, as if she expected some type of treachery.

After a few moments, the Trill passed the damaged rectangle of metal to Bashir, then looked at Nog. "I take it you've run a complete molecular scan to be certain it's not simply a replicated copy."

"I studied it atom by atom," Nog said. "It is the same plaque that is now on display on the bridge of this ship, *except* it is 25,627 years older. And, of course, its condition has been somewhat altered by . . . a variety of mishaps."

Nog's hesitation raised in Jake the desire to know exactly what those mishaps had been. He looked quickly at Centurion Karon, but she didn't seem to have noticed the pause in Nog's delivery.

"So the *Phoenix* crashes on a moon in the Bajoran system," Bashir said angrily. "That could mean this ship was damaged *after* we deployed the deep-time charges and we scuttled it where no one would find it."

Nog laid his hands on the tabletop and spoke forcefully. "Doctor, the Romulans have recovered almost forty percent of the ship. There are components from *all* of the deep-time charges we're currently carrying. That means we did not deploy the charges. And that means our mission will be a failure—because it already was."

"And you believe the Romulans?" Bashir asked, his sarcasm leaving no doubt as to what he thought the answer was.

Centurion Karon responded before Nog could. "Dr. Bashir, I understand your reluctance to trust us. If you were Vulcan, I would call upon your logic. But as it is, I shall ask you to employ that human characteristic known as 'common sense.'

"The mission of the *Phoenix* as planned makes good sense—to stop the Ascendancy without changing the timeline. Surely it is to all our advantages for it to succeed. The Star Empire—old or new—would embrace that result.

"The facts, however, indicate that this mission will fail. That suggests that sometime in the next six standard days the universe will end, as the Ascendancy plans. Our position then becomes, why waste this resource, this magnificent vessel? As much as it distresses us, changing the timeline is preferable to allowing the universe to die."

Jake wasn't an expert, but he had heard his father discuss the terrible equations of the Dominion War with Admiral Ross. And he had come to believe as his father did: There was no escaping the fact that in order to accomplish good, sometimes bad things had to happen.

In the case of the war to save the Federation, that had meant that soldiers had to die. And Jake could see the same inescapable equation at work here. "It makes sense to me," he said quietly, and was suddenly aware of everyone in the room staring at him. "I mean, if I had the chance to take back some tragedy by changing time, I'd do it."

"Even if it meant wiping yourself from existence?" Bashir asked.

"If the tragedy was big enough, I'd have to, wouldn't I? Wouldn't all of us?"

Karon nodded approvingly at him. "This young man is correct. What we are proposing is no different from sending a group of

Imperial Commandos on a one-way mission to inflict terrible damage on an enemy and thereby win a war. Perhaps we will die, but billions more will live because of our sacrifice. Perhaps trillions."

Jake didn't understand why Jadzia hadn't yet offered her opinion, and why Bashir now seemed unwilling to say more.

Karon tried to prompt a reaction from them. "Dr. Bashir, Commander Dax, you and your fellow travelers through time were willing to risk your lives for the mission of the *Phoenix.* Why are you not willing to risk your lives on a plan that has a *real* chance of success?"

"Maybe because it's a *Romulan* plan," Bashir said. "And I'm just not comfortable with taking this ship back twenty-five years into the past and laying waste to an entire world."

At that, Karon rose abruptly from the table, the sound of her chair echoing harshly in the unfinished room, and Jake could see her hands were clenched into fists at her side. "I apologize for being Romulan. But I invite you to work through the problem yourselves. One world and twenty-five years balanced against the universe and infinity. Which would you choose if I had been human, Doctor? Or Andorian, or Klingon?" Obviously upset, the Romulan centurion inclined her head briefly in a nod of leave-taking. "I suggest you discuss your options. Because one way or another, this ship *is* on a new mission, with or without her crew."

Karon headed for the doors, where, as the doors to the corridor slid open, Jake saw two Romulans with disruptors standing to either side of the doorway. Then the doors closed and they were alone.

"What were you thinking?" Bashir snapped at Nog.

"Me? You insulted her." Nog said. "Besides, the mission fails. It doesn't need thinking about. The facts are the facts!"

"The Romulans almost killed Worf!" Jadzia said heatedly.

Jake knew that Jadzia's mate was in the ship's sickbay being tended to by an entire holographic medical team, even though they weren't programmed for Klingon physiology. Fortunately for Worf, his disruptor burns were superficial.

Jadzia's accusation hung in the air. But strangely enough, Nog did not fight back. More than anything, Jake thought, the Ferengi looked sad.

"I am truly sorry for the commander," Nog said, "but I know I did the right thing. If this ship had been taken out on her mission as planned, we would have accomplished nothing. It's as simple as that."

Jake hated seeing his friend so beleaguered, so defensive. Nog was looking twice as old as he had on Starbase 53. Jake tried to remember what Bashir had said about the little capitulations and loss of ideals that accompanied adulthood. How many small defeats had Nog had to endure in the years they had been apart? What had brought him to this state—a troubling and troubled person who had sold out every ideal he had ever believed in?

Unless, Jake suddenly thought, *Nog hasn't changed at all. . . .*

"Nog," Jake said, reaching out for the plaque and holding it up, "what other mishaps?"

Nog looked down the table at him and Jake saw in the Ferengi's sudden wariness that he had hit on something.

The plaque. The plaque was the key. Somehow.

Jake put the plaque down on the table and ran his fingers over its raised lettering. He felt excitement bubbling up in him.

"When you said you conducted tests on this, you said it showed signs of various 'mishaps.' That's an odd word to use."

Nog took a deep breath, and if his friend had still been only nineteen, Jake would have sworn he was gathering his strength to confess some transgression of youth to his father. Then Nog glanced at the closed door, and Jake leaned forward, on the alert. Nog had something he was *hiding* from the Romulans.

Maybe his friend wasn't the traitor, the loser he seemed to have become.

Maybe there was still some of the old Nog—the *young* Nog— locked up in that middle-aged Ferengi's body.

Now Nog leaned forward and dropped his voice to a low whisper.

"Do you know *how* the Ascendancy plans to bring on the end of the universe?" he asked the three before him.

"By merging the two wormholes," Bashir said.

"Yes, but how?" Nog asked. "I mean, really—by what technique can you actually *move* two energy phenomena held in place by verteron pressure?"

Jake, Bashir, and Jadzia all shook their heads.

"Well, Starfleet doesn't know, either. That's one of the reasons we were so slow to react to the Ascendancy's plans. The best scientists just didn't think what they planned to do was possible."

"But . . ." Jake said, grasping for enlightenment, "it *is?*"

"Yesss!" Nog hissed. "Most certainly. And I know what they plan to do, because the evidence is all right here. . . ." He patted the dedication plaque. "My friends, I needed the Romulans to help me steal this ship from Starfleet, but now I need your help to steal it back."

"*Yess!*" Jake thought. *That's* my *Nog.* Then he sat forward even closer to listen to Nog's plan.

CHAPTER 22

"WE'VE LOST, haven't we?" Kira asked.

Sisko stared up at the night sky from his cell. Its narrow window faced north, and the beams from B'hala's space mirrors did not interfere with his view of the stars.

"We're still breathing," he said. As the stars appeared from Bajor, they were almost as familiar to him as the stars of Earth.

Kira didn't sound convinced. "For how much longer?"

"Maybe . . . we shouldn't fight this anymore," Arla said from her corner of the cell.

The enclosure imprisoning them, its walls made of the ancient stones of B'hala, was small, with only three small piles of old rags for beds and a bucket for all other physical needs. But Sisko and the two Bajorans had had no trouble sharing it. There were bigger concerns facing them than mere physical discomfort and lack of privacy.

Sisko turned away from the stars in time to see the look of shock on Kira's face, but felt none himself. After witnessing Tom Riker's appalling death last night, he felt numb to further surprise.

"You can't be serious," Kira said hotly.

"You believe in the Prophets, don't you?" Arla asked.

"Of course I do!"

Arla slowly got to her feet in one fluid, athletic movement, and smoothed her robes around her. "Then isn't what's going to happen here what you've wanted all your life?" she asked.

Kira's head bobbed forward in amazement. "The end of *every-thing?* Why would you believe that *I* would want that?"

Any other time, Sisko might have thought that the secular Arla was merely baiting the religious Kira, and might have intervened. But he recognized a new undercurrent to Arla's questions, and understood that she was trying to comprehend something that had never been part of her own life.

"Isn't it part of your religion that at some time good and evil will fight a final battle?" Arla asked.

"So?" Kira answered.

"So isn't this it? When the two halves of the Temple are rejoined, the Pah-wraiths and the Prophets will fight that final battle and existence will end. That's what it says in your texts, isn't it?"

Kira exhaled noisily as if indignant at Arla's ignorance, but Sisko knew her well enough to sense that she was stalling for time. "Yes. My religion says that sometime there will be a final battle between good and evil. But it doesn't say anything about there being *two* Temples!"

Arla folded her arms inside her robes like a monk. Sisko thought it was an odd gesture for a non-believing Bajoran to have picked up.

"Major, I mean no disrespect, but are you really surprised that your side—the good—has a slightly different version of events than the bad side? Doesn't it make sense that alternate versions of the texts were written to . . . to sow confusion, to lead people from the righteous path?"

Kira narrowed her eyes in suspicion. "Are you saying you *believe* the texts? That you accept the Prophets as gods?"

Arla shook her head, not defiantly, Sisko saw, but in confusion.

"I honestly don't know," she said slowly. "But I saw Dukat and Weyoun fight like . . . like nothing natural should fight. I saw what Weyoun did to poor Captain Riker. I can't deny that there is something going on here that goes beyond any science or history or folklore I know. So . . . so I'm just trying to understand it from a different hypothesis."

"And that would be?" Kira asked.

"That you're right. That the Prophets are gods, not aliens. That the Temples are their dwelling place and not wormholes. That among the texts of Bajor's religions are those that truly are inspired by gods and correctly foretell the future."

Sisko interrupted the uncomfortable silence that followed.

"And is it working?" he asked Arla. "Does it help you accept what's happening?"

The tall Bajoran shook her head again. "What I don't understand is that if everything that's going on *is* what was prophesied in the Bajoran religion . . ." She looked at Kira. "Allowing for some technical discrepancies introduced by purely mortal error in the transcription of the texts through the millennia, or by the deliberate, malevolent interference of the Pah-wraiths . . ." She turned back to Sisko. "Why is everyone against it?"

"The end of the universe?" Kira demanded, as if she still couldn't believe the question.

"But is it really the end, Major? If *your* religion is right, isn't this actually the transformation that Weyoun claims it will be? Isn't this only the end result of linear existence? The ultimate proof of your beliefs?"

Sisko saw Kira's chin tremble in anger. *"I* believe that *when* the real Prophets choose to change the nature of existence, it will be when every being has reached a state of understanding. It will *not* be forced upon us. It will *not* involve war or murder. It will be something that everyone will see coming and will embrace, because they have come to know the Prophets and the time is right."

Arla's calm seemed only to deepen as Kira's temper rose. "Is that what it says in your texts?" she asked. "Or is that just what you'd *like* to believe?"

"It's in the texts!" Kira insisted.

"Where?" Arla asked.

Kira looked dismayed. "I . . . I don't have them here. Weyoun's probably burned all of the real texts, anyway." She turned away from Arla, to end the conversation.

Sisko studied the commander, wondering if she could have some ulterior motive for upsetting Kira, something he'd overlooked. But he knew nothing that disturbed him. Other than the fact that her questions had merit.

Because as far as he knew, there *were* no passages in any of the mainstream texts of Bajor describing the end of time as Kira had.

Time and existence would end for Bajor as it would for the cultures of a thousand different worlds—in a final battle between good and evil, light and dark, blue and red.

"I'm right, aren't I?" Arla asked quietly of Kira and Sisko. "We shouldn't be fighting this."

Kira offered no other answer.

Sisko considered Arla's challenge. "It all . . . it all comes down to free choice," he said at last. "I suppose that we each have to make our own decision in our own way."

"Well said, Benjamin!"

Weyoun was back.

He was standing on the other side of the heavy wooden door to their cell, peering in through its small, barred window.

"I'm *so* glad to see that you're all exploring such important religious issues," the Vorta said. He backed away from the window, and Sisko heard the rattling of the chain that kept it closed. "But if you'll just be patient a few more days, you won't have to trouble yourselves with trying to second-guess the True Prophets. I suggest you do what Commander Arla suggests. Embrace the coming transformation."

Then the heavy door swung open to reveal the Vorta and his five Grigari guards.

"After all," Weyoun said beneficently, "this impending battle is described both in my texts and yours, Major Kira. The only real difference between them is which of us is on the winning side. And since the hallmark of any religion is that the forces of good shall always triumph in the end, I think it's safe to say that whatever we believe now, we'll all be pleasantly surprised then." He pursed his lips in a mischievous smile directed squarely at Sisko. "Wouldn't you say, Benjamin?"

Sisko laughed in spite of himself. "What *I* say is that if the True Prophets are so powerful, so righteous, why do they need to wait so long—and why do they need *you* to restore the Temple? If they're gods, shouldn't they be able to snap their cosmic fingers and reorder reality to their liking?"

Weyoun made a tsk-tsk sound as he wagged a finger back and forth at Sisko. *"That,* my dear Benjamin, is a philosophical conundrum that has puzzled scholars for centuries. If I were you I'd keep it in mind to ask the True Prophets when you next see them, because I'm certain there's a perfectly good explanation." Weyoun bowed deeply and gestured toward the door. "And now . . ."

"Now what?" Sisko said.

"It's time to prepare."

"For what?"

Weyoun rolled his eyes. "Really, Benjamin. Why else are you here?" The Vorta's eyes flickered with just a flash of red light. "Why else have I kept you alive?"

Sisko gathered his robes around him, glanced once at Kira and Arla, then stepped through the doorway and out of the cell.

Weyoun was right.

It was time for the end to begin.

CHAPTER 23

BASHIR WALKED onto the bridge of the *Phoenix,* hands behind his back, whistling tunelessly. He had been chosen for this role because his genetically enhanced capabilities were thought to give him an edge at remaining calm.

Certainly Nog didn't want to risk telling any more lies to the Romulans, not given his track record with Jake.

And besides, Bashir thought, I'm a physician. Which makes what I have to say all the more believable.

Aware of Romulan eyes watching every move he made, Bashir sauntered casually over to Centurion Karon's command chair. On the main viewer, only a computer navigation chart was displayed. Watching the strobing stars passing at transwarp velocities had been too disorienting, for humans and Romulans alike.

The route that was charted took the *Phoenix*—or the *Alth'Indor,* as the Romulans had rechristened her—on a wide galactic curve away from Bajor and into what had once been Cardassian space. This would enable the ship to make her final run toward Bajor from an unexpected direction, and at transwarp speeds even a two-minute lead could translate into a ten-light-year advantage.

Karon looked up from her holographic display as Bashir stopped beside her.

"Any sign of pursuit?" Bashir asked her.

"The alarms would have sounded," Karon said crisply. "In tran-swarp, we are virtually undetectable, just as the Borg are."

Bashir nodded and looked around, hands still behind his back.

"There is something else?" Karon asked, appearing a touch more impatient, exactly as Bashir and the others had hoped.

"Well, it will be four days till we reach our objective . . ."

"Correct."

". . . and I'd like to fill the time with something worthwhile."

"I suggest meditation."

"I was thinking more along the lines of medical research."

Karon stared at him, waiting for him to continue.

"No one's ever traveled through time in this ship," Bashir explained. "There is a slight possibility that there could be some . . . novel physical disruptions in bodily processes. Indigestion. Gas. Diarrhea. Vomiting."

"I am aware of bodily processes," Karon said coldly.

"Well, in order for me to treat these symptoms—if they occur— I'd like to have a baseline medical file on all crew members. So I can compare their readings before and after the—"

"I am also aware of the purpose of baseline readings, Doctor. Get to the point."

"I want to give physicals to your crew."

Karon considered Bashir, her dark eyes unblinking.

Bashir did his best to look innocent, then puzzled, then alarmed.

"Have I said something wrong, Centurion?"

"You really don't expect me to let you take my crew, one by one, into sickbay, where you will be free to inject them with drugs, neural implants, who knows what."

Bashir let his mouth drop open, as in shock. "Centurion, no! I just want to—"

"I know what you want to do, Doctor. This truce between us is strained enough as it is. Don't make it worse by attempting to gain the upper hand."

Bashir affected an air of disappointment and defeat. "If that's what you think, I apologize. It wasn't at all what I was—"

"Is there anything else, Doctor?"

Bashir acted perplexed, then spoke as if he had just had a thought.

"Would it be all right if I ran baseline tests on just the humans and Bajorans?"

"You may vivisect them, if it will keep you off my bridge."

"It . . . won't be that drastic—but thank you." Bashir looked back at the other crew chairs. There were five temporal refugees among the Romulans. "I'll start with them, may I?"

"Just leave."

Bashir gave a deliberately calculated half-bow, then gestured to the humans and Bajorans to accompany him to sickbay.

The Romulan standing guard at the turbolift alcove immediately questioned the fact that the refugees were leaving, but Centurion Karon instructed him to let the doctor proceed with his patients.

Bashir and his party entered the lift. Bashir nodded at the guard and smiled warmly. The guard turned away with a grunt of disapproval.

Then Bashir completed the final, most important act of his deception. As the lift doors began to close, he reached out his hand to make them open again, stepped out into the alcove, and firmly grasped the edges of the ship's dedication plaque and *pulled.*

He felt as if he had sliced open half his fingers, but Nog had been right. The metal plaque released from its mag connectors with a pop.

The Romulan guard turned in time to see Bashir step back into the lift with the gleaming metal plate.

"We're going to make you a new one," Bashir said. "So it says *Alth'Indor.*"

The guard frowned but made no move to stop them as the lift doors closed a second time.

Bashir kept his smile in place until he felt the jolt of the lift car beginning to move. He was no longer startled by it, now that Nog had explained why the dampening fields had been tuned to a slow response time.

When they had descended four decks, Bashir tapped his combadge. "We're on our way to sickbay. I have all the patients."

A moment later, Worf's voice said, "Acknowledged."

Bashir grinned, and this time he meant it.

When the lift stopped on deck 8, Bashir rushed out, heading for engineering, leaving his confused patients to follow on their own. One of them even called out that this wasn't the deck for sickbay.

Bashir burst into engineering, hoping he was in time.

He was. Just.

On the systems wall a large display showed a schematic of the *Phoenix,* all three kilometers of her, a sleek shape most resembling a pumpkin seed bristling with transwarp pods on its aft hulls, ventral and dorsal.

"Here goes," Nog said, with a tense nod at Bashir.

He tapped some controls on the main engineering table. Instantly, a set of system displays turned red and the computer voice said, "Warning: Initiating multivector attack mode while in—" Nog silenced the voice with a sharp jab at the controls.

Also at the main engineering table, Jadzia looked up in alarm. "Would they hear that on the bridge?"

"Doesn't matter," Nog said quickly as his fingers flew over the controls. "They're not going anywhere."

On the schematic, Bashir saw all the turbolift shafts turn red.

Then a communications screen opened on the table and a holographic image of Centurion Karon took shape. "Captain Nog!" she shouted. "You will cease your attempts to override bridge authority and return the ship's dedication plaque at once!"

"Actually," Nog muttered, "that's exactly what I'm *not* going to do." He held a finger over one final, flashing red control. "Hold on to your lobes, everyone," he said, then pressed it.

Instantly the engineering workroom filled with sirens and flashing lights and on the main schematic Bashir watched as a small section of the forward ventral hull become outlined in red.

"Partial multivector mode established," the computer reported. "Prepare for bridge-segment jettison."

The deck shuddered, as the red-outlined section of the schematic suddenly vanished from the board.

"All control transferred to battle bridge," the computer said.

The computer was immediately followed by Worf's triumphant voice. "We are the *Phoenix* once again."

Bashir cheered along with Jadzia. Jake pounded Nog on the back.

Then Worf asked over the comm link, "What are your orders, Captain Nog?"

The doctor heard the passion in the Ferengi's swift reply. "We're going to Bajor."

Bashir relaxed.

The universe had one last chance.

CHAPTER 24

WEYOUN STEPPED OUT onto the balcony of the temple in the center of B'hala and held out his arms as if to show off his new robes of intense, saturated red.

"The blood of innocents?" Sisko asked.

"The flame of faith," Weyoun answered.

Sisko turned back to B'hala, concentrating on the heat of the morning sun, the dry scent of dust, and the silence.

The silence was absolute.

This last day of existence, as reports of riots on other worlds spread across the subspace channels, Bajor was still. Its population had long since been winnowed by expulsion and execution until it was only a home for believers. And this day, even the believers had been sent home, to pray and to wait for their Ascension.

Sisko wondered how many Bajorans were huddled in the stone buildings within his view. He wondered how many were whispering the prayers of the Pah-wraiths and how many were clinging fearfully to the prayers of the Prophets, trusting without trust in one last miracle, one last tear as the Prophets wept for their people.

"Still hoping there might be a bomb or two hidden down there?" Weyoun asked, as he came to stand by Sisko's side as if, somehow, they were equals.

"It would be a nice surprise," Sisko said.

"Ah, but if Starfleet's brave chrononauts *had* managed to plant them and fool our sensors, they would have gone off by now, don't you think?"

"Maybe Starfleet sank a planet buster near the core," Sisko said, baring his teeth in a facsimile of a smile. "Take out the whole planet any time now."

"Benjamin, you know that's not Starfleet's style. Destroy an entire world, just to stop one man?"

"You're not a man, Weyoun. But I am glad to hear the lies have stopped. Starfleet wouldn't destroy a world. Wouldn't start a war. Wouldn't spread lies."

"I wouldn't advise you to take that as a sign of moral rectitude. You should look at it as I do: as a sign of their weakness. *Your* weakness, Benjamin."

"Starfleet's not weak," Sisko said. "There's still time to stop you."

Weyoun's laugh was derisive. "In twenty hours? No. Every attempt has failed—and failed miserably. Operation Looking Glass? That pathetic attempt to attack us in the Mirror Universe—a fiasco. Operation Phoenix? It literally fell apart—a Grigari ship found the *bridge* of the *Phoenix* adrift near the Vulcan frontier, filled with a crew of terrified Romulans. Don't you see, Benjamin? You people wasted too much energy fighting each other. That is your greatest weakness. No self-control."

Sisko refused to be provoked. "Twenty hours. Twenty seconds. I won't give up."

"And that's your weakness, too—refusing to accept the inevitable."

Sisko concentrated on the smooth texture of the worn rock that formed the balcony's edge. This couldn't end. This *wouldn't* end. "You will be stopped, Weyoun."

"Did I mention Operation Guardian?" Weyoun asked.

Sisko shrugged, uninterested.

"Fascinating plan. A sure sign of the sheer desperation rampant in what was left of the Federation." Weyoun leaned forward to be sure Sisko could both see and hear him. "It called for a combined force of Starfleet vessels and Borg cubeships! Can you imagine? The Federation and the Borg acting together?"

Sisko was dismissive of Weyoun and his gloating. "What of it?

It's our way to make our enemies our allies. Always has been. Always will be."

"The combined force—fifty, sixty ships at least—were trying to regain a small planetoid with a strange alien device built into it. Have you ever heard of the Guardian of Forever?"

Surprised, Sisko studied Weyoun. *That might work,* he thought.

Weyoun smiled. "But they failed, of course. The Grigari were ready for them. To Starfleet's credit, or perhaps it was the Borg's—it doesn't really matter which," the Vorta said, "the battle lasted for days. And then, when that noble Admiral Janeway finally managed to get her troops on the ground and within sight of the device—"

Sisko closed his eyes, willing Weyoun to vanish. Willing Bajor to be consumed by a bomb planted a billion years ago. Anything to end Weyoun's vicious prattling.

"—You really should pay attention to this, Benjamin . . . I assure you it is quite amusing. Just at that moment when Janeway thought she had won—*knew* she had won—the Grigari activated a singularity bomb." Weyoun snapped his fingers. "Instant black hole. Borg. Starfleet. The Guardian. Even the Grigari. Sucked out of the universe just like that. A taste of what's to come for all of us, hmm?"

"I *could* throw myself off this balcony," Sisko said, looking down on the silent city far below.

"You could," Weyoun agreed. "In fact, I'm a little surprised you haven't tried it by now. Don't let me stop you."

"If I fall and die, would you just bring me back to life? Or would I just not fall?"

"Why not try it? And I'll surprise you."

Sisko turned around, his back to the city, leaned against the balcony wall. "Tell me, Weyoun. Do you really need me here to . . . to accomplish something? Or are you just desperate for an audience?"

Red sparks danced in Weyoun's eyes. "Oh, I do need you, Benjamin. Two Temples. Two groups of Prophets. Two Emissaries. It all has to be brought into balance."

"How?" The question Sisko had wanted answered for so long hung in the air between them.

Weyoun looked up at the brilliant blue sky and to Sisko, it was almost as if the Vorta were staring directly into Bajor's sun. "Oh, the Temples are easy. And when they come together, the Prophets will know what to do. But the role of the Emissaries . . . you know, that's a puzzle."

Sisko tensed, alert to the first admission from Weyoun that his power and knowledge were not absolute.

"There's something that's not written in your texts?" Sisko asked carefully.

Weyoun shook his head. "That's what's so intriguing, Benjamin. *Everything* is in the texts. Even your name—the Sisko. Your discovery of B'hala. The False Reckoning on your old station. The fall of the Gateway. Your return in time for the joining of the Temples.

"The texts make it very clear that whoever wrote them knew about you. And that you are an absolute requirement for the Ascension to take place as prophesied. But . . . just before the end . . . the text stops—not as if there's a missing page—the narrative simply ends, as if whoever saw this future didn't see its end, either."

"Then maybe it doesn't," Sisko said.

Weyoun waved a hand in the air. "Admittedly there are a few theological loose ends. But, really, physics is physics. Whatever you think about what might be in them, when those two wormholes come together these eleven dimensions of space-time around us will unravel instantaneously and irretrievably."

"What kind of god would want that fate for creation?" Sisko asked.

As if in answer to Sisko's question, an intense red glow flared and then faded in Weyoun's eyes. Then the Vorta reached out to take his arm.

"What do you want of me?" Sisko demanded, drawing back.

Weyoun smiled and shook his head. Then firmly holding on to Sisko, he tapped his chest as if something were hidden beneath his robes.

"Two to beam up," he said.

B'hala dissolved into light as once again, Sisko was transported.

CHAPTER 25

THE *PHOENIX* ripped through a realm of space not even Zefram Cochrane had imagined.

Her engines had the power to change the course of stars and turn planets into glittering nebulae of atomic gas just by passing too close to them. But that power was contained and channeled by technology—technology assimilated from a thousand different cultures, from trillions of different individuals, representing as it did the sum total of Borg knowledge.

But now, only seventeen beings rode within the *Phoenix* as she began her final run. Fifteen of her passengers were already displaced in time. Two others were willing to face the same risks.

The ship's destination was fifty light-years away. But with the incomprehensible power she controlled, she would reach it within the hour.

And that hour might be the last the beings within her would ever know.

"Come with us," Jake said.

But Nog shook his head, his attention riveted on the main viewer of the battle bridge. "The *Phoenix* has to end up on Syladdo, fourth moon of Ba'Syladon," he said.

Without taking his eyes from the viewer, Nog brandished the gleaming dedication plaque he was holding. "Along with this."

"Nog, you can't do this!" Jake said, alarmed by his friend's intentions. "The wreckage wasn't found until *after* we disappeared. You won't be changing the timeline."

Nog stared straight ahead, undeterred. "If the wreckage isn't there, the timeline *will* be changed. I've gone over it with Jadzia and Dr. Bashir."

"Then . . ." Jake struggled to find the right words, the right argument. "Then program the computer to crash the damn thing!"

"No, Jake. There's no guarantee the computers will function after the slingshot maneuver. If they need any significant time to reset themselves, the *Phoenix* could crash somewhere else in the meantime. Maybe even on Bajor. Wipe out a city."

"Come on, Nog. You *can't* kill yourself!"

"I don't plan to. The Romulans' charts of the crash site were very detailed. And as I told you before, they only found forty percent of the ship." Nog flashed a quick grin at Jake over his shoulder, before turning back to the viewer. "Remember, the *Phoenix* is a multivector ship. Not counting the bridge we jettisoned, that means two segments *didn't* crash. I'll be able to go anywhere. Even Erelyn IV."

"Anywhere except home," Jake said. Because that was Nog's plan for the rest of them. Starfleet Intelligence knew that Ascendancy starships would be keeping station at the coordinates where the wormholes would open and merge. Nog was going to beam Jake and the others to the bridge of one of those starships so that it could instantly warp into a slingshot trajectory around the mouth of the *blue* wormhole. The precise temporal heading would be unimportant, because wherever in the past the ship emerged, Jadzia would have more than enough time to calculate a precise trajectory to bring them back to their own time, *before* the Red Orbs of Jalbador were discovered.

It would be an alternate timeline. The past twenty-five years could not be erased. But at least *one* universe would survive. Perhaps.

Jake couldn't hold his emotions in any longer. He and Nog had been through too much together. "I'm going to miss you," he said.

Nog suddenly turned his back on the viewer. "Me, too, Jake. But there'll be another me back in your time." He reached out and gave Jake's shoulder a squeeze.

Jake felt a lump tighten his throat. "Bet he'll be surprised when I tell him how things turned out here."

But Nog shook his head. "Don't tell him. Please."

"Why not?"

"Back then I was just a kid, Jake. I wasn't sure what I wanted. I liked Starfleet. I thought maybe I had a career. But part of me still wanted to go into business. When things got bad after the station was destroyed, that's when I decided to stick it out in the Fleet. But if things are different when you go back . . . well, I wouldn't want some version of myself sticking with Starfleet just because that's what I did. I'd like to think I had a second chance along with the rest of the universe. Okay?"

Jake nodded. He understood. At least he thought he did. "I'm still going to put this all in a book," he told Nog.

"Just make sure it's fiction."

"Absolutely."

"And make sure the brave Ferengi captain has really crooked teeth and spectacularly *big* lobes."

"Gigantic!" Jake had to smile in spite of the way he felt.

"And put in a scene like in *Vulcan Love Slave*—" Nog giggled, just the way Jake remembered he used to.

"Part Two!" Jake laughed out loud as Nog's giggles became contagious.

"The Revenge!" both young men, both little boys, shouted in unison.

"Only this time, the *Ferengi* gets the girls! And they're all . . . fully clothed!"

They collapsed against each other then, gasping in hilarity, laughing as they hadn't laughed in twenty-five years, Jake realized.

Suddenly serious, Jake looked at his friend. "I promise," he said.

"I know. You're a good man, Jake."

Then the door to the battle bridge slid open. Quickly composing themselves, Jake and Nog turned together to see—

Vash.

And Admiral Picard at her side.

"Where's Q when you need him? That's what I want to know," Vash said as she guided Admiral Picard onto the battle bridge, while gently holding on to his arm. The admiral was smiling happily.

"Will! Geordi! Where have you two been hiding?"

Everyone on the *Phoenix* knew the Old Man had his good times and his bad, easily distinguished by the names by which he addressed those he met. So both Jake and Nog respectfully greeted the admiral in turn without correcting him, and Vash helped Picard to his chair, from which all operational controls had carefully been removed.

"Seriously," Vash said to Nog as she joined him by the viewer, "does anyone know what's happened to Q?"

"The admiral's been telling you about him?" Nog asked.

Vash nodded. "He says Q comes to see him almost every day. Is that right?"

"No," Nog said. "I wish it were. A few years ago when all this started, there was a whole division at Starfleet that was trying to make contact with the Q continuum. Q helped out the Old Man once before with time travel. We thought maybe we could ask him to help again. But no one's seen him for . . . well, since DS9 was destroyed. Except for the Old Man's stories, that is."

"And you're really sure Q *isn't* in contact with him?"

"Positive," Nog said. "At the shipyards, we even tried putting the Old Man under constant surveillance. He'd have conversations with an empty chair, then tell us that Q had visited him. Or Data. Sometimes it was Worf. Sorry."

Jake saw how Vash watched Picard in his chair, saw the sudden liquid brightening her eyes. "So am I," she said. Then she squared her shoulders and looked down at Nog. "Okay, Hotshot, listen up. I'm coming with you."

"No, you're not!" Nog sputtered in surprise.

"Yes I am, and you can't stop me because you need me."

"I do not!"

Vash pointed to the admiral. "But *he* does!" She held up a small medkit. "When was the last time you checked his peridaxon levels?"

Jake was surprised by how flustered Nog became under Vash's stern scrutiny. "I've . . . been busy. I was just going to."

"And because you've been so busy," Vash said, "the greatest starship commander in Starfleet history has been calling *you* Will Riker and *him* Geordi La Forge. He deserves better treatment, *Captain* Nog."

"And what makes you think he can get it from you?"

In the midst of this heated exchange, Jake saw Vash become unexpectedly quiet. And the only reason for her change in mood that he could see was that she was again gazing at Picard.

"I owe that man," she said, without anger or hostility.

"You *knew* him?" Nog asked. "I mean . . ."

Vash nodded. "I know what you mean. Ever hear of Dr. Samuel Estragon?"

Nog hadn't. Neither had Jake.

"Doesn't matter. But I'm not leaving Jean-Luc. And I don't care if I have to chew your precious lobes off to make you agree."

Jake saw Nog flush. "Do you know what you're getting yourself into?"

"I do," Vash said simply. "An act of loyalty for one. An appreciation of a great man." She looked deep into Nog's eyes. "Maybe even a chance to help you out because I just know you're going to need all the help you can get."

"You're also risking getting trapped more than two and half millennia in the past."

"I'm an archaeologist, Hotshot. I should be so lucky." Then she tapped Nog's chest with her finger. "And just for the record, I've already been farther back in the past, farther forward in the future, and farther away than this two-credit quadrant."

Nog stared at Vash in disbelief, but Jake thought he knew what she meant.

"How is that even possible?" Nog asked.

Vash grinned. "Jean-Luc and me, let's just say we've got a friend in high places. And maybe he hasn't shown up in this timeline 'cause he knows it doesn't amount to anything. And maybe when we show up a few dozen centuries out of place he'll look in on us again."

"Q," Nog said, distrustful. "And what if he doesn't?"

Vash rolled her shoulders. "I speak and write ancient Bajoran. Maybe we can put on a traveling show."

Nog was wary. "If I do let you accompany us on our mission, I will expect you to behave like a member of my crew and treat me with respect."

"And I'll expect you to act in such a way that you'll deserve my respect."

Vash and Nog stared at each other for a long moment, and Jake could tell that neither one of them wanted to be the first to give in.

So Jake took the initiative.

"I think it's a good deal," he said. "I think you should shake on it before you change your minds." He put his hand on Nog's shoulder. "Think of the admiral. She's got a point."

Nog grudgingly held out his hand. "All right. For the Old Man's sake. But don't make me regret taking you."

Vash's smile was dazzling, and instead of taking Nog's hand she ran two fingers lightly around the outer curve of his ear, ending with a small scratch at his sensitive lower lobe. "Regret taking me? Are you kidding?"

Jake thought Nog's eyes would roll up permanently in his head.

Vash fluttered her long, slim fingers at him, then turned away and went back to Picard.

"What have I done?" Nog marveled.

"I think you've made the best decision of your life," Jake said heartily, not sure at all about what he was saying. But then Nog had never been able to tell when *he* was bluffing.

"Really?"

"Look at it this way," Jake told his friend. "With Vash along, whatever else happens she's going to keep things . . . interesting."

Nog sighed heavily. "That's what I'm afraid of."

Then Jake looked at the time display on the main viewer.

The universe had forty-seven minutes left.

CHAPTER 26

"IT WON'T WORK," Miles O'Brien said.

"Uh . . . I agree," Rom added.

Quark leaned forward and banged his broad forehead against the stone wall of the cell in B'hala. "Perfect, just perfect. Half the galaxy's convinced the universe is going to end in less than an hour, and my idiot brother just *happens* to figure out that this whole War of the Prophets is a big mistake." He banged his head again. "Why not call up Weyoun? See if he'll let us go home now?" Bang.

"Uh, maybe you shouldn't be doing that, Brother. You might hurt yourself."

At that, Quark opened his mouth and screamed and flung himself at Rom with arms outstretched, and for a second it seemed nothing could stop one Ferengi from crashing the other into solid rock.

Except me, Odo sighed to himself, as he reluctantly changed his humanoid arms into tentacles that snaked out across the length of the room to snag Quark.

"Will you settle down!" he said, as he deposited a squirming Quark on the side of the cell opposite Rom. "Maybe the Chief is onto something. What are they going to do? Lock me up? Kill me?"

"We can only hope," Quark said darkly.

Odo grunted, more concerned about the grasping tentacles he'd

566

formed so quickly, which were now becoming tangled in the robes
he'd been forced to wear. He swiftly solved the situation by puddling
faster than his robes could fall, then surging to the side and reforming in his humanoid shape again, his outer layer now a perfect reproduction of a Bajoran militia uniform, circa 2374. "That's better," he
said emphatically.

"Good for you," Quark groused. "Now, why don't you change
into a balloon and float us all out of here? Wouldn't want to be late
for *the end of the universe!*"

Quark, however annoying a cellmate for the past seven days they
had been incarcerated together, was not the real problem, Odo
thought. What was truly unfortunate was that their cell in this partially restored B'hala structure was ringed by the same type of poly-
morphic inhibitor Weyoun had used against him on the *Boreth*.
Behind these walls and barred windows, Odo was as caged as any
solid.

But he refused to give in to self-centered neuroticism as Quark
had done, though. Instead, he walked over to the wall where O'Brien
and Rom had been scratching equations and diagrams into the soft
stone for the past two days.

"Why won't it work?" the changeling asked O'Brien. He had to.
Somehow, he had to believe there was still hope in this universe, that
somehow he would be rejoined with Kira. Because to find love and
lose it in so short a time . . . Odo refused to believe that Kira's
Prophets would allow such agony.

"In the simplest terms," O'Brien said, "it's inertia." Odo watched
as the Chief used a long stick he had peeled off one of the timbers of
a bunk to point to a diagram of the Bajoran solar system and explain
the orbits marked upon it.

Apparently, the entrance region of the blue wormhole of the
Prophets maintained a nearly circular orbit around Bajor's sun, just
at the edges of the Denorios Belt. And sometimes the wormhole
actually crossed into it.

The Chief indicated the entrance region of the red wormhole
which, in contrast to that of the blue wormhole, had a more eccentric
orbit. Reminiscent, he said, of a comet's, travelling from the system's outer reaches and plunging past Bajor's own orbit before it
returned to the realm of the gas giants.

On the Chief's diagram Odo noticed that the red wormhole actually crossed the orbit of the Denorios Belt and the blue wormhole four times each orbit. And in less than an hour, O'Brien said, for the first time since the red wormhole had been reestablished by the three Red Orbs of Jalbador twenty-five years ago in Quark's bar, the orbital harmonics of the Bajoran system were finally going to bring the two wormhole entrance regions to their closest possible approach.

"But that closest approach," the Chief emphasized, "is still going to leave the entrance regions approximately five hundred kilometers apart."

"Uh, four hundred and sixty-three kilometers," Rom corrected him. "More or less."

From the other side of the cell, Quark moaned loudly. He was again leaning his head against the cell wall.

"What's the difficulty presented by that distance?" Odo asked, deliberately shutting out the sound of Quark's complaining. "It doesn't seem very far, cosmically speaking."

"The entrance effect of a wormhole is very constrained, Odo," O'Brien said. "I mean, that's one of the reasons it took so long for the blue wormhole to be discovered. If you're not within a kilometer or so of it when it opens, there's no force acting on you to pull you in. If this thing had been swallowing hunks of the Denorios Belt for the past few thousand years, someone would have noticed pretty early on. But its effect on normal space is very limited. That's why we have to pilot a ship toward it with great precision to actually travel through it."

"In other words," Rom added hesitantly but eagerly, "even if both wormholes open at the precise moment of their closest approach, they're both too far away from each other to have any attractive effect."

From his corner, Quark called out to them. "Before you pay too much attention to that lobeless wonder, did I ever tell you how Rom once stuck a toy whip from my Marauder Mo playset into his ear? He was eight years old, and he was *always* playing with his ears. I was so embarrassed. But here he took this little—"

"Shut up, Quark!" Odo, O'Brien, and Rom said it all together.

"I'm just saying he's not right," Quark said loudly. "Always with the ears. Stop it or you'll go deaf, Moogie kept telling him. But did he listen? Ha? How could he? He had half my toys shoved up his ear canal!"

"No one's listening, Quark," Odo growled. "Please, Rom, Chief O'Brien—go on."

Rom's cheeks were flushed red. "There's, uh, not much more to tell. The wormholes won't move through space. So they won't join. So . . . the universe won't come to an end. That's about it."

"Why didn't Starfleet scientists discover this?" Odo asked.

"Well, it's difficult to chart wormhole orbits accurately," O'Brien said. "They respond to interior verteron forces, as well as to the number of times they open and close in a given orbit. I'm guessing that Starfleet's first reaction was that the wormholes would never come close enough to represent a threat. What do you think, Rom?"

Obviously pleased to have the Chief consult him, especially after such abuse from his brother, Rom quickly nodded his support for this theory.

"Further observations," O'Brien continued, "suggested that the two wormholes *would* open close enough to merge today. But from what the Ascendants told us during those interminable briefings they kept giving us, the orbits are fairly well known for the next few months. And according to their own figures, they just won't be close enough."

"Are you certain there's no way to move them?" Odo asked. "Tow them somehow? Use a tractor beam? Connect them by a charged particle web?"

O'Brien and Rom glanced at each other and both shook their heads. Odo saw little beads of sweat fall from their foreheads.

"You see, Odo, most wormhole entrances are created by verteron particles impinging on weakened areas of space-time," O'Brien explained as Odo listened intently, doing his best to follow the technical language. "The opening they form is bound by *negative* matter, and it's kept open by negative energy, just as they suspected back in the twenty-first century. But not even the Iconians had the ability to manipulate negative matter. It would be like . . ." The Chief frowned as he tried to come up with the most helpful comparison ". . . like trying to outrun your shadow."

Odo stared at the scratchings on the wall. "Then why do you suppose Weyoun's people are so convinced that today's the day the wormholes merge? They're going to look awfully foolish tomorrow."

Quark's indignant voice sounded from just behind him. Odo turned to see the Ferengi pulling out on his robes like a small child about to curtsey. *"They're* going to look foolish?"

They all said it again. Only this time more emphatically. "SHUT UP, QUARK!"

Rom giggled as his brother stomped off with a curse, then recovered himself. "Uh, maybe Weyoun will claim that he interceded with the Prophets on behalf of the people of the universe," he said. "That way, he can take credit for . . . saving us all."

O'Brien nodded. "That makes sense, Rom. The easiest disaster to prevent is the one that could never happen. High priests and shamans have been doing it forever—driving off the dragon that eats the moon, bringing summer back after the solstice."

Odo was feeling buoyed by this revelation. Perhaps he *would* hold Kira's hand again, mold his lips to hers once more. But still, he thought, surely there were easier ways for Weyoun to gain the respect of the galaxy than to manufacture a doomsday scenario that could be disproved by a few lines of mathematics.

"Are you certain there's no way to move 'negative' matter?" he asked O'Brien.

The chief engineer was adamant. "The wormholes are fixed in the space-time metric, Odo, like rocks in cement. Nothing's going to move them. It just won't work."

"Well, then," Odo said with new enthusiasm, "we'd better start thinking what we'd like for dinner tonight."

"There's nothing like an idiot's death," Quark muttered from his corner. "Happy to the end."

Odo walked over to the barred window, felt the warning tingle of the inhibitor field. He looked out at the blazing sun. He wondered if Kira was looking at it, too. He wished he could reassure her that there was nothing to worry about, after all. But Weyoun had been keeping both Kira and Arla with Sisko.

Odo turned away from the window. "I wonder when our jailers will come back," he said to O'Brien. The Bajoran guards that had been posted for them had not arrived this morning. Even the loathsome Grigari were gone.

"I wonder when you'll face the inevitable," Quark snapped.

Odo had just about had it with the Ferengi. "Trust in physics, Quark."

"Ha!" Quark exclaimed. "If I trusted in physics I'd be paying out twice as many dabos and—" He shut his mouth with an audible smack. "Forget I said that." He turned away, face as red as his brother's.

In fact, Odo noticed even O'Brien was more flushed than usual. "Are you all right, Chief?"

"I could use a nice cold beer," O'Brien said with a weary grin. He moved to the window and held up a hand next to it. "That's odd. The breeze doesn't feel all that hot."

"Because it's the wall," Rom said.

Odo and O'Brien shared the same puzzled reaction, and stared at the wall Rom pointed to. It was made of typical B'hala building stones, half a meter square, badly eroded, set without mortar. The only thing beyond it was the outside.

But as Odo watched, the stone wall seemed to waver, as if seen through a raging fire.

"Stand back," Odo cautioned.

O'Brien, Rom, and Odo began retreating from the rippling wall, not taking their eyes off it.

"Here it comes," Quark sniped from his corner position where the rippling wall met the far wall. "Reality's dissolving. I'd say I told you so but what would be the point?"

Odo motioned to the Ferengi. "I'd get over here if I were you, Quark."

But Quark didn't budge. "If I were you," he said, mimicking Odo's way of speaking. "You know what I've always wanted to say to you, Odo?" he announced.

"No," Odo told him.

The rippling wall resembled liquid now, and an oval shape was forming in its center as the heat in the cell air increased.

Quark cleared his throat. "I've always wanted to say, Why don't you turn yourself into a two-pronged Mandorian gutter snail and go—"

A high-pitched squeal rang out as the liquid-like wall exploded inward with a flash of near-blinding red light. Odo and Rom and O'Brien stumbled forward as a rush of cool air blasted *into* the wall opening, kicking up a cloud of sand from the floor and sucking the bunk, the buckets, and Quark all in the same direction.

And then, without warning, the wind ended. The bunks and the buckets and Quark stopped moving.

The sand on the floor lay as still and undisturbed as if in a vacuum.

But Quark wasn't abhorring a vacuum as much as anything else in nature.

"That was the end of the universe?" he crowed, hopping on one foot to shake the sand from his ears. "After all that buildup?"

This time not even Odo bothered to tell Quark to shut up.

Because Odo saw through the opening in the wall that someone else was about to join them.

A humanoid shape was walking toward them from a dark room that Odo *knew* was *not* beyond the shattered wall.

The stench of putrefaction swept into the small cell and infected every molecule of air. O'Brien gagged, Rom whimpered, and Quark protested in disgust.

Then Odo saw a pair of glowing red eyes just like Weyoun's.

"Oh, *frinx,*" Quark said. "Not another one."

"No," a deep voice answered. *"Not another one. The* first *one."*

Odo stepped back as Dukat entered the cell. But the Cardassian's eyes were normal and he was normal, except for the soiled robes he wore and his halo of wild dead-white hair.

"My dear, dear friends," he said. "How good to see you once again."

"How did you get here?" Odo asked Dukat. He had seen enough strange things in this future to not waste time questioning them.

Dukat held up a silver cylinder a bit larger than Weyoun's inhibitor, and looked at it lovingly. "A multidimensional transporter device. A toy, really."

O'Brien stared at Dukat. "The Mirror Universe?"

Dukat lowered the cylinder. "And like all mirrors, what it contains is only a reflection. So when this universe ends, so shall it."

"But this universe isn't ending," O'Brien argued. "The wormholes won't open close enough to each other. And there's no way they can be moved."

Dukat looked at O'Brien as if the Chief were no more than a babbling child. "Miles, that's not very imaginative of you. Of course the wormhole entrances can't be moved through space. But what if *space* were moved. What you might even call a *warp.*"

"Dear God," O'Brien said. "Rom, they're going to change the space-time metric."

"Great River," Rom squeaked. "There's only one way to do that."

"I *knew* it," Quark added. "Um, whatever it is."

"But you have a way out, don't you, Dukat?" Odo said. He for one was not willing to give up just yet.

Dukat beamed. "Odo . . . I always knew there was a reason why I liked you." He held out his hand. "And there is exactly that. A way out. A way to escape the destruction of everything. And all I ask is for one small favor in return . . ."

Odo stared at Dukat's hand as if it were a gray-scaled snake poised to strike. He looked up at Dukat's eyes—at Weyoun's eyes— saw the red sparks ignite.

The universe had thirty minutes left.

It was not as if they had a choice.

CHAPTER 27

THEY WERE ALL on the battle bridge now: Captain Nog, Admiral Picard, Vash, Jake, and the thirteen other temporal refugees.

"Computer," Nog said. "Go to long-range transfactor sensors. Image Bajor-B'hava'el."

Bashir observed the computer navigation graphic vanish from the main viewer, to be replaced by a real-time representation of Bajor's sun. He noted a small solar flare frozen in a graceful arc from its northwestern hemisphere, and a string of small sunspots scattered at its equator. As far as he could tell, it was to all appearances a typical type-G star, securely in the middle of the main sequence.

"What's the time lag with this system?" Jadzia asked.

"With transfactor imaging at this distance? We're seeing the sun as it existed less than half a second ago." Nog's hand moved through a holographic control panel and a spectrographic display of the sun appeared at the bottom of the viewer. Even Bashir was able to see that there were no anomalies present.

"You're sure about this?" Jadzia asked. "Stars don't get much more stable than that."

Bashir could tell the Trill was worried, and about more than Nog's planned maneuver. Jadzia's spotting stood out in high contrast to her pale, drawn face, and the reason for her concern was standing beside her: Worf, his shoulders rounded, restricted by the pressure bandages the holographic medical team had applied to his disruptor wounds. The problem was that this ship had no medical equipment set for Klingon physiology, and what would have required a simple fifteen-minute treatment in Bashir's infirmary on DS9 had become a weeklong ordeal of daily bandage-changings and the constant threat of infection. Jadzia was clearly worried that in his weakened condition Worf might not survive what Nog had in mind. And Bashir had been unable to say much to reassure her. As Vash had earlier pointed out, there were just too many things that could go wrong.

But Nog was a study in confidence. "I'm positive," the Ferengi answered. Then he adjusted more holographic controls, until the image of Bajor's sun shrank to the upper-right-hand corner of the viewer and a new image window opened. Now they were looking at a closeup of the *Phoenix*'s twenty-five-thousand-year-old dedication plate recovered by the Romulans. "Look at the atomic tracings," he said.

Thin lines of artificial color appeared over the plaque. Most of the lines were dead straight. A very few, Bashir noticed, curved and looped like the trail of subatomic particles in a child's cloud chamber.

"Read the isotope numbers, too," Nog urged Jadzia. "And the energy matrix."

This was a more difficult piece of evidence for Bashir to understand. But from what Nog had already told them, it apparently showed incontrovertible evidence that the plaque had been in close proximity to a supernova. In addition, Nog said, to having been subjected to an intense burst of chronometric particles, which suggested it had traveled along a temporal slingshot trajectory.

Furthermore, the Ferengi maintained, the distinctive mix of elements and isotopes that had left their trails through the plaque's metal structure were an exact match for Bajor-B'hava'el—a sun that should not be at risk for even a simple nova reaction for more than a billion years.

Which apparently left room for only one conclusion.

The Ascendancy was going to deliberately trigger the sun's explosion.

And the reason was, again according to Nog, perfectly logical: When the two wormholes opened at their closest approach to each other—something which would happen in just over fifteen minutes, relative time—the portals would be too far away from each other to interact.

The supernova detonation of Bajor's sun, however, provided it was properly timed, would create a high-density, faster-than-light subspace pressure wave. And that pressure wave would be followed minutes later by a near-light-speed physical wall of superheated gas thrown off from the surface of the collapsing sun.

As far as Bashir had been able to understand from Nog's explanation, the combined effect of the two near-simultaneous concussions in real space and subspace—when added to the gravity waves generated by the sudden disappearance of the Bajoran gravity well around which the wormholes orbited—would actually cause the underlying structure of space-time to warp.

Nog told them that the effect would be a natural version of what a Cochrane engine did on an ongoing and far more focused basis in every starship that had ever flown. And then the Ferengi had shown the math to Jadzia that described an incredible event. For approximately four seconds, the space between the two wormhole openings would relativistically decrease from almost five hundred kilometers to less than five hundred meters.

And, Nog insisted, there was nothing in the universe that could keep the two wormholes apart at that distance.

Thus would the Ascendancy end the universe.

"Commander Dax," the Ferengi captain said with finality. "Like it or not, we're running out of time. We'll be at our first insertion point in . . . seven minutes."

"Are you certain you don't want to attempt to place the deep-time charges?" Jadzia asked.

"If we had planted them, they would have detonated by now," Nog said. "There's only one more thing we can do."

Bashir could see that Jadzia's concern was now shared by everyone else who would be beaming from the *Phoenix* at . . . at transfactor twelve, whatever that meant in recalibrated warp factors.

And with Nog claiming that modern transporters could handle the task by using something called "micropacket-burst-transmission," who among the temporal refugees from the past could argue with something so incomprehensible? Certainly *he* himself couldn't, Bashir thought.

Nog turned from the viewer to address his apprehensive passengers. "Trust in the River," he said. "It might not take you where you want to go, but have faith that it will always take you where you *need* to go. Good profits to you all. Now please report to your assigned transporter pads."

Having faced death many times on this strange journey, Bashir himself felt rather unconcerned about soon facing it again. Besides, if anything went wrong with Nog's plan in the past, he and all the others simply wouldn't exist. So they wouldn't even be dead.

As the others left the battle bridge he approached Nog, who was in the middle of saying his farewell to Jake, at least that's what it seemed to Bashir that the Ferengi was doing. What he overheard of their exchange did not make much sense to him.

"Remember," Nog warned his friend, "don't tell 'me.' "

Jake's answering smile was rather mournful, Bashir thought. "But I'll make sure you get all the girls," Jake said. "Fully clothed."

As Jake stepped back, he bumped into Bashir, awkwardly pinning Vash between the two of them.

"Don't look so glum, boys," she said, separating them with a playful push. "This is going to work. I know it." The archaeologist manifested none of the nervousness possessing everyone else.

"How can you be so sure?" Bashir asked her, curious, and rather envious of her upbeat, invigorated mood.

She winked at him. "Let's just say I've seen how the River flowed."

Bashir frowned at her. What did she mean? Had Vash learned something—about the past? Frustratingly, there was however no time left for questions—no time even to express his regret that he and she had not had the opportunity to follow up on the promise of that kiss they had shared on the *Augustus*. More than anything else— if only to bring completion to his time with her—Bashir wished he could kiss Vash again.

The woman was a mind reader. But it seemed she had read the wrong mind. She pushed past Bashir to grab *Jake's* face between her hands and kissed Jake with a passion that could have melted duranium.

When she released him, Jake looked dizzy, and shocked, and pleased—incredibly pleased—all at the same time. And incapable of coherent speech. Horridly jealous, Bashir felt a hundred years old. He remembered feeling that way himself. And hoped he would again.

"You know," Bashir heard Vash say to Jake, "people are going to tell you that you always remember your first love."

Jake nodded silently, still dazed.

"But you know what the truth is?" Vash didn't wait for an answer. "The truth is, the one you really never forget is your *best* love."

Then she looked past Jake at Bashir, who felt his heart skip a beat. But then he, too, was dismissed by her gaze, which now settled on another: Admiral Picard, sheltered in his command chair.

Vash flicked her finger under Jake's nose. "And what I want *you* to remember is your twenty-fifth birthday. I'm buying."

"Okay," Jake mumbled hoarsely, "I'll be there."

Then Jake left, and Bashir felt uncomfortable staying in Vash's presence without him. He crossed quickly to Picard's side, unwilling to leave without one last chance to speak to the living legend.

"Dr. Bashir!" Picard said as Bashir approached his chair.

Bashir was startled at Picard's recognition of him. Through most of his time on the *Phoenix,* the admiral had thought he was someone called Wesley.

"You remember me," Bashir said, pleased, as he shook the admiral's hand.

"How could I forget? Between you and Admiral McCoy, I lived in constant fear that my wife was going to leave me for either one of her heroes. She was a doctor, too, you know."

"I didn't know you had married," Bashir said.

"Damned Grigari took her. Battle of Earth. Good thing we can stop them with this bloody marvelous ship, eh?"

"A very good thing," Bashir agreed. He looked up to see that he was the last of the passengers in the battle bridge. It was time to go. "A real pleasure to meet you again, Admiral Picard. I hope—"

"Oh, don't call me that, young man. I'm not Admiral Jean-Luc Picard anymore."

Bashir blinked in confusion. He felt Nog's hands on his back.

"Doctor," Nog said, with some urgency, "you really have to get to your transporter."

"We're going undercover!" Picard called after Bashir. "A critical mission!"

"Are you sure his medication is under control?" Bashir asked Vash, as she took over from Nog and pushed him toward the doors.

"Absolutely," Vash said. "You have to hurry."

"My new name is Shabren!" Picard shouted proudly.

Bashir stared at Vash in horror. "You can't be serious! You three?"

Vash patted his arm. "Don't know if we have to yet. But who else is gonna know how to spell the Sisko's name twenty-five thousand years ago? Now *run!*"

The battle bridge doors slid shut before Bashir could say another word. So he ran as instructed. And as he did, he tried not to picture the convoluted timeline that might emerge if the archaeologist actually carried out what it seemed she was planning.

For the truth was, unless Nog could accomplish the first part of his mission in the next three minutes, its second part would mean nothing at all.

Because none of this would ever have happened.

And nothing would ever happen again.

The universe now had ten minutes left.

CHAPTER 28

"Does it feel like coming home?" Weyoun asked.

Sisko looked around the restored bridge of the *Defiant*, almost unable to believe he was really here. It had been a shock when the transporter effect had faded and he had realized where he was. And the shock wasn't fading. He had never expected to see this ship again.

But he refused to accept returning here under any conditions but his own. "I won't play your games," he warned Weyoun.

The Vorta slipped into the command chair, examined the controls on either arm. "I wish I knew what games those might be," he said. "I'm certain they'd be amusing."

Sisko could feel his heartbeat quickening, nearly to the point of euphoria. Two weeks ago, O'Brien had clearly explained that there was only one way back to their own present, and that was by taking the *Defiant*—and only the *Defiant*—on a reverse slingshot trajectory around the the mouth of the red wormhole.

Two weeks ago, with the *Defiant* battered and being towed by the *Boreth,* even the possibility of such a return trip had been unthinkable.

Yet here was a chance. It didn't matter how slight.

In only minutes, he knew, the red wormhole would open again.

So a reverse flight *could* be attempted. And even if he had to face the terrible prospect of leaving his crew behind, if he *could* return to his present, then there *was* a chance he could slingshot back to this future with a full task force to rescue them in the minutes remaining.

Sisko shot a glance across the bridge to the engineering station, trying to see if—

"I know what you're doing," Weyoun said. "I know what you're thinking. What you're planning. What you're hoping. And I assure you, none of it is going to happen."

Sisko faced facing the Vorta, hating the way his own robes dragged on the *Defiant*'s carpet, wanting more than anything to be in uniform again. He wanted to belong on this bridge as a Starfleet officer, as he was meant to be.

Apparently untroubled by his own red robes, Weyoun steepled his hands, elbows on the arms of the chair. "Benjamin, I know you'd like nothing better than to go back to the past. To stop the Orbs of Jalbador from ever being brought together. And I know that this vessel following a reverse temporal trajectory is your only way of doing that. So, not being the fool you take me for, when I had this ship repaired I gave specific orders that her warp engines were to be . . . gutted."

Weyoun leaned forward. "Go ahead, check the engine status. You'll find you don't have any."

Sisko crossed quickly to the engineering station, called up the status screens, to make his own confirmation.

Weyoun was right.

No impulse engines. No dilithium. The warp core had been jettisoned.

The *Defiant* had as much chance of traveling at warp as a falling rock.

"No going back," Weyoun said. "Only forward." He glanced over at a time display on the science station. "At least for about the next sixteen minutes."

Sisko's pulse continue to pound, but with rage now. "Damn you, Weyoun! Why are we here?"

Weyoun seemed genuinely surprised by the sudden show of emotion. "In the absence of any definitive guidance, I thought it would be fitting—somehow in keeping with this all-important theme of balance that runs through the texts of the True Prophets. The *Defiant* after all was the first ship to enter their Temple. I thought there would be a certain poetry in having it be the last, as well. Surely you of all people see that?"

Sisko strode off to Weyoun's left, swinging his arms, shaking his head, struggling to keep his mind clear.

"I asked you a question, Benjamin."

Sisko strode back, turned, then whirled around, and abandoning all thought he lunged at Weyoun and smashed his fist into the Vorta's placid, hateful face.

Weyoun was thrown back in the command chair, then sat forward, looking down at the carpet, a small drop of blood escaping from his nose.

Sisko caught his breath, expecting to be consumed by endless fire any moment.

He would welcome it.

But nothing happened.

After a few moments, Weyoun sat back again and rubbed his face, that was all.

"There," the Vorta said as if nothing of much importance had just happened. "Did that help? Do you feel better?"

Pulse still pounding, Sisko checked the time readout. Fourteen minutes. How could he or anyone else have anything to lose at this point, so close to the end of everything? What was to stop anyone from doing *anything?*

"Yes," he said. "And I'm sure I can feel even better!"

He swung at Weyoun again and the Vorta didn't dodge his blow. There was a loud crack, a gasp, and Sisko saw blood gush forth from the Vorta's nose.

"You . . . you broke it," Weyoun said thickly, his fingers gripping the bloody bridge of his nose.

"Then kill me," Sisko taunted.

Weyoun used the back of his hand to wipe the bright red liquid that dripped down his upper lip, held out his blood-smeared hand and looked at it with a bemused expression. "It's not my decision."

"Then whose is it?" Sisko demanded.

"As you would say," Weyoun replied, "your fate is now . . . in the hands of the Prophets."

"Which ones?"

Weyoun pursed his lips as if Sisko had asked a trick question. "Why, the winners, of course."

Then he tapped a bloody finger against the comm control. *"Defiant* to *Boreth.* I believe we are ready to depart." He looked ahead. "Screen on, please."

The *Defiant*'s main viewer came to life. On it, Sisko saw the *Boreth* slide into view just as a shifting purple tractor beam shot out from it.

Then the image on the screen changed, as the *Defiant* was realigned in space. Bajor appeared, most of it in darkness, only a thin crescent showing the light of day.

Next, slowly, the planet began to recede as the *Defiant* was towed at warp.

"A lovely planet," Weyoun said wistfully. "Would you like to say good-bye?"

Sisko checked the time display again. "Not for twelve minutes."

"Oh, no," Weyoun said. "It's not for Bajor to see the end of the universe. Watch."

And then Sisko cried out in shock as on the viewer the crescent limb of his adopted world blazed with blinding light and what seemed to be a vast wind of white steam shot all around the planet and the atmosphere on the dark side glowed with fire and the oceans boiled and the continents rose and—

—in a flash of light that hurt his eyes despite the safety overrides in the viewer, Bajor became . . . dust and . . .

. . . disappeared.

"Bajor . . . what . . ."

"Supernova," Weyoun said matter-of-factly. "Don't worry though. I understand the first pulse of radiation is enough to instantly kill any living being before the shockwave hits. Your crew felt no pain. I know that was important to you."

With a roar of primal rage that startled even him, Sisko threw himself at Weyoun and was suddenly flat on his back by the science station chair, each breath he took stabbing him.

Weyoun's eyes glowed. Red. "We've played that game, I believe. And I don't like it anymore."

Sisko got to his feet. Started for Weyoun again. "You have no choice!"

A bolt of red struck Sisko's chest.

Sisko froze in place. He could not move. The lance had come from Weyoun's hand.

"Neither do you," the Vorta said. "Now be still. And perhaps . . . perhaps . . ." For a single heartbeat, the red light in Weyoun's eyes flickered, then vanished. "Perhaps we can both find out what's supposed to happen next."

Sisko stood transfixed on the bridge of his starship. There was a bigger conflict here than he had ever imagined.

Not only was the universe about to be destroyed, the one person responsible didn't even know why.

The real adversaries were still in hiding.

The universe now had nine minutes left.

CHAPTER 29

GRIGARI WERE deactivated by the millions, and equal numbers of living beings died in those final minutes, as a thousand battles raged through space in the vast cubic-parsec sphere that surrounded the Bajoran system.

But the Grigari lines held.

The last Starfleet vessel attempting to reach Bajor—to destroy whatever remained of the Ascendancy—was blown apart with less than eight minutes left.

The loss of that ship marked the Federation's end.

And with such a glorious dream lost forever, perhaps the universe no longer deserved to exist.

Inward from the chaos of those battles, at the center of the calm eye of the galactic storm, the *Boreth* towed the tiny *Defiant* at warp factor five. Easily outpacing the protomatter-induced supernova of Bajor-B'hava'el, both in real- and subspace.

Total transit time from Bajor to the required coordinates near the Denorios Belt was three minutes, twelve seconds.

The universe had just over five minutes of existence left.

It was then that the *Boreth* came to relative rest and fired a small impulse probe at the exact coordinates of the Bajoran wormhole, and for the first time in twenty-five years the doorway to the Celestial

Temple blossomed in a majestic display of energies unknown to normal space-time.

Soft blue light bathed the pale hull of the *Defiant*. And in that same radiance, five hundred kilometers distant, a trio of hourglass-shaped orbs of a translucent red substance equally alien to this realm orbited together, sparkling from within as they responded to that first verteron bloom, then matched it.

A second opening appeared against the stars and the shifting Denorios plasma ribbons. Radiating red energy as if every wavelength from the first wormhole had just been reversed.

And then, with only two minutes remaining until there would be no time at all, exactly as had been prophesied by the three great mystics of Jalbador, the doors to the Temples opened together.

Both Temples.

One Temple.

The reason why the Prophets wept.

Still immobile, in place, Sisko struggled for breath as he saw both wormholes expanding on the *Defiant*'s main viewer. Weyoun had left the command chair to stand closer to the screen, his weak Vorta eyesight robbing him of the grandeur of the spectacle before him.

"*Defiant* to *Boreth*," the Vorta breathed. "You may release us now." He turned back to Sisko. "Almost time." He open his mouth in a soundless laugh. "Almost *no* time."

The ship's collision alarms sounded abruptly.

"What is it? What's happening?" the Vorta exclaimed, cringing, his hands over his ears.

"Let . . . me . . . go. . . ." Sisko's words were little more than a rasp.

Weyoun gestured impatiently and whatever cord of energy had kept Sisko bound, he was suddenly released. He ran.

Toward the tactical station, where he saw a reading that he didn't understand.

"It looks like a Borg ship," he said to Weyoun, his voice stronger, freer by the moment. "Coming in at transwarp velocities."

"Is it headed for us?" Weyoun gasped in alarm.

Sisko did an instant, rough analysis of the vessel's trajectory. A slingshot. *Good,* he thought.

"Are we in danger?" Weyoun cried.

"No," Sisko lied. "It looks like it's out of control."

Weyoun had turned back to the viewer. The two wormholes remained open as a subspace distortion wave made them ripple. Fine filaments of energy tentatively splashed out toward each other, but still too far away to connect.

"Why aren't we moving?" Weyoun wailed.

"Where to?" Sisko asked. Why should any location matter now?

"We have to get inside the Temple," Weyoun explained despairingly. "That's the only place to escape what will happen." He looked up again. *"Defiant* to *Boreth.* This is Weyoun. Release the tractor beam."

And then, finally, a voice replied from the *Boreth.*

"Never."

Weyoun's white face betrayed his utter shock.

"Who is that? Identify yourself."

The viewer switched to a new image, and both Sisko and Weyoun flinched back as Dukat's features overwhelmed them, red eyes glowing, thin-lipped gray mouth twisted in a terrifying grimace of victory.

"You?!" Weyoun cried out in disbelief.

"You lost before, you'll lose again," Dukat gloated. "The true War of the Prophets is not your fight. It is *ours!"*

Suddenly, the *Defiant's* bridge rang with even more collision alarms, weapons-lock sirens, and intruder alerts—all sounding at once as Weyoun twisted back and forth, his hands pressed tightly over his sensitive ears.

And then the bridge pulsed with multiple flashes of light as three brilliant starbursts exploded around Sisko, and from each of them a human figure seemed to unfold.

Sisko shouted out in recognition.

It was Worf and Bashir—and a young ensign who had just arrived at DS9 only a few days before the station's destruction. All three looked disoriented. They gestured at him, urgent, their mouths open in entreaty. But Sisko couldn't hear a word they said over the blaring alarms.

He ran to join Worf, who staggered over to tactical, hampered by thick bandages wound around his torso. As soon as he was by his side, Sisko heard Worf's voice clear and victorious: "They all made it!"

"Jake?" Sisko cried out, his only thought. His only hope.

Worf nodded vigorously. "All of them! All through the ship!"

Then Sisko saw the time readout. Only a minute remained.

"We have to get into the wormhole!" he shouted to Worf.

Worf stared down at his station. "We have no engines!"

But Sisko refused to be beaten. Could no longer be beaten. Not when his son had been returned to him. Not when the Prophets were finally showing he was right to have hope.

"The tractor beam!" he yelled at Worf. "Steal momentum from the *Boreth!* Use all the station-keeping thrusters at once!"

Then the alarms cut off and Sisko saw Bashir. At the conn. Frantically trying to call up any set of controls that might let him guide the ship.

"Now can you hear oblivion approaching?" Dukat declared, triumphant, from the screen.

"Madman!" Weyoun screeched.

"Loser," Dukat cackled. "Remember that, pretender . . . remember that, *forever.*"

Then, laughing maniacally, Dukat vanished from the viewer, and Sisko looked up to see the two wormholes again, both wavering as space shifted around them.

Then the *Boreth* appeared, heading toward the blue wormhole.

"Worf!" Sisko commanded. "Everything we've got! *Now!*"

A shaft of purple light sprang forward and gripped the Klingon ship.

"He is attempting to use shields to disengage us," Worf said.

"Keep us attached as long as you can," Sisko urged.

"Nooo!" Weyoun screamed as the view of the wormholes began to shift and the *Defiant* was pulled forward by the ship it had caught.

"Dr. Bashir!" Sisko ordered. Commanded. Demanded. "Stand by on thrusters. Get us into that wormhole!"

Sisko checked the time readout.

Thirty seconds.

Worf reported. "The *Boreth* is swinging off course."

"Are we going with it?"

"Not if we detach . . . *NOW!*"

On the viewer, the *Boreth* tumbled toward the red wormhole.

As the blue wormhole grew larger.

"... *No* ..." Weyoun sobbed. "This wasn't supposed to happen."

Twenty seconds.

"Full thrusters, Doctor!"

"Hydrazine is exhausted," Bashir cried. "All we've got now is momentum."

Dazed, crazed, Sisko checked their rate of approach. Checked the time.

They weren't going to make it.

Fifteen seconds.

"DAD!"

Heart soaring, Sisko wheeled. Saw Jake run for him.

Caught him in a wordless embrace, stricken with horror at what he had brought to his child, felt the same inexpressible feelings in his son.

Jake.

Ten seconds.

Worf reported again. "Supernova shockwave approaching."

The *Defiant* trembled.

Sisko looked up. "What was that?"

The young ensign—at the science station. "Subspace pressure wave! It's caught us."

Sisko heard Worf's voice. "Distance to wormhole is decreasing."

Five seconds.

On the viewer, long tendrils of red energy. Snaking. Twisting. Engaging blue tendrils.

Sisko heard Worf again. "The wormholes are merging as predicted."

"The Temple!" Weyoun was raising his red-robed arms to the ceiling. "The Temple is restored!"

Three seconds.

Sisko appealed to everyone. And no one. "Are we going to make it?"

Two seconds.

"Are we—"

Worf said, "Impact."

Weyoun screamed.

One second.

The bridge went dark, the viewer died.

Gravity shut down.

Sisko felt the *Defiant* fall away from him. Felt Jake fall away from him.

Felt everything and everyone and nothing and no one in the universe streak away as if he and they and it had plunged from an infinite cliff and were tumbling toward the infinite—nothingness—never to land.

"I did everything I could," Sisko cried into the silence that engulfed him.

But everything he had ever done was for nothing.

For everything that had ever been was for nothing.

Zero seconds.

It was over.

$$t \; = \; \Omega$$

IT WAS SO SIMPLE a reaction, the equation describing it could fit on a leisure shirt.

What had been broken was made whole again.

The dimensional wound—upon whose fractal edges something called reality had grown like random frost—closed seamlessly in an instant. Healed at last.

And where there had been eleven dimensions of existence, there now were none.

Perfect unity had been achieved again.

In that last eternal moment before the illusion called time ceased to be, the expansion of what had been called space-time abruptly stopped. All at once. Throughout the full extent of its reach.

Some sentient intelligences might have been aware of something gone awry, a sudden slowing of the worlds around them, a sluggishness to the atmosphere or the liquid from which they drew life. But that moment of disquiet was all that they would know. For there was no more time left to explore the reason for the slowing.

If a vantage point had been possible within another realm, then the cessation of expansion would have been apparent. Followed not by an explosion from the point at which the ripped dimension had been rejoined, but by a sudden condensation. A condensation of existence.

Matter did not move through space. Nor did energy change over time. But space-time itself shrank.

Instantly.

A bubble bursting.

A dream vanishing upon awakening.

Not even a black hole extinguished existence as swiftly, as absolute as the effect of total nothingness.

There was not even a place for there to be an absence of anything.

There was not even a place for nothing to exist.

The human adventure had come to its end.

The universe was gone.

EPILOGUE

At the Doors of the Temple

SISKO OPENED HIS EYES, half expecting to see nothing, half expecting
to see white light.

Instead he saw a room.

Familiar.

Comforting.

An observation lounge. On a starship.

He shook his head, clearing it of the disturbing dream he had
had.

That's it, he thought with relief. It was all a dream. A simple disruption in his sleep during the journey out here. The journey to . . .

He looked out the curved viewports of the room.

Bajor.

A beautiful planet, he had to admit. Though he didn't want to stay
here. Not really. A space station was not the place to raise his son.

But his eyes kept turning back to Bajor, so perfect and green and
blue.

A dream . . . ?

Had he even had a dream?

He closed his eyes a moment, rubbed them, saw again the disastrous ruin of the Promenade of Deep Space 9.

He had just been on it, touring his new command.

He had been awake twenty hours, between reviewing reports and briefings, even to squeeze in an hour with Jake at the fishing hole.

So when had he managed to have a dream? Let alone a nightmare?

The door slid open. Another man entered.

Or maybe he had been there all along.

"Commander, come in," the man said. "Welcome to Bajor."

He pronounced it in the old way, with a soft *j*.

Sisko reached out to shake the man's hand, thought the man looked better than he had just a few . . .

Sisko recognized him.

"It's been a long time, Captain."

Picard! Sisko thought. *Of course . . .*

Picard looked at Sisko with a puzzled expression. "Have we met before?"

Sisko grinned with relief, all the pieces coming together.

"That depends," he said to Picard. "What does 'before' mean in nonlinear time?"

Picard did not answer the question, said what he had said before. "I assume you've been briefed on the events leading to the Cardassian withdrawal."

"It's all right," Sisko insisted. "I know what's happened. I know where we are. This is the Celestial Temple. We've met before, or will meet, or have always known each other."

It isn't over, Sisko thought in excitement. Some realm beyond the universe still existed. There was still hope. . . .

"Incorrect," Picard said. "Even here, there's a first time for everything. . . ."

Through the viewports, Bajor suddenly dissolved like a child's sandcastle, flying into billions of fragments as the shockwave of the sun's detonation hit.

Sisko shrank back from the heat of that destruction. The viewports cracked. The top surface of the conference table curled up and ignited.

Sisko looked for Picard, saw him at that table leaning forward, appearing to be falling—but no—he was—

—growing.

—transforming.

Eyes now afire with the same flames that were consuming the ashes of Bajor.

Sisko stepped back, hit something, turned to see—

—his command chair.

He was back on the *Defiant.*

The bodies of his crew around him.

All dead.

Because of him.

Everything—everyone—dead because of him.

The thing that had been Picard loomed over him, and whether it was the admiral or Grigari or Weyoun or Dukat, Sisko had no way of knowing.

All he did know was that it was coming for him, its eyes ablaze with the insane fury of the Pah-wraiths.

The creature leered down at him, slime dripping from its yawning maw. "Welcome to Hell, *Emissary!*"

The flames reached out for Sisko and their heat seared his flesh.

The universe had ended.

But in the Temple of the Pah-wraiths, his punishment had just begun.

BOOK III
INFERNO

As for the sand of that hourglass we sailed through, each speck an infinite echo of the Temple of All That Had Been and Was Still to Come, I walk through it still, today, among the stones of that city out of time that in these words is called V'halla, the one place and the true place where all paths lead. And even now, as I stand—a man far older than He Who Found This City ever was in this realm—my hand on the ancient blocks that bear his name, he is with me, and his hand guides mine, even as does his heart. ANSLEM, I whisper in that soft sweet tongue of this world we have adopted. FATHER, I say in the language of our first home. And on all of those paths that stretch out from this moment, I hear his answer, telling me that what we leave behind continues, and that our Journey, still, is without end . . .

—JAKE SISKO, *Anslem*

PROLOGUE

In the Hands of the Prophets

"*THIS MUST END,*" *Captain Jean-Luc Picard says.*

The Sisko laughs as he pushes back his catcher's mask and strides toward the pitcher's mound. The scent of fresh-cut grass explodes within him, bringing with it every summer day he's ever known.

"But that's just the point," the Sisko says. "It didn't *end!" He throws the baseball to Picard.*

Admiral Ross angrily gets to his feet in the Wardroom of Deep Space 9 and catches the baseball. "Because it does not *begin!"*

Beside him, General Martok says, "Because it does not *happen."*

The Sisko points at the casualty board where the names of the Dominion War dead appear and disappear in endless nonlinearity. As an unseen crowd chants for a hit, the baseball leaps by itself from Ross's hand and the Sisko swings and the baseball drives through the casualty board which shatters into a sparkling, glittering comet's tail, and again they are all on the field, under the stars, as the night game begins, the scent of fresh-cut summer grass mingling now with a crisp autumn chill that carries the delicate smoke of burning leaves.

"No," the players protest. Vash and Rom and Kira and Lwaxana and Dulmer and Lucsly and Ezri and Arla—they are the Sisko's team, unhappy, staring at the images on their hats and shirts—the

Station and a baseball? Juxtaposition is lost on them. "No!" *they say.* "No!"

But "Yes," *the Sisko says as he holds up the baseball.* "This is the essence. This is why you brought me here. This is what I am here to teach you." *He tosses the ball straight up into the air. He swings the bat. A line drive to the right of second base. No one runs for it.*

"You throw the ball," *the Sisko says.* "You hit the ball. You throw the ball. You hit the ball. And each time, everything is different."

Base swings his bat'leth *and knocks the bat from the Sisko's right hand.* "Adversarial," *the tiny Ferengi squeaks.*

Satr snatches a new baseball from the Sisko's left hand and gives it to her sister, Leen. "Confrontational," *the Andorian sisters say together.*

Interruption.

In the light space, Kai Winn stands before the Sisko. "He must be destroyed," *she says.*

"You've said that before," *the Sisko reminds her.*

"I always say that," *the Kai replies.*

"But why destroy your Emissary?"

The Kai spins around and the Sisko falls through the flames of the Fire Caves with Gul Dukat at his side.

"Pay attention," *Dukat says as his gray flesh crisps away from his bones and then is restored in cycles without end.* "Deep Space 9 is not destroyed. The* Defiant *is not in the future. There is only one Temple."*

The Sisko thinks of a time, of a moment, makes it real, takes them all to the bridge of the Defiant *as Bajor is consumed by the super-nova of that world's sun.*

"This does not happen," *Kai Weyoun says.*

"Then why do I remember it?" *the Sisko asks.*

"You are linear," *Kai Opaka says.*

"I realize now that so are you," *the Sisko says.* "In a different way than I am, but linear just the same."

Jake stands before the Sisko, twelve years old, the legs of his overalls rolled up, a fishing pole on his shoulder. "Explain," *he says.*

The Sisko smiles, reaches out to rub the boy's head, walks with him through the torchlit tunnels of B'hala, Ranjen Koral at their sides.

"Here," *the Sisko says. He points to the stone on which his name* *is carved.* "This is the past." *He turns around on the bridge of the* Defiant *to point to the main viewer on which the red and blue wormholes reach out tendrils of negative energy to entwine and combine and end the realm of linear time forever.* "This is the future." *He turns around on the dark and deserted Promenade and points toward Quark's bar where the Red Orbs of Jalbador float in alignment, the red wormhole beginning to open.* "And this is the* now *which followed from the past and from which the future* might *follow in turn."*

The Sisko's father stops in midstep on Bourbon Street, the sounds of a dozen jazz bands blending in the night, each from its own club on the rain-slicked streets around them. "Might?"

The Sisko understands the Prophets' confusion. "Might," *he says. He inhales deeply, drawing in the sweet, damp scent of New Orleans.* "You throw the ball. You hit the ball. And each time . . ."

"Everything is . . . different?" *his father says.*

"It* might *be a pop fly,"* the Sisko says. "It* might *be a line drive. It* might *be fair. It* might *be foul. It* might *be caught.* Might *be fumbled.* Might *go over the fence or the batter* might *even miss and strike out."*

Worf walks up a narrow set of stairs, carrying a saxophone. "So the wormholes—the two wormholes—they are a 'might'?"

"A possibility," *the Sisko says.* "One result or another. One time or another."

They stand on the Promenade, on the first day the Sisko steps onto it, his path blocked by debris, by work crews cleaning and repairing.

At the door to the temple, the monk bows his head to the Sisko and says, "Another time."

"Another time," *the Sisko agrees.* "It* might *be this time. It* might *be the next time."*

"Different times?" *Kasidy asks.*

"Different possibilities?" *Odo asks.*

"Always," *Sisko says.* "You throw the ball . . ."

Jake swings and the crack of the bat echoes and the ball soars and—

Jadzia swings and the crack of the bat echoes and the ball bounces foul over the third base line and—

Nog swings and misses and—

Vic swings and the crack of the bat echoes and the ball drives straight at Solok on the pitching mound who ducks and—

Keiko swings and the ball ticks and—

They all *swing and each time—*

Another thing happens. A different thing happens.

"A different time," Jennifer Sisko says.

Sisko nods, the lesson taught. "Another time."

An infinity of eternities in just two words. An infinity now within the understanding of the Prophets.

The Sisko rides the turbolift down with Worf and O'Brien and Jake and Nog. They are in the unmapped section, standing before the door that opens into the hidden room of Deep Space 9.

The Sisko looks around at the Prophets. He does not bring them here. He does not know who does.

The door to the hidden room remains closed.

The Prophets wait.

"Do you want me to open this door?" *the Sisko asks.* "Is that why you brought me here?"

"This is the Emissary's door," *Quark says.*

"My door?" *the Sisko asks.*

"Uh, no," *Rom says.* "Not yours. The Emissary's."

The Sisko smiles suddenly, another mystery revealed. "You still don't know, do you?" *he asks.* "When I first came to you, you didn't know who I was. You wanted to destroy me. You didn't recognize me as your Emissary."

Kira puts her hand on the Sisko's shoulder. "You are not our *Emissary. You are* the *Emissary."*

The Sisko stops smiling. "Is there another?" *he asks.*

"Open the door," *Curzon Dax says.*

The Sisko faces the door to the hidden room in the unmapped section of Deep Space 9. He thinks of it opening, makes it real.

The door remains closed.

As if he is in a linear realm, the Sisko puts his hand on the door control, inputs the 'open' command.

The door opens.

Inside, a wormhole tunnel of slowly pulsing light—full white, the perfect blending of blue and red and all the other colors of the spectrum.

The white tunnel is open, waiting.

The Sisko doesn't hesitate. He steps through the portal.

There are walls to either side of him, glittering with every color of light, sparkling, not like a comet's tail, but in a pattern of regular, repeating . . . shapes.

Hourglass shapes.

The Sisko is in a tunnel with walls made of Orbs.

Countless. Endless.

He turns to—

—a human in clothes that are centuries old, with transparent lenses held over his eyes by a frame of thin metal that—

The Sisko gasps, for even here, there can be surprise. "Benny?" he asks.

Benny Russell takes off his glasses. "Welcome, Messenger. The Gods of the Spacewarp Passage await you."

The Sisko thinks he understands. "I know what you're doing. You're showing me another possibility. Another time."

Benny shrugs. "It . . . might be."

The Sisko looks at the endless tunnel of Orbs. "But what about these? Are they real? So many of them?"

"Yes," Benny says.

"Why did you make so many of them?"

"We don't," Kai Winn says.

"They are here," Kai Opaka says.

"In another time . . . before us," Kai Bareil says.

The Sisko looks at Bareil and the robes he wears. "You were never Kai."

Bareil bows his head. "Another time."

The Sisko looks back at the Orbs. "You didn't make the Orbs? You didn't build the Temple? They were already here when you arrived?"

"Possibilities," Solok says.

"But leading where?" the Sisko asks.

Curzon points ahead, past the Orbs, to the end of the new Temple.

The Sisko peers in that direction, unable to picture himself travel-ing there, but able to see . . . to see . . .

Jake, older, in the excavations of B'hala, carefully brushing soil from a stone carved with ancient Bajoran glyphs which the Sisko can almost recognize.

Beside Jake, Kasidy waits. Unthinkingly, the Sisko reaches for her. She is watching Jake, cradling a young child, no more than three years old, but with wisdom far older reflected in attentive eyes—

"My child," the Sisko says, arm outstretched. "Kasidy—our child."

The dust of B'hala swirls around Jake and Kasidy and the Sisko's child. The three turn as if sensing his presence.

The walls of Orbs come together. The end of the Temple. The new wormhole an infinity away now.

"Why bring me here?" the Sisko demands.

"You brought us here, Lieutenant," Captain James T. Kirk says.

The Sisko is on the bridge of the first Enterprise. *He feels the old-fashioned warp generators vibrating through the deck, smells the faint odor of tetralubisol from the air circulators.*

"What is this?" the Sisko asks.

"A possibility?" Kirk asks.

"I don't understand," the Sisko says.

"Then finish your story," the Sisko's mother says from behind him.

The Sisko turns around at his desk in his office above Ops. His mother stands framed by the viewport, the white light from the opening Temple refracting through her lustrous hair.

"That is why you are here," his mother says. "And when you have finished your story . . ."

At last, the Sisko understands. "Then you will tell me why you are here."

Gul Dukat steps up to the plate, taps his bat on home. "Throw the ball," he says.

The Sisko laughs as he winds up on the mound, no longer merely describing the game to the Prophets, but at last playing the game with them.

"Hit the ball!" he calls out to Dukat.

The baseball speeds through the bright summer air of Ebbets Field.

Dukat swings his bat beneath the dome of the Pike City Stadium. The crack of the bat echoes and—

—in a superposition of infinities, all possibilities happen at once. And the Sisko's story continues . . .

CHAPTER 1

CAPTAIN BENJAMIN SISKO of space station Deep Space 9 fell backward as the flight deck of the *United Space Ship Defiant* burst into unholy flames around him. Then, huddled, panting, gasping, he saw bank after bank of calculating tubes and visi-screens detonate in response to the spectacular heat, saw Jean-Luc Picard rear up on mightily thewed reptilian legs, completing his incredible transformation into a six-limbed Venusian Firebeast!

Because what had at first appeared to be the legendary captain of Starfleet was in reality that hideous energy life-form known in the whispered legends of a hundred fantastic alien worlds as an Antigod of the Spacewarp Passage.

Ben Sisko willed himself to his feet, his proud African features glistening in the hellish light of the awful surrounding flames of destruction. As a child growing up in New New Orleans on Venus, he had once been chased by a Firebeast and almost devoured alive—a singular experience which to this day brought him pulse-pounding nightmares.

I must assume the Antigod is able to read my mind through some advanced telepathic technique, Ben Sisko thought urgently. *That might explain how it has been able to reach into my subconscious mind and*

extract a frightening memory from my childhood. It
wants to disorient me--make me incapable of fighting
back.

"You will never withstand me in this timeless void without
dimension!" the Firebeast thundered, its cavernous voice still eerily
echoing that of the genteel starship captain whose form it had
assumed. "The Moibius Effect has destroyed the universe. Now you
must do battle with me for all eternity!"

"If that is my fate, then I shall face it like the Starfleet officer I
am!" Ben Sisko exclaimed proudly as he raised the only weapons he
had against the loathsome creature that towered above him—his two
bare fists!

"Bravely said, Earthman," the Firebeast hissed, each breath a
sibilant sussuration of reptilian evil. Then, in a motion too quick to
describe, it launched itself and flew swiftly by means of telekinetic
atomic projection to land on Ben Sisko, and with hind claws the size
of a strong man's forearm, rip open his chest and—

"Damn," Benny Russell muttered.

He stared at the typewriter on his rickety desk. The typing paper
curled up in it stared back, the incomplete sentence describing
Captain Sisko's fate taunting him. Through his open window rumbled the sounds of midnight traffic in Harlem, in the summer of
1953. An almost nonexistent breeze merely teased his open curtains,
making his cramped apartment as hot as he imagined the flight deck
of the *Defiant* to be.

"Okay," Benny sighed. "Firebeast is too powerful. Unless . . .
Sisko's dagger collection!"

He snapped the crisp white paper from the typewriter, making the
platen whirr. Along with it came a nearly exhausted sheet of carbon
paper and a crinkly, semitransparent sheet of onion skin. Benny
slipped the carbon out from between the other two sheets, then
balled them up and—

Sisko screamed as all the dimensions of space collapsed upon
him at once, twisting the bulkheads and deck and ceiling of the
Defiant's bridge, crushing the bodies of his fallen crew, leaving him
compressed and forcing him into an inescapable, dimensionless

point, a singularity in which his only thought and knowledge was that his life had been from its beginning an illusion, mere letters on a page, now discarded.

He screamed in despair and frustration and outrage until there was no more room to move or to fight or even to breathe.

He was nothing now. A figment of a dead man's imagination. A fleeting dream. Meaningless.

And then Starfleet met the Borg at Wolf 359 and the whole senseless story began again . . .

Bashir calmed himself. After the lights of the *Defiant*'s bridge had flickered into darkness, he had experienced a momentary flash of panic. As a Starfleet officer, he had had to contemplate the possibility of his own death on numerous occasions. In the abstract, he felt confident he could face the actual moment with composure.

But to experience the destruction of the *universe?* The obliteration of *everything?* Bashir was not sure that was something he was prepared to face with a stiff upper lip and the determination to do his duty.

Yet even now, after the light had fled, he was aware of sensation. The *Defiant*'s artificial gravity generators were still working. He could hear the compact vessel creak softly around him—the normal sounds of the ship as far as he could tell.

And then the emergency lights switched on, dim but steady.

"It didn't happen!" Bashir said to the empty corridor. He grinned. Rom's and O'Brien's calculations had been wrong. Existence continued. Everything was going to be—

"Julian!"

The urgency of that shout struck him like the crack of a whip in his ear, and Bashir wheeled to see Jadzia Dax motioning him into the *Defiant*'s engineering section. As he was, she was dressed in the standard-issue Starfleet uniform of the year 2400—ribbed black-fabric trousers and jacket, the shoulder of which was blue to designate Jadzia's science specialty, with her lieutenant commander pips vertically centered just below the jacket's collar.

Bashir raced down the corridor, through the open doors, and skidded to a halt as he saw who was waiting for him with Jadzia and Captain Sisko.

His parents.

They were holding on to each other, obviously upset, both wearing Federation penal uniforms. Bashir was startled to see that his father's once-black mustache was almost all white now.

"Mother? Father? How—"

Sisko didn't let him finish. "There's no time, Doctor. Show him, Dax."

At once, Jadzia pulled him over to what seemed to be a large power converter in the center of the deck, which Bashir couldn't remember having noticed before.

"But how did *they* get here?" Bashir glanced over his shoulder at his parents. Sisko had an arm around Richard and was holding Amsha's hand. All three looked extremely worried.

"Converging realities," Jadzia said crisply, annoyed. "Twisted timelines. I don't know. We can work it out later. But right now, the only thing that's keeping the universe from ending the way Starfleet feared is this singularity-containment generator." She pointed at what Bashir had taken to be a power converter. "The *Defiant*'s been pulled into the red wormhole and the presence of the black hole fueling our warp engines is preventing the final collapse of normal space-time."

"But . . . singularity containment is a Romulan technology . . . and this is a Cardassian control interface."

"Exactly," Jadzia said. "Just like in the Infirmary on Deep Space 9. You know how to operate Cardassian controls in your sleep, Julian. All you have to do is adjust this interface to stabilize the singularity-containment field, and the universe will be saved."

She swung him around to face her, catching him off guard as she pulled him tight and kissed him. "I know you can do it," she whispered, her breath warm in his ear. "We all know you can do it." Intensely blue, her eyes captured his. "And then we'll have the time we need to be together, the way we're supposed to be."

Jadzia stepped back then, leaving him shaken and stirred and at the controls.

"Save us, son," his mother cried out behind him.

"We're counting on you," Sisko added.

"Yes, yes," Bashir muttered as he studied the controls. Jadzia was right. They *were* simple, grouped in the same standard Cardassian logic patterns as the medical equipment in his Infirmary. All he had to do was to—

The deck pitched and the *Defiant* groaned.

"Hurry, Julian!" Jadzia urged him. "The field will hold for only fifty-two seconds!"

Bashir put his fingers over the master-sequencing control surfaces. He saw exactly what he had to do to stabilize the field—the equations were identical to those he used with medical isolation forcefields. He tapped the surface that would tell the power converter to stand by to receive a new command string.

But sirens wailed first.

"What did you do?!" Sisko shouted.

Bashir stared down at the controls in disbelief. They were different from what he had thought. Everything was shifted. He had hit the wrong control and—

"You dropped the field!" Jadzia said.

"Julian!" his father pleaded. "Save us!"

Jadzia yanked Bashir away from the controls. "You idiot! You've killed us all! The whole *universe*, Julian!" She slapped him hard across his face as tears streaked her own. "How stupid can you be?!"

"No! Jadzia! I know what I did wrong! I can fix it!" Bashir turned back to the controls.

But shafts of unbound energy were already beginning to puncture the control surfaces as the *Defiant*'s singularity began to unravel into useless cosmic string.

"No!" Bashir said.

"It's your fault!" Jadzia railed at him. "It's all your fault because you're so stupid!"

"Stupid!" his mother and father cried.

"Stupid!" Sisko echoed.

Now all the controls were melting, becoming unusable as the bulkheads of the engineering section began to fade into nonexistence. And in those last moments of awareness as all light vanished, Julian Bashir realized that the one thing worse than being present at the end of the universe was being present at the end and knowing it was all his fault . . .

Then, after darkness enveloped him, all around the compact vessel creaked softly—the normal sounds of the ship as far as he could tell. A moment later, the emergency lights switched on, dim but steady.

"It didn't happen!" he said to the empty corridor. He grinned again. Everything was going to be—

Then Jadzia called to him from engineering. And everything began again . . .

Elim Garak sneezed, and when he opened his eyes, his customer was laughing at him.

"Can't take the heat, hmm?"

"I'm sorry?" Garak said politely. He looked down at his body. The last thing he remembered was being clothed in the stultifyingly unfashionable robes of the Bajoran Ascendancy, monitoring the computers of the bridge of the *Boreth,* trying to understand exactly what was happening. Gul Dukat—at least, the crazed maniac who claimed to be the Dukat of the year 2400—had not been particularly forthcoming.

"Are you all right?" the customer asked. "I know we prefer the temperature to be higher than you do."

Garak looked up, nodded. "Quite fine, actually. I was merely—"

"Then get on with it."

Garak looked down at his body again, trying to recall what was wrong with what he saw. Instead of the loose-fitting robes, he was now garbed in a rather dull gray tunic. And he was kneeling on the floor of . . . he glanced around, then relaxed. He was in his tailor shop on DS9. Home ground. Safe.

But then he caught sight of the small piece of tailor's chalk he was holding in one hand and the measurement sensor in his other. He frowned, puzzled, as he tried to remember exactly how he had come to be here. Then a vicious backhand blow hit his temple and he rocked back with a gasp.

"Oww," Garak said as he placed his hand to the smooth side of his head. He looked up at the customer and—"Father?!"

He fell to the floor as Enabran Tain, chief of the Obsidian Order, Garak's father, and dead two years in Garak's own time, kicked his son in the shoulder.

"You insolent filth!" Tain exclaimed. "You think being a trustee is a gift that cannot be taken back?"

Garak pushed himself upright, overwhelmed by confusion. "Trustee?"

"Typical," Tain grunted. He tugged off the pinned-together, half-made jacket he'd been wearing, crumpled it into a ball, threw it to the floor. "Dukat finally finds one of you with a steady hand and an eye for detail, and you've got ore poisoning."

Garak leaned back against the purchasing counter for support. For an instant, he looked past his father to the Promenade. But it was wrong, somehow. Dark, its few lights too blue, the air clouded with the aromatics as the Cardassians preferred.

"Pay attention to me!" Tain commanded.

I've traveled through time again, Garak guessed, *to the time of the Occupation of Bajor.* Just as the *Defiant* had been thrown forward when the station had been destroyed, something must have happened when the *Boreth* reached the wormhole. But now, he decided quickly, instead of going forward in time, he'd gone back— far enough to warn everyone about the Red Orbs of Jalbador and the second wormhole in the Bajoran system. Far enough back to prevent the destruction of Cardassia Prime by the Ascendancy, and save the universe.

"Father," Garak said, "I apologize for my seeming confusion, but I have just had a most remarkable experience which—"

"You're mistaken," Tain said. He reached behind his back to get something from his belt. "What you mean to say is that you're *about* to have a remarkable experience."

"I beg your pardon?"

"Too late for that," Tain said as he aimed a small disruptor at his son.

Garak held up his hands. "No!" Then at once he realized what had seemed so wrong. His skin was pale pink, his nails clear.

He ran those alien hands over his neck, felt something distressingly scrawny, no sign whatever of a strong, doubled spinal cord. He touched his face—no eye ridges, no forehead umbilicus, that proud circle of flesh worn by every Cardassian since the creators had raised Ailam and Neeron from the swamps of Cardassia. Since a spark of divine lightning had imbued them with souls, leaving the sign of their elevation on their foreheads for all to see.

Instead, in the midst of unbearably smooth flesh, the only texture Garak could feel was on the bridge of his nose, and that was a small series of . . .

Garak wheeled to face a fitting mirror, then stared in horror as he saw himself. "I'm . . . a Bajoran."

"And a bad tailor to boot," Tain said in disgust. "Dukat must have chosen you to insult me on purpose."

Garak whirled to face his father. "No! Father, wait! I can explain!"

But all Tain did was to press the firing stud on his disruptor and Garak saw everything in his shop, in the station, and in the universe shrink back from him at warp speed as he fell into darkness.

Only to be prodded painfully awake by an overseer in the ore-processing chamber. "You can sleep when you're dead, Bajoran!"

Mind numb, body aching, Garak loaded ore all that shift, until Gul Dukat himself had him pulled aside to ask if he had ever considered being a tailor . . .

Miles O'Brien opened his eyes and for a moment thought he was back in the half-excavated city of B'hala. The sand he lay upon was searing hot. The air dry. The sun blinding.

But as he stood up, trying to recall what had happened in those last moments of consciousness on the *Boreth,* he realized there were no ancient stone-block buildings nearby. Nor any randomly scattered rocks, nor mountains in the distance.

Only an endless plain of flat sand stretching out boundless and bare in all directions.

"That doesn't make sense," O'Brien said. His voice sounded odd to him. The air was far too still, not even a hint of a breeze to stir the sand.

His engineer's mind sought the pattern and made the connection at once.

"No wind," he said. "That's why there're no sand dunes." He peered around again, trying to see how far the horizon was. But it melted into the soft distortion of rippling heat, unseen and unmeasurable.

"That's not right," O'Brien said. All that heat radiating from the sand should warm the air, form convection currents, drive winds. "What kind of planet is this, anyway?"

He squinted up at the pitiless sun, trying to judge its color. Too white for Earth or Bajor-B'hava'el. He held up his hand to cast a shadow over his eyes, tried to find evidence of clouds or any other type of atmospheric disturbance.

Then, despite the omnipresent heat he shivered. Because what he *was* able to see was so unexpected, so impossible, yet so obvious.

There was a structure in the sky.

He could just make out the vast geodesic pattern of its framework, some beams gleaming in the sunlight, the thickness and colors of others subtly changing as they neared the horizon and the angles of their shadows changed.

"No . . ." O'Brien said as his eyes, attuned to the structure, now traced it all through the sky, reaching down to every point on the surrounding horizon and stretching up to the sun—

—and *behind* it.

He was in a Dyson Sphere.

An artificial structure built *around* a star.

And if this was anything like the Dyson Sphere the *Enterprise* had discovered near the Norpin Colony, it had to be the greatest feat of engineering that could ever be attempted in . . .

"The universe," O'Brien whispered. He shook his head in confusion, felt sweat break out on his scalp. *The universe was supposed to end,* he thought. *We were heading into the wormhole . . .*

He looked around again in growing panic. There were too many unanswered questions.

How had he come to be here? Who had built the sphere? How was such a structure even possible?

He needed to make notes, to plan, to organize the thoughts cascading in his mind. Automatically, he patted the robes he wore, trying to find something, *anything* to write with.

But his flowing garments held nothing, no matter how many times he searched their folds.

O'Brien stared out for a long time at the unchanging vista, and when he ceased, there was nothing else he could do but begin again.

Because there was nothing to come to an end here. No action to take and then to repeat. He was alone and useless, an engineer without tools, trapped in a structure not even Miles O'Brien could comprehend, not even if he took forever . . .

Jake Sisko input faster, causing the words of his novel to appear on the padd at superhuman speed.

But the delete cursor was gaining on him, only eleven lines

behind, devouring the words he wrote almost as fast as he could input them.

Jake's fingers ached, his eyes blurred, his mind swam with words as he struggled to lay down his thoughts and emotions in some intelligent order.

But the cursor was only seven lines away now, erasing all his thoughts and emotions before they were a minute old. Soon, he knew, each word would vanish as he wrote it.

Jake felt a cramp building in his wrists. Blood from his fingernails smeared the input controls, making his fingers slip, slowing him down.

He had almost run out of thoughts, out of words, of life . . .

He input faster yet.

But with a certainty that horrified him in its inevitability, he knew he could never input fast enough . . .

For his part, Quark was almost blinded by the shocking radiance of pure latinum as the doors to the Divine Treasury opened before him. Here at the celestial source of the Great Material River, there was no need for that oh-so-precious metal to be debased by being pressed with gold. The stairs he ascended, the coins he used to bribe his way to the head of the line, even the robes he wore, all were pure latinum, gleaming, somehow liquidly solid, and endlessly beguiling.

A choir of accountants burst into song as Relk, the Chief Auditor, opened both sets of books in which Quark's life was recorded.

Quark waited as he faced his final audit. He told himself he had nothing to fear. That the ledgers of his life would balance and the threat of spending eternity in the Debtor's Dungeon was nothing to be concerned about.

And it wasn't.

Relk shut his books with a double thump as he congratulated Quark, informed him he had shown a most admirable return on investment and would be admitted to the Head Office to take his place at the Counting Board of the Divine Nagus himself.

Quark felt as if he were floating, every care of his past life lifting away from him. Dimly, he now remembered something about being beamed aboard the *Boreth* with Gul Dukat. Something about the . . . what was it now? Oh, yes, about the universe ending.

But why should he have to be concerned about the universe ending when he was this close to his final dividend?

The Junior Assistants in their latinum robes hovered around him as he stepped onto the executive floor.

He followed the latinum-paneled corridor until he came to the solid latinum door that awaited him.

Overwhelmed, Quark gazed at the shining door before him. Every childhood fantasy he had had about the Divine Treasury was turning out to be true.

It all worked out, Quark thought as he surrendered to bliss. *Life makes sense—or, at least,* made *sense after all.*

He had lived a good life of greed and self-absorption, and now he was to be rewarded for all time.

He lifted his hand and knocked on the Divinely Nagal door.

The booming voice that addressed him by name bade him enter.

If possible, it seemed to Quark that the light inside was even brighter, issuing forth from latinum even purer than he could imagine, surrounding . . . *Him.* The Divine Nagus. Sitting in his executive chair behind his executive desk, mounds of latinum coins waiting to be counted before him.

It was all too much. Quark dropped to his knees, hung his head in supplication with only one quick glance around to see if anyone before him might have dropped a spare coin or two, or anything else of value. Then he abjectly thanked the Divine Nagus for granting him an eternal position here.

To which the Divine Nagus replied, "Uh . . . sorry, but there appears to have been . . . a mistake, brother."

Quark's head snapped up at once, and his appalled gaze fell on—

"ROM!?"

And no matter how loudly Quark squealed in that small dark cell that was forever his in Debtor's Dungeon, it was never loud enough to drown out the mocking laughter of his idiot brother—mocking laughter that echoed forever . . .

Arla Rees struggled through mud that stung the raw wounds on her arms and legs and mixed with her blood.

Phaser blasts crisscrossed the air around her, each shot coming closer, making it harder and harder to run.

She fell to her knees in the mud. Looked back.

The Cardassian soldiers were still advancing, implacable, sure of their victory.

Arla tried to stand, but the thick mud held her hands and feet prisoner. Fighting panic, she concentrated on reaching one hand forward to grab a rock and pull herself forward. Instead, the rock broke free of the mud and came away in her hand.

And it wasn't a rock.

It was a head.

Bajoran.

Unseeing eyes wide with terror.

She dropped the grisly object.

"Help me," Arla cried out, hopeless. "Please . . . in the name of the Prophets . . ."

And before her plea had ended, a shaft of warm protective blue light fell across her, and she looked up from the mud to see Kai Opaka, as she had been when she was but a simple prylar, young and slender, come to New Sydney to raise funds to aid the resistance on Occupied Bajor.

Arla sobbed with relief and happiness as she realized that the light was not shining *onto* the figure, but was shining *out* from her. Now she knew exactly what was happening. "You're not Opaka, you're a Prophet!"

Opaka nodded with a beatific smile, and Arla held out her hand to that light and to that comfort.

"Save me," she whispered, at last sure of the Prophets' love.

The shining figure shook her head. "If only you had believed in us while you were alive, my child. If only you had believed . . ."

And then the light vanished.

And with it, Opaka.

And Arla screamed as Cardassian hands grabbed her from behind and ripped at her clothes and . . .

Days later, when the soldiers were through with her, she was thrown into the mass grave and buried alive with the others from the camp, all the while fighting for breath as the dirt covered her, until she awoke to find herself struggling through the mud of the battlefield, pursued by Cardassians, forsaken by the Prophets, by her own choice, again . . .

• • •

Worf, son of Mogh, battled unceasingly upon the flat black rocks beneath the storm-filled sky and felt the thunder of the fire geysers as they shot upward transforming the landscape with flame.

He did not know what had happened to the *Defiant* or to his captain or to his wife or to his universe.

He was not sure where he was or how long he had been here.

But none of those questions concerned him now because in his hands he held the Sword of Kahless, and whatever had happened to him, that weapon's edge was true and sliced through the flesh and bone of his enemies as if the fire of Kri'stak still burned within it.

On this endless battlefield, Romulan warriors fell like wheat before his scythe, and the rocks were slick with steaming green blood.

Worf could taste the coppery tang of the mist it formed as he roared his battle cry, swinging, slicing, thrusting forward to twist and disembowel, wading through the Romulan invaders as did Kaylon at the battle of the Straker Dome, when the two Empires had ended their first war with the Romulans so deservedly crushed.

Worf savored the power of Kahless in his arms and back and legs as he endlessly pressed his attack. From time to time, he would have a moment's respite as the Romulans regrouped, their numbers never seeming to diminish. In those moments, Worf would wonder if this was *Gre'thor,* the land where the dishonored were consigned upon their deaths. But then he would lose himself again within the pure and absolute sensations of combat, and he would know that in some way, he had arrived at *Sto-Vo-Kor.*

All he had to do was to vanquish enough Romulans, and he would arrive at the doors of the Great Hall where Kahless himself would greet him and invite him to join the honored dead and the bloodwine would flow for all eternity.

Yet even if that bloodwine were never to flow again, even if Kahless were an infinity away, Worf suffered no remorse or frustration at his fate.

Endless battle.

What better use for eternity could there be for a Klingon?

He intensified his attack and swung his *bat'leth* so swiftly the edge of it glowed and sparks flew as it carved through his enemies' armor.

A Centurion flew apart in a spurt of bright green.

Two Proconsuls spun into each other, spilt blood and entrails mixing.

A female with Trill spots raised her hands as if to beg for mercy. But Worf cut her in two as well and charged on.

Now humans came before him, but since they wore the earliest uniforms of Starfleet, Worf knew they were from the time of the atrocities of their first contact with the Empire, and that they deserved death even more than did the Romulans.

Now the alien blood that flew was red, and his *bat'leth* blurred in frenzied action, its blade beginning to thrum.

Humans fell by the scores, by the hundreds. Another Trill female rose among them, and she also carried a *bat'leth*. Her mouth opened in a soundless cry, her face turned toward him, as if she wished him to hear her above the constant roar of battle.

But Worf could not be fooled by his enemies' tricks and he brought his weapon down across her shoulder to fling her head from her lifeless body.

Now his boots crushed chittering tribbles with every step. Wild *targ* nipped at his legs as Romulans and humans and Breen massed before him. Until every enemy of the Empire he fought here and now. Fought and vanquished.

And the Sword of Kahless no longer thrummed—it *sang*.

Now Worf added his voice to that of his weapon's, chanting the Warrior's Anthem, keeping time with each deadly stroke of his blade.

Now his boots splashed through an ankle-high basin of blood, and the flickering tongues of the fire geysers reached higher and the Trill female *blocked* his deathblow and made him stumble.

For a timeless instant, Worf knelt, braced for the inevitable impact of a dozen blades as his enemies took advantage of his fall. But death did not come.

Someone was keeping his enemies at bay.

He looked up to see the Trill female fighting in his place.

Worf leaped to his feet, raised his *bat'leth,* profoundly troubled. He had no doubt that a female could be a warrior bound for *Sto-Vo-Kor.* He knew the Trill species to be valorous and fully expected to find warriors of other worlds honored at Kahless's table. But though this female was fighting bravely and fiercely, it seemed wrong to him that she fought at all.

Somewhere, deep in the memories of whatever his existence had been before this time, it was as if he knew this one female should not be placed in danger, ever.

He responded instinctually.

With a roar of unbridled passion, Worf swept his *bat'leth* through a mass of Breen and from the thick mist of their venting coolant he jumped to the Trill's side, then brought his weapon into perfect synchronization with hers.

She took the upstroke, gutting a Romulan centurion, and as she withdrew her blade, Worf covered with a sidesweep that dropped two humans. As he brought his weapon back to strike again, the Trill's blade flashed up to deflect a Breen's cryodagger.

They were in perfect balance, she and he, Trill and Klingon. Aligned, finely tuned, two warriors fighting as one. What higher ideal could there be? What greater eternal reward could be bestowed?

Turning for an instant from the battle, Worf bared his teeth in a full-throated growl of victory at the blood-drenched face of the female. "I am Worf, son of Mogh, warrior of the House of Martok! Identify yourself!"

The female lifted her weapon high to brush her arm across her face, for a brief instant wiping away the blood of their enemies so that Worf glimpsed her pale skin, her dark spots, her pale blue eyes so familiar.

"I am Jadzia, symbiont of Dax, warrior of the House of Martok!"

The female's words echoed so loudly in Worf's mind he no longer heard the roar of battle. How was it possible that she—an alien—had been admitted to Martok's house?

Then Worf became aware that somehow time had slowed. His enemies still advanced on him, yet they no longer moved closer. Even the fountainhead of fire geysers hung motionless against the dark sky's unmoving storm clouds.

"Jadzia?" Worf repeated.

The Trill female's *bat'leth* melted from her hands as some bright light shone upon her from a source Worf couldn't see, the glare stunning him so he was no longer aware of the frozen battle around him.

"Worf!" the Trill cried out. "Look at me!"

But Worf shook his head, tried to step away. It had to be a trick, an illusion to break his fighting spirit. The only way a Trill could ever join a Klingon House would be through marriage to—

The female slapped Worf so hard his ears rang.

"Look at me!" she commanded.

The blow was proof enough for Worf. She was no illusion. She was another of his endless, infinite, eternal enemies, no different from the hundreds of other female Trills he had killed in this battle. Female Trills that looked exactly like—

"Jadzia," he breathed again as he raised his *bat'leth* to dispatch her.

But then, before his weapon could descend, in that one split second in which she might have escaped, the Trill rushed forward and took his face in her hands and she kissed him so hard that his bottom lip split and he tasted his own blood as he remembered he had on his wedding night when his bride had—

A light of piercing intensity struck Worf as he felt himself lifted, then propelled through a tunnel of darkness until he was someplace else where he fell to his knees and there before him, her face slick with tears, not blood, was . . . Jadzia.

Jadzia of the House of Martok.

His bride.

"You're safe now," she whispered, reaching out for him.

And with that, Worf remembered.

Everything.

And was the second of them to be free.

CHAPTER 2

AFTER THE FIRST thousand years in the Dyson Sphere, O'Brien noticed that something was moving on the horizon. A dark shape, indistinct, shimmering, flickering in and out of existence in the turbulence of heat that rose from the level sand surrounding him.

Part of him wanted to cry out and run toward the illusion, to beg forgiveness for whatever he had done that had brought him here. But another part, the reasoning part, the engineering part bludgeoned into submission by the mere fact of this Dyson Sphere's existence, saw no reason for moving.

This part of him had remembered the old legends of Earth and that the point of this place, this hell, was that there was no point to anything. At first, O'Brien had been surprised that the old legends had turned out to be true. But after a century or two of simply standing in the sand, not even able to die, the surprise had left him, along with logic.

He had even given up his last hope that eventually he must go mad.

After another thousand years had passed, O'Brien noticed that the dark shape no longer shimmered as much as it had. It was more distinct. And larger.

Someone was walking toward him.

The engineering part of him tried to calculate the interior surface area of a sphere with a diameter approaching three hundred million kilometers. This part of him wanted to comprehend the incredible length of time it would take for someone walking on the interior of that sphere to randomly meet the only other being in the sphere. But his consciousness could no longer handle the numbers. Zeroes fell away from the pictures he built in his mind like infinite particles of sand.

He could no longer think or reason, except for whatever faculties were required to understand that he could no longer do so.

Within another century, at most, the person approaching was almost within earshot. O'Brien thought if he concentrated he might be able to hear the crunching of the sand under the person's feet. But after millennia of hearing only his own heartbeat, his own breathing, the sound of those footsteps proved almost painful. Even to focus on something other than an infinity of sand hurt his eyes.

A year went by. The person stood before him, dressed in robes that were . . . O'Brien couldn't even recall the names of their colors. The person, however, had gray skin and a wide neck, and O'Brien knew he was from another world, though he was unable to remember which one.

"Miles O'Brien," the visitor said.

O'Brien understood that that was his name. He wanted to say something in greeting but only got as far as opening his mouth. Whatever he was supposed to do after that—and he knew there was something—he had forgotten.

The visitor looked around at the desert, at the overwhelming ghostly lattice work that stretched through the sky and arched behind the blazing sun, as if he hadn't spent centuries walking through this same unchanging landscape, as if he were seeing it for the first time.

"I understand," he said. "And I can take it away. Would you like that?"

Only one thought formed in O'Brien's mind: *Yes . . .*

The gray-skinned figure smiled as if he had heard O'Brien's reply. "There is a price."

Pain ripped through O'Brien's throat as he forced himself to gasp out, ". . . yes . . ." The first word he had spoken in thousands, perhaps millions of years.

"Do you know who I am?"

O'Brien thought he should know. There were many things he thought he should know. But he didn't. He shook his head.

"You've just forgotten. Just from the look of this place, I'd guess you think you've been here for a long time, isn't that right?"

O'Brien couldn't answer. He had forgotten all the names he had once known for the units of time.

"But it's only been a few minutes. Remarkable, isn't it?"

O'Brien squinted, frowned, stretched his facial muscles, licked his lips as if waking up after a late night drinking Romulan ale with . . . "Julian," he said.

"I presume you mean Dr. Bashir." The visitor sounded amused. "He's not with us, but I am heartened to see that your memory might still function. I have need of an engineer."

O'Brien felt a shiver of recognition along his back, across his arms. *"Chief* Engineer," he corrected.

The visitor grinned. "You'll be fine." He held out a hand to O'Brien, a gray hand with black nails. "Now remember what I said. I will take you away from here, and in return, you will serve me."

O'Brien reached out to take that gray hand. He heard the sinews of his arm creak in protest after so many centuries of absolute immobility.

"That's right," the gray-skinned man said as he gave O'Brien's hand a hard squeeze. "Now, can you say that? Can you say, I will serve you . . . ?"

O'Brien's words were little more than escaping voiced breaths, but in his mind, he said what must be said. "I . . . will . . . serve . . . you . . ."

The gray hand squeezed O'Brien's harder. "Louder," the visitor said. "I *will* serve you, Kosst *Dukat.*"

"Dukat," O'Brien croaked, as if that word had been about to be spoken for millennia. "Kosst Dukat, I will serve you . . ."

Dukat's face took on an expression of bliss, even as his dark eyes momentarily seemed to flash with the color of the armband he wore on his robes. "Then you are free," he said, and he pulled O'Brien forward, and with that single step—

—O'Brien was on the bridge of the Klingon battleship *Boreth.*

And he remembered.

Everything.

O'Brien took a step forward and swayed, dizzy, overcome by the instantaneous transition from millennia of damnation to reality. At least, some type of reality.

"Dukat?"

"No questions," the Cardassian ordered. "Get to work!" He pointed to the engineering consoles to the side of the bridge. On the deck by most of them, O'Brien registered the unconscious forms of his friends and coworkers, six in all, including Quark, Odo, and Garak.

"Doing what?"

Dukat hissed, "It's not going the way it should! The way *he* promised."

O'Brien stared at Dukat, completely baffled. He remembered being in a prison cell in a restored ancient building in B'hala, with Rom and Quark and Odo. In nearby cells were Garak and the ten others rescued from Deep Space 9's destruction by the *Defiant,* then transported twenty-five years into the future to become prisoners of the Bajoran Ascendancy. Only Captain Sisko, Commander Arla, and Major Kira were not among them, apparently held prisoner at another location on Bajor. O'Brien hadn't seen any of them since the terrible day they had all been forced to witness the public execution of Tom Riker.

Then O'Brien remembered working with Rom on what was supposed to have been the universe's last day of existence, to prove that when both Bajoran wormholes opened together, they would *not* be close enough to merge and unravel the hidden dimensions of space-time, instantaneously destroying the universe.

But then the wall of their cell had somehow melted, and Dukat had walked through some kind of dimensional portal from the Mirror Universe to join them. This version of Dukat, twenty-five years older, white-haired, and completely mad, had then told them that Weyoun and the Ascendancy were planning to induce a nova reaction in the Bajoran sun. Their goal: To distort the space-time metric so that the two wormholes *would* move close enough together to merge when they opened.

And then Dukat had offered them a way out—what O'Brien and the others had mistakenly taken to mean a chance to stop the nova detonation and save the universe.

But Dukat had had no intention of saving anything. He had only needed a crew to operate the *Boreth* long enough to keep Weyoun from entering either wormhole in the *Defiant,* so that the *Boreth* could enter instead.

O'Brien's mind pictured the destruction of Bajor as it had been shown on the main viewer of the *Boreth*'s bridge. Three Bajorans from DS9 had left their positions then, to charge Dukat in fury, only to be incinerated by the blasts of fiery red energy that sprang from the Cardassian's outstretched arms.

And now Dukat was holding out his hand to *him* just as he had to those three Bajorans. "Do not defy me, Chief."

O'Brien forced himself to remain calm. The last thing he remembered before waking up in the Dyson Sphere from hell was hearing Weyoun and Dukat scream at each other as the undulating mouth of the red wormhole grew larger on the viewer. Now he needed to know what had happened *after* that, to him and his friends, and to the *Boreth*. Not to mention the universe.

"I have no intention of defying you," O'Brien said. "But I'm not a mindreader. If you need me to do something, you have to *tell* me what it is."

Dukat's eyes flared red for a heartbeat, the betraying flash of unearthly energy uncomfortably reminding O'Brien of the events on DS9 which the Bajorans had called the Reckoning. He cautioned himself to remember that Dukat was still somehow possessed by a Pah-wraith, perhaps even the same one that had taken control of the captain's son.

"I need full power restored to this vessel," Dukat began calmly enough, though each subsequent word grew disturbingly louder and came faster. "I need weapons and sensors brought on line. I need to restore the Amojan for all eternity!"

O'Brien quickly looked around the bridge, taking what relief he could from the fact that Quark and the others sprawled by their stations still appeared to be breathing. Also, he noted, the Klingon displays and the retrofitted Bajoran control surfaces indicated that the ship was on standby reserve—the condition he would expect the ship to automatically establish in the event of the sudden incapacitation of its crew. That suggested that the *Boreth* was not heavily damaged. A positive sign.

But before he could act, there was still a major question he needed to have answered.

"Are we in the wormhole?"

"You just spent two thousand years in a sand-filled Dyson Sphere. What do you think?"

O'Brien hesitated, unsure. "Was that . . . an Orb experience?"

He flinched as Dukat reached out to him to put a heavy hand on his shoulder. "Chief O'Brien, what you experienced was your own personal hell. And now that I know what it is, I can put you back there any time I please. Do you understand?"

"I'll get to work at once."

Dukat lifted his hand.

O'Brien hurried to the main flight console where he called up the sensor controls. Swiftly, he reset the primary sensor net and ordered the ship's computer to reestablish an optical environment on the main viewer.

"Tell me what you are doing," Dukat warned.

"I'm making sure we're safe. No sense starting repairs if we're about to be attacked or—"

As if he were some primal beast, Dukat raised his voice in a bellow of rage as the viewer came to life.

"He's still there!"

O'Brien looked up to see the last thing he expected to see.

Deep Space 9.

Against a roiling red backdrop of twisting, glowing, pulsing verteron strings.

"We *are* in the wormhole," O'Brien said wonderingly. *But how did DS9 get here?* he thought.

"Of course we are," Dukat snarled. "The universe has ended. This is the only reality that exists now. But *he's still here!"*

"Who?" O'Brien asked. He took a deep breath as he waited for Dukat's reply and then wished he hadn't. He could almost taste the acrid odor of burned flesh that still filled his nostrils.

"Weyoun," Dukat raged. "He's out there. I know it."

"On the station?"

"No, you fool!" Dukat swept over to O'Brien and angrily stabbed a finger at the top-right corner of the viewer. "There!"

O'Brien peered into what appeared to be a shimmering verteron node. But as the hyperdimensional energy artifact wavered in and out of view, he saw that there was another shape occupying the same area.

"The *Defiant*," he said.

"Weyoun isn't supposed to be here," Dukat fumed, spittle flying from his mouth. "He was *supposed* to fade into nonexistence. Never to be. Never to have been."

O'Brien tried running a structural scan on the station in the center of the screen. "The ship must have entered the blue wormhole." It was the only explanation. At least, to account for the *Defiant*. As for what appeared to be DS9, its twin, Empok Nor, had been in orbit of Bajor. Perhaps that station had somehow been swept into the wormhole as well.

"Destroy the *Defiant!*" Dukat commanded.

O'Brien looked at the weapons status display. "Sorry, all weapons are off-line."

"Then we'll *ram* her!"

O'Brien pointed to the propulsion systems display. "Not like this, we won't. The warp engines are off-line, and the impulse engines need to be restarted."

O'Brien was yanked into the air as easily as if he were wearing an antigrav. Dukat had him by the front of his robes. The engineer tried to turn away from Dukat's foul breath as the madman whispered very softly into his face, "Then restart them."

Dukat abruptly released O'Brien, and he dropped awkwardly to the deck, almost falling backward over his chair.

"Look, Dukat, you need an engineer, and I'm willing to be that engineer—" O'Brien saw the telltale red flashes of light flicker in Dukat's narrowed eyes. He began speaking more rapidly. "—but for me to do my work, I have to know what I'm starting with. I don't know what the ship's been exposed to. I don't know how long we've been in here. I don't know how much longer we can last. So unless you want the *Boreth* to fall apart around your ears, let me do my job the way it's supposed to be done!" O'Brien stopped then, half expecting to be blasted by Pah-wraith lightning on the spot.

But Dukat stepped back. "Work swiftly," was all he said.

O'Brien pushed his luck. "It'd go faster if I had some help."

"Who?"

"Rom," O'Brien said. He searched Dukat's face for any sign of hesitation or resistance. Didn't see it. Pressed on. "And Garak, he can handle the computers." O'Brien saw Dukat's face darken. "That should do it," he said quickly. "For now."

"That's all there is in here," Dukat reminded him sharply. "The endless, eternal *now*. We are completely outside linear time."

O'Brien had never been able to accept that part of the story regarding the wormhole environment, and he still couldn't. As far as he was concerned, in a true realm of nonlinear time, even the simplest conversation would be impossible to conduct.

"If we're in nonlinear time," he asked daringly, "then why haven't I already finished my work?"

"You can be sure that somewhere in this wormhole, you have," Dukat warned. "And unless you begin your work now, you can be equally sure that somewhere in this wormhole, I am already standing over your lifeless body."

O'Brien sensed he had gone right to the limit. He sat down at the main console and began queuing the diagnostic routines he wanted to run.

"Who do you need first?" Dukat asked harshly.

"Rom."

"Keep working."

O'Brien felt a sudden breeze disturb his robes, and when he realized he couldn't hear Dukat's ragged breathing any longer, he risked looking over his shoulder.

Dukat was gone. Rom must be somewhere else on the ship.

And though O'Brien wished nothing bad for the Ferengi, for the sake of the universe he found himself hoping Rom's torment was awful enough to keep Dukat busy for at least another thousand years.

Then O'Brien turned back to the viewer with renewed purpose: to restore the *Boreth*'s communications systems. Because, before he could do anything to change the situation, he needed to find out if DS9 and the *Defiant* were really in the wormhole with the *Boreth*.

And if so, who was onboard them.

CHAPTER 3

"THERE WERE too many hells," Jadzia said.

Sisko wasn't sure what she meant. He was still having difficulty concentrating, and the flickering emergency lights in the *Defiant*'s sickbay weren't helping. Beneath his Bajoran robes, his ribs continued to ache from the crushing and compressing that he—

"Benjamin? *Are* you all right?"

"I'm fine, Old Man." It was unimportant to Sisko whether or not he would ever find time to reflect on his own experience of hell. He had a ship. He had a crew. His duty was clear. "But for an illusion, the, uh, Venusian Firebeast . . . packed quite a wallop, as Mr. Russell might say."

Jadzia's smile indicated her commiseration. She had crossed into Sisko's illusion, and he knew she had seen exactly what he had experienced. In fact, when she had first appeared, she had been part of it, complete with a bizarre outfit that appeared to be comprised of an extremely abbreviated two-piece bathing costume incongruously made of hard, gleaming metal, in combination with a spherical, transparent breathing helmet. The mid-twentieth century had certainly given rise to some odd ideas about environmental suit requirements.

Sisko reached up a hand to the side of the diagnostic bed that had just examined him and pulled himself to his feet. "You were saying something about too many hells?"

"Think of it, Benjamin. You had to face the realization that you were only an imaginary character in a series of twentieth-century scientifiction stories. Julian felt responsible for the universe's destruction. Jake couldn't write. You all had a single worst nightmare hidden in your psyches, and that's what . . . what I presume the Pah-wraiths focused on and brought to life, creating an individual hell for each of you.

"But for me—" Jadzia placed her hand over her abdominal pouch. "—for *us*, there wasn't one hell, there were eight. One for each of Dax's hosts, plus one for Dax. And because we experienced our night-mares all together, all at the same time, it turned into one huge con-fusing jumble. Which reminded me exactly of what you and I experi-enced the first time we entered the wormhole six years ago."

Sisko understood at once. "Of course. That first trip. You saw a paradise . . . I saw a raging storm and barren rocks."

"Exactly. The wormhole was a completely subjective experience for both of us. And as soon as I made that connection, I woke up on the bridge of the *Defiant,* surrounded by the rest of you." She looked over to the main treatment bed and the patient still physically strapped to it—with the ship's primary power grid shut down, the confinement field generator was inoperative. "And him."

The patient, the prisoner, was Weyoun. Of the sixteen others onboard the *Defiant,* he alone remained in whatever subjective hell to which the Pah-wraiths had consigned him. The bed's diagnostic display indicated his lifesigns were within Vorta norms, except for the confused tracings of his brainwave patterns that revealed him to be in both deep sleep and a hyperalert state of consciousness at the same time.

"What do you suppose his nightmare is?" Jadzia asked.

"I don't want to know."

Sisko looked up as the sickbay doors scraped, then opened awk-wardly as they were forced apart by powerful hands. The corridor beyond was almost pitch black, lit only by two palm torches.

Worf's tall form filled the doorway, moving stiffly. The Klingon was still suffering from the disruptor shots he had taken from the Romulans while on Admiral Picard's *Phoenix.* Immediately behind the Klingon was Ensign Ryle Simons, a young human from Alpha Centauri whose skin was as startlingly white as his hair was flame red. Sisko recalled that Simons had graduated the Academy two weeks before arriving on DS9 to await the arrival of his first ship, the *Destiny*. But only a few days later, the lost Orbs of Jalbador had been found and brought into alignment in Quark's bar.

Then, as the Bajoran system's second wormhole—or Celestial Temple—had opened *inside* DS9, destroying the station, the young human ensign had been one of the thirty-three Starfleet personnel, Bajoran militia, and handful of civilians beamed to the *Defiant* and subsequently tossed twenty-five years into the future. When Jadzia had entered young Simons' personal hell, she had found him floating in deep space, abandoned by his Academy classmates during a zero-G evacuation drill, his environmental suit improperly sealed, perpetually within three minutes of losing all life support.

Since Ensign Simons had taken a minor in Warp Theory, he had been the closest thing to an engineer the *Defiant* had—which explained why Sisko had dispatched Simons with Worf to assess engineering.

Though it was at the very bottom of his list of priorities, in addition to restoring power, Sisko hoped the young ensign would also be able to do something about bringing the ship's replicators online. Sisko was more than ready to discard the Bajoran robes Weyoun had forced him to wear. He envied Worf, Jadzia, and Simons their Starfleet uniforms, even if they were wearing the versions adopted in the year 2400.

From the look on young Simons' face, it seemed to Sisko that the ensign had something to say. Simons was just as clearly waiting for Worf's permission to speak. Until the ship's internal communications system was restored, all reports had to be delivered in person.

Sisko turned to Worf, but the Klingon's attention was focused firmly on Weyoun.

"If we have indeed experienced the end of all existence," Worf said, "the Vorta must be killed."

Appealingly simple and direct as that Klingon approach to their situation was, Sisko did not agree with it. "He might be the only one who knows what's happened to us."

Worf kept his attention on Weyoun, took several cautious, shallow breaths as if even the slightest movement of his chest was painful. "Perhaps. But it might be that our fate is not in question. Under the circumstances, it is possible that we are in *Ko'th*. Limbo. A state of non-being between *Sto-Vo-Kor* and *Gre'thor*. In human mythology, it is the equivalent of being the damned."

Sisko was uncertain if Worf truly believed in what he was saying, or if he was just describing a Klingon tradition which held no special significance for him. "Is there anything that those in *Ko'th* can do to change their fate?"

Worf's tone and expression remained neutral though he held himself unnaturally rigid. "They must commit an act of vengeance, for right or for wrong, in order to proceed to one destination or another—*Sto-Vo-Kor* or *Gre'thor*. Killing Weyoun could be our act of vengeance. If we are the damned."

Sisko suspected that Worf himself did not know the answer to the question he had raised. "Are you that eager to proceed to eternity, Commander Worf?"

"If the universe has ended, Captain, what else awaits us?"

"But we don't know it's ended for certain," Sisko argued.

"Actually, Benjamin," Jadzia interrupted, "we do know. Our sensor net is still down, but I checked the logs for what was recorded just before we lost power. According to those logs, the *Defiant* entered the blue wormhole three point two seconds before it completely merged with the red wormhole. From the final readings of conditions outside the wormholes at that moment, subspace had already degraded by more than eighty percent. Basic astronomical observations showed wavelength disruptions entirely consistent with the emergence—the unraveling—of the hidden dimensions of space-time.

"While it's true we can't be certain that the incident of broken symmetry that triggered the vacuum fluctuation that became our universe was *initiated* by the splitting of this wormhole pocket we're in, it *is* certain that—based on the sensor logs and the Starfleet research I reviewed on Mars—when the two Bajoran wormholes were rejoined, our universe's originating vacuum fluctuation was *negated*. Space-time just . . . rolled in on itself, compressed to a singularity, and ceased to exist—returning to the quantum foam that underlies any concept of reality."

The elegant explanation might have made sense to his old friend

Dax, but Sisko still felt a connection to reality. "Then why are *we* still here?" he asked, slapping his hand against the side of the diagnostic bed to physically emphasize his point. "This ship *exists*. We still *exist*."

Jadzia nodded in understanding but not acceptance. "Only as an echo, Benjamin. Think of this ship as one last reverberation of mass and energy from our universe. In time . . . whatever time means now, we'll fade out, too."

Sisko thought of his son. "How much time?"

Before Jadzia could answer, sickbay was plunged into darkness as the emergency lights abruptly cut out, only to flash on and off and on again as the *Defiant* shuddered violently in the grip of some unknown new assault.

In the harsh, pulsing light, Sisko saw Jadzia grab hold of Worf's arm as the decks and bulkheads creaked and groaned, then fell silent as the ship steadied and the emergency lighting stopped flickering.

Sisko tried to focus on the impossible situation. "Does anyone know where Jake is?" The last Sisko had seen of his son had been on the bridge, just before entering the wormhole.

"He is on the bridge," Worf answered. "Working on restoring the computers."

"Thank you," Sisko said. He looked at Jadzia. The Trill had released her husband's arm. "What we just felt—a theory? Anything?"

The Trill sighed. "Benjamin, every wormhole Starfleet has ever charted, every wormhole for which records exist, is a *tunnel*. A tunnel that joins two separate points in four-dimensional space-time. What we're in now, it's not connecting anything. I can't even make a wild guess about how *verterons* can exist in an unconnected environment, let alone normal matter and energy."

"*Something* exists other than us, Old Man. For what we just felt, there have to be other forces at work on us."

Jadzia shook her head. "Until we restore some kind of sensor capability, we're blind."

Sisko turned to Simons. "What about it, Ensign? What shape are we in?"

Pale cheeks blotched with red, the young human was still staring upward at the sickbay ceiling, as if fearing it would crack open. He lowered his eyes, cleared his throat. "Uh, there's no warp core—"

"Weyoun had it removed so we couldn't slingshot around the red wormhole's maw and go back to our own time," Sisko explained.

"That makes sense, sir. Without warp capability, temporal relocation is impossible. But we still have all our power converters. And about thirty percent of our matter/antimatter reserves. If it's true we don't have anywhere to go in here and we can use all that power for life support for the eighteen people onboard, my, um, estimate is the *Defiant* can easily function for at least . . . twenty years."

Sisko grimaced at the thought that they were all trapped in a single hell now. Twenty years in a starship with nowhere to go and no hope. No crew could last that long under those conditions.

"Twenty years is out of the question," Jadzia said, making it clear that in her opinion Simons's estimate wasn't going to be an option. "Whatever bubble of space-time we're protected in for now will . . . evaporate. That's the best analogy I can think of. And then . . . then there won't be anywhere for us to exist, so . . ." She shrugged. She didn't have to finish.

But Sisko was tired of talk, anyway. "This isn't doing us any good," he said, starting for the sickbay doors. "We need to know what the conditions are out there. We need to know how long we have so we can look for a way out."

But Worf stood between Sisko and the doors.

Sisko halted. He faced the Klingon. "A question, Mr. Worf?"

"What if Jadzia is correct, and there *is* no way out?"

Sisko didn't want to even consider that question. But he wasn't going to lie to Worf and suggest it wasn't possible. "I don't know."

"But if she *is* correct," the Klingon said slowly, as if considering each word before saying it aloud and bringing more pain to his chest. "And if our existence ends before we have killed our enemy—" He glanced at Weyoun's still form. "Then we will remain in *Ko'th* forever, knowing neither victory nor defeat." He held Sisko's gaze now. "Captain, even *Gre'thor* is preferable to limbo."

Sisko didn't intend to argue with Worf. But he also didn't intend to endanger Weyoun when the Vorta might be needed to provide information. So long as Worf remained true to his Starfleet oath, Sisko knew no officer more loyal, even in the face of death. But under the extreme conditions they faced now, Sisko also knew a point could come where Worf might feel he had to choose between his duty to an organization that no longer existed in any meaningful form and the needs of his Klingon heritage. Indeed, in the same situation, Sisko did not know if in all good conscience he could order his crew to place duty before their deepest spiritual beliefs. So he decided to make it a bit more difficult for Worf to choose to harm Weyoun, in case that conflict arose.

"Dax," Sisko said, "you're responsible for Weyoun."

"I'd be able to do more on the bridge," Jadzia replied.

Sisko glanced at Worf, whose expression remained neutral as he stepped outside, out of Sisko's way. "Commander, you will accompany Ensign Simons and me to the bridge." He looked back at Jadzia. "As soon as we're there, together, I'll send Commander Arla down to watch over Weyoun, and then you can join us. Until then, Old Man, whatever happens," Sisko concluded with a nod to Weyoun, "don't leave his side."

Jadzia pursed her lips as if to remind Sisko that if anyone had seniority in this situation, it was she with her three hundred years of experience. But all she said was, "Where would I go?"

"Maybe I'll find out on the bridge," Sisko said grimly.

Then the ship creaked again, and he wrenched open the sickbay doors and waited for Worf to switch on his palm torch and step into the corridor. The Klingon did so, without hesitation, though his heavy brow was more deeply furrowed than usual with thought.

"Um, what should I do, sir?" Simons asked, switching on his own palm torch as he followed after Sisko and the sickbay doors rattled shut behind them.

All three officers were now standing in the dark corridor, along which only the faint glow of emergency lights could be seen.

"First, get the lights on so we can restore the sensors." Sisko looked down at his Bajoran robes. "Then do what you can to get at least *one* uniform replicator working."

"Yes, sir!"

Simons's palm torch quickly disappeared around the curve to the left.

Worf led the way to the right, halting when he reached the first intersection. With only emergency power available, they would have to use the access ladder by the central turbolifts to get to Deck 1.

But Sisko stopped at Worf's side, not as his commanding officer but as a fellow being facing the same overwhelming, almost impossible-to-comprehend disaster.

"Worf, I do understand your concerns. I'm just not willing to admit defeat until we know more."

In the scattered uplighting from his palm torch, Worf's heavy features took on an ominous appearance. "I understand, sir. But if we discover that no other options are available, remember that there is no shame in accepting the inevitable, provided we behave honorably. And there is no honor in refusing to acknowledge that events have gone past our ability to control them."

"I'm not refusing to accept that. I'm just not convinced it's true."

Sisko sympathized with Worf. Starfleet protocol had little meaning in this era.

Because Starfleet—the epitome of life's best intentions—had come face to face with life's worst fears—total annihilation and meaninglessness. And in this future, in Starfleet's long deep stare into the abyss, those fears had won. Even the Prime Directive had been abandoned.

But in this future, Sisko had not been part of the battle that had raged during the past quarter century. As this time's Starfleet and its Federation had made concessions to the Ascendancy, small ones at first, only in the last years becoming an unstoppable movement toward appeasement and defeat, Sisko and his companions had been insulated—out of time—traveling in a single instant within their frame of reference from the year 2375 to the year 2400.

The optimistic hope for the future that had once been the cornerstone of the Starfleet known to him and the other temporal refugees from 2375 had been slowly crushed by 2400 during the war with the Ascendancy. But that dream still was alive within Sisko, undiminished. And he had to believe that in some way it still existed in his crew.

Even Worf.

"When the time comes, Worf, I will not stand in the way of you doing what your beliefs demand. But I will ask you to consider if the murder of a defenseless being is truly an act of honor, whether vengeance is required or not."

Worf studied Sisko for long moments in the darkness of the corridor, clearly wrestling with the difficult decision to place his fate for all eternity in the hands of an alien who could never truly understand his Klingon heart. "Captain, how will you know when that time has come?"

"I have faith that we will arrive at that decision together."

Sisko held out his hand.

"If we don't have hope, Worf, if we don't work together, then the Pah-wraiths really will have won for all time. The greatest battles demand the greatest risk."

Warrior to warrior, Worf reached out and clasped Sisko's hand.

"Heghl'umeH QaQ jajvam," he said gruffly.

Then, together, through the darkness, Sisko and Worf ran for the bridge.

CHAPTER 4

ON THE *Defiant's* bridge, Jake Sisko told himself his fingers did *not* hurt. The painful sensation was just something left over from the illusion.

But as he forced himself to concentrate on the basic task of resetting the ship's computers, he couldn't help thinking about how limitless the illusion was—had seemed—within the hell in which he had been lost.

One moment, he had been *there*—twenty-five years in the future, in the transporter room of the *U.S.S. Phoenix,* the monstrous starship conceived by this era's Admiral Jean-Luc Picard for travelling back twenty-five thousand years, to a time before the founding of the fabled Bajoran city of B'hala. And the next moment, he had been *here.*

In that nightmare future, the original mission for Picard's ship had been to place ultrastable explosive charges beneath those sections of B'hala that would not be excavated by the year 2400 C.E., guaranteeing that they would not be detected. Those charges were to be set to explode during the final Ascendant ceremonies on the day the universe was scheduled to end. The expected result was the death of Weyoun and most of his followers, as well as the destruction of a sizable portion of Bajor—a small price to be paid for the safety of all existence.

By setting the explosives to go off *after* the *Phoenix*'s departure, Picard's plan had ensured that the universe's timeline would not be altered and that no paradox would be created.

But unknown to Starfleet, a paradox had *already* existed. A team of Romulans had discovered the 25,627-year-old wreckage of the *Phoenix* and its explosive charges on the lifeless moon of one of the Bajoran system's gas giant planets. Thus, before the *Phoenix* had even set off on its mission, that mission could be proven to be a failure.

So Jake's best friend, Captain Nog, now twenty-five years older and Admiral Picard's assistant and supporter, had devised a *new* plan.

To maintain the timeline in which Nog and Deep Space 9 and Weyoun and the Orbs of Jalbador existed, Nog intended to travel back to Bajor's past and allow enough sections of the *Phoenix* to crash on the lifeless moon to account for the wreckage the Romulans would find.

Then just before the *Phoenix* had entered her temporal slingshot trajectory around Bajor's sun, Nog's programming activated the ship's advanced technology transporters, beaming Jake, Worf, Jadzia, Dr. Bashir, Ryle Simons, and their nine fellow refugees from the past to a starship near the opening Bajoran wormholes, so they could safely slingshot back to their own time.

That moment of transport had been unlike any other beaming experience Jake had ever had, even his most recent, when he had been plucked from his own time onboard the *Defiant* and taken twenty-five years into the future onboard the Vulcan ship, the *Augustus*. This time, he had felt a sudden chill, and at once the unfinished walls of the *Phoenix*'s transporter room had been instantly replaced by the corridors of the *Defiant*. He had felt no quantum-dissolution effect, nor any temporary loss of sight of his surroundings as his nervous system had been tunneled from one point to another. All Jake could remember now was that one moment he had been *there*, and the next he had been *here*. It had been like being in a dream.

And right now, he was still confused about just when it was that dreamlike experience had become his nightmare.

First had come the elation of being back on the *Defiant*. He'd quickly determined where he was in the ship and immediately raced for the bridge. The intensity of his excitement had been matched by the bedlam around him. On his run through the ship, he had heard shouting as all the *Defiant*'s alarms—collision and weapons lock and intruder alerts—sounded off at once.

Then the bridge doors had opened before him and he'd rushed in, caught sight of his father, called out to him.

Bajoran robes fluttering, Sisko had wheeled to face him, and he and his father had thrown their arms around each other, their embrace saying more than words ever could.

Then someone had called out, "Ten seconds."

And even if Jake had been able to explain why he and the others had come back to the *Defiant,* he'd known from the look of horror on his father's face that there was no time to follow through on the rest of Nog's plan. No time to follow through on their own escape.

They'd run out of time. Everyone had. Literally.

After that, Jake remembered hearing Worf report a supernova shockwave was approaching.

He remembered feeling the *Defiant* tremble. Hearing his father call out for some—any—explanation. Seeing Ensign Simons at the science station. Hearing the young Centaurian identify the impact as a subspace pressure wave catching the ship.

On the main viewer, he'd seen the two wormholes about to merge, red and blue energy tendrils reaching out like the warring tentacles of two incomprehensible creatures.

He'd seen Weyoun, dressed like a Bajoran kai in bloodred robes, shouting out that the Temple was restored.

He'd heard Weyoun screaming just as Worf said, "Impact," as he himself . . .

At the *Defiant*'s computer station, Jake shook his head. He rubbed at his face as if he had slept for days. He remembered falling away from his father at that moment of impact. He remembered the lights going out, just for a moment, and then . . . he was in his room on the *Saratoga,* sitting hunched over his tiny, child-sized desk, inputting into his padd, seeing his words deleted almost as fast as he wrote them, somehow not questioning the sudden transition to a starship that in his frame of reference had been destroyed almost ten years ago.

Jake shivered. There had been *nothing* at the time that had made him even suspect the nightmare had not been real, not logical. Even now, he still couldn't shake the feeling that he had actually been on the *Saratoga,* fingers bleeding, absolutely certain that the moment he stopped inputting, the moment the cursor caught up with his words, it would be the moment he ceased to exist.

How long his nightmare had lasted, Jake didn't know. He couldn't even remember what he had been inputting. *Anslem,* he suspected. For all his detours had taken him into crime novels and thrillers and even Quark's attempts to talk him into a lurid collaboration about the Red Orbs, *Anslem* was the book he always came back to, always regretting ever having put it aside. Which is why, he decided now, it most likely *was* the book he had been frantically inputting in his personal version of hell.

But for however many years or hours or centuries he had existed within that room, his nightmare had ended the moment Jadzia's hand had slipped past his shoulder and her finger had lightly touched the POWER control on his padd.

At once, the all-devouring cursor had stopped moving, his words had been stored, and the padd's screen had winked out.

The next thing Jake could remember was staring at that blank screen until he'd finally become aware that Jadzia had stepped in front of him. He'd looked up to see that she had on the deep red sweater he remembered his mother wearing on the *Saratoga* that final day. He'd loved that sweater. It was the last real memory he had of his mother.

Dressed like that, her spots almost invisible against the dark hue of her skin, now the same color Jennifer Sisko's had been, Jadzia had held out her hand to Jake. "This is just a dream," she'd told him, "and your father's waiting for you to wake up."

An instant later, Jake had found himself in the *Defiant*'s sickbay.

And now he was here, on the bridge, desperately trying to dredge from his memory all the basic procedures Chief O'Brien had taught him in those years when everyone had expected Sisko's son to follow in his father's footsteps and attend the Academy.

A series of status lights turned green before him.

Jake sighed. Maybe his whole life was an illusion. Maybe the whole universe he lived in no longer existed. So what did the color green mean anymore, without suns to shine on plants that grew on worlds to be explored? What did anything mean anymore?

"Computer," a familiar voice suddenly said behind him, startling him.

Jake felt a hand pat his shoulder and looked up to see Major Kira. He didn't know what the major's hell had been, but her eyes were still deeply shadowed, and he hadn't seen her smile since he had come to the bridge. Although he had heard her use a rather raw Bajoran expletive as she had ripped the sleeves off her Bajoran robes.

"Working," the computer replied, indicating that its most basic operating system had been reloaded.

"Good work, Jake. I'll get it up to speed now." From the way Kira looked down at him, it was obvious that she wanted him to get out of the duty chair.

"Right, sorry," he said. He moved out of the way as Kira took over.

For the moment, Jake realized, he had nothing to do but watch the others on the bridge take action while he stayed out of their way. Commander Arla was on her back under the combined flight and operations console, an access panel on the deck beside her. She was adjusting something inside the console's base with a pulsewrench.

"How's that power supply coming?" Arla called out, her voice echoing within the depths of the machinery she worked on.

The bridge lights suddenly brightened to full intensity.

"We're on-line," Kira announced. "Let's try internal comm. Bridge to engineering."

Jake heard Ensign Simons's high-pitched voice over the bridge speakers. "Simons here."

"Good work, Ensign," Kira told him. "Now . . . is it going to last?"

"It should," Simons answered. "We have plenty of antimatter, and we'll have the second power converter operational in twenty minutes. That'll give us full backup power, too."

"What about propulsion?" Kira asked.

"Um, you should probably talk to Captain Sisko about that. He's on his way up."

Jake's spirits lifted. He knew it probably wasn't the most mature reaction, but in a situation like this, he felt more secure when his father was nearby. Then the bridge doors opened and his father and Worf stepped onto the bridge.

Sisko nodded at him once, and Jake understood from that terse acknowledgment that his father was deep in his "Starfleet" mode. He wasn't anyone's father right now. Nor was he anyone's friend. Not even to Dax if she were here. For now, he was a starship captain whose only concern was his crew and his ship.

Sisko stopped by Kira's station. "What's our status, Major?"

"No significant damage. Jake reset the computer. Ensign Simons has restored power. And between me up here and Dr. Bashir in the replicator bay, full life support has been reestablished. All we need are exterior sensors and propulsion."

Worf was at his tactical station. "And weapons," he said.

"Sensors first," Sisko said. He went over to Arla. "Commander, how close are we to having the main viewer operational?"

Arla's head was still deep within the console and her voice was muffled. "Two more circuits to replace . . . one more . . ." There was a sudden spark of light from within the console. "Got it." The tall Bajoran commander pulled herself out of the console and sat up, shaking one hand as if she'd received a jolt of transtator current. "Major, give it a try now."

Jake watched as Kira left the engineering station and went to science to call up the ship's sensor operations system. The viewer instantly filled with a rippling pattern of blue light, bringing a cold glare to the bridge.

"Can you adjust focus?" Sisko asked.

"All the adjustment subroutines are functioning," Kira said as she studied her controls. "What we're seeing is what's out there. Or at least an optical extrapolation of the local energy environment. Seems to be mostly tachyon-based." She glanced up at the screen and said what Jake was thinking. "It looks like the inside of the Celestial Temple."

But Sisko didn't agree. "Not exactly. I don't see any verteron nodes. No energy strings." He scratched at his beard. "Commander Arla, go to sickbay and take over from Dax."

Arla was on her feet at once, no outward sign visible of the emotional aftereffects of her own Pah-wraith-induced hell. Jake didn't know what type of subjective experience Arla had been trapped in, but, unlike the others, she appeared fully recovered.

"Take over how, sir?" With Starfleet efficiency, Arla asked the question as she headed for the doors, already on her way.

"Just standing by Weyoun."

At that, Arla stopped. "Sir?"

"We've left him in his . . . Pah-wraith experience. Just monitor his lifesigns, let me know if he shows any change or any sign of coming to. And tell Dax to get up here right away. The turbolifts are working."

Jake knew that his father had just ordered Arla to place herself in the same room as the man who had destroyed her people's world. But all Arla replied was, "Yes, sir." And then, without any other reaction that would betray her true feelings to Jake or anyone else on the bridge, she went through the open doorway in a run. Jake found her self-control astounding.

Then Jake saw his father's stern expression soften as he put a hand on Kira's shoulder. "How are you, Major?"

"Truthfully? I've been a *lot* better."

Sisko nodded, an understanding friend for one brief moment, before his Starfleet mission took control once more. "Run a full sensor sweep, maximum power and range. I want to find out if there's anyone else in here with us."

"You mean Dukat."

Jake saw the shudder that ran through Kira, just once, as she said that name.

Sisko confirmed the major's conclusion. "He was heading for the wormholes, too."

Kira's face hardened, but she began calling up the required controls to run the sweep.

Then his father's gaze finally fell on him, and Jake knew that Sisko was his father again. Saying nothing, Sisko walked over and hugged him again before making a point of tugging on the collar of Jake's twenty-fifth-century Starfleet uniform. "So this is what it took to get you to finally join up," he said, a half smile on his lips.

"Hey, this is a *civilian* specialist uniform," Jake said. Unlike the black uniforms given to Worf and the others, Jake's was gray. And where the other uniforms had single shoulders set off in a specialty color, Jake's shoulder was black. When he had first put it on, it had reminded him of a cadet's uniform.

"What kind of specialist?" Sisko asked.

Jake did his best to fill in his father about everything that had happened to him since he had been beamed off the *Defiant* right after the ship's arrival in the future. He recounted the story of Admiral

Picard, Captain Nog, and Vash, and their mission to the past. And how Nog had hoped that he'd be able to send his friends back to their own time by beaming them to a starship near the opening wormholes.

"I'm surprised by that," Sisko said, frowning slightly. "There's no way any of us would have been able to return to our own time except by reversing the slingshot trajectory that brought us here. And that would have been possible only by being on the *Defiant* and looping around the red wormhole as it opened."

"Nog knew that," Jake said quickly. "We all did. But . . . because of everything else that happened, there was no way to save the timeline the way Admiral Picard had planned. So the best we could do was to create alternates. Wherever we ended up after our first slingshot around the blue wormhole, Dax was going to work out the trajectory that would bring us back to Bajor the day *after* DS9 was destroyed. That would've at least preserved *our* subjective timeline, and we could've stopped Weyoun's expedition into the red wormhole *and* given Starfleet enough time to figure out a way to destroy the Red Orbs."

Sisko's frown deepened. "Nog should have worked out a way to take the *Phoenix* back twenty-five years instead. Not risk trying to reach Bajor at the last moment."

"Dad, he had to make sure the wreckage of the *Phoenix* reached that moon twenty-five thousand years ago. Otherwise . . . well, I don't understand it all, but Dax confirmed the theory. Something about the paradox causing this timeline to collapse like a black hole, so that there'd be no one who could stop Weyoun in the past."

"In theory," Sisko said. "Does Nog have any way of coming back?"

Jake shook his head. "Vash said maybe . . . maybe Q would come looking for them."

Sisko's skeptical expression let Jake know how likely he thought that possibility would be.

Jake hadn't believed Vash, either. "I think she meant it as a joke."

"What did Nog think he and Admiral Picard and *Vash* of all people could accomplish that far in the past? Other than crash part of their ship?"

"I . . . don't know. We didn't have a lot of time to talk about it. Nog was mostly interested in what he missed on DS9 the day . . . the day it was destroyed. Dax might know what he was thinking."

"Well," Sisko said, "whatever Nog thought he could do, it obviously didn't work. Not in this timeline."

Jake felt confused. "Uh, does this even still count as a timeline?"

Sisko's pain was obvious. Jake had always known his father would never lie to him, and he wasn't lying now. "I don't know, Jake. I—"

"Captain!"

Sisko and Jake instantly turned to Kira.

"There *is* someone else in here!"

"Onscreen, Major. Is it the *Boreth?*"

Jake saw Kira working frantically on her controls. "No, no. The mass is at least ten times greater. Whatever it is, it's huge, it's . . ."

She muttered something under her breath. To Jake, it almost sounded like she was praying. And then she simply turned her head to stare past Jake and Sisko at the viewer.

Jake turned to see what she saw. Felt the hair bristle on his arms, on the back of his neck.

For at the end of the universe, in the last pocket of existence that remained, Deep Space 9 was waiting.

CHAPTER 5

QUARK DRUNKENLY reached across the counter of his bar on the Promenade and his gold-pressed-latinum sleevebinder caught the edge of the curved, leather-wrapped flagon of Saurian brandy.

Vintage Saurian brandy. 2215. One hundred bars apiece.

Behind the counter, by the sink, Rom watched in horror as the costly flagon rocked back and forth. Rushing forward, he slipped on the filthy floor and vainly stretched out the gnarled fingers of his injured hand full-length until his knuckles popped and shocks of pain skipped along his arm. But the instant before he could make contact with it, the flagon tipped over and shattered. The suddenly worthless amber-gold liquor swept across the bartop like a miniature tidal wave, taking with it what little remained of Rom's dreams.

Rom groaned as Quark reared back and cried out grandly, "Put it on my tab!" And then, whooping with laughter, he fell into his companion's arms.

"Oh, Quarky," Leeta giggled.

Rom stared in open-mouthed, abject despair as the beautiful dabo girl who had once been his wife pulled "Quarky" closer, then slowly circled his lobe with a single suggestive finger as she whispered something unintelligible that made Rom's brother giggle and lick his lips appreciatively.

"B-but," Rom stammered, "y-you never pay your tab, brother."

Quark merely grinned at him. "You were always telling me you could run this place better than I ever could. Here's your chance to prove it."

Just then, in the far corner of the bar's main floor, two outraged Klingons tossed a flailing, screaming Bolian through the air to land headfirst on the dabo table which promptly collapsed, the appalling damage clearly beyond repair.

Quark sniggered as he made a mock grimace. "Ooo, there go your dabo profits for the *month*. Ouch." Then he blew a farewell kiss to Rom as he left with Leeta hanging on his arm, heartlessly taking her up to the holosuites as he did every night, to enjoy the holocylinder for *Risian Ear Clinic—The Jamaharon Continues*. That had once been Rom's and Leeta's favorite, too.

Mournfully watching Leeta leave without him, Rom felt his chest ache almost as painfully as the deep cracks that furrowed the skin of his hands—the cracks that never healed anymore. Because he was forced to wash the dishes in scalding water every night now. Because he no longer had time to repair the sonic sterilizers.

"Hey! Ferengoid! Some service over here!"

A table of rowdy Nausicaans hurled their empty glasses at him—five at a half-slip each. One even struck Rom's bandaged ear where he had lost a lobe in the unfortunate altercation with Grand Nagus Nog.

"NOW!" the Nausicaans screeched, fangs nastily clicking to emphasize their threat.

Rom lurched forward to dab up what he could of the Saurian brandy with his already stained jacket, then quickly began pouring shots of steaming bile wine as more and more customers shouted out for immediate service.

But in the entire bar, there was only Rom to serve them. All the others who had once worked for Quark had walked out on strike, demanding such high wages that every day Rom bitterly wished he had never organized the union in the first place.

Even thinking about the union, Rom felt his hands tremble and he spilled more bile wine than he poured into the glasses, guaranteeing there would be no profit on this transaction. Even worse, there was no profit on any of the transactions he made these days, and his debt was growing faster than a black hole.

Then Rom jumped as the glasses on the bartop began to rattle rhythmically. Nervously, he looked up to see his absolute best customer—Morn—pounding his tankard, insisting on another round. Now!

Rom picked up a jug of draft Romulan ale. "H-how's it going, Morn? H-how're the brothers and, uh, sisters?" Morn had seventeen siblings in all. The question was a surefire conversation starter with the big guy. He usually went on for hours, consuming high-markup beverages all the while.

But these days, not even Morn was speaking to Rom. He simply sat in unnerving silence, as if he didn't have a word to say.

"I'm . . . I'm sorry!" Rom blurted, because in truth he was sorry for *everything*. He practically upended the jug into Morn's tankard, then winced as the ale's pale blue foam promptly bubbled upward and cascaded onto the bartop.

Morn's small dark eyes narrowed as he *growled* at Rom.

Rom shrank back, dropping the jug of draft on the counter. "S-sorry, sorry, sorry." The jug spun around in the foam and then slid off the counter, exploding spectacularly as it hit the floor beside Morn's feet.

Rom's voice rose high in a squeal. "Uh, I'll . . . I'll get you a bottle of *vintage* ale, all right? No bubbles?"

Morn growled again. Louder. Meaner.

"And on the house!" Rom squeaked, then rushed back to the replicator because dirty plates and platters were now raining down from the second-floor railing. The impatient Tellarites on the upper level were on a snorting, grunting rampage for more tribble pie.

"What kind of hell is this?" Dukat asked. Rom was so startled, he misentered the last digit of the tribble-pie code and then cringed as a hundred-count of brain-stuffed ravioli sprayed out from the mouth of the replicator. The filthy mess was an illegal dish his brother Quark had programmed years ago when a contingent of Medusan navigators had been onboard. The unsettling eating habits of the noncorporeal life-forms were a closely held secret known only to the top levels of Starfleet and a few select suppliers in the hospitality services. When Captain Sisko found out about the contents of that ravioli, Rom knew for a certainty he'd lose Quark's lease on the station. He was always losing Quark's lease.

"And what is that disgusting smell?" Dukat asked.

Rom's boots squished as he trudged through the mound of replicated pasta and Vulcan brain tissue that now covered the deck behind the bar. There were holes in the soles of his boots, so the body-temperature mass slurped up horribly between his toes.

"Uh, would you like some *kanar?*" Rom asked miserably. Then he blinked in confusion at the Cardassian.

Dukat was out of uniform. He was wearing what seemed to be the robes of a Bajoran religious order. And his hair was white, his face deeply etched.

"Uh, Gul Dukat . . . are—are you feeling all right?" Rom asked, peering at him more closely. It was as if the Cardassian had suddenly aged a quarter century or more.

Dukat looked around the chaos of the bar. More fights were breaking out. Dishes and furniture were being destroyed at an accelerating rate. A group of Cardassian soldiers had just won their eighth consecutive dabo at the table that no longer seemed to be in pieces. And even more impossible, Quark and Leeta were locked in a seamless, impassioned embrace at a tiny table off to one corner.

"How is this *different?*" Dukat asked.

"Uh, different from what?" Rom couldn't be sure, but for a moment it seemed Dukat's eyes had glowed red.

"From the way it used to be. When all this was real."

Rom stared at the gul. His eyes *were* glowing red.

"This *is* real . . . isn't it?" But even as Rom said those words, there was something in Dukat's eerie eyes that made him doubt them.

Dukat held out his hand. "If you come with me now, I promise that when you return to . . . this realm, you shall be in whatever passes for Ferengi heaven, not this hell."

"I . . . don't understand," Rom said. He looked past Dukat and goggled at what he saw and heard. The crashes and screams of the bar's mayhem were rapidly fading. A Bolian was suspended, midair, about to crash headfirst into Quark's perfectly intact dabo table. All the other customers in the bar were similarly frozen in place, including . . . *Gul Dukat?* Younger, in uniform, treating those at his table to the most expensive *kanar* on the menu, just as he always did at this time of night, telling Rom to bill it to a Cardassian trade mission that had gone out of business years ago.

Rom wanted to ask how there could be two Dukats in his brother's bar, but he didn't. He didn't want to say a single word to break the spell the bar was under. For the first time in . . . in centuries, in millennia, it seemed to Rom, the place was blissfully quiet.

"You don't have to understand anything," Dukat said. "Just take my hand, and promise to serve me."

Rom stared at that hand, hesitant.

"Rom," Dukat said, "really. How much worse could your life get?"

Rom considered the question seriously. "It . . . it couldn't. This is the worst it's ever been."

Dukat nodded once, held his hand higher. "So, what do you say?"

"I, uh, promise to serve you?" Then Rom took hold of that cold gray hand and at once—

—arose from the deck in the *Boreth,* in the engine room, hand in hand with Dukat.

Rom gazed around him in confusion, stared down at his hands, no longer cracked and gnarled. He lifted his one free hand, felt for his lost lobe, and found it intact. He looked up at Dukat, at last remembering what had happened.

"The universe?" he asked weakly.

"This fever called living is over at last," Dukat intoned. "There is no more universe."

"Then how . . ." Rom swallowed hard as he made his realization. "We're in the wormhole, aren't we?"

"Where else is there?" Dukat suddenly squeezed Rom's hand hard enough that Rom was sure he heard his own bones grate as the Cardassian hauled him into the air with one hand.

"And when I was in the bar?" Rom gasped.

Dukat's eyes flared with red energy as he excruciatingly tightened his grip on Rom's hand. "You were being toyed with," the Cardassian said. "Punished for no other reason than to satisfy those driven mad by their *own* punishment."

"Wh-who?" Rom hoped he wouldn't faint from the pain before he heard Dukat's answer.

"Chief O'Brien needs you on the bridge," Dukat said abruptly, dropping Rom to the floor. "If I were you, I'd do what he says. Otherwise . . ."

Rom nodded vigorously as he swayed on his feet and clutched

his throbbing hand. He didn't want to go back to the bar. He would do anything to avoid that. He looked around the vast engineering section of the advanced-technology Klingon ship. "Uh, where is the bridge?"

Dukat dragged him toward the doors, never letting go.

Not that there was anyplace left for Rom to run to.

At the engineering station on the bridge of the *Boreth*, surrounded by the motionless bodies of the other temporal refugees, O'Brien stared at the displays on his sensor screens and tried to make sense of them.

At the least complex level of interpretation, there was little to question in the results he had obtained.

Just as the main viewer made clear, it was Deep Space 9—and not Empok Nor—which was within the wormhole environment in some sort of proximity to the *Boreth*. O'Brien could only conclude that instead of being gravitationally crushed by the opening of the red wormhole, the station had, instead, been swallowed by it. Judging from the fact that all its docking arms had been restored, Weyoun had apparently had repair crews in here to restore it.

In the same indistinct fashion, O'Brien could see that the sensors confirmed that the *Defiant* was also here, and also apparently without major damage.

But none of that solved O'Brien's key problem: In this realm, what did the term "here" mean anymore?

He touched a control that would give him access to the *Boreth*'s external communications array. As the comm keypads appeared on his board, he glanced again at the bridge's main doors. Dukat had been gone for ten minutes and there was no way to be sure how much longer O'Brien would have to work undisturbed. But if ever a situation called for taking a chance . . .

He set the communications transmit options to full subspace spread, no encryption, maximum power. "O'Brien to *Defiant*. O'Brien to *Defiant*. Come in, anyone." Then he put the message on automatic repeat and watched as the status lights showed it being transmitted up and down the subspace spectrum.

But there was no reply. In fact, the feedback sensors indicated that the message had not even been successfully sent.

O'Brien blew out his breath and called up a sensor diagnostic subroutine. And even allowing for the extra time it took to translate the controls and readings from their odd mixture of Bajoran and Klingon technical glyphs, it took less than thirty seconds to see what the problem was.

The message had not been transmitted because there was no subspace through which it could travel. The local environment was the equivalent of a subspace vacuum.

"Impossible," O'Brien muttered to himself. "We used to transmit subspace messages through the wormhole. We . . . oh." The chief engineer paused as he realized that the subspace environment that had allowed messages to be transmitted through the Bajoran wormhole was an artifact from the normal space-time metric which existed at each end of the wormhole.

But there were no ends here. Normal space-time no longer existed. The *Boreth,* Deep Space 9, and the *Defiant* were no longer in a wormhole tunnel, they were within a wormhole pocket. *Though how can you have a wormhole if there's nothing for that hole to pass through?*

Rather than torture himself over trying to answer the maddening question, O'Brien decided then and there to accept the fact that he missed Dax. He could always count on her to come up with an equation or two to help give him a direction for his more practical, hands-on approaches to various problems.

But for this problem, without Dax, he was reduced to tapping his fingers at the side of the console, trying to think of what to do next. Then the ship trembled and the deck pitched as if the *Boreth* were an ancient ship at sea.

For whatever reason, the movement lasted only a moment. The lights didn't even flicker.

In fact, the only aftereffect the chief engineer could note was that the background of red energy and glowing verteron strings and nodes against which DS9 and, most of the time, the *Defiant* had been hung had changed.

Now it was blue. The same rippling, icy translucence that the chief engineer remembered from his trips through the first Bajoran wormhole.

O'Brien checked his sensor readings of the *Boreth's* environment again but saw no appreciable change resulting from the switchover from red to blue. But the fact that color could change out there made him think of simple, ordinary photons. Unlike subspace transmissions which had to travel through a subspace medium as sound traveled through air, electromagnetic signals could propagate through a vacuum. O'Brien smiled in relief as he ran through a set of seldom-used Klingon communications settings until he found what he was looking for.

Radio.

The primary reason a ship like the *Boreth* even had that capability was in the event contact was made with an emergent, pre-warp technological culture. But in this case, primitive radio was just what he needed to conquer the unfathomable conditions of the wormhole pocket.

With a series of quick commands, O'Brien redirected his spoken message so it was relayed over the simple electromagnetic spectrum. He even adjusted the *Boreth*'s transmitter arrays so that the message was aimed at the *Defiant*.

But, frustratingly, even though the feedback indicators showed that this time the message was indeed being transmitted, there was still no response.

O'Brien sighed, turned his attention to Deep Space 9. Under normal conditions, the station constantly transmitted automated navigational signals in a variety of energy spectrums, even radio. If he could measure how those signals were being transmitted from the station to the *Boreth,* perhaps get an idea of what kind of interference might be at work in here, he might be able to make adjustments to his own transmission to the *Defiant*.

He checked the bridge doors again. Still no sign of Dukat. "Keep 'im busy, Rom," O'Brien said under his breath. Then he scanned all frequencies he knew the station would be transmitting on.

Nothing.

"Bloody hell," O'Brien said. He looked at the viewer. Deep Space 9 took up the middle quarter. He knew it had power because he could see the glow of its fusion reactors and its running lights were . . . "Wait a minute." Tapping a finger each time the station's hazard-warning lights blinked on and off, O'Brien started to count off seconds out loud like a first-year engineering student. "One millicochrane . . . two millicochrane . . . three millicochrane . . . *that's it!*"

The hazard lights atop each docking arm were cycling on and off too slowly. "It's in a different temporal frame of reference!"

He ran a quick series of calculations based on how fast the lights should be blinking versus how fast they actually were. The offset was approximately twenty-eight percent. Fortunately, Starfleet encountered enough antique space probes traveling at sublight, relativistic speeds that any junior engineer could handle the Hawking transformations necessary to bring timeshifted communications into synch. The realignment of the *Boreth*'s Klingon communications array took less than a minute.

O'Brien listened again, then smiled in triumph as familiar patterns of automated acquisition signals beeped over the bridge speakers.

"Ah, I've missed you, too," he said wistfully. Then he entered the transposition code that would translate the beeps into Federation-standard alphanumerics.

At that, his display screen changed to show three message windows. One was for DS9's Starfleet identification codes. One was for the codes required for in-system use by the Bajoran Transportation Commission. And the final one was a basic Cardassian location signal. One that Starfleet had elected to keep in operation for the benefit of any ships or automated probes that might have left the Bajoran system before the Cardassians withdrew and that might someday return to a different political situation.

But O'Brien's focus was on the Starfleet codes. These included time-alignment data, navigational positioning updates, and, of course, like any other Starfleet installation, local stardate calculations. He made some final adjustments in the selectivity of the *Boreth*'s electromagnetic receivers, then began working out his strategy for applying what he had learned to his next attempt to raise the *Defiant*.

As a final check of his calculations, he also applied the same adjustments to the radio channel on which the stardate information was being transmitted.

And then he sat back in shock, "No . . ."

The stardate was wrong.

That wasn't Deep Space 9 that faced the *Boreth*.

It was Deep Space 9 as it had existed on stardate 51889.4. Twenty-five years ago.

After having given up all hope of ever escaping his future, Chief Miles O'Brien found himself looking through a window into his past. And the first thought to burn through his engineer's mind was: *If light particles can pass through that window, then so can I.*

But before he could do anything about it, the bridge doors slipped open, and Dukat, red eyes ablaze, swept in, towing a baffled-looking Rom.

O'Brien erased his communications screens.

This wasn't the time, nonlinear or otherwise.

But soon it would be, and with that realization, hope returned to him.

Escape *was* possible.

But without Dax, it was all up to him.

CHAPTER 6

EYES CLOSED, Garak slumped down against the sharp rocks of unprocessed uridium ore piled by the slag cars. Each six and half hours, his labor cohort was permitted a ten-minute food break, and the last time the break signal had sounded, everyone in his group had rushed through the disk door like a herd of ravening *volekra*. But Garak hadn't joined them because he was conducting an experiment.

He no longer ate on any of his breaks. Neither did he drink water. And after more consecutive shifts than he could count, interrupted only when Gul Dukat made his regular appearance to take him to the Promenade to tailor a suit for Enabran Tain, Garak no longer even slept, though he was desperately weary.

For him to be able to withstand those deprivations, there was something wrong here. He knew it.

He just didn't know what.

The premonition took hold in him that soon he would no longer be able to even conceive of the notion of 'wrong.' That the sum total of his existence would be reduced to handling ore, half-making a suit, and then dying at his own father's hand. Again and again and . . .

Garak still retained one half-remembered idea that suggested dying was once the way all things were supposed to end, and that it only happened once. But for a reason that remained gratingly out of reach, life on Terok Nor seemed to allow no such escape. It continued forever in its bleakness, devoid of meaning or of hope.

"It's time for you to leave." The voice of the gul who commanded the station penetrated Garak's mental fog.

But Garak didn't even bother opening his eyes. "You're early," he murmured. "I've only been here for a shift. I remember too well what you're going to ask me to do. The same thing you always ask me. But you're supposed to let me work down here until I can't be sure what happened the last time was real, or a dream, so it can happen all over again."

"You think this is *real?*" Dukat asked. "Garak, I had thought that of all people, you might know better. Or, at least, have harbored some modicum of suspicion about its true nature."

Garak blinked, staring now at the high ceiling. Dukat had never said those words to him before. Usually, he simply escorted Garak along the station's corridors and discussed his dossier. At least, the dossier of a Bajoran resistance fighter who had once apprenticed to a tailor in Tohzat Province and with whom Garak had apparently been confused by the Cardassian bureaucracy.

Garak was honest enough with himself to admit that he couldn't really remember how he had actually come to occupy his current position on Terok Nor, or what he had been or done before coming here. But without question he knew he was not a Bajoran. And that knowledge did help him keep from accepting at least some of what he experienced here as unquestionable reality as Dukat seemed to suggest he should.

"Don't you wish to leave this place?" the gul asked.

Another question that had never been asked. Garak opened his eyes. Looked over at Dukat—

—and shot to his feet in surprise.

This Dukat was *different.* Not the same one who had been coming to him for . . . for centuries, it seemed. This Dukat was clad in the robes of a Bajoran religious order. His weathered features bore the mark of age. His hair was white. His strange eyes those of a fanatic.

And on his arm the red band of a Pah-wraith cult that—

Garak's breath came short and fast. "Of course! That explains it! This is an Orb experience."

"Close enough," the older Dukat allowed. He held out a hand. "But I can free you from it."

Fatigue lost its hold on Garak as relief unleashed a discomfiting torrent of memories. "Free me? Then there *is* something else that exists outside of . . . of this personal hell, I suppose we could call it." He gestured around him, at the ore-processing facility, its realization more detailed than the best Starfleet holodeck technology could produce. "I truly am impressed," Garak said. "Even I had no idea my issues with my father were so deep-seated. Here I had always thought that my personal hell would be to be confined in a narrow space with ravenous *marklars* gnawing on my flesh. But this *is* much more harrowing. On an emotional level, that is."

Dukat stared, wild-eyed, at him, hand still outstretched. "What are you talking about? I said, I can *save* you from this. Say after me: I will serve you."

Garak ignored the gul, or whatever rank this Dukat was. He really had no patience for such bizarre posturing. "This is most remarkable. Obviously, the *Boreth* entered one of the wormholes before the universe was destroyed." He peered intently at Dukat. "The universe *was* destroyed, wasn't it?" He held up a hand to forestall Dukat's answer as he continued excitedly. "Forget that I said that. Of course it was destroyed. But somehow . . . somehow this ship must have maintained a small island of stability in the midst of . . . whatever conditions exist here. Wherever here is. And clearly—"

"Take my hand and serve me!" Dukat's voice rose in anger.

Garak nodded, not listening, as he linked his hands behind his back and began to pace beside the slag cars and their piles of unprocessed ore. "And since the Pah-wraiths came after me by subjecting me to this . . . this illusion of Terok Nor, in reality, or in whatever passes for it now, we somehow must be physically protected in the ship."

Garak stopped pacing and looked questioningly at Dukat, who still stood with outstretched hand. "Is everyone consigned to their own version of hell? Were you?"

A sudden wind set Dukat's robes fluttering as he withdrew his hand and then threw both arms open wide, declaring, "I am Kosst Dukat, ruler of this realm! And in Amojan's name I damn you to—"

"Oh, do be quiet and let me think," Garak said. "If you could do anything to me in here, you would have done it by now."

Dukat dramatically pointed both his hands at Garak, red sparks of energy flickering the length of his long black-nailed fingers.

"Dukat, are you really willing to throw away your one chance at eternal victory?" Garak asked, completely unintimidated.

The robed Cardassian stiffened, enraged, but he did not strike. "Why are you not afraid?"

"For the same reason you *are* afraid," Garak said, lifting his own hands before him, remembering in detail how they used to look. At once, his clear nails became black and pink skin that had been as repellently smooth as that of a gas-distended corpse became gray and lightly plated, neither black nor white but a perfect aesthetic balance of the two—the Cardassian ideal.

Garak put his restored hands to his neck, felt his proud dual spinal cords restored to their proper location.

"Consider what's happening here," Garak said with satisfaction. "This wormhole—or the Temple, if you prefer—is obviously a place with rules. A place with limits."

"I am without limits!" Dukat shouted. "I am absolute power— Amojan without end!"

"And if that were true," Garak said, "for my insolence, I would not exist, and you would not need me." He smiled pleasantly at Dukat. "Because that *is* why you're here, isn't it? You *need* me."

"O'Brien needs you!" Dukat sputtered. "As for me, I leave you here in your hell for all time!"

"Dukat, have you forgotten who I am? Is there anyone you have ever known who was better at . . . circumventing the rules? Finding exceptions to the limits?"

Dukat's eyes bulged as they pulsed with red energy, but none of that energy spilled out to strike Garak down.

"When you're ready to talk," Garak said, his argument confirmed by Dukat's inaction, "I'm certain you'll know where to find me."

Then, with absolute certainty about what would happen next, he closed his eyes for less time than it took him to blink, and when he opened them again, he was looking up at the ceiling of the *Boreth*'s bridge, less than a meter from the last place he remembered standing when the ship had spun into the wormhole and all the lights had gone out.

"How utterly remarkable," Garak said, getting to his feet. He nodded to the two people watching him: "Good day to you, gentlemen." He added a smile to his greeting, but the expressions on the faces of Miles O'Brien and Rom remained stern and slightly confused.

"Come now," Garak teased them. "We did survive the destruction of the universe. I believe that's worth a small round of self-congratulations, wouldn't you agree?"

"You'll pardon us if we don't join you," O'Brien said stiffly. "*We* were in our own personal hells."

"Indeed."

"Uh," Rom said as he looked back and forth like some type of agitated avian, "wh-what happened to Dukat?"

"Oh, the last time I saw him," Garak said, "he was in *my* hell." He shrugged at O'Brien. "It wasn't a very good one, though. No logic to it. I think . . . in fact, I'm sure I would have found my way out soon enough. How about you?"

"This isn't the time," O'Brien said. "Dukat might be back any moment."

Garak smoothed his robes, all that remained of his Bajoran captivity, then looked up at the main viewer and was startled by what he saw there. "The station? In here with us?"

"More than that," the chief engineer said. "According to its navigational time code, that's the station as it existed about the time it was destroyed."

"You don't say."

"This isn't a game!" O'Brien exclaimed with a nervous glance to either side of him. But except for himself and the two engineers, Garak knew there was no one else who was awake. The others, including Quark and Odo, were all unconscious.

"I assure you, Chief, I am quite aware of the situation. But given that the universe is gone and we can't possibly survive for long in . . . wherever we are . . . there really is little else to do but marvel at the fact that of all the trillions, perhaps quadrillions of sentient beings ever to have lived, it is *we* whom fate has chosen to be present at the end."

"Uh," Rom tried again, "I think what the Chief is trying to say is that this might not *be* the end."

Garak hid a smile. Ferengi were *so* amusing. Always trying to find an angle so they wouldn't have to admit defeat. "And how would that be possible?" Garak paused. *Unless—"Is* Dukat able to be about on the ship?"

"Yes," O'Brien said tersely. "He can be on this ship, *and* he was in my hell, and in Rom's."

"He . . . brought us out," Rom added. He peered at Garak suspiciously. "How did you get out?"

Garak hesitated, conducting his usual estimation of what he had to lose and/or gain by telling the truth and how he might alter that particular trade-off one way or another with a judicious act of misdirection. But, he decided, in the end there was nothing to lose because everything was already lost.

"Yes. Dukat came to see me, as well," he said. "That visit was a change in the pattern that had been established, you see, and his presence fit with suspicions I had already entertained. After only a few minutes of conversation, it became apparent to me that he needed me more than I needed him, and I resolved to return here."

Garak enjoyed the way O'Brien and Rom exchanged a look of disbelief.

"It musn't have been much of a hell," O'Brien said, confirming Garak's long-held belief that humans had little resilience and even less imagination.

"Honestly, Chief," Garak replied amiably, "after the obliteration of my world, my people, my culture, and my universe, how could any concept of hell be worse than what I had already experienced?"

O'Brien grunted as he turned back to his engineering station. "Ask me when we're out of this."

"I would appreciate hearing what you're planning."

O'Brien turned around in his chair. "You mean you'll help?"

"When have I not?" Garak said.

Rom held up a finger. "Well, there was that time when—"

"Since the universe came to an end, I mean," Garak added.

O'Brien ignored them both as he got up and crossed from the communications station to what passed for a Klingon science station. As far as Garak could tell, the science station was about half the size of the flight console and, in true Klingon tradition, about one-fifth the size of the weapons station.

"The science of what's happened—and what's happening—is beyond me," O'Brien said bluntly. "But I've got a theory."

"I'm sure you do." Garak saw the flash of anger that passed through the human's features and realized once again that not everyone shared his ability to view adversity as an amusing diversion. A pity, really. "I'm sorry, Chief. That was uncalled for. Perhaps my illusion had more of an effect on me than I realized. Please, continue."

His apology, though insincere, had the desired result.

"All right," O'Brien said gruffly as he adjusted incomprehensible controls. "I think what we're seeing is some side effect of those bloody Red Orbs of Jalbador."

"The ones that opened the red wormhole in the first place," Garak said helpfully.

"Right," O'Brien agreed. "I think that . . . well, we're in nonlinear time, so one way to look at it is that in here, where we are, everything happens at once."

Garak nodded and tried to look interested.

"So," the Chief continued, "we're here, on the *Boreth*, existing in some sort of leftover bubble of space-time that originated in the year 2400. But Deep Space 9, as we see it out there, is in its own space-time bubble from the year 2375."

"I'm afraid I don't understand," Garak said kindly but truthfully. "Why from twenty-five years ago? Why not from last week? Or, for that matter, forty years ago?"

"It's the Orbs," O'Brien explained. "When they opened the wormhole, it's as if the maw *swallowed* a section of space-time. In 2400, the Orbs opened the wormhole, and it swallowed us on the *Boreth*. Back in 2375, the Orbs opened the wormhole, and it swallowed the station." He pointed to the viewer. "And see up there? Upper right-hand quadrant?"

Garak looked up as directed and reacted with appropriate surprise. "Is that the *Defiant?*"

"I'm certain of it," O'Brien said. "I just can't tell if it's the *Defiant* as it was when we entered the wormhole twenty-five years ago or as it was when it entered the wormhole with us at the end."

In spite of himself, Garak was intrigued by the possibilities. "As I recall, there was a great deal of confusion in those last minutes. Are you certain the *Defiant* did enter the wormhole with us?"

"Dukat seems to think so," O'Brien said. "He's convinced Weyoun's on her."

Garak chuckled softly.

O'Brien reacted crossly. "How can any of this be amusing?"

"Not this," Garak said quickly. "I was just thinking of a line from some old Klingon play. About 'the evil that men do' living after them. I mean, can *you* imagine continuing any sort of conflict after the *universe* has ended? What possible point could there be to it?"

"Uh," Rom piped up unexpectedly, "I think that the conflict Dukat and Weyoun are involved in actually started in here and not in our universe. But . . . I might be wrong."

"You are," Garak said. "The conflict isn't between Dukat and Weyoun, it's between . . ." Garak waved his hand at the screen. ". . . whatever dwells out there."

"The Prophets and the Pah-wraiths," O'Brien said.

"Among others," Garak agreed. "Remember, Dukat says he represents those Pah-wraiths imprisoned in the Fire Caves, which I understand are different from those Pah-wraiths who dwell in the second Temple."

For just a moment, Garak allowed himself to sigh at the inconsequential wonder of it all. "Just imagine . . . is it possible that all of existence—*our* existence—was simply a random by-product of a war between beings we can never comprehend?

"To think that we were created by those superior beings, just as the religions of a thousand worlds maintain, but then to discover that those superior beings created us *accidentally*. Really, Chief, Rom, how can you not find amusement in that possibility? Surely, it's either that or madness."

O'Brien shook his head. "Garak, I'm a simple kind of guy. I leave science to the scientists and philosophy to the Vulcans. All I know is that I *liked* my existence. I *miss* my wife and children. And if there is one chance in a . . . a quadrillion that something I can do now might take me back to them, even for a minute, you can bet I'm going to do it.

"Now, are you going to help? Or are you going to stare into your navel and contemplate infinity?"

Garak allowed no offense to seep into his voice. "Seeing as how what passes for my navel is centered on my forehead, I believe my only choice is to help you. What would you like me to do?"

Then he listened carefully as O'Brien described his discovery that time was passing at a different rate on the *Boreth* than it was on Deep Space 9. The Chief's assumption was that the *Defiant* was also caught in a unique pocket of temporal progression, and that for communication to become possible between the two ships, that rate had to be calculated and compensated for.

Unfortunately, it seemed the *Boreth* was not able to create an image of the *Defiant* with enough resolution to measure the blinking of her navigational lights. Assuming, of course, that those lights were actually functioning.

Thus, what O'Brien needed Garak to do was to undertake a tedious set of scans of the *Defiant.* He was to look for any kind of timeshifted emanation from her, whether it was the venting of hydrazine from her station-keeping thrusters or the standard signals from her Starfleet automatic Identify Friend-or-Foe transmission.

"And how, exactly," Garak asked, hoping O'Brien took the question as seriously as he meant it, "will any of this enable you to return to your wife and children in the past?"

The chief engineer took a deep breath before answering. "Garak, when DS9 and the *Defiant* went into the wormhole the first time, none of us knew what was happening. No one knew how to take steps to reverse the process. But now the three of us do. So if one of us—" O'Brien looked over at the unmoving forms of Odo, Quark, and the others. "—*any* of us, can get over to the station or to the *Defiant,* or even transmit what we know to them, there's a chance we might be able to do something to change what happened."

"In other words," Garak said, "change the past to eliminate this future. Which means we won't exist." He didn't like the sound of that.

"Look at it this way," O'Brien said earnestly. "If you could save Cardassia Prime from being wiped out by the Ascendancy, would you do it, even if it meant you'd die?"

All sense of amusement drained out of Garak. "Without question."

"And I'd do the same for my family, my world, and my universe," O'Brien said. "And what might make it interesting is, considering we're in a realm of nonlinear time, even if the past *is* changed, maybe we'll still exist anyway."

For a moment, Garak's mind fastened on the fascinating notion of being able to have dinner with himself. Then he recovered, bowed politely. "I am at your disposal, Chief."

O'Brien set him up at the communications console and showed him how to begin his scans. Garak hesitated before beginning his assignment, glancing over at Odo on the deck. "Is there anything we can do about them?"

"I don't think so," O'Brien said grimly. "Rom and I have both tried to wake them up. I don't know how Dukat does it, but he's the only one who can enter their illusions."

"It must be horrible," Rom said, shaking his head over his brother.

Garak smiled encouragingly at Rom. "If their illusions are crafted as mine was, they'll be more superficial than terrible. Your brother is probably in Ferengi Hell . . . what is it? Ah, yes, the Debtor's Dungeon. And knowing him, he probably thinks that *you* put him there. And Odo . . . well, wherever he is, you can be sure he believes he can't change shape. And he's alone."

"Those don't sound very superficial to me," O'Brien said. "And neither was mine."

"Chief," Garak countered, "I'll be the first to admit I don't have deep knowledge of Earth's religious beliefs, but how could you possibly think that you are important enough to the creator of the universe that he, she, it, or they would go to enough trouble to craft a hell specifically for you? Does the term 'delusions of grandeur' mean anything on your world?"

O'Brien muttered something Garak couldn't decipher, then pointed at the comm console. "Just start your scans," he said.

Garak turned to the controls. And that was when Gul Dukat said, "Better that you don't."

As Rom squealed as only a Ferengi could, Garak spun around in his chair to see Dukat now on the bridge beside Odo. The changeling, conscious, was sitting up, rubbing at his neck, obviously disoriented.

"Welcome back," Garak said, his interest sharpening. Dukat had not arrived on the bridge through any door. Apparently his ability to enter others' illusions involved some sort of self-generating transporter effect.

"I know what you're doing," Dukat thundered at O'Brien. "And I will not allow you to continue."

"Look—you can do whatever you want in here," the Chief said with admirable defiance.

"You're right, I can," Dukat hissed.

"All we want to do is go back to our own time and leave the wormhole to you."

Dukat shook his head. "My realm can't be whole while your realm exists. So, you see, it's one or the other. And, understandably, as I'm sure you'll agree, I choose mine." His eyes flared with red fire.

O'Brien fell silent as if he had nothing more to say, and Garak waited, watching, wondering if the Chief would actually have the courage to charge Dukat and physically overwhelm him. But O'Brien made no such move.

Not surprisingly, Rom appeared to be in the same inactive, ineffectual mode. Though Garak could see that at least the Ferengi's gaze was frantically darting around the bridge, presumably seeking some kind of weapon.

But in the absence of the others' initiative, Garak could not deny his own role any longer: What happened next would be up to him. As it usually was when indecisive humans and calculating Ferengi were involved.

He stood up from his chair and started toward Dukat.

Beside Dukat, Odo was on his knees, staring at his own hands as if he had never seen them before. Or had not seen them for centuries.

"What do you think *you're* doing?" Dukat demanded as Garak moved closer, until they were only centimeters apart.

"This," Garak said simply. And then he brought his open hand up to smash into Dukat's jaw, cracking the old Cardassian's brittle yellow teeth together and sending him tumbling back against the life-support station.

Even as Dukat regained his feet and stretched out his arms and the murderous power of the Pah-wraiths rose in his glowing red eyes, Garak stood his ground.

"I will crush your soul!" Dukat shrieked.

"Not likely," Garak calmly replied.

And then O'Brien finally acted, launching himself into the space between Dukat and Garak. *"Run!"*

Rom followed with an ear-splitting squeal.

But Dukat stepped back as he expertly flipped the Ferengi and deflected O'Brien's charge, knocking both of them over the life-support-station chair and onto the deck behind Odo.

Typical, Garak thought.

Then Dukat pointed his finger at O'Brien.

A halo of red energy enveloped his gray hand.

On the deck, O'Brien drew back, grimacing in expectation of what would happen next.

But nothing did.

Garak moved in on Dukat. "Don't you understand *yet?*"

Dukat backed up against the life-support console. He pointed both hands at Garak. Both hands glowed red, as did his eyes.

But there were no deadly discharges of red Pah-wraith energy. No attack of any kind. Dukat whimpered with incomprehension.

"You were only a *vessel,*" Garak said brutally. "A puppet for Kosst Amojan."

"He gave me power!" Dukat wailed.

"*Gave* you power," Garak agreed. "Certainly, while you were out there, in the universe of suns and planets and fragile linear beings and had something to offer him in a realm where he could not easily exist. But *think,* Dukat! What did Kosst Amojan want from you? What was his goal?"

Dukat looked at his outstretched hands and turned them both palm upward in a supplicating gesture. "To . . . to reclaim his realm."

"This realm?" Garak asked.

Dukat looked up, the first glimmer of understanding dawning on his time-ravaged face.

"And so what did you do?" Garak persisted. "You *brought* him here. Back into the realm from which he had been expelled."

Dukat nodded. Blood trickled from his slack mouth, a splinter of broken tooth adhered to his lip.

"So why does he need you any longer?" Garak asked. "Don't you see? This isn't your battle. It never was *your* battle. You were just . . . transportation. The real fight is out there!" Garak pointed to the viewer, to the pale blue glow of the nonlinear realm. "The simple truth is, you have no power here. Not anymore."

Dukat swayed as he pulled himself upright. He spread his arms. "I *am* Kosst Dukat! I *am* the Emissary of the Amojan!" he cried.

Garak put a swift end to such nonsense. He grabbed Dukat's

robes in both hands, hoisting the old man into the air. "You are *nothing!*" he shouted. And then he twisted around and hurled Dukat's frail form across the bridge to land by the empty command chair.

Garak looked down at O'Brien. The engineer seemed stunned by what had just happened. "Well, what are you waiting for?" Garak asked him. "The Prophets and the Pah-wraiths have their fight, and we have our ours."

Nodding wordlessly, O'Brien got to his feet.

Open-mouthed with shock, Rom followed suit.

"Gentlemen, it is time to go home," Garak told them.

Then he went back to his console to begin his scans, wondering if they had the slightest chance in anyone's hell of actually accomplishing what he had promised.

CHAPTER 7

WEYOUN'S STORAGE TUBE was located at the far end of the main storage chamber on Rondac III. Since the nutrient-stasis fluid was colorless and the tube cover transparent, from his upright position he could stare out and see the entire facility. On one side, bank after bank of tubes just like his stretched out to the vanishing point. On the other side, the tube banks soared upward and plunged downward for kilometers.

There were so many storage tubes, he was unable to count them. But he did know what lay inside each one.

Another Weyoun.

Every few centuries, a team of Jem'Hadar would walk past his tube, usually escorting a Founder. Occasionally, Weyoun would see another Vorta in their company—an Eris or a Keevan or a Marklar. And always, he would see another Weyoun, freshly awakened, the nutrient fluid still dripping from his glistening body, his eyes bright with the prospects of the new life he was about to embrace.

But over the millennia that Weyoun had spent motionless, expectant, in his own tube, not one Founder, not one Jem'Hadar, not one other Vorta had come for him.

Slowly, in the sporadic bursts of thought that surfaced at random in a mind lacking stimulation, it occurred to Weyoun that though he had been brought to the brink of life in this cloning facility, it might not be his destiny ever to partake of it. Instead, he might spend eternity in his tube, neither dead nor alive, simply waiting . . . forever . . . without ever being—

Weyoun suddenly realized—a few decades later—that his view of the storage facility was blocked by a person standing in front of his tube.

No, not a person, Weyoun thought—eventually—*a female.* His eyes registered flowing dark hair and dangling ear jewelry. His artificial memory began piecing together disparate, disconnected images from half-remembered lives of all the decanted Weyoun clones who had preceded him.

Kilana. It was Kilana. Or, more precisely, a Kilana. A female Vorta whose third incarnation had once shared passion with Weyoun's sec—

The female Vorta placed her hand on his storage tube's cover.

Her hand *passed through* the cover.

The cover was gone!

The weight and thickness of the tube's nutrient-stasis fluid left Weyoun, spilling away from him, splashing noisily on the floor. The sound thundered in his ears. The overhead lights seared his eyes. He shivered as the slick coating of the fluid evaporated from skin that had never been exposed to a change in temperature.

Weyoun's lungs expanded and he drew in a huge gulp of air and he *lived!*

Driven by instinct, Weyoun stepped from his tube. But his legs were not ready and they buckled beneath him.

Kilana caught him, steadied him.

Weyoun heard his own voice as it moaned with delight. To be embraced by solid arms, to sense the delicious change of pressure and gravity bearing down on his limbs, to be in a position other than floating upright in his tube—it was so marvelous and so confusing and so overwhelming, all at the same time.

"Shhh," Kilana whispered, and Weyoun thrilled to feel her fingers gently brush his sodden hair from his forehead. "You're free now."

Weyoun stared into the face of the incarnated female who had meant so much to his own previous incarnation.

It was then that he noticed that something was wrong.

The female who held him was dressed like Kilana. Quite properly, she wore the standard deep-red gown of a Vorta negotiator—the color to imply the threat of violence. Quite properly, her shoulders were cloaked in the blue of authority—the color to imply the rewards of cooperation. And, quite properly, the gown itself was cut low and pulled tight to distract male eyes and attention.

But her ears—they were missing or mutilated. Weyoun saw no sign of Vorta amplifying nodes ascending from her jaw.

Instead, he saw what appeared to be some lesser form of sense-amplifying structure covering the bridge of her nose.

"Who are you?" Weyoun gurgled. Voicing that question made him cough up thick clots of nutrient fluid that he realized he must have been breathing during the millennia he'd spent in his tube.

"Arla Rees," the female said.

Weyoun gasped as the storage chamber melted away, replaced by the cold sterility of a Starfleet sickbay. In the same instant, his memory was restored, and he realized he was on the *Defiant*.

"How did you find me?" Weyoun asked. He tried to pull his hand from hers, but she wouldn't relinquish her grip.

"The True Prophets guided me to you," Arla said, "so that I might give you your freedom, and you might grant me my release."

Weyoun knew exactly what she meant, why she wouldn't let go of his hand.

"Of course," Weyoun said. "I gladly share the gift of the Grigari."

He squeezed the flesh of her hand then, pinching it between two nails until the skin broke and blood welled.

She gave a small moan, then did the same to him.

And when their wounds met, blood to blood, the gift of the Grigari *was* shared.

"But what if *everything* that's happened since we entered the wormhole has been an Orb experience?" Dr. Bashir asked. "Including this conversation? Right now?"

In his command chair, and finally wearing a newly replicated Starfleet uniform, circa 2375, Sisko stared at the main viewer of the *Defiant*'s bridge. He couldn't take his eyes from the image of Deep Space 9 displayed there, now floating against a violent red background of rippling light, glowing verteron nodes, and shifting verteron strings.

No, that's wrong, Sisko thought. Despite Jadzia's discovery about why she couldn't receive any signals from the station and her subsequent adjustment of the *Defiant's* communications systems to account for two different temporal frames, he still could not make himself believe it. *That is* not *Deep Space 9. Not yet.*

Sisko roused himself from his thoughts of the past. Returned to the present. Or to the future. "Doctor, this is *not* an illusion," he said firmly. He looked away from the screen and over at Bashir, who was seated at the ship's auxiliary life-support station. Worf was at tactical, Jadzia at science, Kira at flight. Appreciatively, Sisko noted that Jake was sitting at the back of the bridge by the situation table, trying to stay out of the way. Off the bridge, Commander Arla was watching over Weyoun in sickbay, and Ensign Simons and the remaining eight members of the crew were on duty in engineering. "That you can be sure of."

"But how?" Bashir persisted. "The illusion I was trapped in was indistinguishable from reality."

Sisko knew each one of his crew was waiting for the answer to Bashir's question. After what they each had experienced, how *could* any of them be certain what reality was anymore?

Sisko knew his answer wasn't good enough as he gave it, but it was the only thing he could think to say. "This moment we're in, Doctor, it doesn't *feel* like an Orb experience." He held up a hand to stop Bashir's protest. "It doesn't *feel* anything at all like the individual illusion of hell I was trapped in. And if you think about it, I'm certain you can identify the differences between what you feel now and what you felt . . . before Dax came for you."

In the silence that followed his challenge, Sisko knew everyone was daring to revisit his and her own experience of hell.

Jadzia spoke first. "He's right, Julian. I remember my first Orb experience. Right in my lab on Deep Space 9. I opened the Orb Ark and the next thing I knew, I was with Curzon, in the transference bay, as Dax passed from him to me."

"That was an actual memory being replayed," Bashir argued. "Of course you knew it wasn't real because it had happened before."

Sisko intervened to take control of the discussion. They had decisions to make and, if Jadzia's estimates were correct, they would have to make them soon.

"Doctor, in your illusion, after the first time you . . . you fouled up the singularity containment field and the universe . . . ended, didn't you have some small question in the back of your mind when the experience began repeating?"

"Well, yes, but . . . it was more like an unsettling sense of *déjà vu*. It was nothing that made me think, 'Oh, right, this is just an illusion. Everything's going to be all right after all.' "

"But the point is, you *knew* something was wrong. When I had my first Orb experience, I found myself suddenly walking on the beach where I had met Jennifer. And I met her again, then and there, fully aware that I was in the past, even though I gave no thought to how I had arrived at that moment." Sisko spread his arms to encompass the bridge. "But *this* is different. Through the Orbs, or being in the presence of the Prophets, things feel altered. Time moves in fits and starts, back and forth. The . . . the light comes from outside *and* from within . . . the sound is something you feel as much as hear . . . the quality of *existence* is different.

"Having experienced the Orbs, having met the Prophets, and having been trapped in a Pah-wraith hell, I say what we're experiencing *now,* on this ship, is the *same* reality we all remember from our past. And I believe Dax's sensor scans bear me out."

Sisko looked to Jadzia, who nodded her agreement, then took up his argument.

"Julian," she said, "at some point we have to draw the line. Sure, maybe we're all still stuck in the wormhole from back in our first trip through it. Maybe everything that's happened to us in the past six years is an illusion. But if that illusion is indistinguishable from reality—*truly* indistinguishable and not just a convincing reproduction—then we have no choice but to *accept* it as reality and deal with it as best we can. Otherwise, we might as well sit in a corner, doubt the existence of everything, and just . . . do nothing."

"This is why I prefer medicine," Bashir grumbled. "Physics always ends up colliding head-to-head with philosophy."

Jadzia's smile was pointed. "Not quite. To test the postulates of physics, you can design experiments. Trust me: Domains of linear reality *can* exist within the nonlinear realm of the wormhole pocket." She turned to Sisko. "And Benjamin? My experiments show we really are running out of time."

"I'm convinced," Sisko said. He looked around the bridge for any other questions, but all attention appeared to be focused on what Jadzia would say next. For however it was that the *Defiant* and the station could exist in here at all, the Trill had clearly determined that they would not be able to exist much longer.

Then the ship pitched again and everyone on the bridge grabbed the closest chair or console to steady themselves. Sisko kept his eyes fixed on the main viewer. And just as before, by the time all movement stopped, the image on the viewer had changed. Now DS9 appeared before a background of undulating *blue* energy, with *no* verteron phenomena observable. Sisko turned to Jadzia for her report. "Old Man?"

"Another equalization wave. And it came . . . one hundred seventy-seven seconds faster than the last one."

"So they are accelerating," Sisko said.

"As predicted," the Trill confirmed. "Along a perfect geometric curve."

"Any change in the time required to equalize the pressure difference between the two wormhole fragments?"

Jadzia had discovered that when the wormhole pocket split in two, the resulting halves were not identical. The blue wormhole had extended from the Bajoran system through a hyperdimensional realm to emerge seventy thousand light-years away in the Gamma Quadrant. The red wormhole, though, had joined two regions of space more than one hundred thousand light-years apart, stretching from Bajor to the farthest reaches of the Delta Quadrant. To her, that implied that each wormhole contained a different energy density, so that when they were rejoined, that difference had to be evened out, just as when two spacecraft docked and their differing atmospheric pressures had to equalize when the airlocks were opened.

Sisko listened intently now as Jadzia read the displays at her station. "No change in my first calculation. Other than now I can be precise to five decimal places. The equalization waves will keep passing over us at an accelerating rate during the next . . . fifteen hours, twenty-seven minutes. Just like water sloshing through a pipe, trying to find its level. And after those nine hundred twenty-seven minutes, the delay between each pass will have shrunk to something on the order of the Planck interval so that the wormhole environment will effectively become homeostatic, and . . ."

Sisko completed her analysis. "The space-time bubbles containing the station and this ship will follow the universe into nonexistence."

"Exactly. The wormhole pocket will not only be nonlinear in time the way its two fragments were, it will also become dimensionless in space. And that, I'm afraid," the Trill concluded, "is as close to nothingness as the Heisenberg Uncertainty Principle will permit."

"Fifteen hours, twenty-seven minutes," Bashir repeated glumly. "So much for philosophy. And physics. And everything else."

Sisko stood up, alarmed by the doctor's sudden embrace of defeat, and also acutely aware of his crew watching him, looking to him for strength, and for leadership.

"That's enough, Doctor. It's not over yet." Sisko made his decision. *Their* decision. "We're going to cross over."

"What?" The startled response had come from Jake at the back of the bridge. His son had obviously reached his limit for remaining a silent observer. "Dad, are we really going back to Deep Space 9?"

Sisko shook his head. It wasn't as simple as that. If Jadzia was correct, then, technically, that *wasn't* Deep Space 9 out there. In its current temporal frame, it wouldn't become Deep Space 9 for at least two more weeks. Because, according to the navigational signals that Jadzia had received from it, the station before them existed at a specific time in the past.

Like everyone else on the bridge, Sisko could not look away from the main viewer and the achingly familiar shape that was slowly turning on it, waiting. The home they had lost. Before it had become their home.

A time in which it had been known as Terok Nor.

Stardate 46359.1.

The Day of Withdrawal.

The day to which Sisko now had to return, to save his life, his crew, and his universe.

Odo, like almost all the others on the *Boreth* who had been "rescued" by Garak, didn't want to talk about the hell in which he'd been trapped, and O'Brien wasn't inclined to force the issue. Mostly because he had finally determined the nature of the periodic waves that had struck the *Boreth* and caused the huge Klingon ship to buck as if hit by a phaser volley. It appeared that the quantum structure of the blended wormhole fragments was equalizing, and as best as the chief engineer could determine, once equilibrium had been achieved, the space-time bubble containing the *Boreth* would no longer have any dimensions in which to exist.

By entering the red wormhole, those aboard the *Boreth* had *not* escaped the end of their universe. They had only postponed it, and not by long, either.

"How much time?!" Quark bleated, incredulous. Except for Dukat, who still lay unconscious, bound, and gagged on the deck beside the unused communications station, only the Ferengi barkeep among the twelve others on the bridge of the *Boreth* seemed not to have heard what O'Brien had just announced.

"I *said,* to our frame of reference," O'Brien repeated, "we have thirty hours and . . . some odd minutes. I can't work it out any closer than that."

Quark whirled to confront Garak, who as usual, O'Brien noted, looked unperturbed in the face of the Ferengi's extravagantly expressed emotions. *"You* should have left me in Debtor's Dungeon!"

"Believe me, if I had known how disagreeable you were going to be about being saved, I would have preferred to have left you there myself," Garak said.

"Then send me back!" Quark demanded.

O'Brien knew they didn't have the time for this. "That's enough, Quark. Settle down."

Almost comic in his bulky Bajoran robes, Quark drew himself up to shout at O'Brien. "You're not in charge!"

But any further protest from the furious Ferengi was quickly quashed as Garak clamped a hand on Quark's shoulder. "Yes, Quark, he *is* in charge. Chief O'Brien is the *only* one among us who understands the unique nature of our predicament. And I, for one, am content to hear his conclusions and act accordingly."

Indignant, the Ferengi shook off the Cardassian's hand. "Don't you understand?! You dragged us out of our afterlives! *Eternal* afterlives! To face absolute extinction in thirty hours!"

Odo, the only person on the bridge to be in proper garb—because he had formed his Bajoran uniform from his outer layers of mutable flesh—made a futile attempt to get Quark to listen to reason.

"Quark, we were not experiencing *real* afterlives," the changeling said. "The Pah-wraiths created illusions *for* us. Presumably because they couldn't get at us any other way."

"Uh, that does make sense, brother," Rom added.

"SENSE!" Quark all but screamed at Rom. "Have you grown points on your ears all of a sudden? What do *you* know about things making sense?"

O'Brien did not intervene in the exchange between the siblings. He was confident that Rom could handle himself.

"Well," Rom said, as if his brother had asked him a reasonable question, "according to the Chief, as long as normal matter and space-time exists in the wormhole pocket, the pocket's domain is disrupted. So it seems to, uh, make sense that if the Pah-wraiths, or whatever, didn't want to be . . . disrupted, they would have destroyed us when we first entered. But since they didn't, I agree with Garak. It's because . . . they can't."

"Well said, Rom," Garak added in an approving tone of voice; just to provoke Quark, O'Brien was sure.

"So how does that explain them putting us to sleep with illusions of the afterlife?" Quark asked acidly.

Garak took over. "Quark, it might help if you would start thinking less like a condemned prisoner and more like a Ferengi." The Cardassian ignored Quark's shocked, insulted gasp. "Why don't you consider what we're involved in as a business deal? What would your response be if you were trying to get the better of a potential customer—one who didn't realize he had some method of gaining an advantage over you?"

To O'Brien, it seemed clear that the glowering and dark-faced Quark knew the answer Garak was going after, but he didn't want to give the Cardassian the satisfaction of saying it.

So Garak did. "I believe," he said helpfully, "you would attempt to *distract* your client. Perhaps provide him with an expensive yet potent bottle of bloodwine. Introduce him to a fetching dabo girl or two. Keep him occupied until the window of opportunity for exploiting his advantage over you has fled. And then, for the cost of a small distraction, you would no longer be at risk. At least, as *I* believe."

"So?" Quark said, surly.

"So," O'Brien said, impatient with the both of them, "the afterlife illusions we experienced were distractions. To keep us from attempting to get out of here."

His huge ears flushing perceptibly, the Ferengi lifted his hands up toward the ceiling in a dramatic gesture of frustration. "Am I surrounded by idiots?! There's nowhere else to go!"

O'Brien's displeasure with Quark's antics sharpened his voice. "Not *where*, Quark. *When*." He pointed to the main viewer. "That's not just Deep Space 9 out there. That's Deep Space 9 on the day it was swallowed by the red wormhole. If we can somehow get onto the station on that day, we can stop the Orbs of Jalbador from being opened in your establishment."

Quark's pale eyes bulged with shock. "That's—that's *time* travel!" he quavered. "And from the first *frinxing* day we popped up in this nightmare future, every one of you has said—" His voice now under more control, Quark adopted a high-pitched singsong voice, his impression of human, O'Brien guessed. "—'The only way we can go back in time is if the *Defiant* slingshots us around the red wormhole.' "

"In *normal* space, Quark," O'Brien said. "And we're not in normal space anymore. Normal space doesn't exist anymore. And under the circumstances, I don't think anyone here is terribly concerned about what the Department of Temporal Investigations has to say about avoiding the creation of alternate timelines."

Quark slapped his hands to his face. "How in the name of all that's profitable can you have alternate timelines if *time* doesn't exist?"

O'Brien was suddenly aware of everyone, even Garak, looking at him, waiting for his answer. For all the Ferengi's panicky, self-obsessed bluster, something in Quark's last outburst had resonated with the others on the bridge. And O'Brien knew that if he was to somehow keep this group together, make them capable of at least attempting his admittedly desperate survival plan, he had to come up with something convincing, and fast.

But for a moment, he just stared blankly back at them, the only thought running through his mind, *What would Captain Sisko do?* Followed almost instantaneously by, *What would Captain Picard do?*

Garak broke the silence. "Though I am loath to admit it, Chief O'Brien, our Ferengi friend does raise an interesting question."

And then, as if a phaser burst had struck him directly between the eyes to fill his mind with blinding light, O'Brien had it. Thanks to Captain Picard.

"Look, like I said, the multidimensional physics of what's going on here are completely beyond me. We'd be a lot better off if Dax were with us, that's for sure. But what I can tell you is that I *know* for an absolute fact that alternate timelines do exist."

By the silence that greeted his pronouncement, O'Brien understood that what he had to say next would be made infinitely easier by the fact that everyone *wanted* to believe him. Even Quark, it seemed, for all his negativity, was not yet ready to abandon all hope.

"Twice," the chief engineer began, deliberately making eye contact with everyone on the bridge of the *Boreth*, "when I was on the *Enterprise*, we had encounters with beings or technology from a time period beyond the year 2400. Once we picked up a time-transport pod from the twenty-sixth century. Another time, Captain Picard himself had a run-in with two unsavory types from the twenty-seventh century. And Vash was with him. So, *somehow*, in De Sitter space or the multiverse or some undefinable phase space in which time has more than two dimensions—and which Dax would be able to talk about for days—timelines exist in which the universe did *not* end in 2400.

"Now, I'm not Dax, so I can't tell you how. Or why. But I do know that it's possible the way one of those timelines came into existence is because some of us managed to get back to Deep Space 9 in 2375—and *stopped* the red Orbs from opening the red wormhole."

O'Brien stopped, having made his point as best he could, satisfied that he had done what every good leader was supposed to do: Show his followers a direction to go. And he was flattered to see that even if he had never delivered a speech like it before, this one seemed to have been effective. His audience was looking encouraged, even excited by his words.

Now only one last element remained to be put in place.

Captain Sisko and Captain Picard, O'Brien knew, would have taken care of it at once, out of instinct. The same instinct that likely had made them Starfleet captains in the first place.

But O'Brien wasn't working from instinct, but rather from his experience—first on the *Enterprise* and then on Deep Space 9, where he had observed great leaders in action, and those observed examples told him what he had to do now.

"I'm going to give it a try," O'Brien said in a ringing voice that sounded more confident than he felt. "Who's with me?"

He felt his face grow warm, and he knew his cheeks were red, as one by one every member of his crew stepped forward and vowed his or her support.

Even Quark.

His proud moment was brief.

"So it would appear," Garak said drily, "since we are all in agreement, that only one last detail remains to be worked out." The Cardassian nodded pointedly in the direction of the viewer and the tantalizing destination it still displayed. "How *do* we get over there?"

Relief swept through O'Brien.

"Now you're talking engineering," he said gratefully. "And that part I've got all worked out."

On the viewer, Deep Space 9 turned slowly, waiting, just as it had on the day it was destroyed.

The day to which O'Brien now had to return, to save his life, his crew, and his universe.

CHAPTER 8

THE TINY SHUTTLEPOD, designation Alpha, rose slowly from its landing pad in shuttlebay 2. Above it, the pressure door slid open to reveal the chaotic blue energy flux of the wormhole pocket. Capable of carrying up to six personnel, Shuttlepod Alpha, for this mission, was empty. Lifted by the expert manipulation of the shuttlebay's variable gravity fields, the shuttlepod continued its ascent until it was five meters above the *Defiant*'s ventral hull and well out of range of any localized, artificial-gravity fluctuations.

As precisely as if it were on a mechanical turntable, Shuttlepod Alpha then rotated in place until it faced its destination.

Deep Space 9.

On the bridge of the *Defiant*, Sisko gave the order and the main viewer switched from the optical view as seen from the starship to that seen from the shuttlepod's sensors.

"What's the distance?" he asked.

Ignoring the viewer, Jadzia focused her attention solely on her science station. "Well, as we thought, no sensor ranging data are available. Not even a radar return. Going just by apparent size . . . Alpha's holding at fifteen kilometers from the station. Just as we are."

"All right, then," Sisko said. "Give her a nudge. Station-keeping thrusters only." The speed of the shuttlepod would be no more than thirty-six kilometers per hour. A cautious approach that would enable Jadzia to probe the structure of the space-time bubble in which the *Defiant,* for the moment, existed.

"First thruster fire," Worf announced. "Delta vee of one centimeter per second."

Sisko waited for the first report. It came in seconds. "I don't believe it," Jadzia said with a laugh.

"What is it, Old Man?"

"As soon as we stopped the thrusters, the shuttlepod stopped moving relative to us."

"*No* inertia?" Sisko asked, surprised.

"Not out there," Jadzia said, still sounding amused. "Absolutely incredible." She picked up a small padd from her console, then tossed it to a startled Dr. Bashir, who recovered quickly enough to clap two hands together to catch it. "At least we've still got inertia in here," the Trill scientist concluded.

"So what do we do?" Sisko asked. "Go to constant impulse? Or use the tractor beam?"

"Tractor beam," Jadzia said. "That way, we'll be able to measure any noninertial resistance to the shuttlepod's motion, so it'll double as a measurement of the density of space out there."

Sisko nodded. They had fifteen hours, three minutes remaining until the pressure waves peaked and the *Defiant* ceased to exist. Time enough to transfer the eighteen passengers on the ship to DS9, provided they could determine a way to do so.

"Activating tractor beam," Worf confirmed.

"Let's see the shuttlepod," Sisko said.

The viewer switched over from the shuttlepod's sensors to display a new angle from the *Defiant*'s hull. The Alpha was suddenly bathed in a shaft of pale purple light.

"Start her forward, Mr. Worf."

As the angle of the tractor beam changed, Sisko watched the shuttlepod slip away from the *Defiant,* propelled by the gentle pressure of the tightly focused gravitons. When the tiny craft had cleared the bow of the ship, the viewer display changed again to a new forward angle.

"No resistance," Jadzia reported. "It's moving just as if it's in a normal vacuum."

"Speed?" Sisko asked.

"Twenty kilometers an hour," Worf said.

"Go to fifty."

"Aye, sir."

The shuttlepod grew smaller on the viewer.

"Still no anomalous readings," Jadzia said.

Sisko couldn't suppress his smile. "You sound disappointed."

"Just surprised that there're no surprises."

"Take her to five hundred kph, Mr. Worf, and stand by to bring her to a relative stop, fifty meters from the station."

"Aye, sir," Worf acknowledged. "Estimated time of arrival from current position is ninety seconds."

Just then, Sisko became aware of his son standing to one side of his command chair.

"It can't really be this easy, can it?" Jake asked.

"I think we're allowed to win one every once in a while," Sisko said with a smile. "How're we doing, Dax?"

"No distortion in the tractor beam. And no mass anomalies. Frankly, Benjamin, I'm at a loss to explain it."

"Maybe the shuttlepod's stretching the space-time bubble we're in," Bashir volunteered. "Dragging space-time with it."

Sisko glanced over at Jadzia, saw her thoughtful expression. "That's possible," the Trill said. "Certainly it would explain the fact that there are no detectable anomalies in the structure of space-time along the shuttlepod's path."

As Sisko returned his attention to the viewer, he caught sight of Jake's expression, recognized it.

"Go ahead, Jake. Ask your question."

Relief in his voice, Jake spoke hesitantly. "Well . . . if we can see the station, can anyone on the station see us?"

"Unlikely," Jadzia said. "We're so far out of temporal alignment with the station's local frame of reference that at most we'd be showing up as a very faint chroniton shadow. Even then, someone would have to be specifically looking for that kind of phenomenon and adjust the sensors precisely. And I don't know why anyone would."

"But, then," Jake continued more strongly, obviously thrilled to be taken seriously, "how come we can see the station?"

"Good question." Jadzia smiled at Jake, pleasing Sisko by her encouragement of his son's curiosity, even under these conditions. "I think part of it has to do with the station's being much more massive than the *Defiant,* so in a way it's putting out a stronger signal. Not to mention the fact it's also still connected to normal space, which we're not." The Trill shrugged. "If I had to give a name to the phenomenon, I'd say the station had more temporal inertia, so it's easier to detect."

Jake nodded, but the confusion on his face suggested to his father that Jake had understood little of Jadzia's explanation. "I'll take your word for it," was Jake's only comment.

"Coming up on destination," Worf announced. "Fifty meters . . . and holding at relative stop."

"We're in good shape," Jadzia said. "Switching over to shuttlepod sensors. We should be able to look right through the station's viewports."

The viewer flickered, changing from the optical view of DS9 from the *Defiant* at a distance of fifteen kilometers to a close-up from the Alpha at fifty meters.

Sisko leaned forward in his chair, expectant, but the viewpoint did not change.

"Old Man . . . ?" he said, turning to Jadzia.

Jadzia and Worf both made rapid adjustments on their controls, but the image on the viewer didn't change.

"It seems Jake was right," the Trill finally said. "It's not going to be easy. According to all our readings, DS9 is the same distance from the shuttlepod as it is from us. Fifteen kilometers."

"I won't even ask how that's possible," Sisko said. From the corner of his eye, he saw his son retreat back to his previous position at the situation table.

"Thank you," Jadzia replied.

Sisko stood up and walked over to the science station to see Jadzia's displays for himself. "How do we proceed?" he asked.

The Trill scientist didn't waste time. "Since we have full power reserves, I think we should take a few minutes to beam a test cylinder over to the shuttlepod, then retrieve it. We still need to know if we can actually establish a transporter beam in an environment without subspace, and now without inertia."

Sisko felt the unwelcome stirrings of concern. If they could not physically approach and board the station, the transporter would be absolutely critical to their plan.

"Do you foresee any problem?" he asked.

The Trill sat back in her duty chair with a sigh of finality. "I just don't know, Benjamin. When it comes to theory, I could spend the next week telling you all the ins and outs about what we're seeing here. But when it comes to implementing those theories . . ." She looked up at him, serious. "All I can say is I wish Chief O'Brien were here."

Sisko nodded. Jadzia was speaking for them all.

Odo stood by the empty command chair on the bridge of the *Boreth* and wondered what it was about Miles O'Brien that kept the engineer from taking his place there.

There could be no question the Chief was in command of this ship. Not by rank but by ability. Not even Quark questioned him anymore.

But O'Brien was adamant in his refusal to assume the trappings of command, even though such action would make it much easier for him to monitor the rest of his irregular crew.

"Odo, I think he's afraid," Quark said under his breath.

Odo was momentarily startled. He hadn't heard the Ferengi come up beside him at the engineering station.

"Who's afraid?" Odo demanded.

Quark impatiently gestured toward the side of the bridge. "The Chief. Who else?"

"Why would *you* say that?"

Quark stared up at him crossly. "I know you were wondering why Chief O'Brien wasn't taking the command chair. He's afraid, that's why."

Odo folded his arms. "I was wondering no such thing."

Maddeningly, Quark folded his own arms in mocking parody, the movement twisting up his Bajoran robes. "You can't fool me," the Ferengi smirked. "You think because you keep your face so smooth and . . . and unfinished, people can't see what you're feeling, or what you're thinking. But I've been watching you, Odo. Almost ten long years. I know you better than you know yourself."

Odo moved swiftly in verbal counterattack. "Quark, I've never seen you so nervous."

Predictable as always, Quark sputtered in immediate, indignant protest. "I'm not nervous. I'm never nervous."

Odo shrugged. "Aren't you? You're talking quickly. Your ears are flushed. And if you really were able to peer inside me and know what I'm thinking, you certainly wouldn't tell me about it."

Quark bit his lip, eyed Odo skeptically, then spoke extremely slowly. "And—why—wouldn't—I?"

"Because," Odo said with great satisfaction, "you're giving away a trade advantage. The next time I catch you smuggling something and haul you in for questioning, I'll stand behind you, and you won't have any idea what I'm thinking."

Odo enjoyed the way Quark's mouth fell open, then snapped shut. The Ferengi really hadn't been thinking clearly.

"Well," Quark stammered, "well, I don't care. Because there won't be a next time."

Odo smiled as coldly as he could. "I see. Your experience in Ferengi Hell has finally convinced you to change your ways."

"What ways? I don't need to change my ways. What I mean is, there won't be a next time because . . . because we're *doomed*. That's why. We're *doomed*. Not that *you* care." Quark gave a little sob and turned away, his back to Odo.

Odo grunted and took the chance to check again on Dukat. The aged Cardassian was still lying stretched out on the deck by the communications console, legs bound at the ankles, hands bound at the wrists. Someone had rolled up a blanket from a medical kit and compassionately placed it under Dukat's white-haired head, but Odo didn't think the Dukat of the year 2400 was someone who was concerned with physical matters, and certainly not with compassion. The Cardassian had remained unconscious since Garak's assault, and it was Odo's impression—or, perhaps, wish, he admitted to himself alone—that Dukat was now immersed in his own Pah-wraith-inspired hell. With any luck, he'd never bother his fellow passengers again.

Reassured that Dukat still posed no threat, the changeling walked over to watch O'Brien and Rom at the operations station as they worked with the crew members in the main transporter room to switch manual control to the bridge.

"Well . . . ?" Quark said.

Odo sighed. The Ferengi was right in front of him.

"Well what, Quark?"

Some of Quark's bluster appeared to be gone. His ears were definitely looking paler. "Well, I . . . I just poured out my heart to you. This is . . . this is when you're supposed to say something supportive."

Odo nodded in understanding. "Ah, of course. This is supposed to be a moment of bonding between us. Two old adversaries facing what might be their final hours. At last breaking down the barriers between them so they can finally admit their admiration for each other, reach some kind of common ground and mutual understanding in the face of oblivion."

"That's it, exactly," Quark said with a hopeful smile.

Odo returned the smile. "Good idea. I'll go talk to Garak right now."

The changeling walked away from the Ferengi, knowing precisely the sequence of emotions that would flash over Quark's face: shock, disappointment, and fear.

Garak had positioned himself at an auxiliary control console near to the entrance doors. Somehow, in the few minutes that had passed since Chief O'Brien had come up with his plan to cross over to Deep Space 9 of the past, the Cardassian had managed to find and change into an Ascendancy uniform—a poorly fitting cross between Odo's own Bajoran uniform and a Starfleet design but a much more practical garment than the robes Weyoun had made them all wear in B'hala.

Garak looked up and gave Odo a slight nod of acknowledgment as the changeling joined him at his console. Then the Cardassian's gaze slid off Odo and settled on Quark, a forlorn and lonely figure standing in the middle of the bridge.

"Is he acting up again?" Garak asked.

"Nothing more than usual," Odo said. He peered over Garak's shoulder to see what was on his screen. But in a quick, careless gesture, Garak's hand brushed across the controls, erasing the screen before Odo could glimpse more than a fraction of its heading.

"Klingon Planetary Defense Analysis?" Odo asked. That was as much as he had been able to read.

Garak blinked at his console's blank screen. "Is that what was there? I was merely passing the time by randomly scrolling through the ship's library. And I appear to have lost my place."

Odo studied the guileless Cardassian. He quite understood if Garak wanted to find out how Ascendancy forces had defeated his world. Though he would never admit it to Quark, Odo thought, the Ferengi was right in thinking that in these final hours, some accounts should be settled.

"Is there something I can do for you?" Garak asked politely after several seconds of silence.

It was a difficult moment for Odo, but he forced himself through it. He cleared his throat. "I—I don't think I thanked you properly. For saving me from . . . from where you found me."

Garak held up a hand as if refusing a gift. "It was the least I could do."

Odo appreciated Garak's quick acceptance and desire not to exaggerate the nature of his gratitude. But he hadn't finished. "And . . . I was hoping that we might be able to come to an understanding that . . . well . . ." Odo wasn't sure how to continue.

But Garak was. "Rest assured," he said smoothly, "I will never speak of it. Where you were, what you experienced at the hands of the Pah-wraiths . . . that shall be a secret between us." The Cardassian allowed himself a small smile. "Indeed, considering the techniques that enabled me to enter into the Pah-wraith illusions of yours and the others, I could say that what I found comes under the heading of doctor-patient privilege."

Odo was puzzled. "What techniques?"

Garak regarded him in wide-eyed innocence. "Oh, this and that."

Odo rearranged his own expression into a stern glare.

"Well," the Cardassian said as he shifted forward in his chair, "if you must know, I once made a suit for a . . . person who I had reason to believe was a member of the—" Garak dropped his voice to a sibilant whisper "—Obsidian Order, Special Investigations Unit."

So it's like that, Odo thought. "I see. You made a suit . . ." he said.

"A very nice one, as I recall. It took many fittings. And, as you may or may not know, a man has very few secrets from his tailor."

"And this . . . man, just happened to tell you all about the Obsidian Order's techniques for interrogating prisoners by entering into induced illusions."

Garak nodded gravely. "I was as shocked by his candidness as I see you are. But as things turned out, it appears that what little I remembered of the techniques he described did come in handy. Wouldn't you say?"

"Handy," Odo repeated. And all at once the changeling no longer felt disturbed that Garak had penetrated his hell to find him eternally wandering the barren world upon which the Great Link had once existed, forever fixed in his quasi-liquid state, unable to become any sort of shape or solid. Instead, he became concerned about any other secrets Garak might have obtained from the others he "rescued."

"I know what's worrying you, Odo," Garak said.

"You and everyone else, it seems," the changeling said gruffly.

"But you needn't worry. A mind is not something to toy with. Especially not those of one's friends and allies."

Odo didn't know whether or not to believe Garak, but for now, there seemed to be little point in thinking the worst. The worst was doing quite well on its own, and coming closer to them each minute.

"It worked!" O'Brien suddenly said joyously, and at once Odo, like everyone on the bridge except for Dukat, turned his full attention to the Chief and Rom at the operations console. "There are no more surprises about the structure of space in here."

Odo felt distinctly heartened to see the Chief smiling broadly. "We were able to beam equipment and biosamples to the probe we sent out to the station and beam them back with absolutely no loss of information."

"So what?"

Odo scowled as Quark dared challenge the Chief.

"Ten minutes ago," the Ferengi charged, "you told us it didn't matter how far that probe traveled. It was *always* going to be twenty-two and a half kilometers from the station, the same as the *Boreth*. There's *no* connection between the two space-time bubbles, you said. So what good does being able to beam out to a probe and back do us?"

"Quark, it's not important where we beam to," O'Brien explained, his good humor not diminished one whit by the Ferengi's rancor. "It's the fact that we can beam at all. Since we can't get to the station physically, the transporter is the only way we can get from here to there."

"But *how?*" Quark demanded fretfully. "It could be a trillion light-years away, for all we know."

Now Odo saw O'Brien's smile fade. But then, Quark could do that to anyone. "It's not a trillion light-years away, Quark. In absolute terms, its distance is probably only a few hundred-thousandths of a light-second."

Even Odo was surprised by that, though he left the questioning to Quark.

And Quark didn't disappoint him. "That's *impossible*. You said yourself you sent that Klingon probe five hundred kilometers away and that its distance to the station didn't change from our distance."

"Physically, no," O'Brien agreed testily. "But look at the viewer, Quark. We can *see* the station right there, plain as day."

Garak spoke up next. "Which raises an intriguing conundrum, Chief. Just how is it that photons are able to pass between the two bubbles of space-time if physical objects remain trapped in them?"

"Old-fashioned relativity and a bit of quantum physics, Garak." Regaining some of his previous elation, the chief engineer warmed to his topic. "You see, on average, all photons travel at the speed of light—the absolute top speed for a physical object in normal space. But individually, each photon is actually a probability packet—not an object, but a probability wave.

"Now, if you send out a thousand photons at a target at the *exact* same time, most of those photons will reach the target also at the same time—that time, corresponding to the speed of light. *But* it's been known for centuries," O'Brien said with a stern look at Quark, who shrugged and rolled his eyes to indicate his disinterest, "that a handful of those photons will arrive at the target slightly *ahead* of the others. That's because, when their probability waves impinge on the target and collapse into a photon, the photon, just by sheer quantum chance, is at the very front edge of the packet. So, there'll always be a few photons out of every bunch that manage to travel slightly faster than light.

"And *those*," O'Brien emphasized with a smile, "are the very photons our sensors are picking up to create the image on the viewer."

The chief engineer waved at the image. "And by exceeding light-speed in their local frame of reference, those photons have popped out of their space-time bubble and entered ours. Just like a surface-launched space probe breaking out of the gravity well of one planet and traveling through space to another."

"Jadzia Dax could not have explained it better, Chief," Garak said silkily. "Yet you raise another intriguing possibility. Is it possible that whoever's on the station can also see us?"

But O'Brien shook his head dismissively. "No. First of all, this

ship is much less massive, and second, our local rate of time is too different from the station's. If someone worked at it, reconfigured the
main sensors, knew where to look, they might be able to pick up
enough to know that *something* is nearby. But they wouldn't be able
to resolve us with any greater detail than we can resolve the *Defiant.*"

Odo turned to look at the viewer again to locate the small and
indistinct gray disk that was the station's starship. Like DS9 itself,
the *Defiant* was occupying its own space-time bubble, approximately
forty-five kilometers away, judging just by its apparent size. But
O'Brien had been unable to make any estimates of what era the ship
was from. In fact, the Chief said it was likely they were seeing the
ship as it was during one of its many trips through the blue wormhole. And since the *Boreth*'s sensors could not establish the ship's
apparent position with the required accuracy, O'Brien had ruled out
any attempt to beam to that craft.

The changeling was still studying the *Defiant*'s image when he
heard the irrepressible Quark sound off once again.

"Would someone please tell me why all of you people are so
pleased with yourselves?" Quark complained. "Even *I* know transporter beams don't travel faster than light."

Odo watched sympathetically as O'Brien took a deep breath
before he answered. The changeling admired the Chief's resilience.
"For our purposes, they don't have to," O'Brien said. "They just have
to travel through something other than normal space."

Quark wasn't finished. "But even if they can go from . . . from
'here to there,' our time scales are *still* out of synch. You still haven't
told us how can we possibly survive the trip."

"Uh, brother—"

Odo saw the grateful look that Chief O'Brien gave Quark's
brother Rom. Quark just closed his eyes as if to ask, "Why me?"

Undeterred, Rom offered his own explanation. "Uh, almost every
time someone beams from one place to another, the time frames are
slightly out of synch. I mean, if you're in standard orbit of a planet,
you're traveling more than thirty thousand kilometers per hour. And
if you beam down to the surface? Suddenly, you're only traveling a
few hundred kilometers per hour as the planet rotates."

Quark opened his mouth as if to say something, but Rom pressed
on earnestly. "It's the transporters that do that, brother, by automati-

cally compensating for changes in kinetic energy and temporal acceleration. I mean, Starfleet transporters can even manage near-warp transport at relativistic speeds. We might feel a bit dizzy sometimes, but the transporters have been doing what we need them to do for centuries."

"Thank you, Rom," O'Brien said. "Now, if there're no more questions?" The chief engineer looked around the bridge.

Beside him, Odo heard Quark mumble something that seemed to imply some natural connection between Rom and being dizzy, but that was the extent of Quark's effort. The Ferengi barkeep was back to looking glum and depressed.

"All right, then," O'Brien said, "let's go on to the next step."

"Uh . . . beaming a test pallet to the station?"

O'Brien gave his assistant a sideways glance. "Well, not really, Rom. That won't tell us anything."

Quark roused himself enough to snort at his brother's confusion.

"Uh, why not?"

"Because we won't be able to beam it back."

Odo saw Rom blink in surprise.

"No carrier wave," O'Brien said simply. He made his hand move up and down and forward like a small boat on rough water. "A transporter carrier wave propagates through subspace. But there is no subspace in here. So we're going to have to transport the way they did in pioneer days. Dead reckoning. One at a time."

"I knew 'dead' would come into it somehow," Quark sighed heavily.

"It's not that bad, Quark." O'Brien tapped a finger to his temple. "After six years, I've got all the key DS9 coordinates up here. There won't be any trouble finding a place to beam to. It's just that, well, without subspace, there's no way I'll ever be able to get a fix on anyone to bring them back. So it's going to be a one-way trip for all of us."

His panic revived, Quark's voice rose in a wail. "But . . . but what if you're wrong? What if that version of DS9 is a mirage? Or it's only five seconds from being destroyed by the red wormhole? Or—"

Odo had had quite enough. He wheeled abruptly and placed a hand firmly over Quark's mouth.

"That's why we're going to send just one person first," O'Brien interrupted. "A volunteer. To see if—"

"Mmmmph—I'll go!" Quark cried as he tried to bite Odo's hand and the changeling jerked it sharply away from him. Even if he couldn't be bitten, Odo found the mere thought distasteful.

Everyone stared at Quark. Odo thought he heard a chuckle and knew it had to have come from Garak.

"*What?!*" O'Brien said, giving voice to everyone else's reaction.

"What's wrong with that?" Quark snapped. "I want to do my part, too."

"But . . . ," O'Brien said, almost choking, "you're a coward."

"I am not!"

O'Brien looked as if he were in sudden pain. "Well, not about some things," he conceded. "I'll give you that. But all you've been doing for the past half hour is complaining about how everything I've been saying won't work."

Quark held up his finger like an orator making a final point. "I've been . . . testing the hypothesis."

"You've been quaking in your boots, is what you've been doing," O'Brien said hotly.

Quark's face grew sober, as if he were trying to rise above his sense of outrage and hurt feelings. "I am sorry you feel that way, Chief, but your misperception of me, and, perhaps, of all Ferengi, in no way changes the fact that I am volunteering for this dangerous experiment in order to help my fellow. . . ." Quark looked around at the others on the bridge. ". . . uh, fellows," he concluded.

O'Brien ran his hand over his head, clearly nonplussed.

Odo snorted. This fiasco had to end. "I'll take care of this for you, Chief," he said. "You're not going, Quark."

"*je SoH,* Brute?" Quark said sadly.

"I beg your pardon?"

Quark waved his hand with a world-weary sigh. "It's Klingon. You wouldn't understand."

"No, but what I *do* understand is that you are *not* volunteering to be the first on DS9." Odo looked over at O'Brien. "Chief, think about it. The first thing he'll do if he actually shows up on DS9 twenty-five years in the past is to make sure he's safe and his bar is protected. And if the rest of us run out of time while he's attending to his own business"—Odo shook his head—"well, then, I'm sure he'll raise a toast to us on Ferenginar, or wherever he retires to after profiting from his knowledge of the future." He smiled grimly at Quark to let him know just who had won here. "How many years did you say we'd known each other?"

"You don't know me at all," Quark said in his most wounded tone, then spun around and marched away to sit by himself at an unused station, two down from Dukat's prone form.

Odo looked over at O'Brien. "I'll go," he said.

"You're sure?" O'Brien asked.

Odo nodded. He had no doubts. "When I get to the station, if time's of the essence, I can take on a liquid form and move more quickly than anyone else. And, perhaps most importantly, security won't be a problem."

"Why would it be?"

Seeing the worried look on O'Brien's face, Odo pointed out the obvious—at least, it was obvious to him. "Chief, what do you think Captain Sisko's response is going to be when what he'll take to be a duplicate Odo shows up and tells him to close Quark's, arrest Vash, and lock down the station until the Red Orbs are found and neutralized?"

O'Brien nodded, at once seeing the point. "You'll have a better chance convincing him if we're *all* over there backing your story, giving Dr. Bashir DNA samples to confirm we're not a bunch of Founder spies." Then O'Brien gave an unhappy sigh.

"Chief?" Odo asked.

"We won't belong there, will we? I mean, Keiko will be married to the other me."

Rom's gasp was immediate. "Leeta!"

"Anyone think about *me?*" Quark whined. "I'm going to be a half-partner in a solely owned business!"

"But we *will* be saving a universe," Garak said as he finally left his console to join O'Brien and Odo. "I daresay that will bring more than enough personal rewards to make up for whatever personal sacrifices we might have to make."

"Easy for you to say," Quark said. "With two of you, you'll make twice as good a spy."

"If I *were* a spy," Garak said pointedly, "I could see where you might have a point."

"So how do I signal back to you that the transport was successful?"

Odo asked, to bring the discussion back to what was really important.

"Oh," Rom said, "I already worked that part out."

Odo waited patiently.

"When you get to the station, go to one of the upper pylon docking ports."

"Which one?"

"Uh, doesn't matter. Whichever one you can get to. Right by the manual controls for the airlock, there's a small control panel that activates the visual docking lights—for ships that have lost their guidance systems. There are three banks of three lights each—"

"How Cardassian," Odo said as Rom continued.

"—by the outer airlock door. All you have to do is turn them off and on by hand."

"Presumably in some sort of code?" Odo asked.

"Uh, I hadn't thought of that," Rom said.

"Idiot," Quark sneered. But no one was listening.

"Starfleet binary?" O'Brien suggested.

Odo recalled having studied it. "With the long and short signals?"

O'Brien now picked up a small Bajoran padd, input a command, then showed Odo the screen. It held a simple chart showing the long and short codes for the standard Federation alphabet. "Start with ten or so rapid flashes so we'll know which port to watch, then give us the local time. That'll let us know how quickly we have to get the rest of us over there."

It all sounded reasonable to Odo, which left him with only one final question. "What if I don't make it?"

O'Brien nodded at Rom, and the Chief's assistant held up another padd.

"I'm going to record a warning message for Captain Sisko," Rom said. "We'll store it in as many padds as we can replicate, then transport the whole lot to the Promenade ceiling *and* to Ops and let them rain down on whoever's there. One way or another, we'll get them—*us*—to do the right thing."

Odo was satisfied. Everything was covered.

"Then I'm ready anytime you are," he said.

"We'll transport you directly from the bridge to the target coordinates," O'Brien explained. "I'm sending you to that unfinished habitat area on Deck 4."

"Good choice," Odo agreed. He knew the location. It was a section in the lower personnel levels that the Cardassians had never completed as designed. In an area where up to ten individual living units might have been installed, a large room had been left instead. It was such a tempting storage area, so far from the cargo bays and the station's regular security patrols, that Odo had made it a point to inspect the area personally at least once a week. "The last time I checked it, it was completely empty."

"That's what I'm counting on," O'Brien said. "Without sensors or a carrier wave, none of the transporter's automatic positioning safeguards will be operational. I'm going to set your coordinates for a meter and a half above the deck, so brace for a drop."

"Understood," Odo said. "Shall I just stand here?"

"Maybe back up a bit," O'Brien suggested, "so we can get a clean fix. And I'd crouch down."

"Why don't I just do this?" Odo asked. He formed a picture in his mind, and became that picture, settling on the deck away from the others with a fluttering of coppery wings and feathers. Quark made a clucking noise but moved away hastily when Odo's form advanced on him with hissing beak.

"Perfect," O'Brien said. "Admiral Picard would be pleased."

Odo nodded his avian head in acknowledgment. He had taken the form of a Regulan phoenix, not much larger than a Terran hawk. In this form, a sudden drop would not be a problem.

He took advantage of the moment to enjoy the sensation of being in a different form, while O'Brien and Rom made the final adjustments to the transporter controls now accessible from their console.

"Ready?" O'Brien asked. "This'll be a slower transport than you're used to. Could be disorienting, the way they used to write about it back in the old days."

Odo spread his wings. He even enjoyed the odd way O'Brien's voice sounded to avian ears and how clear and sharply focused everything looked with avian eyes. He fixed his intent glance on Quark, who retreated even farther from him.

"Stand by, then," O'Brien said. "Three-second countdown for the autosequencer . . . coordinates input . . . and energize."

Odo took a breath, thankful for the chance to finally be taking action, and only in the last second of the countdown did he realize that he was not the only one who had been waiting.

Because, just as the cool tingle of the transporter effect began to spread through him, with his heightened avian senses he felt the deck shake under pounding footsteps, heard ragged shouts of surprise, and then felt the tight grasp of powerful hands as he was lifted upward.

To stare directly into glowing red eyes.

And with that, the *Boreth* dissolved around him, and Odo beamed into the past.

Taking a monstrous demon there with him.

CHAPTER 9

THE *DEFIANT* SHUDDERED as the pressure wave disrupted its inertial dampeners and artificial-gravity generators, then forced both systems to reset. In the power surge that immediately followed, the ship's primary internal lights flickered, and everyone in the transporter room froze, expecting something worse to happen. Though what could be worse than the end of the universe was something beyond even Jake Sisko's imagination.

The young man's stomach lurched with the seeming rise and fall of the deck. But he really wasn't sure if it was because of the sudden physical disorientation or because in the midst of that disruption he had seen his father step up onto the transporter pad with Major Kira, ready to beam through whatever type of phenomenon it was that was only hours away from destroying them all.

Jadzia Dax, however, from her position at the transporter control console, sounded unperturbed as she announced, "Right on schedule. Next one won't be for another hour and three minutes."

Jake watched his father take his place beneath the dematerializer lens. "Dax," Sisko asked with a sudden thoughtful expression, "will we be able to feel the pressure waves on the station?"

"You shouldn't be able to," Jadzia answered.

"Shouldn't," Kira repeated with a small smile. "I've heard that before."

Once again Jake marveled at how, in the face of the ultimate disaster, everyone around him was still able to display a sense of humor, even confidence.

Jadzia returned the major's smile as Sisko gave Jake a nod of acknowledgment. They had already said what amounted to their good-byes, both maintaining that they would see each other again within a few hours.

Jake was well aware that his father and Kira were about to attempt something that had never been done before—beaming out of a pocket of space-time that was trapped in an unknowable domain of existence, into the past. And unlike any other Starfleet temporal mission he had ever heard of, Jake knew his father's stated goal this time was to *change* that past, *not* maintain the status quo.

For their mission, both Sisko and Kira were dressed in replicated costumes as Bajoran trustees. Since the *Defiant*'s historical records suggested that only a handful of humans might have been on Terok Nor at the time of the Cardassian Withdrawal—crew members of neutral merchant ships, for the most part—Jake's father also wore a stained bandage across the bridge of his nose, to disguise his lack of Bajoran epinasal folds. For expediency, Sisko had chosen the bandage over surgical alteration by Dr. Bashir. Besides, Starfleet Command was going to have a difficult enough time accepting the story that a duplicate Sisko would be telling them, and that difficulty might be reduced if his appearance was relatively unchanged. Though Jake had noted that his father hadn't elected to dissolve his beard or use follicle accelerators on his scalp to completely return to his appearance of the past.

"This is as ready as we'll be," Sisko told Jadzia.

"All right," the Trill said. "Benjamin, I'm sending you first. As ordered," she added pointedly. "You'll be materializing about a meter off the deck in Holosuite 2. After you drop, roll to the side and stay down. Major Kira will follow in thirty seconds."

Sisko and Kira nodded, but Jake saw that this time their smiles were absent. There had been a great deal of discussion about where to beam into the station. Without the system's subspace-mediated sensors and safeguards, it would be impossible for the operator to be certain the target coordinates weren't already occupied by a bulkhead, a piece of furniture, or even another person.

Jake knew that modern transporter technology had made all those concerns negligible, if not nonexistent. In fact, he couldn't remember a single transport he had ever experienced in which his feet had not rematerialized in perfect contact with the floor or ground.

Fortunately, the basic quantum-transporter effect itself created a weak repulsion force sufficient to clear the target volume of air molecules and dust particles. It just wasn't strong enough to clear away any denser matter.

Thus, based on almost everyone's recollections of Quark's complaints about how the Cardassian Withdrawal had almost bankrupted him because of a drop-off in business, Jadzia and Dr. Bashir had chosen the holosuites in Quark's bar as the safest possible beam-in point. Chances were good that the suites would not be in use. And, in the event they were, Bashir's surprisingly deep knowledge of holo systems made him confident that the suites' own safety subroutines that prevented the transport of replicated props into the same volume occupied by visitors would also deflect the incoming transport beam to a clear area, if necessary.

Whatever happened, Jake knew that he and all the others onboard the *Defiant* would have the answer within a few minutes. Both Sisko and Kira had radio communicators replicated from plans used by Starfleet in the first decade of its operation. Both were wearing shoulder straps to carry the bulky devices, each the size of a large book. To Jake, the communicators looked like antique tricorders, though considerably more awkward in design and size.

It had been Jadzia who had suggested the radios' use because, since photons could obviously travel between the pocket of spacetime containing DS9 and that containing the *Defiant*, she believed it was likely other forms of electromagnetic radiation could as well.

However, the Trill had cautioned, for Sisko and Kira to have the best chance of sending a radio signal via the old-style devices, they would have to transmit from as close to the station's outer hull as possible. Transmitting through a viewport would give even better results. And if they had the time and opportunity, patching into the station's own radio transmission system would improve their chances most of all.

The moment had arrived. Jake held his breath.

"Get set for a drop," Jadzia warned Sisko. "Energizing . . ."

Jake watched as his father shimmered, then dissolved into a quantum haze of light. The process was much slower than usual, the result of Jadzia's having to coordinate the entire fifty-eight-step process manually.

Then Sisko was gone.

"No feedback fluctuation," Jadzia reported.

Jake slowly exhaled as he stared at the spot where his father had been. He knew enough of basic transporter theory to understand Jadzia's observation. It meant there was no sign the transporter beam had been deflected or dispersed. But again, in the absence of a subspace dimension, he also knew the Trill could not be sure if any transport fluctuation would feedback to the transmitters at all.

Jadzia tapped a control on her console. "Thirty-second countdown starts now."

The transporter room doors slid open a moment later, and Jake was surprised to see Commander Arla step in.

Kira spoke first. "Commander, who's watching Weyoun?"

"Ensign Simons," Arla said. "He and his team are finished automating the controls in engineering, so he's spelling me for thirty minutes. Has the captain beamed over?"

Jake saw but did not fully understand the flash of alarm that momentarily tightened Kira's face. The major continued to question the commander. "Does Worf know you're here?"

Must be something to do with the chain of command, Jake thought. In his father's absence, command of the *Defiant* had passed to Worf, who was now on the bridge.

Jake could see that Arla had registered Kira's concern, though she was controlling any defensiveness she felt. "I'm just stretching my legs, Major. I'm going to visit the head, get some soup, and go back to my station."

Ah, Jake thought, *that's why the major's upset.* Sisko had ordered Arla to watch Weyoun in sickbay, and by leaving her post, Arla was technically disobeying that order. For a moment, Jake speculated about what might have happened if Arla had come into the transporter room a few minutes earlier, when his father was still here. *Dad probably wouldn't have made a big thing out of it,* he decided.

As long as Arla had made sure someone else was covering for her, his father was flexible enough to allow the commander her break.

Arla walked over to the console to look over Jadzia's shoulder. "You're doing it manually?" she asked the Trill.

"Fifteen seconds," Jadzia announced to Kira. Then she replied to Arla. "Just the first time. The major's transport will be easier because I'll just repeat the process, with a minor deflection to account for the station's rotation." She looked back at Kira. "Five seconds."

Jake saw the look of annoyance that Kira directed at Arla, but neither Bajoran said anything to the other.

"Energizing . . ." Jadzia said.

Jake watched as Kira dissolved into glowing light about twice as fast as his father had, though the process still took more time than usual.

A few seconds after the last sparkle had faded, Jadzia reported, "No feedback. It's a clean transport." She stepped away from the console then and bumped into Arla, who seemed to have been paying closer attention to the controls than to Kira.

"Sorry," the commander said to Jadzia. "I'll be back in sickbay in a few minutes. Should I send Simons up to the bridge?"

Now Jake sensed an undercurrent of tension between Jadzia and the commander, just as he had between Kira and the commander, and again he didn't understand it.

"I'll ask Worf," Jadzia said crisply. She glanced at Jake. "Let's go. I can use you at auxiliary communications."

Jake headed toward the doors. When they slid open, he continued through and into the corridor before he became aware that Jadzia was not behind him. He looked back to see her waiting for Arla to leave with her.

Then, as the transporter room doors closed behind the three of them, Jadzia turned to Arla and said, "All we can do now is hope for the best." The innocuous words were so unlike anything Jadzia might usually say that Jake stared at the Trill in puzzlement.

"Hope for the best," Arla said in agreement, "and trust in the Prophets."

The two women held each other's gaze for a moment, then Arla headed to starboard and the lift that would take her back to Deck 2. Jadzia and Jake took the corridor forward to the bridge.

As soon as he was sure Arla was out of earshot, Jake pressed Jadzia to find out what was really going on. "Since when does Arla believe in the Prophets?"

Jadzia waved his question aside as if it were unimportant. "Have you ever heard the Earth expression 'There are no atheists in a foxhole'?"

Jake shook his head, not grasping the connection, if any, between a small Terran animal's den and religious beliefs.

"Then how about what the Klingons say: The *bat'leth*'s blade always points toward *Sto-Vo-Kor?*"

"Oh, that one," Jake said. "Sure." He'd written the saying down as a useful example of tough-guy dialogue for the heist novel he'd been writing before the Orbs of Jalbador had come to the station. "Basically, it means people are more likely to turn to religion when they're facing death. You think that Arla—"

Jadzia nodded. "Arla didn't talk about her Pah-wraith hell, but maybe whatever it was she suffered through was enough to make her reconsider her interpretation of the Prophets."

They had reached the bridge and the door slid open before them.

"But Major Kira doesn't seem to have become more religious or . . . anything," Jake said.

Jadzia paused in the doorway. "On the contrary, that's what's made her so strong in all this."

Jake frowned. "She's always strong."

"Strong-willed, Jake. There's a difference. It's not inconceivable that some people might have had their faith diminished by what we've all been through. I mean, from a theological viewpoint, what's happened here could be interpreted as the final battle between good and evil . . . and evil won."

"Is that what Major Kira thinks?"

Jadzia shook her head. "Absolutely not. In fact, she doesn't believe this has anything to do with the Prophets at all. As far as she's concerned, the Prophets might test her people from time to time, but they would never be responsible for something as . . . as evil as the end of the universe and the deaths of so many innocent people."

Jadzia stepped onto the bridge and Jake followed her to her science station. "Then what does she think happened?" he asked.

"You know," Jadzia said as she took the seat facing her console, "the major doesn't have any answers, and she's comfortable with that." Then, the way the Trill shifted in her chair to look directly at him, Jake knew she wanted to emphasize the importance of what she said next. "Kira is a devout believer in the Prophets as her gods. And for all her . . . personal combativeness, when it comes to religious matters, she has a certain ease that comes from her absolute faith. That's why she never tries to force her religion on others, why she never judges those who don't agree with her, and why she's not troubled by what's happened—at least, in a religious sense. Faith is a wonderful thing, Jake, especially when it's pure like Kira's and not just a façade covering up unadmitted doubts—and fear."

Jake looked to the main viewer and the image it carried of Deep Space 9. "What do you believe?" he asked.

The Trill didn't hesitate. "That sometime in the next thirty minutes, we're going to pick up a time-shifted radio signal from your father and the major. That we're all going to be able to transport back to the station. And that we are going to be able to change our present so that the future we saw will never come to pass."

Jake regarded the Trill scientist as if seeing her for the first time.

"What is it?" Jadzia asked, but her compassionate smile told Jake she already knew the answer.

"Nothing," he said slowly. "It's just that, sometimes you sound like my dad. When he makes up his mind about something. And you just know that whatever he says is going to happen is *it*. You know?"

Jadzia placed a hand on his arm. "I think that's why your father and I are such good friends. We're a lot alike."

Jake blinked. "Yeah, but . . . you know . . ."

Jadzia smiled. "Right. Part of me's a three-hundred-year-old slug and—"

"No, no!" Jake said quickly, waving his hands. "I didn't mean—"

But Jadzia just patted his arm. "Jake, it's all right. I understand exactly. Admittedly, your dad and I do have differences, but in a lot of ways, well . . ." Her gaze fixed on the image of DS9 on the viewer. "What it comes down to is, out in space, *everyone's* an alien."

Now Jake did understand. "And if everyone's an alien, then—"

Jadzia completed his statement. "—then that's what makes us all the same."

Jake suddenly became aware of an imposing presence at his side. Worf.

The Klingon's deep voice rumbled. "I do not wish to intrude on this stimulating discussion of Vulcan philosophy, but is it not time to scan for radio signals?"

Jadzia winked at Jake. "Almost all of us." Then she swung her attention back to her controls and activated the ship's seldom-used Starfleet radio communication displays. "Jake, I'll need you to monitor the time scans on the auxiliary console."

"Right," Jake said as he stepped back to move carefully around Worf, who sported an extremely gruff expression and who was obviously still in pain from his Romulan disruptor wounds. He decided that if it was true what Jadzia had said about everyone being the same, then Worf's famously blunt manner was a lot like Sisko's "Starfleet mode"—just a specialized way of behaving when the situation warranted it. Jake hid a smile as he thought about how hard it would be even for Worf to maintain such an attitude for long in private with someone who liked to laugh as much as Jadzia.

As he sat at the console Jadzia had set up for him, Jake realized, odd as it seemed, that he was almost beginning to enjoy this mission. He was learning new things about people he had lived with for years.

But the realization was immediately supplanted by a feeling of horrible conflict. *What's wrong with me?* How he could possibly derive any sort of pleasure from such a terrible situation?

Jake's troubled gaze settled on his console screens as the ship's sensor net scanned for time-shifted radio signals, similar to the ones that might have come from a pre-warp ship traveling close to light-speed. Except, in this case, he thought, that ship was carrying his father, and it existed thirty-one years in the past.

The *only* thing that was making this whole mess bearable for Jake was his suspicion that, in some way, everyone else on the *Defiant* was feeling the same sort of apprehension and confusion he was. Even Commander Arla. That might even account for some of her newfound religious feelings.

Jake shook his head, tried to take control of his own emotions. It was essential not to think of the consequences of this mission. So he did what his father had so often taught him—he focused on the job at hand.

And his concentration became so intense, that when the transport alarm chimed and Worf rushed off the bridge, it took Jake several precious moments to realize that for some reason unknown, someone else had just beamed off the *Defiant* to follow his father into the past.

Sisko fell through a blizzard of light, its dying radiance lasting just long enough to reveal to him a familiar wall of banked holo-emitters, and then he hit the cold, hard deck in darkness and sprawled awkwardly onto his side.

Though there was now absolutely no light, Sisko didn't need to be able to see to know where he was. He could smell it: the faint undercurrent of overcooked popsnails that pervaded Quark's bar like methane in a swamp; the slightly acrid ozone twang contributed by Cardassian air filters; and the wholly artificial scent of the Bajoran industrial adhesive used to keep squares of friction carpet in place. Give most people a day in this unique atmosphere, and they would never notice any of those odors. But to Sisko, who had lived with them for so many years, then been away for weeks, their sudden reappearance was as welcoming as a fresh spring rain in New Orleans, as the salt air on Gilgo Beach.

He was home.

And then he remembered he wasn't the only one making the trip. Staying as flat as he could, he quickly crawled away from the point where he had fallen.

When he reached a bank of holo-emitters, he stopped, stretched out, head down, arms and legs flat, still in complete darkness. With his ear pressed against the deck, he could hear the thrumming of the station's air circulators and fluid pumps. The hum of the power system was there, as well, so it was unlikely the entire station was dark. And he was almost able to convince himself that he heard distant voices coming from the bar below, even though he knew the holo-suites were heavily soundproofed.

Then golden light blazed in the room again, and Sisko relaxed as he saw the transporter effect take shape two meters away, a meter and half above. Moments later, Major Kira tumbled gracefully from mid-air, and the darkness returned.

"Major," Sisko whispered, "are you all right?"

"Nothing broken," Kira's voice came back softly. "How about you?"

Sisko let her know he was fine and that he was moving toward her. When their hands made contact, they stood up together.

"Sure smells like Quark's," Kira whispered. "Probably the same pot of popsnails he was trying to sell the last time I was there."

Sisko heard her rustling in the layers of her Bajoran clothes. "Do *you* have a light?" he asked. For all their preparations, he hadn't thought to bring a palm torch.

"No, but maybe we can get something from the control panel on the radio. Unless . . ."

"Unless what?"

"Let's try the obvious first." Kira spoke normally. "Computer, restore room lighting."

Reflexively, Sisko half-closed his eyes, expecting to be blinded. But nothing happened. He opened his eyes. "Knowing Quark," he said, "if the suite isn't booked, then he's not about to waste power that someone else isn't paying for."

Sisko heard a soft click, then a blue glow appeared from the control surface of Kira's radio. The major held it facing up so they could see each other's face.

"Well," Kira said with a wry smile, "all your parts rematerialized in the right place. I guess Jadzia knew what she was doing." Then she aimed the pale blue light to the side, and slowly turned in a circle, dimly illuminating the suite. "Can you make out the door?"

Sisko squinted, saw a dark shadow between two panels of holo-emitters. "Over there." He moved toward it, and the major did the same, both of them walking slowly and quietly. But the door didn't open at their approach.

Kira frowned as she studied the door. "So how does Quark's security system work? If we open the door, is it going to trigger an intruder alarm downstairs?"

"It might," Sisko said. "But Quark is the least of our worries. We just have to avoid the Cardassians till they've all left, and after that . . . wait for Starfleet to arrive."

Even in the pale blue light, Sisko could see Kira was not convinced by his assessment. "So we open the door?" she asked.

"We have to," Sisko said. "We need to find out the date and time so we'll know how and when to proceed."

"Since we know the transporter works, couldn't we just beam everyone into the holosuite with us?"

In Sisko's opinion, that possibility had already been dealt with.

"Major, what happens if Quark's is subjected to one last sweep by Cardassian security forces? We have to beam everyone to a place we *know* is safe. And we won't know what's safe until we know what time it is and how many Cardassians are still aboard."

Sisko sensed Kira still didn't agree with his reasoning, but she offered no further argument. She gestured to the door, inviting him to go first.

Sisko found the door control panel and pressed the 'open' control. Nothing.

"Quark *really* likes to save money," Kira said drily.

Sisko was puzzled. "Why would he lock the door from the inside?" He tapped in his commander's override code which he had used in his first few months at the station, before the initial stage of the Starfleet computer retrofit had been completed. It had been Gul Dukat's code.

The door opened at once on the brightly lit corridor on Quark's top level.

And before Sisko's eyes had adjusted to the change in light levels, he heard the sounds of running feet charging up the metal staircase.

With identical movements, he and Kira instantly reached inside their clothes to withdraw their phasers—palm-sized Type-1s. Both weapons had already been set to stun.

"Only if they're Cardassians," Sisko cautioned.

Kira stood ready at his side as the footsteps came closer. Sisko heard their sound change as when the people approaching—two, at least—topped the stairs, raced across the metal flooring, and reached the corridor leading to the holosuites.

He held his breath, kept pressure on the phaser's firing stud, then—

—released that pressure and his breath as two Bajorans rushed around the corner with Cardassian hand phasers pointed ahead.

Sisko and Kira immediately raised their hands above their heads.

"We're with the Resistance!" Kira shouted.

But the Bajorans didn't seem to care what Kira said and continued their charge, unabated, as if they intended to run directly into Sisko and Kira.

"Wait!" Sisko said, then pulled Kira to the side as—

—the Bajorans ran through *her and into the holosuite.*

The emotions that swept over Sisko in that instant were too inter-twined to make sense to him. Surprise at the impossible action he had just witnessed, relief that he and Kira had not been attacked. But also despair that his hopes for a quick solution were doomed because of some unexplained side effect of their travel into the past.

Kira's face betrayed her own shock. "What happened?"

"Did you feel anything?" Sisko asked.

"No, but . . . he ran through me?"

Sisko nodded, his glance darting back to the Bajorans who were sweeping the holosuite with phasers ready to fire.

"I don't understand," the taller of the two men said angrily, his voice deep and booming. "The computer picked up Dukat's code in use."

Then Sisko realized he had heard that voice before.

"Obanak," he said.

The prylar with the body of a plusgrav powerlifter looked directly at Sisko beyond the doorway, then turned away, clearly hav-ing heard nothing.

"He was in the Resistance with me," Kira said wonderingly. "But I never knew he was here for the Withdrawal."

"That's not important." Sisko was suddenly aware of the ache in his knees from his fall to the deck from the transporter effect. He pushed his hand against the doorframe. *Solid.*

"Of course, it's important," Kira snapped. "He's a member of a Pah-wraith cult. And the whole reason this version of the station exists in the wormhole pocket is because somewhere on it, some-one's opening a Red Orb."

Sisko made the connection he'd been seeking. "So Obanak is looking for the Orb! We can work with him to—"

"No!" Kira said emphatically. "We don't know why he wants it. He could be here because he wants to open the red wormhole *now.*"

Now Obanak and the second Bajoran freedom fighter walked cautiously back to the holosuite's door, their Cardassian phasers con-cealed beneath their tattered clothing.

Sisko's natural reaction was to step out of the Bajorans' way, but he forced himself to stand his ground, and once again the two men passed through him, just as they had through Kira.

"Somehow," Sisko said, "we're not in phase with this reality."

In answer, Kira rapped her knuckles against the wall. Loudly.

Obanak and his companion stopped in the corridor and stared back, hands reaching for their weapons.

"We're in phase with part of it," Kira said. "Look at them!"

"Did you hear that?" Obanak asked.

Sisko raised his voice to a shout. "Prylar Obanak! Can you hear *me?*"

The two men gave no reaction to show they had heard anything.

Kira slammed a fist against the bulkhead.

At once, both men ran to the wall panel she had hit and pressed their ears against it. Needlessly, instinctively, Sisko and Kira jumped back to give them room.

"Any suggestions?" Sisko asked, perplexed.

"Other than we're *borhyas?*"

Sisko knew the Bajoran term for ghosts and rejected that explanation swiftly. "We're not dead, Major. This is a wormhole effect, nothing more."

Moving as if he were certain someone was hiding in the wall, Obanak edged slowly back, then subjected the wall to a wide-field phaser blast. Two ceiling lights winked out, but there was no other result.

"One of the Ferengi's smuggling tunnels?" Obanak's companion asked nervously.

The prylar shook his head. "Not in this wall. Maybe a service bay for the holo-emitters." He led the way back into the holosuite.

"So what do *we* do?" Kira asked Sisko.

"We have to get a message back to Dax. Maybe there's something she—"

"LOREM!"

Obanak's shout of warning came from the holosuite.

Sisko and Kira immediately ran into the suite to see the glow of a transporter effect shimmering in mid-air in the center of the enclosure.

Obanak and his partner could see it, too; they aimed their phasers directly at it.

Sisko didn't understand. "Why would Dax send—" And then he recognized the figure that fell from the light to the deck of the holosuite.

Weyoun. Still wrapped in his kai's robes of blood red—the same color as the Vorta's glowing eyes as he got to his feet to face Obanak and Lorem. And from their reaction to the sight of an alien whose species in this time had yet to visit the Alpha Quadrant, Sisko knew that the two Bajorans saw Weyoun. The Bajorans dropped their weapons.

"Serve me," the Vorta said to them.

And to Sisko's horror, Obanak and his companion fell to their knees and together whispered the one word Sisko did *not* want to hear in these circumstances.

"Emissary . . ."

CHAPTER 10

IN THE BLACKENED dust of his homeworld, Odo felt his wings melt and his feathers retract as he reverted to his true form, oozing like liquid despite all his efforts to create a solid form of any kind.

Dukat stood over him, his wild-haired, leering image repeated a thousandfold among the individual optical-perception cells that covered the changeling's amorphous body.

"That's right, Odo," Dukat said, and his harsh voice was multiplied by Odo's specialized acoustic cells, just as was his image. "We have returned to that place which you fear most."

Helpless, Odo could only watch as Dukat leaned over and scooped up a handful of him. Odo's essence dripped down Dukat's arm like thick, golden tar.

"Or should I say," the Cardassian sneered, *"you* have returned. Because *I* may leave any time I want."

Odo fought to create tentacles to wrap around Dukat's wide neck and strangle the Cardassian into silence. But physical control had left him. All he could do was to flow uselessly in the grip of gravity, powerless, just as when he had first experienced this personal and private hell—when the two wormholes had merged and he had flowed across the lifeless surface of this planet for millennia.

"Unless, that is," Dukat continued, "you make the right choice."

Odo felt tiny flakes of carbonized ash and debris adhere to his outer surface, and he knew those flakes were all that remained of his people after the Great Link had been incinerated by whatever disaster had struck this world.

But when the end had come here, Odo had been selfishly absent. His people had perished while he lived among the solids, adopting their ways, deliberately suppressing and ignoring his heritage. So that now he was even more alone than when he had been a solitary freak of nature on Terok Nor. Then, he hadn't known about his past or his kind. But now he knew exactly what he had lost, and he would know that loss forever.

"Do you have something—anything—to say?" Dukat asked. He shook the last of Odo from his arm. "Perhaps I can help." He gestured and a red glow of energy formed over the gray flesh of his hand. Suddenly, Odo felt reconnected to his form and to his abilities.

At once he pictured himself as a humanoid and within an instant his dispersed vision and sense of hearing coalesced into the localized regions of a humanoid head as he took shape and rose up from the ashes of his people.

"Is that better?" Dukat asked.

Odo controlled himself. He would not attack the madman. Not just yet. This experience was not real in any physical sense. But though Garak had not had any difficulty in extracting him from it, Odo wasn't certain how Dukat's manipulation of reality might have been affected by the process of their being beamed onto the changelings' homeworld. All Odo could remember of his transport from the *Boreth* was his shock when Dukat had leaped at him on the bridge.

"*Do* you have something to say?" Dukat asked again.

Odo cleared his throat, then spoke. "By adding your mass to the transport beam, it's most probable you've thrown off O'Brien's coordinate calculations. This time, we likely are dead."

But the Cardassian madman shook his white-haired head and his eyes glowed red with the fire of the Pah-wraiths. "Odo, really, can't you feel the difference? On the *Boreth,* it seems Garak was right. The Amojan had departed from me to do battle against his betrayers, leaving me with only a pitiful reminder of the power I once had." He held his hands before him, and weak scarlet sparks crackled from open palm to palm, sullying the dry air with the stench of burning flesh.

"But now," Dukat went on, "I exist in a temporal frame in which the Amojan has not yet returned to his Temple."

An almost dreamlike reverie come over Dukat, and Odo guessed the Cardassian was caught up in some memory of where he had been twenty-five years ago.

"At the time you and Sisko were tampering with the secrets of the Orbs of Jalbador, I was returning from my . . . sojourn in the Gamma Quadrant," Dukat said. "I was eager to meet with Weyoun and Damar, to retrieve the ancient fetish doll that had contained blessed Amojan's spirit. But now that I am returned to this time, the Amojan walks within me once again, needing no release." Dukat's eyes blazed with sudden red energy so searing in intensity that his features seemed to melt away and Odo was forced to shield his own eyes.

"He is a timeless being," Dukat chanted, as if reciting some ancient catechism. "All barriers fall before him. Accept this gift as you have always accepted him, now and forever, Amojan." The light faded and Dukat stared soulfully at Odo. "Can I hear an Amojan from *you*, Odo?"

"Why not?" Odo said.

Dukat blinked in happy surprise. "Truly?"

"Truly," Odo said. Then he morphed his right hand into a ten-centimeter cube of elemental iron and thrust it forward as fast as his nerve impulses could travel.

There was a satisfying crunch as the iron cube struck Dukat's face, and the Cardassian fell onto his back as if he were an android whose powerpack had been deactivated.

Odo knew this was an illusory realm and that nothing he could do would bring on Dukat's death. But even the illusion of pain might be enough to make the madman careless. And an enemy's carelessness usually brought with it opportunity. Odo changed his left hand into another cube of iron and swung it around like a hammer to crush Dukat's rib cage. The madman's arms and legs kicked out, twitched, then lay still.

Odo reduced the length of his arms, drawing the cubes away from Dukat's twisted body, savoring the illusion of dark blood that pooled around the illusion of a mangled face. He held his cubefists ready to strike again.

But the pooled blood faded as if evaporating and Dukat's face reformed from the battered ruins of his skull as if a melted statue had entered a pocket of reversed time. Then his chest reinflated, its ribs whole once again.

"Say hello to your eternity," Dukat spat at Odo, once his teeth had reformed.

Odo shut out all else as he concentrated on a critical alteration of his body, then sent out both fists—

—which missed Dukat because he was no longer there.

The Cardassian had vanished from Odo's reality.

But he had not vanished quickly enough.

For even as Dukat escaped the dimension within which this illusion existed, something else went with him—tiny barbed tendrils no thicker than a single human hair, identical to those of the Trelbeth grabber tree that had once flourished in Keiko O'Brien's arboretum on Deep Space 9. Odo had projected then outward from each cube-fist of iron to snare the robes covering the madman's still re-forming body.

And Odo, whose morphogenic molecules shifted mass through other dimensions as easily as they altered their appearance and alignment, was suddenly in contact with both Dukat's position and his own. In one simple action, he now pulsed the bulk of his mass along those linking tendrils.

In that other location to which Dukat had fled, the changeling opened his eyes in his solid, humanoid body, just as the Cardassian ran from the large, unfinished storage room on DS9, exactly where O'Brien had beamed them.

Instantly, Odo withdrew the tendrils that connected him to Dukat. There was a momentary burst of disorientation as he puzzled over what had happened to him and where he had been—someplace that had been a psychic dimension for himself yet a physical one for Dukat. But the sound of Dukat's footsteps receding down the corridor made Odo quickly put the paradox aside.

His mission was plain to him. If the transport had gone as planned, and if Dukat's extra mass had not proved too disruptive, both he and Dukat were on DS9 twenty-five years in the past, at the time Sisko had returned from Jeraddo with two of the three Red Orbs of Jalbador. In slightly less than four hours, the third Red Orb would be discovered in Quark's bar, and the red wormhole would open, destroying the station and propelling the *Defiant* into the future.

Odo knew Dukat would do all he could to see that history played out exactly as it had before.

It was now up to Odo to prevent that from happening.

Odo rushed for the corridor, determined to use all the resources at his disposal. And as chief of security for DS9, his resources were considerable.

It only took him a few seconds to find a communications node at the intersection of two corridors, and he hit the emergency access control. "Odo to Security. Gul Dukat is on the station in the lower levels. He must be found and captured at once. Use heavy stun on sight. Acknowledge."

Odo paused, half expecting to hear his own voice in reply, demanding to know who was impersonating him.

But no response came.

He hit the control again. "Odo to Security, acknowledge." Nothing. He entered his personal ID code. "Computer, this is Odo. Put me in contact with the Security office." Again, nothing. "Odo to Ops, this is an emergency. Acknowledge!"

With a growl of frustration, Odo realized the node must be out of service. He was about to hurry to another intersection, when he took a closer look at the panel. Though he could not have articulated his suspicions—he was acting more on a feeling than any logical conclusion—he pressed the tab on the side of the terminal node and swung up the trapezoidal cover.

Inside, a tiny, isolinear status display screen glowed pale lavender; precisely, Odo knew, as a fully functioning node on this level should.

Recalling an action that seemed to be a habit with Chief O'Brien and Rom, Odo carefully held down the subsystem diagnostic key to the left of the display. Before anything else, the two engineers had always checked the status of the equipment they had been sent to repair, from the equipment's own perspective.

The self-check of the tiny terminal took less than three seconds. The Cardassian symbols that appeared in the display window indicated the device was operating at efficiency level 729—the Cardassian equivalent of 100 percent.

Yet the device had not transmitted his communications.

Odo tapped more controls, then stared at the new display line that appeared, this time in Federation alphanumerics.

O'Brien had miscalculated. Odo and Dukat had *not* been beamed to DS9 on the day the three Red Orbs had been found and brought together.

The stardate was 51884.2—almost *five* days earlier.

"How is that possible?" Odo said to himself. O'Brien had been certain that the bubble of space-time containing the station existed in the wormhole pocket because it had somehow been 'swallowed' by the red wormhole when it opened in Quark's bar. The fact that the time signal the Chief had measured on the *Boreth* seemed to originate from a few hours before that event was easily explained by the non-linear temporal nature of the wormhole. *But five days?* Odo thought. *What's connecting the station to the red wormhole in this time?*

As quickly as he had asked himself that question, he knew the answer.

With no time to waste this second time around, Odo stretched into a pseudopod of golden liquid and surged through a ventilation grille.

Before he could save the universe in the future, he would have to stop a crime in the past.

Sisko and Kira followed, appalled, as Obanak and Lorem reverently ushered Weyoun from the holosuite as if they were his acolytes.

"Why can they see *him* but not *us?*" Kira demanded. "Why can we interact with the station and not people?"

"There's an answer," Sisko said.

"For Dax, maybe," Kira replied worriedly.

They came to the metal staircase that led down to the main floor of Quark's where Sisko was surprised to hear a hum of conversation, even the familiar clacking of the dabo wheel accompanied by its usual chorus of cheers and groans.

Sisko looked over the staircase, down toward the main floor. Quark's was packed. Almost every customer was a Cardassian.

"Quark said business was dead in the days before the Withdrawal," Kira said.

For Sisko, there was only one explanation. "Then we're in the wrong time frame," he said.

"But how?" Kira asked. "Dax picked up the time signal for the Day of Withdrawal."

Sisko shook his head. "Maybe that's not the only day that connects the station to the red wormhole. Remember what Leej Terrell said. She studied the first Red Orb on the station. Hooked it up to some sort of device. Created what she called a 'wormhole precursor field,' and it allowed her to see *into* the red wormhole. It even allowed some of her researchers to step into it. That could be why we're here before the Day of Withdrawal—this might be one of the days Terrell conducted her experiments."

Sisko and Kira took the staircase down to the main floor. Weyoun had pulled up his hood to hide his features, and before him, Obanak and Lorem were moving politely through the crowd of Cardassians, heads bowed like nervous trustees grateful for even the small amount of freedom their position offered them. The three were heading for the main entrance. The Promenade beyond was bathed in cold blue light, heavily misted.

"We have to keep following them," Sisko said urgently. He started through the crowd, automatically trying to shift and twist to avoid colliding with the passersby who simply slipped through him without awareness of his presence.

Halfway to the entrance, Sisko looked over to the bar to see Quark serving drinks. The Ferengi, though younger in this time frame, paradoxically seemed older: his face haggard, his eyes deeply shadowed, his brightly colored jacket wrinkled and spoiled by a large stain. Sisko had forgotten how Quark had changed over the time the station had been home to a Starfleet presence. After six years, for all his complaints and occasional misadventures, the Ferengi barkeep Sisko knew had become a successful businessman, obviously getting more sleep than he had in this time.

Sisko and Kira reached the Promenade, and now the changes between Terok Nor and Deep Space 9 became even more pronounced.

Half the storefronts were shuttered, closed for more than just the evening. They were out of business. And there were none of the small sales kiosks set up by optimistic entrepreneurs. This was a dying place.

"That way," Kira said, and she pointed to the right, where Obanak and Lorem remained to either side of Weyoun, walking toward the security fence that cut the Promenade in two—one side Cardassian, the other Bajoran.

Weyoun passed through the narrow gate without being troubled by the Cardassian guards, but Sisko saw a look pass between Obanak and a heavily armed glinn and guessed that bribes were paid on a regular basis.

"I suppose we just walk through," Sisko said as he moved beside the lineup of Bajoran trustees returning to their quarters or carrying out assignments on the Bajoran side.

"Why not?" Kira said, and with a tight-lipped look of trepidation, stepped into the line and walked through the people ahead of her.

Sisko matched her movements, and the experience was definitely unsettling. He found it easier to only open his eyes every few seconds, to avoid the disorienting strobe-like flicker of darkness that accompanied each figure he passed through.

Penetrating the security gate required waiting for a Bajoran to approach it and then moving through the briefly open gate at the same time as the Bajoran. Kira went first, then Sisko.

"Did you see that?" Kira asked. She was pointing to a Cardassian in a security booth set back from the fence.

"See what?" Sisko asked.

"When we passed through, the guard monitoring the sensors couldn't see us but he acted as if he knew there was more than one person going through the gate."

Hope flared in Sisko that he and Kira might be able to use a computer terminal to transmit written messages. "Which confirms we're able to interact with the station's equipment at different levels. At least some of it." He peered around the darker and more crowded Bajoran side, trying to catch a glimpse of Weyoun's red robes. "Over there," he said.

Obanak was leading Weyoun into the Bajoran Temple.

"Not a good sign," Kira said flatly.

Sisko looked at her, waited for an explanation.

She gave one promptly. "The Resistance usually tried to avoid involving any temple in their activities, so the Cardassians wouldn't have an excuse to close them. So the one place on Terok Nor where you could almost guarantee there would be no Resistance members present is the Promenade Temple."

"But would the prylars have allowed it to be used by a Pah-wraith cult?"

Kira shook her head. "Until I saw Obanak go inside, I would have said no."

"Well, it won't do any good to try to signal Dax until time catches up with us and we're in the station on the same day the *Defiant* is observing it from the wormhole."

Kira understood. "So, first we follow Weyoun."

Together, they approached the Temple, and once they moved closer, Sisko noticed how threadbare the carpet was at the base of the steps leading inside. And how the elegant Bajoran carving which represented the gateway to the Celestial Temple appeared to be darker than he remembered, a result of the ore soot that the Cardassian filters couldn't totally eliminate from the station's air supply.

Kira paused at the entrance, also inspecting its tattered condition. "We really made a difference here these past six years," she said softly. "We can't let it all have been for nothing."

Sisko regarded her somberly. "We won't," he promised.

They stepped through the doorway and entered the Temple.

And were instantly struck by a solid blast of blue light.

Sisko gasped as its impact crashed down upon him like a wave. But the force of it hit from all directions at once so that he remained on his feet.

He staggered as the light faded, leaned in toward Kira who had doubled over, trying to catch her breath. "What was that?" she said as she coughed.

"An explosion?" Sisko suggested. But there had been no sound to accompany the flash. He straightened up with some difficulty, to peer into the Temple's worship area, to see if Weyoun and his Bajoran followers had been similarly affected.

But the Vorta was gone, along with his acolytes.

The only occupant of the Temple now was a tall, distinguished prylar with a neatly trimmed white beard.

And his eyes were fixed on Sisko.

Sisko stared at the old prylar.

"Can you see me?" he asked.

The prylar bowed in acknowledgment. "I have been waiting to see you all my life, Emissary."

The way the prylar said that word brought a sudden memory to Sisko. The man before him was the *first* prylar he had ever met.

The first Bajoran to call him Emissary.

On the first day he had set foot on the Promenade when he had arrived on Deep Space 9.

And now the paradoxes begin, Sisko thought, fighting bewilderment. In his original timeline, he had met this prylar days, perhaps months from now, two weeks after the Cardassians had left the station. But now, when Sisko's earlier self arrived on the station for the first time, this prylar would already have met him, in a way.

"Prylar Rulan," Kira said in greeting.

The Prylar nodded again. "Nerys."

"You know each other?" Sisko asked, realizing how foolish the question was as he said it. He forged on. "Prylar, there were three men just here. Two trustees and an alien in red robes."

A small smile played across Rulan's placid features. "There has been no one here today but me, Emissary. And there are no more trustees, thank the Prophets."

Sisko looked at Kira, about to ask if she knew of any hidden passages connected to the Temple. He knew of none.

But before he could ask his question, Kira had one of her own.

"Prylar, *why* are there no trustees anymore?"

"Not since the Cardassians left, my child. All of Bajor are free now." The prylar fixed his calm eyes on Sisko. "And you, too, are of Bajor now."

Sisko felt the skin of his arms rise up in gooseflesh. *The light,* he told himself. *That's what the light was.*

"Prylar," he asked, "when did the Cardassians leave?"

"Two weeks ago."

"We've shifted to a new temporal frame two weeks *beyond* the time we wanted," Sisko said to Kira.

"How?" she asked. Then answered her own question, just as Sisko had. "That light?"

"It has to be. I asked Dax if we'd feel the pressure waves on the station. We must still carry with us some connection to the *Defiant*'s frame of space-time so that each time an equalization pressure wave goes past, we get tugged along with it.

Kira took it to the next logical step. "So when the next one passes, we'll be tugged back into the past."

Sisko nodded. "Just not as far. Then we'll come forward again."

Kira looked at him. "What do you want to bet that the one place we'll finally settle is the Day of Withdrawal—the same time frame the *Defiant*'s observing."

Sisko rubbed his hand over his face. "And by then it'll be too late." He saw Kira's puzzled expression. "Major, if we're still linked to the *Defiant*'s temporal frame, when it ceases to exist, we probably will, too."

"Or else . . . the link will cease, and we'll be left here."

"Are you willing to risk that?"

Kira gave him a grim smile. "Do we have a choice?"

"The Emissary has many choices," Prylar Rulan said quietly.

In the back of his mind, Sisko tried to work out the difference in the rate of time passage between the *Defiant* of the future and this station in the past. Knowing that might give him some idea of how much longer he and Kira had before the pendulum of time swept them back into the past. But he had another, more personal question burning in him as well.

"Prylar," Sisko asked, "how do you know that *I* am the Emissary?"

The prylar smiled, as if to indicate he knew more than anyone could ever suspect. "You are the Sisko. You have just appeared before me from within the light of the Celestial Temple itself. There are those among us who have always known that just such a person will be the Emissary."

Sisko didn't understand how that could be possible. In this past, when he had first seen Rulan, Rulan had also called him Emissary at once, even though Sisko had merely stepped out from an airlock on the Promenade and not from a flash of wormhole radiation. But when Sisko had first met the Prophets, only a few days after that, those beings had seemed to not recognize him as anything except a disturbance in their environment. Indeed, at first they had seemed to have a difficult time even recognizing him as a corporeal being and had said they wanted to destroy him.

"You've always known?" Sisko asked, truly baffled. "How is that possible?"

Prylar Rulan shook his head as if the question had no meaning. "I know because those who came before me knew, because those who came before them knew, all the way back to the first writings of the great mystics in the time before Lost B'hala."

"The mystic Shabren?" Kira asked.

The prylar smiled. "And Eilin and Naradim."

Kira frowned. "But those are the mystics of *Jalbador.*"

Sisko was fascinated to see the serene prylar bristle at Kira's use of that term.

"Some have called them that," Rulan said sharply. "But they are mistaken. To those who *know* the Will of the Prophets, they are the mystics of *Jalkaree.*"

"But, Prylar, in all the lessons you've taught me," Kira said, "in all the lessons I've learned in all the Temples I've worshipped in, not you, not one prylar or monk, has *ever* taught me of Jalkaree. Or said the name of the Emissary."

The prylar's smile returned, this time like that of an indulgent parent. "Oh, my child, think what would have happened if those who knew the truth so many millennia ago had named the Emissary for all the world. Do you not think that every generation would then have hundreds, if not thousands of people coming forth to say that they were the Sisko? And do you not think that if the full prophecies of Jalbador and Jalkaree were known to all the world, if the history of the future were laid out for all with the mystics' precision, there would not be those who would attempt to change that future?"

The prylar stepped closer to Kira, placed a hand on her shoulder, looked directly and deeply into her eyes. "My child, I know your faith is pure and absolute, and as part of your faith, I ask you to accept that there is a reason the Will of the Prophets must sometimes be seen as difficult to interpret for the many, even while it is understood perfectly by the few."

"But who chooses those few?" Kira asked.

The prylar's expression revealed nothing. "In the end, who chooses the Emissary?" He looked over at Sisko. "I sense that you are not entirely accustomed to your role."

The prylar's understatement was overwhelming. Sisko held his true reaction in check, simply said, "That's true."

"Naradim spoke of that, in the same text in which Eilin states the danger inherent in revealing too much of the prophecies, that the revelation of the one direction of time might contain within it the seeds of another outcome."

"Another time," Sisko said.

The prylar studied Sisko carefully, as if looking through him, into the melee of thoughts that filled his mind. He reached out to Sisko's ear. "May I?"

"As long as you realize that Eilin is correct and some of what you learn must never be revealed."

Rulan nodded, then tightly, almost painfully, squeezed Sisko's left earlobe between his thumb and forefinger.

Rulan closed his eyes, turned his head up, opened his mouth—not in fear, Sisko thought—but in awe.

Sometime later, seconds or minutes, Sisko couldn't be sure, he felt the prylar's grip lessen, then his hand slipped away.

From outside the Temple, on the Promenade, Sisko heard a sudden clang of metal. He and Kira glanced back over their shoulders.

"The repair work," Rulan said. "But then," he added, "you know that."

Sisko nodded. A subtle though familiar tremor vibrated through the deck.

"That's an airlock cycling," he said.

Rulan nodded, as if hesitant to say much more. "Since the *Enterprise* arrived, there have been a great many comings and goings."

Sisko held Rulan's gaze for a few moments, knowing that the prylar would know—knew—or at least sensed—all that he did.

And then Sisko couldn't resist and spun around and walked quickly to the Temple's entrance.

He peered cautiously around the edge of the doorway. The Promenade beyond was even darker than it had been under the Cardassians. It was littered with debris and ruined components that had been too bulky to loot and so had been destroyed in place.

Fusion torches sent sparks through the shadows. Metal rang under the impact of molecular saws. And spinward, past Quark's, an inner airlock door opened.

A younger Chief Miles O'Brien stood before the disk door as it rolled to the side.

And Commander Benjamin Sisko set foot on the station for the very first time.

Captain Sisko, in the doorway to the Temple, was suddenly aware of Kira and Prylar Rulan at his side.

"This probably isn't the best idea in the world," Kira said.

"No, it's not," Sisko agreed. He stepped back; Kira followed. Prylar Rulan stayed in place, gazing out at the second Sisko now approaching.

"Remember, Eilin was right," Captain Sisko said.

Rulan looked back into the Temple. "Of that," he said, "I have no doubt."

Sisko understood the prylar's unspoken promise. Rulan would not tell Commander Sisko that he had just been visited by a future version of him. What would happen here on the Promenade in the next minute would be what had happened before.

"You must understand as well," Rulan said. "There can be no other time, or all is lost."

"*I* understand," Sisko said as he moved farther back into the protection of the Temple. "But *he* does not."

Rulan nodded as if to put Sisko's mind at ease. "Shabren is very clear about that in his text about the Emissary's first visit to the Gateway to the Temple. There were—there will be—many things the Sisko did not understand that day. This day."

Sisko thought back to his beliefs and his attitudes of six years ago. Had he ever been that naive? "In time, he will," he told the prylar.

"In this time," Rulan said emphatically. "Not another time." He looked back to the Promenade, then turned to bow his head to Sisko in the Temple. "If you will excuse me, I must go welcome the Emissary. For the *first* time."

Then Rulan left the Temple to await Commander Sisko, just as he had awaited him before. *Just as he will* always *await me,* Sisko thought.

And with an unexpected flash of insight, the concept of nonlinear time became clearer to him. It wasn't that to the Prophets their realm of nonlinear time was without past, present, and future, it was that the past and present coexisted interchangeably within a third dimension of time, with only the future in flux.

"Are you all right?" Kira asked, and Sisko was surprised by the intense concern in her being. Then he realized that he could hear a conversation outside the Temple. A conversation that included his own voice.

"Fine," Sisko said. "I was just thinking that if I ever get the chance to see the Prophets again, maybe I'll have something *I* can teach *them.*"

Kira's voice sharpened. "Be careful who you say that to. Some might think it heresy."

"Believe me," Sisko said, "if I ever do get a chance to spend that much time with the Prophets, I don't think I'll be too worried about what other people think."

Kira looked around the Temple as if searching for another way out. "Well, we can't stay here while . . . we're both out there."

Sisko didn't understand. "Why not?"

"You heard what Rulan said. The danger of changing time. We can't just walk out there and warn ourselves about the future. We have to let everything proceed just as it did the first time."

"Major," Sisko said, stunned by Kira's abrupt change of heart. "We will *not* allow the Pah-wraiths to win. I have no intention of allowing the universe to end, simply because that's what happened before."

Kira stiffened in anger. "That's not what I meant at all. I just mean, we can't change what happened *before* the Red Orbs were brought together. But we can *stop* that from happening just before we were pushed into the future—if we get rid of the one Orb hidden in Quark's right now. Nothing else would change for the next six years."

"But we'd still be changing the timeline." The nuance of the major's argument still escaped Sisko.

"If we stop the red wormhole from opening on DS9 in the last few minutes before we left on the *Defiant,* maybe we won't be changing time, we'll be restoring it."

At last Sisko saw what Kira meant. "Of course," he said. "Leave the past alone, but affect our present in order to create a new future."

"The same as we do every day," Kira added.

"So . . . all we have to do is get to Quark's and take the Orb from its hiding place inside the stained-glass portrait of the Tholian general."

The plan was just that simple. Its execution even simpler. At the back of the Temple, there was a wide selection of monks' attire, and in minutes, both Sisko and Kira were unrecognizable in large hoods and bulky robes.

Side by side, they crossed the cluttered Promenade, their passage met only by smiles from the Bajoran workers, clearly pleased to see religious figures using their newfound freedom to move about the entire station.

The noise and commotion all around him brought back to Sisko the heady sense of victory and celebration that had existed in the station's first days as Deep Space 9. At the same time, he remembered the tension that had equally been present, because no one had known how Bajor's provisional government would survive the next few weeks, let alone years.

But now, knowing that it *had* survived, Sisko continued with Kira to Quark's, easily resisting the opportunity to tell those around them that for the next few years, at least, their world would make great strides.

Once they were in Quark's, Kira brazenly stepped up to the bar and, with her head bowed and hood pulled forward, informed Quark in a low, muffled voice that they understood he was leaving the station and that the prylars were considering asking the station manager to have the Temple relocated to this larger area.

"We'd like to look around," Kira said.

Quark, still as careworn in this timeframe as when the Cardassians had been in charge, waved his hand dismissively. He was in the middle of packing up what few items remained that weren't broken. "Be my guest," he sighed. "You can even use the holosuites to guarantee mystic visions for the faithful. Ha." Then he turned his back on his visitors.

Kira and Sisko made their way slowly around the ruined bar, only gradually moving toward the large, yellow and orange glass mural that was about the only source of light at the moment.

Then they both stepped behind it where they couldn't be observed.

Sisko pointed at the access panel in the back of the mural's thick housing, flush to the floor. "There," he said.

Kira nodded, then knelt beside it, pulling out a small pulsedriver she had found in a maintenance toolbox at the back of the Temple.

Six years from now, Sisko knew that he had been led to this same spot by the glowing interior light from two Orbs of Jalbador, because hidden inside was the missing third Orb, protected from years of maintenance sensor sweeps by an unusual low-power Andorian sensor mask.

"Leave the sensor mask turned on," Sisko whispered. "Just take the Orb." What they'd do with it was something he work out later.

The mostly likely possibility was to "borrow" a runabout and launch the Orb into the Bajoran sun.

The final fastener came out of the panel and Kira carefully pulled it free. From inside the service alcove, no larger than an Orb Ark, Sisko saw the pale blue glow of the sensor mask device.

He exhaled, abruptly aware that he hadn't taken a breath for the past half minute.

Kira smiled up at him, then bent forward and reached inside.

She kept her hand in for a long time, methodically moving it back and forth, then leaning down close to the floor to peer inside.

She pulled back and stared up at him.

Before she could utter a word, Sisko knew what she would say.

"It's not there!"

Sisko even knew why.

Weyoun.

CHAPTER 11

LIKE A LIVING current of blood, Odo propelled himself through the *tiyerta nok,* what the Cardassians called the lifeflow of iron—the arteries of the machine.

But to Odo, they were DS9's complex, interwoven network of Jefferies tubes, air conduits, and even Quark's smugglers' passageways—a gift of the Obsidian Order.

Faster than a security team on turbolifts, the changeling unerringly flowed along those hidden paths through the vast station, their unrecorded layouts long memorized, a simple matter for someone who could effortlessly recall the three-dimensional molecular structure of virtually every solid object he had ever studied.

From the intersection where he had realized what was about to happen to the lower-level corridor where he knew Dukat was intending to go, Odo's swift liquid race took less than fifty seconds and ended when he streamed from a wall-mounted air vent, reforming into his familiar solid shape from his boots up, as if he were a wave of honey being poured into a transparent humanoid-shaped container.

At once, he looked around to be sure of his location: the side corridor leading to the false wall that cut off the long-concealed section of DS9. For six years, Leej Terrell's secret Orb research lab had escaped detection by Starfleet engineers and teams of retrofitters.

Before that, not even Gul Dukat had known of its existence during his control of the station.

It had taken Jake Sisko and Nog, as boys playing in the Jefferies tubes, to accidentally discover the walled-off section of corridor and the hidden lab. The two youngsters had used it as their private holo-suite, never suspecting that what seemed to them to be holographic environments were actually illusions created by the Pah-wraiths—illusions intended to tempt corporeal beings into the Pah-wraiths' realm.

But by the time the three Red Orbs of Jalbador had been brought to the station, the secret of the hidden section was known to Sisko's command staff. In fact, for Odo, only three mysteries had remained when DS9 was destroyed.

Why were his memories of the Day of Withdrawal, along with those of Quark and Garak, inaccessible?

Who had killed the two Cardassian soldiers in civilian clothes who had been discovered fused into the station's hull as if they had been deliberately beamed to their deaths?

And who had murdered Dal Nortron, the Andorian merchant of dubious ethics whose arrival on DS9 had preceded all the events leading to the destruction of the station?

Now, standing on the spot where Dal Nortron's body had been discovered—or would be discovered in just a few hours in this time-frame—Odo felt certain he was about to solve the third mystery. With luck, he hoped that he might even stop it from ever coming into being in the first place, simply by saving Dal Nortron's life before it could be taken.

He paused, listening carefully, but heard no one else nearby. Feeling confident he had arrived well before Gul Dukat, he moved to the false wall that hid the small intersection leading to Terrell's lab and pressed his hand to the seam between the false panel and the real one beside it. Taking advantage of the near-microscopic space between the two panels, Odo flowed through the crack and reformed on the other side like a crystal growing on a cave wall.

There was light in the hidden section, spilling out from the open door to Terrell's lab.

Odo temporarily changed his eyes from humanoid-normal to those of a nocturnal Vulcan primate, enabling him to see the dimly lit corridor as if it were high noon.

The corridor was empty.

Odo returned his eyes to their usual size and construction as he moved quickly toward the open door. Pausing on its threshold, he beheld the laboratory's flawless recreation of an ancient village of the Bajoran moon, Jeraddo, as it had existed almost one thousand years earlier at the dawn of Bajoran space travel. It was the same illusion that Jake and Nog would discover two days from now, when Jake's research for his latest novel would inspire the two friends to revisit their childhood playground.

The details of the Jeraddan village were derived from the Cardassian memory rod that Dal Nortron had brought with him to DS9. But unlike the Andorian, who Odo knew was inside the lab's reconstructed village right now, convinced he was using a Cardassian holosuite, Odo understood that since the village was what Nortron most wanted to see, it was what the Pah-wraiths were showing the Andorian in order to bring him closer to their realm.

Stepping through the open door, Odo sensed the subtle change-over to the slightly weaker gravity of the moon as his foot crunched into gravel.

It was night here. To the west, the Bajoran stars formed summer constellations like spilled jewels. To the east, the horizon was beginning to glow with the blue-green light reflected from Bajor itself, still unseen on the moon's dayside. A soft breeze blew, and in the village of stone buildings about a kilometer distant, Odo could see flickering candlelight in small windows.

But he saw no sign of Dal Nortron.

"NORTRON!" Odo kept his hands cupped to his mouth and shouted twice more. But not even an echo came back to him. He would have to go into the village.

Odo knew that Sisko had found the third Orb of Jalbador hidden in a mural wall in an underground chamber of a large structure in the village, as it really existed in this time: battered ruins on a world that had been transformed from Class M to Class Y as it had been converted into a seething power source for the hungry world it circled. Though the map had not shown the Orb's exact location, Odo decided the Andorian would be close to it. Because the map was incomplete, whoever had given or sold it to Nortron must also have given him verbal instructions for interpreting it. Otherwise, it would have been worthless.

Odo began to run, then leaped into the air and became a Kalari lightning hawk, flying the kilometer to the village in only a few seconds of hyperfast wingbeats.

Settling to the stony ground on the outskirts of the wide plaza at the center of the village, the changeling returned to his humanoid shape. The glow on the horizon was becoming brighter. Again Odo cupped his hands to his mouth and called Nortron's name.

Still no response.

But a shadow darted past a small building at the far corner of the plaza.

Odo recognized the rotund form of the stubby-antennaed Andorian in his bulky fur vest. Odo called out once more, but Nortron merely hurried on, head down, eyes fixed on what Odo took to be a small map reader, and then disappeared around a corner.

Odo sighed, thinking that solids could be so typical. *Try to save their lives, and what do they do . . .*

He began to run again, deciding against changing shape to avoid startling Nortron, or possibly offending the Andorian's solid sensibilities.

Odo raced around the corner where Nortron had disappeared, then skidded to a stop, sending small rocks flying. The Andorian stood facing him, the metallic blue gleam of a small, knife-shaped stinger gun clutched in one hand.

"What are you?" Nortron said shakily. Odo had encountered panic enough times to recognize its presence when he heard it.

"I'm Odo, Chief of Security for DS9. Your life is in—"

"I said, what are you?!" Nortron gasped in a thin, rising voice.

Odo realized that for whatever reason, the Andorian was in no condition to listen to reason. He had to be disarmed first, warned second.

"I'm here to help you," Odo said firmly as he took a step forward and—

An incandescent stream of relativistic ions shot forth from the Andorian's stinger, striking the ground where Odo's foot crunched into the gravel.

Sharp, glowing stone fragments sprayed up into the air.

Startled, Odo stared down at his foot, fully expecting to see his boot sliced in half faster than his restorative autonomic reflexes would have been able to act.

Instead, his boot was intact. But it rested in the center of a small glowing pit of melted rocks.

Odo snorted in exasperation. "Now we do it *my* way," he growled as he shot out his hand to cross the two meters to Nortron, to grab the stinger.

But then shock caused Odo's hand to snap back to him like rubber. His hand had passed *through* the Andorian's. Suddenly, Odo understood why he had been unable to get a response from the communication node in the corridor.

His footsteps in the gravel prompted the Andorian to fire at him again, once at the ground, then once above the sounds of his footsteps, directly through his midsection.

But Odo felt nothing. The beam had no effect on him.

"Out of phase," Odo said to himself. Somehow, he could interact with the solid, nonliving elements of this timeframe. But for living beings, or anything directly connected to them like Nortron's weapon, Odo had no way of making his presence known.

As Nortron backed up, blue face glistening with sweat, short antennae fairly vibrating with tension, Odo wasted precious moments wondering how it was he could crunch gravel yet not make air molecules vibrate to produce the sound of his voice.

But, ever practical, the changeling abandoned the finer points of temporal physics to lean down and pick up a rock so he could scratch a message on the stone wall of the building beside him and Nortron. The Bajorglow was bright enough to allow such a message to be read, and surely the sight of a rock floating in air would hold the Andorian's attention.

But the instant he picked up that rock, Odo saw Nortron's eyes bulge and his mouth gape open, and the Andorian spun around and ran off screaming.

Odo tossed the rock away in disgust, then chased after him.

Panting and wheezing, the out-of-shape Andorian took almost five minutes to reach the improbable open doorway that hung suspended in midair a kilometer from the village, framing a corridor that was in distinct contradiction to the rocky landscape surrounding it.

Nortron scrambled up and into that doorway, then frantically twisted around to push the door sideways, sliding it shut in Odo's face.

But Odo liquefied to flow through the narrowing opening,

re-forming beside the Andorian even as Nortron, gulping for air, placed his shoulder against the door to seal it more swiftly.

Then the door closed, and Odo and Nortron were plunged into blackness. At once, Odo heard footsteps hastily scurrying away.

With a sigh, Odo altered his form to that of a Ferengi mudbat, his humanoid eyes merging to form a dark membrane of thermal-imaging cells, perfect for identifying prey on dark Ferengi nights when stormclouds cut off all starlight and perpetual thunderstorms had made the evolution of echolocation a rare event.

In the narrow, shimmering spectrum of infrared, Nortron was a blazing white blob moving rapidly away from Odo, toward the false wall. Odo glided after the Andorian, flying over him halfway. Peering down, the changeling caught sight of a dark band around Nortron's face and identified it most probably as a portable thermal viewer.

Then Nortron slid open the false wall and the heat spectrum of the corridor changed, as did Odo, back to his humanoid form. The amount of shapeshifting he had undertaken since arriving on the station was beginning to take its toll on his energy. Except when absolutely necessary, he customarily avoided switching from form to form as quickly as he had today.

The false wall slid shut again and Odo saw Nortron standing in the ordinary DS9 corridor, peeling a pair of thin, dark goggles from his eyes. The Andorian shook the goggles once, and they self-folded into a small, square packet which he stuffed under his fur vest. The stinger gun, though, he kept in his other hand.

Aware that Nortron had only a few minutes to live, Odo came up with a simple but adequate plan. By using his limited ability to interact with the nonliving, mechanical parts of DS9, he would drive Nortron away from the site at which he had been or would be murdered.

As Odo fully expected, Nortron began hobbling on obviously strained legs toward the main corridor leading toward the turbolifts. The Andorian's free hand grasped his ample belly as if to help hold it up and make breathing easier. In his other hand, he gripped the stinger as if he were drowning and it was his lifeline. Every few steps, Nortron glanced behind himself, his fleshy blue face still streaked with sweat, no sign of his panic decreasing.

This time, Odo didn't need to change form to pass Nortron and stay ahead of him. Reaching the first intersection, the changeling stretched up to grab the overhead vent grille just beyond. When Nortron reached the intersection, Odo yanked the grille free and sent it crashing to the deck in front of the Andorian. Odo's expectation was that Nortron would wheel to the left, heading away from the site of his murder.

But instead, Nortron instantly fired his stinger. Unfortunately, he also fired without thought or aim and with his weapon pointed to the side. Instantly, an ODN conduit erupted in sparks and smoke and flung the doubly startled Andorian into a spin that made him stumble through Odo and continue on in the same direction he had been going before, only now wheezing horribly.

Odo kicked the useless grille to the side and ran past Nortron again to set up another diversion. This time, he decided not to drop the grille. He'd hold it up so that to Nortron it would appear to be floating. Then Odo planned to push against the Andorian with it, physically *forcing* him to go in another direction.

But before Odo could set his new plan in motion, Nortron lurched to a stop in the corridor, staring ahead in even greater alarm.

"Did . . . did Atrig send you?" Nortron stammered.

Odo looked in the same direction Nortron did.

Dukat was there. Just as Odo had anticipated. Complete with robes and wild white hair. And for whatever reason, the Cardassian was in temporal phase, meaning Nortron could see Dukat, but Dukat, apparently, could not see Odo.

"Give me the Orb," Dukat said.

"I . . . I don't have it," Nortron stammered.

Dukat raised his left hand as if making an idle gesture. "You will be rewarded."

"No one else has arrived," Nortron explained in a shrill, anxious voice. "Quark says I have to wait."

"Or you will be punished," Dukat concluded. His left hand began to shimmer with red energy. "I should think it would be a simple choice."

"I have latinum!" Nortron pleaded. "I won three dabos! It's in a dimensional safe in my—"

Dukat's eyes sparked with red light. "Do I *look* like I want *latinum?*"

Nortron dumbly shook his head.

Odo thought furiously. As long as Nortron held his position, the Andorian was safe. His body had been found ten meters away, showing no obvious sign of having been moved. Odo just had to keep him from going that extra ten meters.

"Quark's little scheme was merely a smokescreen." Dukat held out his hand. "The Orb."

Nortron swallowed audibly. "Please . . . whoever you are, I *don't* have it. I was only given a map."

Dukat's face darkened with temper, puzzling Odo. The Cardassian apparently didn't know his history. Vash had brought the first Red Orb of Jalbador to Deep Space 9, while it was Nortron who brought the map that showed the rough location of the second Orb. And the third Orb had been hidden in Quark's bar since the Day of Withdrawal. So why would the Dukat of the year 2400 think the Andorian had one of the Orbs, when the historical record would indicate otherwise?

"You *are* Dal Nortron, are you not?" Dukat asked angrily.

The Andorian nodded.

Odo looked around for something heavy he could detach from a wall or the ceiling and use as a club.

"You have been in contact with Leej Terrell, yes?"

Nortron shook his head in denial.

Dukat's voice became acidic. "You spoke of Atrig."

"Yes," Nortron said hurriedly, frantic to please his interrogator. "Atrig came to me. Gave me the map. Told me to contact Quark to arrange an auction."

"Atrig works for Terrell," Dukat hissed.

"I . . . I didn't know."

"And she has the third Orb."

"I . . . I don't know about that, either."

Dukat advanced on the cringing Andorian. "Oh, she's had it since *I* ran this station. Right under my nose. Can you understand the betrayal I felt?"

Nortron backed up, nodding vigorously, clearly desperate not to do anything to further provoke Dukat.

Odo grunted with satisfaction as he spotted a section of an ODN conduit that hadn't been completely closed. It appeared he could rip down about a meter-and-a-half section of the composite, half-walled pipe that contained the optical cable. The pipe would make a good club to knock Nortron unconscious, so the Andorian *couldn't* move the ten meters to his place of death.

"You aren't what I had hoped for," Dukat mused in an almost dreamily singsong voice. "Of course, in this time, I wasn't hoping for much . . . only a chance to serve the Amojan. And so many years from now, when I found out about you . . . the summoning of the Orbs . . . your murder . . . the station's destruction . . ."

"Mmmurder?" Nortron gibbered.

"You're a shadow, my friend, a ghost of what was, never to be again. But I *was* hoping that this time around, you would tell me what I need to know to serve the Amojan . . . so I can retrieve the Orbs for his power and his glory. . . ." Dukat peered at the Andorian. "Can I have an Amojan from *you?*"

"Ama . . . Ama . . ." But in his horrorstruck state, Nortron couldn't form the name of Kosst Amojan, the Evil One, the Pah-wraith Dukat served.

"Last chance," Dukat warned. "Then I shall let history resume its flow, Amojan be his name. Who has the Orbs now?"

Odo decided he had waited long enough. He had hoped he might learn something useful, but he wasn't the only one who knew about Nortron's fate. Dukat did, and he was preparing to speed him to it. The changeling reached up for the loose ODN conduit.

"Oba—Obanak!" Nortron abruptly blurted.

Odo hesitated mid-reach at the mention of that name, looked back at Dukat, saw the Cardassian's dark eyes widen in surprise, a slight smile touch his gray lips.

"*Prylar* Obanak?"

Nortron wiped his face. His white hair lay in damp, flattened tendrils against his blue forehead. His antennae now twitched incessantly. "I . . . I don't know if he's a prylar. Just the name. That's the name Atrig used. Obanak—he's the one who . . . who gave the map to Atrig."

Odo held his hands over the conduit, ready to take action the instant before Dukat could strike but also alert to learn more, especially about the prylar. In this time, Odo knew, Obanak had been involved in a Pah-wraith cult. The prylar had come to DS9 at the same time as Leej Terrell and her associates, Atrig and Dr. Betan.

Those three had proclaimed themselves to be humanitarians come to retrieve the bodies of the Cardassian soldiers found fused within DS9's hull plates.

But since Obanak had accused Terrell of being a mass murderer, a war criminal, why would he have provided Atrig, a member of Terrell's team, with the map that led to the second Orb?

Dukat loomed over Nortron. "I beg your pardon," he thundered. "But am I to understand that Obanak is *already* aware of the second Orb's location?"

Nortron almost gagged in his terror, clearly not knowing how he should answer such a question. "I . . . well . . . he had the map . . . so maybe he looked at it . . . maybe . . . I don't know." Then, in a single stream of fear, Nortron wailed, *"Pleasedon'tkillme!"*

Dukat reared back. "What can I say? To me, you're dead twenty-five years. And who am I to argue with history?" Imperiously, he raised his left hand. It began to radiate with red energy even as Nortron began to whimper mindlessly.

And then Odo snapped the conduit cover loose and in a single movement swung it through the air to impact not Nortron but Dukat, in a stunning blow to the side of his head.

The Andorian squealed like a stuck Tellarite and ran off, thick legs pumping like a prime athlete's.

Dukat was slammed into a bulkhead, then whirled around, dark blood running from his mouth, his red eyes literally afire.

"Too late, Odo!" he cried out, ducking. the changeling's second wild swing to charge down the corridor in pursuit of the shrieking Andorian.

Odo raced after him, joining the chase, rushing around the next intersection in time to see Dukat direct a blast of red energy from both outstretched hands.

The double energy discharge struck Nortron square in the back, stopping him instantly.

Enveloped in a scarlet haze, the Andorian's corpulent body rose into the air, tossed violently back and forth in the grip of a power Odo had never witnessed before.

Odo raised the conduit cover above his head to swing it down again on Dukat.

But without turning, Dukat swung one hand away from his attack on Nortron and pointed it behind him to fire energy not at Odo but at his improvised weapon.

The conduit cover splintered, useless; shards of it dropped from Odo's hands.

Then the energy glow surrounding Nortron faded. The Andorian's body stilled, dropped to the deck, and lay there, unmoving.

Odo stared at Nortron's body. Its position exactly matched that in which Odo's security team had found it, when the Andorian was discovered killed by an energy blast of some unknown type.

The power of a Pah-wraith from an impossible future . . .

Now Dukat spoke directly to Odo, but without looking at him, letting the changeling know that his presence was suspected, although the Cardassian still could not see him.

"Don't you understand, Odo? You don't belong in this time anymore. So there's nothing you can do to change it."

"You seem to think *you* can," Odo muttered, not caring if Dukat heard him, as he looked about him for a new weapon.

"But," Dukat continued, moving his head back and forth as if addressing an audience of thousands, "I do belong here. Because the Amojan is a timeless being. Vengeance without end." Dukat sighed as if he still had more to say but had run out of time to say it. He looked down at Nortron's lifeless body. "From the few station logs remaining from the fall of Deep Space 9, I know you never solved this crime. But as you can see, it was *always* me. I hope you feel better now. Your perfect record will no doubt bring you much solace when you find yourself back in your own private *hell*."

With that, Dukat's hands flared with energy as he abruptly lifted them and thrust them forward, and Odo barely had time to twist his body out of the way of the blindly aimed attack that sprayed along the corridor.

"Amojan, your will be done in the Gateway, as it is in the True Temple," Dukat vowed, then turned and stalked off down the corridor.

Odo slowly got to his feet, wondering if Dukat truly thought he had been successful in banishing him from this timeframe. But if that's what the Cardassian *did* think, then Odo wasn't about to object. He remained motionless so as not to make any sound, only moving when he was certain Dukat was gone.

Then Odo hurried over to Nortron. At the very least, he'd change the body's position to make it look more like the murder it was. *In fact,* he realized, *this is the perfect place to write a message to Captain Sisko.*

A long-missed feeling of relief came over Odo. All he needed to do was to find a shard of the shattered conduit cover, then use it to scratch a message into the bulkhead. Odo was certain his own security staff would notice it when they recorded the crime scene, and within hours, he could be communicating with Sisko—and even this timeframe's version of himself—over a computer link.

Odo picked up a shard from the conduit cover, judged the sharpness of it with his thumb. It was perfect, easily able to mark the soft decorative metal used in sections of the wall panels on this level.

He returned to Nortron's body, already composing his message. *Such a simple thing to change history,* he thought. Then he held the shard to the bulkhead and—

—was struck by a flash of red light so powerful it felt distinctly like a physical blow.

Odo fought to keep his balance and then noticed with dismay that both his hands were pressed against the bulkhead for support, the shard gone.

He stepped back unsteadily, looking down at the deck for what he had dropped. And then he realized it wasn't the only thing now missing.

Nortron's body was also gone.

In its place, the telltale crime-scene seals and forensic markings of his security investigation of Nortron's murder.

"I've gone forward," Odo said aloud. It was the only explanation. But how far?

He stumbled as he ran through the corridors to the turbolift, too exhausted to propel himself in his fluid form.

He staggered off onto the Promenade, intending to go to his office.

But there was no need to search for his answer there.

It was right before him.

In the flickering, shifting bands of red-colored light that played across the Promenade's deserted expanse.

Odo lurched forward, bitter with the realization that he had come too far into the future, *past* the moment of DS9's destruction.

Through the overhead viewports on the Promenade's second level, he saw the energy displays of the red wormhole.

His mission had *failed*.

The Pah-wraiths had won.

Again.

CHAPTER 12

SISKO AND KIRA left Quark's, heads bowed, faces hidden by the robes they wore, to find a place to talk.

"The one good thing about the Orb being missing is that it tells us that the timeline *can* be changed," Kira said. "That means we can do it, too."

"But how?" Sisko asked her. "If we do get swept back to an earlier time on the station, then it's obvious we *don't* succeed, because if we had, the Orb would have been back in its hiding place." Hearing his own words, Sisko sighed. The grammar of Federation Standard was not equipped to deal with time travel.

He and Kira came to a tangle of fallen metal that was all that remained of the old security fence that once had bisected the Promenade into its Bajoran and Cardassian halves, and carefully stepped through it. The stores up ahead were dark, but at least the deck itself had been cleared of major obstructions. Sisko vaguely recalled that the initial clean-up crews wouldn't return to deal with the minor debris until the rest of the big pieces elsewhere had been cut up and carted away.

"Then maybe this is an alternate timeline," Kira said. "I mean, with the Orb missing from the place we found it, or will find it, six years from now, it's sure not the timeline we started in."

Sisko risked looking up to the viewports on the Promenade's second level. Bajor was bright in them, and close. Somewhere higher up, he knew, he himself, six years younger, was now in Ops, taking the stairs to his new office, listening to Kira give all the reasons why Starfleet's mission here wouldn't succeed, why Bajor would succumb to civil war in weeks, why . . .

He couldn't stop the ironic laugh that escaped his lips.

"We've had this conversation before," he said to her. "Except the last time, you were the negative one."

Sisko saw the major's confused expression, so he glanced up again, lifting a hand in the direction of Ops. "Remember what was going on about now?"

At that, startled, she gave a sharp laugh as well. But a tight one and only for a moment.

"So now I'll think positively," Sisko said. "Given current conditions, how do we accomplish what we set out to do?"

Kira shrugged. "Find Weyoun. Take the Orb from him. Put it back into its hiding place in Quark's."

"No, Major," Sisko said. "That *restores* the timeline. Somehow, we have to change it."

"All right. We put a message into the computer," Kira said. "Encrypt it, bury it in some database with a time-release code, so it . . . it shows up on your padd the day before those Andorians arrived and all this started."

But Sisko shook his head. "I thought about that, but remember all the work we've done on these computers in the past six years. More than half the components have been replaced. The programming has been lost and restored more times than . . . than I can remember. We can't count on anything we input today remaining accessible or executable when we need it to be."

Kira ran a hand through her short auburn hair. "So how else can we leave a message to warn ourselves?"

"Maybe," Sisko said, ". . . maybe we should just go up to ourselves now."

But even before he had finished uttering his suggestion, Sisko saw the major's objection register on her open face.

"Captain, you heard Prylar Rulan. Eilin was clear about the dangers of altering history."

"How could it be *history*, Major, if Eilin wrote his texts in the time *before* B'hala? That's more than twenty millennia ago."

"Twenty-*five* millennia ago," Kira corrected. "Eilin wrote his texts at the same time Shabren wrote the Prophecies. And the Fifth Prophecy came true, *exactly* as written."

"Not exactly," Sisko corrected her in turn. "The Prophecy said there would be a thousand years of peace if the Prophets defeated Kosst Amojan during the Reckoning."

Kira nodded vigorously. "That's right—*if*. The Prophecy said the confrontation *would* take place. It said *where* and *when* and *who* or *what* would be involved. And all those details fell into place precisely as foretold. But the one thing Shabren didn't say was who would *win* that confrontation. Don't you see? When the Prophets gave Shabren the gift of the Orb of Prophecy, they held back just enough to ensure that free will would still be the deciding factor. We're not their puppets or their playthings—"

Bridling, Sisko interrupted her. "I have never suggested that we are, Major."

"Maybe not said it. But you're feeling it now. I can tell by the way you're thinking about what we should do. As if . . . as if we should abandon the Prophets."

Sisko hesitated. He knew that at any other time, his instant response—and the response Kira would expect of him—would be to state emphatically that he would never abandon the Prophets. But this time, something held back his words, and he didn't know what it was.

"You see, you don't even know what choice to make, do you?"

Feeling overwhelmed, experiencing it again the way he remembered he had when first seeing it, Sisko looked up and down the Promenade. "Why . . . why would the Prophets make that choice so difficult?"

"You made a more difficult choice, once," Kira reminded him. "When you let the Reckoning proceed, even though your own son's life was at risk."

Sisko nodded. That day, that decision, still woke him from his sleep. "But that was different," he said slowly. "The conflict was clear-cut, well defined. I had no doubt what it was the Prophets wanted." He spread his arms to the ruins of the Promenade. "But this . . . how can linear minds comprehend what we're facing now? Isn't it easier to be a Starfleet officer? Because my duty here *is* clearcut. To save Starfleet, the Federation, and the universe."

Kira raised a skeptical eyebrow. "By breaking every temporal translocation regulation in the book?"

Now it was Sisko's turn to remind her. "The regulations of *today,*" he said. "Not of the future, Major. Even Starfleet recognized that drastic action must be taken. That's why they built Picard's *Phoenix.*"

But Kira was already shaking her head. "They didn't build it to *change* the past. They wanted to put in position a weapon that would let them *save* the present. There *is* a difference, Captain. I believe Starfleet was being true to its ideals, even then."

"And if so, what did it get them?" Sisko asked angrily. "Nothing!"

Kira responded to his outburst with equal passion of her own. "Which tells me that if you think there's a conflict between following the Prophets and being a Starfleet officer, then you're wrong! In this case, we know what being a Starfleet officer means: failure."

Now Sisko felt the touch of Kira's hands on both his arms, as if she worried that he might be getting ready to storm off, which he was. "I'm not saying that for you choosing the Prophets is always the right choice, or the only choice. Sometimes, I know you've *had* to choose Starfleet. And I'd argue that even those decisions ended up serving the Prophets eventually, in ways we couldn't foresee at the time. But here and at that moment. . . ." Sisko had never seen a look of such desperation or of such hope on Kira's face as she stared up at him at that moment. ". . . Emissary, if ever there was a time to trust the Prophets and their servants, this has got to be it."

Having delivered her speech, the major dropped her hands from Sisko's arms and stepped back, awaiting his answer.

Sisko looked away, unthinkingly adjusted the strap of the heavy radio he carried under his robes, trying not to think that the fate of the universe itself might rest on what his decision would be. Eventually, he turned back to face Kira.

"Major," he began, "my one hesitation, my one doubt that I just . . . can't overcome is that the *Bajorans* recognized me as the Emissary, but the Prophets did not."

"I know," Kira said. "Not at first. But it seems like the Prophets' acceptance of you . . . that changed, didn't it?"

Sisko nodded, not sure what her point was.

"Because, in time, the Prophets came to trust *you.*"

"In time," Sisko agreed.

Kira stared at him fiercely. "The Prophets are *never* wrong."

"But is that the same as *always* being right?"

It was clear to Sisko that even Kira had no answers left for him. Just as clear as his own knowledge that he would be asking no more questions.

It was time to take action. To exercise free will.

To save the universe, or destroy it.

Sisko made his decision.

Odo walked slowly to his office, still feeling disoriented by his latest transfer, shielding his eyes from the blinding blasts of red energy that lit up the Promenade's upper-level viewports. He had concluded that the flash of red light that had propelled him from the time of Dal Nortron's murder to this time in which the station existed within the red wormhole was related to the pressure equalization waves measured by Chief O'Brien.

Somehow, Odo thought, when those waves had washed over the *Boreth*'s bubble of space-time, they had affected him, as well, like flotsam on an ocean swell being pushed toward shore and then pulled away.

If that were the case, then there was hope that soon another flash of light—blue, this time—might shift him back into the past, before the station's destruction, when he could access a computer node to send urgent messages to Sisko and the command staff, telling them how they could change their present so this nightmarish future could never come to pass.

But as he walked around the Promenade's curve to see Quark's bar open and empty, and even his own security office apparently left unattended, the changeling realized the significant flaw in his reasoning.

When the Red Orbs had opened the red wormhole, he himself had seen the gravimetric effects rip apart the Promenade. Onboard the *Defiant,* he had witnessed the station's docking pylons buckle and the station's hub begin to deform like a wagon wheel twisting.

Yet everything here was intact. Perfect.

There had to be some explanation. But since he was a constable, not a temporal mechanic, if he was ever to find out what was really happening, he would need to contact an expert. Jadzia or O'Brien or—

"Hey, Stretch! Are you a sight for sore eyes!"

Odo whirled around in shock.

Shock that was multiplied a thousandfold as he said, "Vic?"

Vic Fontaine, a holographic representation of a quintessential Las Vegas lounge singer, circa 1962 Earth, elegantly clad in a formal tuxedo of his era, lifted a hand to wave happily at Odo as the singer quickened his approach.

Vic was a character in one of Dr. Bashir's role-playing programs. A clever combination of synthetic intelligence algorithms, holographic imagery, and micro-forcefields that could exist only within a holographically generated environment. It was impossible for him to be on the Promenade, or anywhere else on Deep Space 9, except for the holosuites on the top level in Quark's.

"How . . . how can you be here?" Odo asked.

"I was going to ask you the same thing," Vic said. The holographic singer tugged on his collar and looked up at the viewports that seethed with red wormhole energy. "And I gotta tell ya, in person, space sure looks different from those photos in *Life* magazine."

"No, Vic, I'm serious. You're a hologram—"

"Thanks for noticin'."

"You can't be here."

"You don't have to tell me."

"So . . . *how* can you be here?"

Vic shook his head. "Okay, here's the story so far. I was doing my thing at a matinee. The power goes out. I find you and your pals locked up in some twenty-fourth-century hoosegow and spring the lot of ya. Then I amble back to my half of the program and let you guys take care of business."

"Yes, yes, I know all that," Odo said. That's exactly what had happened the day before the station had been destroyed. When Terrell had taken Sisko to Jeraddo to search for the lost Orb, she had imprisoned Odo and the others in a holographic version of Odo's security holding cells. Vic, perhaps the only holographic character with the ability to cross between programs of his own volition, had entered Terrell's simulation and set them free. "But what happened then?"

"Near as I can figure, one of those A-bomb tests the military runs out in the desert took a left turn. Big flash of light, thought it was an earthquake, then the power's out again and . . ." Vic's face took on an uncharacteristic grim expression. "Everyone sort of disappeared, Stretch. Like one moment I'm in the middle of panic city, telling the audience to walk not run to the nearest exits, and the next . . . I'm like Belafonte in *The World, the Flesh, and the Devil,* only there's no Inger Stevens, if you know what I mean."

"No," Odo said in bewilderment. "I don't."

"Everyone else *vanished,* Stretch. Everyone. And the other thing that's not kosher is that all of a sudden there's this crazy door in the middle of the casino that's got all these flashing lights and . . . where it leads to ain't exactly there, you know?"

"A holosuite arch?" Odo asked.

"Maybe it was the penthouse suite. How'm I supposed to know? But I step through it anyway. Y'know, maybe the little green men have come for me or something. But I figure, what've I got to lose?

"So, I step through, find myself on the top floor of what has got to be Ming the Merciless's favorite bar and grill, and when I ditch that joint"—Vic looked around again and shrugged—"I'm here in this circular shopping mall, with no doors to the parking lot. But with what's outside those big picture windows up there, I'm going to take a wild guess and say there *aren't* any parking lots. Am I right or am I right?"

From his reading of twentieth-century detective novels, Odo knew that a parking lot wasn't really a park of any kind. The hologram was right, and Odo told him so.

"So," Vic said, "my next guess is that this is that deep-space station you guys are always talkin' about."

"That's right."

"Whoa. Well, I can't stop now. I'll turn over all the cards and say, 'Something's gone haywire.' "

Odo tried to remember if that was a reference from a cowboy novel.

"You know—screwy," Vic said. "Messed up. SNAFU."

"Not right," Odo suggested.

"Now you're cooking."

Odo took that as agreement.

752   JUDITH & GARFIELD REEVES-STEVENS

"So," Vic continued, "from what I remember, this station of yours is supposed to be crawling with crew members, visitors, a regular McCarran in space."

Odo understood what Vic meant if not his exact words. "Everyone's vanished from here, too."

"So . . . I'm no Einstein, but that makes me think that somehow what happened to your joint and what happened to mine are connected."

Odo nodded, remembered a phrase Captain Sisko liked to use. "You're batting a thousand."

Vic smiled and cocked a finger at Odo as if firing a phaser. "Good one, Stretch." But the smile was short-lived. "So, any twenty-fourth-century ideas about what we can do about the whole megillah?"

Odo suddenly had an unnerving thought. "Vic, how long have you been walking around the Promenade?"

"The mall?" Vic asked. "I don't know. Twenty minutes or so. Is it important?"

Odo didn't know the answer to that question. But he felt confident that he hadn't been thrust into some Pah-wraith-generated hell concocted expressly for Vic Fontaine. Otherwise, the hologram would have thought he had been walking for centuries, if not millennia. Still, there had to be some explanation for how Vic managed to exist where there were no holo-emitters. Just as there had to be an explanation for how this once-ruined station was now intact and, judging from the lights and the breeze from the circulating air, fully operational.

Then Odo had it. "This is an illusion," he said.

"Hey, hold on, Stretch. A guy could get a complex from talk like that."

But Odo shook his head. He was beginning to make sense of his surroundings. "No, *you're* not an illusion, Vic. But everything around us . . . it's not what we'd normally call reality."

"Speak for yourself, pallie," Vic said. "My reality is Vegas. And this place is definitely not normal. Not that Vegas is all that normal to begin with."

Odo suddenly held out his hand. "Shake," he said.

Vic gave him a 'Why not' look, took his hand, and pumped it. "Was that supposed to prove something?"

"I think so," Odo said. "Let's go to my office."

"Lead on, MacDuff."

Odo knew things would be simpler if he ceased asking Vic to explain himself. So he just nodded at the hologram and continued on to the security station.

"You see," Odo said as they walked on together, speaking more to help himself understand his situation than from any expectation that Vic could follow his reasoning, "I was just in another version of this station. As it existed a week ago, more or less."

"Whatever you say, Stretch."

"And while I was there, I could touch the walls, I stood on the deck, I could even press controls on a communication node. But I couldn't touch anything that was alive or that was closely connected to anything that was alive. I couldn't even make anyone I saw or heard see or hear me."

Vic stopped at the entrance to Security. "I can tell you right now, I don't like where this is going."

Odo stopped as well. "I don't understand."

"Hey, you made me shake hands with you. And I can hear every word you say . . . even if a lot of them don't make all that much sense."

Odo stared blankly, waiting for some clue to what Vic meant.

"It's like you're saying because I can see you, hear you, and feel you, I'm not real—like I don't exist."

"Ah," Odo said, at last understanding Vic's concern. "You're seeing things from a twentieth-century viewpoint."

"Like I have a choice?"

"In this time, we recognize that life comes in many different forms. The majority of those forms are biological, and they're what I was referring to. You're a special case."

Vic looked skeptical. "Don't humor me."

"I'm not. You're what we call an isolinear-based life-form." In fact, Odo admitted to himself alone, he really didn't know if Vic actually *was* a life-form or not. At the one extreme, he knew there were artificial entities such as Lieutenant Commander Data of the *U.S.S. Enterprise,* who was unquestionably a living being under Federation definitions. At the other extreme, there were the Starfleet Emergency Medical Holograms, some of whom, like Vic, were prone to exhibit characteristics and behaviors that had never been intended by their programming. Dr. Bashir had told Odo of the debate raging within Starfleet Medical over whether or not the EMHs were evolving into true self-awareness, or were simply uncannily accurate reconstructions of the irascible Lewis Zimmerman.

But given current conditions, the changeling saw no need to hurt Vic's feelings, real or simulated as they might be.

"I was only pointing out," Odo said in conclusion, "that I seemed to have no connection to *biological* life-forms. But since your consciousness—" *If that's what you have,* Odo thought. "—arises from the station's computer system, it's as easy for me to interact with you as it is with this door." At that, Odo tapped his code into the door of the security station and it slid open. Then he gestured for Vic to step in first.

Vic maintained his skeptical expression. "You're pretty smooth, Stretch. So I'll take what you said under advisement. But the big question still remains: How come you and I are the only two cats on the station?"

To Odo, the answer was simple. "Everyone else was either evacuated or . . . or died, I imagine, when the station entered the red wormhole. I escaped on the *Defiant* and, to make a long story short, came back. In your case, well, obviously, since the station still exists and all its equipment is functioning, entering the wormhole wasn't harmful to you, either."

Vic blew out a deep breath, as if giving up. "You any relation to Rod Serling?"

To Odo, the name Rodserl had a Romulan sound to it, but he guessed he was safe simply shaking his head.

"Coulda fooled me," Vic said, then walked into Odo's office. "So where does all this fancy gobbledygook leave us? Are things ever going to get back to normal or a reasonable facsimile thereof?"

Odo sat down behind his desk, saw that all his computer systems were on-line. "There's a chance."

Vic sat on the edge of the desk. "Enlighten me."

"All right," Odo said as he began to access the station's main science logs, "we're in a wormhole."

"Let me guess. That's the twenty-fourth-century way of saying we're up the creek without a paddle."

"Exactly," Odo said, not knowing if it was or not. But time was of the essence. "And the first time Sisko and Dax went through it, they ended up together but in two different realities." Odo glanced up at Vic, wondering if he was making any more sense to the hologram than the hologram was making to him.

Vic had tilted his head to one side and was regarding him with narrowed eyes. "You keep going. I'm just trying to imagine how'd you look with a beret and goatee." The hologram paused. "Ever think of playing the bongos?"

"Not . . . really." Odo looked back at his security screen, accessed the station's last hour of sensor logs. "Anyway, what Sisko's and Dax's experience seems to suggest is that a great deal of what we experience within a wormhole environment is subjective. But the fact that . . ." Odo hesitated, thinking of how Dukat had appeared to him on the desolate surface of the world that had once held the Great Link. How could he convey that to Vic? "The fact that you and I are both sharing this subjective reality of the station tells me that somehow there is an underlying reality to everything that's happening in here."

"Okay. Ya lost me back at that wormhole thing, pallie."

Odo called up the sensor log's gravimetric profile of local space and watched it play back at ten times normal speed. Keeping the record was a standard function of the station's sensors, one of the several dozen methods used to track and measure the opening and closing of the Bajoran wormhole. "Think of Las Vegas," Odo suggested as he watched the display.

"All the time," Vic sighed. "All the time."

"But where you live isn't really Las Vegas."

"Ooo, you don't pull any punches, do ya, Stretch?"

"But it's still Las Vegas to you. Just as it's Las Vegas to me when I go into the holosuite. And to Dr. Bashir. And Kira . . . it's a shared illusion. And the fact that it's shared means that something independent of the people visiting it is responsible for creating that illusion."

"Whatever you say, Stretch."

Odo persevered. "So the same principle is at work here in the wormhole. It's full of illusions, but because you and I can share this one, it must have some kind of independent reality."

"So basically you're telling me that we're just in some kinda big holosuite in the sky?"

"That's one way of putting it," Odo agreed. Then he saw what he'd been waiting for: The first gravimetric fluctuations that corresponded to the alignment of the three Red Orbs of Jalbador in Quark's bar. "Got it," he said.

Vic craned forward to peer at Odo's screen for himself. "Got what?"

Odo slipped a memory rod into an access port to copy the sensor log onto it. "This is how the . . . the doorway to this particular holosuite opened. It shows how the structure of local space-time was deformed when the station was swallowed by the wormhole."

"And that's a good thing?"

The moment the screen went dark, Odo held up the memory rod. "This is the equivalent of a map. It shows the way *in,* so if we can somehow reverse the deformations . . ."

". . . it'll show the way out," Vic concluded.

Odo nodded, inexplicably pleased that a hologram could follow his logic.

"So?" Vic asked after a few moments of silence. "How do you reverse the deformations and get us outta here?"

"I . . . don't," Odo said. "I have to get these data back to Chief O'Brien."

"Is he evacuated or . . . you know?" Vic asked.

"Evacuated." Odo stood up.

"So . . ." Vic pointed to the ceiling. "He's out there?"

But Odo shook his head. "Actually, he's in the past. Or in the future, I suppose. From this frame of reference."

Vic held up both hands and shook them back and forth. "Okay, that's it. Now you're being just plain nuts."

Odo smiled, then pressed the memory rod to his chest, concentrating on an entirely new modification to his humanoid body. The rod sank into him like a log disappearing into quicksand.

Vic's eyes opened wide. "Man oh man, if that's legit, you could give Blackstone a run for his money."

Odo knew he *was* in a race, though not the kind Vic might mean. At any moment, he suspected a new equalization pressure wave would strike the *Boreth* and somehow fling him back to the station's past. And if he was correct about the special nature of biological lifeforms within the wormhole, then he was confident that the memory rod would survive the transition encased within the newly formed pocket inside his body as if it were a standard medical implant. He stood up.

"What happens now?" Vic asked, without moving from Odo's desk.

"We wait."

"For what?"

"For me to be sent back in time."

Vic stared at Odo. "Okay for you, but . . . what about me?"

"If what I'm planning works, you'll be fine."

"So what's 'fine' mean in the twenty-fourth century?"

"You'll remember rescuing us from the Security holding cells, just as you do now. Then you'll remember singing to the matinee audience. And then . . . we'll all come in, just like we usually do, and none of this will ever have happened."

Vic's eyebrows arched. "You don't say?"

"You should be happy," Odo said.

"Why? You think I don't know what happens to the regular-type light bulbs around here? Push a button, and pow! Lights out, pallie. No memory. No life. Just reappearing back at the start of the program and carrying on like it's the first time all over again. Odo, that sort of thing . . . scares me, okay?"

"I had no idea," Odo said truthfully. "But you *do* remember what happens from one run of your program to another, don't you?"

"I do now. But if what you're saying is true and none of this will ever have happened . . . then I *won't* remember it, will I?"

Odo shook his head.

"Which is sort of like . . . being erased, wouldn't ya say?"

Odo nodded.

"I don't want that to happen to me."

Odo understood. "No living being does."

"Living." Vic's wistful smile was full of irony. "What a way to find out you're alive—the day you find out you're going to die."

"No, no. You won't die," Odo said hurriedly, trying to reassure the hologram. "Your life will continue—"

"But from back then. Not from now."

"That's right."

"So *that* Vic Fontaine will live." Vic tapped his chest. "But this one, *me,* the *putz* who stepped out onto your fancy space station, won't."

"That's right," Odo reluctantly agreed.

Vic took a deep breath, got to his feet. "You know, I probably shouldn't know this about myself, but, well, you know the guy who programmed me?"

"Felix."

"Yeah. He sort of . . . set it up so I could get away with a few things here and there."

"So I've noticed."

"So I figured out what these memory cylinders are." Vic nodded at Odo's chest. "Like the rod you just 'disappeared' into your chest."

Odo was amazed by what he knew Vic was about to ask. But he also knew there was no answer he could give that would satisfy the hologram.

"Vic . . . I can't take you with me."

"But you're taking that map."

"Well, yes, but when I give the information on it to Chief O'Brien and *if* he's somehow able to use it to knock this station out of the red wormhole back in the past, then *none* of this will have happened. Not for you. And not for me."

Vic stared at Odo. "What? *You* get erased, too?"

"That's right."

"Well, ain't that a kick in the head." Vic sat down again on the edge of the desk and fixed his unfocused gaze on the wall.

"Are you all right?" Odo asked.

"Well, yeah . . . it's just that . . . well, I never really thought that you guys could, you know, *be* erased, or die, or whatever ya call it when you're biological."

Odo was thoroughly puzzled by Vic's sudden confusion. "Vic, exactly what do you think *we* are?"

Vic looked over at Odo with haunted eyes. "C'mon, Stretch. Ya come and go like ghosts. You're always talking about living in space, and in the future, and . . . well, between you and Spots and Worf and the little guys with the big ears, you sure don't look like any of the cats I grew up with back in Hoboken."

"So what does that make us?" Odo asked. He was absolutely baffled by the idea that any hologram might have a belief system that was different from the worldview created by its internal programming.

"You tell me," Vic said. "I mean, what do you and your friends think *I* am?"

Odo didn't even have to stop to think about the answer. "A friend," he said.

"I like that," Vic said. "Don't get me wrong—being erased really bugs the hell outta me. But being your friend, I can . . . I can live with that."

"I'm glad," Odo said. He checked the time readout on his desk. When he had beamed onto the station from the *Boreth* on the day Dal Nortron had died, he estimated he had spent approximately thirty minutes in that timeframe before jumping ahead to this one. Since O'Brien had noted that the waves would come closer and closer together, Odo had assumed he would have less than thirty minutes to spend in this timeframe, and he was almost at twenty-five minutes already.

"So, how do you go back?" Vic asked. Then he laughed as if it was the most ludicrous thing he could say. "In time, I mean?"

"I'll see a flash of light," Odo answered.

"Any idea what I'll see?"

"No."

"Will you be back?"

"Not to this timeframe."

"So, it'll just be me and . . . nobody."

Odo suddenly realized the paradox Vic had stumbled upon. Certainly, if everything worked out as Odo now hoped, and O'Brien *was* able to change the past, *that* version of Vic would have no knowledge of the events following the destruction of the station, because that destruction would never have occurred.

But in that case, *this* Vic would inhabit an alternate timeline, completely alone.

"Talk to me, Stretch. This just ends, right? I forget all about it? Go back to the ways things were?"

Odo didn't know what to say to comfort the worried-looking hologram.

Vic got back to his feet. "Hey, c'mon, pallie. This is Vic. Ya gotta talk to me. Ya gotta tell me this is going to work out."

"I . . . I really don't know," Odo said. "There're so many possibilities . . ."

"Are you telling me I might be stuck here by myself forever?"

"But there'll be other Vics . . ."

Odo winced inwardly as the hologram's voice rose with his concern. "I don't care about *other* Vics. Hell, Felix has probably sold copies of my program halfway to Timbuktu and back again. I care about *this* Vic."

"So do I," Odo said, struggling to think of a way to help the hologram. Could it be possible to copy him onto a memory cylinder? Was Vic's consciousness purely digital and totally transportable from computer to computer? Or was there an analog component to it that meant the hologram would not remain 'Vic' when copied from the computer system he inhabited at this moment?

"Stretch . . . ?" Vic said, plaintive. "Don't leave me here."

Odo opened his mouth to say something, anything that might ease Vic's growing fear of loneliness. But the instant he did, a flash of blue light of unbearable clarity struck him with a physical impact that shot pain through his body, focusing like a laser on the center of his chest.

When the light faded, Odo was still in his security office, but Vic was gone.

Odo checked the time display.

Stardate 51885.9. A day and a half after Nortron's murder. Three and a half days before the station would be destroyed.

Odo placed a hand on his burning chest, focusing on flexing muscles not naturally found in most humanoid bodies.

The memory rod passed through his simulated Bajoran tunic and into his hand.

He went to his security desk and slipped the rod into the access port.

The data—detailing an event that would not happen for another eighty-seven hours—downloaded perfectly.

But Odo knew that if he provided these data to O'Brien today, or to Dax, then the chances were that they wouldn't have need of them.

Instead, Sisko and his staff would make certain that the three Red Orbs of Jalbador would never be brought aboard this station, let alone brought into alignment.

"But what happens then?" Odo asked himself.

He thought of Vic stranded on an empty station in an alternate reality.

He thought of O'Brien and Garak and, yes, even of Quark on the *Boreth*. And the seven others with them, including Rom, waiting in a tiny bubble of space-time for a communication from him—for a sign that they would soon all be saved.

And in this time, Odo knew, they would all be saved. They would never travel into the future. The universe would not end in twenty-five years when the two wormholes were aligned and the Bajoran sun destroyed.

But in an alternate timeline, there would always be those whom he had consigned to an endless existence in an endless nothingness.

He stared at the gravimetric sensor log on his desk's display screen. Sometime in the next twenty to thirty minutes—however long it would be until the next pressure wave struck in a flash of red light—he could save the universe simply by inputting a warning into the station's computer system.

But if he did, then who would save his friends?

Odo struggled to think of a third possibility.

Because, for now, taking one path at the cost of the other was a choice he could not—would not—make.

CHAPTER 13

JAKE KNEW BETTER than to get in Worf's way, so he stayed in position at his auxiliary console while the Klingon thundered from the bridge.

But even though he had seen his father transport safely from the *Defiant* with Major Kira, Jake couldn't help imagining the worst.

"Dax?" he called out over the harsh staccato of the transporter alarms.

The Trill scientist had also remained at her station, and her eyes were fixed firmly on her displays. "It'll be all right, Jake. Worf can handle it."

"But handle what?"

"Someone probably got tired of waiting," Jadzia said reassuringly, "so they had themselves transported over on the same settings I used for your father and Kira."

"But what if whoever it is gets caught by the Cardassians or . . ." Since arriving in the future, Jake had learned more than he'd ever known about the potential consequences of creating new timelines. And what he'd learned was worrying him. What if his father and Kira set up one alternate past, and whoever had transported after them inadvertently set up another? That particular scenario could lead to the *Defiant*'s being unable to maintain contact with *any* version of DS9.

But Jadzia didn't seem interested in leading him through another discussion of temporal physics. "Jake, right now, our job is communication. Just watch your board. Let Worf deal with security." As if to underscore her instructions, the alarms stopped just as she finished speaking, their cessation suggesting the situation had come under control.

Jake sighed, and for a moment his concentration diverted to his hand which he saw trembling above the controls at his station. It was time he got himself under control.

"Are you cycling for different time signatures?" Jadzia asked him.

Jake sprang back into action and input the sequencing code that would start the process. "Yes, sir," he said. *Focus,* he thought. Jadzia was searching for a radio signal from DS9, timeshifted by the same degree as the navigational timecodes the station was transmitting from the Day of Withdrawal. His job was to look for any other unexpected temporal perturbations generated by the wormhole environment that might obscure his father's attempt to communicate.

The overhead speakers hissed into life. It was Dr. Bashir from elsewhere in the ship. "Dax, I'm going to need your help in sickbay."

Jake looked over at the Trill, caught her eye. Someone was obviously injured. "Who is it, Julian?" Jadzia asked.

"Commander Arla. Weyoun came out of his trance or whatever it was. Beat her up badly. Then transported off the ship."

"Sorry, Julian. I can't leave my station."

"She has internal bleeding in her skull. I need an assistant."

"Then you've got at least nine other people to pick from." Jadzia did not look at Jake as the comm circuit went dead.

"Dax—Weyoun could change everything, couldn't he?" Jake asked nervously.

"I'm sure Worf is taking that under consideration." Jadzia's terse tone turned suddenly angry as Jake saw her hit her combadge sharply. "Dax to Bashir."

Bashir answered promptly, considerably calmer than before. "It's all right, Dax. I've got one of Simons's engineers to assist me."

But the Trill brushed his assurance aside. "I need to talk to you in private—immediately. Can you come to the bridge?"

Bashir's reply was indignant. "I'm not leaving my patient any more than you'll leave your station."

"Oh, for . . . Julian, step into the corridor."

Wondering what was going on but hesitant to interrupt Jadzia in her present mood, Jake studied his display, watching the spray of individual datapoints as they undulated up and down across the center screen. Out of the corner of his eye, however, Jake actually saw Jadzia's spots darken—he'd never seen her so upset before. But still, Jadzia kept her eyes on the console before her, and her hand moved rhythmically over the controls, continuing to carry out her duty.

"All right," Bashir replied a few moments later, exasperated. "I'm in the corridor. Now, what's this about?"

Jake's fingers continued to work at his own assignment, but his ears strained to catch Jadzia and Bashir's exchange for any clues to the Trill's concerns about Commander Arla.

"Arla came into the transporter room and watched me beam out Kira."

"So?" Bashir asked.

"So . . . she seemed too interested in the process," Jadzia said.

Jake immediately thought back to Arla's demeanor when she was in the transporter room, recalled the way the Bajoran commander had looked over Jadzia's shoulder with such close attention.

"As I recall," Bashir replied, "Arla's a Starfleet officer with limited starship experience. I would hope she would show some interest in procedures outside her field of—"

"Julian! Weyoun couldn't have beamed himself off the ship without help! There are no automated subroutines to handle transport in the absence of a subspace carrier wave."

Jake sat up straighter, not sure if he had heard Jadzia correctly.

"You're saying *Arla* beamed Weyoun off the ship?" Bashir asked.

"Well, *someone* had to have helped him."

Bashir didn't sound convinced. "So then who came up behind Arla and fractured her skull from behind *after* she operated the transporter?"

"I don't know," Jadzia admitted to Bashir. "I'm just suggesting you be careful with her."

"Suggestion noted," Bashir replied drily, then the circuit went dead again.

Jake heard Jadzia mutter something under her breath, knew it wasn't intended for him, but asked anyway to see if he could get her talking to him again. He had to find out if she had said what he thought she had.

"I'm sorry?" he asked.

"Nothing," Jadzia answered shortly. "I'm just surprised that given the situation, people aren't more concerned than they are."

Gathering courage for his next question, Jake visually tracked the sensor-scan advance to the limit of receptivity, then tapped in the sequence that told the sensor subroutines to begin again.

"Dax?"

"I'm here."

"The transporter . . . you said you couldn't set it on automatic?"

Jadzia's reply seemed unnaturally even-toned to him. "It's all right, Jake. I'm the most qualified transporter operator. I'll stay behind."

Jake stared at the Trill, unbelieving. "Does . . . does Worf know?" He couldn't imagine Worf allowing his wife to stay behind, to be lost with the ship.

Jadzia half-turned to meet his gaze. "What are you suggesting, Jake? That Worf would order someone else to stay behind and die so I could live?"

Put that bluntly, Jake knew she was right. There was another option. But Jadzia dealt with that one before he could even voice it. "And he won't stay behind, either. Worf knows he's not proficient enough to handle the beam manually under these conditions. If he even tried, he'd probably end up killing the last person to beam off. Besides," she said, "Worf has Alexander to think of. All my children—*Dax*'s children, at least—have already had full lives of their own. And I have lived seven lifetimes, while Worf hasn't even lived one. I know what I'm doing, Jake. So we don't have to talk about it anymore." She turned back to her console.

Jake looked back at his own display. A yellow spike flared out of the random noise.

"Dax! A signal on timeshift forty-seven!"

"What?"

Jake froze the sensor scan's progression before allowing himself to glance over at Jadzia, who was rapidly inputting a long string of commands.

"That's way out of bounds," she said. "Almost like it's a reflected signal instead of . . ."

The bridge speakers crackled with interference so intense that the computer couldn't remove it. But a new voice could still be heard within the cacophony.

"... *shifting with each ... lization wave ... days before With-drawal ... weeks after ... Weyoun in phase but ...*"

A long hiss of static blanked out the rest of whatever was being said. But Jake had heard enough.

"Dax! That's my dad!" he said just as Worf entered the bridge.

"Have you made contact with the captain?" the Klingon asked.

"We're definitely getting something," Jadzia said. "But according to the timeshift on the signal, it's not coming from the time we sent him to."

Jake heard his father speak again through the harsh static. "*Repeating ... Major ... and I arrived safely ... on target day. At first, we ... phase ... on living ... to the day I arrived on ... first time. We're ... equalization wave through time. ... First arrival, several days before With ... then ... when Starfleet ... but doesn't get caught in the waves like we ... other time signals ... over at once ...*" Then interference swallowed the transmission again.

Worf stood beside Jadzia. "The captain said he was repeating his message. Have the computer overlay each transmission we receive to build a complete version."

"Already on it," Jadzia confirmed.

Elation and anxiety in equal parts filled Jake. He turned toward Worf and Jadzia, unsure if he could—or should—leave his own station now. "That means he made it, doesn't it?"

"And Kira *and* Weyoun," Jadzia said. "But it sounds as if each time the *Defiant* gets hit by an equalization wave, they get moved through time by a few weeks or days."

"What does that mean?" Jake asked.

"I don't know," Jadzia confessed. "Clearly, we can beam off the *Defiant* to the station, but if we're somehow still connected to this pocket of space-time when the wormhole environment finally stabilizes, I can't be sure we'll stay in the past. We might get snapped back here and ... disappear."

"What will it take to make you sure?" Worf asked.

Jadzia looked up at her husband. "I'll need to have readings taken during a temporal shift on the station, then compare them to the readings I already have from this side."

"Then you will beam over now," Worf said. The short statement sounded a great deal like an order to Jake, despite what the Trill had said earlier about what her mate would do in these circumstances.

Jadzia stood up. "Sorry, Worf. I'm the best transport operator on the ship. Julian can take the readings I need and radio back the results."

From his own station, Jake tried to observe the two without being obvious. He understood they were dealing with something other than a Starfleet command decision. They were also a wife and husband. And perhaps the last hope the universe had of surviving in some form, in some timeline or another.

But for all the complexities of their conflict, Jake decided there must be advantages to their multilevel relationship as well. Because their argument ended before it had even begun.

"I will inform the doctor," Worf said gruffly. "Assemble whatever instruments you require him to take, then report to the transporter room."

Before Jadzia could respond, the main viewer flashed blue, and the *Defiant* pitched violently. Jake held on to his console to maintain his balance. Worf and Jadzia steadied each other.

The lights on the bridge flickered briefly before the ship's artificial gravity field returned to trim. And when Jake next looked up at the viewer, Deep Space 9 now hung against a shifting field of red energy, not blue.

"The waves are speeding up," Jadzia reported. "Just as predicted."

"How much longer?" Worf asked.

"For the *Defiant,*" Jadzia said as she glanced down at her console, "seven hours, three minutes. But the last twenty minutes are going to be rough, with waves hitting us every few minutes, then every few seconds."

"Then we will abandon ship before that happens," Worf said.

Sharing a brief, intense look at her mate, Jadzia nodded. "I'll . . . go get what Julian will need."

"And," the Klingon added, "when you have beamed him to the station, you will then work with the computer to automate the transport sequence so that—" Worf harshly cleared his throat before continuing. "So that . . . when the time comes, the last crew member will be able to beam off as well."

Jake could see that Jadzia wanted to argue about that, but again it was as if a burst of micropacket communications was exchanged between the couple, relieving them of the necessity of arguing with spoken words.

"I'll get on it," Jadzia agreed. She leaned down to tap some controls at her station. "Jake," she glanced over to his station. "The computer will continue to record anything your father transmits. But you stay here and listen for any changes we should know about right away."

Jake nodded.

Then Jadzia left the bridge, followed by her Klingon mate. Just at the door, Worf stopped and turned to Jake. "I must talk with Dr. Bashir." The Klingon looked around the otherwise empty bridge. "It would seem that you have the—"

"Oh, no, I don't," Jake said, though he knew his reaction differed from the one everyone else onboard the ship would give in his position. He pointed to the twenty-fifth-century uniform he wore. *"Civilian* advisor, remember? I'll watch the viewer and monitor communications, but . . ."

Worf nodded. "Carry on."

Then Jake was left alone on the bridge of the *Defiant.*

With its empty center chair.

Where his father belonged.

Where Jake *knew* he would see his father again.

As far as Jake was concerned, no other choice was possible.

Julian Bashir dropped easily from midair, rolled once, and was instantly on his feet in total darkness, knowing exactly where he was. The smell of Quark's was quite unmistakable.

"Computer, lights please."

At once, he found himself standing within a flickering pool of light coming from a series of wall-mounted torches, looking out through a dramatic marble arch at a set of wide stairs descending to a small garden.

Bashir's stomach tightened. The holosuite was in use. He wondered how close he had come to being beamed directly into one of the suite's occupants or replicated props.

A deep snorting sounded behind him, and he spun around to see who else was with him.

Bashir's mouth dropped open. "Morn?"

The big Lurian was sound asleep, huge mouth agape, in the midst of a mound of red pillows on which sprawled the softly breathing forms of four or five, perhaps even six, web-fingered Laurienton spa girls wearing . . . not much, as far as Bashir could tell.

"Computer," Bashir whispered urgently, "lights down, please. Intensity one."

Half the torches were suddenly extinguished and the others reduced to the glowing radiance of coals.

Undisturbed and unaware, Morn snored on in the arms of his holographic companions.

Bashir looked around the suite as he shifted his radio under the ragged Bajoran trustee clothes he wore and tried to guess where the holosuite's arch might be. It wasn't self-evident.

"Computer," Bashir said in a low voice, "please indicate the exit."

A green square of light flashed on the far side of the mound of red pillows. But at the same time, a computer voice warned, loudly, "Credit will not be given for any unused time."

Bashir cringed and began running for the flashing green light, but it was already too late.

Morn stirred, sat up, rubbed at his eyes. His movements woke the spa girls as well.

Bashir was almost at the hidden arch when the Lurian caught sight of him.

Morn's blank look of alarm betrayed no personal recognition, and the doctor realized that meant he had arrived in a timeframe before his first arrival on the station.

Bashir put his finger to his lips. "Shhh," he said quietly to Morn. "Don't say a word."

Morn's tiny eyes narrowed in brief suspicion, but then a mighty yawn struck him and the Lurian shrugged as if to say he had no argument with his unexpected guest's suggestion. Morn's eyes began to close as he sank back into his soft pillows and the giggling spa girls, who once more curled up against him, their holographic contentment a mirror of his own.

Bashir nodded with a relieved smile, hoping that the bandage he wore over the bridge of his nose had been enough to disguise him in the low light, so that the Lurian wouldn't recognize the younger Dr. Bashir when *he* arrived on the station.

Then, casting off any worry about what could not be changed now, Bashir approached the flashing green light and asked the computer to show him the arch.

Seconds later, he was standing in the corridor outside the holosuites, releasing a deep breath as the door closed behind him.

From what Jadzia had been able to piece together of Sisko's garbled message, the doctor understood that he had most likely arrived on Deep Space 9 in a timeframe different from the one seen by the *Defiant,* though still connected to it. However, from his current position, it was impossible for him to know precisely which timeframe he was in. Morn, for instance, had been a customer of Quark's before the Day of Withdrawal, as well as after it. About all he could be certain of, Bashir thought, was that this day was *not* one of those on which the station had been plunged into chaos.

Now he moved cautiously along the corridor, heading for the balcony overlooking Quark's main floor. Creeping up to the railing, he looked down and saw—

Cardassians.

"Wonderful." Bashir sighed.

He had arrived *before* the Day of Withdrawal. And judging from the raucous laughter down below, the station's Cardassians were in no hurry to leave.

He backed away from the railing, trying to remember if there were any nearby Jefferies tubes he could escape into.

But his thoughts of escape ended when he felt the emitter node of a phaser dig into his back.

Without being told to, Bashir slowly lifted up his hands to show he was unarmed. Rough hands efficiently patted him down, located his Starfleet radio and modified tricorder, relieved him of both.

Then a deep voice said, "Turn around. Say nothing."

Bashir did as he was told but couldn't hide a flicker of recognition as he saw Prylar Obanak.

"You know me, don't you?" the prylar said.

Though Bashir knew that each interaction he had in this time could cut him off from his own time, he also knew he had to reply. "You . . . look familiar."

Obanak regarded him doubtfully. Then he reached behind himself to a bulkhead panel, pressing something the doctor could not see, until the panel popped open a few centimeters, revealing an access port.

Obanak waved his phaser—a segmented Cardassian model, Bashir noted—to make it clear that the doctor was to go first.

Bashir complied and found himself looking into a narrow service-access tunnel. The node of the phaser again prodded him in the back. Obviously, Obanak wanted him to proceed.

Squeezing through the opening, Bashir could see the tunnel ran for about four meters to a poorly lit Jefferies tube. Quickly guessing it would take the broad-shouldered prylar more time to squeeze through the tunnel behind him, Bashir began formulating a plan to escape. But the instant he poked his head into the Jefferies tube, another phaser node found his temple.

"Slowly," was all the second voice said. But that was enough for the doctor to put his plan on hold.

The Jefferies tube was unlike any other Bashir had encountered in his time on DS9. More than half its lights weren't working. Of the few that were, most were flickering on and off erratically. The customary, pristine ODN conduits installed by the Starfleet Corps of Engineers were nowhere to be seen. And somewhere off in the shadows, a liquid badly in need of recycling dripped noisily.

The Bajoran who held the phaser node to Bashir's temple pushed the doctor to one side as Obanak twisted out of the narrow access tunnel with surprising agility for someone of his bulk. Crouching down beside Bashir, the prylar handed his phaser back to his partner. Then, with shocking, almost unnatural, speed, he leaned forward and ripped the bandage from Bashir's face.

"Human," Obanak said. He made the statement sound like an accusation.

"I'm not here to make trouble," Bashir said quickly. If Jadzia's reconstruction of Sisko's message was correct, sometime in the next hour—adjusting that timespan for differing rates of temporal flow—an equalization wave would pass over the *Defiant*. All he had to do, the doctor reminded himself, was stay alive for that time, and the wave would snap him into a timeframe on the other side of the Day of Withdrawal. *If* Jadzia's reconstruction was correct.

"Does that mean you support the Cardassians?" Obanak asked sharply.

"Of course not!"

"Then what are you doing here?"

Bashir's genetically enhanced intellect whirled through and considered all his options at an accelerated rate. Most of all, he knew, he had to be sure not to introduce any changes into the past. But he also had to find Sisko and Kira. And, Bashir knew, since Kira had said that Obanak was part of the Bajoran Resistance, his best strategy was to trust the man. The only question was how little information could he reveal and still earn Obanak's trust in return.

"Can you tell me the date?" Bashir began.

Obanak and his partner exchanged a look.

"The Third Feast Day of Tral," Obanak said.

"I mean . . . the stardate."

Obanak squinted at him, judging him. "Who is the Emissary?"

Bashir froze. How could he reveal that information in the past, before Captain Sisko had been identified by the Bajoran people? "I . . . I can't tell you."

Obanak nodded as if he had expected that answer. "But you know him?"

"Prylar Obanak," Bashir said, "you have to trust me. For the good of your people, you—"

He fell back as Obanak lunged at him. The prylar's massive forearm shoved against his throat, under his jaw, pressing with shocking strength, cutting off his flow of air.

"What does a human know about what's good for Bajorans?" the prylar growled.

". . . I'm on . . . your . . . side . . ." Bashir wheezed.

Obanak did not reduce the pressure. "Then tell me—*Who is the Emissary?*"

The light in the Jefferies tube became even dimmer to Bashir as his field of vision shrank and darkened. Bashir's hammering pulse filled his awareness. If he died here, then nothing would change. He had to take a chance. It was the only choice.

". . . *Sisko* . . ." he gasped.

The constriction on his throat was gone. Bashir gulped in a burning rush of air and his hands flew to his bruised throat.

Obanak rocked back on his knees. "You see?" the prylar said. "That's all we needed to know. To give us a common ground."

"For what?" Bashir coughed as he took another deep breath and flexed his leg muscles as best he could in the cramped space.

"This is what *you* need to know," Obanak said firmly. "In five days, the enemy will leave the Gateway abandoned. The Temple will be in disarray. The Prophets will weep no more. Fourteen days later, the Sisko will arrive from the stars. Three times he will deny that he is the Emissary. Then even the Prophets will deny him. But that will be a test. For the Emissary will come to the Gateway not once on that day but twice. And the Temple at last will open its doors for all to see."

Bashir staring intently at Obanak, saw only resolve in his eyes, heard only conviction in his voice. "How do you know that?" he risked asking.

Obanak stared back. "I know how I know. The question is, how do you?"

But Bashir had done with taking chances. "Truly, all I can say is that I will be gone in less than an hour. If you give me back my radio and tricorder, I'll stay right here, won't cause any trouble, and events will unfold just as they . . . just as they should."

Obanak's partner's glance went to the radio and tricorder on the floor of the Jefferies tube.

Obanak frowned. "I'm disappointed in you," he told the doctor. Then he shoved Bashir to the side, forcing him to start to crawl forward down the tube. "Turn left at the fourth intersection," the prylar instructed Bashir. "And remember, the moment you make noise is the moment you die."

The crawl through the Jefferies tubes took ten minutes at least, and by its end, Bashir couldn't be certain which level he was on. But Obanak knew. Shoving past Bashir, the prylar unlatched an access panel, then dropped through into a large room beyond. Bashir, then the prylar's partner, followed immediately after.

To Bashir, the room seemed to be a storeroom of some kind, smaller than a cargo bay, perhaps one of the supply lockers on the level directly under the Promenade where storekeepers kept their stock.

Two small emergency wall-mounted fusion lamps provided light. Bashir also noted a cot against the bulkhead between two stacks of shipping containers. Almost everything appeared to be labeled in

Cardassian radians. Bashir guessed the most likely explanation was that this was a hiding place for resistance members on the station.

"I'd really like my tricorder and radio back," he said.

Obanak took them from his partner, held them out of Bashir's reach. "And I'd *really* like some answers."

"Look," Bashir said, "you've told me that you know about events in the future. How the . . . the enemy will leave the Gateway, how the Emissary will arrive from the stars. Is it really so difficult for you to accept that maybe I know something about what's going to happen, too? Can't you just accept that . . . that we both obtained our knowledge from the same source?"

"That is not possible," Obanak said, handing Bashir's tricorder and radio back to his Bajoran partner. "I know what my source is. The source of my people and of my order since time began. But you are not of my people. You are not of my order."

"Yet I know what you know," Bashir insisted, looking at Obanak's partner, wondering whether or not, when the pressure wave came, he would have enough of a warning at least to retrieve his tricorder.

"Only two types of beings know what I know," Obanak said. And now Bashir heard the conviction in the prylar's voice begin to turn into threat. "Bajorans and Prophets. Are you a Prophet, human?"

"No."

"And you're not Bajoran. So . . . I'm at a loss."

For all his superior reasoning powers and abilities, Bashir couldn't see how he was going to get out of this. "Prylar Obanak, I promise you, someday I will be able to explain everything to you. But . . . I just can't explain today."

"Because you don't know, or because you won't?"

Bashir struggled to project conviction equal to that the prylar had shown him. "For those of us who have . . . knowledge of what is to come, we know the danger of revealing too much. And that's what I face now. If I reveal too much, I might change what I know must come."

For once, Obanak did not have a ready reply. Instead, he simply contemplated Bashir with a thoughtful expression on his broad, weathered face.

"Will you," he asked at last, "at least reveal the source of your knowledge?"

Bashir shook his head. Even that information might be enough to change the history he knew. "I'm sorry."

Obanak looked over to a corner of the storeroom, and Bashir suddenly had the shock of realization that there was a fourth person with them in the storeroom.

A person who now stepped from the shadows into the cool blue light of the fusion lamps, his bright red robes the color of freshly spilled blood.

"I've heard enough," Weyoun said.

Obanak bowed reverently. "Yes, Emissary."

Bashir almost choked. *"He's* not the Emissary!"

"He is the Sisko," Obanak warned. "Even you knew his name."

"He's Weyoun! He's . . . he's possessed by the Pah-wraiths!"

Obanak took a step toward Bashir but stopped obediently at a gesture from Weyoun. "The Prophets are known by many names," the prylar said. "And dwell in many places. Reconciliation of all Bajor and her Prophets is—"

"Obanak!" Bashir said forcefully. "I'm from the future! Do you understand? That's how I know what will happen. And I'm telling you that *this* creature is *not* your Emissary. He is—" Bashir's tirade ended in a cry of pain as a bolt of red energy slammed into his chest, driving him back against the storeroom bulkhead.

"That, good doctor," Weyoun said softly, "is quite enough of that." The Vorta moved forward until he stood over Bashir, looking down at him with a pious expression of dismay. "Tell your friends, whatever they try to do, I will undo. There are no alternate timelines. There is only the one True Temple and those who dwell within it. And unfortunately for you, Dr. Bashir, you are not in their number."

At that, Weyoun raised his hand, and a nimbus of red energy crackled across his fingers.

"Damn you," Bashir whispered, still almost completely paralyzed by the first blow Weyoun had struck, knowing what the second blow was likely to do.

Weyoun smiled with real amusement at the doctor's choice of words.

Then a blast of light obliterated Bashir's consciousness.

And his last thought was to wonder why the light was blue, not red.

CHAPTER 14

O'BRIEN FLUNG HIMSELF at Dukat, but he was a second—a life-time—too late.

The Cardassian wrapped his arms around the Regulan phoenix that Odo had become even as the transporter beam dissolved them both into their fundamental quantum essence.

O'Brien's arms wrapped around nothing, and he tumbled to the deck of the *Boreth*'s bridge, skinning his chin on the rough Klingon carpet, the air knocked out of his lungs.

"That was not a good thing," Garak said.

"No kidding," Quark muttered.

"But . . . Dukat can't win in a fight against Odo," Rom said hesitantly.

"It's not just Dukat," O'Brien huffed as soon as he could breathe again. "It's that Kosst Amojan thing, too." He rolled over and awkwardly pushed himself up from the deck, straightening the annoying robes he wore. Then, limping slightly and feeling every year of his age, he returned to his science console, where Rom was checking its display.

"No sign of beam dispersion, Chief," Rom informed O'Brien.

"So we may assume they survived transport?" Garak asked as he strolled over to O'Brien and Rom.

O'Brien thought about that for a moment, uncertain. Maybe it would be better if his coordinates *had* been off, or if smugglers had filled the supposedly empty room with supplies. Maybe it would be better if Dukat had been beamed into solid matter and—

Suddenly, he moaned. "Why didn't I think of that before?"

"Think of what?" Garak asked with interest.

But O'Brien didn't waste his time answering. He glanced over at the main viewer. Deep Space 9 was perfectly centered against a sea of shifting blue energy. The chief engineer focused his attention on the station's navigation lights. Each one he could see blazed without interruption or blinked on and off as it was intended to.

"Chief?" Garak prompted.

"Look," O'Brien said quickly. "Let's say the transport went wrong—"

"Why not?" Quark groused from the other side of the bridge. "Everything else has."

"What I mean is," O'Brien continued, "if Odo and Dukat had materialized in a bulkhead, there would have been a hell of an explosion inside the station."

"Of course!" Rom said excitedly. "We'd see a power fluctuation in the navigation lights! Uh, *did* we see a power fluctuation in the navigation lights?"

On his console, O'Brien played back the last sixty seconds of the viewer's automatic recorded image. The lights didn't vary. "No, but that wouldn't have been the only effect."

"Uh . . . there'd be a minor subspace distortion caused by the superposition of fermions in conflict with the Pauli exclusion principle?"

Quark had stalked over to see whatever was on O'Brien's displays for himself. Seeing nothing that made sense to him, he shrugged, then rolled his eyes at his brother's suggestion. *"That* sounds reasonable."

But that kind of distortion wasn't what O'Brien was looking for. "No subspace out here, Rom." The chief engineer couldn't resist the opportunity to be a teacher. "But you're right—there would be a different sort of energy signature produced by a matter interference explosion."

"Uh . . . another signature which we could detect . . . ?" Then Rom suddenly shouted, "Electromagnetic pulse!"

Quark stuck a finger in his ear and shook it back and forth, as if he had been deafened by Rom's outburst.

"That's it, Rom!" O'Brien said. "If visible-light photons can jump out of their space-time bubble and cross the wormhole environment to reach us, then any type of electromagnetic radiation should be able to do the same. That's how we detected the navigation time codes in the first place."

O'Brien checked the broad-spectrum radio-scan subroutine he had set up when he had tried to communicate with the *Defiant,* still a blurry gray disk in a corner of the viewer. When the technique hadn't worked, he had put the idea of radio communication to the side. But now he realized that he should have sent Odo over with a radio communicator—it would have been a far easier way to receive a message from the changeling than by having him switch docking lights off and on in code.

"No spikes," O'Brien said. "They made it."

"Poor Odo," Rom sighed.

"Chief O'Brien," Garak said, "I think our next step is obvious."

O'Brien gave the Cardassian a curious look. "Are you volunteering?"

"Present company excluded, Chief, you have your choice of the seven Starfleet crewmen in engineering, only two of whom have experienced regular duty on Deep Space 9. I believe I am the most qualified for what needs to be done."

O'Brien took Garak at his word. "All right, you're next. Rom, see if you can coax a high-powered radio communicator from one of the replicators."

"Right away, Chief!"

"Excuse me," Quark complained as Rom hurried off to the back of the bridge. "But Garak's next for what?"

"Beaming to the station," O'Brien said.

"Why him? If it's safe," Quark protested, "why can't we all go?"

O'Brien paused, sternly regarding the Ferengi. "Quark, all we know is that it *looks* safe. We won't *know* it's safe until Garak goes over there and radios back a signal to us."

"And in the meantime," Garak added politely, "there is the small matter of Dukat allowing Kosst Amojan to run rampant on the station." He held out his hand to Quark. "But if you insist on going over first . . ."

"Never mind," Quark said, then walked away.

O'Brien lowered his voice. "What *will* you do about Dukat?"

Garak shrugged noncommittally. "At the very least, he'll have to deal with *two* Odos, so the odds will be in our favor. And I'm certain Captain Sisko won't have forgotten that little trick of flooding the station with chroniton particles to . . . persuade the Pah-wraith to move on."

"In case he has forgotten," O'Brien said, "remind him."

"Oh, I'll do more than remind him, you can be sure." Then Garak lost his usual expression of equanimity.

"What is it, Garak?"

"I take it that we are officially giving up on any plans we had of trying to preserve the timeline in some semblance of how we remember it."

O'Brien nodded. "I know. That went by the boards when Odo beamed over. And Dukat cinches it."

Garak responded with an expression of sadness O'Brien couldn't remember seeing before. "While I'm no expert in these matters, Chief, I feel obligated to point out that with so many opportunities for changing the timeline in. . . ." The Cardassian looked over at the viewer and the station it displayed. ". . . that past, it is conceivable that at some point the *Boreth* will . . ."

"Disconnect from the Feynman curve linking it to the station," O'Brien said.

"Exactly," Garak agreed.

"A chance we'll have to take."

"No," the Cardassian said gravely. "It is a chance *you* have to take. I daresay the others—" Now he looked back at Quark and Rom arguing beside the replicator slot. "—have no understanding of the ramifications of what you're planning."

O'Brien knew Garak was right, but that didn't stop him from being surprised by the Cardassian's concern for the rest of his fellow temporal refugees.

"You're a decent man," O'Brien said.

Garak smiled with an expression of delight, quickly repressed. "How kind of you to think so."

"After you go, I'll explain it to them. If we hear from you, I'll beam everyone over."

"And if you don't hear from me?"

"I'll beam the rest over anyway. At least . . . at least they might have a chance at turning up someplace else. They certainly won't have one here."

Garak nodded, then paused, looking O'Brien directly in the eyes.

"Now what?" O'Brien asked.

"Just the way you said that, about beaming the *rest*. You *will* be able to beam yourself over, won't you?"

O'Brien chuckled, surprised once again by Garak's concern. "You're damn right. Now, if this had been a Starfleet ship, I wouldn't be able to take manual control of the transporter in the absence of a subspace carrier wave. But the Klingons, they don't see the need for the same sort of safety protocols we do."

Garak leaned forward conspiratorially. "Personally? I find it one of those traits that makes Klingons rather endearing."

Sometimes, when Garak shared opinions such as that, O'Brien found himself wondering if the man really saw things so differently. But this time, he realized that Garak was simply making a joke. So O'Brien just smiled, wondering how many other times he might have misinterpreted Garak's intentions.

Garak nodded graciously. "I'll just stand over there, shall I?"

O'Brien nodded back. "All we need is the radio," he said. "Rom?"

Over at the replicator slot, Rom and Quark jerked guiltily at the sound of his voice. They both looked flushed. "I almost have it, Chief!" Rom cried out.

"Is there a problem?"

Rom shot a sideways look at the replicator, where a Klingon device clad in a light-brown metallic casing suddenly materialized. "Uh, not really . . ." Rom grabbed the device and hurried over to Garak with it.

O'Brien joined Garak to check the radio. The chief engineer glanced back at Quark, who had remained beside the replicator. "What's he all worked up about?" O'Brien asked Rom.

"Uh, the replicator," Rom said. "I guess in the future . . . uh, they've figured out how to replicate gold-pressed latinum."

O'Brien groaned. Quark and latinum. But lacking the strength to yell at Rom's brother for delaying the replication of the radio, O'Brien turned his attention to the device. Like most Klingon technology designed for field use by warriors, the Klingon radio's controls were simple and intuitive.

"Just remember," O'Brien began.

Garak completed the warning. "Brace myself for a drop."

At his console, O'Brien called up the transporter controls. "Stand by . . ."

"I will see you all on the station," Garak said.

But before O'Brien could energize the transporter, an unexpected voice cut in over the bridge speakers, breaking up and full of static.

"Repeating . . . Major Kira and I . . . arrived safely, but not on target day . . ."

O'Brien stared at the sudden radio spike on his broad spectrum scan, afraid to say the words already on his lips, scarcely believing they could be true.

But in the end, nothing could stop him.

"That's the captain!"

Bashir wasn't frightened. He had experienced death uncountable times in his Pah-wraith hell. What more could Weyoun do to him?

But then he realized his chest hurt. And his head hurt. And the bare metal deck was icy cold.

He opened his eyes. A single fusion lamp, almost exhausted, provided the only light.

He was still in the storeroom.

But Weyoun and Obanak and the other Bajoran were not. They had vanished, along with most of the crates.

I've shifted, Bashir thought.

His aches and pains forgotten, Bashir jumped to his feet. If Jadzia had interpreted Sisko's message properly, then he should be on the station sometime *after* the Cardassians withdrew.

Bashir took the fusion lamp from the bulkhead and peered into the corners of the storeroom, searching for any sign of his radio or tricorder. Nothing.

But that couldn't stop him from creating a plan. First, he had to sneak up to Ops to set up a radio link. Then he had to beg, borrow, or steal a tricorder that he could set to record during the next equalization wave event.

Everything would be fine—as long as he didn't run into Obanak and Weyoun . . .

"Oh, no," he said aloud.

Weyoun would have had days, if not weeks, by now to alter events on the station. Bashir shook his head. For all he knew, with Weyoun present to reveal the existence of the Bajoran wormhole, the Cardassians might not have withdrawn at all.

Bashir headed straight for the storeroom's door, put his ear to it, then tapped it open.

The corridor beyond was also poorly lit, but empty. Judging from the corridor's size and the tight curve it followed, Bashir decided he was correct in thinking he was in the shopkeepers' storage area, one level down from the Promenade.

Entering the corridor, he turned to his right for no particular reason, then set off at an easy run until he came to a Cardassian radian indicator. The sign revealed he was beside Turboshaft 3, which told him exactly how far away his Infirmary was. Bashir decided to go there first. Homeground was always best.

During his tenure on the station, he hadn't used the storage area beneath the Infirmary, primarily for security concerns. But Bashir knew there was a narrow stairway that led up to a supply locker off his small back office, and as he climbed it now, he was relieved to see the narrow doorway hadn't been sealed. That meant that he hadn't arrived on the station *after* he had first arrived on it, because one of the first things he had had the work crews do was to block off this doorway, which they hadn't yet done. Despite the seriousness of his situation, Bashir couldn't help smiling: The confusing thought actually made some sense to him, in a time-bending sort of way.

Bashir reached the top of the narrow flight of stairs. The small door before him operated by means of a manual lever, and he pushed against it, making the door squeak open.

What would eventually become his office was littered with debris, and all the lights were out. But light from the treatment areas filtered in through the half-opened main doors.

Bashir carefully picked his way over the mounds of trash on the deck and peered out through the doors, trying to catch a glimpse of who might be on the station. If he saw any Cardassians other than Garak, he'd know he'd have to stay hidden.

But all he saw was another blinding flash of light. Not red or blue, but white.

"What're you doing back there?"

Bashir realized that he hadn't been shifted through time again. He still had twenty minutes before that could happen. Shielding his eyes with his hand, he tried to look past the blinding light to see who was addressing him.

"Get out of there," the annoyed voice repeated. "Hands where I can see them."

Bashir squeezed out through the inoperative doors and felt a moment of unreality as he found himself standing in the middle of his Infirmary as he had never seen it before—looted, trashed, and not yet even marginally cleaned up as he had seen it on his first day.

"I said, who are you?"

Relief flooded through Bashir. The Cardassians *had* left. His questioner was a Bajoran wearing an old-style militia uniform.

"Are there any Starfleet personnel onboard?" Bashir asked, blinking in the glare of the Bajoran's palm torch.

The Bajoran moved closer, keeping his torch centered on Bashir's face, specifically on the bridge of his nose.

"You're human?"

"I'm with Starfleet." Bashir guessed that would be a safe enough admission to make.

"Dressed like that?"

Bashir looked down at his trustee's rags. "I was . . . undercover."

The Bajoran muttered something that was obviously a curse but which Bashir didn't hear clearly enough to understand.

"Don't you people have any sense?" the Bajoran growled. "The Provisional Government is tying itself in knots trying to decide whether or not to invite the Federation in as observers. And the biggest thing you've got going for yourselves is that you've been neutral through the whole Occupation. But if the opposition finds out there are Federation *spies* in the system, the next thing you know, we'll be inviting the *Romulans* in to keep the peace."

Bashir's mouth went dry. If his presence here could lead to such a profound change in the timeline . . . if the *Romulans* discovered the wormhole . . . made contact with the Prophets . . . with the Dominion . . . the whole history of the galaxy and of the universe would change. And if the Romulans and the Cardassians formed an alliance and shared what they would undoubtedly learn about the wormhole and the Tears of the Prophets, it wouldn't take six years for the Red Orbs of Jalbador to be brought into alignment. It would take months.

"I'm not a spy," Bashir protested, but even he could hear the tension that thinned his voice. "I only just got here. On a . . . a fact-finding mission."

"Dressed like a Bajoran slave?" the Bajoran said suspiciously. "We all burned those clothes a week ago."

A week, Bashir reasoned rapidly. *The* Enterprise *hasn't arrived yet. Starfleet is making contingency plans in case the invitation to observe the peace is actually made.* His mind raced as he thought back to where he 'was' in the week after Withdrawal: at the medical conference on Vulcan, torn between attending a lecture to be given by Admiral McCoy himself or contacting everyone he could think of back on Earth to lobby for the position of Chief Medical Officer on the mission to Bajor, should it come to pass.

"Is there any way I can at least *talk* to someone from Starfleet?" Bashir asked, urgent. "I know I can straighten this out without . . . without harming relations between Bajor and the Federation."

Obviously, the Bajoran was a Federation sympathizer, because he now took a moment to consider Bashir's request.

"Well, they've got some huge starship standing by outside the system."

"The *Enterprise?*" Bashir asked with hope in his voice. Captain Picard would be the perfect person to tell his story to. Starfleet would listen to him.

"I think so," the Bajoran said. "It's been sending in shuttles with humanitarian aid. I could maybe talk to one of the pilots."

"That would be best," Bashir agreed quickly. "And the quieter we can keep this, and the faster I can talk with someone, the less disruptive my presence here will be."

The Bajoran lowered his palm torch. "I'll see what I can do. But I'm still going to have to take you to Security. The constable has to—"

"Odo?"

"You know him?"

Bashir didn't want to give away more than he had to. "We . . . have friends in common."

"Maybe that'll help." The Bajoran gestured with his palm torch. "Walk ahead, and don't try anything."

"I won't," Bashir promised, thinking once more that everything might still work out after all.

Until Major Kira blocked his exit, dressed in her old uniform, hands on her hips.

"What the hell is going on here?" she demanded.

"Major," Bashir said in resignation, knowing the paradox he was about to create, "my name is—"

"I don't care who you are," the major interrupted. "You keep your mouth shut until I deal with *him*." She pointed at the startled Bajoran militiaman. "Is this human your prisoner?"

"Uh . . . yes, Major."

"I don't see any restraints. I don't see your weapon drawn. I don't recall having heard anything over the security channels. Is this your idea of an arrest?"

The Bajoran's face flushed. "I thought . . . he said he was with—"

"I don't *care* what he told you. You're on security patrol. *You* round up suspects. *I* do the thinking. Is that *clear,* Mister?"

"Y-yes, sir."

Kira waved her hand at the door. "Then you go do your job, and let me do mine."

The Bajoran nodded vigorously, then bolted for the doors leading out of the Infirmary, halting abruptly when Kira put a hand on his shoulder.

"We're all new at this," she said in a low voice. "So I'll let this go without a formal report. If you don't talk about it, I won't talk about it. I don't want anyone thinking I'm getting soft. Understood?"

"Understood, sir," the Bajoran said as if he couldn't believe his good fortune. A moment later, he was gone.

"How long have you been here?" Kira asked Bashir.

So many complications filled the doctor's mind that he remained silent.

"Julian, it's me," Kira said. "I'm *your* Kira, from the *Defiant.* Six years from now. From the end of the universe."

There was only one thing to do, and Bashir did it. He reached out and hugged her. Hard.

But Kira pushed him away. "Things are very complicated. We have to talk quickly. How long have you been in this time?"

"Ten minutes?"

"How much longer do you have?"

"At least ten more," Bashir said, still marveling at the sudden turn of events. "I came in before the Withdrawal. Weyoun told Obanak that he was the Emissary."

"I know," Kira said with a grimace. "Weyoun is somehow anchored in this timeframe. He doesn't shift back and forth, so he has a lot more time than we do."

"Time to do what?"

"To get the Red Orb from Terrell's lab. The captain and I are trying to get it, too. But . . . in the past, before the Day of Withdrawal, the lab is under heavy guard, completely unapproachable. And in this timeframe, it's abandoned."

"Then we'll have to get in *on* the Day of Withdrawal!" Bashir said. "That's the key time signal we're getting on the *Defiant*. So that's when the Orb effect must be strongest—the timeframe we're all settling toward."

"You've been talking with Dax?" Kira asked.

Bashir nodded. "Look, I need a tricorder and a radio. Jadzia needs readings from a timeshift event, and then I have to be able to radio back the results."

Kira frowned. "I've only got about five minutes left before I go back." She hit her communicator. "Major Kira to Ops. I need emergency transport for two from the Cardassian Infirmary to Cargo Bay 4. Lock on my signal."

A Bajoran voice answered. "Did you mean emergency transport *to* the Infirmary?"

"I meant what I said!" Kira snapped. "There might be Cardassian saboteurs still on the station. Now, *energize!*" She gave Bashir a rueful smile as she took his arm. "Back then, I really was a b—"

But the transporter effect muffled whatever else she was about to say.

A moment later, Bashir and Kira materialized in Cargo Bay 4.

"—wasn't I?" Kira concluded.

Merely smiling, Bashir offered no comment. Instead, he directed his attention to the gleaming shipping containers that surrounded them, containers marked with the Seal of the Federation. He found what he was looking for at once. General science kits designed to help in the construction of emergency shelters, to dig for water, to check for unexploded ordnance.

Kira helped him shift the crates and tear open the science kits. "You find a tricorder," Kira told him. "I'll check out the communication gear."

Bashir located and pulled out a Mark VII tricorder, which he hoped would be a satisfactory replacement for the Mark X Jadzia had given him. At the same time, Kira cracked open a communications package and brought out a Vulcan radio wand. She passed the thin green cylinder to him. It was no more than ten centimeters long. "This is intended for ground-to-ground communications, but since you only have to broadcast for under a hundred klicks . . ."

"It'll do," Bashir said, satisfied. "Where's the captain?"

Before Kira could reply, a familiar voice crackled from her combadge.

"This is Major Kira to Cargo Bay 4. What the hell is going on down there, and who the hell is saying she's me?"

Kira looked at Bashir, grabbed hold of his arms to emphasize what she had to say. "Julian, this is important. We will *not* change the timeline. Understand? It is crucial that you do nothing that will change how events took place the first time."

Bashir was puzzled. He didn't understand.

"I said," the other Major Kira demanded, *"who's down there?"*

"But Weyoun must be changing things," Bashir said.

Kira shook her head. "As far as we can tell, he's keeping a low profile, too. All he wants is that Red Orb in Terrell's lab."

"That's it," the other Kira said over the combadge. *"Whoever you are, you are now encased in forcefields and under transporter lock. If you have weapons, I'd strongly advise you to throw them away and put your hands on your head."*

"Why can't we change the timeline?" Bashir asked *his* Kira. "What do you know?"

With a troubled look, the major gave Bashir's upper arms a squeeze. "Julian, trust me. It's the Will of—"

She looked to the side. Three columns of transporter light sparkled into being.

"Just trust me!" Kira said.

Then, once again, Bashir was blinded by light. And this time, it was red.

CHAPTER 15

THE UNIVERSE SEETHED, chaotic, and for Garak, there could be no greater pleasure than to study that confusion for the sole purpose of teasing out such random bits of order as the cultivated mind might discover.

The stuff of a sublime opera here. An intricately crafted novel there. The delicate composition of a landscape captured on an unknown artist's canvas. Even the meticulously orchestrated sequence of political upheaval following a flawless assassination.

All order was fleeting, which is why, Garak supposed, it brought such joy to civilized beings. And joy without despair was, of course, utterly meaningless, for one could not exist without the other.

That was why each snick of his scissors was as deeply satisfying to Garak as the pruning he had undertaken in the gardens of Romulus—pruning both that world's indigenous flora *and* fauna, as it were. To take a formless plane of cloth, each portion of it identical to the rest, and by a precise series of cuts and stitches create a three-dimensional structure that would, for a moment at least in the affairs of Cardassians, define his world's epitome of style and culture and civilization, was, for Garak, a way to achieve profound personal peace. Surely the ancient explorers of Cardassia's past could have felt no greater happiness upon first glimpsing the beacon of a lighthouse on the shores of the homeland to which they returned. So it was with Garak and the simple craft, the exquisite art of the tailor.

Thus, it was with contentment that Garak was engaged in cutting a particularly fine bolt of Remarlian wool to make a handsome hunting jacket when the chime of his tailor shop's door sounded, and he rose from his work to meet whatever new visitor, customer, perhaps even appreciator of art, whom chaos had selected to cross his threshold this day.

At first glance, the stranger was commonplace, as from the plain cut of his traveler's robe it was apparent he was a Cardassian civilian of limited means. But that was not surprising, given that fully eighty percent of Terok Nor's inhabitants were of Garak's species. It was only on rare, fortunate occasions that a glinn made arrangements to bring by one of the slight, pale-skinned Bajoran females that the Cardassian command staff seemed to hold in such high regard. It was always a particular challenge for Garak, and one he enjoyed for its novelty, to fashion flattering gowns for beings with such pathetically thin necks, unsettlingly smooth skin, and ill-hued complexions that warred with any reasonable color palette, so unlike the universal harmony of pure Cardassian gray.

"Welcome to my shop," Garak said with a gracious bow despite the poor amusement value the stranger offered. "May I offer you some refreshment? A cup of Linian tea, perhaps?"

Most delightfully, the stranger did do something quite surprising then. Without removing his hood, he glanced furtively over his shoulder, as if looking out to the Promenade to see if anyone were following him.

Garak felt a flash of anticipation. He did appreciate a day that began with an unexpected touch, and actual intrigue would go a long way to brighten his mood.

Eager to make his mysterious visitor at home, Garak moved quickly past him to lock the door and tune the windows to their holographic display mode.

"As a matter of fact," he said cheerfully, "I was just going to close for a mid-morning break. Perhaps you might be more comfortable if you knew no one could disturb us. Or see into the shop, for that matter."

Garak turned his back to the sealed door and smiled in welcome to his visitor. And then it took all his powers of self-control to keep that smile in place as his visitor lifted his hood to reveal his identity.

"You're right," the second Garak said, "it would be best if we weren't disturbed."

Garak the tailor paused for the briefest of moments and then asked the most obvious question. "Odo? Is that you? If it is, I am most impressed with your new mastery of fine detail."

"Alas," the new Garak replied, "that *would* be the simplest explanation. Unfortunately, in this case, we are facing something much more complex."

"And that would be?"

"Exactly what it seems to be," the new Garak explained. "I *am* you."

"If that's the case, then you'll understand my skepticism."

"Oh, absolutely. I know exactly how I would respond to such a situation, so I am certain that is exactly how you are responding."

Garak the tailor felt his heart rate increase. It was most unlikely that the duplicate across from him was really himself, but what if he was? What a thrillingly puzzling conundrum *that* would be.

"If you know how I will respond," the tailor said carefully, "then you must know what my first suggestion will be."

The visitor returned the tailor's smile. "In the back room, third shelf, beside the tea jars. There is a dimensional safe with a . . . shall we say, medical kit."

The tailor beamed. "I *am* impressed. Though, of course, there is a flaw in what you're proposing."

"Correct," the visitor said. "If I know about the medical kit, then it's very likely I have altered its contents in order to return a false DNA match."

The tailor nodded, entertained beyond measure. "And is there a way out of that difficulty?"

"I believe so. For I am not just you, I am you from the future."

Outwardly, Garak gave no reaction. But his heart wasn't just racing now, it was fluttering. "You'll forgive me for taking a moment to try to organize the . . . the . . ."

"Possibilities?"

"My thought exactly. The possibilities of the situation that has brought you here. *If*—"

"What I'm saying is true."

"Of course."

"Naturally."

The tailor regarded the visitor with narrowed eyes, secretly hoping that he truly was who he said he was and not some tired psychological gambit initiated by the—

"And no," the visitor said, "this has nothing to do with the Obsidian Order."

The tailor grinned as he held up a finger. "Which is precisely what someone from the Order would say!"

"Which is why I must insist you check my DNA and my chroniton levels. And in the meantime, I can think of a few questions which only I could answer, and I suggest you ask them."

Finding the visitor's suggestion to be reasonable, Garak the tailor led the way to the back room of his store. He paused on the threshold of the doorway. "But then, if you're me from the future, you must already have a memory of this meeting."

Garak the visitor shrugged. "That is, shall we say, where things might get confusing."

"I certainly hope so," Garak the tailor replied. Then he entered his back room and went directly to his dimensional safe, withdrew the interrogation implements which could also, in a pinch, double as a fairly complete emergency medical kit, and began the analysis of his visitor's molecular and temporal structure.

During the procedures, the two Garaks continued to test each other. They began with the memories of a certain young upperclassman at the Bamarren Institute who had been most generous in her enthusiastic initiation of Garak into certain adult pleasures. Then, on a more somber note, there were the hurtful contents of the final encrypted communication from his father. And on the professional side of things, the exact and inspired molecular modification to the untraceable poison used on the Gentleman Usher to the Romulan Assembly.

Before ten minutes had passed, Garak the visitor was rolling down the sleeve of his tunic, having not complained about any of the necessary tissue excisions. *"I would be convinced by now."*

Garak the tailor nodded, even as he struggled to think of any detail or additional test he might have overlooked. "Transporter accident?" he asked. "I have heard such things are possible."

"But would that explain the chroniton levels showing I am from six years in your future?"

Garak the tailor sighed, accepting defeat—for the present.

"That's the right decision," Garak the visitor said. "Reserve final judgment, but go along with the moment, see where it leads."

"I must say I find it tremendously refreshing to speak with someone—"

"—who understands exactly how you think?"

Garak the tailor offered his visitor a chair as he took one himself. "As your host, you must allow *me* to begin," he said. "Frankly, I must admit, as I try to think of what might possibly inspire me to travel back into my past and speak to myself, I can only imagine the most grave of events."

Garak the visitor nodded, his mood now one of deep sadness.

"The survival of Cardassia?" Cardassia's defeat was the gravest event Garak the tailor could imagine. Nothing meant more to him than his world and his people, despite the flawed leadership that currently blighted both.

"Even graver, I'm afraid," the visitor replied. "Though I have seen . . . I have seen Cardassia Prime laid waste and our people . . . our people erased from existence."

The tailor leaned forward, eyes wide. "All this in six years?"

"Longer than that," the visitor allowed. "But six years from now, I—you—*we* will be afforded a chance to look even further into the future. And it is a future that cannot be allowed to come to pass."

"And the answer is here?" the tailor asked, greatly curious. "In this time?"

"In a sense."

"Do you have any memory of this meeting in your past?"

The visitor shook his head.

"I'm no expert in such things," the tailor said, "but does that not mean that you are setting in motion an alternate timeline?"

Now the visitor leaned forward and lowered his voice conspiratorially. "There are those with whom I am working today—*my* today," he added, "who have despaired of saving the . . . the universe—"

Garak the tailor felt the unfamiliar thrill of shock at that first mention of the catastrophe that lurked in his future.

"—*without* changing the timeline."

"But you have not despaired of that?" the tailor asked, matching his visitor's low voice and intense manner.

"As long as I see that I have a choice in the matter," the visitor replied. "For example, I'm sure that if you think of it, the very fact that I have returned to you from six years in the future informs you that you will survive the next six years."

The tailor nodded, grateful. "I have taken heart from that."

"Not that there haven't been a few close calls," the visitor warned.

"Then I will have survived *and* not have been bored," the tailor said with a smile.

"And six years from now, our Cardassia is not in the finest state it could be."

"War?" the tailor asked, not the least bit surprised.

"Several, I'm afraid."

"With what you know, couldn't we stop them before they start?"

"But that's my quandary," the visitor said with a slight frown. "I *know* how the next six years transpire. I *know* that if I am successful in undertaking an extremely difficult task in this time, the next six years won't change, yet the future I have seen beyond that will. And Cardassia and the universe will be saved."

"I think I understand," the tailor said slowly. "On the other hand, you could take drastic measures now, change the outcome of the next six years, and by your knowledge of the future make Cardassia stronger and more secure than it ever has been before. Yet if you choose that course of action, you can't be certain that the disaster you saw even further in the future might not come to pass through some other means."

Garak the visitor nodded appreciatively. "I couldn't have said it better myself."

Then both Garaks laughed lightly, together, in perfect synchronicity.

The moment passed. Then the tailor asked, "Six years from now . . . are we happy?"

The visitor folded his hands, looked down. "When have we ever been?"

"But we do live in hope, do we not?"

The visitor nodded. "Always. How can we do anything else?"

"A final question, then," the tailor said. "If we make no changes in this time, six years from now, as best as you can see the new future you'll create, will Cardassia survive?"

The visitor studied him before answering, truly considering the question.

"Yes," he said at last. "Our people face a most challenging set of circumstances, led by rulers who have lost their way, who have chosen the path of expediency. But . . . over the next six years, we will make many new friends. And . . . quite unexpectedly, in their way, they will care for Cardassia's fate as well. With the help of those friends, I do believe that Cardassia will return to her rightful glory in time. Though at great cost. Great cost."

The tailor studied the visitor, carefully considering him and his story, then got to his feet, his decision made. "So what may I do for you—for us?" the tailor said. "Bearing in mind that I trust your judgment as much as if it were my own. Above all else, Cardassia must survive as a *great* world, not merely survive."

The visitor got to his feet, his decision apparently made as well. He reached into the open interrogation kit, withdrew an ampule of straw-colored liquid, and held it out to the tailor.

The tailor understood at once. "I had already guessed that was the other possible reason you have no memory of this meeting. Not because it takes place in an alternate timeline but because . . ." The tailor accepted the ampule from the visitor—from himself. ". . . because the memory of it no longer exists."

"But you're not to take the inhibitor yet," the visitor said. He slipped a hand into his robe and withdrew a padd. "I've recorded a series of instructions I would like you to follow in the next few days."

The tailor studied the padd, didn't like what he saw. "This is Klingon, is it not?"

"I arrived here from a stolen vessel," the visitor explained. "One makes do with the tools at hand." He pressed the padd controls that accessed his instructions. "Try your best to accomplish everything, but whatever else happens, take the inhibitor *before* the Withdrawal begins."

"So we *do* withdraw?" The tailor had seen the signs of Cardassia's unrest, but to his understanding, those signs might just as well have foretold a further escalation of the noble attempt to bring peace to the fractious Bajorans.

"We withdraw," the visitor confirmed. "Very soon, now."

"And what happens then? The Bajorans destroy themselves?"

"Let us just say that your life—our life—will become more interesting than you could possibly imagine. For the first year, I promise you, you will live in a state of perpetual delighted surprise."

"How pleasant." The tailor looked at the ampule. "Tell me, six years from now, will the technique exist to reverse the inhibitor? I would enjoy having some memory of this encounter."

The visitor seemed never to have considered that possibility before. "I'll look into it. You will come to make a very good friend in the weeks ahead. A human, of all things."

The tailor rocked back in surprise. "A human? A *friend?*"

The visitor held up a cautioning hand. "Now, now. He has been genetically engineered to enhance his intellect. I assure you he is the equal of any Cardassian—a condition which I must say puzzled me for the first few years of our acquaintance, until I learned the truth. However, he is quite clever in medical matters, so I shall put the task to him. I, too, share your desire to remember this meeting."

"How fascinating to remember it from both sides." The tailor started for the door, then stopped as he saw that his visitor did not follow. "Am I wrong to assume that you will have to leave soon?"

"I'll take my leave another way," the visitor said.

The tailor guessed his counterpart referred to a transporter of some kind. "Soon?"

"Any minute, I think. Neither the process nor the timing is completely under my control."

The tailor nodded. "I look forward to the day I will understand what you mean."

"It's well worth the wait," the visitor assured him. "I envy you your—"

And the visitor was gone. Simply and abruptly. Without so much as a flash of quantum dissolution or even subtle harmonic hum.

"How absolutely fascinating," Garak said. Whatever had happened, it was not a transporter that was responsible.

He looked down at the padd he held. He pressed the activate control.

On the small device's display, an image of himself appeared. An image that spoke to him.

"There is a hidden laboratory on Terok Nor," his future self said calmly, "and within it is a most remarkable artifact. An artifact that represents the gravest of dangers to our world and our people . . ."

Once again, Garak the tailor sat down to listen in his empty back storeroom. He had his own complete attention. Six years from now, it was obvious, he still knew how to tell a story.

But what Garak was about to find out from himself was whether that story could have a new ending.

CHAPTER 16

ODO STOOD AT the door of his office in Security, gazing out at the empty Promenade. The station was on its night cycle, so the lighting was subdued, and the only indication of activity was coming from Quark's across the way.

It was peaceful, Odo thought, and he liked Deep Space 9 this way. The station was, in a very real sense, his adopted home. And he knew from the time display on his desk that in less than a week it would be gone, destroyed by the red wormhole.

Unless he took action in the next thirty minutes. But what action?

His brief peace vanished suddenly as a small cloaked figure stepped out from a turbolift, looked both ways, then quickly ran for Security.

Odo felt a momentary twinge of panic. Right now, he knew, the Odo of *this* time was in Kira's quarters but would soon receive an urgent call from his second-in-command, delivering the preliminary findings on the cause of Dal Nortron's death. Odo remembered that only minutes after that, he had come up to check on his 'prisoner,' Quark.

The Ferengi barkeep, for now under protective custody, was in a holding cell behind him. But before morning came, he would be under legitimate arrest for Nortron's murder. Odo's specialists had just not been able to identify the Pah-wraith energy Dukat had used on the Andorian for what it actually was. So Quark had been left as the only likely suspect in the murder.

Odo knew it would be simple enough to make a similar call to his other self this evening, to rouse his other self out of Kira's bed and tell the whole story of the Red Orbs, one of which, even now, was hidden in Quark's, awaiting its discovery by Sisko in just a few days.

But just where would that leave Vic, Odo asked himself, *and all the others stranded in the wormhole pocket?*

For their sakes, at least until he had had more time to consider all the possibilities, he did not want to make that call and set in motion an alternate timeline. And for the same reason, right now, he didn't want to be caught in Security by whoever was running toward it. Since the other Odo had not been in the office at this time, history might change if he were found here now.

With nowhere to run without drawing attention to himself, Odo stepped back against the textured security wall and spread himself over it, careful to duplicate every feature and still leave openings through which the security scan lights could continue to shine. Only the most observant eye would notice that the texture on one wall was a centimeter thicker than that on the others.

The small cloaked figure raced up the steps to Security doors, pressed his face against a transparent section, hands cupped to either side.

Then the figure whispered a single word: "Odo?"

Odo was puzzled. Whoever this was seemed to be in urgent need to find him. Yet the changeling had no memory of anyone having sought him out at this time. As he recalled it, Dal Nortron's murder investigation had been the only business of concern that he had undertaken that final week.

"Odo," the figure said more loudly, barely muffled through the doors. "It's me!"

With that, the figure pulled back his hood for just a moment.

But the moment was long enough.

Odo poured from the wall and re-formed into his humanoid shape, swiftly opening the doors and hauling Quark inside.

"What do you think you're doing?" the changeling said harshly. He began dragging Quark toward the holding cells. "You're supposed to be under protective custody."

But Quark struggled and slapped both hands against Odo. "You moron! That was a month ago! I'm *me!*" He pointed ahead through the door leading to the cells. "Not *him!*"

And Odo stopped abruptly, one hand still gripping Quark's arm, as six meters away another Quark slept in his holding cell.

"Why did they send *you?*" Odo said in disgust, letting go of Quark's arm.

The Ferengi backed off at once, indignantly straightening his cloak. "Garak's at another version of the station, six years back, trying to get Sisko and Kira and everyone from the *Defiant* back to this time."

Odo stared at Quark, as if having to translate from the original Ferengi traders' tongue himself, and not rely on a universal translator. Quite clearly, other things had been going on while he had been swinging back and forth through time.

"Are you able to explain *any* of this?" Odo demanded, not really expecting a useful answer from the Ferengi.

But just then, from across the holding room, the other Quark suddenly cried out, *"Moogie!"* and sat up in his Cardassian sleeping ledge so suddenly he slammed his head against a utility shelf.

Odo started as he heard the dull thump echo in the bulkheads. From his experiences when he had been imprisoned in solid form, he knew that had to have hurt.

The Quark of the past sat up on the side of his ledge, rubbing his head, cursing colorfully to himself.

The current Quark tugged on Odo's arm. "Unless you want to ask *yourself* what's new, let's go!"

Quickly comprehending their situation, Odo grabbed Quark's arm and pushed the Ferengi out of Security onto the Promenade. The changeling understood that his own past self must already be on his way up here. He remembered walking in on Quark as the Ferengi stood in front of the replicator slot.

At the same moment as the doors closed behind him and Quark, Odo heard the hum of a turbolift arriving. Though he could not recall having seen anyone suspicious that night as he returned to his office, the changeling took no chances on untimely discovery. Slightly changing his form to something more feminine, he slipped an arm around Quark and strolled onto the quieter half of the Promenade without looking back.

As soon as he and Quark had passed by Garak's shop, closed for the evening, and were beyond the Shipping Office, out of sight of Security, Odo felt Quark twist out of his grip. The Ferengi stared at him in equal parts fascination and horror as Odo returned his body to its usual male form.

"Odo, sometimes you frighten me."

"I assure you," Odo said, "the feeling is mutual. Now, how much time has passed since I left the *Boreth?*"

"An hour, maybe. Garak was all set to beam over and help you out with Dukat—" Quark suddenly looked up and down the Promenade. "Where *is* Dukat, by the way?"

Odo scanned the Promenade as well. The last thing he needed was for one of his security officers to come across him talking with Quark here, while he was also talking with Quark in his office. He pointed over toward the barber shop. "This way. And I don't know what happened to Dukat. He beamed over with me, tried to put me back in an illusion of Pah-wraith hell, then murdered Dal Nortron."

"Ah ha!" Quark exclaimed. "I told you so!" The indignant Ferengi jabbed a finger into Odo's chest for emphasis.

Reflexively, Odo lessened his molecular cohesion in reaction to violent contact and Quark's finger sank deep within the changeling's torso.

"Ewww, I keep forgetting," the Ferengi said, cringing at the sucking sound that accompanied the reemergence of his finger.

Odo pulled the barkeep into the entrance of the barber shop and punched in his security override code on the doorplate. "Keep it down, Quark."

"Anyway. Told you so," Quark said sulkily as he needlessly shook his finger to cleanse it. "Arresting *me* for murder . . ."

The door to the barber shop slipped open, and Odo shoved Quark inside. As a general rule, there was little in the station's barber shop and beauty salon that was worth stealing, so it had one of the simplest security setups on the Promenade. Most important, Odo knew it had no interior sensors that would record his presence.

"Then what happened?" Quark demanded. *"After* you found out that I was innocent—just like I told you."

"Look," Odo said, "I don't have much time in this . . . timeframe, and I'm guessing you don't, either."

The Ferengi scowled. "Oh, right. Sisko's radio message talked about that, all of us jumping back and forth in time whenever one of those waves goes over the ship. I think O'Brien's just about figured out what the captain was talking about."

"What do you mean, 'figured out'?"

"Figured out whether or not we'll be yanked back to the *Boreth* when the last wave hits or left where we are in the past." Confusion twisted Quark's face. "I mean, in the present. Or . . . or . . . oh, wherever it is we are when it—"

"Quark, just tell me what O'Brien *thinks* will happen."

"Well, supposedly, we'll be okay *if* no one changes the timeline for the places we're in. The Chief mentioned something about more 'temporal inertia' or something . . . I don't know. But the important thing, Odo, is if we change anything and an alternate timeline splits off, we're in trouble. O'Brien says we won't stay with the new timeline."

Odo frowned. "We'll go back to the ship?"

"Not exactly. I mean, we do, but we get there just in time to . . . to evaporate into *nothingness*. No, it's even worse than that. The Chief says if we somehow cause that new timeline, there won't even *be* any more nothingness. Talk about the story of my life."

Odo checked out the silent, darkened shop. Past the hair dryers, scale buffers, and cosmetic replicators, the narrow windows offered a restricted view of the still-deserted Promenade. "Does the Chief have a plan?"

"He thinks he does." Quark sighed heavily. "Unfortunately, my idiot brother is helping him with it, so—"

"Quark, what *is* the plan?"

"Okay, see if this makes sense to you." The Ferengi reached under his cloak and brought out a padd. As Quark rattled off his explanation, Odo listened carefully, trying to find the pattern in the events.

"When the *Boreth* fell into one of the wormholes, just before they merged, it somehow established a link with that moment just when the wormhole opened on the station. In my bar, I might add. And from what the Chief got out of the captain's message, he says it looks like the *Defiant*'s also got a timelink to DS9, back around the time when the Cardassians withdrew from Bajor."

"Terrell must have been conducting experiments with her Red Orb back then," Odo said.

"Whatever," Quark said, hurrying on with his account. "Anyway, Sisko and Kira have to deal with Weyoun, so O'Brien sent Garak to the timeframe they're in to help them out."

"Are you saying O'Brien can beam us back to another time?"

"Not *us*, Quark said in a tone suggesting the changeling was a Pakled. "Anyone on the *Boreth*. The Chief . . . triangular . . . ized the hyper-something-or-other radio whatsit from Sisko. And that let O'Brien lock onto . . . another DS9. The one that's linked to the *Defiant*."

Inwardly, Odo marveled at O'Brien's ingenuity. Outwardly, in the interests of time, he confined himself to a simple question of Quark: "So what happens next?"

Quark rechecked his padd, ran a black-nailed finger over the text until— "Here it is. Garak gets word to Sisko and Kira. Sisko and Kira transmit messages to the *Defiant*." Quark looked up. "We can only communicate in one direction, y'see."

"Believe me, I get the point, Quark. Go on."

"So everyone from the *Defiant* beams to *this* station, the one that the *Boreth*'s linked to, and—"

Odo interrupted the Ferengi. "What about Sisko, Kira, and Garak?"

"*And* Weyoun," Quark said, picking up where he left off.

"Well? What happens to them in the past?"

"O'Brien's still working on that. I believe that if all else fails, they turn themselves into the Department of Temporal Investigations and . . . sit out the next six years. Which, I don't mind telling you, is a real waste of an opportunity in the interplanetary futures market. I mean—"

"That's enough, Quark. Now, specifically, what are you and I supposed to do?"

"Well, the first thing is, you and I don't change a thing. We have to stay linked to this timeframe."

"Up to what point?"

"Uh, O'Brien's still working on that, too."

"And then what?"

Quark looked down at his padd again. "Second thing . . . second thing . . . oh, here—make sure Dukat doesn't change any-thing, either."

Odo turned away from the Ferengi, looked around the shop for a time readout, concerned that he didn't have much more time here. "That might be difficult. Dukat doesn't seem to be affected by the equalization waves. I can't be sure what he's been doing here while I've been bouncing back and forth."

Quark looked at him anxiously. *"Is* anything different from what you remember?"

"Not so far."

"Then . . . maybe . . . maybe he's gone off to Cardassia or something."

"Two Gul Dukats," Odo said darkly. "I'm sure *that* won't affect the timeline."

"I'm just the messenger," Quark said, self-pity etched on his broad face. "None of this would have happened if—"

A flash of red light blinded Odo. By now, the changeling knew what it was and what had happened.

When his vision returned a few moments later, he was still standing in the barber shop, which now appeared to have been abandoned during business hours. All of its lights were on, Bajoran music played softly in the background, and the strong, acrid aroma of over-brewed *raktajino* cut sharply through the shop's varied chemical scents and perfumes.

Odo stepped out of the barber shop onto the Promenade, looked up, and saw the blazing cauldron of red wormhole energy beyond the viewports. Once again, he had jumped forward to a timeframe *after* the station's destruction. The changeling hesitated, tempted to go to the other side of the Promenade to see if Quark's had been completely restored by this time, but just as quickly thought better of the idea. It wouldn't do to encounter Vic before the moment the holographic singer met this timeframe's Odo for the first time.

Instead, the changeling sought out the nearest turbolift and selected his next destination: Ops. As the turbolift rose to the deck of Ops, Odo discovered that it, too, was abandoned, though every piece of equipment appeared to be in perfect working order.

Odo stepped out of the turbolift and headed for Jadzia's science station. Its sensor display was frozen at the moment the first gravitational anomalies were recorded in Quark's. Seated before the console, Odo studied the fixed display for a moment, then decided that the sensor's readings described DS9 as the station had existed the moment *before* it had begun to deform. But why that should be, Odo had no answer. During his earlier conversation with Vic, which would actually take place *later,* the changeling recalled concluding that there was an underlying reality to this destroyed version—this illusion of destruction—of the station. But who or what had created that illusion, Odo did not know.

It took a few minutes more of silent contemplation before the changeling abruptly remembered that in twenty minutes or so, he'd swing back through time again and reappear at this spot *before* the station's destruction. The realization spurred him on to setting his next priority: finding an out-of-the-way place to wait, so that when he reappeared in the past, he would do so without witnesses who could then ask bothersome, perhaps potentially history-changing questions.

Returning to the turbolift, the changeling reviewed what Quark had told him, and he felt inordinately pleased that his own purely emotional reluctance to change the timeline had been backed up by O'Brien's careful consideration.

He halted before entering the turbolift again, remembering something else Quark had mentioned: Sisko and Kira had used radio to communicate with the *Defiant,* and it was those signals O'Brien had intercepted.

Odo turned back into Ops, approached the equipment replicator, and entered his security codes to order a Bajoran militia ground-to-ground radio communicator. The replicator obediently produced and delivered a device the size of a padd, though about twice as thick. Included with the device was an equipment belt and holster. Odo retrieved the radio and its accessories and carried them back to a library terminal, where he called up the setting for a Starfleet emergency-channel radio frequency. He adjusted the communicator accordingly.

Two minutes later, the changeling was safely ensconced in a dead-end Jefferies tube above the main habitat ring, waiting for the next wave to strike. Only then did Odo begin his transmittal to tell his story.

He wondered who might be listening—not just in space but in time.

• • •

On the bridge of the *Defiant,* Jake turned to Jadzia, and though they both opened their mouths to speak at the same time, Worf beat them to it.

"That's Odo!"

At once, the Klingon was out of his command chair, heading for Jadzia's communication console. Since receiving Sisko's first message, the Trill had made refinements to the *Defiant's* antenna simulators, and the message Jake heard was the clearest one yet, with far less static and interference than the first.

". . . *right now, I am in . . . as it exists after being swallowed by the red . . . I have been here once . . . later time. I have also been in the station prior to its . . . first visit, Dukat killed Dal Nortron, but . . . not seen him since. In my last visit to . . . Quark, who told me Sisko and . . . on the station around the time of the Day of Withdrawal. From what they've said and from . . . O'Brien has concluded that as long as we do not change the timeline, we . . . on the station when the final equalization waves destroy what pockets of space-time remain in the wormhole pocket. . . . Garak back to Sisko and Kira's time, . . . wants everyone from . . . Boreth to beam over to the station of this time at once.*

"*This is Odo. Right now, I am . . .*"

The speakers went dead. A moment later, the *Defiant* shuddered as another equalization wave passed over it.

Jake saw Jadzia and Worf exchange a glance.

"I think we got the whole message," Jadzia said.

"Does that mean everyone else is all right?" Jake asked her. "I mean, everyone on the *Boreth?*"

"Sounds like it," the Trill said. She made further adjustments to her console. "And it sounds as if O'Brien's making more headway than I am."

"Does his hypothesis sound reasonable?" Worf asked.

"That we not change the timeline?" Jadzia said. "I'm not sure. I mean, if we do absolutely *nothing* to change the past, then the future will unfold as we saw it, and everything will come back into this same endless loop. So, assuming that we *can* all get back to the station before it was destroyed, we're going to have to do *something.*"

To Jake, it was as if a small photon torpedo had burst in front of him. The answer was that clear to him. At least, it seemed to be.

"This is the same thing that Nog and Admiral Picard faced!" he said excitedly.

Jake's sudden assurance wilted in the blast of intense scrutiny that Worf and Jadzia now directed at him.

"Uh, you know," Jake faltered. "Time traveling to the past to make a change that won't show up until *after* the point at which the journey to the past took place. So the past won't be changed, only the future."

Jadzia and Worf turned their attention from Jake to each other.

"He's right, Worf," Jadzia said. "If we can do something that results in history unfolding just as it did up to the point at which we traveled into the future, and then see to it that we return to that time-line even an instant later, we won't have changed *anything* in the past. So if Chief O'Brien is right—and he usually is—we'll stay in 2375, and not in the wormhole."

"But the station will still be destroyed?" Worf asked.

Jadzia nodded reluctantly. "We can't press the reset button on that one, I'm afraid. If we change the past, we die."

Worf looked as dejected as his mate but for a different reason. "But if we do *not* change the past, then the universe dies."

"Which is why," Jadzia concluded, "we'll have to choose the moment we change something with . . . great precision."

"You know . . ." Jake suddenly said aloud without thinking, then stopped as quickly as he had begun.

"Continue," Worf said, the suggestion issued Klingon-fashion, as an order.

But Jake only shook his head, feeling foolish, struck by the ridiculousness of what he had been about to say. "It's nothing. Really."

Jadzia gave him an encouraging look. "Jake, this isn't the time to hold back. The worst that can happen is that we'll listen to you, then go on to another idea."

Jake sighed and steeled himself for ridicule. The Trill scientist was right. How could a minute's worth of embarrassment compare to the end of the universe? "Okay. Before . . . before any of this happened, the Orbs and . . ." He saw Worf's brow begin to furrow, and he picked up the pace. "I was working on a new novel. *The Ferengi Connection?*"

"Time *is* of the essence," Jadzia advised calmly, even as Worf grunted his impatience.

"The point is, for the heist to work and Quark and Morn—uh, for

Higgs and Fermion, the bad guys—to get away, they had to set up a diversion. So what they did was, they rigged a runabout to take off into the wormhole, so that Odo—uh, Eno—would chase after them, but they actually hid under the runabout pad and didn't go anywhere until after Eno had gone into the wormhole, too."

"And your point would be?" Worf asked.

"We do the same thing. Get back to the station just before it's destroyed, then hide." Jake held up his hand to cut off Worf's almost immediate rejection of his idea. "Not on the station, Commander Worf. On a *ship*. And we don't come out until *after* the station's been destroyed. That way, the timeline we're connected to now doesn't change, but we'll be in a position to stop the future we saw by warning Starfleet about the Ascendancy."

Jadzia and Worf looked at each other once more, and again Jake sensed the strange current of unspoken communication between the two.

"Check our logs to see if you can find a suitable ship in range of DS9 on the day it was destroyed," Worf said.

Jadzia nodded, then glanced up at Jake. "A fallback plan," she explained.

Not being privy to the secret mode of communication Jadzia and Worf appeared to share, Jake didn't understand. "Why a fallback?"

"If it is in *our* best interests not to change the past," Worf said, "then we must assume that it will be Dukat's and Weyoun's intention to do the opposite."

"Which means," Jadzia said as she completed Worf's assessment, "we have to be prepared for making drastic changes of our own. Assuming we can actually figure out how to get ourselves into the *Boreth*'s timeframe."

Jake felt Worf's and Jadzia's eyes upon him, measuring, wondering if he truly understood now.

He did. He met their gazes unflinchingly. If the only way to save the universe was to change the timeline, then change the timeline they must. Even if the result would be their own deaths.

Jadzia had already faced that decision when she had chosen to remain aboard the *Defiant.*

Jake hoped he could face his own decision as bravely.

He also hoped he wouldn't have to make it.

CHAPTER 17

BASHIR GRUNTED as he slammed his shins into a dark shipping crate.

He was still in Cargo Bay 4, though it was almost empty now, without a trace of Starfleet supplies.

The woman still gripping his arms, squeezed them, twisted him around.

"Julian?"

"Major!"

"I was holding on to you," Kira marveled, staring at her hands on his arms. That's what must have done it." She beamed at him. "We're in phase! The two of us!"

Bashir wasn't certain what she meant, but Kira dispensed with his confusion as she told him about the first trips back and forth which she and Sisko had taken. "The captain started thinking about what was happening to us as if we were on a pendulum, swinging back and forth," Kira said. "In the beginning, we were so far out on the end of the swing that we weren't keeping in step with everything that was around us. So the first time we arrived, people couldn't see us. But the more often we got caught in the back-and-forth, the more in phase we became. And that just continued until it was as if we finally belonged here."

The major's last words provoked a sudden memory in Bashir. He looked down at his tricorder—it had accompanied him on the transport through time as well.

Even better, he had remembered to switch it to record mode.

"I've got the readings!" He held up the green cylindrical Vulcan radio. "I've got to send them to Dax!"

Kira's response was to hold out her hand. "Give me your jacket." She pointed to her uniform. "We've gone back. I can't wear this out there."

"Of course," Bashir said, and quickly slipped out of his tattered trustee's coat. "But wouldn't you be better getting rid of the uniform?"

Kira pulled the jacket over her shoulders. "In twenty minutes or so, I'll need it again, when we get swept back to the other side of the Day of Withdrawal." She started for the main cargo bay doors. "Let's move it," she said, without waiting to see if he would follow. He did.

"Move it where?" Bashir asked.

"Dax thought the original radios we had would work best if we used them by a viewport. We should be able to get over to one of the ore-transfer docks from here without running into too many Cardassians."

Bashir preferred not to think what running into *any* Cardassians might mean to the timeline. Nor did he wish to think of how his and Kira's presence here and now could do anything *except* change the past. But then it hit him, and he stopped in mid-stride with one thought churning his stomach: *They had already failed.*

"Major, wait!"

Kira stopped just as she was about to open the main cargo bay door.

"We might already have altered the timeline," Bashir said.

"How?" Kira demanded, alarm widening her dark eyes.

"Just a moment ago, when you called yourself on your combadge. Do you remember that having happened? That someone impersonated you?"

Kira looked troubled, as if Bashir had brought up an unwelcome memory. "Julian, that week before the *Enterprise* was finally invited to the station, this place was a madhouse. Sabotage. Impersonations. At least five people claiming to be in charge of the station under the orders of the Provisional Government. I was just getting over Lake flu. I don't think I slept for a week once I came up here. I was beaming everywhere, trying to do everything at once—at least, whenever the transporters were working. Which wasn't all that often."

"But do you remember someone claiming to be you, requesting transport from the Infirmary to Cargo Bay 4, and then you beaming in to find that two people had escaped from forcefield confinement?"

Kira took a quick breath. "I don't know. Maybe. I can't remember exactly."

"Because you've forgotten? Or because it never happened?"

"What's the difference? Either way, the event couldn't have had any effect on the timeline."

"What if *our* presence in the cargo bay just then made you spend time in it investigating our disappearance, when you should have been doing something else that *would* affect things?"

Bashir could see the major struggle to control the same agitation he was experiencing. "Look, Julian, either we altered the timeline or we didn't. All we can do now is get those readings to Dax!"

Bashir abandoned his argument. The major was right: They had failed, or they had not. Time, like everything else in the universe, was quantum. "Let's go," he said.

Kira opened the door, checked both directions in the corridor beyond, then ran off to the left. Bashir ran after her. Much to his surprise, they almost made it to a docking port before they met their first guard—a gorr, one of the lowest of the named ranks in the Cardassian military. Her uniform, though, clearly showed where two insignia had been removed, indicating that up till recently she had held the rank of glinn. That act of discipline, Bashir decided, could explain the grimace of ill humor that twisted the guard's face as she caught sight of what she probably thought were two Bajorans on the loose outside a designated work area.

"Transit forms, *now!*" the gorr barked at Bashir and Kira. For emphasis, she brought out her phaser.

Bashir quickly ducked his head, holding a hand to his nose as if he were in pain, hoping that the major would know what to say.

"We were robbed!" Kira wailed, cringing as she edged closer to the soldier, both hands held up to make her plea, blocking the Cardassian's view of Bashir. "A glinn took our ration rods, our idents, *and* our transit forms. He said he'd sell them back to us, but—"

The gorr shoved Kira to the side, ignoring her. She pointed her phaser at Bashir. "You! What's your problem?"

"The glinn beat him!" Kira cried. "I think his nose is broken! If we don't get to sick call, our cohort will miss its quota! And you know what Gul Dukat said last—"

"*Quiet!*" the gorr commanded. She stepped closer to Bashir. "Look at me."

Bashir gingerly bobbed his head up and down as if moving it was excruciatingly painful.

But the Cardassian soldier didn't seem to care about what a Bajoran might feel. "Put your hand down or I'll phaser it off your wrist."

Bashir lowered his hand. The gorr's attention fixed on the bridge of his nose.

"The glinn must have *crushed* his nose!" Kira sobbed. "We'll never make it back in time!" Then she rushed to Bashir to try and cradle his head in her arms.

But the gorr grabbed Kira by her hair and yanked her back, throwing her to the deck.

"You're *human?*" the Cardassian asked Bashir in amazement. She looked down at Kira, whose coat had opened in her fall. "And you're in *uniform?*" The gorr sounded as if she were about to start laughing. "I think I just won my rank back."

Bashir rapidly considered the odds. No one else was in the corridor. If he and Kira both took action at once, the guard could only get one of them. But if they were arrested and then disappeared in front of their captors, it was anybody's guess what the temporal ramifications would be.

His eyes met Kira's. He saw her almost imperceptible nod.

They would have to take the chance and—

"Oh, good, you found them," a familiar voice suddenly said. "I'll take over now."

The gorr jerked her head to the side. "What?"

Garak had just rounded the intersection and confidently approached the gorr with a pleasant smile. "You have done excellent work. These two have been eluding security patrols all day. And as you might imagine, they are wanted for questioning."

Bashir was confused. Had he and Kira previously been spotted on another swing through time? Or was Garak actually trying to save them from the gorr? The doctor quickly glanced at Kira, but from the surprised expression on her face, it seemed she was just as bewildered as he.

"Garak," the gorr said tersely, "you have no authority here."

Garak's smile faded, becoming an expression of stern reproach. "Oh, but I'm afraid I do. You see, this is not a matter of concern to the *military.*"

The gorr narrowed her eyes. "Then who is it of concern to?"

Garak locked his eyes on hers. "Do you really want to know the answer to that question? Or would you rather I report that you were most cooperative and deserving of a return to your rank?"

Bashir could see the Cardassian soldier hesitate, and it took no great insight to guess exactly what she was thinking: Of course, Garak was only a civilian tailor, but what if the rumors about him were true?

The gorr backed down. "Do you . . . do you require any assistance, sir?"

Garak's contented smile returned. "No, thank you. But I do appreciate the offer, and I will make my appreciation known. And now, if you would be so kind . . ."

Realizing she was being dismissed, the gorr promptly holstered her phaser and left.

Kira was the first to speak. "Garak, how long have you been here?"

But Garak shook his head as he produced a Cardassian tricorder from his jacket and directed it at Kira and Bashir. "I'm afraid that your chroniton levels indicate I am not the same Garak with whom you're acquainted."

Bashir was shocked and knew his voice revealed it. "But . . . you know about us?"

"As little as possible. Suffice to say that two days ago, I had the most remarkable experience of being visited by myself."

"Oh, no," Kira said. "That's it."

"Now, now," Garak admonished her. "I am well aware of the dangers of changing anything that you remember as the past. I assure you, precautions have been taken."

Bashir didn't know whether or not to believe that assurance, given its source. "What kind of precautions?"

But Garak was in no mood for conversation. "I am also aware," he said briskly, "that you are both pressed for time. I believe you will have a radio communication to make? Yes?"

Bashir nodded.

"Very good," Garak said. "If we go this way, we won't be disturbed."

Garak led them along a short corridor, then up a service ladder to a level just above a docking port. A series of small, square viewports ran along the outer bulkhead. "I believe this should be suitable," Garak said.

Kira opened her mouth to ask a question, but Garak interrupted. "Please, the less information exchanged between us, the less we will have to fear that the 'precautions' are not entirely adequate."

Because it was the simplest decision to make, Bashir had no difficulty in accepting Garak's suggestion. He took up a position next to the center viewport and had the tricorder relay its data to the Vulcan radio, which, in turn, transmitted them to . . . wherever, whenever, the *Defiant* was.

After a minute, Bashir sensed Kira's presence beside him and felt the touch of her hand on his arm once again. "Just in case," she said in a low voice.

"This is all you need to do?" Garak asked Bashir.

"That's right," Bashir said. "We need information about exactly what's—"

"Ah-ah-ah, but I don't," Garak interrupted.

Bashir smiled. "Sorry, Garak." Then he noticed the Cardassian tailor's puzzled and curious regard of him. "Yes?"

"Nothing," Garak replied pleasantly. "I was just . . . tell me, by any chance, are you involved in medical matters?"

Bashir couldn't think what harm that innocuous information might cause. "Yes, I am. Why?"

Garak smiled, shook his head. "No reason. But I do wish you good fortune. For all our sakes."

"Thank you," Bashir said.

"No, thank *you.*"

Bashir laughed, then added for Garak's enlightenment, "Well, at least, *you* haven't changed."

"How reassuring."

Before Bashir could say anything more, a blinding flash of red light erased the scene before him, and when the brilliance had faded, Garak was gone.

Someone else stood in his place, though.

"It's about time," Prylar Obanak said. "I've been waiting for you."

"Nonlinear time!"

On the bridge of the *Defiant*, Jake looked up from his auxiliary station to see to whom Jadzia was talking. Worf was at the ops console, and three of Ensign Ryle Simons's *ad hoc* team of engineers worked at the life-support, engineering, and science stations. Off the bridge, three other crew members were on duty in main engineering, and two civilians stood watch over Commander Arla in sickbay. The commander was still recovering from Dr. Bashir's treatment of her subcranial bleeding, and Worf had ordered that no crew member be alone until he could determine who had helped Weyoun beam off the ship—though given everything else the crew faced, that was a mystery that seemed destined to remain unsolved.

But Jadzia, who was still at the communications console, was only talking to herself.

"That's it!" she said, more loudly than before, and Jake could hear real excitement building in her voice. "Worf, look at this." Then, surprisingly, she added, "Jake, you, too."

On Jadzia's main display, Jake saw an unusual graph that to him looked something like a spider's web with its center point pushed off to the right. The skewing of the rectangular segments that the crisscrossed strands defined made it seem as if he were looking at a net made of rubber. About a dozen of the strand intersections were marked by blue Starfleet symbols; about half as many others were tagged with yellow Klingon tridents. At the center of the warped web was a single red Bajoran emblem.

"I was trying to trace the Feynman connections among our bubble of space-time, the *Boreth*'s, and all the other bubbles that hold different versions of DS9," Jadzia explained to Worf, and to Jake. "But I couldn't find any pattern that made sense, especially—"

A pressure equalization wave enveloped the *Defiant* and disrupted the ship's gravity generators. Like everyone else on the bridge, Jake lurched as the deck seemed to pitch, but he managed to hold on to the back of Jadzia's chair. He also felt Worf's large hand on his back, helping keep him in place. The faster the waves came now, the more powerful their impacts were. At least with the extra crew manning key bridge stations, the *Defiant* was recovering more rapidly as well.

At the same moment the deck felt level again, Jake became aware that the constant background chorus of voices coming from the bridge speakers had once again increased in number. Over the past hour, as Jadzia had begun reconfiguring the sensors to respond to greater timeshifts in any detectable radio signals, the *Defiant* had begun to pick up multiple messages being transmitted from all the different temporal versions of DS9.

Jake's ears caught the repetition of his father's first message, as well as his second and third, together with Bashir's spoken messages and data transmissions, all of them layered in with Odo's and Quark's and even Garak's multiple transmissions. Fortunately, the ship's computer was capable of extracting all the pertinent information from each message, because with each new wave that swept over the *Defiant,* even more transmissions became detectable, and the old ones invariably repeated as if some eddies of time were caught in a loop.

On Jadzia's console, Jake saw that the center of the web was now distorted to the left, instead of to the right as before. He guessed the change was in response, somehow, to the passage of the wave. There also appeared to be even more Starfleet and Klingon symbols at additional web intersections.

Jadzia picked up her wave-interrupted explanation where she had left off. *"Especially* because those equalization waves keep changing temporal conditions. Until I realized my problem was that I was trying to include too much information."

Jake was lost, so it was a great relief to hear Worf say, "Explain."

Jadzia pointed to her display, touching the Klingon tridents first. "According to the time signatures on the radio transmissions we've been receiving from Odo, and Odo and Quark, these are all the relative positions of the *Boreth.* Both from *before* the station's destruction by the red wormhole and *after* it.

"And these," she said, indicating the Starfleet emblems, "according to the time signatures of the transmissions from Captain Sisko, and now from Julian and Major Kira, and Garak, are all the relative positions of the *Defiant*—from before the Day of Withdrawal and after."

Once again, Worf asked the question Jake thought. "I do not understand. How can the *Defiant* be in so many different positions when movement is not possible?"

"At the risk of sounding old-fashioned," Jadzia grinned, "it's all relative. You see—" She tapped the central Bajoran symbol. "—this is the station, the one unchanging element in the wormhole pocket."

"But shouldn't there be many stations," Worf asked, "each accounting for one of the timeframes experienced by the personnel that we and the *Boreth* have beamed to it, and from which we are continuing to receive radio transmissions?"

"That's just what I thought," Jadzia said. "And *that's* what made it impossible for me to connect all the different Feynman connections, even using Mannheim transformations."

Jake sighed. He hoped the discussion did not become so technical that he would be unable to follow it. He really wanted to understand what they were in the midst of.

"But then it hit me," Jadzia went on. "In this wormhole pocket, Deep Space 9 *itself* is the object, the location, the timeframe . . . whatever you want to call it . . . that's most strongly connected to the wormhole environment. And the wormhole itself is a domain of nonlinear time! So I took all the hypermaps I had been trying to assemble and compressed them so that all the different versions of the stations occupied the *same* coordinate positions, making station time nonlinear. And there it is." The Trill's smile of triumph was bestowed equally on Worf and on Jake. "A complete hyperdimensional map of all possible space-time interconnections between the station and the two ships, reducible to only two dimensions."

Jake felt like the odd man out. It was clear that Jadzia was incredibly pleased and relieved at her breakthrough, and Worf might know why. But Jake certainly didn't.

Then Worf's next question made Jake feel much better. "Does this knowledge provide an advantage to us, or is it simply interesting?" Worf's tone left no doubt about what the Klingon position was regarding applied versus pure research.

"An incredible advantage," Jadzia said. "The *Boreth* is an advanced-technology ship, twenty-five years ahead of the *Defiant*. I had no idea it was in here with us, but according to Odo, they can see the *Defiant* on their viewer. And one of Garak's messages said that Chief O'Brien will be able to set the *Boreth*'s transporter for automatic use."

This time, when Jadzia smiled up at Worf, Jake felt certain he understood the meaning of the unspoken message that passed between them: If everyone from the *Defiant* could get to the *Boreth* as Chief O'Brien had requested, then the crews of both ships could be saved. Without requiring an operator to stay behind and sacrifice himself—or herself—for the others.

With new hope, Jake listened closely to Worf's next query.

"Jadzia, can the personnel on the *Defiant* be beamed to the *Boreth?*"

"With this map, yes," the Trill said. "We just have to get the information to the Chief, and he should be able to lock onto us."

Worf completed the plan. "Then, to get the information to O'Brien, we must send it with someone to DS9. So it can be transmitted from the station."

"Exactly," Jadzia said. "And we still have four hours and—" She checked her console. "—twelve minutes. More than enough time."

But Jake thought he saw a flaw. Reminding himself that fear of embarrassment could not stand in the way when so much was at stake, he spoke quickly. "Hold it," he said. "The *Boreth*'s connected to the day the station was destroyed. So . . . what happens to my dad? And Major Kira and Dr. Bashir? And Garak? Do they just get left in the past?"

His heart sank as he saw the compassionate look that settled on Jadzia's face. "If they can contact the Department of Temporal Investigations, they can be relocated to an isolated community to wait six years before rejoining the timestream."

"*If?*" Jake asked. "What if they can't contact the Federation in time? What if the Cardassians get them? What if . . . if *anything* goes wrong?"

"Then the past *will* change," Worf said.

The Klingon looked at Jadzia, and Jake once again understood the question that was being asked.

Jadzia sighed. "The transporters on the station—*if* they properly reconfigured to resonate with the gravimetric distortions of the Red Orb hidden in Quark's bar—*might* be able to transport our people from the station in the past to the station the *Boreth*'s linked with in 2374."

"Might?" Worf repeated.

"It would depend on the skill of the operator," Jadzia said.

Worf folded his arms. "Could *you* make the necessary modifications?"

"Yes," Jadzia admitted, then quickly began to add, "but if I beam over, there won't be anyone here to—"

"Then you *will* beam over," Worf said, cutting off all further discussion. "You will then transmit the dimensional map to Chief O'Brien, so that he may attempt to rescue us from the *Defiant*. And then you will reconfigure the station's transporters in order to send Captain Sisko, Major Kira, Dr. Bashir, Garak, and yourself six years into the relative future."

"And if O'Brien can't rescue anyone from the *Defiant?*" Jadzia asked tightly.

"In the end," the Klingon said firmly, "there will be less disruption to the timeline if this ship is lost with all hands than if the captain and the others remain in the past. It is a risk I am willing to take."

"What if I'm not?" Jadzia said with more than a trace of challenge in her voice.

"In this case," Worf growled, and Jake shivered at his tone, "your concern is not of importance. I am the commander of this vessel. You will beam to the station at once."

But Jadzia didn't give up easily. She shook her head. "No one can operate the beam manually the way I can."

"Jadzia, I have reviewed the procedure you have followed for the three previous transports. *I* can handle the beam manually."

"Worf! I am the only—"

"That is the end of the discussion," Worf interrupted, sharply. "You will accompany me to the transporter room."

The tension between officer and crew, husband and wife, was so explosive, Jake didn't know where to look, and he was sure everyone else on the bridge felt the same. Right now, more than anything, Jake wanted to know his father would be safe with the others. Just as strongly, he wanted the timeline to remain unchanged. But he couldn't see any way both situations could come to pass. If the decision were his, Jake didn't know if he'd be able to make it.

But his problem was not Jadzia's. She *could* make the decision that was required, however much it troubled her. She took a tricorder from the utility compartment under her console, downloaded her map, then stood up. "Let's do it," she said curtly.

"Good luck," Jake said, knowing it was not enough, but it was all he could think of in the time that was left.

"You, too, Jake," Jadzia told him. Then she and Worf were gone.

Jake turned back to Jadzia's communications console. He focused his attention on the multiple time displays showing estimated elapsed time on the *Defiant,* the *Boreth,* and the most recently contacted versions of DS9. The closer the waves came to one another, the smaller the time distortion became among the different timeframes, and Jake saw that in two hours and two minutes, all the different rates of temporal flow would become identical—at the exact same moment as the temporal pressure between the two wormhole fragments equalized and all time stopped.

Jake decided to return to his own station because he didn't know what else to do. But then a new thought came to him.

Thinking back to what Jadzia had said about Arla's renewed interest in her people's religion, Jake found himself wishing he knew more about the Prophets, too. Because all too soon, it seemed, his fate and the fates of everyone he cared about would be in their hands.

Jake made a new decision: to see if Arla was awake.

He wanted to know how Bajorans prayed.

CHAPTER 18

EACH TIME SISKO was swept into the relative future, past the Day of Withdrawal, he took the opportunity to rest, and he had found the perfect site to do so.

Cannibalized over the years by Cardassian engineers, an antiquated fifty-year-old Cardassian ore hauler had remained undisturbed beside an unused ore-processing bay in Deep Space 9's outer ring for six months after Sisko had originally arrived to take command of the station. In a timeframe several days prior to the Withdrawal, Sisko had located the hulk again and saw that its condition *then* was no different from what it would be six months later, when Chief O'Brien would finally arrange to have it carted away as scrap.

Since nothing had disturbed the hauler in all that time, Sisko felt secure hiding in its cargo hold, in no danger from departing Cardassians searching for plunder or—depending on which timeframe he was in—zealous Bajoran militia searching for saboteurs.

Now, on this latest transfer into the future, Sisko carefully set down the two cases he had brought with him that held his work. He had learned from experience that he could carry through time anything he could hold that was not in direct contact with the station. Next, he recovered the Cardassian tricorder he had concealed behind a loose baffle plate in the past and checked the local time and date.

Once again, he had been swept past the actual events of the Day of Withdrawal, though not as far as on his previous jumps.

According to the tricorder's readout, he was now approximately fifty hours past the departure of the last Cardassian from DS9. From the reports he had read when he had taken command, he knew that confusion would still reign on the station. In the next few hours, a minor general from the Bajoran Resistance, whose name Sisko could no longer remember, would declare the station the Star of Bajor and begin to organize the transport of orbital weapons to its cargo bays, in order to enforce what he termed a just peace on the planet below. That general's term of office would last a little more than one day before he was taken into custody by an assault team sent from the hastily formed Provisional Government, whose hurriedly elected members even now were struggling to make their way across their ruined world to hold their first assembly.

As for himself, Sisko recalled that he had been on Earth at this time, his visit to Rutgers University cut short by an urgent recall order from Starfleet Command. He had been considering a teaching position, and when the recall had arrived, he was standing in the backyard of a quaint mid-twenty-second-century cottage on Moravian Lane, smiling as he watched his son Jake eye the towering maple trees, already imagining himself climbing them.

With that, Sisko's thoughts inevitably turned to Jake in this present, a young man now, off somewhere in time with the *Defiant*. Though Sisko knew he couldn't be sure that the action he had decided on would result in his own individual survival or Jake's, the certainty at least would exist that *a* Ben Sisko and his son would live on in another timeline without the threat of the Bajoran Ascendancy and the end of the universe it would bring.

The decision itself had not been an easy one for Sisko to make, but he felt that somehow Jake would understand. If their positions were reversed, he even thought there was a possibility that his son might make the same choice.

In Sisko's last face-to-face exchange with Kira, after the two of them had left Quark's knowing that the Red Orb had already been removed, the Bajoran major had not supported his decision. Kira was convinced that they had to follow the admonitions of Eilin, the ancient mystic of Jalbador, and of Prylar Rulan, who had first welcomed Sisko to the station: No change in the timeline was to be permitted; everything was to be left in the hands of the Prophets.

Sisko had told the major he thought her choice *was* the better one, and the one he would prefer to see prevail, but that even if he put his duties as Emissary first, he could not stop thinking like a Starfleet officer, and that every aspect of his training was demanding that he consider what might happen if the Prophets remained silent to their plight.

"If faith fails us," Sisko had argued, "then science must not."

He and Kira had agreed to separate. Kira told him she would do all she could to establish further communication with the *Defiant,* to track down Weyoun, and to obtain the Red Orb of Jalbador from Leej Terrell before whoever stole it from Quark's hiding place was able to take it from the station.

"You know," Kira told him in that last conversation, "maybe the people who stole the Orb were *us.* I mean, if we took it two days after Quark hid it, that would explain why it wasn't there when we tried to find it two *weeks* later. Right?"

Sisko allowed the possibility of that scenario but pointed out that if he and Kira *were* responsible for the Orb's disappearance, then surely they would have left some sort of sign to themselves, so they would know what actually happened.

"Maybe not," Kira said. "That would be like telling ourselves the future, and that might mean we'd be careless and miss the opportunity to steal it. Or maybe we intended to leave a sign or message for our future selves to find, but we were being chased and didn't have the time."

"The truth is," Sisko said, "this is like every other life-or-death situation we've been in. We have no idea what will happen next."

"I believe the Prophets do," Kira said.

"I hope you're right."

Then a flash of light had swept the two of them into the past, more than a week before the Withdrawal.

Fortunately, they materialized in the Bajoran half of the Promenade, and their sudden appearance in a shadowed alcove was barely noticed by the exhausted slave workers who huddled together during the station's night, the fabled Cardassian efficiency having failed to provide them with berths.

Sisko and Kira had gone their separate ways then, Kira stead-fastly determined to do what she had to do, telling Sisko that if—when—she succeeded, she would seek him out where she knew she could find him, no matter the timeframe, in the abandoned ore hauler. On his own, Sisko managed to steal a Cardassian tricorder and reach the hulk within a half hour, after which he was swept ahead into another post-Withdrawal timeframe.

By now, Sisko was spending less than ten minutes in each time-frame, and it had taken him multiple timeshifts to nearly complete building the device that, if necessary, could take the place of Kira's faith: a chroniton pulse-emitter which he now carried with him through each new timeshift, along with his assorted borrowed tools. To assemble the simple emitter, he'd made use of various compo-nents left behind in the Cardassian ore hauler, as well as key isolin-ear circuits and a spare sensor-resonance chamber which he liberated from the Starfleet materiel that had arrived from the *Enterprise.*

He knew the emitter would be a crude device, unlikely to operate for more than a few minutes once the power supply was attached. But Sisko was betting that at the appropriate time, even the brief cas-cade of chronometric particles the emitter produced would destroy the worm hole-precursor field that Leej Terrell had created with the Red Orb in her secret lab deep within DS9. That destructive cascade would have the added benefit of driving whatever entity possessed Weyoun from his body—presuming, of course, that Weyoun was still on the station. As yet, Sisko had seen no sign of the Vorta, other than when Weyoun had been greeted by Prylar Obanak as the one true Emissary, the first time Sisko had arrived with Kira.

Weyoun, however, was not all that important now. The actions Sisko planned to take would still change all of the history that unfolded from the Day of Withdrawal, with or without the Vorta's presence on the station.

Sisko knew the chroniton cascade would be easily detected on Cardassia, only five and a quarter light-years distant. Undoubtedly, the Science Directorate of the Obsidian Order would ask pointed questions, and Terrell, in particular, couldn't help but suspect a con-nection to wormhole phenomena. That could lead her to return to the station more quickly than she had in Sisko's original timeline. If she did so, Sisko thought, at worst, the Red Orb would be discovered years earlier, perhaps when the Cardassians were destined to retake control of the station at the beginning of the Dominion War. At best, the Orb would remain hidden, and there would be no secret 'Cardassian holosuite' for young Jake and Nog to discover. The consequence of that would be that it would take more time for the Sisko and Odo of that day to realize what Quark and Vash and Dal Nortron, among others, were planning almost six years later.

In the end, Sisko knew, the new future he would bring into being was unpredictable. After all, from the moment he and Kira discovered for themselves that the Red Orb had been moved from Quark's, the timeline had already changed. At least, Sisko reassured himself, the strategy he had decided upon would introduce a *different* set of changes and would thus create a greater chance that the three Red Orbs would not be brought together.

Beyond that, Kira was right. All their fates would be in the hands of the Prophets.

Sisko carefully replaced the Cardassian tricorder behind the baffle plate, picked up his cases with his tools and his almost-completed emitter, then stood expectantly to one side in an area of the cargo hold he knew he had left clear in the past.

When the next equalization wave struck, Sisko estimated he'd be arriving in the past about the time the first troop transports had left Bajor. At first, he knew, those departures would seem to be no different from a normal troop rotation. But as soon as word began to spread that fresh troops had not arrived to replace those who had left, the first uprisings would begin among the Bajorans, and battles for the Cardassian-controlled spaceports would rage across the planet. Since the first uprising had occurred about two days before the Cardassians evacuated the station, Sisko guessed it would take him another three or four more time oscillations to reach that specific timeframe. When he did, he would activate his emitter. Then, one way or another, the nightmare would end.

Sisko was prepared when a flash of blue light blinded him. He had learned that closing his eyes did nothing to lessen the light's intensity. At least, he thought, wincing, repetition served to blunt the physical shock of timeshifting.

But this time, the moment his vision cleared, Sisko was struck by a shock of a different kind.

Kira was in the cargo hold, and so was Dr. Bashir, and both were bound and gagged and kneeling before their captor.

Weyoun.

In the *Defiant*'s sickbay, Jake nodded to the two crew members watching over Arla. Each was a civilian, garbed in the same style of gray and black advisor uniform he wore. Briefly over the past few weeks, Jake had talked to both of them. They were agricultural technicians, human, from Deneva, who had been returning from a Federation exchange program to Ferenginar. When the red wormhole had opened both had been on DS9 waiting for transportation because they had lost all their personal belongings and equipment in an all-too-common misunderstanding of Ferengi hotel laws. Neither had been aware that those laws equated the offer of shelter with imputed ownership of whatever was then placed in that shelter unless money changed hands first—a minor detail Ferengi hoteliers regularly neglected to share with off-worlders. Since the technicians were the only personnel onboard the *Defiant* with anything close to training in biology, Bashir had deputized both of them as his nurses.

"How is she?" Jake asked, looking down at Arla's still form on the sickbay treatment table.

But Arla herself replied before the technicians could. "Jake?" The Bajoran commander lifted her head and looked over at him.

Jake went to her side as she slowly sat up on the treatment table. "I wouldn't move too much. Dr. Bashir said you might be dizzy for a few days." At the time, Jake had considered the diagnosis optimistic, considering they might only have a few hours of existence left.

But Arla merely stretched her neck from side to side, arched her back, and a moment later slipped off the table to stand unaided, without any unsteadiness. "Actually, I feel fine." She looked around sickbay. "Where *is* the doctor?"

"A lot's happened," Jake said. He enjoyed the novelty of talking with someone who was almost his height. Arla was definitely one of the tallest Bajorans he had ever met.

"Um, excuse us," one of the technicians interrupted. "But Commander Worf . . . he wanted to be informed the moment Commander Arla woke up."

"Why?" Arla asked.

"You should let him know," Jake told the technicians. To Arla, he said, "Do you remember who hit you?"

"Hit me?"

"Your head," Jake said, repeating what Bashir had told him. At the same time, the technician who had just spoken with Jake fumbled with his combadge, achieving contact with Worf only after several false starts.

As the technician informed Worf of her condition, Arla gingerly touched the top of her head. "What happened?"

"What do you remember?" Jake observed her action, puzzled. Bashir had said Arla had been struck on the back of her head, not the top. Couldn't she feel the injury? Or was the doctor's treatment that good?

Arla wrinkled her face in concentration. "I . . . I went on a break. Ensign Simons sent someone up from engineering to watch Weyoun." She snapped her fingers. "I saw Major Kira beam out to the station. Are she and your father all right?"

"So far," Jake said. "What else?"

"Well . . . let's see . . . did I come back in here?"

"The engineer who spelled you said you did."

Arla nodded. "That's right . . . that's right . . . I did come back. I was carrying a coffee . . . Weyoun was on the table . . . and . . ." She shook her head in frustration. "All I remember after that is a red flash." She smiled apologetically at Jake. "Do you think there's any coffee left?"

"Sure," Jake said with a shrug, deciding she wasn't used to starship food replicators. The coffee was always on.

Then, after asking the technicians to tell Worf that he and Arla would be in the mess hall, he left sickbay with her.

On the short walk to the mess, Jake filled in Arla on what she had missed. But the best news of all was that Jadzia had managed to contact O'Brien and that the crew of the *Defiant* were already being beamed to the *Boreth*.

But as they entered the mess hall and went straight to a replicator, Arla didn't seem particularly interested in their pending rescue.

"So all the times are converging?" she asked, then instructed the replicator to give her coffee, black, New Berlin blend.

Jake nodded, watching as a gray mug of steaming dark liquid

appeared in the replicator bay. "Dax said it's inevitable. These pockets of space-time we're in, they're the last remnants of linear time, and basically they're going to dissolve into the nonlinear environment of the wormhole."

Arla picked up the mug. "How much more time is left?" she asked.

"It's different for each pocket," Jake said. He gestured to the closest table and accompanied her to it, taking a seat directly across from her. "As if we were all traveling at relativistic speeds, back before inertial dampeners. Dax set up a time display at her station. We've got about three hours. The *Boreth* has about two and half. On the station, they have just over two."

Arla stared down into her coffee, warming her hands around the mug.

Jake didn't know if there would ever be an easy time, so he decided to be blunt. "How do you feel about the Prophets?" he asked, mortified by the sudden betraying catch in his voice.

He thought he saw a brief smile lift Arla's mouth at the corners. "You mean, do I believe in them?"

"Yeah. I guess that's it."

"I didn't used to."

"I . . . I know. That's what Dax said."

"You were talking about me?"

Jake flushed. "Well, I heard what you said about, you know, hoping for the best and trusting in the Prophets."

Arla again raised her coffee mug, but it seemed only to touch her lips. She set it down again without drinking from it, as if just going through the motions.

"I heard what the Pah-wraiths did to you," she said. "The hell they put you in."

Jake shivered, recalling the whole all-too-real experience of inputting as if his life had depended on it.

"Do you know what my Pah-wraith hell was?" she asked, stroking the side of the coffee mug.

Jake shook his head, said, "No," almost too softly to be heard.

"I didn't have one."

Jake stared at her, not understanding. "But . . . everyone else did . . ."

"I didn't believe in Pah-wraiths, either." She looked up at him then, so suddenly Jake was startled. Her large eyes were bright, gleaming. She gave him a half-smile. "My parents didn't even tell me stories about them to scare me when I was a child. They were very practical people. No Prophets. No Pah-wraiths. No absolute good. But no absolute evil, either. Funny how that works."

"So . . . so what happened to you?" Jake asked. "Did you experience anything?"

Arla nodded. "Oh, yes. I *was* punished."

Jake was startled by the intense pain in Arla's voice. "But . . . not by the Pah-wraiths?"

"By the Prophets." The Bajoran spat out the last word as if it were the foulest substance in the universe. "They put me in a camp. With Cardassian soldiers. I was their . . ." She shook her head, unable to continue.

Jake waited. He thought again of what the doctor had told him, about how people were the product of their experiences, and he knew how much of life was still before him. At least, he hoped it was.

Arla spoke again. "There was only one way out left to me. One way. The Prophets. And I begged for them to help me. I prayed to them. And the soldiers . . . when I was no more use to them, they'd throw me in a pit and bury me alive with all the others, and then I'd wake up and I'd be crawling through the battlefield again, and the Prophets . . ." Arla bent over her mug of coffee, and her voice became little more than a whisper that Jake could barely hear. "The Prophets *would* come to me then. And they'd say, 'Sorry, Arla. You had your chance. Now this is what you get.' And then the soldiers would come again, and . . ." Arla's hands tightened around the mug until Jake could see the bones in her knuckles. "We *all* had our chance."

Jake sat silent, unsure what reassurances a nineteen-year-old could offer a Starfleet commander. If Arla had been his age, maybe he would have put his hand on hers, to try to tell her that things would be all right, that she had had a Pah-wraith experience after all, that the Prophets wouldn't abandon Bajorans. But he didn't know if any of that were true. All he did know was that he was as confused as she was.

"But . . . you said, 'Trust in the Prophets,' didn't you?" Jake finally asked.

Arla let go of her coffee mug, pushed back on her chair, stood up. "I should go talk to Worf."

Jake quickly got up to follow her. "Uh, Worf says we should all go around in pairs."

Arla stared at him, frowning.

"Until . . . until we know who beamed Weyoun out."

"Don't worry," Arla said with a brief laugh that made the hair on the back of Jake's neck bristle. "I'm sure we'll see him again."

Then the ship seemed to drop out from beneath Jake's feet as the lights brightened and dimmed and everything about him shifted abruptly to port. *Another pressure wave.* The violent movement slammed Jake's head—which was level with Arla's—directly into hers, his forehead smashing into her upper lip, the recoil of the collision tossing them both to the deck.

A moment later, Jake was sitting up, a hand to his head, looking over at the Bajoran. "Are you all right?" he asked over the ringing in his ears.

Arla was sitting up as well. She had lifted one hand and was touching two fingers to her already-swelling split lip. A bright red smear stained her teeth; a trickle of blood ran down her chin.

"Commander—I'm sorry," Jake said. He got unsteadily to his feet. "I can get a medikit and . . . and . . ."

"No need," Arla said, her speech slurring as she licked the blood from her fingers.

Then her split lip knit itself back together and deflated until it was its normal size. Unbelieving, Jake watched as the trickle of blood on Arla's chin broke into small, distinct beads which then disappeared as if they were being reabsorbed into her skin.

"Now you know why I don't have to believe in the Prophets," Arla said as she came for him. "I have something even better . . ."

Jake didn't even have time to scream.

On the bridge of the *Boreth,* Rom delivered his confirmation: All transporter settings had been realigned according to Jadzia's specifications.

The transporter was ready to energize.

But energize what? O'Brien thought. He knew he was dealing with a more sophisticated transporter technology than he was used to. He knew that Jadzia understood the theory of temporal mechanics much more thoroughly than he did. But as far as the chief engineer could see, the coordinates to which he had set the transporter contained *imaginary* numbers. Frankly, he was surprised the computers—even Klingon ones—had even allowed him to do so.

"Uh, Chief?" Rom prompted. "We're ready to . . . go."

"All right," O'Brien said, feeling a touch apprehensive and not too proud to show it. "You might want to stand aside, because I have no idea what we're about to bring in here."

Rom and the two other crew members—Starfleet personnel who had just happened to be on DS9 between assignments when the red wormhole had opened—immediately moved to the back of the bridge.

Though the main transporter rooms were on other decks, it still remained easier for O'Brien to keep transporter controls switched to the bridge because wormhole conditions continued to limit targeting to one person at a time. With the *Boreth*'s warp engines unusable in an environment without subspace dimensions, the massive Klingon vessel had power to spare for such energy-intensive, point-to-point beamings.

"Energizing," O'Brien said.

Because the coordinates didn't seem to correspond to any physical location in local space, on his display O'Brien saw no gravitational deviation in the transport beam's propagation. Instead, as the Chief expected, it remained as coherent as a laser, until it snapped back as quickly as if he had initiated an intraship transport.

Then, to O'Brien's complete surprise, the resulting cylinder of sparkling light in the center of the bridge resolved into a form, and that form became solid—a living, breathing, redheaded Starfleet ensign whom O'Brien hadn't seen since the battle with Tom Riker's ship, when the ensign had been transported from the *Defiant* in the midst of the action.

"I see it, but I don't believe it," O'Brien marveled.

Ensign Simons looked down at his hands as if to count his fingers, then said excitedly, "It worked! It really worked!"

"Rom—set the controls for another go."

"Aye, aye . . . Chief."

It took O'Brien only ten minutes more to beam over all but five of the *Defiant*'s remaining crew, with the chief adjusting the coordinates of each transport in precise accordance to the detailed instructions that Jadzia had transmitted from the station, along with her remarkably simple dimensional map.

Ensign Simons had made the process even more efficient by providing the up-to-date figures Jadzia needed to compensate precisely for changes to the *Defiant*'s navigational deflector shields—changes that had been brought on by the ship's fall into the wormhole.

"Uh, that only leaves Commander Worf," Rom said happily as he checked off Jadzia's manifest, "Commander Arla, the two agricultural technicians, and . . . Jake."

O'Brien frowned. He was having a hard time believing that beaming through *time* and space—as he had once done in Earth orbit—could be this simple. Not to mention accepting that in only about two and a half hours, if his calculations were correct, even a truly amazing accomplishment like this might amount to nothing. What good would it do to rescue people from the *Defiant* if the end result was merely that everyone then died together instead of alone? The chief engineer shook off his dark thoughts. There was nothing to be gained by dwelling on what might go wrong. Beam everyone to the *Boreth,* then beam everyone to the station. Those were his orders, so that was what he would do.

"The transporter has recycled," Rom announced.

"Here comes the next one," O'Brien said crisply. "Energizing . . ."

On O'Brien's transporter display, the beam shot out once more to the new, impossible coordinates, but this time it didn't snap back.

O'Brien watched, unconcerned at first. The beam was showing no feedback ripple to indicate it had dematerialized anyone, so no immediate danger existed. To compensate for target drift, the chief engineer did what usually worked. He increased the power by eight percent and widened the focus by two.

Nothing happened.

"The coils will time out in ten seconds," Rom called out in warning.

After first making sure the beam was still clear, O'Brien forced it back to rematerialize anything it might have found but that might not be showing up on the display.

But nothing appeared. O'Brien didn't understand. He had Rom reset the system.

The hum and pop of the Heisenberg compensators echoed through the deck as O'Brien rapidly worked out the new degree of Jadzia's coordinate drift, basing his calculations on this minor delay alone, then energized the beam again.

Still nothing.

Beads of sweat began dotting the Chief's brow as he tried five more times until the coils timed out for quantum-phase realignment.

O'Brien swore under his breath. He had no choice but to shut down.

"What happened?" Rom asked, worried.

O'Brien had no answer other than the most troubling one—the one now shown on the *Boreth*'s main viewer.

"The *Defiant*," O'Brien said. "It just . . . isn't there anymore."

CHAPTER 19

"Is THIS EVERYONE?" Odo asked.

Rom looked around the crowded storage room with Ferengi exactness, then rattled off the count. "Uh, not yet. There are still five unaccounted for on the *Defiant.* Chief O'Brien's on the *Boreth.* And . . . five people on the station back at the time of the Withdrawal: Captain Sisko, Major Kira, Lieutenant Commander Dax, Dr. Bashir, and . . . Garak." Rom gave the constable a quick, nervous smile. "That means *we* have eighteen out of twenty-nine possible retrievals, or sixty-two percent . . . rounded."

Odo was not pleased with the news about the *Defiant.* When the first of that ship's rescued crew and passengers had started arriving on the station from the *Boreth,* he had thought it would only be a matter of minutes before everyone was finally reunited after their harrowing trip through time. Everyone, that is, except Vash and the three Bajorans killed by Dukat on the bridge of the *Boreth.* Those four absences were responsible for the reduction in the number of temporal refugees from thirty-three to twenty-nine. Still, the changeling decided, the combination of Jadzia's scientific skills and O'Brien's engineering expertise had worked better than he, for one, had dared hope.

"Any idea what's happened to the *Defiant?*" he asked.

Rom shook his head. "Not really. The wormhole conditions are changing so rapidly now, the ship might have experienced a phenomenon we've never even seen before. Or else . . . well, the Chief thought it might even be cloaked."

Odo looked sharply at Rom for an explanation. "Why?"

But the Ferengi could only shrug. "Equipment failure, probably."

"Constable Odo?" Ryle Simons broke into their discussion. "You asked for a one-minute warning." The redheaded Starfleet ensign held up his tricorder.

Odo nodded, then turned to face the seventeen others who were sheltered in the storage room which now existed in a timeframe just over a day after the station's destruction by the red wormhole. It was the same storage room into which he and Dukat had first timeshifted. "Everyone, your attention! We're going to transfer again."

Most of the rescued crew and civilians had already been through enough time transfers to know what to do, and within the space of ten seconds, each held the hands of those to the right and left, until all eighteen people were linked in a circle. No more than thirty seconds later, a flash of red light engulfed them, and they found themselves still in the same storage room, but now *before* the station had been destroyed.

At the moment of their materialization, a murmur swept through the group as everyone stumbled, losing their footing, shuffling a step or two forward in the direction of the far end of the room, which was now decidedly downhill.

Odo knew at once that in this timeframe, DS9's gravity generators were still unbalanced, a direct result of their infection by the Bynar computer virus. The virus had been introduced into the station's computers by Satr and Leen, the two Andorian sisters who had accompanied Dal Nortron.

At a nod from Odo, Simons switched on the handheld Klingon communicator O'Brien had beamed from the *Boreth,* which the chief had modified so it could eavesdrop on Deep Space 9's internal communications network. The first words Odo heard this time were especially welcome. They came from Kira, though it was the Kira of this timeframe.

"—from the Rio Grande. *They found the captain!"*

Bashir's voice answered. *"What's his condition?"*

"Exhausted," Kira replied. *"But he's uninjured. And he found the Orb!"*

Those events were very clear in Odo's memory, and they told the changeling that he and his group were now approximately twenty-six hours away from the red wormhole's opening.

Odo glanced around the storage room. "Everyone still here?" he asked.

When he received no reports of anyone's missing the transfer, Odo concluded that once again the mere act of remaining in physical contact had been enough to keep everyone—with all their initial individual time differences—in joint phase.

"We should stay here about nine minutes, ten seconds," Simons advised.

"Thank you, Ensign," Odo said. "Give us a one-minute warning as before."

"But what do we do for . . . eight minutes?" Rom asked hesitantly.

"How about saying hello to your brother?" Quark said indignantly, pushing Simons aside.

Rom turned and smiled happily at Quark. "Hello, Brother."

Quark snorted. "Good to see you, too. Well, so much for family reunions. Now, here's *my* plan—in eight minutes, we can get to a runabout and get off the station."

Odo sighed as he shook his head. "Quark, we've been through this. All the runabouts were employed in the evacuation when the red wormhole opened. If we take one now, the people who originally used it to evacuate won't get off the station, and that will change their timeline. *And* when *we* jump through time again, we'll have no guarantee that the runabout will still be around us when we reappear."

"Odo, really," Quark snapped. "The station and this room are always around us!"

"Because this station and this room are linked to the red wormhole. And O'Brien doesn't know how far that linkage extends."

"He's right, Brother," Rom added quickly. "If we try to fly away from the station, why . . . there's a chance we might be snapped back to the wormhole, or to the *Boreth,* or to . . . nothing."

"Which is what's going to happen to us in—" Scowling, Quark

turned to Simons. "You, how much 'relative' time do we have now?"

"Altogether? Maybe ninety minutes," the ensign said.

The red blotches mottling the young ensign's pale face were the result of simple exhaustion, Odo knew, but continued exposure to Quark might make them permanent.

Odo frowned as Quark pointed at the communicator. "Odo, c'mon. One lousy message to Major Kira, telling her not to take the Orbs into my bar. That's all it would take."

"You heard what Ensign Simons told us about O'Brien's and Dax's conclusions, Quark. That's all it would take to shut down our timeline and snap us back to the *Boreth,* too."

"So we just wait here till we *die,* is that it?" Quark asked incredulously.

"No," Odo said for at least the thousandth time, it seemed. Surely no amount of timeshifting could be as bad as the endless repetitions Quark required. "We wait here until the red wormhole begins to open, and then we leave with all the rest of the evacuees. Then, once the station is swallowed by the red wormhole and the wormhole closes, the Chief and Dax both agree that we'll be stable in this time-frame, and we can do whatever we want to change the future we saw. And that's exactly what we're going to do, Quark—*when* the time comes and *not* before."

Quark's barrel chest began to swell, and his enormous earlobes darkened dangerously. *"Frinx* time travel!" he sputtered.

Rom nodded brightly. "That's pretty much what Chief O'Brien thinks, too."

And as if he had heard his name spoken, O'Brien's voice was the next to come over the communicator. *"O'Brien to Odo."*

Odo's first thought was that O'Brien's modification to the Klingon device had made it very sensitive. The Chief had taken part in the search for Sisko on Jeraddo, while Odo had remained on the station. Thus, whatever they were hearing now had been a long-range transmission. Though Odo couldn't recall having spoken to the Chief until he had returned with the search parties.

But then his confusion cleared as O'Brien said, *"This is O'Brien on the* Boreth *to Odo in the storage room. This channel is encrypted, so reply using the communicator I gave Simons if you can."*

Simons instantly thrust the communicator at Odo, and the

changeling touched the transmit control. "Odo to O'Brien, we can hear you!"

Everyone else in the storage room ceased talking. Until now, all communication had been from the station to either the *Boreth* or the *Defiant*, but neither ship had been able to transmit messages back.

"*Wonderful,*" O'Brien's voice said. "*I'm picking up a bit of timeshift distortion, but we're almost in phase now, so the channel will get clearer. What's your status?*"

"Eighteen safe and sound," Odo reported. "Any word from the *Defiant?*"

"*Nothing yet,*" O'Brien said. "*But in about five more minutes, the phase difference between the* Boreth *and the past version of the station should reach the point where Dax can contact me directly, so I'll put her to work on it, too.*"

"What about you, Chief?" Odo asked.

"*Not much I can do except stand by here till you get closer to the opening of the wormhole. I'll . . . transport in at the last minute so . . . I can join you.*"

But Odo had registered the hesitation in O'Brien's voice and understood with sadness that the engineer intended to stay at his station until it was too late to save himself. Just for the chance of making contact with those still on the *Defiant.*

"Whatever you think is best, Chief."

"*Well, I'm going back to sensor sweeps,*" O'Brien said. "*Every time you transfer into a timeframe before the wormhole opens, contact me so we can keep everything synchronized. The next time we talk, I should have a report from Dax.*"

"Thanks, Chief," Odo said. "We'll stand by. Odo out."

"And cheerfully wait to die," Quark muttered, "like good Starfleet soldiers."

Odo looked past Quark to Simons. "Time, Ensign?"

"Three minutes and counting."

Then hammer blows of pounding shook the storage room's main door—the one connecting it to the corridor.

All heads turned toward the closed door. Odo immediately gestured for everyone to remain silent, and everyone had the good sense to comply, even Quark.

Rom caught Odo's eye. "Is that you," he whispered, "making a security check?"

Odo shook his head. He had last inspected this room for contraband the day before he had placed Quark in protective custody. Someone else was pounding on the door.

The changeling held out his hand, palm up, to Simons, and the ensign promptly passed him the tricorder. Odo switched it over to detect life-forms and aimed it at the door.

Nothing.

The pounding stopped, then started again.

Altering the soles of his boots to air-filled pockets of soft, spongy flesh, Odo soundlessly made his way to the door, then used the tricorder again.

But even as another sequence of heavy blows rattled the door, the device detected no lifesigns. In frustration, Odo set the tricorder to register any energy phenomenon, and the small display screen suddenly turned bright red as all intensity bars filled their scales.

Two more blows hit the door, this time deforming it.

Odo backed up, just in time to avoid being struck by the door as a final, immensely powerful blow burst it from its tracks, and it spun forward, clanging as it skidded across the bare metal deck.

But Odo's attention had already shifted from the door to the creature who had dislodged it.

Dukat.

The madman whose white hair twisted away from his gray scalp as if charged with electricity, whose wild eyes pulsed with red energy. Who rushed into the storage room as if his bare scaled feet no longer were in contact with the deck and whose scarlet robes floated around him like the trailing fronds of water plants caught in a boiling ocean's currents.

"*I want QUARK!*" Dukat roared. And as he raised his hands encased in red fire, all Odo could hear was the high-pitched squeal of a Ferengi.

"Emissary," Weyoun said amicably in the hold of the old cargo hauler. "It's been such a long time." He smiled at the chroniton emitter that Sisko grasped in one hand. "And I see you've been busy."

Sisko's other hand dropped his tool case, and he quickly reached inside the emitter to close the circuit that would set it off, knowing full well that because the device wasn't yet complete, the resulting explosion would probably kill him. But with any luck, it would also kill whatever entity possessed Weyoun, ending this here and now.

But the Vorta merely flicked his hand as if waving off an airborne pest and the emitter flew from Sisko's grip, sailed over the heads of Kira and Bashir, and shattered against the bulkhead.

"But I'm afraid it was a waste of time," Weyoun said. "Especially when there is so little of it left."

"What do you want?" Sisko asked through gritted teeth.

Weyoun folded his hands back inside his bloodred robes and smiled. "I'm sure you can guess."

The Vorta paused, expectant, a solicitous expression on his face, but Sisko did not intend to play his game.

"Or perhaps not." Seemingly untroubled by Sisko's refusal, Weyoun looked down at his two captives—Kira and Bashir, on their knees before him, wrists and ankles bound with red cloth. Mouths gagged with narrow strips of the same fabric.

It took Sisko a moment, but then he recognized the strips. They were the same as the arm- and headbands worn by adherents of the Pah-wraith cults.

"That's right," Weyoun said, apparently noticing Sisko's gaze. "I am not without supporters here." He raised his hand. "Allow me." Red sparks haloed one upraised finger, and the gags dropped from Kira and Bashir at the same time.

"Obanak!" Kira gasped.

"He was waiting for us," Bashir added. "After Withdrawal! He took us to an airlock, and when we jumped back, Weyoun was waiting for us."

"Obanak thinks Weyoun is the Emissary," Sisko told them.

"Because I am," Weyoun said serenely. "True Emissary to the True Prophets, as Obanak and his people believe. As they have always believed. As has always been true, I might add, Benjamin."

Sisko took a step toward the Vorta, hands becoming fists.

But Weyoun stood his ground, smiling. "Do you really think you can accomplish anything like that?"

"Afraid I'll break your nose again?" Sisko taunted him. He had struck Weyoun when they had been together on the bridge of the

Defiant—before the universe had ended. He had savored Weyoun's look of shock and pain as the Vorta had gingerly touched his flattened nose.

But this time, Weyoun merely placed two fingers alongside his own nose, no longer damaged, and laughed. "A *human* actually hurt the *Emissary?* Never."

Whatever the reason behind Weyoun's denial of their last encounter, Sisko understood from the eerie glow of red energy now animating the Vorta's dead eyes that attempting another physical attack on him was impossible. In any case, in a little more than eight minutes, Sisko knew he'd be shifted again into the future and would be able to escape the ore hauler. Beyond that, he wasn't sure what to do. But he was ready to do anything—*anything*—before he'd let Weyoun win. And right now, that meant keeping the Vorta talking. For at least another eight minutes.

Weyoun studied Sisko like a disapproving parent. "You're being unusually quiet, Benjamin. I have come to expect a more spirited response from you."

"You won't win," Sisko said.

"But you forget, I already have. You were there, remember? The year 2400. The joining of the Temples. The battle between the True Prophets and the Pretenders at last under way." Weyoun shook his head as if overcome by the wonder of it all.

"I don't mind admitting to you, especially, Benjamin, that I do regret not being present for the culmination of eons of effort. Those 'pressure equalization waves' you're experiencing? What they really are is the waves of battle. True Prophets surging forward for the attack. Pretenders desperately struggling to push back the assault. The True Prophets regrouping and charging forth again. That's what your ship was caught in. A war beyond your comprehension. A war that can have only one conclusion. Victory. The end to all conflict. Forever."

"I don't believe you."

Weyoun pursed his lips. "I never took you for the masochistic type. Do you enjoy suffering? Do you know how many *billions* of inhabited worlds were in your universe? Do you know how many more billions of intelligent species arose, looked at the stars, felt the pain of that enormity they would never conquer, faced the bleak, meaningless prospect of not only their own individual deaths but the deaths of their cultures and their worlds?

"Is that kind of torture humane by your standards, Benjamin? Would you truly prefer to allow the universe to continue without end, condone another *trillion* races to such pathetic despair, all for the sake of your personal continued existence for, at best for a human, another few *decades?* How petty of you. How selfish. In fact, how perfectly *evil* of you."

Sisko did not reply. *Another four minutes,* he thought. *Keep talking . . .*

Weyoun nodded as if Sisko's failure to respond was not unexpected. "I can see I'm making some headway. The old headstrong Captain Sisko would have engaged me in a scintillating argument by now, forcefully renouncing my statements, trying his best but in vain to establish that he speaks for all living beings on behalf of the stalwart Starfleet and the venerable United Federation of Planets. But your silence tells me you're finally beginning to understand. Aren't you?"

"Whatever you say," Sisko said curtly.

Weyoun shook a finger at him. "Now, now. When I hear that tone from you, I know you're thinking about something else. But believe me, Benjamin, there is *nothing* else to think about. You can do nothing to stop me now, because this moment has already come and gone in your history.

"That's what I want, you see. Nothing. I want the Cardassians to withdraw from the station, Leej Terrell to shut down her secret lab within it, the Red Orb to find its way to its safe hiding place in that Ferengi's bar, exactly as it happened before."

Sisko tried but couldn't completely contain his surprise at what Weyoun had just said. For whatever reason, it seemed the Vorta had not experienced any oscillations into the future just beyond the Day of Withdrawal. He didn't realize that Kira and Sisko had discovered that the Red Orb was not in its hiding place where it had been found in the hour before the station's destruction.

The Vorta's voice continued on, in response to Sisko's sudden spark of interest. "Ah, I see I've intrigued you at last. What did you think? Surely not that I came back to this time in order to *change* the past? To find the Orbs ahead of schedule? To try to bring on the joining of the Temple earlier than 2400? Oh, Benjamin," Weyoun chuck-led, wiping a false tear from his red eye, "I will miss you, you know."

Sisko had only half listened to the Vorta, caught up in thought about his one advantage over Weyoun. Between this moment and a time two weeks after Withdrawal, the Orb upon which all of Weyoun's mad dreams depended had been stolen—and without Weyoun's knowledge. History had already been changed. But by whom?

"Weyoun, if the end of the universe is such a good thing," Sisko began, trying his utmost to keep his growing excitement hidden from the Vorta, "why *not* end it early? Think of all the suffering that would never take place."

"Ah, but that would add variables to the equation, don't you think?" From Weyoun's relaxed manner now, it appeared that the Vorta was in no hurry to do anything. And Sisko wondered why. Surely, Weyoun had to know about the swings through time, despite all that talk about the equalization waves being only the waves of battle. The Vorta had been waiting in the ore hauler for Sisko to appear, after all.

"I don't know what you mean," Sisko said, guessing he had fewer than three minutes left in this timeframe.

Weyoun snickered as if he had thought of a private joke. "Why change perfection?" he asked airily. "If things proceed as they did, unchanged, then we know what happens for a certainty: The universe ends. All sentient beings are freed from the suffering of their exis-tence. But if I were to take the Orb from Leej Terrell now, try to locate the one hidden on Jeraddo, somehow locate the Orb that Vash secured before she originally obtained it . . . well, who knows what might happen? Perhaps the Bajoran Ascendancy would arise more quickly and the Temple would be restored a few years earlier. But perhaps not. At best, we would gain six years. At worst, we would lose everything. So why risk it?"

"Six years times trillions of beings is a lot of suffering," Sisko said, keeping up his mental count of the time remaining in this time-frame. *Less than two minutes now.*

Weyoun walked over to a dented, unpainted bulkhead, leaned against it nonchalantly. "Benjamin, I can see your interest waning. Perhaps it's time we changed the topic of our conversation."

Sisko shot a glance at Kira and Bashir, made eye contact with both. But there was no information they could communicate to him in a glance. Just their frustration.

"A good choice," Weyoun said approvingly. "Let's talk about Dr. Bashir and Major Kira. Temporal refugees, I believe was the term they used. Like you, Benjamin. Caught in time, thrown backward and forward in the wake of the Prophets and the False Prophets. Tell me . . . as you sit there now and plot your escape, did you take a moment to ask yourself how it is these two came to be my prisoners for longer than the few minutes they might otherwise stay in this timeframe?"

The effect of Weyoun's question was as strong as if Weyoun had struck Sisko. Since Kira and Bashir had been here before Sisko had appeared, of course they should have vanished to another timeframe by now. But they hadn't. Why?

"Oh, Benjamin, really," Weyoun hooted. "Stop it. You'll make me die of amusement. You're so transparent. You honestly thought that you would simply *vanish* like a character in a child's morality tale?"

Sisko tried to think of some reason he wouldn't. Rapidly, he scanned the cargo hold. Had Weyoun installed some kind of force-field?

"Here. Let me explain," the Vorta said, and suddenly he was at Sisko's side, one hand gripping Sisko's arm, the other Sisko's neck.

Sisko fought against Weyoun's grip, struggling to strike back, but in the starburst of red energy that lanced forth from Weyoun's eyes, his body went rigid, unmoving.

"It's all about being in *phase,*" Weyoun crooned, his face only centimeters from Sisko's. "About being in harmony. Remember how, at first, you didn't belong in this time at all? How no one could even see you? And how, later you could stay a few minutes now, a few minutes then, as you searched to find the one time in which you would finally belong?

"Trust me, Benjamin. You've found your time. You belong here, and you belong now. With me. No more oscillations. No more chances for escape. You will stay in here with me, and with your friends, for a few more hours. And then, when Leej Terrell runs her final experiment and the barest glimmer of the one True Temple opens on this station in her lab, all times will become one, and you will return to your ship in the restored Temple, and there even you will melt into oneness with the final oblivion."

Weyoun suddenly released Sisko from his grip and paralysis. Sisko staggered but stayed on his feet, swaying from the draining residual effects of Weyoun's red energy.

He could only watch as Weyoun began walking away from him, returning to the bulkhead. The Vorta's smug voice floated back to Sisko. "It's over, Benjamin, and it was over before you were even born. In the realm of nonlinear time, the end of the universe was always there, always waiting for you. You saw it happen once. And you will see it happen again."

There was no logic to the fury that erupted in Sisko then, freeing him from his stupor, and finally propelled him into action. Without a sound, Sisko rushed not at the departing Weyoun but at the hatch leading to the hauler's command cabin.

Sisko leaped up the short ladder and had rolled into the small cabin before Weyoun had even turned around.

The cabin hatch cover had been removed long ago, and Sisko jumped through its opening, dropping two meters to the deck of the ore-processing bay. All his concentration and all his energy were focused on crossing the ten meters to the main corridor exit before Weyoun could scale the ladder behind him and get within striking range.

Sisko ran across the deck as if he were possessed himself, not looking back, seeing only the exit.

He had to find Cardassians or Bajorans or anyone to whom he could shout out his story. Thirty seconds would be all he would need to alert someone—anyone—to the traitors, the saboteurs, the spies, whatever, hiding in the ore hauler. All he had to do was to cause enough chaos to bring on what Weyoun did not want at any cost—a change in the way things had been in the past.

Sisko reached the exit and its half-open disk door. Breathing hard, he twisted sideways and lunged through it, not quite fitting, ripping his jacket and badly scraping his chest and back in his haste.

He stumbled forward into an airlock, tripped, slapped the deck to break his fall. He kicked his legs free of the disk door behind him, then began rolling back to his feet.

The next disk door opened onto the corridor. Sisko had time only to give the airlock status panel one fast look. But that was enough—it was not locked. He threw himself at the controls, slapped his hand against it.

The door began to roll open.

In the agonizing seconds the door's movement took, Sisko risked a half second to look behind him, which is when he learned that he had lost.

Weyoun was nowhere in sight.

Sisko's heart sank.

The only reason Weyoun would not pursue him was that no pursuit was necessary.

The disk door was open enough that Sisko could run through it.

But it was also open enough for Obanak and Lorem to enter, weapons charged and aimed.

"We serve the Emissary," Obanak said.

And then he fired his phaser.

CHAPTER 20

JAKE FELT as if he were twelve years old again, running with his mother through the shaking corridors of the *Saratoga,* with no comprehension of the nightmare playing out around him. He felt that helpless, that useless, as Arla held an emergency medikit protoplaser to his neck and pushed him onto the *Defiant'*s bridge, shouting out her warning: *"Move away from the controls or he dies!"*

At the ops console, Worf instantly jumped to his feet, but Jake could tell the Klingon's action was not in response to Arla's threat. Worf was preparing to attack.

"Don't even think about it!" Arla ordered. "The plaser's set on high, and that means his head comes *off.*"

"There is no need to harm him," Worf said, his voice level and controlled. "We can all be safely on the *Boreth* within the next five minutes."

"Nothing can change," Arla said as she moved to the back of the command chair. "Nothing *will* change. All we're going to do is remain on this ship until the war comes to an end."

Jake could see Worf's confusion at Arla's mention of 'the war.' "She must have been infected by Grigari nanomachines," Jake said to Worf. "She's—"

The swift, increased pressure of Arla's arm against Jake's throat ruthlessly cut off the air to his lungs. He gasped for breath.

If Arla had had no weapon, he knew he would have had at least a chance of breaking the grip she had on him. Nog had shared with him several good Vulcan self-defense moves from his Academy lessons. Even if Arla had just been holding a knife to his throat, it would have been worth the risk to struggle to escape. But not against a protoplaser. All Arla had to do was touch the device's activation switch once, and the resulting force beam would shoot out faster than Jake could move to deflect it. Realistically, that left him with only one choice: remain passive.

"Commander Arla," Worf said firmly, "you are a Starfleet officer who has been infected with an alien contagion. The contagion is affecting the performance of your duty. You must fight its influence and—"

"Be quiet!" Arla shouted. "I am Bajoran! And I will serve the True Prophets *before* I will be a slave to Starfleet!"

"Arla," Worf tried again, this time making his appeal more personal, "what has happened is not the Prophets' doing. You—"

Arla jabbed the tip of the protoplaser deeper into Jake's neck. "I will kill him!"

Worf issued his own ultimatum. "Then you will have no protection against my attack. And I promise you I will rip your heart from your chest."

But Arla did not give way. "Spoken like a true Starfleet officer, Commander. Now, cloak the ship."

Jake caught Worf's questioning look, obviously trying to understand some reason for Arla's wanting the *Defiant* to cloak. But Jake could only stare back, mute. He had no idea what Arla wanted or why.

"That system is off-line," Worf bluffed.

"I might not know starships as well as I know starbases," Arla said, "but I know how to read status displays. The cloaking device works. You will activate it."

"I am unqualified, and there are no cloaking specialists left aboard," Worf said stonily.

"In five seconds, I will take off the boy's head, and then you can try to take the protoplaser from me. Five seconds . . . four . . . three . . ."

Jake braced himself for the assault. He had to give Worf a chance. Maybe the Klingon could—

But Worf gave in. He started for the cloaking console. "I will require approximately twenty seconds. We are not at battle stations."

"Twenty seconds, then," Arla said. "Nineteen . . . eighteen . . ."

When her countdown hit three seconds, the ship's cloaking device switched on.

"We are cloaked," Worf said. "Release Jake."

Arla shifted Jake to the side, and he realized it was so she could see Jadzia's console. The action caused her arm restraining Jake to relax by a fraction. His breathing steadied and Jake began to think more clearly again.

"Not for another eighty-two minutes," she told Worf.

Jake stared at the time displays on the console. Eighty-two minutes was when all the pressure waves would achieve equilibrium. When everything would end.

"Now, move away from the console," Arla ordered.

The Klingon did as he was told, until he was facing her from the front of the command chair.

Despite her control of the situation, Arla's anxiety was making itself felt to Jake. He could hear the shallow rapidity of her breathing, feel the sporadic tremors that struck her body. He quickly reassessed his situation. He might still not be able to do anything physical against her, but that didn't mean he was *completely* helpless. Especially if all Worf needed was about a second—more than enough time for Klingon reflexes to act.

Jake decided to give Worf what he needed: a diversion.

He twisted his head around to look at Arla. "You beamed Weyoun over to the station, didn't you, Arla?"

"I serve the True Prophets," Arla said automatically. "They gave me the power to save the kai from his unjust punishment. Their will is my will." The Bajoran commander's attention was still on Worf. Obviously, she did not consider Jake a threat.

"And that head wound you got—that was Weyoun, because—"

Arla's arm pressed harder on Jake's neck. "*Kai* Weyoun, Emissary to the True Prophets."

"Right." Jake coughed and rolled his eyes in warning at Worf, to let him continue without interruption.

Arla's arm lessened its pressure. Jake went on. "Kai Weyoun . . . he's served by the Grigari, so the Grigari also serve the True Prophets. I bet it was their nanites that worked on your head—made it look as if you'd been attacked when you hadn't. You've probably got millions, maybe billions of tiny machines inside you right now. Pushing around your individual brain cells. Changing you."

Arla said nothing, and Worf held his position, so Jake pressed ahead, hoping Arla's silence meant there was some part of her unchanged that still remembered being part of Starfleet.

"So you can see why Worf thought you were like someone who'd been infected by an alien contagion. A natural mistake. I mean, because you have things in you that can change the way you think. Maybe even put thoughts in your head."

Arla's thumb flicked on the protoplaser's adjustment setting, and the device hummed. Jake stiffened.

"I know what you're trying to do, Jake, and this is what I think of it!"

"Owww!" Jake cried as an electric jolt of pain shot through his cheek. He twisted away from her in a reflex motion and surprised himself by suddenly discovering he had slipped out of her armhold.

In the same instant, Worf let out a roar that shook the bridge and Jake dropped and flattened, making himself deadweight just as Nog had taught him.

Jake's practiced fall threw Arla off balance when she didn't let go of his jacket. And just as she stumbled sideways, Worf hurtled over the command chair, one forearm expertly deflecting her hand holding the protoplaser, his other slamming into her throat.

Now Jake felt Arla's grip release on his jacket and he immediately rolled to the side to stay out of Worf's way, then scrambled to his feet and ran to a weapons drawer under the closest console.

But the *Defiant*'s computer didn't recognize him as an authorized crew member and the drawer would not open.

Only then did Jake look back at Worf and Arla wrestling on the deck. The Klingon's face was awash in bright blood, his left arm flopped uselessly, his one good hand still strained to hold both Arla's arms in check.

Then Jake saw the protoplaser's force-beam shoot out to a length of at least ten centimeters. Arla had obviously decreased its reach to inflict the warning cut on his cheek, but now Worf faced the glowing equivalent of a Romulan fusion blade.

Untrained to react instinctively to battle situations, without any real experience in the tactics of hand-to-hand combat, Jake did the only thing he could think to do: He asked himself how Nog would respond.

As if he were writing a scene in one of his stories, Jake visualized Nog's probable actions then carried them out, charging across the deck with an earsplitting roar of his own, and kicking Arla's shoulder where it touched the deck as hard as he could.

Arla cried out and Jake fought down the automatic urge to apologize for hurting her. *The whole idea is to disable to win,* he told himself. He spun around, prepared to strike again.

But Arla was on her side now, Worf right above her. And just as the Klingon brought his huge fist down on her face, she swung up with the plaser.

At one and the same moment in time, Jake heard the dull crunch of breaking bone and the sizzle of plased flesh.

Arla's body arched and went limp, the protoplaser rolled from her hand. The left side of her face appeared to have been crushed by the force of Worf's blow.

But Worf, too, fell to one side, moaning.

Jake ran to Worf, remembering to kick the protoplaser away from Arla.

Then he stopped and stared in shock at the gaping wound in Worf's chest. The plasing beam had sliced deep into one of Worf's hearts, and every beat sprayed more blood from the wound.

Worf looked up at Jake with clouded eyes. Tried to speak. But then slumped, head down, as if dead.

"No . . ." Jake protested, furious at his inability to help. A simple wound was something any medic could treat in seconds. But what could a writer do?

Jake slapped at his combadge. He called the agricultural technicians in sickbay, told them to get to the bridge with a full medikit at once.

They arrived within a minute, and by then Jake had used the bridge's emergency supplies to spray a coagulant into Worf's wound and hypo him with electrolytic stabilizers, metabolism blockers, and the three other drug ampules marked for emergency use in cases of BLEEDING, MAJOR: KLINGON.

The agricultural technicians helped Jake apply a self-constricting pressure bandage to Worf's chest, and with only a brief bout of squeamishness, Jake found he was capable of following the moving illustrations on the medikit's instruction padd to assist in setting up intravenous delivery of TRIOX FLUID REPLACEMENT: KLINGON in a vein in Worf's inner elbow. But the instruction padd ended with the warning to get the patient to medical facilities at once.

"The *Boreth*," Jake said. "O'Brien's got to beam him over." Then he remembered the cloak. As the technicians assembled an antigrav stretcher for Worf, Jake went to the cloaking console. But the console was unusable. Half the controls were in Romulan, and when Jake asked for translations to be displayed, the computer asked in turn for his command authorization codes. He couldn't shut it off.

Desperation impelled Jake to think back to everything O'Brien might have told him about the *Defiant,* about cloaks—which was nothing—about anything at all that might—

"Emergency transporter beacon!" Jake said. He turned to the technicians, told them to float Worf to the transporter room.

"Uh, what about her?" the bald technician asked. He looked over at Arla's still form.

Jake couldn't even look at the Bajoran, remembering the way Worf's fist had crushed her skull. "She's dead."

The technician held up his medical tricorder. "Not according to this."

"Oh, man," Jake said, forcing himself to look again at Arla. He frowned—her injury didn't seem as bad as he had first thought. He looked back at Worf, on the stretcher. *Make a command decision,* he thought, remembering a lesson from his father. *In the heat of the moment, when people are depending on you, don't waste time trying to think of the* best *decision, just make any reasonable decision and be open to correction.*

"Stay here," Jake instructed the technician. "Uh, stabilize her. And . . . tie her up or something, just in case."

The technician knelt beside Arla. "Okay, but I don't think this one's going anyplace soon."

Jake nodded without really listening. His mind was already one step beyond his next task. He gestured to the second technician to lift Worf with the antigravs and then hurried from the bridge to the transporter room.

"Can you even beam through a cloak?" the technician skeptically asked as he floated Worf's stretcher onto the transporter pad.

Jake bit his lip as he stared intently at the transporter control console, knowing just enough to bring up the printed menu of command options—the sort of information that was built into the system primarily for instruction and diagnostic purposes. "I don't know for sure," he said. "But I do know that my dad always said that a cloaked ship couldn't risk making any transmissions. So if O'Brien's still trying to find us . . . and I can get this thing to put out an emergency transport beacon . . . *yes!*"

He had found the command line. And, he noted gratefully, it wasn't dimmed, which would have indicated he'd need to input a command code to access that function. But the emergency beacon was something that was used for disasters, when a ship's crew had to be evacuated. And in cases like that, the system had to be accessible to anyone—even civilian advisors like him.

"I don't know if this is going to work," Jake cautioned, "but you should probably move off the pad."

"Right," the technician said, then jumped down, away from the stretcher. "What now?"

Jake looked at the console and the display that showed the emergency transport beacon was in operation. "I don't know," he said truthfully. "I guess we just have to wait."

That was when his combadge came alive with a call from the technician who had stayed behind on the bridge with Arla.

The technician was screaming.

The crowd in the storage chamber scattered before Dukat as the crazed Cardassian pushed through them.

Odo repeated the tactic that had worked before and changed his arms into heavy battering rams. But before the changeling could make contact with Dukat, a sphere of red energy pulsed around the Cardassian's robed form and Odo was thrown back as abruptly as if he had tried to breach the security field of a holding cell.

By the time Odo regained his feet, Quark was within Dukat's energy sphere, stubby legs kicking as the Cardassian held him up by the throat, his airway squeezed shut. The Ferengi's lavender-rimmed eyes goggled and bulged outward as his lungs ran out of air.

"Where is it?!" Dukat demanded.

A handful of others threw themselves against the glowing sphere and were repelled with the same crackling flares of red energy that had attacked Odo. Most gave up after two or three tries. But Rom kept mounting his charge over and over again with heartrending squeals of despair.

Odo quickly and gently blocked Rom, who was half-dazed by now, to discourage him from attempting yet another useless charge, then passed the distraught Ferengi over to the care of others. Only then did the changeling begin to circle Dukat's shimmering force-field, searching for any sign of an opening.

Within the forcefield, Dukat loosened his grip on Quark's throat and lowered the frantically, flailing Ferengi to the deck, to give him a chance to answer the question.

"I don't know . . . what you're . . . talking about," Quark wheezed as soon as he had sufficient breath to speak.

"Wrong answer," Dukat said. His gray-scaled hand closed around Quark's neck and the hapless Ferengi was swung high again.

Odo didn't think Quark could last a minute more without air. But with the thought of that time limit came another. The changeling turned to Simons, silently mouthed his own question: *How long?*

Simons looked at his tricorder, held up one finger.

One minute, Odo thought. That's all it would take, and Quark would survive to disappear from Dukat's grip as everyone else in the room swept into the future again. Odo was sorry he wouldn't be present to see Dukat's face when that happened.

But another thought occurred to him. Although Quark had been in phase with the rest in the group for so many oscillations already, what if, because he was in Dukat's grip, he did *not* sweep ahead with all the others?

Just to ensure that the proper transfer took place, Odo decided that Dukat should release his grip on Quark.

"Dukat!" Odo shouted, his voice echoing against the bare metal bulkheads and deck. "Put him down!"

Dukat whirled to glare at the changeling.

"I know where it is," Odo said.

Dukat suddenly grinned. "Tell me, or he dies."

"Let him go, and I'll tell you."

Dukat vigorously shook his head, and Quark. The Ferengi's eyes were closed now. Odo doubted Quark would survive much longer.

"Let me into your forcefield; let Quark out," he quickly said. "Then, if I don't tell you, you can kill me instead."

Odo stood steady as the section of the spherical forcefield directly in front of him flickered, then winked out.

He stepped forward, knowing there could only be seconds left. The forcefield reformed behind him.

"Now I can kill you both," Dukat crowed as he reached for Odo. "Tell me where the Orb is, because it's not in Quark's bar!"

But before Odo could even think of a new bluff with which to respond, blue light flashed around him—

—and he was in the storage chamber, the gravity gradient perfectly level, with everyone else but *one*. Quark hadn't made the transfer.

Odo called out to Simons. "Get me O'Brien!"

The young ensign switched on the Klingon communicator and called for the *Boreth.*

But there was no response. Odo felt Rom's pleading eyes upon him.

"It could be the Chief can't reach us when we're in the wormhole environment," Simons suggested.

"Odo," Rom pleaded, "what are we going to do?"

"The only thing you and the others can do is wait to go back," the changeling said gruffly. Then he started for the door.

As a changeling, Odo had other options.

CHAPTER 21

"Now, where were we?" Weyoun said.

Sisko opened his eyes. He focused blearily on the stained metal plates that formed the roof of the ore hauler's cargo hold.

"Ah, yes," Weyoun said. "Back to the *beginning*. Where everything *ends*. Poetic, don't you think?"

Sisko sat up, queasy. A wave of post-phaser nausea rumbled through him, though he couldn't remember when he had last eaten.

"Captain, how are you feeling?" Bashir asked.

Sisko looked away from Weyoun and saw Kira and Bashir, still tied up, sitting with their backs to the far bulkhead.

"I'll survive," Sisko said.

"Now, now," Weyoun cautioned him. "Let's not have that conversation again."

Sisko took a deep breath and slowly registered the fact that his own arms and legs weren't tied. He wondered why Weyoun would trust him not to make another escape attempt.

Then he heard a slight scraping sound behind him, looked over his shoulder, and answered his own question.

Obanak and Lorem were there, phasers in hand.

"*I* am the Sisko," Sisko told them. It was worth a try.

But Obanak looked unimpressed. "*A* Sisko, perhaps. Not *the* Sisko."

"That would be me," Weyoun explained for Sisko's benefit.

Then all the loose baffle plates in the ore hauler began to rattle at once.

"So," Weyoun said with great satisfaction, "it really has begun. That will be the transports leaving. We're in the final hours of the Day of Withdrawal."

Sisko made an attempt to construct a list of what few options remained to him but came up with none. Rushing Weyoun, or Obanak and Lorem, was out of the question. Before he even got to his feet, he'd be blasted by Pah-wraith energy or by phaser fire. And even if the blasts were meant only to stun, Sisko estimated that in the hour or two remaining before all time would end, he might never wake up.

"Are you satisfied yet, Benjamin?" Weyoun asked solicitously.

"How can I be? You're not dead."

"Droll, Benjamin. Droll. I was referring to your escape options. Are you satisfied that you have none?"

"Oh, I have at least one."

Sisko enjoyed seeing the brief flash of apprehension on Weyoun's face. "And that would be . . . ?" the Vorta asked.

"All I have to do is to convince one of you three to turn against the other two."

Weyoun chuckled in relief. "You are a rare and singular being. The twenty-five years in which you were missing from the universe were dull indeed."

Sisko looked back at Obanak. "How well do you know your texts, Prylar?"

Obanak shook his head. "This discussion isn't necessary."

"But it is. I want to know what your texts say will happen in the next thirty-one years. I'm from that time. I experienced the Reckoning. I can tell you about—"

"*Benjamin!*" Weyoun said sharply. "You can be conscious for the end of the universe, or you can be dead. The decision is yours. And the way you're talking now is one way to make it."

Sisko was encouraged that Weyoun didn't want him describing the future to Obanak and Lorem, who still had to live through the next thirty-one years. If he could say the right thing, maybe these two could make changes in that time.

"You won't kill me," Sisko challenged Weyoun. "You need an

audience. And when the three Red Orbs of Jalbador were opened in Quark's bar six—"

A bolt of red energy crackled against the deck plate beside Sisko. Weyoun glared at Sisko.

"It's all right, Captain," Obanak said unexpectedly. The prylar's thick-soled boots rang on the bare metal deck of the ore hauler as he walked around Sisko so they could see each other clearly. "If you think about it, there is nothing you can say to convince either Lorem or me to act against the Emissary. After all, in five days, we will capture your friends—" He glanced over at Kira and Bashir. "—and deliver them to Weyoun. If you *had* changed anything with what you say here, then they wouldn't be captives."

Sisko fought the growing surge of desperation swelling inside him. "Not in this timeline. But in another! Another time!"

Weyoun sighed. "Benjamin, Benjamin, Benjamin . . . haven't you realized it yet? There are no other times. No alternate realities. No mirror universes. Everything is interconnected and intertwined— like tributaries branching off from the main river. Some fall over escarpments, some dry up in thirsty ground, others rejoin the river again. But in the end, all that water, all those different ebbs and currents of cause and effect, they all spring from the same source and empty into the same sea.

"What we're about to experience isn't the end of just a *single* timeline in which the True Prophets have just happened to win. It is the end of *everything*. Oh, I grant you, other timelines might have arrived at the same moment with different timing, some sooner, some later. But just as all the pockets of space-time in the restored Temple will finally converge on the same exact eternal moment, rest assured, Benjamin, that *every* universe that ever was or ever might be will reach that moment at the same time, too."

Obanak respectfully moved to one side as Weyoun came forward until he stood over Sisko. The Vorta's gaze was full of pity. "You really must accept it, Benjamin. You simply must accept there is nothing you can do, nothing you will do, and nothing you might have done to change the inescapable fact that *this* is the *end* of *everything.*"

Sisko kept his eyes locked on Weyoun's. "I don't believe you."

Weyoun clapped his hands together in frustration. "Honestly. The one negative aspect of the end of everything is I won't be able to see the expression on your face when you realize I was right."

Sisko made up his mind then. Attack Obanak. Even if Weyoun struck him with a lethal blast of energy. Perhaps the blast would also be lethal to the prylar, and that would certainly prevent his capturing Kira and Bashir five days from now. That, along with the fact that the Red Orb would go missing from Quark's, still might be enough to change everything.

"May I stand up?" Sisko asked, then started to get to his feet anyway.

"No, you may not," Weyoun said crossly.

With a gesture from the Vorta, Sisko felt his legs go numb and he fell backward, to the deck.

"Accept it, Benjamin," Weyoun said with finality. "Who knows? You might even find it enjoyable."

Sisko vigorously rubbed his legs to bring back feeling. He wouldn't give up. There had to be something . . . something he could do, or might do, or had done . . .

And then he looked up as a transporter harmonic chimed in the close air of the cargo hold and a handheld communicator resolved from quantum scintillations in the middle of the deck.

Obanak and Lorem stepped forward and aimed their phasers at the device.

"It's Klingon," Weyoun said, perplexed.

Then the communicator buzzed to life. And with that sound and the voice that followed it, new life—and hope—took hold in Sisko.

"O'Brien to Sisko. Can you hear me, sir? I can't beam you off the station, but we have figured out a way to shut down the wormhole in Quark's before it can open. All I need from you are your personal computer override codes. Are you there, sir?"

Weyoun gave a soft laugh, leaned down to pick up the communicator, then turned it around in his hand until he found the transmit control.

"Miles O'Brien," Weyoun said sweetly, "however did you survive the destruction of Bajor, you clever, clever man?"

"Is that Weyoun?" O'Brien asked in shock.

"I prefer that you think of me as the last voice you'll hear," Weyoun said with a chuckle. "As for Benjamin, he won't be giving you any codes, because he never gave them to you in the first place. Don't *any* of you understand that—"

And then Weyoun looked up in indignant outrage as he began to dissolve into a stream of sparkling light.

Sisko was on his feet in seconds. He wanted to cheer even as Obanak and Lorem rushed forward but were unable to do anything but watch their leader disappear.

Except he didn't disappear.

For just as the transporter effect reached the final moment when all within it should have vanished, the glittering light began to intensify again.

Sisko didn't wait to see more. He jumped Obanak and fought for the phaser. If he could fire one blast through Weyoun's still forming body, it would be enough to disrupt his rematerialization.

But Obanak would not relinquish his grip and even as Sisko wrenched the powerful prylar's arm around to try to force him to fire the shot that would kill Weyoun, Sisko abandoned the struggle.

The figure in the beam was not Weyoun.

It was O'Brien.

"Chief!" Sisko shouted in joy. Then he remembered the Bajorans. "Look out!"

But the two prylars with phasers did more than alarm O'Brien. They rushed to Kira and Bashir. And untied them.

"What's going on here?" O'Brien asked Sisko as the prylars helped Kira and Bashir to their feet.

"I'm . . . not sure, Chief."

Obanak approached Sisko. "The events that are occurring," the prylar said, "are exactly those which are supposed to occur."

"I don't understand," Sisko said, now completely baffled, convinced that more than physical timeshifts were responsible for the utter confusion in this nightmare existence he was in.

"Your understanding isn't necessary, Captain." Obanak beckoned to Lorem. "You merely have to play out your role and do exactly what the false Emissary wanted us all to do—make no changes." Then the prylar left Sisko to go with Lorem to the hatch that led up to the hauler's flight cabin.

"The false Emissary?" Sisko called after Obanak. "Then you *knew* he wasn't the Sisko?"

The prylar paused before ascending the hatch's short ladder. "Of course," he said. "But in case you're wondering, neither are you."

As Lorem started up the ladder ahead of him, Obanak delivered a last message to Sisko. "Your friends will be with you soon. Leave this time; make no changes." Then he followed Lorem.

But Sisko didn't want them to go. He still had so many questions for them. "We *will* meet again," he called up after them.

He could see the prylar pause in the opening to the flight cabin. Obanak was in shadow, and Sisko couldn't be sure, but it almost seemed as if the grim prylar was smiling as he said, "Another time, Captain." Then he and Lorem were gone.

"What was that all about?" O'Brien asked as Sisko turned away from the hatch and walked toward him.

"I don't know," Sisko said. He gave in to impulse and gathered the engineer into a bear hug. "Where's Weyoun?"

Clearly discomfited by Sisko's show of emotion, O'Brien mumbled, "Um, Dax did a sensor scan that told us he was here. So I made up all that nonsense about stopping the wormhole from opening so he'd pick up the communicator. And as soon as he did, I did a transport swap, used the same beam pathway. He'll be on the *Boreth* now, all by himself, and . . . the transporter coils . . . they should be shorting out right about now."

Sisko beamed. "Chief, you're a genius!"

"Thank Dax. She talked me through it."

"Where is she?"

"She's up in Dukat's hideaway, right under the Prefect's office, still shifting through time. You know how the transporters were always so touchy when we first got here?"

"Yes?" Sisko said encouragingly. He was so pleased to see O'Brien, he just wanted to hear him talk, even if the chief's timing for reminiscing was not entirely appropriate.

"I think it was because of all the modifications Dax is making to them now. I didn't understand it back then, but it's starting to make sense."

"What kind of modifications?" Sisko asked sharply, his attention now firmly on O'Brien, whose ramblings had suddenly become much more relevant.

"Well, software changes, mostly. And if it works the way Dax says it will, she'll be able to adapt to the wormhole distortions and beam us six years into the future, to just before the station got destroyed. Then we can all evacuate, and as long as we don't interact until after the station's swallowed by the wormhole, we'll be stable in this timeline and be able to change the future."

"We can *all* evacuate! Even Jake?" Sisko's heart soared with the unexpected change of fortune.

But his all-too-brief exhilaration was quickly crushed as O'Brien painfully added, "I lost contact with the *Defiant,* sir. Jake, Worf, Arla, the two agritechnicians from Deneva. They were still onboard."

O'Brien continued his explanation, but Sisko had already begun walling off his heart again. He barely heard the Chief's next words.

"Captain—Dax is still scanning for them. I . . . would have kept trying from the *Boreth,* too. But Dax ordered me to get rid of Weyoun and not risk being on the same ship with him."

Sisko nodded like an automaton. "You did the right thing, Chief. Dax knows what she's doing. And we did need Weyoun off the station." He turned to Kira. "It's what you wanted, Major. What we both wanted. Now nothing will change but the future."

But Kira's haunted expression stopped Sisko and he remembered then the one detail he had forgotten in the excitement of seeing O'Brien and the torment of losing his boy once again.

"Six years from now," Sisko said, "the red wormhole won't open."

"Why not?" O'Brien asked, looking from Sisko to Kira.

"The Red Orb in Quark's bar," Kira said quietly. "Two weeks from now, we went looking for it. But it was gone."

O'Brien couldn't accept that. "Well . . . we have to find it. Unless *everything* goes as it originally went, we'll get snapped back to the wormhole when all the different timeframes converge."

"Where's the Orb now?" Bashir asked. "In this timeframe, I mean?"

Sisko had the answer, but it wasn't reassuring. "This is just about the time Terrell told me she sent her men looking for a Ferengi—to enter her lab and retrieve the Red Orb."

"Quark," Bashir exclaimed, his eyes alight with realization. "He doesn't remember anything that happened on the Day of Withdrawal. And neither do Odo or Garak."

Sisko was getting used to thinking in terms of effect and *then* cause. "Then let's hope it's because the three of them were helping us," he said.

O'Brien checked his tricorder. "Well, if they are going to help us, they've only got fifty more minutes to do it," he said.

Sisko looked over at the ladder that led out of the ore hauler. "Then let's give the Cardassians a hand leaving our station," he said.

The last day of the Occupation had begun.

Quark was awash in *déjà vu.*

A mad Cardassian was dragging him through the crazily tilted, deserted Promenade. By his throat. Which was almost crushed. He could hardly breathe. And worst of all, there was absolutely nothing he could do except wait for the final darkness to descend. So he would once again bribe his way to the doors of the Celestial Treasury and—

The sudden memory of the Pah-wraith hell in which he had seen the face of the Divine Nagus inspired Quark to struggle anew. He *couldn't* die. Not if it meant he'd spend eternity charting profit-and-loss statements for Rom.

"Settle *down!*" Dukat snarled at Quark, digging his long, black-nailed fingers even deeper into Quark's bruised throat.

"Ehcanbreef," Quark gasped.

Dukat's exclamation of disgust was still ringing in Quark's ears as his cruel captor threw him to the steps in front of his own establishment.

"My bar. It's still here." Quark nearly sobbed in relief.

"For seven more hours." Dukat sneered. He kicked Quark as if to keep his attention focused. "Now, show me where the Orb is hidden."

Wincing, Quark stood up, looked up and down the Promenade, but saw no one. It was the middle of the station's night, and all the excitement with Dal Nortron and the Andorian sisters had inspired his idiot brother to close early. *Just when people needed a chance to relax most,* Quark thought, still indignant at the lost opportunity for profit.

"Now!" Dukat commanded.

Quark pushed slightly against the closed doors of his bar. "Oops. Locked. We should come back—"

A bolt of red energy traced the frame of the doors, and they slid open noisily.

"—or go in right now," Quark said.

He stepped inside, looked around his beloved bar, so peaceful, so quiet, almost everything in it paid for. "Can I offer you a drink?" Quark asked cheerfully, desperate for any type of delay that might help him think what to do next.

But he was suddenly looking into eyes like dying suns and breathing the air of a charnel house.

"O-on the house," he added weakly.

Dukat's slap hurled Quark five meters across the main room, until he collapsed in a heap beside the covered dabo table.

Quark sat up more slowly this time, heart racing, limbs trembling, unsure how much longer he could keep up this foolhardy attempt to laugh in the face of danger, and absolutely furious at Rom for squandering latinum on a new cover for the dabo table when the old one was perfectly serviceable as it had been for the past eleven years. But for the matter at hand, Quark was sorry for everything bad he had ever said about time travel. More than anything, he longed for a blue light or a red light or any color light the Prophets might choose to scoop him up and put him down in any time other than *now*.

"Are you that eager to die?" Dukat shrilled at him angrily.

"Of *course* not," Quark snapped back, surprised anew by his own impressively inexhaustible temper. "But . . . but I don't know what you want from me!"

Dukat advanced on Quark, forcing the Ferengi to back up until he hit the dabo table and could go no farther.

"In approximately six and half hours," Dukat thundered, "history records that your Captain Sisko discovered the third Red Orb of Jalbador in a hiding place in your bar. When that Orb was found, it was brought into alignment with the other two, and the doorway to the Second Temple was opened."

"I'm with you so far," Quark whispered nervously, holding his hands over his ears.

"That cannot happen," Dukat hissed, spraying spittle. "That *will not* happen. Do I make myself clear?"

Quark turned his face away, closed his eyes, and nodded.

"Because the denizens of the Second Temple don't deserve to be free," Dukat intoned. "When the time came to battle the False Prophets in their Temple, when the Pah-wraiths rose in vengeance, where were those of the Second Temple?"

Eyes still tightly shut, Quark shook his head, not wanting to do anything but agree with the madman, wishing he knew how.

"They *hid*," Dukat spat at Quark, who distinctly felt drops strike him but was too frightened to wipe them away. "Cowered in their Temple as Kosst Amojan fought the good fight and *lost. Lost* for the many because of the cowardice of the few." Dukat put a hand on Quark's shaking shoulder. "So there's really only one thing left for us to do, isn't there?" he asked.

"What-whatever you say," Quark agreed tremulously.

"We find the third Orb. We destroy the third Orb. And the Second Temple will never open." Dukat leaned in close to Quark, his frightful breath hot in Quark's ear. "Can I have an Amojan from *you?*"

"Amana-Amana- . . . what you said."

Quark moaned as Dukat's hand began crushing his shoulder. "Then tell me where you hid the third Orb, Quark. Because I've already looked in this timeframe, and it's *not* where Captain Sisko will find it."

And that, Quark told himself, *is that.*

There was nothing more to say. No other options to explore.

A mad Cardassian from the future, possessed by who knew what kind of evil alien being, was set on killing him, and there was nothing more Quark could do to save himself or the universe.

There was only one last thing to do, and that was to go out like a Ferengi.

Quark opened his eyes and faced his adversary.

"Dukat," Quark said, beginning to recite the traditional last words of a Ferengi facing certain death. "This is my final offer . . ."

Dukat stared at him as if he had no idea what Quark meant.

And then, with pure Ferengi aplomb, Quark brought up his hand, extended two fingers, and poked Dukat in his red glowing eyes as hard and as fast as he could.

Dukat's otherworldly screech of shock and rage stung Quark's ears as the Ferengi ducked down and dove away from the dabo table, not sure of where he was going but determined to run away till the end.

Ahead of him, a hellish red glow crept up the walls and was reflected in all the glasses and bottles on the shelves behind the bar. Feeling most ill used, Quark braced himself for a final bolt of energy, and then—

—as quickly as if a curtain had been drawn, the red glare faded, disappeared.

Quark had bolted to the entrance but sighed, unable to help himself, and looked back.

"Huh?" Quark said.

The brand-new dabo table cover now fully covered the fallen form of Dukat's body.

And then the cover rose up by itself.

Quark drew back in horror.

But the cover re-formed into Odo.

The changeling ran at Quark. "Hurry! We don't have much time!"

"Tell me something I don't already know!" Quark wailed, horridly confused and upset.

But as usual, Odo didn't show any concern for how Quark felt, and Quark groaned as the changeling grabbed his arm to drag him back along the Promenade. Uphill against the slope of the malfunctioning gravity generators. In the opposite direction from the way he had just come.

As far as Quark was concerned, it was *déjà vu* all over again.

Jake had one last hope.

He looked up at the ceiling of the transporter room and called out, "Computer! This is an emergency!"

"Please state the nature of the emergency," the calm computer voice replied.

"The commander of the *Defiant* has been attacked by an intruder."

"No intruder alert has been authorized."

Jake struggled to think of some way to get through to the system that had the ability to control almost every piece of equipment on the ship.

"Can't you hear the screaming on the bridge?" He could. The vibrations from the tiny speaker in his combadge were awful.

"No request for specialized security functions has been received from an authorized member of the ship's crew," the computer replied.

Jake looked at the technician by the transporter pad on which Worf lay in his stretcher. The technician looked even more frightened than Jake felt.

Jake pounded his fist on the side of the transporter console, as if that might make it easier to get the computer's attention. "There *are* no more authorized members of the ship's crew! Worf's dying! Arla's infected by nanites. And everyone else is a civilian!"

"Civilians are not permitted in the transporter room without authorized personnel. Please leave at once."

The screams from Jake's combadge stopped. "If we go out there," Jake said, "Arla will kill us!"

"No request for specialized security functions has been received from an authorized member of the ship's crew."

"Because they're all *dead!*" Jake shouted. "Now, help us!"

"Please state your command authorization codes."

Jake uttered a strangled cry of rage.

"Your response was not understood. Please state your command authorization codes."

"Jake?" It was Arla on the combadge now. "Are you still there?"

"Computer, please . . ." Jake pleaded. "Use your scanners or your sensors or whatever you have to examine Commander Arla for yourself. She's infected by nanites! She tried to kill Worf!"

"Bioscan facilities are not available on the bridge of this vessel."

Suddenly, a curtain of sparkling blue energy sprang up around the transporter pad, cutting Worf's body off from the technician.

Jake stared at the shimmering blue barrier. "Computer—what did you just do?"

"A class-four security screen has been erected around the transporter pad."

"Why?"

"Authorization codes were received from Commander Arla Rees, now in command of this vessel."

Jake didn't want to give up. He couldn't just sit down and wait for Arla to kill him. But what was the point of trying anymore when not even the ship would back him up?

In desperation, he looked down at the transporter console. At least the emergency transporter beacon was still operating. If O'Brien was out there, maybe he could—

"Jake! Look!" the technician cried out.

Past the security screen, Worf's prone body was dissolving into light.

Jake looked back to the console. None of the *Defiant*'s transporter systems was in use.

"It's the *Boreth!*" Jake said. "O'Brien saw the beacon!"

"What do we do now?" the terrified technician asked.

Jake thought wildly, knew they couldn't get through the security screen to the pad where O'Brien could find them. He caught his breath. There was another option. "Transporter room 2!" he said. "Deck 3, forward!"

The technician started for the door, but Jake ran to him, stopped him, pulled off both their combadges. "This is how the computer tracks us!" He sprinted back to the aft bulkhead, pulled open the Jefferies tube access hatch, then leaned in and threw the combadges as far down the tube as he could.

"Now," he said. He raced back to the doors. They opened. Jake looked directly to the left and saw the aft ladderway that linked all decks. He waved the technician down first, checked for any sign of Arla in the corridors, found none, then followed.

They reached Deck 3 in seconds. Transporter Room 2 was only a few dozen meters ahead. Breathing hard, Jake slowed as they ran past the escape-pod hatches.

"Go ahead!" he urged the technician. He had just thought of the perfect diversion to distract Arla. Just in case she saw the second emergency transporter beacon switch on and decided to try to stop it from the bridge.

Working as fast as he could, Jake armed three escape pods with two-minute countdowns, then raced off to catch up with the technician.

Jake saw him waiting outside the transporter room, clearly afraid to even try to open the doors.

Jake ran up to them. They opened. He rushed in first.

"Get on the pad," he ordered the technician, then called up the same basic command menus as he had before.

Jake held his finger over the control that would activate the second beacon. He sent his thoughts to Chief O'Brien on the *Boreth*. *Keep scanning for the beacon . . . keep scanning . . .*

Then the deck thudded with the launch of the first pod. Then the second and third. Jake hit the control. The beacon began transmitting.

"Get up here!" the technician called out in a panic.

But Jake shook his head. "Worf said the Chief could only handle one at a time. I'll jump up as soon as—" Jake whooped with victory. The technician was already dematerializing. The Chief had come through again!

Jake ran for the pad as soon as it was empty.

And fell back as the security forcefield hit him.

"Very clever, Jake," Arla said from the overhead speakers. "I can see that you know this ship better than I do. Unfortunately, I have the command codes, and you don't."

Without stopping to argue, Jake was out of the transporter room before Arla could think to seal it off as well.

He ran aft again, remembering the time-honored truism every Starfleet officer he had known had insisted on quoting: *Whoever controls engineering controls the ship.* Chief O'Brien called it Scott's First Law.

By the time Jake reached the antimatter storage facility and ran between the frost-covered, supercooled magnetic field generators, Arla's voice was coming over every speaker in the ship. But that only improved Jake's spirits. It told him Arla had no idea where he was. With any luck, she might even believe he had already beamed off with the technician.

But luck was not completely with him.

"I know you're still onboard, Jake," Arla's voice echoed around him. "Worf got away. But I raised full shields in mid-transport—only half of the technician got through to Chief O'Brien. I ran a DNA analysis on the other half. It wasn't you."

Jake found another ladder, took it up a deck and crossed into the Jefferies tube that connected with engineering.

"You can't stop what's going to happen, Jake. So why be alone?"

Jake squeezed through the last hatchway, then shut the cover behind him and ran to the master console.

"I was alone," Arla said. "But then I found out I didn't have to be."

Small droplets of sweat fell from Jake's forehead to spatter on the glossy control surface. At least these controls were familiar to him. Thanks to O'Brien and Nog, he knew at least half a dozen different tricks to disable a starship—until now, strictly research for his novels. The Chief had cautioned him that any good engineer could work around the tricks in a minute or two. But Jake was confident that Arla wasn't any kind of engineer, good or bad.

"Ah," Arla's voice said. "I see excess computer activity in engineering. Is that where you are, Jake?"

Jake hit the controls that activated trick number one and vented a small amount of radion isotope gas into the air feed for engineering. The gas was slightly radioactive, used for calibrating the engineering tricorders that tested for leaks. The gas was also harmless, but in the words of Chief O'Brien, the safety systems onboard a Starfleet vessel jumped to warp first and asked questions later.

"Warning!"

A siren began wailing, and red flashing lights appeared on the room's cavernous ceiling.

"Radiation leak detected in engineering. All personnel must evacuate."

Within seconds, all possible entry points into engineering had been sealed, and Jake knew they would remain that way until the ship's Chief Medical Officer instructed the computer that there was no more danger of contamination. Now Arla couldn't come in after him.

"Jake?" Arla said over the sirens. "What have you done? What sense is there putting yourself in danger so close to the end?"

Jake initiated trick number two: He forced a primary bus overload.

A heavy shipwide thud announced the initial cutoff of direct power to every part of the ship except engineering. Jake knew that batteries would instantly provide backup power and could do so for days. But he also knew that a side effect of the process was that the bus overload had to be reset manually. And until it was, Arla would not be able to switch engineering control to the bridge.

Unless she knew exactly which Jefferies tube to go into, and exactly how to manually reset a bus, Jake had just effectively cut off Arla's control of propulsion, weapons, and life support.

Arla's voice was almost plaintive on the speakers. "Jake? What are you doing? It doesn't matter if you have control of the ship. There's no place to go. Nothing to do with it."

But listening to her, feeling breathless, exultant, determined, Jake knew Arla was wrong. Everything he had just done had a very specific purpose—to protect him from her. And now, undisturbed, he intended to do everything he could to figure out how he could create an emergency transporter beacon. So Chief O'Brien could find him in engineering instead of a transporter room.

And from this console, Jake had the resources of one of the most powerful starships ever built by Starfleet and access to the ship's complete engineering library.

He knew the answer he needed was in there.

Somewhere.

But he had less than one hour to find it.

CHAPTER 22

IT HAD BEEN years since Sisko had been on the emergency escape stairs that led from the lower levels of the station all the way to Ops. He had almost forgotten the enclosed circular staircase existed. But he flew up it now, with Kira, Bashir, and O'Brien close behind.

"Fifty-five minutes," O'Brien panted. "Dax should just about—"

Sisko swung to a stop on the stairs, held on to the railing, looked down past Kira and Bashir. "What was that, Chief?"

"He's gone," Bashir told Sisko. "The timeshift!"

Sisko groaned. *Of course,* he thought. O'Brien hadn't been "grounded" in this timeframe by contact with Weyoun. So as the pressure waves swept over the *Boreth,* he'd still be subject to being drawn back and forth through time.

"He's probably gone two hours ahead," Sisko said. "Major, the Bajorans didn't know about this escape passage, did they?"

Kira shook her head. "Not till O'Brien started looking for a place to put new ODN conduits."

"Then he'll be safe in here till he gets swept back. Maybe eight minutes or so," Sisko said. "Let's go." He began running up the stairs again, up the final levels to his intended destination: Gul Dukat's private safe room, just below the Prefect's office overlooking Ops.

When Sisko had first seen the secret chamber—just before

O'Brien had turned it into a secondary computer installation—his first thought had been that Dukat must, at some level, have lived his life in constant fear.

The small enclosure, nearly the equal in size of the office above it, contained resources suggesting someone with great concerns for his own safety: a sensor-masking generator, a month's supply of food and water, a chemical waste-disposal unit unconnected to the station's main plumbing lines, a cot, encrypted communications gear, and a single emergency transport pad for rapid evacuation. In the event of a real emergency—or slave worker uprising—Dukat would not even have to risk running to an airlock or runabout pad. He merely had to duck through a panel in his office upstairs and conceal himself one level below until a suitable Cardassian ship came within transporter range.

Sisko had often wondered what the gul's reaction had been when, upon regaining control of the station under the Dominion, he had discovered his secret escape route had been jammed full of backup computer cores.

At this moment, though, Sisko expected the hidden chamber would be as Dukat had left it—with the exception now that it was Dax, and not the Chief, who had claimed it for a workroom.

But as Sisko entered the safe room through the half-height door at the top of the emergency stairway, he saw something unexpected.

At the far end of Dukat's private chamber, the single transporter pad that rested on a small raised platform was covered in bright pink blood.

"Worf's been hurt!" Sisko said as Kira and Bashir pushed in behind him.

"The Chief said Worf was unaccounted for on the *Defiant,*" Kira said.

"But look at the blood. It's Klingon." Sisko scanned the empty room. "And where's Dax?"

"She's still shifting, too," Bashir said. "Her schedule will be slightly different from—"

"Julian!" The Trill's cry came from the transporter platform as she and Worf suddenly appeared on it.

Bashir sprang toward Worf, lowered the unconscious Klingon to the deck, and quickly told Jadzia what to bring him from the medical supply cabinets on the wall.

Without any hesitation, the doctor tore through Worf's already gashed jacket, grabbed a Cardassian scalpel to remove an improperly applied pressure bandage, and exposed a badly closed wound even now spurting blood. Sisko had never seen Bashir work so swiftly.

"He was treated by a butcher," Bashir said tersely as he turned away from Worf to rifle quickly through the contents of a Cardassian surgical kit, looking for supplies he could use.

In less than sixty seconds, Worf's wound was securely sealed, and from the combination of drugs Bashir had employed, the Klingon's deep brown skin was no longer ashen.

Bashir complained to himself as he studied the intravenous fluid pack on Worf's arm. "Well," he allowed, "maybe I was too hard on his first doctor. This fluid replacement pack saved Worf's life." He looked up at Sisko. "And it came from the *Defiant*. He must have been treated there."

"That's right," Jadzia said, her face still unnaturally pale from her ordeal. "O'Brien said the *Defiant* had disappeared from his sensors—almost as if it had been cloaked. So I kept scanning for it, and I finally picked up an emergency transport beacon. And then . . . on my first try . . . I got Worf . . . like this . . . and . . ." She stopped to take a steadying breath, still shaken by discovering her husband moments from death. "A few minutes later, I got a second beacon. But . . . it wasn't a successful transport."

Jake. Sisko steeled himself. "Who was it, Old Man?"

"Not Jake. Not Arla. It had to have been one of the two agritechnicians from Deneva."

The words *not Jake* echoed in Sisko's mind. But his profound gratitude was dampened by the death of another. "Was Worf able to tell you what happened?" he asked.

Jadzia shook her head as she looked from Sisko to Bashir, her own need to know etched on her face.

"He'll be fine, Jadzia," Bashir said as he got to his feet. "But I can't risk speeding up his metabolism to wake him. He's lost too much blood to survive that." Bashir looked at Sisko. "Sorry."

"Is that transporter set for beaming ahead?" Sisko made himself ask.

"Yes." Jadzia looked down at her husband's blood on her hands. "Yes, it is." She looked up again, at Sisko. "This pad doesn't exist six years from now. But I *can* send everyone from here ahead six years to the transporter in the *Rio Grande,* the night before the second wormhole opened. And if the first person I send uses the right override code on the pad airlock, we won't alert security."

"And everyone else is present in that timeframe?" Sisko asked.

"Everyone," Jadzia repeated. "Everyone except whoever's left on the *Defiant.* And Garak . . . can't seem to find Garak anywhere . . ."

Sisko saw how Jadzia was struggling to maintain her self-control. He had never seen her so upset. "Old Man, are you going to be all right?"

She nodded. "It's just that Worf . . . he was always afraid that I would die first, and now . . . now I know what he meant . . ."

Sisko put a hand on her shoulder, gave it a squeeze. "He'll be fine. You heard Julian. We've all got long lives ahead of us."

Jadzia gave him a smile, and Sisko saw the old fire in her eyes. "You're right. We do." She wiped her hands on her jacket. "So—who goes first?"

"Send Bashir," Sisko said, "so he'll be there when you send Worf through. Then Kira. By then, O'Brien should come wheezing up those stairs. Can you set it for automatic?"

"First thing I programmed into it," Jadzia said. She held up a tricorder. "Just set the timer on this."

"All right, then you go next."

Jadzia stared at him. "Benjamin, what about you?"

"I have to go find out what happened when Terrell sent Quark in after that Orb."

One look at his friend's face told Sisko that wasn't answer enough. "It's missing, Dax. Somehow, I have to make sure the Orb gets put back where I'm supposed to find it six years from now, or . . ."

Jadzia continued his statement. "The timeline's changed, and the instant we create an alternate history . . ."

"This history's over," Sisko said in conclusion. "And so are we."

"Isn't this risky?" Quark whispered far too loudly.

But Odo was in no mood for either argument or explanation. "I know what I'm doing, Quark." He dragged the Ferengi through the doors of Security.

At once, Artran Mage—the young Bajoran security officer on night duty this week—jumped to his feet behind Odo's desk. "Constable!" Artran quavered. "I thought you were taking the night off."

"So did I," Odo growled. He pushed down on Quark's shoulder to let the Ferengi know he shouldn't budge from that spot if he valued his life, then went behind his desk to the storage drawers.

Artran vainly tried to change over a computer screen before Odo could see the tongo cards displayed on it, but he was too late.

"Slow night?" Odo asked as he entered his code for the enforcement equipment drawer.

"Uh, I was just taking a break, sir."

"Mm-hmm," Odo said, not really caring one way or another. Right now, in this time he knew, he was in his quarters, meditating. And Quark was in his own quarters, snoring, most likely. So everything around Odo and Quark at this moment could almost be considered a dream of the past.

The drawer slipped open and Odo took from it the equipment he needed, safely packaged in a hard-composite shoulder case.

Artran's eyes widened at the sight of it. "Trouble, sir?"

"Not yet. Carry on, Artran."

The young officer nodded, quite confused. "Y-yes, sir. Thank you, sir. Good night, sir. Good night, Mr. Quark."

"Whatever," Quark said as Odo dragged him through the door again.

Once outside his office, Odo got a more secure grip on the Ferengi and then broke into a run as he started back toward Quark's bar.

"I—thought—you—didn't—want—to—change—anything," Quark complained as Odo's long strides bumped him up and down.

"I didn't," Odo said as he charged through the bar's doors, dropped Quark, and stopped in front of Dukat still sprawled on the floor. "You and I are both sound asleep in this timeframe."

Quark straightened his jacket grumbling. "And what happens when you take over from that kid tomorrow morning and find out you paid him a visit tonight?"

Odo knelt by Dukat and opened the case. "That's just it, Quark. I didn't. Tomorrow morning, I'll have breakfast with Major Kira, go up to Ops to see how the computer repairs are coming, then get called back down here when the Orb is discovered. I never find out that I was in two places at once, and neither do you."

"Oh, you think you're so smart," Quark snorted.

"You'd better hope that I am. Now, stand back." Odo snapped confinement forcebands around Dukat's ankles, then pulled the Cardassian's arms together to secure another set of bands around his wrists.

Dukat stirred, mumbling.

"He's waking up!" Quark warned.

"I can see that, Quark." Frankly, Odo was surprised at Dukat's premature recovery from the concussive blow he had given him. The changeling had used a technique he'd learned in the Great Link. First, he had swiftly flowed around Dukat's body like a rubber membrane, then instantly compressed against every square centimeter of the Cardassian at once. To a solid, the changeling had been instructed, the effect was similar to being caught in the blast wave from an explosion.

Odo pulled another, wider forceband from the restraint kit, tuned it to half strength, then slapped it over Dukat's eyes. Even if the Cardassian came to full consciousness now, he wouldn't be able to see a thing. Odo hoped that might reduce the effectiveness of whatever Pah-wraith powers he could wield while restrained.

Quark didn't look impressed by Odo's elaborate precautions. "Why don't you just kill him?"

"Because he doesn't annoy me even half as much as you do."

Next, Odo chose a clear cylinder from the kit and snapped it in half, activating the tiny device inside—a general-purpose neurocortical stimulator, preset to induce deep sleep, authorized for application only by law enforcement officials. As a further safeguard against misuse, Odo knew, the device would only remain active for half a day after opening. It was an extreme, though safe, method of capturing potentially dangerous suspects and much more humane than even a phaser stun in Odo's opinion.

The moment the stimulator was fixed on Dukat's temple, the Cardassian ceased his restless muttering and lay still again.

Odo allowed himself to sit back with a sigh. "I think I did it."

"You did it?! What about me?!" Quark said.

Odo straightened up with a sigh. "You know, Quark, when it comes right down to it, none of this would ever have happened if it hadn't been for you."

"That's not true," the Ferengi protested.

Odo bent down, hooked his hands under Dukat's arms, and hoisted him up with a grunt. "Get his feet, Quark. And yes, it is true."

Scowling but complying, Quark lifted Dukat's feet and began backing up toward the bar's entrance. At the same time, Odo began walking backward in the opposite direction, with their opposing actions threatening to tug Dukat in half. But Odo had the advantage of height and changeling strength.

Quark promptly dropped Dukat's feet with an exclamation of disgust. "Aren't we taking him to Security?" Quark demanded. "And if you ask me, this is all Vash's doing."

"Pick him up, Quark," Odo growled so fiercely the Ferengi instantaneously obeyed. "If I take him to Security, then as soon as I wake up tomorrow morning, the report will be on my personal padd. And since it wasn't on my padd, we're not taking him there. Besides, it's a bit crowded with all your friends and business partners already locked up in it. Base and Satr and Leen. And aren't you ashamed, blaming your shortcomings on a woman who's no longer here to defend herself?"

Quark huffed in his struggle to keep his end of Dukat in position as Odo directed them toward the bar's backroom. "We're not putting him into *my* storage room?!" Quark gasped.

"As a matter of fact, we are," Odo said as he shouldered open the storeroom door.

Having lost the battle, Quark was anything but gracious in defeat. "Well, anyway, don't forget Sisko brought the other two Orbs in here. It's his fault if it's anyone's."

Odo lowered Dukat to the deck. Once again, Quark simply let go of Dukat's feet, and they fell with a thud.

"Now what?" Quark sighed.

"Now we let time catch up with us," Odo said. "Any moment now, we're going to be swept into a timeframe after the station's destruction—"

"Speak for yourself, Odo. You all disappeared last time, remember? But *I* stayed put with Dukat."

Odo paused and thought about that. Quark was right. Everyone in the storage chamber had shifted to the future timeframe, leaving only Dukat and Quark behind. Odo himself had hurried through the empty station to become a cover for the dabo table, so that when he had been swept back to the same timeframe Odo and Dukat occupied, he had been ready to attack in the bar, where he had strongly suspected Dukat would come.

Could it be possible that Quark was permanently in phase with this timeframe now?

Odo reached out and took Quark's arm.

"Now what?" Quark exclaimed in total frustration as he tried to wriggle out of Odo's grasp.

"Now we find out if—"

A flash of red light burst around the changeling, and when it faded, Odo was alone in the backroom of Quark's deserted bar.

Poor Ferengi, Odo thought.

It had happened again.

Quark and Dukat were alone in the past with each other.

It was a toss-up to Odo which one would be more dangerous.

Jake looked up from the main display screen on the master console in engineering and checked the time readout.

Forty-seven minutes.

And he still hadn't found what he needed.

"Think, Jake," he said aloud. "Think!" Still talking to himself, pacing back and forth by the console, he suddenly came up with an approach. "What would Higgs and Fermion do?!" He shook his head, quickly chose another scenario. "No! What would . . . Marauder Mo do?!" At least he knew the answer to that one. Mo would call for help from Nit, his comic sidekick, and Nit would come bumbling in, crash an aircycle into the villain's warship or, better yet, stumble and knock poison into the vat of slicerfish his partner was slowly being lowered into, or otherwise end up freeing Marauder Mo by accident.

Mind racing, thoughts tumbling, Jake discarded the idea of an accident—that was too much to hope for now.

He stopped pacing. *Then again, the idea of calling for help . . .*

He brought up the emergency communications screens on the master console. Everything he wanted to do was already built into the ship's comm system!

"Jake? Are you still there?"

Arla's voice was huskier, as if she'd been shouting. Or coughing. Or weeping. Jake didn't reply to her. There was no reason to.

"If we're together when the end comes, Jake, then maybe we can end up in the next realm of existence together. Would that be so bad? We wouldn't be alone then."

Great offer, Commander, Jake thought. *That's just how I'd like to spend eternity. In a Pah-wraith hell with someone infected by nanites.* He pressed his hand to the large red square that appeared on the console and immediately a new screen confirmed that he was transmitting a Starfleet general distress call on all subspace and electromagnetic frequencies.

The response was almost immediate, as if someone had been listening specifically for his signal. Jake almost whooped in his excitement, in his relief.

"Dax to *Defiant!* I am receiving your distress signal. Come in, *Defiant!*"

Jake leaned forward, staring at the screen, almost unable to believe that after all he had been through, the solution to his nightmare had been so simple. But the emergency comm system was designed to be used by people with no experience with starship procedures. Now all he had to do to reply was touch the command line indicating the preferred mode of communication—in this case, ordinary radio.

He touched the control with one trembling finger. "This is Jake! Dax, where are you?"

"Jake, we're all on the station."

"Is my dad there?" Jake held his breath as he waited for Jadzia's reply. As he waited to hear if his nightmare was really over.

And it was. Sort of.

"He's here," the Trill said, "but . . . you know about the timeshifts. Right now, he's back at the Day of Withdrawal. But the rest of us, we're back full circle, Jake. Right on the day the red wormhole opened."

Now Jake needed to know why his father was alone in the past. "Can you bring him forward? Are we going to make it? And what about Worf?"

"Worf's stable," Jadzia answered. "Julian says whoever treated him on the *Defiant* saved his life. But Jake, now we have to get you and Arla and the last tech off the ship. Can you get to a transporter room?"

"Can't you beam me off from here?" Jake asked, his voice rising, unwilling to let hope slip so soon from his grasp. Quickly, he filled Jadzia in on what had happened to Arla. What she had done to the tech. Why he couldn't leave engineering.

Jadzia's answer was heartstopping. "I can't beam you out while your shields are up, Jake. Can you drop them?"

"I don't know," Jake said, despairing. "Can I?"

A new voice came on the circuit, and Jake's spirits rose again at its capable, practical sound. "Jake, it's Miles. Where are you exactly?"

Jake told him *everything*. What was on the displays. The tricks he had used to seal engineering and block Arla from taking control of most of the ship's subsystems—most but not all.

On the bridge, Arla still controlled the shields.

"And I'm not going to let them down," Arla's voice suddenly said as she intruded into the circuit. "If that's what it takes to make you people accept the inevitable, I am *not* going to let them down."

Jake heard something else on the circuit then. Something he had never ever heard before.

Chief O'Brien swearing.

And that told Jake there was no use in struggling anymore.

If the Chief couldn't get him off the ship, no one could.

CHAPTER 23

FROM THE second level of the Promenade, Sisko stared down into the hell Terok Nor had become—a tumultuous pocket universe of heat and noise and anarchy.

The security gates that had bisected the Promenade were collapsed, twisted by hammers and wirecutters and the frantically grasping hands of slaves set free. The glowing restraint conduits that once had bound the gates now cracked and sparked and sent strobing flashes into the dense blue haze that choked the air, still Cardassian-hot.

Hull plates resonated with the violent release of multiple escaping shuttles and ships. A thrumming wall of sound sprang up as departing soldiers phasered equipment too heavy to steal.

Decks shook as rampaging looters forced internal doors and shattered windows. Turbolifts whined and ladders rattled against their moorings. Officers shouted hoarse commands. Soldiers cursed their victims. In counterpoint, a calm recorded voice recited the orders of the day: "Attention, all biorganic materials must be disposed of according to regulations. Attention . . ."

But the only response to that directive that Sisko could hear was the high-pitched shriek of a Ferengi in fear for his life. A Ferengi whose shriek Sisko recognized.

"A compelling display, wouldn't you say, Captain?"

Sisko jerked away from the safety railing as another familiar voice whispered unexpectedly in his ear.

"Garak! Where have you been?"

The Cardassian knelt beside Sisko, the mangled decorative wall panel that leaned against the railing providing the two of them a semblance of cover from the combatants one level below. Sisko saw that Garak wore a uniform obviously replicated from the *Boreth*—an odd combination of Starfleet and Bajoran militia designs that was completely out of place in this time.

"Oh, here and there, reliving history, as it were."

Sisko had no patience for Garak's infamous perversity right now. "Get up to Dukat's personal shelter, beneath his office. Dax set up a transporter that will beam you to the *Rio Grande,* six years into the future."

"Ah, good," Garak said. "Then everything's working out."

"What do you mean?"

But Garak ignored the question and pointed past Sisko to the level below. "Look, there's Quark and Glinn Datar."

Sisko looked down to see Quark's struggling form being lifted by an ODN cable that was wrapped around his neck and attached to a rising antigrav cargo lifter. All around Quark's suspended form, a crowd of angry Cardassian soldiers chanted and jeered.

Sisko's automatic reaction was to try to do something to stop the outrage. But Garak put a hand on his shoulder.

"Don't do anything foolish, Captain. You know as well as I that our Ferengi friend survives this day."

So Sisko forced himself to remain hidden, flinching as Quark kicked so desperately hard that one of his boots flew off.

"The soldiers didn't like Quark," Garak explained. "They decided to use the absence of the command staff to obtain some justice of their own."

Sisko was appalled by the treatment Quark endured. No wonder the Ferengi had been packing up and eager to leave when Sisko had arrived on the station.

Then a lance of blue phaser fire sliced into the antigrav. The machine burst in two and fell, dropping Quark flat on his back in the middle of the Promenade. At the same time, another round of phaser bursts killed Datar and scattered the soldiers who had gathered to see Quark punished.

"What now?" Sisko asked, sickened.

"Ah," Garak said, "this is where it gets interesting. I believe you know the group approaching just down by the gem store? Leej Terrell's associates?"

Sisko caught a glimpse of three Cardassians through the haze, and though he couldn't recognize them at this distance, he remembered Terrell had told him what she had sent three Cardassians to do on this day.

Right now in this timeframe, the Red Orb that the Cardassian scientist had studied was in her hidden lab in the station's lower levels. And whatever equipment she had connected to the Orb to amplify its powers was at this moment creating a precursor field that would eventually lead to the opening of the red wormhole. Sisko knew that several of Terrell's scientists had already stepped through that field and had disappeared, tempted by the red wormhole entities themselves.

So, to retrieve her Red Orb safely on the Day of Withdrawal, to keep it from the Bajorans without sacrificing any more of her staff, Terrell had decided she needed a Ferengi to fetch the Orb, because Ferengi brains were resistant to most forms of telepathy—including, Terrell hoped, the influence exerted by wormhole entities.

More phaser beams shot forth below. Sisko peered down through the railing. A Cardassian soldier was crouched protectively by Quark, but he was drawing heavy fire from Terrell's three cohorts.

"Now someone's trying to *save* Quark," Sisko told Garak.

"Glinn Motran," Garak said with an unconcerned nod. "One of Dukat's personal bodyguards. There is considerable bad blood between Terrell and Dukat. And many others, I might add. In any case, from the communications I've managed to intercept today, it appears Motran's assignment is to delay Terrell's departure by any means possible."

"Why?"

"So she'll still be on the station when the self-destruct countdown reaches detonation."

Sisko turned to Garak in amazed alarm. Terrell had told him that Dukat had set the station to self-destruct. But why the system had failed was still unknown.

Garak misread Sisko's reaction. "Why so surprised, Captain? Of course Dukat set the self-destruct timer when he left. I believe there is something on the order of slightly less than two hours remaining."

"Who stops it?" Sisko asked.

"Ah," Garak said with a smile. "That remains to be seen. *So* many mysteries to be solved this day." He pointed down again as if commenting on a passing parade. "Oh, look, there goes Motran . . ."

Glinn Motran was suddenly hit by multiple shafts of disruptive energy and his body flew backward across the Promenade. At the same moment, Quark scurried into his bar and out of sight of the second level.

But Sisko knew the Ferengi barkeep wouldn't remain there for long. The three Cardassians who served Terrell were marching forward, shoulder to shoulder, along the ruined Promenade toward Quark's bar.

"I can handle it from here," Sisko told Garak. "Go up to the transporter and get out of here."

But Garak shook his head. "Remember, Captain, you're on my station now. For the next few hours, this is still Terok Nor, and I would be most remiss if I did not do all in my power to see that you survived your visit."

Six years after the Cardassians withdrew from Bajor, in the back room of his bar, Quark stared at the empty space where Odo had been just an instant before. Then he looked down at Dukat, sprawled on the floor at his feet.

Gingerly, Quark rapped his foot against Dukat's arm.

No reaction.

Quark escalated from a tap to a kick.

Still nothing.

With a sigh of relief, Quark realized he could walk out of his storeroom, leave Dukat behind, and not feel the slightest bit guilty. The insane Cardassian had been removed from the equation by DS9's own constable. If he woke up later and caused any trouble, then it definitely would not be Quark's fault.

"Thank you, Nagus," Quark said softly, then returned to the main room of his bar.

He knew exactly what he was going to do.

First, he was going to clean out his floor safe. True, the Quark of this timeframe might be upset at losing his working capital so mysteriously, but it belonged to Quark as much as it belonged to Quark. "Or . . . however that works," Quark told himself. "It's all mine no matter how you calculate it."

Then Quark planned to open up the long-hidden, long-forgotten alcove behind his towering, stylized, stained-glass portrait of what Gul Dukat had once believed to be a Tholian general but Rom had identified as that part of a Tellarite not to be mentioned in polite company. And *then* he was going to take out that *frinxing* third Red Orb and . . . and . . . throw it into Bajor's sun.

That way, the red wormhole would never open. The station would not be destroyed. And everyone *and* the universe would be saved. All because of one selfless Ferengi, Quark.

Quark repeated the description to himself, relishing the sound of it. Really, he mused, it was a mystery how the people on this station could ever think they could get along without him.

Cleaning out his floor safe was a simple matter. He had rehearsed the operation often enough, and he always kept inside the safe a variety of belts and a vest with custom pockets for latinum bars and slips so he'd be able to carry as much as he could.

The only unfortunate thing, Quark thought as he now retrieved his vest and belts, was that he could carry a lot more than he had in the floor safe.

But what he did have would be enough to put him on an equal footing with the second Quark who already inhabited this timeframe. Perhaps they could even become partners. Quark filled his vest pockets to bursting with latinum and then paused for a moment before fastening his belts. It was an absolute certainty he'd make a much better brother to himself than Rom had ever been.

With that self-satisfied thought, Quark closed the empty floor safe. Then he leaned behind the bar counter and took out a small deconnector tool and ran—actually, with the tightly belted, latinum-stuffed vest, it was more like waddled—over to the large frame that held the orange, yellow, and red mural that was the centerpiece of his main room. Making his gait even more awkward was the slant of the deck caused by the still-unrepaired gravity generators.

Quark awkwardly squatted down behind the mural's frame and

removed the connectors holding an access panel in place. The opening it revealed and the space it protected within were no larger than those of a typical Bajoran Orb Ark.

"Marauder Quark *saaaves* the universe," Quark cackled as he reached inside, past the sensor mask.

He reached a bit farther, hit the back wall.

Moved his hand back and forth. Hit the side walls. The deck. Even the top of the compartment.

"I know you're in there," Quark said. "I saw Sisko find you six hours from now."

But even as he frantically waved his hand back and forth until it moved like the clapper of a bell, no Red Orb was found or magically materialized.

"Odo," Quark said in growing outrage. The changeling was the only one on this station who would deliberately change history in order to make life more miserable than it already was for Quark.

"When he comes back . . ." Quark vowed hotly. "I am—"

He heard someone move behind him. Froze. Cringed. Turned slowly, barely breathing, expecting to see the mad Dukat reaching out for him.

But it was someone else.

Quark let out his breath. He patted down his vest to be sure that none of its precious cargo showed.

"I'm sorry, but I'm not open yet," he said politely as he got to his feet, never one to annoy a customer—unless the customer deserved it. "But I'm sure the cafe just down the—"

Quark never finished his sentence.

Because the third Red Orb of Jalbador, swung like a club by his unexpected visitor in prylar's garb, smashed against his head much too fast and too hard.

Quark's body hit the floor and stayed there, every bit as limp as yesterday's *gagh*.

Jake read the master console's time display.

Thirty-two minutes.

O'Brien had thought of nothing that could be accomplished in the time remaining. Not that the Chief hadn't been trying, endlessly suggesting ways to gain control of the *Defiant*'s shields.

If Jake had been elsewhere on the *Defiant,* the Chief might have been able to induce a minor matter-antimatter explosion, disabling the ship's entire power grid so the shields would drop and Jadzia could attempt to blindly beam Jake from the unprotected vessel. But even Jake knew that while he was sealed in engineering, any attempt by O'Brien to explosively damage the *Defiant'*s generators would prove fatal.

Even Bashir had tried to save him. The doctor had provided his authorization codes so Jake could report to the computer as the ship's chief medical officer. But that hadn't worked, either. The computer was not that easily fooled.

"How's my dad?" Jake asked, needing a short break from the relentlessly hopeless attempts.

"He and Garak still aren't here," Jadzia radioed back. "But we've got a little time."

Then Kira's voice came over the channel. "Commander Arla, are you still there?" she asked firmly.

"Major Kira," Arla answered breathily, her voice continuing its gradual decline that Jake had noticed earlier but could not explain.

Jake was guessing that Arla was still on the bridge. Though with a combadge, he knew, she could be anywhere else on the ship. He shivered.

Kira's voice was commanding, persuasive. "Arla—why won't you let Jake go? You've heard what's going on. If Sisko and Garak don't return to this time, history will change. You'll have won."

"And what if they do return?" Arla asked.

Jake was troubled by Arla's deep, rough tones. It was as if her throat had changed in size or configuration. He didn't want to think about what the Grigari nanites might be capable of doing to her. And perhaps, soon, to him.

"Then Jake's death accomplishes nothing but to add to the sorrow of the universe," Kira argued. "I know there's enough of you left inside, beyond what the Grigari have done, to know I'm right. Let him go, Rees. Please. As a Bajoran. For the sake of our people."

"You are the dead," a new voice said.

Jake jerked back from the console in a reflex action.

Weyoun was back. But where?

"Oh, yes," Weyoun continued in a voice that froze Jake's ability to think. "I'm still here. On the *Boreth.* Exactly where you placed me against my will."

Jake heard the change in Kira's tone. "Is that what this is going to take?" she demanded of Weyoun. "A trade? Your life for Jake's?"

Jake stared at his communications screen, listening, hoping, dreading. He didn't want to die on this *Defiant.* But he didn't want Weyoun to go free because of him.

"What life, Major?" Weyoun said over the comm link. "There's less than an hour remaining by whoever's timeframe you measure it. Arla is doing the right thing." Then he added for Arla's benefit, "You *are* doing the right thing, Commander."

"It is the will of the True Prophets," Arla chanted tonelessly.

Jake leaned over his console, rested his head in his folded arm. He'd been right before. There was no way out of this.

"Weyoun," Jadzia suddenly suggested, "I could beam you from the *Boreth* to the *Defiant.* You and Arla could be together at the end."

Jake did not lift his head, but he listened in spite of himself.

"What a splendid idea," Weyoun answered. "Then, when the *Defiant's* shields drop to let me beam onboard, why, you could beam Jake off, too. Do you really think that's going to happen?"

Jake lifted his head. He had heard that tone of voice before, back in his school days on Earth. It was the sound of a bully. Someone who enjoyed creating pain because he drew strength from it. "You're not talking about the will of the Prophets anymore," Jake said accusingly to Weyoun. "You're just mad at my father."

"I assure you, Jake, I am quite beyond such petty emotions."

"You want me to die out here because you want to hurt my father."

"Jake, it doesn't matter to *me* where you die. The whole universe is coming to an end."

"But not because you want it to!" Jake said. He sat up in his anger.

"Jake, it is the will of the True Prophets. I am sorry that—"

"It's *not* the will of the Prophets!" Jake cried out. "Don't you understand, it's the will of those lousy little nanites in your skull. Rearranging your brain cells. Making you think whatever the Pahwraiths want you to think."

Weyoun's voice hissed with menace. "If you were within my

reach, Jake, I would settle this now. You would die for your blasphemy."

"Blasphemy," Jake muttered. "Ha! Don't you remember anything about the 'discussions' you used to have with me on DS9 when you were in control? You never used to care if I didn't agree with you. You might have clamped down on what I could write, but you never had a problem just listening to me!"

"That was another time," the Vorta said. "And another Weyoun."

"Why? Because the Grigari nanites have . . . have reconfigured you! Just like they crushed Arla's skull and rebuilt her brain in their image!"

"Jake, I can tell you're working yourself into a regrettable emotional state. It would be a shame if you were to miss what is likely to be the defining moment of your life's experience."

"You know what my defining moment is?" Jake shouted at the console. "I love my father! Who the hell have you ever loved?!"

There was no reply on Weyoun's channel. Nor anything from Arla on the intraship link.

Jake rocked back and forth as he breathed deeply to steady himself.

He checked the readout.

Twenty-four minutes.

The end wouldn't be so bad, Jake thought, if only he could talk to his father one more time.

If he was a condemned man, that was his last wish.

CHAPTER 24

"OH, LOOK," Garak said with satisfaction. "Now I'm here, too."

Sisko looked in the direction Garak indicated and saw—

Garak.

This timeframe's version of him, dressed in civilian clothes, huddled behind the twisted wreckage of a collapsed air channel on the second level of the Promenade.

"It would appear all the players are now in the game," Sisko's Garak said.

"Do you know what you were doing here?" Sisko asked. He looked down through the railing to the main level, to see Terrell's three agents marching Quark and Odo out of Quark's bar. They were heading for a turbolift.

"No doubt the same thing I'm doing now," Garak said. "Trying to make sense of a very confusing day for the Cardassian people. Oh, look again—Quark's seen me!"

Sisko saw the Ferengi below look up in their direction, his attention caught by something he saw on the second level—Sisko's Garak, in his hiding place.

But atypically silent, the Quark below walked on without giving any other reaction.

"We should go down," Garak said behind Sisko.

Having already made up his mind to accept the Cardassian's lead, Sisko now followed him, quickly reaching the first level via a winding metal stairway.

With Sisko close behind him, Garak edged out onto the Promenade, then ducked a moment later into a half-opened airlock. Once again, Sisko stayed with him.

Garak stayed a step back within the shelter of the airlock's entrance. He held up a cautioning hand. "Well, that should confuse the poor fellow," he said. "I believe Quark just saw me again."

Sisko peered past Garak. But if the Quark of this time had seen the Cardassian, again he was not giving any reaction to confirm the sighting. All Sisko could confirm for himself was that Quark and Odo had stepped into a turbolift car with the three Cardassians, then descended.

"Now where?" Sisko asked his guide.

Garak gave him a look of reproach, and Sisko realized how obvious the answer to that question was.

Over the next few minutes, Sisko and Garak's task of following Quark and Odo and their captors was made immeasurably easier by knowing where they were going—to Terrell's hidden lab.

The most delicate aspect of the operation for Sisko and Garak was ensuring they wouldn't be spotted by Garak's past self, as he also followed the other Cardassians for reasons of his own.

"This is all so new to me," Sisko's Garak said as they ended up crawling through a Jefferies tube on the same lower deck as Terrell's lab. "I must have already been suffering from some sort of memory lapse—because of the inhibitor I had asked myself to take. Afterward, since I undoubtedly suspected that I had been subjected to a memory-altering drug developed by the Obsidian Order, I, of course, must have suspected Terrell."

Sisko attempted to make that causal loop make sense. "So . . . you followed Terrell's agents in the past," he reasoned, "because you came from the future to give yourself a memory inhibitor, because you couldn't remember why you followed Terrell's agents."

Garak paused for a moment and looked back at Sisko with a good-natured smile. "Isn't time travel remarkable? Such an invigorating challenge!"

A minute later, Sisko and Garak hit the end of the same dead-end conduit that Sisko recognized as the one Jake and Nog would discover a year or so from now, when they first located Terrell's lab and believed it was a Cardassian holosuite.

Through the air mesh of the conduit's cover, Sisko had a direct view of the door to that lab. The door itself was pulsing in and out in what Sisko recognized was a manifestation of Pah-wraith energy—something that Terrell had not yet learned to identify, quantify, or fear.

But because of the rumble of other sounds that now echoed deep within the conduit—explosions, alarms, the thrum of departing shuttles—Sisko couldn't hear what Terrell was saying about Odo and Quark, who were right beside her. He could see her face, though, and its expression revealed to him that she wasn't happy. Sisko's assessment was confirmed as in the next moment Terrell shot Odo.

Sisko tensed as the changeling collapsed, but Garak only whispered, "Easy. Remember—Odo survived this day, too. Though I'm afraid the same can't be said for those two young men in the brown suit and the blue."

All three Cardassians with Terrell were civilians—at least, their clothes were.

And the tailor was right. Sisko had seen those two suits before.

They'd been on the two soldiers whose bodies would be found fused into the hull plates of the station—at the same time as Odo investigated Dal Nortron's murder.

And Terrell's three agents weren't the only Cardassian civilians in the corridor below. Because now, the blue-suited Cardassian held onto a third captive—Garak.

"I must say, it's beginning to make some sense to me now," Sisko's Garak said.

Sisko watched and tried to listen through the conduit cover's airmesh as Terrell said something to the Garak held captive before her, then turned and had a separate word with Quark.

"She's telling him she wants him to go into the lab and get the Orb," Sisko said.

Quark's reluctance was apparent.

Tendrils of red energy had begun to snake out all along the doorframe, as if outlining a miniature wormhole that was already beginning to form inside.

"That must be what's linking us to this day," Sisko said in a low voice. "And what's linking the station's timeframe to the wormhole six years from now. Terrell almost succeeded in opening a wormhole just with one Orb and her equipment."

"A sobering thought," Garak said quietly beside him.

Suddenly, in the scene beyond the conduit air-mesh, Sisko saw Odo come back to consciousness and then begin to shout out something. Almost immediately, the changeling was drawn to the distorted, pulsing door to Terrell's lab, moving toward it as if compelled.

"A telepathic summons," Sisko whispered to Garak. "That's what Terrell said happened to some of her scientists."

Now the third Cardassian—perhaps Atrig, Sisko thought, younger and unscarred—jumped between Odo and the lab door. He pointed a weapon at the changeling, then stunned him again, preventing Odo from entering the lab.

Meanwhile, Terrell pushed Quark closer to the door.

Sisko instinctively recoiled as a huge strand of red energy unfurled from the opening upon the door and then lashed out at Terrell, who was saved at the last moment when Atrig leaped in front of her. This time, the Cardassian was struck by a tendril on his back and was hurled forward across the corridor, falling facedown on the deck, red energy snapping over the length of his body.

Then two more coils of energy darted out and Sisko saw Quark duck as they shot over him to strike the two Cardassians—the same two who would be found six years later, merged halfway into the DS9 hull.

Sisko and Garak watched as red light crept over the Cardassians' flailing forms as if it were alive and ingesting them. Then, like a whip being cracked, the coils snapped back to the door, and the bodies of the two Cardassians were pulled through solid metal.

Terrell's small phaser was now pressed against Quark's temple.

Sisko saw waves of indecision sweep over the Ferengi's face and could almost guess at his thoughts: Accept a clean death here? Or face whatever lay beyond that door that might be worse?

But as Sisko knew Quark must, the feisty Ferengi gathered up his courage, wrapped his head in his arms, ran straight at the door, and—

—disappeared.

"A remarkable display of character," Garak commented. "I wonder what convinced someone like Quark to make the attempt?"

Sisko didn't know. He accepted that he never might. Whatever had driven the Ferengi forward, though, Sisko knew it hadn't been cowardice.

"And now we wait?" Sisko asked Garak.

The Cardassian nodded. "There can't be much time remaining, but if we wish to know how Quark obtained the Orb, then wait we must."

A moment later, though, the waiting was over for the versions of Odo and Garak who stood below in the corridor. Two more red coils whipped out from behind the door and pulled them both back into the realm of the red wormhole, even as Terrell finally gave up her vigil and shouted for her people to withdraw.

Sisko's eyes tracked the Cardassian scientist's retreat, not to return for six long years, abandoning her research and her lab. Without ever learning what now transpired behind its pulsing, glowing door.

Sisko's eyes remained fixed on the door.

He wondered if he would ever learn its secret.

And if so, who would tell him.

In a timeframe six years later, Quark awoke. And wished he hadn't. His head throbbed as if Morn was performing his favorite toe-tapping, crowd-pleasing Lurian fertility dance directly on Quark's skull.

He tried to get up, but something—someone—held him back. Someone behind him.

Quark groaned as he twisted his neck to look back over his shoulder.

Then he squeaked to see Dukat's unconscious form slumped behind him.

He and the mad Cardassian were tied together, back to back.

Quark lurched forward in his desire to get away, but his legs were tied together, too. He struggled to do more than squeak, but he was gagged.

He took a deep breath to quell his panic, forced his racing heart to settle down, exactly as Odo would undoubtedly instruct him. He looked around.

Wherever he was, the dim light was coming from a single fixture overhead. Slowly, his eyes adjusted to the insubstantial light and then, with a start, he realized he knew where he was: tied up in his own storage locker under his own bar.

And from the sounds of the footsteps overhead, his bar was opening up for business.

Quark's eyes widened. If whoever had hit him had placed the Red Orb in the hiding place where it belonged . . . He began to struggle against his bindings again. In only an hour, maybe two, he knew the red wormhole would open and the station would be destroyed, exactly as it had been before.

Except this time, *he'd* be trapped on it, bound and gagged and facing certain death with his only company a madman.

There was only one way out.

Even as Quark sent a silent entreaty to the Divine Nagus, he knew how utterly ridiculous he was being.

Yet what else could he do?

So he said the words he would never in a millennium have believed he would ever utter.

Squeaking full volume through his foul-tasting gag, Quark cried out: *"Dukat! Dukat! You have to wake up!"*

On the *Defiant,* Jake leaned with his back against the master console, arms folded, thinking about Mardah. Thinking about all the things he had left undone, the books unwritten, the secrets never shared.

"Still there?" Jadzia asked over the comm link.

"Yeah," Jake said. "Any word from my dad?"

"Not yet." Jake could almost picture the Trill's smile as she spoke. "But you know your father, Jake. He likes to push his deadlines to the very last second."

"Yeah. Maybe he'll surprise us." Jake shook his head at his own words. A surprise was about the only thing that *could* save him now.

He twisted around to look at the time readout.

Nineteen minutes.

Jake turned back.

Just about time for the universe to end.

Again.

CHAPTER 25

"FIFTEEN MINUTES," Garak said as he looked at his tricorder. "Ah, well. Perhaps there are some things we are not meant to know."

"Five more minutes," Sisko said. He had peeled off his ripped jacket in the close confines of the conduit. It was enervatingly hot in here. The air circulators were off-line, along with most of the other equipment on the station.

"It will take five minutes for us to reach the transporter in Ops," Garak reminded him. "And then there will be two of us to beam out. Even for you, that is leaving precious little time."

"Do you want to go ahead?" Sisko asked.

But Garak declined the offer. "What I might do, however, is move back to the Jefferies tube. I find the conduit is a bit . . . closed in for my liking."

Sisko shifted out of the way and Garak crawled back to the Jefferies tube to which the conduit connected.

Quark, Odo, the past Garak, and the two Cardassian soldiers had been gone from the corridor outside Terrell's lab for almost ten minutes. If time in the red wormhole was nonlinear, anything could have happened by now, Sisko knew.

Then Garak called out in an urgent whisper, "Captain! Quickly!"

Sisko slid along the conduit to join Garak in the Jefferies tube.

"Quark!" the Cardassian whispered. He pointed ahead. "He just crawled through that intersection. And he was carrying the Orb!"

Sisko immediately began crawling down the tube with Garak following behind.

At the intersection, Sisko carefully looked around the corner, saw no trace of Quark, and pushed on.

After two more turns, it was clear where Quark was headed—his bar.

"This is it!" Sisko said to Garak. "Somehow, Quark got the Orb, and he's taking it up to hide in his bar, exactly where we'll find it six years from now!"

"Except," Garak pointed out, "didn't you say someone else will steal it?"

"Not if we steal it first!" Sisko said decisively.

He was positive there was a chance his last desperate plan could work. *If* he could get the Orb from Quark. *If* he could take it into the future. And *if* he could then hide it again in Quark's bar just before he himself went to search for it after returning from Jeraddo. If he could make that chain of events work out, everything else would, too.

Sisko, with Garak still following, proceeded as quickly as he could through the tubes for one more deck, until he saw an open hatchway. He leaned forward to peer through it, just in time to see Quark hurrying along a corridor, Orb in hand.

Sisko jumped down after his quarry. Garak dropped in pursuit an instant later.

And then, two levels below the Promenade and what Sisko *knew* was Quark's final intended destination, everything changed.

Sisko charged around a corner to find Quark rolled up against a bulkhead, blood trickling from his mouth, completely unconscious.

And the Red Orb of Jalbador was gone.

"No," Sisko gasped, leaning forward, hands on knees, breathless from the long pursuit. "How could it have been stolen already?"

"Unless it was stolen to begin with," Garak said, wheezing slightly as he arrived at Sisko's side a moment later.

"But how?"

"This might not be the time to explore that question, Captain. We have barely enough time to reach the transporter, let alone—"

"GET THE FERENGI!"

At the far end of the corridor, a group of Cardassian soldiers had appeared and now began running forward, eager to complete the lynching that had almost occurred on the Promenade.

"We can't leave him!" Sisko said.

"Captain! We *know* he survived this day!"

"No one could survive *this!*" Sisko cried as he swept up Quark's limp body and began to run back the way he had come.

"You're going the wrong way!" Garak called after him.

But Sisko didn't stop.

He had finally accepted that there was only one thing left that he could do.

What Kira had told him to do from the start.

Trust in the Prophets.

CHAPTER 26

WITH ONLY eight minutes remaining, Sisko finally stopped in front of the door to Terrell's lab. His chest heaved. His lungs burned with each breath. Quark's body was a dead weight in his arms.

But the door to Terrell's abandoned lab still glowed faintly with the power of the Orb.

The power of the Temple.

Garak stumbled to a stop beside him. "You . . . can't be . . . serious," he gasped.

"They entice corporeal beings by offering them what they want most," Sisko said. He shifted Quark's body once again. "I know what I want most. What about you, Garak?"

Garak's weary smile brightened with his understanding. "By all means, then. May I?" He held his hand over the doorplate.

Sisko nodded. Without the Orb, they would have to enter the lab just as Jake and Nog had, not by passing *through* the door but by opening it.

"If it *is* an illusion that we find," Sisko said, "you *can* get us out, can't you?"

Garak cocked his head to one side, looking intrigued by the possibility. "Assuming there *is* someplace else to go, I believe I am well versed in the techniques Dukat used."

"Good enough," Sisko said.

The door opened.

Sisko stepped through it with Quark in his arms.

Thinking only of what he wanted most—

"Captain!" Odo shouted.

Sisko spun around to see that he was exactly where he had wanted to be.

Deep Space 9.

In Quark's bar.

Surrounded by all the rescued crew and passengers with whom he had traveled through time.

Almost all.

Odo stepped forward to take Quark's unconscious body from him.

Then Sisko saw Worf on a stretcher, badly injured.

He saw Jadzia seated at a table far off in the back, working intently at a communications terminal.

"What timeframe is this?" Sisko asked.

Then Garak appeared beside him.

Sisko looked but could detect no obvious portal or distortion that might indicate a wormhole or its precursor field. He and Garak had simply both materialized in the center of the bar's main room.

"We're about ten minutes *after* the station was destroyed," Bashir explained quickly. "And in about two minutes, we'll be swept back to just about ten minutes *before*."

"The evacuation is about to get under way back there," Odo said. "We've got a chance."

Sisko didn't know how that could be possible. He didn't understand how the timeline could continue unchanged. Not without the presence of the stolen Red Orb. But he had an even more important question to ask them all. "Where's Jake?"

Bashir's expression was not reassuring. "He's still on the *Defiant*," the doctor said. "It's Arla . . . she's been infected by Grigari nanites, and she's a follower of Weyoun now. She won't drop the shields to let us beam Jake off."

Bashir led Sisko to Jadzia, who looked up at him with surprise. "Jake!" she said excitedly. "Your father's here!"

"*Dad!*"

Sisko felt a heartrending surge of joy tinged with sorrow as he heard his son's voice crackle from the small device on Jadzia's table.

"Jake! It's going to be okay. We'll get you off the ship!"

Sisko saw Jadzia's silent shake of her head, but he couldn't—he *refused* to—believe there was no hope. Not when he could hear his son. And his son could hear him.

"We'll get you off the ship!" Sisko said again. There had to be a way, and he would find it.

Then Weyoun's voice obnoxiously intruded. *"Oh, Benjamin, you shouldn't lie to your son."*

"You can stop this, Weyoun!" Sisko said. "Tell Arla to drop the shields!"

"Why?" Weyoun asked. *"So the pain of life can continue forever?"*

"No!" Sisko exploded. "So the joy of life can continue! You were alive once! You know what—"

"I assure you, I am alive now as well," Weyoun coolly interrupted.

"Are you?" Sisko demanded. "Remember when I hit you, Weyoun? I broke your nose! And now it's perfectly restored, isn't it? Rebuilt by those damned nanites. They're in you, Weyoun. They're making you forget what it even means to be alive. They've programmed you just the way your Founders did! They've turned you into a soulless machine, and *that's* what wants this universe to end!"

"Coming up on ninety seconds!" someone in the bar called out. The earnest young voice sounded like Ensign Simons.

Jadzia lifted the communications device under one arm. Sisko held out his hand for it—it was his only contact with his son. But instead, the Trill held out her other hand to him. "We have to link hands, Benjamin," she said. "It's the only way we can overcome the temporal inertia or whatever it is that kept Weyoun and Dukat and everyone they touched locked in a specific timeframe."

Jadzia took his hand in hers when Sisko made no motion of his own. "We'll come back to this timeframe at least once more," she said softly. "I promise you'll be able to talk to Jake again."

Sisko heard the unspoken words at the end of her sentence. He'd be able to talk to his son one last time.

"All right, everyone," Odo shouted. "It's going to be getting dark on the other side. Lots of confusion. Stay to the back wall and out of sight so we don't interfere with anything!"

In a daze, Sisko saw all the temporal refugees in the bar begin to move to the back wall of the bar's main room. Jadzia used her grip on his hand to move him in the same direction, to join the others.

"Why's Odo saying that?" Sisko asked in sudden alarm. "We have to be *evacuated* on the other side. *Before* the station's destroyed."

"No, sir," O'Brien answered as he hurried over to join Sisko and Jadzia. "Dax and I, we've worked out the equations. If we leave the station too soon, all bets are off. Our one chance to not create an alternate timeline is to reenter our own timeframe at the exact moment the wormhole fully opens."

"Is that even possible?" Sisko asked. He saw the way Jadzia and O'Brien looked at each other. It meant they both had their doubts.

"I'm going to have to blow the station's reactors," O'Brien gruffly admitted. "A full explosive overload."

"What?"

"For what it's worth, Benjamin," Jadzia pointed out, "the force of the explosion might have been what threw the *Defiant* into the future in the first place. I did the calculations, and between the wormhole opening and Terrell's ship firing at us, there wasn't enough energy hitting our ship to put us into a slingshot around the wormhole's mouth."

"But what will blowing the reactors do to this part of the station?" Sisko asked.

"This part of the station's destroyed anyway," O'Brien said. "We all saw it implode. But if the next time we come back to this timeframe *after* the station's destruction—if we can run up to Ops so when we switch back, it'll be completely evacuated—and if I can blow the reactors then, with any luck, all the airtight doors will seal, and the whole Ops module will pop free of the wormhole."

"That's a lot of ifs, Chief," Sisko said.

"It's all we've got, sir. Short of setting off a trilithium planet-buster outside the habitat ring."

"Ten seconds!" Odo shouted. "Everyone link arms!"

Sisko stood, arm in arm with Jadzia and Kira against the back wall with the others, linked arms with them, and was suddenly blinded by a flash of blue light.

But when the flash faded, full visibility did not return as it had so many times before.

Instead, like everyone else, Sisko staggered to one side in the skewed gravity field. Staring in disbelief at the three floating Orbs of Jalbador, now in perfect alignment. They were suspended in midair, just a meter or so above the deck, spinning and glowing, each just like an Orb of the Prophets, except that the energy they shed was the hellish hue of blood and fire.

"But the third Orb was stolen!" Sisko said.

"I don't know how it got back," Kira told him, almost yelling to be heard over the wail of the pressure alarms, "but the last time we were in this timeframe, we were watching from upstairs, and we saw you find it again. Right behind the mural."

Now, just as Sisko had witnessed six years in the past outside the door to Terrell's secret lab, coiled tendrils of red energy began to unfurl. This time, they curled away from each Orb to link up with tendrils sent forth from the others, until they merged and defined an equilateral triangle of shimmering crimson light.

And in the middle of that formation, a distortion was growing.

The doorway to the Second Temple.

And to DS9's destruction.

To Sisko's profound amazement, *everything* was as it was before. It was as if *all* the actions he and the others had taken in the past had had no effect on the present. Unless, as Garak had said, what had happened in the past was what had *always* happened in the past. What was *supposed* to have happened.

On the other side of the room, Sisko observed the O'Brien of this timeframe try to touch an Orb, only to be thrown back in a flash of red lightning.

He observed the growing wind generated by whatever dimensional forces the Orbs were unleashing that blew at the other Jadzia's hair as she tried to take readings with her tricorder.

He heard that other Jadzia shout, "We've got intensive neutrino flux! A definite wormhole precursor!"

And then Sisko was electrified to hear his *own* voice shout back, *"Here?!"*

There was a flash of phaser fire as someone tried to disrupt an Orb but was disintegrated by his own beam's precise return.

Then Kai Winn and Kira appeared in the entrance to the bar, astonishment stretching their mouths open wide even as the howling wind attempted to drive the women back.

Sisko watched, mesmerized, as these earlier versions of himself and his crew began to withdraw.

And then he remembered . . .

"Chief!" Sisko shouted to the O'Brien of his own timeframe. "You wanted to shut down the reactors! To cut off the power you thought the Orbs were using!"

Sisko saw the sudden fear that struck his engineer. "But if I do that, I won't be able to set them to overload!"

Sisko knew there was no more time to waste.

He ran away from the others, away from the back wall, skirting the glowing triangle of light to race out onto the Promenade, just as the power grid failed and the station was plunged into darkness.

This is it! Sisko thought. This was when O'Brien made his suggestion to shut down the reactors.

And in the halflight, Sisko turned, remembering he himself was just about to give that order, until . . .

The Sisko who had survived his journey into the future ran up to the Sisko who had yet to depart, pushed the Quark of the past to the side, and with all his strength punched *himself* as hard as he could.

Even as his past self fell to the deck, Sisko took command.

"Abandon station!" he cried out, exactly as he remembered hearing himself say so many days, so many years, so many millennia ago. "Chief! Jadzia! Pass the order on to abandon station!"

He checked on himself on the deck, saw himself rubbing his jaw, beginning to get up. He remembered how he felt momentarily confused at the time. As if he had missed out on something important.

He heard O'Brien of the past urgently call out a question. "What about the reactors?"

"Now, Chief!"

The Sisko of the future saw that his order had just the same effect on O'Brien now, as he remembered. A moment later, the station's siren wailed with two long bursts, two short. Over and over.

The order to abandon station.

Sisko watched, fascinated, as his past self got to his feet, looked around in confusion and then tapped at his combadge to issue more orders.

At the time, Sisko remembered, he hadn't known who had given the order to abandon the station, but he had assumed it was in response to something that had happened when he had been hit and half-conscious. So he had not countermanded it.

The Sisko of the future ran back into Quark's bar, felt the floor already beginning to buckle, evaded the debris that was flying everywhere.

He ducked bouncing chairs and rolling tables, went charging for the back wall, reaching out his hand to grab Kira's as—

A red light flashed over him, and he was back in a silent restored version of Quark's bar.

The sudden calm was jarring to Sisko, almost physical.

"We're eight minutes past the destruction of the station!" O'Brien shouted. "Everyone up to Ops!"

Sisko watched in confusion as the others began to run past him, out of the bar. He didn't understand. "Why is the station restored in here? Why aren't we floating in imploded debris?"

"I wondered the same thing," Odo told him as he hurried past to join the others. "Even Vic is operational in this version of the station. I met him walking around the Promenade."

Sisko decided to think about the implications of that later. It was time to run. Time to try Jadzia's and O'Brien's last-ditch plan to return them all to their timeline.

And then Jake's voice called out to him from Jadzia's communicator.

"Dad! I know what to do! I know what to do!"

Jadzia stopped so Sisko could speak to his son.

"Are the shields down?" Sisko asked him.

"No—Arla's not saying anything. But I can save the station!"

"What? How?"

"By blowing up the Defiant."

Sisko's blood turned to ice. "No!"

"Dad, it'll work. All I have to do is cut the power to the magnetic bottles, release the matter and antimatter, and, according to the computer, the explosion will have enough force to create a subspace compression wave."

"There is no subspace in the wormhole," Sisko said.

"*I know!*" Jake answered. "*But the explosion will create it, and that's what'll push the station free.*"

"You will not blow up the *Defiant!*" Sisko raged. "That is an order!"

"*Dad, the channel was open. I heard what you were talking about with O'Brien. The reactors. The planetbuster. I worked it out with the computer. Tell him, Dax.*"

Sisko looked at his friend in sudden hope, but she had none to give him. "He's right, Benjamin. A subspace bubble generated by the *Defiant* would be enough to push us from the station, with far less risk than overloading the station's reactors."

"Less risk?" Sisko cried. "What about my son?"

"*Dad! I'm trapped here! In seven minutes, I won't exist!*"

"I'll get you out!" Sisko promised, pleaded.

"*Dad, please. Let me help!*"

"Don't, Jake . . ."

"*Dad, I have to. I know . . . I know you'd do it for me . . .*"

Tears burned Sisko's eyes.

He had raised his son too well.

"*I love you, Dad . . .*"

"Jake . . . I love you . . ."

Sisko swayed on his feet. He couldn't go on. He just couldn't believe that after all he and everyone he loved and cared about had been through, after he had trusted in the Prophets to deliver him and his people and his universe, that *this* would be the price they would demand.

"Benjamin," Jadzia urged as she tugged on his arm. "We have to go."

Sisko let his friend guide him to safety.

But what did it matter that a universe was saved, if the cost was the life of his son?

In the engineering room of the *Defiant,* Jake finally felt at peace. This was something he could do. Something that would matter.

He touched the command lines that would make the computer think the ship's matter-antimatter fuel had been vented—one of O'Brien's tricks for interfering with a starship's operational readiness.

Then he activated the commands that would permit him to order a powerdown of the magnetic coils—the ones that generated the containment fields in which the matter and antimatter were stored.

Three seconds after he entered that command, the ship would explode. But the timing had to be precisely right.

Jake watched the countdown on the console. Three timeframes gradually coming into phase, only a few seconds off right now.

He was surprised at how good he felt.

He thought of his father.

He was proud to be Ben Sisko's son.

Sisko lost track of timeframes and elapsed time and whether the light that flashed over him was blue or red.

Because nothing mattered anymore.

It was all confusion anyway.

And then he was in Ops with all the others.

A perfect Ops, with gravity level and restored.

"Thirty seconds," Odo said.

Everyone joined hands.

Almost everyone. Three Bajorans had died on the *Boreth.* Two Denevan technicians on the *Defiant.* Vash had escaped to the past. Quark had simply vanished, leaving his past self alone.

And Jake—Jake was somewhere beyond time and space.

In the hands of the Prophets.

"Fifteen seconds," Odo said.

Jadzia squeezed Sisko's hand.

"This will be the final transfer," she told him. "We'll be switching to a timeframe about five seconds before the station was destroyed. We'll actually be on the station as it falls into the red wormhole. And then, just before the wormhole closes, just as the *Defiant* of that time is attacked by Terrell's ship, the subspace bubble will push us out again."

And Jake will die, Sisko thought, remembering the accusations he had hurled at Weyoun. Now he felt like a soulless machine himself, beyond all care, beyond emotion.

"Five seconds," Odo intoned. "Four . . . three . . . two . . ."

The flash was blue, and when it faded, the others cried out in terror as they toppled to the side, the gravity more off-balance than it had ever been before.

Every alarm in Ops was screaming. Distant explosions echoed through the deck. Consoles exploded in sparks and flame.

And then a red glow infused everything in Sisko's field of vision, as if the very air had combusted.

"We've entered the wormhole," O'Brien shouted.

Jake, Sisko thought—one final time.

And then he was in—

—the light space.

"What happened?" the Sisko asks.

He is by the reflecting pool in the meditation garden.

"What happens," *Kai Opaka corrects him. She smiles at him as she reaches for his ear.*

"No," the Sisko says. "This isn't right. This isn't what was supposed to be."

Captain Picard turns away from the table in the conference room of the Enterprise. *Behind him, Bajor is resplendent in full sunlight, a world reborn. "Supposed?" Picard asks.*

"I trusted in you!" the Sisko laments.

He falls to his knees in the ruins of B'hala. "I trusted in you."

"You always trust in us," Opaka says.

The Sisko looks up at her, and even on the Promenade as it is on the first day he sets foot on it, he feels the tears run down his face.

Not the tears of the Prophets.

His tears.

The tears of a father.

"I hate you," the Sisko says.

His own father stands behind him in the kitchen of the restaurant in New Orleans, holding the Sisko's hand in his as he guides the whisk through the eggs that swirl like galaxies.

"Hate? What is this?" the Sisko's father asks.

The Sisko stands behind Jake in his own kitchen in his apartment in San Francisco, Jennifer looking on as the Sisko holds his son's hand in his as he guides the whisk through the eggs that swirl like galaxies.

"No . . . ," the Sisko says. "This isn't fair . . ."

"Yes," Opaka tells him. "It is."

The Sisko walks the paths of the Academy as a student.

"Just as there is no time—" Boothby says.

The Sisko is under the stars of Earth, outside the tent in Yosemite, cradling Jennifer in his arms the night Jake is conceived.

"—there is no hate," Jennifer says.

The Sisko stands on the deck of the Saratoga *as it burns.*

"But there is death!"

Prylar Rulan bows his head outside the Temple on the Promenade. "Another time."

"Not another time," the Sisko says. "This time! This time Jake died! Not because of time! Not because of anything at all except for you!"

The Sisko expects to be taken to the light space, where he is always taken when his emotions overwhelm the Prophets.

Instead, he is on the pitcher's mound in Ebbets Field.

The Sisko does not understand.

"You brought me here?"

"We always bring you here," Jackie Robinson says.

The Sisko looks around the perfect field, inhales the rich scent of the grass, hears the growing tumult of the crowd.

They are on their feet, cheering. He hears a cowbell ringing in the outfield stand, a ragtag band plays Dixieland off-key.

The Sisko turns again, sees the scoreboard.

"Someone pitched a no-hitter," the Sisko says.

He looks at the baseball in his hand. The Prophets, for once, do not correct his incorrect use of tense.

"I don't understand," the Sisko says.

"You throw the ball," Picard says.

"They hit the ball," Opaka says.

Twelve-year-old Jake points to the scoreboard again. "This is what happens."

Sisko turns back to the board, reads it carefully.

"The home team won?" he says.

The Sisko is in the Wardroom on Deep Space 9.

"The war ends," Locutus says.

The Sisko is in Vic's.

"You threw the ball, pallie. Heckuva game."

The Sisko stands on the bridge of the first Enterprise, *a glimmer of understanding beginning to grow in him.*

"The War of the Prophets," he says. *"You* won."

Captain Kirk turns in his command chair, holds out his hands. *"We* always *win, Lieutenant."*

The Sisko hangs his head, in the ruins of B'hala, alone.

"But I have lost," he says.

He grimaces as Opaka's thumb and finger squeeze his earlobe, feel his pagh.

"What is this?" she asks.

In the light space, the Sisko hears the answer to the question she has asked.

The voice is Jake's, but the boy cannot be seen.

"It is, quite simply, your journey, Dad, the one you've always been destined to take."

"What is this?" the Sisko asks.

And the Prophets answer as they always do.

CHAPTER 27

SISKO STUMBLED over the deck and opened his eyes to see—

Ops.

Everyone who had been there before was there again, even Worf on his stretcher.

Sisko tapped his foot on the deck. The gravity *felt* right, but . . .

"Chief?" he asked.

O'Brien looked up from an engineering console, shook his head. "We're not in the wormhole, if that's what you mean."

Sisko wasn't sure what he meant. Nor what he was looking for.

He saw Kira watching him.

"You were with Them, weren't you?" she asked, no question as to whom the word 'them' referred.

Sisko nodded. Touched a communications control on the console beside him.

And instantly a squeal of subspace static raced through the speakers surrounding Ops, until a single voice rang out.

"Dad? Are you there?"

"Jake?!"

And then father and son both spoke together, asking the same question at the same time.

"What happened?"

• • •

They knew the answer in minutes, provided by Captain Halberstadt of the *U.S.S. Bondar* and Captain S'relt of the *U.S.S. Garneau*. The two *Akira*-class starships had been dispatched to Deep Space 9 when the Bynar computer virus had degraded its defensive capabilities. That deployment had proved invaluable when the time came to evacuate the station as the red wormhole opened.

But what had happened at that time was most easily understood by viewing the visual sensor data the *Garneau* transmitted to the main viewer in Ops.

At first, Sisko had trouble concentrating on the images he watched. *His son had been returned to him!* The *Defiant* was powerless but intact, safe within the protective grip of the *Bondar*'s tractor beams. Jake would be beamed back to DS9 within the hour. Once some routine radion isotope decontamination had been performed on his section of the ship.

The *Garneau*'s sensor log showing the fate of Deep Space 9 was no more than ten minutes old, and it began exactly like the one Sisko had been shown almost twenty-five years in the future.

A glow began on the Promenade as the red wormhole opened in Quark's. The station was deformed by the tidal stresses of the wormhole's immense gravitational well. Escape pods misfired and were drawn to their destruction. Docking pylons collapsed toward the opening mouth of the wormhole as the *Defiant* released her docking clamps and pulled away.

And then, like the familiar Bajoran wormhole seen through a colored filter, the red wormhole opened in just the same way, and Deep Space 9 shrank faster than the sensor log could smoothly record, as if the station had suddenly plunged into a bottomless pit.

This was where the record Sisko had seen in the future had ended.

But here on Ops, the log continued.

The *Defiant* suddenly swung past, gyrating wildly, taking phaser fire from an unseen enemy.

Terrell's ship, Sisko knew.

The *Defiant* spun on its *y* axis like a sailing ship in a maelstrom. It shrank just as Deep Space 9 had, into the still-seething energies of the red wormhole.

An instant later, Terrell's *Chimera*-class vessel—a Cardassian warship engineered to resemble a Sagittarian civilian liner—blurred into view as its illegal cloaking field failed, and the craft followed the *Defiant* into a hyperdimensional realm.

Yet this time, unlike the fall of Deep Space 9 or of the *Defiant,* as soon as Terrell's ship vanished within the red wormhole, an enormous gout of energy burst from its mouth, and the wormhole collapsed far faster than its blue counterpart ever had.

Sisko watched as the background of stars and the Denorios Belt suddenly shifted, although the timecode at the bottom of the log continued to count without interruption. That told Sisko the transmission from the *Garneau* had switched from one visual sensor to another to show events as they occurred in quick succession.

From this second viewpoint, Sisko saw the Bajoran wormhole open slowly and majestically as always, and when its mouth was open and the passageway revealed, he saw Deep Space 9, intact, tumble out of the blue wormhole like a child's toy rolling out of a funnel.

And just behind the station, the *Defiant* followed, the ship slowly spinning, out of control, but out of danger, too.

Then the image on the Ops viewer changed again, this time to show Captain S'relt on the bridge of the *Garneau.* If Sisko didn't know better, he'd swear the elderly Vulcan was smiling.

"Captain Sisko, were the events clearly depicted?" S'relt asked.

"Clearly depicted," Sisko agreed. "But what exactly were we seeing there at the end? When Terrell's ship entered the red wormhole?"

The captain referred to a padd he held. "According to spectral analysis of radiation and debris ejected from the red wormhole at the moment before its abrupt collapse, we were observing the result of a high-speed collision between two vessels. Molecular samples recovered positively identify one vessel as the *Chimera*-class ship observed entering the wormhole immediately prior to the collision. Additional molecular samples and fragments of unusual hull debris suggest the second ship was of some undocumented Klingon design." The captain looked up again. "My science officer has so far been unable to identify the class."

For Sisko, however, the picture was complete. "The second ship was called the *Boreth,* Captain. An advanced-technology Klingon vessel. We will provide a full report."

"I am certain I will find it fascinating," the Vulcan replied. *"Garneau* out."

The viewscreen looming over Ops became an empty frame.

Sisko's silent contemplation of it was broken by the voice of his chief engineer.

"Am I getting this right?" O'Brien asked. "Terrell's ship *collided* with *Weyoun's,* and *that's* what pushed us out of the wormhole?"

"More likely, it was the subspace bubble formed by the explosion of the two ships that pushed us out of the wormhole," Jadzia said.

Sisko had no real interest in the details. All that was important to him was that *something* had pushed them out of the wormhole before Jake had been able to follow through on his plan to sacrifice himself by destroying the *Defiant.*

And then a different puzzle came into Sisko's mind. His brow became furrowed as he searched for an explanation he wasn't at all sure he had.

"Captain?" Kira asked in concern. "Is something wrong?"

"I was just trying to remember who shut off the—"

"Benjamin!"

Everyone in Ops instantly stopped talking and turned to see Jadzia at her science station, absolutely dumbfounded.

"Benjamin," she said again, "you are not going to *believe* the life-signs readings I just found."

Two minutes later, Sisko sympathized with Jadzia's amazement. He, on the other hand, had the experience of punching himself in the jaw. Compared to that, what was waiting for them in Quark's was just another day on Deep Space 9.

This time, the temporal refugees numbered four. Five if Sisko included the still unconscious version of Quark whom he had rescued on the Day of Withdrawal.

Two of the refugees, dazed and considerably confused, were the blue- and brown-suited Cardassians whose autopsies Bashir had performed no more than a week ago.

The other refugee was a less dazed but even more confused Odo, accompanied by a remarkably calm Garak.

Wherever these people had been taken on the Day of Withdrawal, when Sisko had seen them pulled into Leej Terrell's lab, the collapse of the red wormhole had now deposited them in this place and time.

Sisko couldn't help noting that all four of them were gathered in the center of the main room, in the same location where he and Garak had also appeared after their passage through Terrell's lab.

The same site had been the center point of the triangle formed by the Red Orbs of Jalbador as they had floated together in perfect alignment.

Now the Orbs were scattered widely in the bar, all three glowing but not near enough to each other to cause any dimensional effects. To ensure this secure state, before Sisko even approached the disoriented group of time travelers, he instructed O'Brien to delegate a team to gather the Orbs, one at a time, then take them to three different and widely separated storage sites on the station, in the constant company of armed security officers.

Sisko still couldn't be certain who among the group of travelers had stolen the Orb from Quark's bar six years ago and then replaced it just before Sisko had searched for it, but he did have his suspicions.

He was certain that none of those present was a suspect, though.

In the debriefing that followed, the Odo from the past doubted everything he was told, even when he was told it by his counterpart of this day. Sisko thought it might actually benefit Odo to see his stubborn streak through his own eyes, the way others usually did.

The Garak from the past easily accepted what had happened to him, and from what Sisko could overhear of his conversation with the Garak of this time, it seemed that someone had 'forgotten' to take a certain neural inhibitor. Sisko made a mental note to discuss that with Dr. Bashir.

From the first, there was no question that Odo, Garak, and Quark would have to be returned to their own time. Since they had already lived through those intervening years, it was obvious that they *had* been returned, though with their memories of what had happened carefully excised.

As he considered the Quark of the past, who had finally regained consciousness with Bashir's help, Sisko realized he would be sorry to see this version of the Ferengi go back. The Quark Sisko knew in his own timeframe appeared to be the one casualty of the journey through time whose fate wasn't known. The last time the barkeep had been seen by anyone was by Odo, after Dukat had been neutralized. And where Dukat had ended up was anyone's guess as well.

But the most problematic decision Sisko had to make was what to do about the two Cardassian soldiers.

For now, they both conveniently believed that they were the victims of an elaborate Bajoran plot, one whose purpose was to make them think the conflict between the two worlds was long over and that they should feel free to reveal military secrets.

These two sat together, apart from the others, stoutly refusing to talk with anyone except to supply their names, ranks, and DNA samples.

To send them back, Sisko knew, would be to condemn them to death. Their bodies already had been found, merged with the hull of the station. Yet if Sisko didn't send them back, how could the investigation of Dal Nortron's murder ever be linked to their deaths? The past would be changed.

Sisko could see no way out of the hard decision he must make soon.

Until Bashir came up with a solution.

"I could clone them, and we could send the clones back," the doctor suggested. "The clones wouldn't have to be perfect. I'd make sure they had no nervous tissue so they wouldn't really even be alive. But after six years in hard vacuum fused to the hull plates, even I wouldn't be able to tell the difference between them and the real soldiers, so the past could remain unchanged."

Sisko gratefully accepted Bashir's audacious plan and told him to begin work right away.

As for Odo, Garak, and Quark, everyone was in agreement that the less time these three spent in their future, the better. So, on Sisko's instruction, Bashir set to preparing the memory inhibitors he would need to wipe out their entire experiences of the Day of Withdrawal.

"At least now I know why I was so impressed by the way their memories were erased," the doctor said with a chuckle.

Within the hour, Sisko was satisfied that all the plans were in place. The Cardassian soldiers would remain on the station for another two weeks while Bashir engineered their pseudo-clones. But Odo, Garak, and Quark would be sent back at once.

And the technique to use was one Sisko already knew would work.

He would carry the third Red Orb of Jalbador to Terrell's lab himself.

"Are you ready?" Sisko asked the three time travelers.

Odo looked from Sisko to his present-day self with dour skepticism. "Can you at least tell me if by now I know where I come from?" he asked.

But the Odo of the present crossed his arms and shook his head. "No one told me," he said.

Garak, on the other hand, appeared to be having immense fun. "I shall enjoy going back, knowing how much I have to look forward to."

"Undoubtedly," Garak of the present agreed. "Except this time, I shall watch you take the memory inhibitor myself."

The Quark of the past, however, was not enjoying himself and had moved well beyond skepticism. "If this is my bar," he said suspiciously, "then where am I?"

"Uh, don't worry, Brother," Rom tried to reassure him. "It all works out."

"Don't be too sure," Quark snapped. "As soon as I get back, I'm changing my will, and *you* are out."

"What . . . ever you say," Rom agreed.

The past Quark threw up his arms, perplexed. "All right, what's the deal? Who's this pushover, and where's my real brother?"

Sisko had called ahead to security to make sure the way to Terrell's lab was clear. "Rom's right," he assured the travelers. "We just have to—"

And then a Ferengi squeal shook the few unbroken glasses behind the bartop as Quark of the present came flying out of his back room as if chased by a demon.

"I'msorryI'msorryIdidn'tmeantolethimgoRUNNN!" Quark screeched.

A heartbeat later, Sisko knew exactly what Quark meant.

Dukat was behind him.

Red sparks flew from every centimeter of exposed gray skin as he floated over the deck, both outstretched hands encased in writhing globes of red energy.

"You are the dead!" he proclaimed in a voice that seemed to come from everywhere at once. *"Give me an AMOJAN!"*

Then, with his white hair flying out in all directions, he raised his hands as the fires intensified, and just before he could release his first blast of energy—

—a phaser beam struck him from behind.

An attack Dukat had not expected.

His personal forcefield briefly flared into life but faded just as quickly.

The phaser beam stayed in operation, and once the red glow left Dukat, the blue haze of phased dissolution began to spread over his body.

Dukat hovered for an instant in front of the openmouthed victims he had intended to immolate.

But then what life he had left him, and he fell dead to the deck, his dark eyes dulled and empty, a curl of blue smoke rising from the back of his robes.

Only then did Sisko see who had shot him.

Jadzia.

She was shaking.

Sisko went to her. He took away the phaser she had grabbed from one of Odo's officers.

"He would have killed us all," she said.

"I know," Sisko told his friend, understanding her remorse at taking the life of even a monster like Dukat. "But that's the end of it, Old Man. The Pah-wraiths. The Ascendancy. Kosst Amojan . . . it's over."

Jadzia didn't look convinced.

Later, they assembled by the door to Leej Terrell's hidden lab. The two Cardassian soldiers were part of the group, though under guard, because Sisko wanted them to see the truth of how they had come to this time, to prove that there was no deception. The three other time travelers—Odo and Garak and Quark—were accompanied by their counterparts, for reassurance more than any other reason. O'Brien and Jadzia were also present to take readings with various probes. Two weeks from now, when the two Cardassians' lifeless clones were ready, this procedure would have to be duplicated.

Sisko had the Orb.

With a look to Sisko, Bashir now injected the three time travelers with an inhibitor so sophisticated, he said with a smile, that he absolutely guaranteed it would fool even him.

With the Orb so close to whatever equipment Terrell had installed in her lab, the door began to glow.

"It's still there, Benjamin," Jadzia said as she studied her tricorder. "The wormhole precursor field."

"Don't worry," Sisko assured her. "Once these Orbs are off the station, the whole lab's coming out as scrap." He turned to Bashir. "You give the word, Doctor."

Bashir used his medical tricorder on the three he had injected. "Another minute for the reaction to begin."

Sisko sighed, believing for the first time that it was almost over. Jake and Kasidy were already back on the station. Already waiting for him in his quarters.

"I wish I could leave you with something from this future," Sisko told the three travelers. "You will all survive. And Quark, you will prosper."

The past Quark snorted as he looked at his present self. "Not very much, by the looks of it. You call that a suit?"

But present Quark ignored the insult. "Norellian eel hide," he blurted. "In three years, it'll become a fad on half the planets in the Alpha Quadrant. The price goes up by *five thousand* percent in two months!"

"Don't bother, Quark." Sisko laughed. "He'll never remember. You didn't, did you?"

Quark stared at his past self. Mouthed the words *Norellian eel hides*. Gave himself a quick thumbs-up.

The past Odo looked over everyone again, as if comparing each face he saw to a mental file of mug shots. "At least I keep my job," he said. "There's some small comfort in that, I suppose."

The past Quark looked up at him with a sly smile. "And I'm still in business in spite of you doing your job." The past Quark suddenly looked at his counterpart. "Hey—is Odo finally on the take?"

Dejected, the Quark of the present shook his head.

"Keep trying," his past self urged. "He's got to come around sooner or . . . or . . ." He stopped in mid-sentence. Yawned.

"I think we're ready," Bashir said drily.

Jadzia opened the door to the lab.

Sisko concentrated on the Orb just as he would with an Orb of the Prophets.

Red light began to glow within the lab.

"It doesn't look any different," Jadzia said.

O'Brien showed her his tricorder. "But look at the chronometric flux. We're at six years. We've got a link just like when we were in the wormhole."

Sisko nodded. Bashir guided a stumbling Quark to the open door.

Inside the lab, the Ferengi began to swerve left and right like Morn after a party, then fell to one side and was gone before he could hit the floor.

Odo guided himself to the door next. The changeling from the past appeared to have difficulty holding his shape, and when present Odo released him, he seemed to pour into the lab, then disappeared just as Quark had.

"Garak," Sisko said.

Garak also escorted himself to the door, then politely shook hands with himself.

Sisko saw a sudden furtive movement between the two.

"Stop!" Sisko ordered.

The past Garak looked back at Sisko, then ran into the room to vanish like smoke.

"Garak!" Sisko said, furious. "You passed him something! What was it?"

Garak's usual pleasant expression became deadly serious. "A small memory rod with Gul Dukat's personal codes. For switching off the station's self-destruct sequence. Did *you* remember to shut it off, Captain Sisko?"

Sisko hesitated, as if waiting for some part of the present to change as a result of Garak's unwise decision.

"But Garak," Bashir said, "what about the inhibitor I gave him? He won't remember how to use the codes. Or even if he should."

But Garak only smiled. "As expert as you are in the field of memory control, Doctor, rest assured that there are those whose techniques are even more advanced. In fact, I am quite sure that should your inhibitors not function as you had planned, I can be counted on to take one that will do the job required. *After* the self-destruct is terminated, of course."

"And did *you* take the inhibitor?" Sisko asked.

Garak smiled. "Really, Captain, I can't remember."

Sisko shifted the Orb in his arms. "Time to call it—"

"*Look out!*" Odo shouted.

But the warning was too late.

As one, the two Cardassian soldiers jumped away from their guards and barreled past Odo and O'Brien and Jadzia, diving through the open door to the lab to make their escape.

But they didn't vanish as quickly as the first three had.

Their bodies hung in midair for a moment, becoming more transparent, then finally settled through the deck at the far end of the lab where they disappeared from view.

O'Brien moaned. "The field was collapsing."

"Then they wouldn't have been able to punch through on the other side," Jadzia said. "They'd just . . . merge with the . . ."

O'Brien stared into the lab. "And the trajectory they were on . . . with the station's rotation . . ." His shoulders sagged. "Well, at least we know where they ended up, poor devils," O'Brien said. "That makes it full circle."

Bashir nodded. "Then everything's back where it belongs."

The Orb suddenly felt very heavy in Sisko's arms.

"Almost," he said.

Because there was still one last mystery to solve.

CHAPTER 28

THEY MET AT the second-floor safety railing, where they always had met, where they had bedeviled Odo, played too many pranks, shared their dreams and their secrets, planned their futures, and watched the stars.

The awkwardness lasted only a moment, and then they hugged. Not as friends, but as brothers.

That was how Jake felt. And he knew Nog felt the same.

"It's stupid," Nog said as he stepped back to lean against the railing, "but it feels like you were gone for years."

"I was," Jake said.

"But it was only a minute to us."

Jake nodded. "Ten days for us. Not that long." *Only a lifetime,* he thought.

They both leaned forward on the railing, watching the crowds pass below. There were many more Starfleet personnel than usual. Jake had heard the rumors that a major new offensive was being planned, to take the war to Cardassia.

"I saw Commander Worf," Nog said. "Dr. Bashir says he'll be good as new in another day."

"Helps to have two hearts," Jake said.

"Dr. Bashir also says you're a hero. He says you saved Commander Worf's life."

Jake frowned, thinking of the technicians from Deneva. "I had help," he said.

Nog pursed his lips, bobbed his head. Silence returned.

"How is your father?" Nog asked.

Jake thought about the question. "Different. He's going to Bajor tomorrow with Major Kira. He says . . . well, he says he's almost got everything figured out."

Nog suddenly thrust out a package Jake hadn't even noticed he'd been carrying. "I got him this!"

Jake smiled, took the package. "Great." It felt like a book.

"You can open it," Nog said eagerly. "See if he'll like it. It's one of Chief O'Brien's favorites."

Jake slipped the paper wrap from the object inside. It was a book. An old hardcopy of an Academy text from the Starfleet Institute Press.

He read the title. *"On Time Travel: Three Case Studies in Effects and Cause."* He read the author's name. "Admiral James Tiberius Kirk. Oh, my dad likes him."

"I know. Chief O'Brien likes to quote him." He put a hand on Jake's arm. "Do you know what James T. Kirk's first rule of time travel is?"

Jake shook his head.

"Don't!" Nog grinned.

Jake shared the smile. "I think my dad can appreciate that."

The silence returned. Jake wrapped the paper around the book again.

"You met me, didn't you?" Nog asked at last.

Jake had been expecting the question for the past two days, dreading it, but he was relieved now that it had finally been asked.

"I . . . really can't talk about it," Jake said. "All the civilians had to sign all these security oaths about not revealing future technology and politics." Jake had been surprised to learn that even Vic had come under the exacting scrutiny of the unsmiling agents from the Federation Department of Temporal Investigations. Like every other machine-based system on the station, Vic had emerged from the red wormhole in perfect operating condition, which in his case included a complete memory of meeting Odo in a nonlinear future. But for all the intriguing possibilities that fact raised about the nature of time, of the wormholes, and of Vic, himself, it was a detail that Jake and the others were specifically enjoined against discussing. "Basically," Jake said in frustration, "if I say anything about what happened, I could end up spending the next ten years in New Zealand, you know."

"I am not interested in future technology," Nog said. "And that future you saw, it won't come to pass now, correct? Because . . . because the station's still here and . . . the red wormhole's gone . . . and . . . and like that."

Jake was puzzled by how much of the story his friend already knew. "Who've you been talking to?"

Nog squinted at Jake in confusion. He tapped a finger to an ear. "I'm a Ferengi. I hear things."

Jake sighed. He couldn't avoid it forever. "Okay, I met you."

"Well . . . what was I like?"

"Pretty much the way you are now. A big pain in the lobes."

"Jake!" But Nog laughed along with him. Until the silence returned. "Seriously."

Jake knew the promise he had made to Captain Nog of the future. But he also knew the demands of his friendship with Nog in the present.

"You were a great man," Jake said. "You worked at the highest levels with one of the greatest heroes of our time. You were brave. Hardworking. If we hadn't come along, you would have been the guy who saved the universe."

Nog stared at Jake as if he had forgotten how to speak.

"And I really can't say more than that," Jake told him.

"Just one more thing," Nog said, moving closer like a salesman about to close a deal. "Was I happy?"

Jake knew that was always the question. Bashir had told him that Garak's past self had asked the same of his counterpart. Jake wondered that about his own life. The details of what was to come weren't important. But the emotions were.

"No one was happy," Jake said, skirting the truth without really lying. "It was pretty grim. But you were good at your work. People knew it. And . . . and you were the best."

"Was I still in Starfleet?"

Jake almost started to laugh again. He wondered if Captain Nog had made him promise not to tell his past self about his future just to play one last trick on his human friend. After all, who could withstand relentless Ferengi persuasion for a lifetime?

"Nog, just this once. Just this one thing, all right?"

"Of course."

"You, yourself, made me promise not to tell you where you worked or what your job was, because you didn't want your . . . um, you in the future didn't want you in the past to make decisions about your new future based on what the old future . . . this makes no sense."

"But it does," Nog said. "Basically . . ."

"Yeah?" Jake said with a grin. "Basically what?"

"Basically, I didn't want to spoil the surprise for myself."

"Exactly," Jake said.

"But . . . did I happen to give myself any investment advice?" Now Nog laughed.

"Yeah," Jake said. "You told yourself always to be sure to pick up the check when you have lunch with me."

Nog poked Jake in the ribs as he pushed away from the safety railing. "Yeah? Well, today you're buying," he said.

Jake fell into step beside his friend, heading for the stairs that would take them down to the main level.

"Did I mention that you'd put on fifty kilos and your ears had fallen off? Very attractive."

By the time they had reached the stairs, they were both giggling as if they were twelve again, as if nothing had changed or ever would.

Then Nog stopped with his hand on the stair railing. "When the evacuation started, I was in Ops. I . . . I thought I saw you. Like a ghost or something. I thought you were trying to talk to me or something."

Jake put a hand on his friend's shoulder. "Nog, you have to start getting out more often."

But Nog, shook his head, smiling. "No, I don't." He looked all around the Promenade. "I like it right here."

Jake knew what he meant.

For now, at least, the future could wait.

CHAPTER 29

BENJAMIN SISKO breathed deeply of the air of Bajor, picturing the
molecules of it entering his bloodstream, becoming part of his body,
just as his soul was part of this world.

"It's beautiful," Kira said beside him.

Sisko looked out at the vista of the Cirran Mountains—bold,
craggy, snowcapped peaks stretching to the northwest; gentle
foothills to the southeast melting gracefully into green meadows tens
of kilometers away; transparent clouds high brushstrokes on the
scarlet sky as dawn changed to day, red turned to blue.

And the silence of this altitude, Sisko thought. So far removed
from the cities and the farms, the roads and air-traffic corridors.

Perfect stillness. Perfect peace.

The peace of the Prophets.

"Beautiful," Sisko agreed, knowing how insignificant that word
was, how inadequate. "I can see why they built their monastery
here."

Kira nodded. "Not even the Occupation touched it. As if the
Cardassians didn't even know it was here."

They probably didn't, Sisko thought. And if any had discovered
it, he doubted if Obanak's followers would have let them live long
with that secret.

A brisk wind suddenly danced around them, and Sisko and Kira both secured more tightly the heavy coats they wore. Though they hadn't discussed doing so beforehand, when they had met at the airlock for this day's journey, they were both outfitted in civilian clothes. To each of them, it had seemed the right thing to do, coming here to this place of peace on Bajor.

"There," Kira said, and she gestured with one hand toward the old stone path that led from the small parapet they had beamed to, to the entrance of the monastery, where two figures emerged from a small doorway and made their way down the path in a leisurely manner.

As the two figures came nearer, Sisko's gaze traveled beyond them to the monastery behind. The structure was enormous, built of hand-cut stone blocks that seemed to Sisko identical to those that had been used in the construction of B'hala's earliest buildings. Yet the quarries for that fabled city's stones were hundreds of kilometers away.

Sisko tried to comprehend the driving passion that would compel a people to transport the massive stone blocks from such a distance, then carry them up to this mountain peak.

To his surprise, after all he had been through, he found that he could.

The two figures were closer now and Sisko recognized one of them. His identity was unmistakable despite his flowing russet robes. Prylar Obanak's broad shoulders and powerful stride could not be disguised.

The second figure, though, who walked behind the prylar, cloaked in the simpler robes of a monk, was unfamiliar to him.

Sisko sensed rather than saw Kira's glance at him. He adjusted his shoulder bag, felt the Red Orb inside shift slightly to one side. "It's the right thing to do," he said.

She nodded. "I know. I'm just surprised that . . . that you think so, too."

"I'm not a Starfleet officer today."

Kira's smile was thoughtful. "Oh, yes, you are. You were born a Starfleet officer, just as you were born the Emissary."

"Is it possible to be both?"

"If it is, you'll find the way."

Particle or wave. This time or another. His wasn't a quantum condition. Perhaps Kira had always understood that better than he had, Sisko thought. That his choice had never been to be one or the other. It had always been to find the way to be both.

"Captain Sisko," Obanak said as he and his follower came up the path to the parapet on which Sisko and Kira were standing. "Welcome to Cirran."

"Ben," Sisko said. "Not Captain."

"Ben," Obanak said. He looked at Sisko's shoulder bag. "You once tried to give these to Kai Winn."

"Before I knew what they were."

"Do you know now?"

Sisko shook his head. How could he? How could anyone? "If I thought that the entities in the wormhole were merely aliens, and these . . . devices were simply artifacts of an immeasurably advanced technology, I would destroy them."

"And if the entities are gods?" Obanak asked quietly. "And the Orbs known throughout Bajor are their tears? What does that tell you about these Red Orbs and the entities who created them?"

Sisko looked deep into Obanak's eyes but saw only the prylar's conviction.

"Whatever they are," Sisko said at last, "they belong here, because they've been here before."

Obanak's face was unreadable. "Why would you say that?"

Sisko had had a long time to think on the trip from the station, to weave the final strands of the tapestry and complete the missing elements of the picture. "You, your order, are the keepers of these Orbs. You hid one on Jeraddo just before the moon was abandoned, then gave the map to Dal Nortron. And in the chaos of Withdrawal, you stole the Orb from Quark after he had stolen it from Terrell, watched over it for six years, then hid it in Quark's bar when you came back to Deep Space 9 just before all the Orbs were brought together."

Sisko knew it was the only explanation. Where the Orbs were concerned, there were no other times. It all had happened. It all had been real.

"Emissary!" Kira said in surprise. "Do you know what you're saying?"

Obanak held up a hand to assure Kira. "It's all right, Nerys. I'm sure he does."

And Sisko *was* certain, even more so now. "In fact," he added, "I wouldn't be surprised if you had somehow arranged the sale of the third Orb to Vash, knowing it would start the search for the other two."

Sisko heard Kira gasp as Obanak gave him an enigmatic smile before responding. "Oh, we would never *sell* an Orb, Ben." But that was the only part of Sisko's suppositions that he bothered to deny.

"Prylar, I apologize," Kira said hotly. She was about to continue when Obanak stopped her.

"Nerys, really, no offense is taken. But I am curious to know why it is you think what you do, Ben. How you could even consider such . . . manipulation of events to be possible."

Sisko remembered back to his time-bending meeting with Prylar Rulan, in the Temple on DS9, just before he had *first* arrived at the station. To the way Rulan had read his *pagh* and how the prylar hadn't been surprised that the Sisko before him was out of time. *I ask you to accept that there is a reason why the Will of the Prophets must sometimes be seen as difficult to interpret for the many, even while it is understood perfectly by the few.*

"No one thing in particular," Sisko said. He looked up at the magnificent edifice of the monastery, struck by the way it seemed almost to grow from the mountain, attesting to the length of time that had passed since it had been built and the centuries, the millennia, of weathering it had endured to blend its walls and parapets into the natural flow of the existing rock.

"But in that monastery," Sisko said without rancor, without judgment, "I would suggest there exists the complete texts of the mystics of Jalkaree. Every word written by Shabren, Eilin, and Naradim. Not just the fragments known to Bajor at large, but everything—the details that you dare not reveal because if too many people knew the future, that future might change."

Sisko saw Kira look from him to Obanak and back again, her eyes wide with an emotion he was not sure he could identify.

"An interesting theory," Obanak said at last. "They must teach you well at Starfleet Academy." He held out his hand.

Sisko gave him the shoulder bag with the first Red Orb.

"And the others?" Obanak asked.

Sisko reached inside his coat, pressed his combadge. "Sisko to *Rio Grande*. Mr. O'Brien, you may beam down the second Orb."

"*Energizing*," O'Brien replied.

A few moments later, a safe fifty meters farther down the path, a Starfleet packing crate shimmered into existence.

Sisko touched his combadge again. "Sisko to *Defiant*. Dax, you may beam down the third."

"*Energizing*," the Trill said.

The second packing crate took form halfway up the path toward the monastery.

"Thank you, Ben," Obanak said. "They will be quite safe here."

"As I'm sure they always have been," Sisko replied.

Obanak glanced down at the time-smoothed stones of the path for a moment. "If it were true that we had the *complete* prophecies of the mystics, it would also be true that those prophecies extended to a particular time, to a particular set of events, and then . . . ended. As if the mystics could see no farther through the veils of the ages." He looked up at Sisko again. "If it were true."

Sisko nodded. *I know because those who came before me knew,* Prylar Rulan had told him, to explain how it was that he recognized Sisko as the Emissary. *Because those who came before them knew, all the way back to the first writings of the great mystics in the time before Lost B'hala.* "So they set forth their prophecies, and your order made sure they would come to pass," Sisko said.

But Obanak betrayed no inclination either to agree or to disagree. "To respect the mystic texts to such a degree, that would be a worthy undertaking, I believe."

Sisko smiled in defeat, accepting that Obanak would give him little else. "Very worthy."

Obanak bowed his head. "Again, we thank you, Ben. All of Bajor thanks you, even those who cannot know what you have done, or will do."

"Will do?" Kira repeated, eager to finally seize her chance to ask her own question of the prylar. "So there are still prophecies to come?"

Obanak grinned. "The mystics of Jalkaree are not the only ones who have seen the future, Nerys. All you have experienced has been but the first chapter in a book that is still to be written."

"Which book?" Kira asked, frowning.

"The Book of the Emissary."

Kira stared at Obanak, puzzled, confused. "But you don't believe the Sisko is the Emissary."

Obanak looked surprised. "Nerys, I never said the Sisko was not the Emissary."

She waved a hand at Sisko. "But you won't even *call* him Emissary."

"No," Obanak agreed. "Not Ben."

Sisko exhaled, at last understanding. "And not Jake," he said.

Half-smiling, Obanak shook his head, as if to confirm Sisko had finally come to the right conclusion.

"But I don't understand," Kira said.

"It's all right," Sisko told her, and meant it. *Maybe Kas and I will have to talk,* he thought. Then he held out his hand to Obanak. "I look forward to our next meeting, if there is to be one."

"After so many others at such interesting times, you can be sure of it," Obanak said. Then he handed the shoulder bag to the monk at his side. "Rees, if you would. I'll get one of the others."

Obanak started down the path, but Sisko reached out to the prylar's companion, pulled lightly on the hood of the monk's robe.

"Captain," Arla Rees said. She looked at Kira. "Major."

The former Bajoran commander's hair was cut short and ragged in the style of a novice. Her eyes were shadowed, her skin pale.

As if she saw and understood the concern in Sisko's eyes, Arla smiled reassuringly. "I'll be all right, Captain. I'm still taking Dr. Bashir's medications, to be . . . to be sure there's no trace left in me."

"Is this the right place for you?" Sisko asked her quietly.

Arla nodded. "It always has been. I just didn't know it until . . . well, just until."

Kira suddenly stepped forward and threw her arms around Arla and hugged her. Sisko saw the bright tears in Kira's eyes.

Arla lifted a hand to touch one of those tears with her finger. " 'I know why the Prophets weep,' " she said softly, and Sisko recognized the words from an ancient poem.

" 'For joy,' " Kira answered, smiling warmly at her former adversary.

Arla nodded and completed the quotation. " 'In time. In time.' " Then she stepped back from the major, pulled up her hood, turned, and followed after Obanak, who stood waiting for her on the path.

Sisko and Kira watched Arla walk past the prylar, carrying the Red Orb to the doors of the monastery. Then she stepped through those doors and into her new life. Carrying the second Orb a safe distance behind her, Obanak walked the same path up and into the monastery. The crate holding the third Orb remained on the path, awaiting its turn once the other two had been carefully put away.

Sisko took another deep breath of the mountain air of Bajor, each breath linking him closer to this world.

"Time to go home?" Kira asked after a while.

"We already are," he told her, though he knew that until his part of that story still to be told was complete, he could not stay.

He took a final look at the monastery of Cirran, wondered about the mysteries still within it, thought of the Emissary named Sisko still to come, then called to his ship to return to the stars, to the Gateway to the Temple, to Deep Space 9.

EPILOGUE

In the Hands of the Prophets

JAKE SISKO breathed deeply the dry air of B'hala and, as softly as a kiss, blew it out again.

The finest particles of dust danced away from the standing stone, caught in the bright sunlight to swirl like stars in a distant galaxy, swept away by Jake's exhalation and the gentle sweep of his archaeologist's brush.

Jake knelt to examine more closely the last details of the ancient carving he had discovered and now revealed.

Among those details was a single, simple glyph of ancient Bajoran, more familiar to him than his own name.

"There," he said, and the word hung in the still, silent air. He touched his finger to the stone, to trace out the worn but unmistakable lines carved by passionate hands long since turned to dust. Kasidy's shadow fell over him.

"Welcome, Emissary," she said, reading the inscription as easily as could Jake.

Jake turned to her, smiling as he saw the child asleep in her arms. Her child. His father's child.

The child of Bajor, to whom even the kai bowed her head in reverence.

"There's no question now," Jake said.

At the mouth of the cave on the outskirts of what once had been the first and oldest section of the city, Kasidy leaned down to peer more closely at the stone embedded in the rock. "But the way they're depicted, Jake. It's so different from the others."

"Because it's the first time they *were* depicted."

Kasidy's smile lit up her face. The expression came more easily to her face now than it had that first year, before the child was born. Before the new prophecies had been revealed. Before so many things.

"Is it?" she asked as she straightened up. "Or is it someone's idea of a joke?"

Jake understood why she asked the question. He couldn't blame her. Every other representation of the mystics of Jalkaree were almost identical in their presentation of three learned men.

But this carving, buried for millennia, clearly predated all the rest. It had been carved while the mystics had walked this world, before legend and tradition had compromised fact.

"Twenty-five thousand years ago," Jake said, "this wasn't something the Bajorans *could* joke about."

He pointed to the silhouettes beneath the glyphs.

"See? This is Shabren as he's always depicted." The first silhouette showed the traditional stooped figure of an old man; above him, the hourglass shape of a Prophet's tear—the Orb of Prophecy. "But here, beside him, Eilin is clearly a woman." The lines of the second silhouette made that obvious.

"Then how can you be sure it *is* Eilin?"

"Because she's at Shabren's right hand—where Eilin is always depicted. And it really makes more sense when you consider that to the Bajorans who inhabited this area when B'hala was founded, that's the position that would have been taken by an elder's spouse. And see here . . ." Jake lightly drew his brush back and forth across the weathered carving of the second great mystic. "Here's Eilin's bag of knowledge. It all fits, Kas. Shabren stooped with an Orb over his head—the symbol of the knowledge of the Prophets that he gave to Bajor. Eilin with the bag in which she kept her scrolls—the symbol of her knowledge of the world that she gave to Bajor."

"But what about Naradim?" Kasidy asked. "Shouldn't he be carrying his abacus—symbol of the knowledge of mathematics that he gave to Bajor?"

Jake grinned at her formality. "Naradim didn't *need* an abacus. That came much later, as a way the Bajorans could keep up with him."

"But look how much shorter he is. Doesn't that mean he's younger than the other two?" Kasidy asked. "And don't the texts say the three were the same age?"

"They might say that," Jake said. "Or they might be saying that the three *arrived* at the same time. The old glyphs are . . . imprecise. The explanation could just be as simple as we see it here: He's not younger, just shorter. And see here . . ." Jake tapped his brush against the third silhouette.

"His hood is up," Kasidy said. "That's traditional, at least."

"But now we know why," Jake said. "It had to be in that position so the Bajorans wouldn't know he was . . . from someplace else."

Jake laid down his brush, stood up, stretched, scratched at the beard he wore.

The child in Kasidy's arms stirred, half-awake, half-dreaming in this lost city.

Kasidy stroked the child's head and timeless sleep returned.

"This makes things very complicated, don't you think?" she asked. "I mean, not just time travel but circles of events looping from one alternate time to affect events in another . . ."

"Maybe there aren't any alternates," Jake said. He had spent long nights thinking of all this during his time in B'hala, during his voyage through the wormhole. One of his friends in Starfleet had hinted to him that this interconnection among different histories had been suspected before in events involving the Romulan Empire. "Maybe the way we see time as being quantum, as going either one way *or* the other, isn't the way it really is. Maybe all the different timelines are like the planets were to our ancestors. Individual worlds with their own existence. Their own destinies. And maybe . . . eventually . . . we'll learn to travel between them, instead of just stumbling around like we do now."

Jake had no doubt about what could be used to travel among the timelines, the pathway that linked all times.

"Infinite worlds," Kasidy mused. "And infinite times. An infinity of infinities." She looked down at the child of Bajor. "So what about the timeline you saw? The future where everything ended."

Jake closed his eyes and turned his face upward, toward Bajor-B'hava'el, savoring the heat he had come to associate with B'hala. The moment in his life that Kasidy was asking about, the journey into a future that now could never be, it was more like a dream when he remembered it.

"I think that was a warning," he said. "For us or for the Prophets, I don't know. But it was a warning that had to be, so that . . ." Jake opened his eyes and looked down again, at the three silhouettes on the stone—Shabren, Eilin, and Naradim, to be sure. Picard, Vash, and Nog—who could say for certain? "So that the circles could wheel within circles. So that we could see that one time doesn't exclude another."

"Another time," Kasidy said beside him.

The child in her arms gurgled happily, still caught within a dream.

A sudden wind gusted up then, sending the dust at the mouth of the cave into a helix of shifting sparkles, glittering almost like an Orb, Jake thought.

And then the heat of the day vanished, and from deep in the cave, it was as if a light flickered somewhere far off.

A light that was obscured by a figure before it, one hand held out to them.

Kasidy stepped forward to the edge of the cave, its depths now shimmering, radiant, as if its walls were lined with Orbs.

The sleeping child's eyes opened wide, dark and lustrous, their shining surface reflecting the light from the cave.

And then the light was no more and the dust drifted downward in the still air as the heat of B'hala returned.

Jake reached out to Kasidy, took her hand in his.

They both knew what had just happened, who had been with them.

Who would always be with them.

"Another time," Jake said as he released her hand. Then he crouched down to touch his fingers to the silhouette of Naradim, completing one circle, knowing an infinite number remained. "We should go home."

The Station would be waiting for them at the entrance to the wormhole. The Gateway would be waiting at the entrance to the Temple. And for the first time, Jake truly understood that the one definition did not exclude the other. Circles within circles.

Jake gazed one last time into the darkness of the cave, then turned away into the sunlight to follow Kasidy, wondering who had walked this same path millennia before him and who would walk it after him.

But when he reached the campsite, he abandoned all his thoughts of past and future for a time much more important. The child was waiting, small fingers wrapped around a favorite toy.

"Heads up!" Kasidy warned with a smile.

And in that timeless moment, accompanied by the peals of laughter of a mother and a child, Benjamin Sisko's baseball arched into the air of B'hala, spinning gloriously in the bright sunlight, a blur of scuffed white leather and frayed red stitches, launched on an erratic path that might take it anywhere.

As he had a thousand times before, and would a thousand times again, Jake leaped up to try to catch it . . .

And from the Temple, the Prophets watched as they always did.

But in this one timeless moment, as they had learned from their Emissary, even the Prophets wondered what would happen next.

Star Trek: Deep Space Nine—Millennium

Timeline

Compiled by Allyn Gibson

CIRCA 23,600 B.C.E. Agents of the Bajoran Ascendancy bury a transporter sensor beneath the future site of the Bajoran city of B'hala. The sensor's purpose is to detect the deep-time explosive charges Project Phoenix plans to place beneath B'hala to destroy the surrounding region in 2400 C.E.

23,226 B.C.E. The *U.S.S. Phoenix* crashes on Syladdo, the fourth moon of Ba'Syladon, a gas giant in the Bajor system. In the closing years of the twenty-fourth century, nearly forty percent of her wreckage will be discovered frozen in Syladdo's methane seas by the Romulans.

CIRCA 22,600 B.C.E. The Bajoran mystics Shabren, Eilin, and Naradim set down the prophecies concerning the Red Orbs of Jalbador, the conflict between the True Emissary and the False Emissary, and the end of time itself.
    City of B'hala settled on Bajor.

17,627 B.C.E. On Bajor, a painting is made of the sacred city of B'hala.

CIRCA 17,600 B.C.E. Location of Bajoran city of B'hala lost.

CIRCA 12,600 B.C.E. B'hala rediscovered.

Last temple to the Bajoran prophets built in B'hala. Shortly thereafter, the city disappears in a landslide.

7627 B.C.E. The search begins by archaeologists for the lost city of B'hala on Bajor.

2340 Border dispute between the United Federation of Planets and the Cardassian Union. Leads to an ongoing set of skirmishes between Starfleet and the forces of the Cardassian Empire.

2346 A space station named Terok Nor by its Cardassian designers is completed. In orbit around the planet Bajor, the station uses forced Bajoran labor to process ore in horrendous conditions.

2365 The commander of Terok Nor, Gul Dukat, appoints Odo as the chief of security to the station.

2369 The Cardassian Union agrees to leave the Bajoran system. The space station is handed over to the Bajoran Provisional government, which requests help from Starfleet.

Stardate 46379.1. Commander Benjamin L. Sisko is appointed by Starfleet to command the space station located in Bajoran orbit. The station is renamed Deep Space 9. Upon discovery of a stable wormhole that connects the Alpha Quadrant to the Gamma Quadrant, the station is moved to a position just outside the gravitational pull of the wormhole. Commander Sisko's communication with the aliens who live in the wormhole, referred to as the Prophets by the Bajorans, leads to Sisko's being acknowledged as the Emissary of the Prophets by the Bajoran people.

2372 *Stardate 49011.4.* The Khitomer Accords are suspended and the Klingon Empire takes up hostilities against the Federation and the Cardassian Union.

2372 The lost city of B'hala is discovered by Sisko.

2373 *Stardate 50564.2.* Dominion Forces join with the Cardassian Union in open hostilies against the Federation.

The Khitomer Accords are reinstated, and the Klingon Empire joins with Starfleet to defend the Alpha and Beta Quadrants against Dominion-Cardassian agression.

Stardate 50975.2. Deep Space 9 falls to the forces of the Dominion-Cardassian alliance.

2374 Space Station Deep Space 9 is retaken from the Dominion-Cardassian forces.

Stardate 51721.3. Aligning itself with the United Federation of Planets and the Klingon Empire, the Romulan Star Empire declares war against the Dominion-Cardassian alliance.

Discovery of the Red Orbs of Jalbador. Upon bringing the three Orbs together in Quark's Bar, a second Bajoran wormhole opens *within* Deep Space 9. Before evacuation of the station can be completed, DS9 and the *Defiant* are destroyed by the wormhole's gravitational forces.

Cardassian and Dominion forces retake the Bajoran system, gaining access to both wormholes.

2375 *Stardate 52145.7.* Weyoun travels through the second wormhole, accompanied by Cardassian and Jem'Hadar ships. When the *U.S.S. Enterprise* attempts to follow, the wormhole will not open.

Three weeks later. Weyoun returns alone, the joint fleet with whom he travelled having disappeared. Lost are 1,137 Cardassian and Jem'Hadar personnel. In the aftermath of Weyoun's return, Grigari ships emerge from the second wormhole.

The Dominion War ends with the destruction of Cardassia Prime and devastation of all worlds of the Cardassian Union. By 2400, there will be no more than a million Cardassians alive.

Thomas Riker is freed from the Cardassian internment camp at Lazon II by the Grigari. Feeling abandoned by Starfleet, Thomas Riker joins the Grigari forces.

2376 Ensign Nog assigned to *U.S.S. Enterprise,* NCC-1701-E.

Founding of the Bajoran Ascendancy, a political alliance of worlds long denied Federation membership. Chief among the leaders of the Ascendancy is Weyoun, now a kai in a new Bajoran religious order.

2381 Destruction of the *Starship Enterprise* at the Battle of Rigel VII.

2382 Last good vintage of Chateau Picard.

2383 Captain Jean-Luc Picard is given command of *U.S.S. Enterprise,* NCC-1701-F. The first of her class, the *Enterprise* is designed specifically to combat the Grigari threat in the Alpha Quadrant.

2385 Picard is promoted to the rank of admiral and reassigned to Starfleet Headquarters.

Command of the *Starship Enterprise* is transferred to Captain William Riker. Among his crew are Deanna Troi, Geordi LaForge, Thomas Paris and B'Elanna Paris.

2386 The Klingon Empire begins construction of the dimensional transporter pads needed for Project Looking Glass.

2388 A Grigari trade delegation arrives in Sector 001 and, because of an apparent miscommunication, opens fire on Earth. The *Enterprise,* under the command of Captain William Riker, is lost with all hands in the first three minutes of this battle.

Death of Kasidy Yates while running the Grigari blockade of the Terran system.

Project Looking Glass. A massive Klingon fleet commanded by Chancellor Martok transitions to the Mirror Universe and attempts to take the Bajor system by force. However, the Grigari meet the Klingon fleet in the Mirror Universe and decimate it, then go on to destroy the planets of the Klingon Empire and unleash nanoprobes on human colonies, resulting in the deaths of virtually all Klingons and humans in the Alpha and Beta Quadrants.

The Bajoran Ascendancy claims control of Starfleet.

2390 Seven of Nine and Hugh-Borg negotiate an alliance between the Federation and the Borg.

2393 Ascendancy blockade of the Ferenginar system begins.

2395 Construction of the *U.S.S. Phoenix* begins at Utopia Planitia. The *Phoenix* is the brainchild of Admiral Jean-Luc Picard, designed to travel 25,000 years back in time to place deep-time charges that will destroy the Bajoran Ascendancy and prevent the merging of the two Bajoran wormholes *after* the *Phoenix* has departed. Thus, causality is preserved.

2399 Agents of the Bajoran Ascendancy use the Orb of Time to travel to the distant past to place a transporter sensor beneath the site of the city of B'hala to detect the placement of the *Phoenix*'s deep-time charges.

2400 December 17. *U.S.S. Defiant,* NX-74205, reappears in interstellar space in the Bajor sector and is met by the *U.S.S. Opaka* under command of Captain Thomas Riker. Three other Starfleet vessels engage the *Defiant* and *Opaka,* and a number of the *Defiant* crew are abducted. The arrival of the *U.S.S. Boreth* drives away the other vessels, and *Defiant* is taken under tow.

Remnants of the Tal Shiar strike at fifteen Starfleet outposts, hoping to disrupt Project Phoenix and Project Guardian.

At the Utopia Planitia shipyards, a Romulan commando team kidnaps Admiral Jean-Luc Picard and Captain Nog.

Stardate 76958.2. Lieutenant Commander Worf, Lieutenant Commander Jadiza Dax, Dr. Julian Bashir, and Jake Sisko are captured by Captain T'len of the Vulcan ship *U.S.S. Augustus.*

December 18. Nog replicates his last Starfleet uniform. As a result of wartime restrictions, it is his first new uniform in two years.

December 20. Captain Nog arrives at Starbase 53 and meets with the temporal refugees captured by Captain T'len.

December 22. Nog and the temporal refugees arrive at the Utopia Planitia shipyards. Bashir meets Admiral Seven of Nine.

December 23. Captain Nog, with the assistance of a Romulan

commando team, steals the *U.S.S. Phoenix* from the Utopia Planitia shipyards.

December 25. Kai Weyoun recovers the deep-time transporter sensor in B'hala. Death of Captain Thomas Riker.

December 22-28. Project Guardian. A combined Federation and Borg fleet under the command of Admiral Kathryn Janeway attempts to wrest control of the Guardian of Forever from the Grigari. The attempt fails with the loss of all Federation and Borg ships and personnel.

December 28. With the assistance of the temporal refugees, Nog recovers the *U.S.S. Phoenix* from the Romulans and changes course for Bajor.

December 31. Kai Weyoun and Benjamin Sisko beam aboard the *Defiant,* which lies derelict near the Bajoran wormholes.

Bajor-B'hava'el undergoes a protomatter-induced supernova, destroying all planets in the system.

2401 *January 1. Stardate 77000.0**. Merging of the two Bajoran wormholes. Restoration of the Celestial Temple.

The universe ceases to exist.

---

*NOTE: This date also corresponds with the first day of the Fourth Age of Kahless, the beginning of the three hundred and thirtieth iteration of the Orthodox Andorian Vengeance Cycle, and related significant dates in the calendars of fifteen other starfaring species in the Alpha and Beta Quadrants.

ACKNOWLEDGMENTS

When Rick Berman and Michael Piller created the *Deep Space Nine* television series, they accomplished an almost impossible twofold task. Not only did they successfully expand Gene Roddenberry's original *Star Trek* paradigm beyond the limits of stand-alone stories centered on a ship that traveled from place to place, they set in place an arena and an initial set of characters so full of possibilities that they fueled 176 hours of a series that even in its seventh and final season showed no signs of running out of creative energy and new directions.

But simply providing fertile starting conditions is not enough to guarantee success, and Berman and Piller also deserve the highest regard for the way in which they set in place an ongoing creative team—to say nothing of their top-notch production team—that took those starting conditions and lived up to the series' promise, constantly making it even richer and more satisfying.

Dozens if not hundreds of dedicated people need to be thanked for their ongoing contributions to the series throughout its seven-year run, many of which we've drawn on for these novels. Fortunately, in the impressive *Star Trek: Deep Space Nine Companion,* by Terry J. Erdmann with Paula M. Block, the full story of all those contributors through every season is told in detail, and we strongly recommend it.

But because we're limited to just these few words, we must call out only one additional star of that galaxy of talent for special acknowledgement: Just as *Deep Space Nine* would not exist without Berman and Piller, it would not have developed so memorably without Ira Steven Behr.

Moving beyond the television screen, it's important for us to also acknowledge that none of the novels of this trilogy could have been written without the magnificent store of Star Trek knowledge, insight, and good humor contained in the *Star Trek Encyclopedia,* by Michael and Denise Okuda, with Debbie Mirek, and the *Star Trek Chronology,* also by Mike and Denise.

In addition, we have benefited enormously from the exquisitely detailed and brilliantly illustrated *Deep Space Nine Technical Manual* by Herman Zimmerman, Rick Sternbach, and Doug Drexler.

In the spirit of the 33rd Rule, we would also like to offer our thanks and a shameless plug for Quark's own *Legends of the Ferengi,* as told to Ira Steven Behr and Robert Hewitt Wolfe, which offered fascinating insights into Ferengi culture.

For this omnibus edition of *Millennium,* we also pass along our special thanks to Allyn Gibson, who graciously allowed us to include his comprehensive timeline of the novels' events. All writers should be fortunate enough to have such diligent readers.

As always, we're also indebted to our editor, Margaret Clark, and to Liz Braswell, Scott Shannon, and Paula Block, for their ongoing involvement and much-appreciated contributions to the development of the entire *Millennium* project.

—J&G